I0731067

THE
ALIEN GIRL

Must not be a Threat

SJ CARVIL

Copyright © 2022 SJ Carvil .

All rights reserved. This book or any portion thereof may not be reproduced or used in any manner whatsoever without the express written permission of the publisher except for the use of brief quotation in a book review.

ISBN 978-1-957956-02-2 (sc)
ISBN 978-1-957956-03-9 (e)

Rev. date: 02/25/2022

Contents

Introduction to the Collier Family

Along the south coast of Britain, runs the stunning landscape of the South Downs National Park. Among these rolling chalk hills in the rural County of Hampshire, lies the village of Allcott.

One mile out from the village, an old Tudor Cottage, Oakleaves, sits nestled in a valley. This is the home of 58-year-old, retired, well decorated SAS captain Brian Collier. Because of his Welsh parents, and how he would dig his friends out of trouble. He was given the nickname 'Bryn, the miner', which has stayed with him always.

Bryn sister Gwen, five years his elder, with her husband Harold Hobart, live in the village. Both are retired teachers. They were there for him when Bryn needed help to get over the death of his wife Kitty from Breast Cancer. Harold's well-trusted old school friend is Michel Henderson, who is the local Veterinarian. He like Bryn, is a widower.

Bryn's late wife Kitty, that had deep Chestnut hair and green eyes. Many who knew her remarked how she resembled the Pre-Raphaelite Artist Rossetti's model wife, Elizabeth Siddal. Their two children, both married, are now living in different countries. Kit had been a nurse when she met Bryn in the Military Hospital, where Bryn was being cared for. Kitty carried on her career in and around the village, after their children were born.

Catherine, their eldest child, once played for the England's women's cricket Team. She is married to the New Zealander Brent Leany, with their 2-year-old daughter Amy, have settled in Auckland, New Zealand. Catherine's spectacular catches earned her the name 'Cat'. She now works for the BBC Sports Corporation.

Bryn and Kitty's son Thomas, a professional watercolourist, is married to Rachel Turnkey, lives in New York. At present, they have no children.

Bryn was living alone on that fateful day 14th April 2012. When in his garden, suddenly found himself consumed by a beam of light. In the next instant, he was defenceless, fighting for his life in a bear pit arena on an arid planet far out in deep space. Two years later, he is explaining to the world's press, at the Gilmores Park Hotel. Of his abduction.

Bryn does not understand why or how it happened, has undeniable proof that it did. With that evidence, he now faces the world, believing that there are people, who better able, with the right knowledge, might be able to explain the answers, that he does not have himself.

Chapter 1

The Press Conference

Bryn Collier, sitting at the table during the Press meeting, reflected on the reason why he was there. The events of 14th April 2012, were still vivid in his mind. He would never be able to forget, what had happened, would he ever be able to explain why it happened? The proof he had, would make the difference, in terms of the News Media, believing in him; otherwise, this meeting would not be happening. Not only the local press had congregated today at the reception room at Gilmores Park Hotel, all the biggest newspapers and TV broadcasters, from all around the world, were assembled.

Bryn's natural manner was that of a quiet person. He did not like being the centre of attention. When under pressure, or any form of insecurity, he would reach for his wallet. It contained the succour of his late wife's photo. Just to see her face, gave him moral comfort.

That flash of light that taken him away, it was now the flashes from cameras going off all around him, that now brought him back to the present. Catherine his 28-year-old daughter, touched his hand to make him aware that someone was asking a question from him.

Catherine had opened the meeting. She had previously stated the Collier's family's decision, was to explain her father strange revelation.

Bryn faced the ITV science correspondent. who asked what had happened on that morning he was abducted?

'I went to hang some washing on my clothesline. when I was surrounded by light, which instantly turned into darkness. I was unable to breathe, then everything went blank. The next moment as I gasped for air, I sensed warmth, then an acrid smell, that is when I was hit by something very hard, flying through the air, hitting something even harder. The pain I felt was severe, reaching down, my t-shirt was ripped. I had a sticky, warm feeling from the blood that was seeping from a large wound in my side. it was the bone spike, still embedded in me that concerned be the most. For it had penetrated right through me.'

Bryn looked around at the reporters. Their faces told him that they wanted more from him. He nodded, then rose from his chair. Pulled his shirt out of his trousers, lifted his shirt up away from his right side, showing a massive scar, which had been crudely patched up with large, ungainly stitches.

'If this happened two years ago, why did you not come forward earlier?' the reporter from the *Sunday Times* asked.

Bryn knew these questions would be asked. Knowing from the non-response, of his former employers, the British Army. In relation to the full report, he had sent them of his abduction.

Bryn removed his shirt completely, revealing more scars that crisscrossed all over his body. Down his chest and his back, scars that showed three claw marks. The spread across between each claw, could not have been left by any animal that lived here on Earth. There were a few gasps from reporters, that were close to him. Flashes from cameras lit up the press meeting. Bryn now replacing his shirt as he sat back in his chair.

Catherine Leany, Bryn's 28-year-old daughter, placing her hand in his hand, gave him a gentle squeeze. Like her father, five feet, ten inches tall with an athletic build. Her long dark hair that gave her oval face a classic look.

Bryn finally answer the last question. 'I needed time to get myself sorted out, heal the wounds that I had received in that arena. Most of all, I had to recover from the exhaustion I was suffering from, having spent six months away.'

The reporter from the *BBC News*, a stocky man in his mid-fifties, raised his voice so he could be heard over the commotion. 'Cat, it was you who came to us with this story, it was the photograph, that you supplied us, that gave us the most interested. Now we would like you to show us the proof.'

Catherine rose from her chair, leaving the room by a side door. Bryn turned to watch his daughter leave, kept his eyes on the door. Soon Catherine reappeared with her aunt, Bryn's elder sister Gwen. There was no mistaking the two women were related. Gwen looked like she could have been Catherine's mother.

Between them was a young female four feet in height; She had thick rose-gold coloured hair, yellow-pink skin, large eyes positioned slightly to the side of her head, flattish nose like a feline's, thin lips, and protruding trumpet-shaped ears that could move backwards and forwards. When she sat next to Bryn, her hands caught the gathered reporter's attention, for she had three long fingers and a thumb on each hand. Each digit had signs of claws, not fingernails. The Aliens girl's overall appearance was very much as of a human.

Gwen had dressed the alien girl, in a navy-blue pleated skirt, with a white cotton blouse. This was intended to make her look like a schoolgirl in her very early teens; her equivalent human age, which Gwen and her husband, had carefully calculated using all their years of experience, from teaching children of all ages.

The *Sun's* female reporter, sat on the opposite side of the table from Bryn's family. 'Hello!' she said, then paused. The reporter was close enough, to see how the Aliens eyes looked, was taken back by the kaleidoscope of yellows, greens, and blues. 'Wow! What lovely eyes you have.' The mauve vertical slit of the alien's pupils made them more, feline or reptilian, than human. But what the reporter noticed was the way the eyes changed colour.

The alien girl smiled at the reporter, responded. 'Thank you.' Hearing the alien speak, instantly set off a loud reaction from the reporters. Hands and voices raised to get questions in. The alien girl recoiled, looking towards Bryn for protection.

Catherine waited for the fracas to die down, while looking around at all the media attention. 'Ladies and gentlemen, this is quite a frightening ordeal for her. Please show a little consideration. It is the first time; she has encountered, so many people at once. If you are patient; then you may have the storyline that you came here for.'

The *Sun's* reporter sat upright, smiled. 'Have you a name?' She asked gently.

The alien girl smiled back. 'Yes, the group I lived amongst, called me CHARLYYK.'

An American reporter from CNN, raised his hand. 'How would you spell that?' He inquired in a thick Texan drawl.

Charlyyk looked at Gwen. Gwen saw Charlyyk's apprehension, in the way her ears moved, and her eyes kept changing colour. The elongated vertical pupils became enlarged. Gwen smiled at her, trying to ease the tension, passed a piece of paper towards her, Charlyyk looked at it, then slowly spelt out.

'C-H-A-R-L-Y-Y-K.'

'Was that with one Y or two?' The American asked

'Two.'

From the back of the room, a reporter with a French accent asked. 'You mentioned 'the group' called you Charlyyk. Which group was that?'

Charlyyk angled her head to see who was asking the question. The reporter raised his hand. Charlyyk acknowledges him with a nod, timidly said. 'The group who raised me,'

'Did you not know, who your parents were?'

Charlyyk turned to Gwen. They spoke for a couple of seconds, then Charlyyk composed herself. 'No, I do not know who my parents were.' She again turned to Gwen, looking for reassurance that she was doing what Gwen required of her.

Bryn, had tried to prepare Charlyyk, that yes-and-no answers would not satisfy the press. 'You must give them something to write about. Otherwise, they will use their imagination, make up stories, that won't be to your advantage. We need to get people on your side, to see you as a young girl, not as a threat.' Bryn knew that when he had to satisfy his commanding officer, debriefing him on any military action he had been involved in, that had been required to explain the whole truth of the operation. One discrepancy would cast doubt on everything he had achieved previously.

Charlyyk with a nod to Gwen, turned back to face the press. 'Gwen and her husband Harold have helped me, learn about my new home. They taught me to read and write. I read about the...' Charlyyk paused for a few seconds again for reassurance, watched Gwen write something on a piece of paper. Charlyyk picked it up, looking at it, then continued. 'I read about your Earth's history, your Jurassic period, the food chain that existed on this planet at that time. Well, from where I came from, it was similar to your Jurassic period; with my people, that were situated at the bottom of the food chain!' There was a slight pause. Then Charlyyk softly said, 'We searched for food and water every day, which could well be our last, as many beasts were trying hard to eat us.

Bryn was aware of the feelings Charlyyk was having as she relived those moments living among her own people. He moved forward in his chair, touched Charlyyk's arm giving her a loving smile. She responded back with a nod. Charlyyk's eyes relaying her need for him to help her.

Bryn now addressed the reporters. 'That is how I met Charlyyk. She was supposed to be, the evening meal for one of the strange bear-like beasts.' Bryn waited for everyone to settle before he continued. 'Although I was extremely hungry, and in much pain.' Bryn's face tightened relaying to those that it was as if Bryn was there as it was happening. 'I attacked the beast who was holding Charlyyk, that was about to pull her apart, to eat her. For the beast had a weapon, which I needed if I wanted to survive?'

Charlyyk saw the press, in their eagerness to get their stories, as no different than the beast wanting the taste of her blood. Thoughts of what could have happened to her had started to take effect. Tears welled in her eyes, as she trembled. Catherine reached her just as Charlyyk's legs buckled. Seeing the anguish on Charlyyk's face, Catherine cradled her lovingly, like a big sister. Gwen also there with a big comforting arm.

The *Sun's* reporter, seeing what was taking place, walked around the table holding a clean cotton handkerchief. Gwen willingly took the handkerchief, dabbed Charlyyk's face. After making sure Charlyyk was OK, Gwen returned the hanky back to the reporter. 'Thanks!'

A faint smile on the reporter's face, as she received the hanky. 'No problem,' she replied, returning to her seat. Put the hanky into a plastic bag, before securing it in her black leather handbag.

The hotel manager, appeared next to Catherine. Was now talking with her. Catherine nodded her approval. The hotel manager stepped forward, addressed the gathered Press. 'Ladies and Gentlemen, it's been nearly two hours. It would be a good time, for a recess.'

The reporters agreed. With a significant amount of movement and noise, they collected their bits. The hotel manager then pointed. 'If you would all like to leave by the door on your left, the Hotel has arranged some refreshments for you'

As they trundled out of the meeting, there was much to discuss. Many were checking their notes and receiving calls from their Editors, who had been listening in on video links? The American CNN reporter found a quiet corner. His I-phone 5 was on FaceTime. The person he was listening to, had a NASA emblem emblazoned on his shirt pocket. 'Is its real Brad?'

The reporter nodded. 'You received the video?'

'Yeah, we have a team on this at this moment.' The man paused as somebody at his side, spoke to him. 'Can you get DNA samples, Brad?'

'I'll try.'

In the opposite corner of the room, The *Sun's* reporter was deep in conversation with her father. 'Daddy you won't believe this, I have her tears soaked in my hanky! I have sealed it in a plastic bag.'

Her father Professor John Taylor (Forensic Science) was delighted. 'Well done Darling.' He was excited at the prospect, of studying the DNA of an Alien or proving it a fake. 'I'll send my assistant to pick it up.'

The Collier family were giving Charlyyk support, by holding her hands. They were not fusing about her, just being there for her, to get her through the emotional upset she was experiencing. With sad appealing eyes, Charlyyk said 'sorry' to Gwen

'Hey, little one!' Gwen said. She put her arms around Charlyyk, then kissed her on the forehead. 'Experiencing, and showing feelings is what a real person is all about.'

Catherine stroked Charlyyk's hair, as she looked into the Alien girl's eyes. 'And you are, one sweet person.'

As Charlyyk slowly gained her composure she pulled away, looking towards Bryn.

Bryn sitting just a little away from the girls held out his arms. Charlyyk went to him sat on his lap, placing her arms around his neck, her vulnerability showed, a little girl in a big new world clutching at anything that she deemed safe. Bryn watching over her, as any father would, as if Charlyyk was his own child. He was under no illusion that Charlyyk was just as responsible for his safe return

Catherine poured herself a cup of tea, plucked a sachet of white sugar from the bowl provided, tore the end, emptied half the sugar into her cup. As she stirred there was a pensive look on her face. She was looking at the options the family had before them. Catherine had come home specially to get this meeting organised. She knew all the right people to contact, knowing that the authorities would not be able to spirit Charlyyk away, without the world seeing. Her father would not have been happy if that had happened.

Catherine looked at her father and Charlyyk. 'Dad are you both OK with this, or do you want to stop?'

Bryn looked at Charlyyk, asked. 'Well, how do you feel?'

Charlyyk held Bryn's hand with both of hers. 'I'm OK now,'.

'OK.' said Bryn. 'Let the herd in.'

Catherine knowing what it was like to be in the media mix, trying to get a question answered, said, 'Dad they are trying to do a job here!'

Gwen chirped in. 'Don't you forget what we are trying to achieve with this Bryn?'

Bryn, with a sigh, 'This is to put a bit of pressure on the Home Secretary. I know Gwen.'

'We need British Citizenship granted, for Charlyyk.' Gwen quickly replied.

The Collier family had submitted their application three months earlier, yet had received no response from the Home Office. This press meeting was to get the Governments attention. The Collier Family had contemplated the possible repercussions, understood they could not keep Charlyyk's secret forever.

Catherine had spent time working in the media spotlight. She knew how this coverage could backfire and make their lives unbearable.

Bryn was more concerned about how the military would respond. He knew this had to be done on his terms, not something forced upon the Collier family. The authorities might have taken her away, he owed Charlyyk, more than that.

The World's press started to drift back to the meeting room. Three highly respected newsmen approached the table. Each placed before the Collier family written offers for exclusive interviews. The family glanced at the offers on the table, looked at each other, nodded.

Catherine was the one to speak. 'OK Dad, I'll handle this.' She faced the gathered press, pausing to gain their attention. When it was quiet. 'Ladies and gentlemen, let us make it quite clear to you. This is not a money-making enterprise. We know that we can't wrap Charlyyk up in cotton wool all of her life, we are damn well not going to turn her into a freak show either. Charlyyk needs to lead a healthy, normal life, which we as a family intend to give her.'

The American reporter stood up. 'The world has a right to see her,' he retorted.

Gwen was quickest to her feet, anger in her eyes, directed her words solely at the American. 'What! With America's damn stupid gun laws, where any unstable idiot can purchase a gun, even weapons of mass destruction, that could kill us all, believing that they would be saving America from an alien invasion!'

The American reacted strongly. 'America is not like that!'

'No?' Gwen retorted, menace in her voice. 'How many have died, including your Presidents?'

Bryn tried to calm Gwen down. 'Gwen, this is not a political rally!' As he eased her down into her chair with his arm around her shoulder.

Gwen's shook her head mouthing *'sorry'* to everyone.

Charlyyk's face was a picture of confusion. She had never seen Gwen angry before. In the two years, she had been with Gwen, she had learned to read and write, to use a knife and fork, also to wear clothes. They'd had fun as she tried wearing high-heel shoes. Gwen was milk and honey, strawberries and cream in Charlyyk's eyes.

Charlyyk stood beside the seated Gwen, put her arms around her head, cradling the side of Gwen's face to her chest.

Gwen placed her arms around Charlyyk's slim waist, began a rocking motion. Charlyyk kissed the top of Gwen's head. Cameras flashed, recording this act of humanity, by this little girl from outer space. No mystical powers, no mind-bending, just a little girl adapting to a new home, becoming a member of a new family.

The *Sun's* female reporter noticed a sign of movement at the back of Charlyyk's skirt. 'Look! she has a tail!' Camera lenses were changed, video cameras zoomed in on this new discovery. Poor Charlyyk looked embarrassed, for a moment thinking she had done something wrong. Gwen, Catherine could only laugh.

Charlyyk looked at Catherine, who pointed at her tail, and waggled her finger. Charlyyk realised what the press people were taking a keen interest in, could not help a snigger. Then Charlyyk turning to face the press. 'My tail has proved troublesome for poor Gwen.' Charlyyk covering her mouth, as she giggled.

Gwen and Catherine had purchased all types of knickers and shorts in an attempt to accommodate her tail, cutting and re-sewing, to no prevail. So, they let bygones, be bygones; they left it to do as it damn well pleased. Charlyyk had not worn any clothes on the planet where she lived. For there was no reason to do so; survival was the only thing her group had on their minds.

A voice came from amid the gathered media. 'Carlsson of *Swedish News Television*. Charlyyk when you first found yourself here on Earth, how did you feel?'

Charlyyk natural instinct was to pause, to think. 'At first I was very disorientated, not sure how I felt. I was trying to steady myself. Then I noticed that there was so much grass, which I had never seen before, I found myself gazing at how lush it was, the scent was so sweet, the sound, so much different to where I had lived. Bryn was lying on the ground he looked in a bad way, blood soaked his clothes. I shook him, when he moved that's when I smelt the Feeng's blood on him. My defences screamed at me to run, Bryn had come too, he managed to take a good hold of me.

Charlyyk again paused for a moment, the images of Bryn injuries still etched deeply in her mind. Her thoughts at the struggle getting him off that hill. 'Bryn pointed to a nearby cottage. I tried to help him, but the gravity here is stronger, than on my planet. We staggered down the hill, falling many times. When Bryn fell on top of me, it took great effort for me to drag my legs out from under him. I was near to exhaustion. When we finally reached the cottage, Bryn showed me how to use the tap. The water tasted so good.' Charlyyk remembered the struggle it had been to get, a single big mouthful to take back to her group, to quench the thirst of others. 'So much water was here at a turn of a tap!'

The Swedish Reporter, raised her finger, 'The fact sheet, it mentioned that a Vet treated you. Why was that?'

'The vet is a dear old family friend.' Gwen responded. 'He could treat Bryn and Charlyyk without giving Charlyyk's existence away. It would have been hard to have managed the media frenzy it would have caused at that time. With my brother trying to overcome his injuries, we did not know what would be the best way forward.'

'Hardy of the *Daily Mail*. Gwen, you were the first to see Bryn and Charlyyk when they arrived back on Earth. What was your reaction to seeing them both?'

'I was alone at home, when receiving Bryn's call, it had been six-months since we had last heard from him, I dropped everything, jumped in my car, raced to his cottage. I could not believe the state he was in, instantly reached for the phone, Bryn begged me not to phone for the police or ambulance. So, I phoned my husband's old school friend Michel Henderson, he was there in ten-minutes. While Michel was treating my brother, Bryn told us his story. It sounded so far-fetched till Bryn pointed to a chair, that is when Charlyyk appeared from behind it. I nearly fainted. When Michel finished treating and cleaning Bryn's wounds, he examined Charlyyk. Later my husband Harold and Michel organised how we could look after Charlyyk till Bryn was in a fit state of mind to make those decisions.'

Another reporter stood up. 'Rolf Lehmann. *Reuter's*. Cat, many of us know you, with your TV Sports coverage. We must take it you have informed the authorities, what have they said about Charlyyk?'

Catherine picks up a folder off the table, takes out some A4 sheets of paper. This is a copy of an application form, for Citizenship we applied three months ago, but as yet we have had no response.

The meeting ended abruptly when Charlyyk slumped in her chair. The day had taken its toll on her, she was fast asleep.

The Hotel manager, stepped forward and whispered to Bryn, 'Let's take Charlyyk to room 94.' Bryn scooped her up and followed the Hotel manager, pursued by an anxious Gwen.

The press trying hard to get exclusive interviews; surrounded Catherine. As Cat was handing out leaflets detailing the experience that her father and Charlyyk, had encountered, with the contact information for future meetings.

As soon as possible, Catherine followed her father to room 94. There she saw Gwen slumped in an armchair, her father standing looking out of the window. Charlyyk was fast asleep on the King-size bed a lightweight throw covering her. Light from a discreet wall fitting, gave a soft feel to the room. The colours were easy to the eye, as with the light wood furniture, nothing too bright or glaring.

Catherine went to her father, put an arm around his waist, nestled her head on his shoulder.

Bryn slipped his arm around her waist, looked at her lovingly, then gently kissed her. 'What would I have done without you? I'm still trying to adjust to what has happened.'

'I know this is not your thing.' Catherine replied. 'You hate any attention being directed at you.'

Bryn nodded. 'And I'm grateful you were here to take the strain from me.'

Catherine laughed. 'That's typical of you, Dad!'.

Bryn taken back, replied. 'What do you mean?'

Catherine smiled. 'You can face anyone with a knife or gun. A camera, pencil, and notepad? you are hopeless.'

Bryn shrugged his shoulders. 'That bad?'

Catherine put her arms around her father, giving him a big hug. 'No, you were great.'

A few minutes passed. There was a knock on the door. Catherine walked over, opened the door. The woman in her mid-fifties, dressed in an exclusive bespoke charcoal-grey tailored suit, white blouse, a light green silk scarf, loosely draped around inside the collar. Her dark hair, showing a hint of grey, that was pulled back behind her ears, secured with a hairgrip. With a warm, reassuring smile, she said. 'Hello, I am Helen Bennett, personal assistant to the Home Secretary. May I come in?'

Catherine stepped aside to let her enter.

Gwen took a long look at Helen Bennett. 'I saw you standing at the back, during the press meeting; I believed you to be a part of the hotel security.'

'Did you!' Said Helen Bennett with a smile, took two steps forward, raised her hand to Bryn's outstretched hand, shook it firmly, with her other hand, gave Bryn a large A4 manila envelope. 'I have arranged a meeting with the Home Secretary for Tuesday morning, let us say, ten a.m., If, that is suitable for you?' Bryn looked down at the manila envelope. Helen Bennett smiled. 'Details for your security, also arrangements for a prelim at the weekend. As you will see all explained in fine detail.' Helen turned, then headed for the door. 'See you all on Saturday at ten.'

As she walked down the corridor towards the lifts. Helen Bennett, with her phone in her hand was sending out a text to Thames House. '*Target real. No threat. Repeat no threat.*' The smile she gave herself was not smug, more of satisfaction.

Gwen and Catherine looked at Bryn. 'Did not expect that to happen so quickly.' Said Gwen.

A noise caused their attention to turn towards the bed. Charlyyk was making an effort to sit up. Gwen sat on the side of the bed, allowed Charlyyk time to adjust herself.

Catherine touched her dad's arm. 'I am going down to reception and settle up. Then I'll sort out the car.'

Bryn smiled at his daughter; he could not be any prouder of her, than he was at that moment. Watching Catherine walking out of the room. 'See you in the lobby.' Then he walked over to Charlyyk. 'Feeling better for that little nap?'

Charlyyk's eyes were slightly closed. She said dreamily. 'Mmm, that was nice.'

Bryn smiled at her. 'Ready to go home then?'

Charlyyk swung her legs to the side of the bed, slid down, 'You bet.' She chirped. Charlyyk had copied this personal expression, from Gwen's husband, Harold.

Chapter 2

Oakleaves

They met Catherine in the lobby as she was thanking Bill Gilmore and his staff. She had chosen this hotel remembering when the England girl's cricket team had used it for pre-Ashes warm-up. Bill Gilmore's fee to Catherine was modest indeed, as the worldwide media coverage, would put his hotel on the map.

The car was waiting for them. As they walked towards it, Gwen's phone began to vibrate. 'Hi love,' She answered. 'Yes, we are on our way. See you in about...' She looked at Bryn. 'Thirty-five minutes, Love you.' As Gwen opened the rear passenger door, Charlyyk dived in.

Charlyyk loved Gwen's car, a Vauxhall Insignia in charcoal grey. Charlyyk enjoyed playing with buttons. To stop her, Harold had fitted a DVD player, rear of the driver's seat. Charlyyk sat on that side. She could not wait for her favourite movie *Frozen*, and Olaf to appear.

When Charlyyk first encountered snow, Bryn built her a traditional snowman, with a carrot for a nose, and twigs for arms. So, Charlyyk seeing Olaf was like bringing her snowman to life, for she, so loved that first winter with Bryn playing in the snow.

Catherine sat in the driver seat, adjusted her driving position, fitted her seat belt, then started the engine.

Bryn closed his eyes. 'Driving fast doesn't make, for a good driver.'

Catherine gave a haughty laugh, then drove off in a very sedate manner. 'Happy?'

Bryn opened the envelope that Helen Bennett had given him earlier. Shuffling through the pages, he stopped at one, read through it twice.

Catherine noticed the interest he gave it. 'Anything interesting?'

'Yes! It seems that our old friend Toby has been assigned, as our protection.'

Catherine gave her father another quick glance. 'When did that happen?'

'A month ago,'

Gwen leaned forward. 'I was going to tell you, the other day I thought I had seen Toby in the village. Wednesday that when it was, but with all that was going on, it just slipped my mind. Sorry!'

Bryn placed his hand, on his sister's, acknowledging that he had no concerns with her. Gwen sat back in her seat, took a glance sideways. She smiled at the way Charlyyk covered her mouth with both hands when she giggled.

Thirty minutes later. Catherine turned right into Farm Lane. It took them to their Cottage. 'Oakleaves.' The cottage had many additions attached to it over the years. The thatched roof had been replaced by handmade red clay pantiles. It is now a four-bedroom family home, with a wisteria climbing the south facing front elevation of the cottage. In springtime with its distinctive festoon of purple-blue flowers, it looked spectacular, but this time of year just a hint of foliage could be seen as it covered over the cottage like a spider's web.

The extensive rear garden allowed to ramble over time, a six-foot-high flint wall that runs down the right-hand boundary next to the lane that leads to Allcott village. The left-hand border of the garden, where a wooden pole fence with a Hawthorn hedge looked out over grazing meadows. At the bottom of the garden were trees and a gate that opened onto the fields which led north to the copse of trees on the hill where Bryn and Charlyyk was placed by the Light Beam on their return. West side of the cottage a gate that opened onto a tractor track that would lead to the bottom of Bishops Lane.

Halfway down Farm Lane nestled between the trees, they passed a Black Range Rover Vogue. Four men were inside; they made no attempt to disguises themselves. Catherine turned left and guided the Vauxhall Insignia between the brick pillars and onto the shingle driveway.

The door of the cottage opened. Harold, Gwen's husband stood there. He was a lean, sixty-seven-year-old with white hair and a very pleased to see you smile on his face. Charlyyk had to wait till Catherine stepped from the driver's seat, because of Charlyyk's love of playing with buttons they had to put the child's lock on. Soon as her door was opened, she was out like a bolt of lightning, straight into Harold's arms. 'I'm hungry Harold!' Were the first words that Charlyyk spoke.

Gwen picked up the bits and bobs from the car, then started to follow Charlyyk into the cottage. At the entrance door, Gwen embraced Harold. 'Long day darling?' putting his arm around her.

'Can't wait to take my shoes off.'

Charlyyk's nose was twitching, the smell from the kitchen had her attention. 'Salmon Wellington, ratatouille, and chips,' Harold explained.

Gwen looked at Harold with concern. 'You certainly know how to spoil that girl.'

Bryn and Catherine had waited by the car. A figure appeared, walking between the brick pillars...a Clark Gable look-alike, even down to the moustache. Toby had been one of Bryn's recruits, when he'd served in the SAS, and over time they had become good friends.

'Hi, Bryn.'

'Hello, Toby.'

Toby strolled to Catherine, put his arms around her and gave her a big kiss. 'Hi, Cat. How is Amy?'

Catherine's eyes widened. She suddenly remembered she promised to speak with her daughter. She turned and ran into the house.

Toby could only smile. 'Yes, Cat I'm fine!'

He smiled at Bryn, and they followed Catherine into the house.

The commotion in the lounge as the family all positioned themselves for the best view of Amy. The Skype connection was up and running, showing Catherine's husband Brent and his mother Jo, on either side of Amy. Amy's little hand waving. 'Mummy.' Lots of cooing and kisses could be heard. Charlyyk, as always, was right in the middle of them, trying to get Amy's attention.

When Charlyyk had first arrived on Earth, Amy was still a baby, and in that time, she had grown, Charlyyk became Amy's best Skype friend. When Bryn first introduced Charlyyk to Amy, both were learning to talk, yet seemed to understand each other, this had been good for Charlyyk giving her someone she could relate to. As Charlyyk sat there, the facial and eye movement between them both became more like words. Catherine had noticed how her daughter could respond to Charlyyk in this way, and encouraged them wholeheartedly.

Bryn and Toby's hand waving met with a chorus of acknowledgement, from the Leany family. Bryn and Toby continued on to the study. There was much to discuss on the security that Toby was going to supply.

Later they all met in the dining room, bowls of different dishes in the centre of the table to cater for every body's needs. But most prominent was the enormous bowl of chips doubled fried for extra crispness. Charlyyk, had two small bowls, of tomato ketchup, and mayonnaise. She dipped one chip at a time into each small bowl in succession then ate the dripping chip.

Gwen glared at Harold. 'She will get fat on all that stodgy food!'

Harold smiled at his wife. 'She has had a long day darling.' Then to Charlyyk. 'You enjoying those chips?'

Charlyyk replied with her wicked smile. 'You bet, Uncle Harold.'

A little while later, as everyone was talking, Catherine got up from her chair walked around the table to Charlyyk. 'Dad! she has fallen asleep again' With concern in her voice, Catherine picks her up. 'I will take her in with me.'

Bryn placed his hand on Charlyyk's forehead. 'She has not got a temperature.' He shot a glance at Gwen. 'When is Michel coming?'

'I'll check my diary.' Gwen said,

Michel gave Charlyyk medical examinations regularly every quarter.

Bryn waited till it was quiet before watching the late-night news. The playback of Charlyyk, with its over emphasised close-up shots, as the camera looked for the differences. The Science specialist, who were there to give their views, were more excited about her, than wanting to say anything bad about her, they would leave that to others. They have got proof of life on other planets, and the implications they could glean from it, were their main priorities.

A politician who had come talk about climate change, was slightly taken back by what the press meeting had revealed. She tried to add something positive wanting to give a good impression on her knowledge of science. But found herself struggling to convince the real scientist, who showed her, that was the last thing they wanted talk about, was climate change.

The playback of Charlyyk's tail was another big talking point. 'Look at how it moves, I would say no longer than six inches at the most. But its hands, look at the close up, those are claws. Now when we look at the face and the jaw-line we can see how the teeth are positioned that this is not a hunter, but more a gatherer. So, the claws are for digging. The other thing is, we have noticed how her eyes move independently of each other? This is prey not predator.'

Then a roving reporter ask people in the street about their views. This was to Bryn's main concern, had the press-meeting hindered their cause? But the jovial way the interviews were conducted, did not give Bryn any answers. Many people appeared to believe it was all a joke.

Catherine had consulted with a friend of hers in America, who specialised on behaviour studies, she confirmed the percentage of people that objected would be small. 'Catherine, just go with it, when they see she is no threat, curiosity will take over. Just gives it time. England is not America. You are more tolerant in your acceptance of differences in people.'

Chapter 3

Prelim

The morning light breaking through Bryn's bedroom window stirs Bryn into action. As he went to slip out of bed the familiar shape of Charlyyk lying there, makes him realise he must do something about it. But how? He puts on his trousers and a t-shirt, and in bare feet, he walks into the kitchen, picking up the kettle and filling it with fresh water from the tap. He does not need to check the time; old habits are hard to lose. Six o'clock, meant reveille.

The first hint of the kettle's whistle had started to be heard as Toby walked through the door. 'Make mine coffee.'

The men were sitting there with mugs of coffee, when Catherine strolled in. 'Where's mine?' She pulls up a chair and plonked herself down. Bryn pours her a cup. 'When did she?' Catherine, gave her father a stern look.

'Two.'

'It really must stop dad?'

Bryn shook his head.

Toby looked at them both. 'What's this about?' He inquired.

'It's Charlyyk she only goes to bed with dad.' Catherine's words had a bite to them.

Bryn, raised his hands in a 'what can I do?' gesture.

'But dad, she wears no clothes in bed! She's naked! It's not healthy; it has to stop!'

'How's this come about then?' persisted Toby.

'Go on dad explain it... because I don't understand either'

Bryn pours himself another mug of coffee. 'I might not have the right answer for it, but my theory, is when I saved her that day, I became her security. Like with a child's favourite toy she needs to go to bed with it, so that they can sleep at night. I think the real reason Charlyyk does not wear any clothes is that, to keep warm at night, her group cuddled together. Now it a distinctive thing she does.

Catherine poured herself a cup of tea, walked over to the window, and took a couple of sips. 'You could be right, Dad. When Amy has not got her bunny, she can't sleep.' Catherine took another sip of the tea. 'But we can't allow it to continue dad, it's not right. Charlyyk is growing and developing fast it has to stop.'

Toby eyeing his empty mug. 'Yes, I'm understanding what you dad is saying, Cat. As a young lad, I had a mongrel puppy. It would not sleep anywhere but with me. No matter what my parent did to stop it from happening, that puppy always found a way on to my bed. It's not going to be easy to break that habit.'

Catherine opens the top oven door, and turns on the grill, removes the grill pan and places it on the kitchen table. As she goes to open the fridge a naked, sleepy-eyed Charlyyk appears. 'Catherine I'm thirsty.'

Bryn collects a glass tumbler from the wall cabinet, and half fills it with water. 'Here you are, sweetheart.'

Catherine left what she was doing. 'Dad, put some bacon on.' She put her hand on Charlyyk's back, and shepherds her towards the door 'Let's get you sorted my good lady.'

When they returned, bacon sandwiches were waiting on the table, and a bowl of muesli for Charlyyk.

'What do you usually do on a day like this?' Toby asks Bryn.

'We usually do a three-mile jog, before breakfast.' Was Bryn's reply

'Aren't you afraid, you might be seen?' But Toby already knew what they did, he had been observing them for over a month. When Helen Bennett had given him his brief to check if the story was true. Toby had set up surveillance points all around the area. But had ignored the advice to install cameras in the cottage, he knew Bryn would react very fervently if he discovered one. Bryn had already security placed on him, with his reputation as a hero, after his gallantry awards were bestowed on him.

Charlyyk, without looking up. 'You have not seen my tracksuit.' Letting her centre finger down and holding on to it with her thumb, she pushes her hand forward. 'Hoody man.' She gives a giggle and carries on eating her muesli.

The telephone rang. Bryn lifts the receiver. 'Hi, Bryn here. OK Michel.' He puts the receiver back. 'Charlyyk when you finished breakfast, have a shower. Michel will be here at ten o'clock.' Bryn then spoke, to Catherine. 'Would you be a sweetie and open mum's clinic for Michel, he's coming to do some test on Charlyyk?'

Kitty, Bryn's late wife, held a position as a Queens Nurse, covering the surrounding villages and solitary houses and farms. Many farmers saw the benefit of building a Clinic attached to the cottage, so Kit could treat their many farm workers and their families.

The 66-year-old veterinarian, Michel Henderson, who's practice likewise, as Kitty's. covered much of the local area, arrived at 'Oakleaves' at ten o'clock. Michel was thickset and stood five feet eleven. He had sandy coloured hair, with bushy eyebrows, set on a square face, always wore a Harris Tweed jacket, and corduroy trousers. Harold and Gwen were his closest friends.

Michel's regular visits was not just to see Charlyyk, but to make sure that she was not suffering from any dangerous infections, such as alien viruses, that she could have brought to this planet. But his curiosity on how she would develop, outweighed everything else.

As Michel entered the clinic, 'Hi, Charlyyk how are we?' Michel's with his soft reassuring, gentle voice.

'Michel I've been getting very tired lately.' Was Charlyyk's reply.

Michel put his bag on the desk, opened the filing unit and took out her file.

Charlyyk already knew what was required of her. She removed the dressing gown and stepped up onto the scales. Michel entered her weight very carefully into her file. Then he conducted all the routine test he had been using to evaluate her since her arrival.

Charlyyk looked at Michel with a worried expression. 'What do you think it is Michel?'

'I'm not one hundred per cent sure, it could be something normal that all girls go through. It looks like you are going through a change.'

Charlyyk looked concerned.

'We all go through changes Charlyyk.' Stated Michel.

'Am I going to turn into something else?' squeaked Charlyyk nervously.

Michel took hold of her hands. 'Amy is a little girl, but Catherine is a lady. You are changing from a girl into a lady.'

'Is that bad?'

'I suggest you ask Catherine.' Michel smiled, trying to reassure Charlyyk.

Charlyyk puts her dressing gown back on then left. Michel tidies up the clinic, then went in search of Bryn, finding him in his study.

'Hi Michel, what did you find?'

Michel sat down. 'Well, your little girl is turning into a big girl.' The look on Bryn's face showed Michel that he had a problem. 'What's the matter?'

Bryn stood up, went to the door and called for Catherine. Michel was explaining the changes he had found in Charlyyk when Catherine came into the study.

'I've been talking to Charlyyk dad.'

Bryn pulls up a chair for Catherine. He told Michel about Charlyyk getting into bed with him and his theory.

Just as Catherine was about to speak the door opens, Charlyyk entered. 'Am I in trouble?'

Catherine tapped her knee, Charlyyk duly sat on it.

Bryn reached over, and takes her hand, with a fatherly look. 'No, you are not in trouble. Michel has been telling us about the changes you are about to go through, with the changes we are going to have to make.'

Catherine put her arm around Charlyyk's waist, giving her a loving hug. 'I had to make the same changes.'

Looking into Catherine' eyes. Charlyyk asks, 'What changes, did you make Catherine?' her eyes changing colour to a darker blue and green. Her ears pointing straight upwards, this was Charlyyk's inquisitive look.

Catherine grabbed her chance. 'I used to get into bed with my daddy, when I was small. But now I'm older; I don't.'

The expression on Charlyyk's face had turned to sadness, tears forming in her eyes, which had changed back to a softer green and blue, her ears were pointing backwards, and her shoulders drooped.

Catherine's eyes also welled up, at the sight of Charlyyk looking so sad.

Charlyyk's hand still in Bryn's trying to give her some comfort 'Changes take time sweetheart, but it means that you will get to grow into the woman that you would like to be... choose the style of clothes that you will want to wear, listen to the music you would like to hear. To be able to achieve this, we will have to allow you the chance to create your own space.'

Catherine gave Charlyyk an extra squeeze. 'This could mean your own den.'

These words did not help to make things better. Charlyyk left Catherine's lap, flew into Bryn's embrace, wrapping her arms around his neck and sobbing uncontrollably. For Charlyyk felt that she was being pushed away.

Bryn knew he had work to do, to calm Charlyyk down, he had to start right away, he could not leave the situation how it was. 'Sweetheart, you will change not by our say so, but how your body will dictate to you. Michel is keeping an eye on you to see what can be done, to help us, to help you.'

Michel rose from his chair, moving towards the door beckoned Catherine to follow. When they had reached the kitchen, Michel spoke to Catherine. 'It is early days, do not push it so hard. Allow her time to find her own way.'

Catherine realised what Michel was saying that in her anxiety to find an answer to her dad's dilemma she was acting too hastily. 'I do understand Michel I'm returning home on Thursday; I wanted to try and sort out Charlyyk going to bed with my dad before I left.'

Michel collects his bag from Bryn's study, there were no signs of Bryn or Charlyyk. On his way-out, Michel peered into the lounge where he noticed them sitting on the settee with a photo album opened in front of them. Bryn's finger is pointing to the pictures of Catherine in the different stages of growing up. 'This is how Catherine grew over the years, but how you will grow, we don't know, but Michel is going to keep a close eye on you, just in case there are any complication.'

Michel interrupted them. 'I'm leaving now. I promised the Parsons I would look over their new sheep.'

Bryn places the photo album on Charlyyk's lap, then heads for the door. 'I'll see you out, Michel.'

Catherine hearing Michel was leaving, hurries from the kitchen and follows the men out to Michel's car. Michel places his bag inside his car, turns to look at Bryn and Catherine standing together. 'Don't hesitate to call if you need me. These could be delicate times and maybe careful handling will be required.' With that, he gets in with a wave of his hand drove between the brick pillars, turned left and headed for Parson's farm.

As Bryn and Catherine were re-entering the cottage, the sound of a large diesel vehicle was approaching. Bryn turned and went back outside, Catherine waited by the door. Toby's Range Rover turned into the drive, with Toby at the wheel sitting beside him was the village policewoman Sgt Wendy Bailey. The vehicle came to a stop they both step down.

Catherine hurries past Toby, to embraces Wendy. 'Cup of tea Wend?'

As the two women walked into the cottage. Bryn asks Toby. ''What's this all about then?'

'You read your brief, didn't you?' Toby looked surprised.

'Oh, bloody hell! the meeting tomorrow.' Bryn had only managed to read eight out of the ten pages that Helen Bennett had given him in the manila envelope. 'Okay Toby, you better fill us in.'

Sitting in the study, Toby pulls out from his inside jacket pocket two folded sheets of A4 paper. 'Here is the proposed timetable for tomorrow.'

Bryn studied it carefully. 'Ok Toby, this is practical.'

Toby turns over another page. 'This is, the who's who that will be attending the prelim meeting.'

Bryn's slowly read down the page, some names familiar, the others, he would more likely pass them every day in the local supermarket, would still not know them.

Toby leant forward, resting his arms on his knees, one hand over the other. 'Any comments?'

'Yes, where to put them, how do we feed them?'

Toby rose to his feet and heading for the door. 'All in hand, being implemented at this very moment.'

Bryn and Toby walked through the cottage to the rear garden. Where a hive of activity was already underway. Army personnel was erecting a large Army Marquee. From the lane on the other side of the garden wall, the arm of a crane could be seen hoisting the tent materials into the garden.

When Toby discussed with Helen Bennett how a prelim could be organised and where, Toby's prior knowledge of the family, knew that the garden at the cottage would be adequate to house a large tent to accommodate the amount, of people that would be attending.

Catherine and Wendy were standing watching the erection of the tent with great interest, the movement of their lips and eyes, suggesting not what, but whom they were talking about.

Bryn broke away from what was happening; the realisation that he had forgotten about Charlyyk pricked his senses. He had left her in the lounge. He worried, that she would feel neglected. The lounge was a good place to start. Bryn slowly checked through the house. Till there were two rooms left, Thomas's his son's bedroom where Toby was staying, looked as though nobody had slept in there for years. Catherine's room the last one he stopped outside and listened in, he could hear movement, so he tapped on the door then entered.

Catherine's clothes were strewn everywhere, at the epicentre of the maelstrom was Charlyyk, wearing the dress Catherine had worn to her college prom ball; a silk dress, silver blue in colour, the design was beautiful in its simplicity.

Bryn did not want to create any more problems, knowing how Charlyyk had responded earlier. So, Bryn decided to praise Charlyyk. 'Wow, darling you look cute.' Bryn taking her in his arms gazed into her face. 'You look so grown up, a real lady' He carefully moved some of the clothes that were on the bed then sat down. Charlyyk sat on his lap, and they cuddled each other. Bryn remembered the day when Catherine sat on his lap wearing the same dress.

An hour had passed, since Bryn had left Catherine and Wendy, watching the army personnel erect the Marquee. Catherine took Wendy by the arm. 'Come let me show you my baby photos of Amy.'

The scene that Catherine and Wendy walked into, was just utter chaos, and there in the middle of it was Bryn and Charlyyk as though nothing had happened. Catherine turned to Wendy to apologise.

Wendy focused only on Charlyyk. 'Cat she's lovely!' She blurted out staring.

Bryn gave Charlyyk an extra squeeze. 'See what a lovely dress can do, like magic can turn a girl like you into a lady.'

But Catherine could see a more a gentle-approach, of putting her point over to Charlyyk on having her own room. 'Dad, can you leave us please; I think more magic is going to take place here!'

As Bryn left the room, he could tell by the happy tone in their voices that Charlyyk was not going to be told off.

Catherine could now carry out what she had been aiming to do, before going back to New Zealand. 'See Charlyyk. This was my room where I could be me. My own bathroom, wardrobe and where I could do my thing without someone interrupting me. It meant I had to keep it clean and tidy, but it was mine.'

Charlyyk looked around the bedroom, but it was the wardrobe that held her attention.

Bryn headed for the kitchen. To his surprise the kitchen table had gone, new types of catering appliances were being installed. Corporal Tom Smith stood to attention.

'Stand easy corporal.' Bryn said, making the young soldier relax.

'Thank you, Sir... There's tea in the pot. Milk. Sugar?'

'Yes, to all three.'

Bryn accepted a large mug of tea, and walked out to the Marquee. Rattan furniture placed strategically around, tables with communication equipment being installed, at one end of Bryn's kitchen table, had a table cloth draped over it, with an espresso coffee machine and drinks cooler placed at each end.

Toby approached Bryn. By his side was the unmistakable rounded figure of Sgt Wally Brodie, Bryn's old Sergeant, the grin on his face lit up and warmed the whole place like a huge bonfire. 'Hi Captain'

Bryn and Sgt Brodie met in a great bear hug.

'Wally, what are you doing here?'

'Toby told me how thin you were, so here I am to put some meat on them they're old bones.' The Sgt looks at Bryn and with a wicked look on his face. 'Somebody close to us said that you had extended your family, here's me thinking you were too old for that?'

Bryn smiled at Wally's jibe.

'I've been put in charge of looking after you and your guest. Helen and Toby knew we were old pals, so they thought I would be the best person for the job, as some of these people are important and all of them are doing this for gratis. We should give them in return, something special for their services.

Today we can test out the amenities, so tomorrow the service we will provide will be perfect.'

Corporal. Smith arrived by the side of his Sergeant. 'Sarge. I've put the meat on; six chickens, two racks of beef, two gammons, anyone with delicate stomachs?'

Bryn is taken aback, and glanced at Toby. 'Don't look at me; she is your responsibility.' Toby stepping back from any obligation.

'Charlyyk, eats fish, sometimes a little chicken, vegetables, fresh fruit, and nuts.' Bryn said. He had never had to think about what Charlyyk ate before. It had just been a process of what Charlyyk had tried and tested.

Harold had found the fridge open one morning and all its contents spread out on the floor, where Charlyyk had placed what she could eat or not eat in little piles. Pointing at those she could eat, then pointing to her mouth, then gave her agreement nod. Charlyyk had not approved of the evening meal Harold had made the previous night. When she was able to talk, telling Harold point blank that he needed her advice on what she could eat.

Catherine, Wendy, and Charlyyk re-appeared laughing. Charlyyk dressed in some of Catherine's old clothes from her early teens: tight light blue jeans, check blouse, cowboy boots and a 'kiss me quick' hat which was a souvenir from a school trip to Brighton. Catherine seeing Wally Brodie, her smile was of the memories when he would come to the Cottage when she was small. 'Hi, Wally...Wendy meets an old weight problem of my dad's.'

As the two Sgt's shook hands, Wally glared at Catherine. 'You insinuating I'm fat.'

'Of course, not Wally. It's what you use to feed to my dad.' Turning towards her father. 'Oh, dad... Wendy is going home. Brian telephoned. Her dinner will be ready. He is coming to pick her up.'

Kisses all round Wendy said her goodbyes.

Making their way back into the cottage, Charlyyk's nose had picked up the smell of food and had already headed for the kitchen. Poking her head through the doorway, she see's Corporal Smith. She hesitates for a moment before a knowing voice speaks. 'Chips, doubled fried please.'

Charlyyk spun around and threw her arms around Harold's neck. 'Harold.'

'Hi, cowboy.' Harold with Charlyyk still wrapped around his neck carries her into the lounge.

Gwen, surrounded by bags was showing Catherine and Bryn the new outfits for Charlyyk, that she and Harold had purchased that afternoon. Gwen gives Charlyyk a hug and a kiss.

'Are they for me?' Charlyyk looks into the bags, her long fingers feeling the fabric.

'Yes, but only if you like them, I can change any of them if you would like me to?'

'Come on sweetie, give a hand, let's take them to Catherine room where you can try them on.'

Gwen had taken up the task of buying the clothes for Charlyyk. Bryn had given her a budget to work to. It was how Charlyyk was growing that Gwen found hard to keep up with. But now and again Gwen would buy Charlyyk clothes she liked.

A Laura Ashley dress was what Charlyyk found in her hands. The look Charlyyk gave Catherine said it was not to her liking, Catherine eyes told Charlyyk not to say anything.

Harold sitting on the settee next to Toby and Bryn. 'Michel said he had been requested, to give his professional advice on Charlyyk at the meeting tomorrow?'

Toby getting up, he had something to say, as he composed himself, he removed his jacket. The shoulder holster and 9mm Glock 17, worried Harold.

'What's that for Toby? Is that entirely necessary?'

'Sorry Harold but it comes with the job. I babysit those heavy on intellect, though weak on spunk. But this is not what I want to talk about.' Toby was not taking this task lightly, Bryn was his friend, and if anybody was going to threaten Bryn, they had to answer to him first. 'Remember the Sun's reporter Lynn Taylor. Her father Prof Taylor has managed to get onto the VIP list for tomorrow. Helen worries when people do that, we double checked all Miss Taylors movements. When Charlyyk broke down at the press meeting, Miss Taylor offered her hanky. When Gwen gave back the hanky, to Miss Taylor, she put it in a plastic bag. Later was videoed in the hotel lobby passing it to her father's lab assistant.

Toby checked his phone for any new text messages. 'There is another person, we are concerned about. Brad Hoffmann, he claims to work for CN News, he actually works for NASA. His real name is Philip Bradley Lewis.'

Harold was starting to worry. 'What must we do?'

'Nothing Harold, but I would rather Gwen and Catherine stay with Charlyyk at all times tomorrow... she must never be left alone with anyone, and I mean anyone.' Toby was being overcautious but he knew he would be letting

Bryn down if he didn't. 'It's not what I expected to happen Harold. So, it will be better to err on the side of caution, than to be not aware of trouble at all.'

Sgt Brodie and Cpl Smith enter the lounge. 'We have set up a table in the Marquee for dinner. So, when you are ready?'

The chatter from the girls could be heard as they entered the Marquee. Charlyyk with a bounce in her feet trying to get Harold to move faster. 'Come on Harold I'm hungry.' At the table, Charlyyk, could not wait. She kept lifting the lids of the tureens, each one releasing a different smell. She chose a chair nearest to the tureens with the most pleasing aromas.

Cpl Smith came in, carrying a silver platter, placing the tray on the table next to her, lifted the cover of a whole glazed salmon decorated with a mixture of vegetables, piped thick vegetable cream sauce. He took up a fish slice and put a portion on her plate with some Jersey potatoes tossed in butter and freshly picked mixed herbs. The look on Charlyyk's face. She was awestruck; she just sat there looking at her plate. Harold was a good cook but this was different, it was how it was being presented. Charlyyk's little purple tongue could not help but moist her lips, with expectations on how it would taste.

Since arriving here on Earth, food has been one of the high-lights Charlyyk has enjoyed, compared to what she would have eaten on her own planet. Where she would have to scavenged for, and to take what was going at the time. Now mealtime was a pleasure, not a bare necessity.

'What would miss like to drink?' The Corporal asked.

'Sparkling water with a splash of orange juice please.' She said slowly. Still taken, with the look of the food.

There was much conversation between the Colliers and the Army personnel, that were all eating together. When the main course had finished, Sgt Brodie cleared the tables. Cpl Smith brought in another silver platter and again placed it beside Charlyyk, her eyes so wide they sparkled. Cpl Smith deliberately removed the cover slowly revealing a chocolate cheesecake. Charlyyk's purple tongue once again came out to moistened her lips, as Cpl Smith served a healthy portion.

Sgt Brodie placed a cheese platter, with crackers and a fruit bowl on the table. While Toby pulled the cork on a bottle of vintage port. Gwen and Catherine sat with a cafétiere of coffee.

Toby looked at the vibrating phone in his hand. He left his chair, heads towards the entrance door of the cottage. When he returned, Helen Bennett was with him. 'Sergeant, I hope you haven't eaten everything?' Helen's voice had a sense of humour to it.

'No Ma'am, come and help yourself.'

They went to the kitchen. Ten minutes later Sgt Brodie returned carrying a tray. Helen sat with Bryn and Toby; they discussed the events of the day, while Helen ate. Helen also brought Toby up to date on what was happening.

'NASA has confirmed Brad's credentials, have apologised for any misunderstanding it may have caused...I had sent a Home Office letter asking them to explain why an employee of theirs entered the UK on false documents? A direct approach did the job.' Helen sat back in her chair looking pleased.

Cpl Smith had produced a game of Connect Four and was being well beaten, by a smiling Charlyyk. She had made a new friend.

Later Catherine called over to Charlyyk. 'Come on young Lady, big day tomorrow. This is so you can be recognised as a real person.'

Charlyyk understood that by making her existence official, how it would give her a chance to go to school. Bryn had made sure that the situation was discussed, in her presence. This was to give Charlyyk, the knowledge how democratic human beings could be.

Harold and Gwen, could now bid them all farewell.

Bryn checked everyone was okay, then turning to Helen. 'We have already put clean linen on the bed in the guest room for you Helen, please make yourself at home.' Then Bryn put pen to paper. 'This is the password for the Internet? Oh, the door left of the bed is the en-suite.' With that Bryn rose from his chair. 'Good night, everyone thanks for the effort you've put in today... well done.' As he left, the Army personnel all stood up, and saluted him.

Toby smiled, he acknowledged that the soldier had not left Bryn. He was a leader through and through, and that he encouraged good soldiers with respect. Sgt Wally Brodie had told them stories, and Capt. Collier stood out exactly as Sgt Brodie had described him.

**

Saturday morning started early at Six o'clock. The first to arrive were the cleaners, in two minibuses, Bryn showed the leader where to go, making them aware of the no go areas, with red door handle hangers.

Wally and Tom had already started work in the kitchen; instruction had been given that breakfast would be between seven and eight, the cleaners, must vacate the premises by 8:45 am.

Helen walked into the dining area, sat in the first seat she came to, her eyes glued to her iPad. Toby followed five minutes later. 'Seen Bryn?' Toby reached over checked the coffee pot; he poured a cup.

Without taking her eyes away from the screen. 'No... Can I have a cup?'

Ten minutes later, Bryn, Catherine, and Charlyyk came back from their run. Charlyyk hurrying to sit down, close to a large jug of water drinking a full glass without stopping.

Toby pointed his first and little finger at her. 'Hoody.'

Charlyyk removed her tracksuit top her sweatshirt was as dry as a bone, where has Bryn and Catherine's, were wet with sweat.

Charlyyk's bowl of muesli did not take long to finish. As she contemplated having another helping. Tom placed a plate down in front of her; her mouth opened slightly in anticipation of what delicacy he had for her. Egg Benedict, griddled Asparagus, with smoked salmon. 'Madam requires anything else?'

'No thank you, Tom.' Charlyyk was being spoilt, and she knew it. Her eyes glistened with the pleasure it was giving her.

When breakfast was over, everyone leaves to get themselves ready to meet the dignitaries that were going to assess Charlyyk's future.

Professor John Taylor arrived at eight-thirty. Helen was at the door to meet him; she showed him to the Study. Bryn met him there with a handshake.

'I have an apology to make to you Mr Collier.'

'And what makes you think that professor?'

Prof Taylor then explained to Bryn the opportunist way they had obtained the DNA sample. Then he wanted permission to use some equipment to perform a task that sends sound beams through the bone structure, to determine their strength capability without using any X-ray in case it could cause problems with Charlyyk. 'The reason I ask Mr Collier, is that no matches had been made to any other DNA materials known. My test had shown that Charlyyk's DNA was unique, the team became so excited that they all wanted to contributed to finding ways to test Charlyyk. The bone structure of fossils showed that it was the bones that changed in the Jurassic period, that allow birds to fly, so the bones of Charlyyk could be a starting point to find more about the alien species. The photo of Charlyyk's mouth shows how her teeth are arranged. She has six top and bottom incisors where we have four, she has no premolars, the bicuspids follow straight after the incisors.'

Bryn said hesitantly. 'As I know nothing about what you are trying to achieve here, I am leaving those decisions to Michel Henderson who has looked after Charlyyk from the beginning.'

They left the Study and met up with Helen and Toby.

Michel arrived later. Prof Taylor and Michel shook hands, then headed for the clinic.

All the other dignitaries started arriving by ten-o'clock, they were led through to the Marquee. Helen Bennett introduced herself, thanking them for taking the time to resolve this delicate problem for the Collier family and the Government.

Helen then explained the reasoning the Home Secretary needed their help. 'Ladies and Gentlemen, we are here to resolve the right legal procedure for Charlyyk to be accepted as a British Citizen. As there are no existing legal criteria for an alien, we need your guidance.' Helen looked around for any sign, that anyone had issues with what she was asking. 'I have divided you into three groups, Legal, medical and ethical.' She placed forms before each group. 'Your purpose is to fill the required elements, on each of these forms. This will be the primary Legal prerequisite for the Home Office to grant the necessary documents for Charlyyk, so that she can lead as normal life as possible in the United Kingdom.'

Helen's thoughts as she spoke, was when she was at the meeting with the scientist and security chiefs. 'What can we gain from this?' Charlyyk's welfare would be the after-thought when the attendees have worked out what they could gain first. Helen recalled how that felt. She had sensed how her parents had viewed her while they charted their careers in Law, she being the after-thought.

Helen invited Bryn to address the learned Dignitaries and give them good reason why Charlyyk should be allowed legal status.

Bryn knew how important this was, too be allowed to keep looking after Charlyyk. 'What has happened, neither of us can explain. Yet I believe without each other help, we would not be here today. I feel obligated to Charlyyk, and want her to gain legal status, so I may adopt her as my daughter.'

Charlyyk stepped forward to speak. 'I can only say that if you cannot reunite me with my people, you must consider that I have no choice but to live here on Earth. It would be a much-appreciated courtesy if you would allow me to live as normal life as possible.' Charlyyk had overheard Catherine talking with her husband Brent, on what the possibilities that were open to Charlyyk, and these words were a reflection on what Catherine had said.

Bryn did not expect Charlyyk to say this, but agreed with her. He had only seen the little girl, but this was different, Michel was right there were changes happening.

Helen now set up the teams to complete their task.

Catherine, Gwen, and Charlyyk went with Michel, Prof Taylor and the eminent Doctor Sir Edwin Stanton OBE, they headed for the clinic. As they settled themselves, Gwen suggested that first names would be most appropriate to allow Charlyyk not to get nervous. Michel's files on Charlyyk, spread out for Sir Stanton to see how Charlyyk had been tested since her arrival.

In the Marquee, the legal team consisted of Helen's parents. The Chief Lord Justice Sir Edward Bennett and Lady Elizabeth Bennett QC, along with the leader of the House of Lords, Lord Philip Jacobs QC.

On the opposite side of the Marquee, the ethical team consisting of Shelia Morgan MP, Shadow Equalities Minister. Javi Mirzapour, the human rights activist and Lady Janet Morris, the women rights campaigner.

'Charlyyk has rights, unless anyone can prove she is a threat to our civilisation, we must allow her to grow naturally.' Shelia Morgan looked sternly at each one to see what reaction there was.

Lady Janet agreed to Shelia's comments, yet still felt uneasy. 'How do we know; she is not a threat? has anyone done any tests?'

Javi Mirzapour, read aloud from the files that Michel had distributed. 'In the time Charlyyk has lived amongst us no unusual outbreaks of deceases of any description have occurred in this area. Now that tells me, Charlyyk has not carried any alien deceases to our planet. This might sound more logical than scientific, but would you not say that an animal in quarantine is kept under scrutiny over a period of time to test if it carries a threat. Two years is a very long time? I would say that she is no threat?'

Helen moving between these two groups as intermediary, listening to them. Now she said 'Maybe you should ask the medical team that same question, Miss Morris. Sir Edwin will have come to see if Charlyyk's medical condition is safe.'

Then after ninety minutes, the two professional teams joined. They debated each question, until there was nothing left to debate. The medical team put their observation forward, and this too was debated in a deliberate constructive manner.

Bryn and Helen watched together how it was all going. Helen would now and again touch Bryn's hand. The soft touches showed the debate was going well. Helens tender touches, were like a caring mother watching her child, do good. Bryn found them quite endearing.

Lord Jacobs still needed more information about Charlyyk, He looked up from the report of the findings of the medical team. 'Mr Henderson...Michel, you were here with Charlyyk, from the start. Your medical reports are well written. Sir Edwin endorses what you have detailed so precisely, could you describe how you look upon the changes in Charlyyk that have developed to present time?'

Michel was well aware of what he was being asked. 'When I saw Charlyyk for the first time, she was scared, that was understandable. She had trust in Bryn, Charlyyk seeing Bryn accepting me, allowed her to trust in myself. I put a quarantine in place around the cottage. No one was allowed to enter or leave including myself, this enabled me to maintain observation on her for three months. Charlyyk soon adapted. The Hobarts teaching her to talk, we heard more about how she existed on her planet. The changes have been normal very similar to how I would expect to see in the development as any human child. I obtain regular blood test and perform general inspection of her physical condition, mainly out of my own professional curiosity.'

Helen watched their reactions closely, as the three groups carried on debating the finer points, Nods were more frequent than the shaking of heads. Helen's smile showing how pleased she was.

Bryn as ever, kept a keen military observer's eye on everyone. The feedback he was receiving was good. Where Helen's reactions fascinated him, they were similar to his own, of a parent.

The aroma's coming from the kitchen were making poor Charlyyk hungry. Catherine, Gwen, and Harold took her for a walk down the country lane towards Parsons Farm, this was to take her mind off the thoughts of food. Sgt Brodie had given Gwen seven o'clock as the time to return for the evening meal.

The three groups gradually came together in agreement. Lord Philip Jacobs filled in the answers on the forms. With smiles, all around none broader than those on Helen and Bryn's faces.

Lady Janet, was still putting points over. 'We must try and help her to develop into a normal woman, we can see how Charlyyk dresses, how she has started to find what she likes living amongst us. She is no different than any other teenager.'

Lord Jacobs made his summary. 'We were set the task of declaring that Charlyyk is either entitled to have legal rights or not entitled. Helen Bennett has been given the task to supply the security that Charlyyk will require, and the Government have agreed with Miss Bennett terms and conditions that she has laid out to them. So, that Ladies and Gentlemen concludes our advice for the Government, to allow Charlyyk, British Nationalisation Papers.'

When given the nod, the army personnel came in, and in no time at all had set up the long table ready for the evening meal.

Toby was called to the observation vehicle as two unidentifiable cars had been spotted, trolling the area. A search of the databases could not match the registration plates to the vehicles. Checking all the information his team had given him. 'That means they are not the press, put a drone up with an inferred camera let's find where they are.'

Ten minutes later a small drone picks up the tale-tale signs in amongst trees between the Parsons farm and Ford's farm. Toby relays the information to Sgt Bailey, with a two-car team, arrests the drivers. The culprits were two 16-year-old cousins from a traveller's community, joyriding. With that taken care of, Toby decided to stay with his team for the rest of the night.

Everyone was seated around the dining table. Helen at one end between her parents, who faced each other across the table.

Helen had never been that close to her parents because of their careers. Helen had been brought up by various nannies, then had been sent to boarding schools, she had found it hard to connect with her parents. Being around the Collier family and their strong family life, was having a huge effect on her. She felt different inside. Talking to her mother now, there was warmth and affection in the way her mother had touched her hand.

Helen looked down the table at Bryn, who at that moment looked up, seeing her smile at him, then Helen pursed her lips. She had sent Bryn a kiss. Bryn smiled back with a nod.

Charlyyk was in her own mind. For all the attention, she was being given to her, just felt so unreal. If she was still living on her own planet, the attention would have been coming from some beast trying to devour her. How her life has turned around, placing the spoon of soup to her lips and tasting the mushroom and black truffle soup. Closed her eyes as she savoured the pleasure of life of living on Earth.

Bryn sat on the other end of the table either side of him, Sir Stanton and Lady Morris they were discussing the problems of today's teenagers, and how did they relate to Charlyyk's upbringing.

Bryn explained how his sister Gwen and her husband Harold had worked with Charlyyk. 'They used a lot of TV programmes. These were selected to show her how the people of her age group behaved. They discussed situation with her to see what she saw, and how she felt. Harold documenting the progress and any changes, so he and Gwen could make the right decisions in her education.'

The waiters cleared the table for the next course. Catherine, Gwen and Ms Morgan seated in the middle of the table, were enjoying Charlyyk's description of her favourite film *Frozen*. The excitement in her voice, brought tears of laughter from Shelia Morgan.

Charlyyk said, 'When the first flakes of snow fell, Bryn uncovered a red plastic sledge in the garage. We took it up to the top of the hill, the fun we had as we slid down to the bottom, then rushing back up the hill to repeat the fun. When Harold brought me the DVD of Frozen. The sleigh ride where Olaf separated and came back together, just brought back the fun we had in the snow.'

'What did you think of the snow Charlyyk?' Shelia Morgan asked with a glint in her eye.

'I rushed outside trying to catch the snowflakes. Then I began to feel the cold. Bryn made me come back inside the cottage, and sit by the fire till I was warm again. He found some of Catherine's old winter clothes. But the boots were too large. I had to put so many socks on to get them to fit. Still, my feet were warm, then what fun we had!'

Roast beef was being served for the main course. A rather nice Merlot that had been opened earlier, to allow to breath, were poured into clean glasses. Cpl Smith came in carrying a silver platter, placing it next to Charlyyk. When he removed the cover, there were herbed fish goujons, ratatouille parcels wrapped in a filo pastry, with a gherkin flavoured mayonnaise dip. Charlyyk could not wait to get tucked in. Lemon Tart or Eaton Mess followed the main course.

Helen's parents were the first to leave; she promised them that she would make more of an effort to see them. They departed with Lord Jacobs, along with Gwen and Harold, the last to leave Prof Taylor. He could not go until he had Michel's permission to help with the testing of Charlyyk.

Charlyyk said her thanks to them all for coming and waved goodbye. She was so tired, she said goodnight to Helen and Bryn, with a hug and a kiss, went to bed.

Helen sat with Bryn in the lounge, she in the armchair, Bryn on the sofa. 'I'm so pleased how it went today' Helen looked at Bryn with a thoughtful expression. 'Bryn! I have been placed in many difficult situations in my time. I have always been able to solve them. This was never a problem, actually it has been a pleasure; I believe it is going to change the way I'm going to lead my life from now on.'

Bryn had noticed an earlier change in her mood, remembering something that Toby had said how cold and distant she was, due to how she had been brought up as a child. But recollecting the blown kiss, she had sent him earlier, this was still very active in his mind. 'Why how do you feel Helen?'

'Warm... soft and warm.'

Bryn stood up, took one step towards her, held out his hands. She took hold of them, then he gently pulled her to her feet, put his arms around her and gently held her to him. When he released his grip, she stood still for a moment.

Helen looked deeply in to Bryn's eyes. 'I have never been as close to someone, like that before.' She did not look uncomfortable; she looked calm and relaxed. 'Thank you, Bryn... being with your family for even for just a brief time. has made me understand what family life really means. Which I have never known before.' Helen takes Bryn's face in her hands and kisses him on the lips. 'Night Bryn see you in the morning.'

Bryn did not know if he wanted to push his advances towards Helen, the kiss he felt had a softness to it that showed she wanted to kiss him. Bryn had not thought about looking for love. He had just gone along with the flow of events. But the kiss had moved him. Helen's tenderness had warm feelings to it.

Then Helen saying good night had left him unsure how he should respond, his immediate thoughts that he could only leave it as it was. 'Good night, Helen, sweet dreams.'

Bryn strolled around the house, turning off the lights, checking the doors. As he entered his bedroom, he noticed that Charlyyk was not in his bed.

**

Sunday morning Bryn could hear activity outside the house. As he went to slide out of bed, it soon became apparent to him, there was no Charlyyk. He pulled his trousers on, then in bare feet, he looked in on Catherine. Charlyyk was cuddling a pillow no sign of Catherine!

Closing the door very carefully, he went to Thomas's old room. There laying in Thomas's old bed was Catherine not asleep, looking directly at him, she waggled her fingers, placed them to her lips and blew him a kiss. He returned it.

When Bryn looked out of the garden door, the scene was a hive of activity. The Marquee was almost down. The mechanical arm of the mobile crane was swinging materials from the garden onto a parked army truck.

As soon as one of the soldiers sees Bryn, he approaches him. 'Captain, we will replace back all the kitchen appliance and equipment as we found them?'

'Corporal is Sgt Brodie about, could you let him know I would like to see him when it is convenient.'

'Yes, Sir.'

'Still playing at toy soldiers dad?' Bryn turned around when he heard

Catherine speak. She puts her arm into his. 'Come on. I'll let you make me a cup of tea.'

When Bryn and Catherine had settled in the lounge with their mugs of tea, he enquired, 'How did you achieve to get Charlyyk to sleep with a pillow?'

Catherine sipped her tea, looking over the mug at her father. 'I took the sweatshirt you wore on the run yesterday, slipped it over the pillow, then put the pillowslip over your sweaty shirt.'

Bryn's little laugh. 'So, she could sense my scent and think it was me... clever.'

They sat in silence, thinking what had past, these last few days. Catherine pointed the TV controller and switched on the TV. Breakfast News were discussing the event of the past week's events, and Charlyyk was on the agenda. Two groups were there to put their views over, for or against. Prof Patricia Linman was looking at how this was so good for space science. 'We can now focus how to reach out and find new horizons, where before we were hoping for some type of life, now we have proof of life.

The Rev O'Donnell, looked at it with a much different perspective. 'This abomination is the devils work, sent here by Satan himself. Mark my words no good will come by letting this thing loose on this Earth.'

Catherine switched channels, and much the same was being shown on others TV channels. One channel showed parents protesting outside their children's school. 'What is the Government going to do to protect our children, how can they allow this thing to wander around. We must stand up against them giving this alien any type of freedom, it should be locked up.' The Parents waving their fists trying to get as much impact on this as possible.

The camera showed other parents and their children carrying placards with anti-alien words, some not too polite, calling for Charlyyk to be interned. A simple drawn placard implying this group belonged to the flat Earth Society received angry reaction, but the lad did not back down. He just kept reminding them that science had proved these bigots wrong in the past and they should be looking towards the future. 'When this world become so over-populated, we might need these Aliens to assist us to survive.' He kept shouting at the protester.

Charlyyk drifted in settled herself between Cat and Bryn. She felt slightly uncomfortable watching what was being shown. 'Catherine, you said this might happen, I'm seeing angry parents, but the children don't appear to be too concerned. Why is that?'

Catherine put her arm around Charlyyk's shoulders and gave a gentle hug. 'Sweetheart look at the placards in the left-hand bottom corner there is a religious emblem. Those placards have been printed, so I would say pre-orchestrated. The children dragged along to emphasise their importance in the protest. These types of protest are quite common; Political parties, Trade Union, Religious Orders you can go on. They're using the platform of free speech... as they are entitled to do so.' Catherine smiled sweetly at Charlyyk. 'But this is why we are trying so hard to get you legally recognised, this will give you that same freedom to express yourself.'

Fifteen minutes later Sgt Brodie walks into the lounge. 'Ah! Bryn, sorry not to have come sooner, but there's been a lot of flooding up north. I've to set up a field kitchen ASAP!'

'Ok Wally, do what you have to do, we won't get in your way.'

The recognisable sound of a Chinook Helicopter could be heard approaching. 'That's my bus,' Sgt Brodie said, 'Cpl Smith coming as well,' Cpl Daley is remaining here to finish the cleaning up, and follow us when he is ready.'

The two men shake hands and give each other a man hug. 'You know where I am when the opportunity arises don't hesitate to make contact.'

Catherine gave Wally a hug and kiss. 'Take care of yourself, Wally.'

'You to Cat, give a big kiss to Amy for me, when you go home.'

Charlyyk hearing the Helicopter, came out of the lounge. 'Is Tom leaving? I would like to say goodbye.' Grabbing Bryn's hand, she dragged him towards the garden. As they make their way through the debris of the fallen Marquee in the garden, headed toward the garden gate which led out towards the field where the Chinook had landed.

Cpl Smith was handing his kit to Sgt Brodie who was kneeling inside the Chinook. When Wally saw, them he gestured to Tom.

Tom turned and walked towards them. He shook Bryn and Catherine's hands.

A handshake was not on Charlyyk's mind, but a hug and the longest kiss on his cheek she could give him. Then the Colliers watched the big flying beast take off. They headed back into the cottage where they donned their tracksuits and headed off for their morning run.

When they returned, the garden was completely clear. They came across Cpl Daley in the kitchen, loading freshly made filled baguettes, into cooler boxes and tea into vacuum flasks.

'Well done Corporal, good thinking.' Bryn said.

'Thanks, Captain, it's a long drive, we won't have time to stop, the men will need to keep their spirits up...Sir, I have heard many stories about you; it is an honour and pleasure to be able to meet the main man.'

Bryn, shifted awkwardly. 'It's the call of duty Corporal, we must always take the call, and do our best to do the right thing. Many civilian lives depend on us, all around the world.'

Cpl Daley stood to attention. Bryn nodded for him to stand down. Cpl Daly then opened the fridge door. 'Cpl Smith has made a Chocolate Cheesecake for Charlyyk.' Then Cpl Daly picks up the boxes and flasks of tea and heads for the exit.

'Good luck Corporal.' Bryn closes the door behind him, a heavy sigh escapes his lips, 'peace and quiet at last', then heads for his study.

As he entered his study, he notice's a letter with his name on it lying on the seat of his chair. He opens it,

Dear Bryn.

I have been called back to London, sorry not to be able to say goodbye personally.

And it looks like I won't be in England on Tuesday. My thanks, to you and your family for this wonderful weekend. I can only wish that we will meet again.

Helen X.'

Bryn dwelled on the final part of the letter, contemplating any possible hidden meaning. Then he realised there was none. Helen was saying how she felt. He puts the letter in a file, then tidies up the paperwork in front of him; he could hear the whistle of the kettle from the kitchen. He leaves the study and meets the girls in the kitchen. Charlyyk was tucking into a small bowl of Eaton mess. 'That's a stingy portion for you, Charlyyk?'

She gives a little chuckle. 'Don't want to spoil my appetite for dinner.'

Catherine passes a mug of tea to her father. We are expected at Auntie Gwen's, she said about six.'

Bryn sat in the chair next to Charlyyk and with the spoon he had stirred his tea with, attempted to get a little of her dessert.

'Get off! Get your own.' Charlyyk turned her back on Bryn to protect what little she had left. Bryn tickled her. She gave a screech of laughter and wriggled to get away, nearly falling off her chair. He pulled her to him. kissed her cheek.

Catherine watched her father play with Charlyyk. Memories came flooding back. When her father came home from his Army life, how he would play with her. Those days seemed long ago, yet only felt like yesterday. She remembered how sad her father was when her mother died. She thought, *look what this little alien girl as done for him.* That turned her mind to daughter Amy on the other side of the world. *'I must go home.'* She pondered, whether there was more she could do for her father. *'No, I must go home.'*

The three of them walk across the drive towards the double garage that Bryn had Edward Parson build when Thomas was eight. Behind the door to the right of the garage was where Charlyyk's favourite car was housed; a hand built 1990 Morgan four-seater sports; with wire spoked wheels and red leather seats. Bryn had given it to his wife as a fortieth birthday present. It was Catherine's favourite car also; so when ever she came home, she commandeered the car keys. Bryn became the unwilling backseat driver. 'Slow down. Not so fast. Brake-brake' But Catherine just ignored him. Charlyyk meanwhile urged Catherine to drive faster.

They approached Gwen and Harold Hobart's 1673, timber-framed house on the edge of the village green. It had blackened timbers, lime washed wattle and daubed panels, and a thatched roof. Just one of three such houses in the village. Nestled amongst old oaks and beech trees, now with climate change, the ash was becoming more prevalent. With it being an early Autumn and the leaves turning brown and gold, this showed England at its best.

The aged oak-planked door, opened. Gwen had been watching for them, stood there with outstretched arms to greet them. She was extra pleased to see Charlyyk wearing the dress that she had chosen for her. The Laura Ashley three-quarter sleeve, tiny red and pink flowered dress, with the ruffled white lace at the neck. Charlyyk hated it, but its pleased Gwen, and that was what mattered most to Charlyyk.

Catherine, was always encouraging Charlyyk to please her aunt. 'You need her as a friend Charlyyk, for Gwen is the nearest to a mum you will ever have.'

'Hi Auntie Gwen.' The hug and kiss they gave to each other, then Charlyyk spun around to show Gwen how the dress looked on her.

Entering the cottage spacious lounge, with its low timber ceiling, button-backed leather sofas and armchairs, and early Georgian walnut, mahogany and some oak Tudor furniture, gave it a natural, lived-in feel. Prominent were the photos of student classes. The images ranged across all the different years and schools the Hobarts had taught. They did not have children of their own. These photos were the nearest thing to having children.

The combined families moved through to where Harold was working in the kitchen. The greetings were lively. Gwen, Catherine and Charlyyk headed for the study, were soon setting up the computer to be able to speak to Brent and Amy after dinner.

Bryn enters the dining room, sees Michel sitting there reading from some papers. 'Hi, Michel.'

Michel looks up at Bryn. 'Bryn this is a report from Prof Taylor, on some of the tests we did, they are a fascinating read. There are some slight similarities to Charlyyk's blood as to the terrestrial cat. With time we might be able to make a synthetic blood substitute. against any emergencies cropping up. The other thing that he is testing is a substance in her blood that seems to be a self-healing agent.'

Bryn, nodded, then counting the places settings on the table. 'Harold who else is coming tonight?'

Harold was removing the meat from the oven to allow it to stand before carving then puts in the Yorkshire puddings. 'Wendy and Brian Bailey.'

'Will we have enough wine?'

'Brian only drinks Lager, and there's some in the fridge.' Harold goes through in his mind how many glasses to a bottle, how many would be drinking red, how many for white. But with a casual air to his reply. 'Bryn, we can always open another if required!'

Policewoman Sgt Wendy, and her husband arrived shortly after, went to the study. Brian Bailey soon had Charlyyk chuckling. As he describes his sons, George and Mace, they were similar ages to Charlyyk's own age. She was all ears; she could be meeting some new friends. With this in mind the little bite on her bottom lip and eager look in her eyes, showed she had Brian's full attention.

At dinner, Wendy warned. 'Bryn, I have been informed that your security screening has been in place for many years, but I have been asked by MI5 to be aware of any gatherings, in and around any of the villages. Reports of Anti-Alien groups being organised, have given them cause for concern. They stress its early days, but require everyone to be on their toes just in case. Toby has kept me up to date on how the electronic serveillence will operate and the extra monitors they have installed.'

Catherine said. 'We were aware this might happen, once we publicly announced Charlyyk to the world.'

'If you had let me know about Charlyyk earlier, we could have helped.'

Bryn had expected that remark from Wendy. 'Wend, the fewer people who knew, the more chance I could get my head around, what was to happen. You would have been severely reprimanded by your chiefs, if you had tried to help us keep this a secret. The family looked at that as a possibility. We could not let that happen.'

Wendy looked seriously at Bryn. 'You know I use to work for Helen, when I was in the army.'

'Yes, and you had childhood association with Toby. The photos he shown me ...Those were serious gangs in Manchester you hung around with.'

Harold's eyes were on Charlyyk, could see was listening to what was being said, she looked as if to be concerned. 'What do you make of it Charlyyk?'

Charlyyk's solemn look, showing her serious approach to the question. 'Catherine was clear that there could be those that would look at me as some kind of monster. The film industry, has made so many films portraying aliens as unpredictable and violent. Alien, Star Wars and the series of Star Trek, has shown that aliens, as both good and bad.' The news presenter showed their own feelings, not in words, but the facial language. They could not hide their true feelings. I need to let people see who I really am, and let them make their own minds up about me, not to be influenced by what other have to say, or not say. Do I look that much of a threat?'

Michel said thoughtfully. 'No, Charlyyk you are not a threat, I have the scientific proof that you carry no threats. But Cat is right, films don't cast a good light in your direction. I saw the same news this morning and those religious fanatics that fervently believe men were born in God's image, the Earth is flat and the Sun travels around the Earth and not that the Earth travels around the Sun. Unfortunately, they will always be with us.'

Gwen, looked at Michel contemptuously. 'I hope you are not referencing me with that statement?'

Michel winked, when he nodded to Charlyyk. 'Only if you believe the world, is flat Gwen.'

After dinner, the girls went to the study to speak to Amy and Brent on Skype. Catherine told Brent; she was flying back to Auckland. 'The plane departs Thursday evening.' She gave him the flight number, so he could make arrangements to collect her when she arrived.

Back in the dining room for coffee, Catherine tells everyone she was returning to Brent and Amy. Then turning towards her father. 'Dad you are going to be a granddad again!'

Bryn took his daughter in his arms and gave her a gentle cuddle, and many kisses. 'You don't have to be a too soft dad.' With that a big hug was in order, the rest gathered around to congratulate her. Charlyyk had an apprehensive look on her face.

Catherine gathered Charlyyk towards herself. 'You do not look happy Charlyyk!'

Charlyyk put her arms around Catherine looking up at her face, still with that concerned look. 'Will it hurt?'

Catherine cupping Charlyyk's face in her hands, gave her a kiss. 'Yes, but it's going to be a nice pain.'

The drive back to Oakleaves did not lack conversation. Charlyyk asked what was going to happen during the pregnancy, when Catherine explained the procedure Charlyyk looked more concerned, she was still asking questions walking into the cottage.

While Bryn put the car into the garage; Catherine took Charlyyk to the clinic to collect her mother's books on childbirth. This was Catherine chance to thank her for not letting anyone else know of her condition. Charlyyk knew Catherine was pregnant when she first arrived from New Zealand. It was not just Charlyyk's nose that could tell Catherine was carrying a child, but also her acute hearing of the two heartbeats. 'You are two.' She had said, Catherine at that time wanted it to be kept a secret as she hadn't told her husband.

The family went into the lounge together. Charlyyk sat between Bryn and Catherine as they opened the book, that will explain the growth of the baby in all the different stages of the pregnancy, programming for the labour pains, then the delivery. Charlyyk hugged Catherine, said 'I still think you're so brave.'

Catherine cuddled Charlyyk. 'It's mother nature Charlyyk, it is what she does to us, making us want to have more children, to have more it makes us forget the pain we had giving birth previously, so that we go on having more children. It's worth it for the joy we feel, seeing our baby for the first time. It's all in our gene's that how we evolved.' Catherine still convincing Charlyyk it was natural as they made their way to bed

***

The Monday morning weather was overcast with a stiff breeze. The leaves were falling from the trees. Autumn had come early due to the dry summer.

Though the sun was still warm, a cold wind coming down from the north had made the leaves turn early.

When Charlyyk first arrived, finding the right food for her was always going to be a problem. Bryn made porridge for her on one cold morning, it did not go as planned. Charlyyk's looks, as she sampled the first spoonful, then how she spat it out straight away, left him in no doubt how she thought it tasted. Bryn did not want to give up the idea of a warm breakfast so found in the larder a pot of jam and some honey, now Charlyyk likes it so much on cold mornings she makes the porridge herself. Bryn keeping an eye on the amount of honey Charlyyk tries to add.

Once breakfast had finished, the girls cleared away. Bryn collected the post and made some phone calls, then went in search of the girls, they were in Catherine's bedroom, with copies of Country Homes magazines, spread all over the bed. 'Hello, what's this then?'

Catherine gave Charlyyk a friendly push; where she fell on the bed laughing. 'We are making plans to turn my room into Charlyyk's room. But every time I suggest something, 'SHE' says YUCK.' The tickle Catherine gave Charlyyk was the fun they were having.

Bryn smiled at the girl's endeavour. 'We are going to the Home Office tomorrow, have you sorted out what you are wearing?' Bryn looks down at one of the magazines. 'They're a bit old fashion, don't you think?'

Catherine looks at Charlyyk. Who had placed her hands to her mouth to cover her giggling?

At ten minutes to ten the doorbell rang. Catherine answers the door, the 12-year-old son of Wendy and Brian Bailey was standing there. Catherine surprise at seeing Mace, as he was a lot younger the last time, she had seen him. 'Hello Mace, how are you?'

Mace now big for his age, looks more like his father, but his mannerism's more like his mother's. 'I'm fine Catherine, dad was telling me about Charlyyk, I thought it would be good to meet her.'

Catherine opens the door to allow him to enter without any hesitation, for she knew Charlyyk needed people of her own age around her. Now was as good as time, then never. 'Come in.'

As they walked into the lounge, Charlyyk appeared, she had heard a different sounding voice, her curiosity had proven too strong for her to ignore. 'Hello.'

Mace saw Charlyyk, held out his hand. 'Hello I'm Mace, my mum is Sgt Wendy.'

Charlyyk, notice that Mace did not react to their contact, his shake off the hand was firm and steady. The vibes he gave, were good vibes. With a gracious nod Charlyyk beckons Mace to sit on the sofa.

'Would you like something to drink Mace?' Catherine asks.

'Tea would be nice Catherine. Thanks.'

Charlyyk senses were in place putting Maces' scent and its characteristics into logical order. Nothing was missed. Before this James Parsons had been the youngest Earthling she had encountered. As she placed one young male in comparison with the other, she found there was not much difference between them.

Mace, was not shy and was soon talking to Charlyyk. 'My dad spoke about you, saying that you must need to meet others of your own age. There are only three of us, of our age in the village; with myself, there is my brother George and Sarah Martin.'

This was what Brian Baileys had related to her the night before, now Charlyyk could judge for herself, what going to school could mean to her. The smile on her face did not give her thoughts away, she had already put that scenario to her brain, no inner warning sirens had erupted she was safe.

At Eleven thirty, as Bryn passed the lounge, he heard Mace talking, he opened the door and walked in. 'Hello, Mace.'

Mace stood up. 'Hi, Mr Collier.'

'Not at school today, Mace?'

'No inset day, back tomorrow.'

'What's your school like?'

Mace made a slight raised hand gesture. 'It's one of these new Academies, lots of new facilities, and Mrs Landon the headmistress she's nice, easy to talk too. Excuse me, Mr Collier, would it be alright if Sarah Martin comes and meet Charlyyk. I know they'll will get on.'

Bryn looked at Charlyyk she was nodding in approval. She had listened to Mace talk about Sarah and liked the description he had given of her.

Bryn said 'Yes, why don't you both come on Saturday?'

Mace left before one, while Catherine and Bryn were rustling up some lunch. Charlyyk could not stop talking about him. She had picked up some new words. '*Bothered; wicked; awesome; smashed it,*' Catherine handed Charlyyk a plate of baked beans on toast for lunch. With the expectancy of meeting new friends, Charlyyk was in a buoyant mood, her bubbly banter had Catherine and Bryn laughing at the garbled way she was speaking, as if she was mimicking

Mace. As Charlyyk placed her dirty dishes in the dishwasher. 'I must watch X-factor on Saturday as it's awesome.' Then she was gone.

Catherine and Bryn just looked at one another. Bryn shook his head. 'I supposed it was going to happen at some stage.' He did not like the new music of today's youth; in his time, he had preferred big band jazz of Count Basie and Ted Heath, and trad jazz.

At five to three Toby arrives. 'Could have phoned Bryn, but with everything so quiet, I thought what the heck!'

As they sat at the kitchen table drinking tea, they discussed how they would travel to the meeting at the Home Office the next day. Toby leaned on the table. 'Bloody quiet in here!'

Bryn nodded. 'Yeah, the girls have gone up to Parsons Farm. Charlyyk is going to make Catherine's room hers, Jane Parsons is an interior designer. The Parsons combine building work, with the farm work.'

'Does that mean your problem with Charlyyk has been resolved?'

Bryn taps the table. 'Touch wood, I hope so!'

'Almost forgot I met Harold in the village. Gwen's not feeling well! Might not make it tomorrow? Could mean taking a car instead of the transporter.'

By the time the girls returned, Toby had already left. Their high-spirited chatter, and laughter was infectious, Bryn could not help laughing with them although he did not understand what the hell they were talking about. The girls had collected a Chinese takeaway on the way home, they had laid it out on the kitchen table. They could not help laughing at Charlyyk's facial expressions as she sampled the various dishes in front of them. All those she liked she pulled towards her, those she did not like, she pushed away. Her nose told her all she wanted to know.

Bryn inspecting the take-away containers. 'Have you checked the contents, that nothing will affect Charlyyk in any way?'

Catherine looks at her father with a stern face. 'Dad, do you think I'm silly and irresponsible, don't forget I have a daughter of my own. And yes, I checked with the girl, no red meat, she gave Charlyyk a Prawn to sample to make sure she knows how they tasted.'

Chapter 4

Home Office

Tuesday morning, Toby arrived with the Range Rover, one of his men as a driver; Harold had contacted them; Gwen was not up for the trip to London.

Bryn dressed in blazer and slacks, white shirt, regimental tie. Catherine in a rust red and white Karen Millen, striped fitted dress with her navy-blue blazer with the England Women Cricket Team emblem on the top pocket. A silver prancing cat brooch, presented to her by the Jaguar Car Company, pinned on her lapel. Her hair gathered loosely behind with a red ribbon. Charlyyk in black tightfitting trousers, royal blue blouse, loose-fitting white jacket, her favourite white tennis shoes. Her hair like Catherine's, loosely tied back, but with a royal blue ribbon.

The drive to the Home Office was going to be a new big adventure for Charlyyk she had never been to a large town, let alone a City like London. The Home Secretary wanted to make Charlyyk welcome and to give the News to her personally of her acceptance as a citizen of the United Kingdom. Her advisors had warned, that not all people would accept an Alien living amongst them. If she tried to keep this quite it could have serious repercussions. Criticism would be aimed at her decision, also at her department for not being transparent.

As they passed places of interest. Toby pointed them out and told Charlyyk their reasons of interest, or their history. Toby's driver had purposely turned off the M3 motorway at Guilford and travelled through the Country lanes, and villages so to see a close up of Windsor Castle, Charlyyk had seen pictures and some news coverage, the actual building looked magnificent.

On the M4 for the City, she gasped at London's immense size and the sheer mass of people walking the streets. The Range Rover eventually entered Queen Anne's Gate and pulled up outside the Home Office. The press was waiting. The doors of the car opened, Catherine and Bryn stepped out. Charlyyk slipped out behind Bryn on to the road, then stopped and acknowledge the crowd. Keeping close to Bryn as she could.

This situation was different, Charlyyk was not sure of herself. She had never encountered such a number of people before, the look on their faces, the vibes she felt told her to be careful. She saw placards bobbing above the heads of the crowd, what was written concerned her.

Toby was quick to usher them into the building; a very pretty woman of about 30, introduced herself as the Home Secretaries, Private secretary. 'Please follow me.' She led them into a nice room, where leather armchairs and sofas, were arranged in a square with coffee tables placed in front of them. 'Please make yourselves comfortable; the Home Secretary will be here shortly.'

The Home Secretary was as good as her assistant's word. After the introduction, they all sat down and the Home Secretary, in a nice relaxed manner. 'I put this to the Cabinet this morning; everyone was in agreement that all the right criteria have been met. As there were no reasons, not to proceed with issuing Charlyyk with Nationality papers and Passport. A Passport is being processed at this very moment for Charlyyk Collier. Congratulations!... Though I must say, there were concerns. A few leading Church leaders, with other ethical groups had made strong protest. We looked at all the evidence submitted with your application and the advice given by those that came to you on Saturday, the government have not overlooked any details, so we could judge it on its merits.'

The Collier's jubilation lasted many minutes. Catherine, hugging Charlyyk, giving her a big kiss. Cat, looking into her eyes. 'This means you are my sister!'

Charlyyk's grin pushed her cheeks out, she blurted. 'Can I call Bryn, Dad?'

Bryn fondly looking at Charlyyk, said 'You certainly can.'

After the emotional reactions had calmed down, the Home Secretary made a request that they meet the rest of her staff. TV News Cameras, recording the complete meeting. Charlyyk stepped forward and shook their hands, repeating to each one. 'Thank you, very much.'

Toby produced a bottle of sparkling wine so that Charlyyk could have a sip, they all raised their glasses and a toast was given to the Collier family.

The Home Office staff surrounded Charlyyk asking her many questions. What are her favourite foods, TV programs, and music? She spent time with them sometimes seriously but mostly laughing and giggling. After twenty minutes had passed, an assistant stepped forward, announced that the press was waiting.

The Home Secretary presented herself. 'Ladies and Gentleman of the Press: We the Government have granted British Citizenship to Charlyyk Collier. We would like to bring to your notice that all necessary precaution, were taken into account, all objection was looked at seriously.' The Home Secretary knowing that all of her advisors, had taken into account, that there could be more gains than losses in allowing Charlyyk some freedom to live amongst us.

The first reporter in the crowd, was called upon 'Tom Bradbury *ITV*

News; Mr Collier you stated that this was the intention you were seeking at the meeting the other week, could you let us know, what are your plans now that you have achieved this?'

Bryn composed himself. 'We as a family will now debate all the options that give Charlyyk the best chances in life. Finding a good school will no doubt be top of the agenda?'

'Nick Robinson *BBC News*, now that a passport will be issued does that mean Charlyyk could travel abroad soon?'

Catherine stepped forward to answer this question. 'As you know Nick, I live in Auckland, and my brother Thomas resides in New York, if security could be worked out no doubt travel could happen.'

Nick Robinson quickly replied. 'So, you are still concerned about security issues?'

'These are early days.' Bryn said. 'Charlyyk is still adjusting to her new surroundings; much work will be required to build her confidence, so to allow her to be able to take on such a venture.'

The Sun's Newspaper reporter with a wave of her hand got Bryn attention. 'Yes, Lynn.'

'The amount of correspondence we have received from our readers has been unprecedented, they want to know everything they can about Charlyyk, I believe all the other papers have had the same attention? When can we have the chance to interview Charlyyk on a one-to-one basis?'

It was Catherine's turn to answer. 'My Aunt Gwen and her husband Harold have been the ones to educate Charlyyk, as you can tell they have achieved so much in two years, they indicate that the next stage will be the integration of people of her own age group, to allow further progress in her development. This will be carefully monitored. If the press could be a little patient, to give her space, we will respect your interest in her.'

The Daily Mail reporter was next. 'Mr Collier to satisfy our readers would it be possible for maybe once a month we could be updated with Charlyyk's progress; like an in-depth interview possibly some photos?'

Bryn spoke with Catherine then turned towards the press. 'That sounds a sensible solution you the press give Charlyyk some space; we give your readers the chance to be updated?'

Jean Blyth, from the Glasgow-based *Daily Record*. 'Charlyyk, so many of our young readers, are asking, how do you find living in Britain?'

Charlyyk with a big, grin. 'I love it! A short while ago, I was trying to find food or being hunted as food! I have gone from that, to waking up going to the fridge for a meal. I have a soft, warm bed to sleep in, and not to worry that something horrible was trying to eat me while I slept.' She looked at Bryn and Catherine. 'Now, I have a real family and a future, which was not available from where I came from.'

Charlyyk had remembered Bryn advise give them something to write about you or they will make up stories.

'Thank you, Ladies and Gentlemen; our time is up.' The secretary then directs them back to the room where they were shown on their arrival. This gave the Home Secretary a chance to clarify their legal status with regards to Charlyyk.

The conversation in the car on the journey back home was jovial. Catherine teasing Charlyyk the big sister, little sister, family fun thing. Bryn was on the phone with Gwen keeping her informed of the day's proceedings when Bryn noticed they were heading in a different direction. Coming from the opposite direction a large lorry past them then cut across the road to block it. Toby was using a handheld communication device looked at Bryn?

'Three cars have followed us out of London all unidentifiable? We are heading down towards Winchester we will change course in about one mile, which will put us back on track.'

Fifteen minutes later, Toby, checking his communication device. 'Ten men detained, Eastern European.'

His short sentences, reflected how Bryn had trained him. *'When so much is going on keep your communication short and precise.'*

The drive to Oakleaves was quiet. Bryn and Toby went straight to the study. 'Do I need to worry here Toby?'

Toby still looking seriously at his communicator. 'No. Romanian rugby players, heading for Bath.' Toby showed Bryn the device. 'It's like a mobile phone it has no ringtone, just vibrates. It shows text and maps, and the anti-glare screen will not give your position away.'

Bryn reached up and opened a cupboard took out a bottle of Balvenie Caribbean and two glasses with a bottle of still water. He poured a shot into each glass. 'OK Toby, who are you playing with?'

Toby took his device pressed a button held it at arm's length, then turned a full circle, the screen was clear, he sat down, taking a sip of whisky. 'Bryn this device will also pick up any spying equipment.' Toby took a sip of the whisky, rolled it around his mouth. 'Bryn, do you remember Major Danny Walcott?'

Bryn, thought for a moment? 'Yes, Irish Guards'

Toby pulls out a photo. 'As you can see that's Danny on the left; He stumbled on evidence in Iraq that showed America and Russia had infiltrated

MI6. Helen was asked by the head of MI6 to set up a new department.' Toby still checking, his device. 'It took Helen four years, selecting the right personnel. But it was this device that made all the difference. We don't have an office of such; everything goes to a server somewhere. Each device is computer chipped to work only with the person it's issued to.'

Toby took another sip of whisky let it roll around the tongue.

Bryn just looked at him. 'Right, so who's running this operation?'

With a smirk, Toby said. 'MI5 of course, this is internal.'

Bryn, sensing that Toby was still holding back? 'And where do you fit into all of this?'

Toby stroked his moustache. 'I work for Helen!' From the stare Bryn gave him. Toby knew that he was not satisfied. 'Come now, you have signed the Official Secrets Act; it still affects you even though you're retired.'

'Toby, you are trying to show grandma, how to suck eggs.'

Toby now felt a little uncomfortable, he knew Bryn's involvement from his past work while serving in the SAS, and it had been Bryn who had trained him in the first place. 'Ok, I'm assigned officially to MI6, and unofficially to MI9. We do what has to be done. No records, we don't exist. MI9 was set up during the second world war. Their main purpose to invent aids that were like the James Bonds gadgets to assist agents, also for prisoners of war, escape parties. It was disbanded after the war. Helen believed if they the foreign countries got wind of the new department, they may think it was never disbanded and was still achieving the same ends.'

Bryn poured another shot into his glass. 'I'm fine with that.'

They relaxed in their chairs sipping at the whisky. Toby swirled the liquor around in his mouth. 'This is pleasant, yet unusual?... It has a sort of caramel flavour?'

'Matured in Rum barrels. Not Sherry Barrels.'

'Your securty surveillance system has been updated, to cover a two-mile circumference around the cottage, it will be managed twenty-four hrs, a day at the local Police Station. Just one little thing...could we tag Charlyyk. I feel that when she attends school at some stage, it could be something we should consider. Schools are not what I would say as having the best security?'

Bryn nodded. 'I'll talk to Michel about it.'

***

The morning found Bryn looking out of the kitchen window. Catherine was showing Charlyyk how to gather up the leaves. Overnight a stiff breeze had developed and blown many leaves off the trees. Although the sun was warm the breeze still had a chill to it. They had made a bonfire, which fascinated Charlyyk. She had never seen fire before she came to Earth. She liked the warmth of it, but did not like the smoke. She would stand there for hours watching how it flickered. In a way it was like her eyes. For they changed colour like the flames that flickered from the fire. Taarlyyk and Maarlyyk two of her group she lived with could speak with her, in the colour change of their eyes. The look she gave the flame was how she missed her two dead companions.

Catherine was enjoying Charlyyk's company. Bryn joined them; for tomorrow evening Catherine was going home. He was undoubtedly going to miss her.

'Have you packed?' He asked her.

'Yes, in one way I don't want to go, I'm so missing Amy and Brent Dad. Also, cricket season will start in November, I will need to be there for the build-up. I'm signed up to cover it.' Catherine, so enjoyed cricket, so much this to her was a must-do. Brent and his mother Jo would follow her to the matches with Amy, so to keep the family together as a unit.

Catherine places an arm around Charlyyk's shoulders. 'How about lunch, beans on toast?'

Charlyyk with a massive grin. 'You bet.'

They make their way to the kitchen. As they ate their lunch, Catherine explains to her father, what she and Charlyyk had agreed with the Parsons, about the changes to Charlyyk's new bedroom. 'The Parsons are coming tonight with the Bailey's for the send-off. Gwen said she would be here too. I've ordered the food and wine online they are being delivered this afternoon.' The rest of the afternoon the two girls worked together preparing for the evening.

Since Catherine had come home. Bryn had noticed the way she had guided Charlyyk how to clean the house, and improve Charlyyk's cooking skills. Charlyyk was becoming neat and tidy. Compared to the turmoil of those early years, when Charlyyk's thoughts were keeping the bed clean and digging in the garden. When she was able to talk, would say. 'Must keep safe.'

The first guest to arrive were Wendy, Brian, Mace and George Bailey. Charlyyk quickly pulled the two brothers to the kitchen where the food was laid out. George two years older than Mace, could not wait to demonstrate the latest app on his new tablet.

When the doorbell rang, everyone know that the next visitors had arrived. Michel was standing there with Edward and Jane Parsons with their son

James now in his twenties: Fair hair, six-foot, broadly built due to the work he did on the farm.

Catherine greeted them with hugs and many kisses, as they entered the lounge, Charlyyk came rushing in. James picked her up by the waist, held to the ceiling, tickling her at the same time 'Hello twinkle.'

Charlyyk wiggled and squealed with laughter. When James let her down, Charlyyk gave him a big hug and kissed him on the cheek. He went with her to find the Bailey boys. Then Gwen and Harold arrived with Toby.

Catherine held centre stage unwrapping presents and talking about babies with the other women. The men stood back, enjoying the food, drinks and of course a few jokes.

Mace, seeing James was well acquainted with Charlyyk already. 'James! How comes you knew about Charlyyk and we didn't?'

'You know I'm a great friend of Thomas, when Thomas came home to see how his father had survived, he confided with me about Charlyyk.'

Charlyyk Added. 'Thomas sat with me at first, then he would take me up to the farm to meet James, it got me away from the house. I shall never forget what James accomplished. He was the lynchpin that turned my life around, I could see a future for me, instead of being just a prisoner. Don't misunderstand me, I was still living a better life than where I was before, it was just a different restriction that I found myself living in.'

***

Thursday morning the security-tagged mailbag arrived. It came with some local letters. One in particular from the Council's Education Department, informing them that they could offer Miss Charlyyk Collier the choice of three schools to view at their convenience. Would they phone to arrange an appointment?

Charlyyk read the introduction to the letter. 'Miss Charlyyk Collier' The smile on Charlyyk's face spoke volumes, for this meant a great deal to her. The hope of meeting new friends in a different environment built up the feel of excitement inside her. Meeting Mace she could see how she could mould herself to behave as an earthling.

Catherine gave Charlyyk a hug 'Miss Charlyyk Collier...now there's a name that rolls of the tongue.'

Charlyyk, was happy, she had thought of all the possibilities, that it now offered her.

Bryn was most interest a letters from the Ministry of Defence. They asked him to be interviewed by members of the Armed Forces, as soon as possible?

Catherine, putting her arms around her father. 'I'll make some lunch; then I must get myself ready.' Over lunch, the three of them discussed the correspondence they had received.

At three o'clock, Toby arrived driving a Mercedes transporter. Gwen and Harold, were his passengers. After loading Catherine's suitcases into the back, the Collier's seated for the journey to Heathrow. The drive was noisy, as so much was wanted to be said to Catherine before she left them.

They pulled up outside of departures. Toby places a special sticker on the windscreen, that gave him security clearance. The airport security police already know who to contact if there were any issues.

Bryn unloads the suitcases with Harold's help. Charlyyk pulled the hood of her tracksuit over her head, and positions herself between Catherine and Gwen. She had done this before and it had worked--nobody had spotted her.

Catherine drops her luggage at the check-in desk. They make their way to the departure lounge. The farewells brought tears with the hugs. Catherine gave Charlyyk an extra hug that made her hood drop down. A Japanese family passing by noticed her, quickly surrounded her with their I-phones taking as many photos as they could. Charlyyk did not try to hide she joined in with the excitement. Walking back to the Mercedes, she did not ignore those that wanted to see her, but smiled and waved. But still there was those that shied back. Charlyyk registered them with a nod and another smile, trying to win them around. She knew it could be important to do so.

***

Friday morning was tranquil, knowing Catherine had gone home, it gave Bryn and Charlyyk thinking time. They did not speak to each other, a nod or raised eye was all they could muster. An empty feeling now lingered, knowing they were not going to see Catherine for some time.

Charlyyk spent the day clearing out Catherine's old room, sorting out what was to go and to stay. The Parsons are going to start work on Monday, preparing for the changes that the girls had agreed on. The men were going to move the larger heavy things.

Bryn spent the day in his study, sorting out the correspondence and making numerous telephone calls. At mid-day, Charlyyk made him a sandwich and a cup of tea for his lunch. She did not disturb him when she cleaned the house. The smell of cooking brought Bryn into the kitchen; it was late in the afternoon. He found Charlyyk beavering away, a saucepan with an Italian tomato and basil sauce simmering on the hob, she was trying to fill a large pan with water.

'Let me do that.' Bryn filled the saucepan and placed it on the hob for her.

'Thanks, Dad' As Charlyyk tossed some salt into the water. Opening the cupboard, she reached up and found the pasta.

While they ate, they watched *ITV's Southern Meridian News*. The newsreader, was giving out the local news. 'Charlyyk, the Alien girl, was spotted at Heathrow last night to the curiosity of air passengers and members of the airport staff.' Video recordings were shown, witnesses were interviewed.

An elderly couple seeing some family members off, described how slim she was, yet so sweet and polite. The elderly man remarking. 'She was not what I was expecting to see at all, with the way people have described her. I thought, well she is not a different to many of the teenagers strolling around our street today. With their coloured hair and facial studs.'

The national news just repeated the same coverage, with added mixed reaction from some witnesses. One family were very out spoken. The father angerly said, 'We have enough immigrants in this Country already, this has to be given a lot of thought. We should put a stop to it.'

Charlyyk seeing the look Bryn gave her; she smiled back at him. 'Well as Catherine said last night, people will have to get to know me if I'm going to attend school, or go shopping.'

Bryn gave a sigh. 'I do worry.'

Charlyyk picked up the dirty plates. 'At the press meeting you said you can't wrap me up in cotton wool forever, so why don't we make those changes starting from now?'

She put the dirty plates in the dishwasher, picked up some bowls, putting in some ice cream. She gave Bryn his bowl including a spoon, sat down with him.

Bryn was seeing the changes in Charlyyk, she had become more assertive. 'For someone so young as you; you certainly have an old head on your shoulders.'

Charlyyk's hands went to her face. 'Is this one of the changes Michel said would happen to me?'

Bryn laughed out loud. 'No, it means that you have a wise mind, then one would expect for someone so young.'

Charlyyk stopped and pondered. 'Dad we must share the load between us. You are not as young as Catherine. I've watched you, now and again you having to stop to take a breath. The runs in the morning we must keep doing, if at any-time you find a shorter run is necessary, if it is only for one day, you must let me know.'

Bryn reached out to her. 'One moment you are a little girl, now you are like Catherine. How come?'

'There are just the two us, when others are around, I can enjoy being that little girl. When it is just you and me, I have you and you have me to care for each other. I must share the load, do my bit towards us. Dad we need each other this is just the beginning for me, but I don't want it to be the end of you.'

The look Charlyyk gave Bryn told him, Charlyyk was adapting to the circumstances that she was finding herself in. Then like a Chameleon, changing its colour to blend into the surroundings.

Bryn was not troubled with those thoughts, to what Charlyyk had said. He had noticed how Charlyyk adapted to different people in different ways before, though it had not been so noticeable before. The way she had behaved in that Cavern on that damn planet, she had helped him then to survive. His thoughts now, could see her better than he had been able to see her before, the look of pride he was showing, was how Charlyyk was behaving towards himself. A daughter not just in name, but if he had given birth to.

Charlyyk was reading Bryn's eyes, sensing his feeling towards her clenched his hand, just that little bit tighter. Looking down into their hands, then back up to meet Bryn's eyes. 'Dad, I still have a long way to go, many more people to win around, I would like some more time being that little girl. Like Gwen and Harold how they treat me, is how they want to see me.'

'Don't you see yourself as a young girl?'

'Since I've been here, I know I'm growing...but into what? There were no older Lyyk's to take examples from where I came from. I feel these strange behaviour patterns developing within me, that my brain is not sure of the images that flicker inside of it. This tells me there is more I should know; but where do I find the answers?'

***

On Saturday morning, although the sun was warm, that chill wind was still blowing, when Mace, George, and Sarah arrived, Charlyyk welcomed them in.

A very enthusiastic Sarah takes hold of Charlyyk's hand. 'Mace has told me so much about you, when I saw you on the television, I wish it could have been sooner.'

Sarah was a slim girl with a fascinating long pale face, black hair cut in a bob. With her jaunty walk, it bounced up and down, her eyebrows like two thick brush strokes, she liked bright, vibrant colours, which she matched together well. Sarah was a brainy girl, with good sense of humour, Charlyyk liked her a lot.

They went up to Catherine's old room, which Charlyyk had been helping to clear. The boys moved the more substantial items out into Thomas old bedroom. Where they had found a 1980's cassette player and lots of new wave recordings. They were soon dancing to Duran Duran, with a lot of laughter.

At one o'clock. Bryn knocks on the door then pokes his head through. 'Anyone for pizza?'

As they sat around the kitchen table, the conversation, was loud and vibrant. Bryn sipped a coffee and enjoyed their company. His phone vibrated a text message from Catherine *'Leaving Singapore, next stop home. Lv U x.'*

Charlyyk seeing the message, blew him a kiss. She was enjoying the new friends. The way they talked and ate at the same time was amusing, the earnest expressive way putting their point over, was captivating, if this is what school was going to be like, it was exciting her.

After they had finished eating, the conversation turned to Charlyyk going to school. Sarah had the most to say. 'When we first heard about Charlyyk it was all the girls talked about. We were blown away by the way she looked on the television broadcast. The girls are going to flip when I tell them I've actually met her.'

Mace said the boys did not show much interest. 'I did not bother to tell them I had met Charlyyk, I only told you, Sarah.'

George was quiet one, said in a relaxed manner 'Mum and Dad told us about Charlyyk, I did not know what to say? Until Mace visited her on his own. That's when I had to see her for myself. Dad described Charlyyk as being more human than Alien. Mace said that Charlyyk had a couple of issues, but the rest of her was all right'

Charlyyk smiling at the mention of a couple of issues, waved her hands. 'What like these George?'

George nodded. 'And your ears, the way they move'

Sarah, gave George a shove. 'There is nothing wrong there George, at least Charlyyk doesn't exhale flames from her mouth, have horns protruding out of her head, she just has some fingers missing. Even Peter at school can waggle his ears.

Charlyyk loving the conversation aimed at her. 'George are not your hands clumsy, with all those fingers?'

Mace burst out laughing. 'Well said Charlyyk.'

When they were about to leave, Sarah held Charlyyk's hands. 'I live across from your Aunt Gwen. My Mum and Dad would love to meet you, so if you are interested, knock on our door?'

Charlyyk looked at Bryn, who nodded his approval. 'I would like that very much.'

With hugs and kisses, they said their goodbyes.

Bryn had enjoyed the meeting of these teenagers, he was worried at first, but his fears were short-lived as they all seemed to get on well with each other. Mace and Sarah were old friends from their early childhood, what showed was how Mace held the group together, although they were all loud at first, Mace was the one that contained it to a reasonable level. If this is how it was going to be, he could tolerate that. Bryn did not remember much about Catherine and Thomas's teenage years, as he was always away with the army. Bryn could only accept that he would have to allow Charlyyk to blend in, and learn from the other teens.

***

The morning was dry, with a warm sun, with a chill breeze. Bryn and Charlyyk were out for their run; this was what Charlyyk liked most of all that Sunday morning feeling, The ringing of church bells from the village; rabbits scurrying about, the odd fox, with a few pheasants, that scurried about the fields and hedgerows. Then after the run, a hot shower, dressing in fresh, clean clothes then sitting down to a relaxed breakfast, with time to talk.

Bryn asked, 'Charlyyk have you any preferences about school?'

'I think it would be wise, to go with Sarah and the boys. Then I would be with people I know, who could help me settle into a new environment.'

'Yes, that good thinking, I had been thinking down those same lines myself.'

'Mace said a school minibus comes and collects them, returns them after school. Riding the minibus that should help me to integrate with other student from this area.'

Later over dinner. Charlyyk told Harold and Gwen of the meeting previous day with the Bailey's and Sarah; so much more about Sarah. Gwen listened very carefully. 'How about after dinner, we go over to see them, it's just the other side of the village green. A lovely family the Martins.'

Harold remarked, 'Jim, Sarah's dad will love you. He's a real Sci-Fi buff, his wife Liza used to be a make-up artist on film sets. Has worked on the cast of *Star Wars*.'

The five-minute walk across the village green, brought them to a half-timbered, mock Tudor house that Harold said had been built in 1930. The prospect of more new people to meet and, best of all, meeting Sarah again was exhilarating for Charlyyk.

Harold pulled the chain to the old antiquated doorbell. The iron-studded, oak door opened; Charlyyk could hardly control herself, stood behind Gwen.

Standing there was Liza Martin, Sarah's Mother. 'Harold, Gwen, how lovely to see you.' Then from behind Gwen, she saw Charlyyk. 'Sarah.' She called out, 'Come quickly!'

The sound of heavy footsteps coming down the stairs, then Sarah's face appearing from behind her mother.

'Charlyyk.'

Sarah did not expect such a prompt visit from Charlyyk. rushed towards Charlyyk, grabbing her arm. Sarah enthusiasm, made the two families smile.

Liza beckoned them all in.

Jim Martin hearing the commotion, came into the hall. 'Hi Harold, Gwen. Wow, who have we here then.'

Jim thrust his hand out to Charlyyk. 'Sarah has not stopped talking about you since she came home yesterday.'

Charlyyk shook his hand. 'Pleased to meet you, Mr Martin.'

Jim could not wait to ask questions. Even while Liza showed them into the lounge. 'What was is it like on your planet Charlyyk?'

Charlyyk paused before she replied. 'We lived in holes, which we had dug with our bare hands, as deep as possible. For there were beast that preyed on us, that would try and dig us out, their sole intention was to eat us. We lived in small groups, so we were harder to detect.'

These memories gave Charlyyk's sleepless nights. She had nightmares about going to bed, then ending up back on that planet, with beasts, chasing her. Those nights, she clung to Bryn for protection from those night terrors.

Jim did not think that it would be like that; he had a more romantic view of life on alien planets.

Charlyyk replied, 'You could say we lived our lives, like rabbits or Meerkats!'

Liza leant forward. 'So how do you find, living on this planet?'

Charlyyk smiled. 'It is like dreaming of all the nice things, you could ever dream about, then waking up finding it has actually happened.' Once more Charlyyk pauses, reflecting on what she previously had said. 'I once lived with a group; now I have a family.' Tears showed in Charlyyk's eyes. 'Where I cuddled up for warmth, now I cuddle up with love, what more could I ask for?'

Sarah put her arm around Charlyyk. 'Come and see my room.' The girls left the lounge and headed upstairs to Sarah's special place, where Sarah could be Sarah.

Liza and Gwen went to the kitchen to talk freely. Gwen wanted to know how other people saw Charlyyk. Liza was not a stay-at-home mum, her work on film sets had her seeing life, from a different perspective. 'Jim and I have always spoken openly to Sarah about life, that not everything, is what you might seem it to be. She must accept that other people, can be different, not to take people on face value only, to look for the inner person.'

Jim sitting with Bryn and Harold in the Lounge, was still slightly bemused by what Charlyyk had said earlier. 'Bryn, I was not expecting to hear that, I was hoping for a more hi-tech view of another world.'

Bryn responded. 'That Ok. Charlyyk will have to get used to questions like that. Charlyyk knows that she has come from nothing, a desolate, arid planet with no prospect for her, only just to stay alive. Now she lives here amid lush green grass, birds and flying insects that did not exist where she had come from.'

Harold more interested in how Charlyyk would respond to these questioners. 'I thought she handled it very well. This gives me an idea how she will react when she is allowed to go to school.'

Bryn remarked. 'I have had a letter from the councils education department, suggesting three schools for Charlyyk. I have spoken to her about it. She would like to go with Sarah and Mace. Any thoughts?'

Jim replied. 'We are very pleased with Sarah's progress where she is now, the group of girls are a nice mix, that complement each other, I think Charlyyk will fit in quite nicely Mrs Landon the Headmistress has a firm, fair approach to teaching, she prefers debating in groups, the standard is much towards a grammar school education.'

Sarah's room was small and cosy; with posters on the walls. A giant teddy bear on the bed. A computer desk equipped with a printer sat in the corner. Her prized possession was her built-in closet, where her treasured clothes were. 'What do you think?'

With a smile on Charlyyk's face. 'Love it.' Seeing what Catherine had said about her den.

Sarah turned on her computer. When it had warmed up, she pressed a few keys. 'Wake up Jan.'

The screen changed. A blonde, frizzy-haired girl appeared. Sarah said excitedly. 'Jan, meet Charlyyk.'

Jan's eyes widened. 'Wow, is she real?'

Charlyyk waved at the screen. 'Hello, Jan, nice to see you.'

Jan just flipped, falling backwards onto her bed laughing. Jan's mother hearing the squeals, entered the bedroom. Her daughter pointed at the screen. The woman turned, stared at the screen. 'Oh my God, she really does exist.'

When the girls met the others, in the lounge for their tea, they could not resist relating to Jan and her mother's reaction to seeing Charlyyk.

Chapter 5

The Assessment

Monday morning as the students of the Alderbrook Academy were arriving, many girls gathered at the bus stop. The frizzy blonde Jan was in the middle of them, gesticulating. As the village school bus arrived, the crowd converged on it. Sarah, Mace, and George surrounded my schoolmates trying to find out if what Jan had been telling them was true.

The robust matronly figure of Mrs Butler the Maths Mistress, with the rakishly lean looking Mr Waverly the Science Master, pushed their way through the crowd, kept repeating. 'Make your way to your appropriate form rooms. Please.'

Mrs Butler reached Sarah and the Bailey boys. 'You three, stay where you are.'

The crowd soon dispersed when Mrs Landon the Headmistress arrived on the scene. 'Is there a problem here Mrs Butler?'

Mrs Butler looked at the three students in front of her. 'Is there a problem here?' She asked them.

But before they could answer. Jan had come back to explain. She had felt guilty that she could have got her friends into trouble. 'Mrs Landon, it was all my fault, I'm so sorry.'

Mrs Landon, decided her office would be the best place to sort out why this had happened. She guided them into her office. 'Right let us start from the beginning.'

Sarah explained what had taken place at her house, mentioned the Hobarts. The Headmistress responded, 'Would that be Gwen and Harold Hobart by any chance?'

'Yes, they are our next-door neighbours.'

'Ok, back to your lessons, no further action is required, thank you for your time.'

After the students had left, Mrs Landon reached for her handbag. She pulled out a small notebook. Rifling through the pages she picks up the telephone receiver and dialled. 'Harold Hobart? This is Louise Landon, hello, long-time, yes, I would like to meet up with you, this is about Charlyyk. Tomorrow will be fine, seven, great. See you then.'

Harold phoned Bryn to relay the message from Mrs Landon.

***

On Tuesday, at six-o'clock in the evening Bryn and Charlyyk arrived at Carpenters Cottage. Charlyyk went into the kitchen with Gwen, to talk while they waited, for Mrs Landon's to arrive. Gwen telling Charlyyk of her experiences with Louise Landon, at the different schools that they had worked together.

Mrs Landon arrived on time; Harold welcomes her in. Then he introduces Bryn. 'Louise, this is my brother-in-law Bryn Collier.'

After the handshakes, they sat down in the lounge. Gwen came through from the kitchen with a tray in her hands, close behind was Charlyyk, peering around Gwen's back. Gwen smiled 'Hello Louise, may I introduce you to Charlyyk.'

Louise Landon shakes Charlyyk's hand. 'I'm so pleased to meet you Charlyyk. I'm no different than everyone else, I would like to get to know all about you.'

Louise explained the disturbance that had occurred at the Academy on Monday morning. She foresaw problems, if Charlyyk just turned up to attend school. 'Mr Collier, if you are interested in sending Charlyyk to our Academy, I would like set a paper for Charlyyk, just so that we can access her. Could we do that here, say Saturday?'

Bryn agreed with a nod.

Harold had a proposal. 'May I ask you, Louise, could it be possible, when you've accessed Charlyyk that we invite the whole of her year, to spend a day with Charlyyk before she attends school. We have noticed some objections in the national news, that some parents have been voicing strong feeling against Charlyyk attending school.'

The look on Louise's face showed her approval. 'Yes Harold, I have seen the same volume of dissent. I will send a letter to all parents for their views. I can see the merit in your request. We cannot expect parent to just except that an alien would just turn up unexpectedly. I will put it to the teacher's tomorrow and will be in touch on the outcome.'

Louise moved to one end of the sofa. 'Charlyyk, please come and sit with me.' Charlyyk sat tentatively at the other end. Louise did not want Charlyyk to be frightened of her. 'If all goes well and you are able to attend Alderbrook. This will be a big milestone for our school, I want it to be a gentle transition for us all; there could be a few hiccups along the way; I would like us to be able to face them together.'

Charlyyk had listened very carefully to what had been said by everyone. She had the ability to sense, good or bad vibes, it was her way of being able to judge Mrs Landon, by how Louise reacted towards her. It had always served her well; those vibes were telling Charlyyk she could trust Mrs Landon.

'I spoke with Sarah and Mace about when they first attended your school. The first week they felt apprehensive, but after the second week it felt like home to them.' Charlyyk's eyes changed to a soft blue, 'I would be most happy if I could share the same experience.'

Louise smiled. 'Charlyyk, I have seen you on the television, read about you in the newspapers, meeting you tonight I see a very charming well-spoken young lady, who in my opinion will be a great asset to us all, I'm looking forward to seeing how you develop in the coming years?'

On the drive home, Louise could not stop thinking about Charlyyk. As soon as she arrived home, Louise asked her husband, 'If there were going to be problems, where do you think they will come from?'

'Parents...overprotective parents cause the most pain to heads of schools. One, maybe two, will look at Charlyyk and see a Dinosaur, big or small? Will depending on their imagination.'

***

With the morning run over, Charlyyk checked on the progress the Parsons were making in her room. All the walls had been stripped; the rubbing down of the paintwork was well on schedule. James in T-shirt and coveralls with a Filter Spec Respiratory protector pulled up, sitting on top of his head. Was drinking from a water bottle, was listening to his mother Jane explaining to Charlyyk what she was proposing to do.

Charlyyk looked well impressed with what was being achieved. 'Is this all for me?'

James looking pleased. 'The Carpenter is coming tomorrow to install the fitted wardrobes.'

When Bryn poked his head through the doorway. Jane acknowledges Bryn. 'Catherine mentioned you might do something about Thomas's old room Bryn?'

'Yes, I can see some sleep over's happening.' Charlyyk gave Bryn a puzzled look. Bryn smiled 'You no doubt will make friends, you might ask them to come and stay over one night. That is what's called a sleepover.'

Sitting around the kitchen table at mid-day having lunch Jane, James and Bryn, were talking about Charlyyk going to school when the telephone began to ring. Bryn did not look surprised when the caller revealed herself as the secretary to the Chief Constable at Scotland Yard. 'Mr Collier due to a mix up on dates, we have two Policemen from Canada and Russia arriving tomorrow wanting to speak with you. What day would it be possible for you to meet with them?'

Bryn saw no problems. 'Tomorrow, I'll be there, let's say, Ten am.'

Chapter 6

Scotland Yard

Thursday morning Bryn walks into Scotland Yard. At the reception desk. 'Hello, I'm Bryn Collier, to see Superintendent Standing.'

The receptionist pressed a button and spoke into a speaker. 'Mr Collier is here to see you, Sir.'

A young policeman escorted Bryn through the building, 'They are waiting for you, Mr Collier.' As he opened a door.

'Ah… Mr Collier welcome, sorry for the short notice, it was due to a misunderstanding on my part, I somehow miss read the request that was sent to me, had no way to alter their arrival dates, when I realised my mistake. Let me introduce you to Capt. Todd Turner of the Canadian Police, Capt. Victor Tolmoski of the Russian Police.'

Bryn acknowledges them with a handshake. 'How can I help you, gentlemen?'

Capt. Turner spoke first. 'Ten years ago, a man reported that a beam of light vaporised his wife. He was tried for her murder, is now serving time in Prison. What we would like to know is, if what happened to you, could be related to his case?'

Capt. Tolmoski nodded his head. 'We have something similar to that story. A young man witnessed his father walking towards him when a bright light took him away; there was no evidence of foul play the authorities put him in an asylum, we too would like to know the truth?'

A young lady was introduced as a translator, taking down Bryn story. Bryn read it and confirmed it was accurate then signed the statement. The translator then copied them into Russian and French. Both Officers agreeing, they were in order.

Capt. Tolmoski, a serious type of man, explained the interest of the Russian people in the coverage of Charlyyk's story. 'It has been quite intense, due to longstanding interest with the Russian space program that has been a forerunner in the Worlds Space Race. Now that there is proof of life beyond our solar system. there is a great enthusiasm to see what the considerable amount of our investment, will bring us.'

Capt. Turner nodded. 'We are finding many incidents in our old records of beams of lights, mostly classified under UFO's. As we could not confirm if they were true or false. We could not find any evidence at any of the sites where the light beam had been reported, had even occurred. The protest warranted scrutiny. We took some incidents very seriously when a whole Indian tribe were up in arms and threatened reprisals if the authorities did not cease causing them. The Canadian Government built an observatory, manned it for two years, teaching members of the tribe to be able to carry out the research.'

After the Scotland Yard meeting. Bryn caught the train home. Arriving at Carpenters Cottage at five. Where Charlyyk was eager to tell him about her day. Harold and Gwen had taken her to the local Marks & Spencer's, where they had tea in the Café. Many of the patrons had shown some interest in Charlyyk. The very young mums and toddlers gave most attention. With some toddlers had touched Charlyyk's hands, with much fascination. Their mum's, wanting to take photos of their children with her.

Charlyyk was more aware that there were some shoppers, that had moved away from her purposely. 'Dad I noticed the difference in each person's reaction towards me, a few looked frightened, some looked disgusted. Yet there was many that just looked curiously towards me, not knowing what to make of me.'

'The store manager gave us a guided tour.' Gwen said. 'Charlyyk had chosen a winter's coat. When we went to pay, he would not let us, but presented Charlyyk with a bunch of flowers.'

Charlyyk showed Bryn the flowers. 'They do smell nice dad."

Bryn looked at the pink roses. 'Be careful of the thorns darling, they have a tendency of pricking?'

Charlyyk showed Bryn her finger. 'Too late.' She said, replacing the flowers back. She fetched the coat, putting it on, to show Bryn. A duffle coat with a hood, that was made of a waterproofed woollen material. 'It's for when I go to school.'

Over dinner, Bryn explained the reason for the trip to London. Gwen and Harold showed their concerns for two innocent people punished for something they had not done. Harold with some concern in his voice. 'Come to think of its Bryn, how would you have explained yourself if not for Charlyyk?'

'I don't think I could have, if it had just been me, I would have just kept quiet, without proof you are open to abuse. To be honest, I still have problems coming to terms with it even now, if not for Charlyyk, I would have thought it had all been a dream.'

Charlyyk had listened to Bryn. 'If you had not been there at that moment, nor would I be here, and that is what sometimes I wake up in a cold fever, shivering with that thought. If you had not been there to have saved me.' Charlyyk looked down at her hands. The tell-tale sign of them trembling was obvious.

Gwen reached over and placed her hand into Charlyyk's hands, she needed not to say anything as the look in Gwen's eyes said everything to Charlyyk, those eyes that relayed her thanks back to Gwen.

Charlyyk could not understand all that had happened, it concerned her deeply, how at that precise moment Bryn had come to her rescue. A fraction of a moment later, she would have been the beast evening meal. She had felt the tug on her arm from the beast, then nothing as Bryn had found the beast most vulnerable point. Charlyyk kept asking herself, why was Bryn there? She knew why she was there, but why Bryn. It did not make sense, though she was so relieved he had been.

Chapter 7

Visit from the Military

Bryn was finding the early morning run a bit heavy. Charlyyk kept urging him on. 'Do we need to have taken a shorter route she inquired?' The weather had changed it was much warmer, Bryn was noticing the effects.

'No Charlyyk, I've started to show my age.' he laughed.

Arriving back at Oakleaves as usual at the rear of the cottage. Charlyyk rushed through to the bathroom to shower.

Bryn stopped when he heard voices coming from the lounge. As he entered two army officers stood up. One of them was Danny Walcott. He was an old army chum of Bryn's. 'Hi Bryn, excuse us for taking the liberty of coming in, I remembered you have an open-door hospitality, may I introduce you to Major Alan Carter, Army Intelligence's.'

Bryn shook his hand. 'Pleased to meet you Major, Ok Danny what's all this about then?'

Danny Walcott sat down. 'We were passing by, when I remembered you lived nearby so here, we are.'

Bryn sniggered. 'Danny, you have never done spontaneous in your whole life, so why start now?'

Major Carter opened his briefcase, then took out a folder. 'The defence department, NATO and some of the foreign military, have asked permission to brief you on you unexpected journey.'

He showed Bryn the dossier, a list of possible dates. 'There are some big names on this list Bryn, some of them I never thought would ever venture to come together to solve one single issue?' Major Carter allowed Bryn to keep the copy of the dossier.

Charlyyk entered the lounge. Bryn introduce her. 'Gentlemen, this is my new daughter Charlyyk.'

Danny Walcott offered his hand to her.

'I have heard Toby mention you, once or twice.,' She remarked to him.

Danny still holding her hand said, 'Toby told me so much about you, that I had to come and see you for myself?' Then he raised her hand and kissed the back of it.

'Oh Major, Toby told me you were a lady-killer, for a moment I thought you were going to eat my hand!'

Major Carter stepped forward and offered his hand. 'Pleased to meet you, don't be afraid...I'm vegetarian.'

'May I get you something to drink?' Charlyyk asked them.

The three all wanted coffee, then she left them, and headed for the kitchen.

'Capt. Collier'... Major Carter began.

Bryn raised his hand. 'No formalities, Bryn will be okay.'

'All right Bryn, when you sent in your report of what had taken place, HQ had to shake their heads over what you had described, we have your full military history to warrant our knowledge of your integrity not to exaggerate on what had taken place. The video you enclosed of Charlyyk, were repeatedly examined. Now with this in their minds, these high-ranking officers, are concerned that these alien forces could attack us, what chance could we have to protect ourselves?'

Bryn replied bluntly. 'Not a lot.'

By the look on his face, these words were not what Major Carter wanted to hear. 'I hope you're wrong?' He knew what Bryn had said was more likely nearer to the truth than he liked. 'I think you are right Bryn, as you stood no chance to do anything about it when it happened. What chance would others have to respond.'

Bryn had thought about that many times. 'Alan...Danny, let me be honest with you. I don't know what happened, or why it happened. It is something that I have racked my brains over many times, for if Charlyyk had not been there, you would have never have heard a word about it. I would have been so embarrassed to even mentioned it to anybody. It did happen, Charlyyk is the proof of it. These needs explaining, not by myself, because I have no idea how it could have happened in the first place.'

Charlyyk came back into the lounge carrying a tray, with a jug of coffee, cups, with a plate of biscuits. Major Danny Walcott chirped. 'You have her well trained!'

Charlyyk was quick to reply. 'Busy hands, stops you having an idle mind... You came to speak with my dad, not with me. It would have been rude of me not to have offered you both refreshments.'

Charlyyk had not liked the comment that the Major had said about her. She did not feel like a pet that was taught tricks. This was something that James had spoken to her, when she was at the farm, and he explained about how he had trained, his Welsh Collie to help him, herd the sheep.

The officers watch Charlyyk leave the room, then looked straight at Bryn.

Bryn replied. 'It's an aphorism in her translation, of a saying they had on her planet. Another one she says. To slacken; is to be eaten.' Bryn had picked up on Charlyyk's sensitive feelings on how they had thought she was a pet, and not a person. Bryn did feel, the officers warranted an explanation.

Then he explains to them about the meeting he had with the two police officers, on the fate of the two wretched souls who could not make the authorities understand what they had witnessed. 'What we must not do, is to act in haste by clutching at thin air, it needs level headed thinking. The Aliens have the upper hand on this, if we act without any set plan, they the Aliens would know they are more intelligent than us. We must presume that their capabilities with this light force of theirs, have us at a disadvantage. But it's been two years, they have not acted against us. With all these reports of light beam incidences that have occurred over many years, at this moment it does not make any sense at all, why they have not shown themselves?'

Major Walcott stated. 'Bryn, we have read through your reports on what you believe happened. Our best analysist, have dissected the information in order to ask the right questions from you and Charlyyk. Your comments that it happened, so fast not to be able to give us any more detail. We can say we understand what you are saying. We are drawing up some sort of plan how to tackle this and have asked America, Russia and China to share the intelligence on this.'

Then Danny turned to Major Alan Carter. 'Alan, I think we should call it a day, we should return back to HQ. Bryn, as usual, you have put your comments so succinctly, you have made us aware, of what is at stake here.'

Taking the possible dates for a future meeting, Bryn promised to let them know when it could happen. Major Carter, shaking Bryn's hand. 'The sooner, the better!'

Major Walcott, added 'Let's keep in touch.'

Charlyyk opened and closed the doors to the new fitted wardrobes and pulled out the drawers. James could see the excitement in her eyes as she stood back, imagining how her clothes will look hanging there. When Charlyyk saw, Bryn standing by the door she rushed over to him, she wrapped her arms around him and gave him one great big enormous hug.

'Let me show you.' Dragged Bryn by his arm. 'Look at this.' She squealed, it was the tall mirrors that she so wanted to show him, standing there admiring her own reflection. There were two tall mirrors on the inside of the doors; Where Charlyyk was able to see a front and rear view at the same time, when the doors were fully opened.

James could not stop laughing. 'Charlyyk knows she has a tail, she has never seen it, like she has seen it now!'

When Bryn looks at Charlyyk little tail, it was wagging frantically like a tail on an excited puppy. Then Bryn had a good look at the work that James and his mum Jane were doing.

Jane Parsons, placed her hand on Charlyyk's back. 'I have the curtains; they are in the car, come and help me bring them in.'

They collected the package from Jane's car and brought them inside, where Jane unwraps them, shows the curtains to Charlyyk. The patterns were brightly coloured wildflowers, on a cornflower blue backdrop.

Charlyyk drooled over them. 'They are so lovely Jane, Thank you.'

Chapter 8

The Assessment

It was early Saturday morning, the air had a damp, chilly feel to it as they jogged across the fields, neither of them talking to each other. At breakfast Bryn mentions the lack of conversation. 'Are you worried about the test today?'

Looking up at Bryn. 'No, I was thinking about how going to school, will change our way of life?'

'I hope not Charlyyk; I really enjoy what we have going here. You have given my life a purpose, this is just the next stage, with you going to school. It will have some challenges; what kind of challenges, we will just have to wait to find out.'

'Uncle Harold, said that with many of their students, this shaped their thinking, with the friends they made, have helped to mould their characters. I have strange thoughts that come to me, that there is more to me than I know. Oblique images drift in and out, that make no sense. They don't slant in any one direction; showing me why they are there.'

Bryn watched Charlyyk's ears, with the colour changes in her eyes, knew Charlyyk was not worried just unsure of herself. He had noticed this behaviour in her, when something had occurred, that made no sense to her.

After breakfast Charlyyk made herself ready for the assessment. Bryn watched as Charlyyk now dressed started to mentally prepare the mind set she needed to fit the criteria she wanted Mrs Landon to see her as, not to young, not too old. Modelling herself to Sarah's age level, with that achieved, with a deep breath, said she was ready. 'Let's go dad.'

As they drove to the Hobart's 'Carpenters Cottage,' Bryn out of the blue said. 'Do you know...I'm thinking of selling my old Jensen and buying a more practical car, what do you think?'

The 1956 Jenson 541R, was Bryn's very first car. He had found it hard to sell, as it had been a big part of him growing up. Catherine had been the last one to drive it, knew how special it was to her father. She had relayed this to Charlyyk many times, as they had spent time cleaning the two cars.

Charlyyk liked it when Bryn asked her opinion; it made her feel important. 'Let's find how much we'll get for the Jensen first.' She was now brimming with self-esteem. 'Then we can enjoy going around the car showrooms looking at what we could buy.'

They arrived at Carpenter's Cottage, as usual Gwen watching from the window, waiting for them to arrive. Gwen opened the door to greet them. This had stemmed from the earlier days when the they would sneak Charlyyk in without anybody noticing. Now Gwen does it out of habit.

'Hi, Auntie Gwen.' Charlyyk embracing her auntie.

Harold had set out his study as a classroom. There was an old school desk in the centre of the room, a container for pens and pencils placed upon it, even a wooden chair matched the desk. 'This will be how you will find it, on a school exam day.'

When Louise Landon arrived, she remarked. 'This is a bit austere Harold, I'm just going to access her ability; we can do that in a much more relaxed manner than that, don't you think?' Then turning to Charlyyk. 'How about a nice cup of tea?'

They went into the kitchen with Gwen. As they made the tea, Louise talked with Charlyyk, mainly about herself. How did she find life, things in general in a friendly relaxed manner, this was to settle Charlyyk make her feel at ease? Then entering into the lounge, Louise wanted to be sure that Charlyyk was her usual self. 'Make yourself comfortable Charlyyk. I need you to be yourself, so don't worry. If you feel anxious just let me know, we will take a break'

Louise removes some items from her briefcase. She passes a book to Charlyyk. 'In your own time, could you read to me?'

Bryn and Harold stepped out of the cottage. 'I don't think. we will be needed here!' Harold remarked as they strolled around the garden, Bryn talked to Harold about selling the Jensen. Harold agreed with Bryn 'You don't drive it now, so how about we go now and see Bill Symonds he knows all the right people.'

The drive to Symonds garage was fun for Harold. He too loved the Morgan, he remembered when they went to the Morgan factory to order the car for Kitty's birthday, after Gwen had remarked, what Kit had said to her on a retail therapy day, that they shared together.

As they pulled into the garage, a collection of 1930s workshops to the left of the forecourt, an office in the centre, the large showroom to the right, they could see Bill Symonds giving some keys to an elderly chap, sitting in a vintage 1955 red, open top MG sports tourer.

Bill hailed them. 'Bryn, Harold what a pleasure, what can I do for you?' He showed them to his Office. 'Step in guys, take a seat... coffee?'

Coffee in hand, Bryn informs Bill of his idea of selling the Jensen. 'Can you wait for two months?' Bill asked. 'There's an antique car auction being set up, I'll speak to Charley Ross the auctioneer I know him well, I'll get him to place it in the auction at the right time.'

Bill reached for his phone, made a call to Charley Ross, had to leave a message. 'Can I suggest bringing the Jensen here for a check-up, I bet you have not driven it for some time... I'll get Ted Adams work his magic on it.'

By the time Bryn and Harold returned to the Cottage, Louise, Gwen and Charlyyk were in deep conversation. Sitting in the dining room eating lunch, Louise remarked on how well Charlyyk had done. 'She will fit in nicely to the year, for your assessment of her age group fits her well, Harold,'

Louise Landon promised Bryn that she will send written report to him to give to the Education Department. Once he had notified the Education Department of his choice of school, she would then inform all the parents in a letter. Then the students in Charlyyk's year, would be invited to meet her at a weekend, before her first day at school. This was Harold's suggestion to allow more of the students to meet Charlyyk and get to know her prior to going to school.

***

Sunday's weather, cold and very wet. The two runners were working hard to keep their feet from slipping on the muddy track, soaked to the skin it did not deter them from pushing harder. When they finally reached the cottage, Bryn urged Charlyyk to get out of the wet clothes and to have a hot bath.

She was soaking in the bath when Bryn came in with a hot drink, and some more towels putting them on the heated towel rail.

'This will warm you inside' With that, he went to his own bathroom, to take a bath for himself.

Charlyyk soon had drifted into her thoughts, the memories of her own home planet where the temperature was the same all the time due to the many worlds that sat close by. The reflected light from them warmed her planet, warm during the light period, freezing during the dark period; when they slept, the group would cuddle together for warmth. The memories of group members; Taarlyyk, Taar meaning small, Lyyk meaning female, and Maarlyyk, Maar meaning gentle, kind. Then of the Naamnaam shrub, whose leaves they would chew, then spit into their hands, then rub onto their body to take their scent away, so that the beast who hunted them could not detect their scent; when they went in search of food. Digging a hole, putting the broad leaves of the Cruul tree at the bottom of the pit then cover the hole with more leaves, leaving it till after the dark period, and the light time began; to collect the moisture that dropped down onto the bottom leaves.

The demands of survival, did she miss them? No, not at all!... Just her friends.

Strange visions would flash through her mind. Little flickers from another time or place were there, then they were gone. She got up and put on her bathrobe, then went to the guest bedroom where she had been sleeping while her bedroom was being decorated, the paint fumes had been affecting her nose and her eyes.

As she sat at the dressing table drying her hair. Bryn came in. 'Do you need anything Charlyyk?' He asked.

'Yes please, dad -- could you help me dry my hair?'

Bryn, put the hair dryer plug into the socket, brushed as he dried her hair. Although Bryn had strong hands, he was quite gentle with her. He liked the way she called him dad; it made him aware of his obligations to her. His thoughts as he brushed, although at the time he was just trying to survive, there had been no thought of them ever to return together, though as it turned out, he would not have survived without her. This was the bond that they now shared between them, both respecting what each one had done for each other. Bryn looking at Charlyyk's reflection in the dressing table mirror, Bryn could see Charlyyk's contented look beaming back at him.

Once her hair was dry, Bryn left the room to allow her to dress, every Sunday they went to Gwen and Harold's for dinner. To please Gwen. Charlyyk wore the Laura Ashley dress. Though Charlyyk disliked the dress, wearing it meant she could wear the silk underwear Catherine had given her, which she loved the feel off. When she was dressed, she found Bryn in the lounge, 'Come on dad, let's go to dinner.'

It was a very relaxed dinner, Charlyyk loved the banter among Harold, Michel and Bryn as they told tales of when they were young. This was now what she had come accustom to, this gave her a sense of belonging. Especially when they brought her into the discussions; because the talk was of everyday things that exist here and now. This was Bryn's idea to try and engage her into the everyday life on Earth's situations, by involvement.

They had learnt to try and keep away from Politics and Religion, as Charlyyk's logical thinking could cause friction. Gwen's strong religious beliefs made her upset with Charlyyk's dismissal of faith. For Charlyyk it had no rationale. 'Why would anybody believe in asking for help from someone that does not exist, that bordered on insanity.' Yet Gwen, who Charlyyk greatly admired, certainly did believe in this so called, God. This so infuriated Charlyyk to think Gwen could be so gullible, would retort. 'Gwen needs to look at the true picture and see sense.'

***

On Monday, Gwen arrived at ten with the shopping list for Charlyyk's school uniform, Alderbrook was Charlyyk's choice. There were no other School that Charlyyk wanted to attend. The drive to Fosters the official school outfitters for Alderbrook, did not take long. Gwen parked her car in the municipal car park; the short walk took longer than expected, due to shoppers wanting to see what this alien really looked like that had been occupying the news.

In the outfitter's, the staff fussed about making sure every item of School uniform fitted with some growing room: blazer, skirts, blouses, jumpers, ties, a hat, then PE Shorts, T-Shirts, plimsolls, socks the list was extensive but necessary. Bryn could not believe the amount of clothes he had just purchased, then to think when she grows; she will need the same again.

Gwen took Bryn's arm. 'We have not finished, the stationer next!'

They put the clothes in Bryn's car, then head for the stationers, again many local shopper's stop to look at them, then with without any warning one middle aged man stepped forward and spat at Charlyyk.

Bryn's anger bubbled up, made a move towards the man. Charlyyk quickly stepped in Bryn's way. Charlyyk looking at the man, smiled gently with a nod, 'Sorry if I offended you.' Charlyyk knew it was not going to help their cause to be confrontational, it would help their cause to remain calm, showing her passive side to her nature. Then Charlyyk speaking to those that had witnessed the incident, 'I hope he does not believe I would harm him in any way?'

Chapter 9

Freelance Writer

Wednesday found Charlyyk sorting out her clothes. Bryn spent much of his time on the telephone. He had promised the press to keep them informed on Charlyyk's progress. The Editor of 'The *Sunday Mail Magazine*' asked could they send a freelance writer to spend a week with Charlyyk. The writer was a talented girl who he thought, could fit in with Charlyyk very well.

'Mr Collier, the Government have been in touch with the Press Council, they do not want to see a Media Scrum associated with Charlyyk. They have asked for some restraint on how we cover the story. I've spoken with other Newspapers Editors, Janet Stokes has written articles for most of the Media, we have all agreed to use her material on this story. If you can supply us with enough material to keep our readers happy, that could be satisfactory to all our needs, we will assist with the Governments instructions.'

Bryn agreed on meeting with Ms Stokes. Though he suspected, he had no real choice; it was agreement or chaos.

***

At midday on Thursday, Bryn was at the front door talking to the post-lady, when a bright red Mini Cooper with a black and white chequered top, glided to a stop, on the pebble drive. A five foot six, petite young lady, in her late-twenties, with copper coloured hair, dressed in beautiful autumn-coloured clothes, got out of the car. 'Mr Collier... my name is Janet Stokes.' She held out her hand. 'I'm very pleased to have the opportunity to meet you.' She said to him, as she shook his hand.

Bryn welcomed Janet into the cottage, where Charlyyk was sitting in the lounge. 'Charlyyk this is Janet Stokes.' Janet and Charlyyk shook hands. Charlyyk observing Miss Stokes taking every vibe that she gave out, satisfied with the results she received, settled herself.

Janet placed a very large brown leather shoulder bag on the settee. She took out of her bag some magazines; she offered them to Bryn. 'These are some of my previous interviews; I thought you would like to see the type of work I do?

Janet's had studied video of the press conference, which had presented

Charlyyk as a nervous young girl, now seeing Charlyyk in her own environment, the nerves had gone she was more self-confident, even in the way she had welcomed her, she had total control and firm belief in herself. Bryn also showed that he had complete confidence with Charlyyk.

Janet professional approach was to get a clear understanding of who she was going to write about and what type of lead she will need to take. 'Each of my subjects has had a unique lifestyle, that I've tried to capture. Charlyyk is completely different, Charlyyk's is like a blank canvas. For she is someone, nobody knows anything about as of yet, so many will want to know. As each Editor, will want fresh insights about Charlyyk, I must be careful not to exaggerate Charlyyk's existence. This is what makes my work so enthralling, like unwrapping a present wondering what could be hidden in those layers.' Janet's eyes were ablaze with excitement.

Bryn flicked through the pages of the magazines, where Janet Stokes had placed markers. When Bryn was satisfied, 'When would you like to start?'

'I do not expect to start today, would like us all to get acquainted first, however, so we don't feel awkward and worry about saying the wrong things.' If possible, I would like to stay here for the duration of the project and share what I've written before I send articles out for publication?'

Bryn and Charlyyk exchanged looks, each expecting the other to say something. It was Janet that spoke. 'I'm here to tell the public about you: how you think, what you eat, how you see us. I would love to be able to even go with you to school, if the possibility arose. I also want to take lots of pictures, but I want to take it at a pace you find best. Don't let me push you?'

Charlyyk thought for a moment. 'I know we made a deal, that if the press gave us some space, we would keep them updated. I also understand what you are saying, for you to cover this story, we will have to be close, so for you to be able to capture the real me. Will that mean you will be with me all the time?'

'No Charlyyk, I would say a period of time together...then a break, will give me time to write the articles for all the various editors. You will have plenty of time to establish yourself and find new friends. I would like to observe you, but not interfere how you mature.'

Charlyyk looked at Bryn for guidance, 'What do you think Dad?'

'I think we either allow Janet exclusive coverage of your story, or the whole media will be wanting access.'

'May I come Saturday?' Janet asked. 'I have an interview with a lead singer in a very successful boyband, that would give me a full week to be with you.'

Bryn rose from his chair. 'Of course, come and look at where you will stay.'

He led the way to the guest room. Janet inspected the room. 'Could I see Charlyyk's room please?'

'Yes, certainly. This way.' Said Bryn.

Janet stopped at the doorway, looked around very carefully. 'Is there any chance of moving another bed in here?' She asked.

Charlyyk sat down on her bed, the look on her face said she was not happy. 'Why do you want to put another bed in here?' The terse tone of Charlyyk's voice making it clear to Bryn and Janet, that she was not happy. Her room had just been decorated for her needs, now Janet wanted to turn it all around. Charlyyk's ear movement, with the sagging of her shoulders, indicated the deflation of her mood.

Janet sat down beside her on the bed. 'I want to get to know you properly, for you to understand and gain your trust in me. That I must not make up a story about you, but to write about you. So, tell me what's bothering you?'

Charlyyk looked at Janet. 'It feels pushy?'

Janet did not take offence, just smiled at her. 'When I come to stay on Saturday, I will sleep in the guest room, until you get to know me better, would that suit you?' Janet took hold of her hand. 'I will gain a lot of exposure from this assignment. I want it for the right reasons, not the wrong ones. When you are older, I want you to say to me. 'Thank you... not. You bloody bastard'.'

Charlyyk's mouth dropped open. Catherine would use 'bloody bastard' when angry with someone, then humbly apologise, telling Charlyyk. 'Don't you repeat those words.'

Bryn understood what Janet was implying. 'Janet, I understand where you are going with this. I'm with you one hundred percent. You want to tell Charlyyk's story, to do this you need to see the situations that develop and to how she responds to them.'

Janet nodded, facing Charlyyk with a warm smile. 'Do you do housework?... cook?'

Charlyyk nodded. 'Yes of course I do, there are only two of us. It is only right for me to help, with my share of the chores.'

'Then we will do them together...We could go shopping for clothes, food, books even music; all these things will tell me so much about you. I won't be writing about everything you do, but what I want to write will be the real you! If I get this right, the press will get the story, you will have some freedom from their thirst to write anything about you... true or false.'

Charlyyk's apprehension was now gradually fading, a friendly smile had appeared on her face. When they returned to the lounge, Janet gathers up her bits and pieces. 'Thank you, Mr Collier, I appreciate what you are allowing me to do.'

Bryn shook her hand. 'If you are going to spend some time here, let's keep this informal, so please call me Bryn.'

Janet then turned to Charlyyk. 'I'm so looking forward, for us to be friends.'

Charlyyk shook Janet's hand. The mention of Janet being a friend, allowed Charlyyk to relax 'Yes, I would like us to be friends as well, see you on Saturday.'

***

On Friday morning. Bryn and Charlyyk sorted out Thomas's old room after their morning run. It contained boxes and boxes of clothes, books, and old toys, but most of all record albums and cassettes. They were stored in the garage for safe keeping. At the back of the wardrobe, a large sketchbook was found. When it was opened, many sketches of Bryn's late wife Kitty and Catherine at different ages in various poses.

Bryn sat on the bed looking through them, over and over again, one page in particular, with many sketches of Catherine with a rabbit, Bryn remembered it well, he was home recovering from an incident in Angola in 1997, something about a rescue mission due to the Halloween Massacre. Thomas was sitting close to him that day. Bryn eyes had been affected, due to the mortar shell blast that he had been caught in, was having to wear dark glasses, to protect his eyes from any glare.

He told Charlyyk, of those peaceful days, when they had nursed him, recovering from his injuries, none being life threatening, just needed time to get over them. Charlyyk had come to understand this man and his sense of duty. She felt pride him. He was her hero, her champion of champions.

The rest of the day Charlyyk cleaned the house, Bryn tidied the garden and carried out a few small repairs, in the evening they watched Audrey Hepburn in 'Breakfast at Tiffany's.' Charlyyk liked the song 'Moon River' but it was the clothes with the story, that she liked most. Charlyyk was beginning to understand these film represented Bryn's past life, The clothes, the music were of his youth.

Chapter 10

The BBQ

Saturday was hectic Mace, and Sarah arrives on their bikes, with news about the events of the week at school, with letters sent out to the parents. The expectation of those who will come to meet Charlyyk at her home, Mace gave Bryn a letter from Mrs Landon his Headmistress.

Janet Stokes arrived at ten past eleven. Charlyyk, Sarah, and Mace helped her to move her things to the guest room. Bryn ordered pizzas for lunch. Conversation over the meal was more about what happened at school. When at school assembly Mrs Landon announced that Charlyyk was going to attend their school.

Sarah and Mace were in high demand among the other students, to inform them what to expect when they meet Charlyyk. Sarah was determined to tell her school chums that Charlyyk was fun, and almost human, that Charlyyk's hands take a little time to adjust to, but after a while you take no notice of them.

Sarah and Mace left at three o'clock. Janet settled in, then walked with Charlyyk to the village. On the way, back home they walked arm-in-arm. They never stopped talking to each other.

When they reached the cottage, they found Bryn talking to Michel. Charlyyk introduces Janet to Michel, When Charlyyk asks Michel was there a reason for his visit. 'Just a little thing?' Michel said. 'Charlyyk when I did your last test, your blood pressure was a little low, not a lot to worry about. Looking back on your file I see a pattern forming, so I would like to do a test just to satisfy my curiosity?'

Janet listened in on this conversation. 'Can I be there?' she asked.

'Yes, of course, you can.' Michel did not mind, when he answered Janet.

Bryn was cooking dinner. 'Why don't you do it now; dinner will be ready in about twenty minutes.'

In the clinic, Michel carried out the test he required. He went through the details with Janet, to what he had tried to achieve with the test he had performed on Charlyyk. He showed the chart he had maintained with the pattern that was forming. 'She is going through a change Janet, we have no idea, how it is going to affect her, I'm hoping that the blood sample might give some clues?'

Janet with her journalistic trained brain, 'Michel why you, a Vet, is treating Charlyyk, not by a doctor?'

Michel did not flinch, just carried on doing what he had come to do. 'Don't all living creatures have a heart, lungs, kidneys, skin, bones and eyes. When Charlyyk first arrived, it was I that first inspected her. I know more about Charlyyk than anyone else, these tests I have been doing have not just been for Charlyyk's welfare, but for us all. What would have happened if Charlyyk had brought with her some unknown virus?' Michel's raised eyes, were now questioning Janet. 'So, I quarantined all who had been in contact with Charlyyk, including myself, here in this cottage till it was all safe. In that period Charlyyk and myself, got to know each other very well. The trust we formed was as good as a bonding between two equal souls. Since the meeting here, with the two renown medical Doctors, Professor Taylor has since joined me in the testing. I have faith in Charlyyk, for she has taken the test without question, understanding the importance they could do for her wellbeing?'

Janet observed the look Michel and Charlyyk gave each other, confirmed the understanding that they had with each other. Charlyyk's smile was soft and beguiling, her faith in Michel was showing through. Janet made mental notes on these reactions. This was Janet's pathway to understanding Charlyyk more. For how could she write about her unless she could understand the way Charlyyk was feeling, or the moral compass she followed. Then watching Charlyyk's movements as she dressed after Michel's test, were of someone relaxed and carefree. The glance Charlyyk gave at the graph that Michel was making showed her interest was as keen as Michel's in how she was progressing.

At dinner, Janet asked many questions, in between telling some fascinating stories, when Michel was about to leave, he said to Bryn. 'We weren't interviewed, we were interrogated?'

'Yes, she good. I'm looking forward to how the first transcript comes out?'

***

On Sunday morning, Janet was up early. She was going to throw her weight behind Charlyyk's story, by joining in with everything that Charlyyk was involved in. Kitted out in her running gear, she was ready.

The girls set a steady pace, with Bryn close behind. The fields had a low mist to them. Upon the hill, the air was clear. The green and emerging yellow, brown leaves on the trees gave a patchwork feel to the landscape. Just a few rabbits were seen scurrying here and there. The sound of church bells could be heard from the village as they passed the milking sheds, James Parsons gave them a wave. 'Hi, twinkle.' He called out to Charlyyk; She waved back and blew him a kiss.

'Who is that?' There was a knowing smirk on Janet's face 'He looks handsome?'

'That's James. He and his mother Jane, decorated my bedroom.'

Janet's eyes lit up. 'Good looking well developed and handy, *Wow.*'

All the time they were running, Janet would slip in question to Charlyyk with the Dictaphone on record, she was not going to miss any details.

Later the drive to Harold and Gwen's for dinner, all Bryn could hear was Janet pumping Charlyyk for information about James. Then Janet would slip another question about Charlyyk, 'So Charlyyk, if you did not wear clothes on your planet, was it hard to wear clothes here?'

Charlyyk needed no time to think. 'Wintertime, it is too cold not to wear clothes. Gwen did not like me running about naked, would talk abruptly towards me, at first, I did not know what was wrong, then Michel one day took off some of his clothes, in front of me, then quickly dressed again. He looked so funny with no clothes on, I realised what they were trying to tell me.' Charlyyk with a little laugh.

At Carpenters cottage, Gwen and the girls in the lounge, Harold, Michel, and Bryn were in the kitchen.

'When do you get the results from Charlyyk's blood samples Michel?' Bryn enquires.

'Wednesday late in the afternoon. Prof Taylor is working with me on this, so we can double check ourselves.'

Basting the meat Harold was speaking to Michel. 'You've done some more testing?'

'Yes, I'm interested in the changes she is going through, a pattern is evolving, I want to keep up with what happening to her, but let me emphasise to you, it is nothing to worry about, just my curiosity that I'm pleasing.'

Around the dinner table it was Gwen and Harold who questioned Janet, where had she been educated, what were her grades, how did she find Cambridge; the first job she had. Michel and Bryn enjoyed the cross-examined very much. Charlyyk had said nothing just listened. She wanted to know more about Janet and the vibes she gave were still good.

After dinner, Janet learnt more about Charlyyk. As the group settled down with coffees, the conversation relaxed. More was said then, then at any other time. For this is what Janet came for, not to dig dirt, but to discover the real girl in Charlyyk.

Harold directed Janet to his study where he showed her the first papers that Charlyyk had attempted when learning to write. 'You must understand she had never held a pencil before.'

Each sheet was dated. The progress Charlyyk made in the first three months was astounding, even for an 11-year-old girl. Janet had noticed how Charlyyk's name had been spelt on the first sheets, was different to the later papers. She pointed this out to Harold.

'We wrote her name as we thought it sounded, Later she explained how the group had called her; *Char* meaning quick and *lyyk,* meaning girl. We changed the spelling later to the double Y because as Charlyyk was reading a book on *Star Wars* universe, the planet that Chewbacca comes from. It had three Y's, she said the *eee* was too long, and that is why her name has two Y's.'

Maths was the next subject. Janet, was quick to notice Gwen's handwriting. 'So, Gwen taught her maths?'

'And history, her two chosen subjects.'

Seeing Charlyyk had advanced rapidly in those two subjects as well. 'She is no dimwit,' Janet noted.

Harold was quick to reply. 'No, Charlyyk can change very quickly from a little girl, too someone very mature. She is able to soak up what she needs, to be able to survive.'

'Should we need to worry about that Harold?'

'I don't think so. Charlyyk has shown us that she hates injustice. That alone should give us reasons not to worry.'

'How did that manifest itself?'

'When we read some of our classic novels to Charlyyk she reacted to some of the story lines. She would get so engrossed in the story. Without warning, she would rant against what she thought was a wrongdoing towards a character. Later we found her reading law books. If there is something Charlyyk does not understand, she will search hell and high water to find the meaning.'

***

The morning run, then a refreshing shower done, Monday was the time to set out the rest of the week Charlyyk with a bowl of muesli in front of her, confronted Bryn. 'Dad, you haven't told me what Mrs Landon wrote in her letter?'

'Sorry.' Bryn rose from the table and went to his study. He was soon back and placed the letter before her.

Charlyyk read it. 'Saturday that when they will come, then school on Monday, so it's all happening.'

Bryn smiled at her. 'How about a BBQ on Saturday?'

With a thoughtful, smile on her face. 'Dad that sounds fantastic, we could do burgers, veggie sausages and...and I'll think of something I've got until Thursday?'

Janet asked. 'Why Thursday?'

'We will have to order the food beforehand... won't we?'

Taking his dirty dishes to the dishwasher, Bryn said. 'I'll spend some time in the garden, to get it ready, I know the old BBQ needs some attention, we have not used it for a few years, with thirty plus teenagers, and some parents plus teachers... I'll start it today.'

Charlyyk and Janet started to clear up the rest of the breakfast things. That over, Charlyyk looks through the bookshelf for cookery books; she comes across '*Summer Cooking* by Elisabeth David' she pulls it out then takes it to the kitchen.

Janet sits down with her, and they check each recipe, in between the pages were Kits handwritten comments on dishes she had made. Janet observed Charlyyk, she could sense sadness in her. 'You, OK?'

'It's like Bryn's wife is talking to me.'

Janet began to read those pages. 'Oh yes. I see what you mean, she explains alternatives, and why, in such lovely detail.' Janet turned a couple of more pages reading Kits comments. 'I would love to have met her.'

As they went through the many recipes, a list started to take shape. Lunch was simple. During lunch, Bryn tells the girls he will have to build a new BBQ, as the old one would be too small. After lunch, Bryn takes the girls with him to the local builder's merchants, to orders up his requirements. They promised delivery for the next day, with no specific time.

On the way home Bryn stopped off at Parsons Farm, they would need some help with some garden furniture of some sort. 'Edward, could I borrow some of your folding tables for Saturday?'

'Yes, how many do you need Bryn?' Edward moves towards the sheds, inviting Bryn to follow. 'How about some straw bales for people to sit on?'

Charlyyk introduced Janet to Jane. Charlyyk told Jane about the upcoming event on Saturday, with how many would be coming, Jane invites them to go with her to the cow sheds. Where they will meet Josef a Polish Butcher. 'Joe, they have a BBQ on Saturday, about fifty guests.'

Joe had been looking at some livestock; he caters to some high-class restaurants, takes great care to what he selects. 'I'm very pleased to meet you.' He gave Charlyyk his card. 'You phone me, Thursday, I will personally deliver, by Friday night.'

Charlyyk thanked him then returned to find Bryn.

Janet was most despondent that James was not there, kept looking just in case he should turn up.

***

Bryn did not join the girls, on the next morning run. Instead dug the area to lay the base for the new BBQ, the delivery lorry arrived at ten fifteen. The truck had a lifting arm, so was able to drop the pallet over the garden wall, from the lane.

Harold and Gwen arrived later. Gwen checked the list that Charlyyk had prepared, 'How about half and half, of the pork and veggie sausages Charlyyk?'

'Yes, Auntie Gwen, the same with the burgers and veggie burgers? Along with chicken and Steak.'

'Ok, so the meat is sorted, what will you do for desserts?'

Charlyyk face lit up. 'Chocolate brownies, fairy cupcakes and strawberry trifle, also with raspberries and blackberries.' She did not stop for breath, so sure in what she liked.

'What about apple pie to go with it, we could also do, custard and cream?'

Janet sitting close by, making notes how Charlyyk's expression changed with the different question that was asked. How her hands moved and where she placed them; how her eyes turned colour when happy or in doubt, the movement of her ears. There was so much to this young lady, could Janet do her justice?

Harold being Harold, he soon had the kettle on. 'Tea everybody?'

Gwen had seen Janet writing away, positioned herself to see what Janet had written, Janet was already aware of it. Instead of covering her notebook she placed it so Gwen could read it. While Gwen read Janet's notes, Janet opened her laptop, punched in her password, opened 'Words' and clicked on 'Charlyyk Doc's,' then placed her computer in front of Gwen.

Gwen looked at Janet awkwardly.

'No, please Gwen I have nothing to hide.'

Gwen scrolled through the pages, then after five minutes. 'I like what you have written Janet, it's so like Charlyyk, also how she responds to certain situations and people.'

'I'm so pleased what you have said, this is how I like people to read about her... not someone from my imagination, but Charlyyk as a real person.'

Harold overhearing what they were saying was soon reading from the laptop. 'Well done Janet that lovely.'

Closing down her laptop, Janet went on to say. 'Those two articles could be in print this weekend, if you the family approve in what I've written so far. The next transcript will be sent for the magazine publication with pictures, then for general release. You can see how the transcript is written in blocks. This will allow the different editor to put their own take on it.'

Janet produced ten photos and placed them out on the table.

Gwen studied them. 'When did you take these, they are great.' Gwen had her attention to one particular photo of Charlyyk working on a project, total concentration written right across Charlyyk's face. Gwen's memory of Charlyyk in her earlier days on Earth.

Harold liked the other photo of Charlyyk looking out her bedroom window. The pensive look on her face as though she was waiting for something to happen. 'How did you get her to look like that?' Harold asked.

'We were talking about Charlyyk's own home planet, did she know where it was situated. Then I saw that look on her face, I just grabbed the camera, reeled off as many shots as I could. When I send them, I will include the story behind each picture, this allows the Editor his own personal touch.' Janet then picked up a small Leica digital camera, turned it on and showed them what she had taken that morning.

'I like this one.' Gwen looking at the camera's monitor. The image showed Charlyyk pondering over the list for the BBQ. She had a pencil in hand placed near her mouth. Her eyes looking up in deep thought. their colours stood out.

A photo of Charlyyk laughing, brought the biggest smile to Gwen's face; this revoked the way Charlyyk won Gwen over in those early days when she found it hard to understand what was happening to her family. As Charlyyk started to adjust to her new life, her sense of humour began to come out. Gwen began to warm to her. 'Will you send this one too?' Gwen asked.

Janet made no attempt to fudge her answer. 'No probably next time; just in case I don't get another decent picture to send them.' Janet paused for thought. 'I saw in your face that these photos hold a lot of memories for you. Would you tell me about them someday? I would love to hear about those early days. It couldn't have been easy on you.'

Gwen was in a reflective mood. 'I made it hard for Charlyyk. She worried me, I looked at her as a threat to my family.' Shame showed on her face, of those memories. 'I knew what I was doing was wrong, but found it so hard to correct. Then one-day Charlyyk saw something funny, her laughter was so infectious. I found myself laughing with her. From that day on I warmed to her, and each day after that it just became easier and easier. The love just grew between us, as you can see for yourself, she is like a granddaughter to me now, which is the greatest love you can get in any family.'

Charlyyk listened to Gwen's admissions, came to stand beside her. Charlyyk knelt down beside Gwen's chair looked up into her face, with a soft smile. Gwen's hand gently caressed Charlyyk's face. Charlyyk reached up and covered Gwen's hand with her own hand. Janet could see Charlyyk's trust in Gwen.

Harold knew what had been going through Gwen's mind. 'Those first few early days was the hardest for Charlyyk, we had to find the trust to teach Charlyyk to speak English. Charlyyk would look at us, not understanding what we were saying. Her head would turn different ways listening to how we said something, her eyes peering into our eyes looking for acknowledgement.'

The books Gwen and I had in our library were for the older more advanced student, so we brought new books for first-time reader, books that demonstrated the phonetic alphabet. The theory was to repeat words fifteen times to be remembered. 'Then slowly Charlyyk found the key that opened the door to knowledge and then it just went manic. The more Charlyyk learned, the more she wanted to learn.'

This is what Janet wanted; insights to what Charlyyk had done to learn to communicate.

On Wednesday, Bryn did not run with the girls in the morning but was busy in the garden. He admitted to himself that he was not the best bricklayer, but he was going to give it his best effort.

With the Butcher's card in hand, Charlyyk phoned her order. Josef's wife reassured her of their vegetarian sausages and burgers. 'We can guarantee, no contamination with meat, or any nuts.'

Charlyyk, Janet, with grocery list at the ready, headed off in Janet's red Mini. Charlyyk strolled into the supermarket, choose a shopping trolley. Some shoppers took photos, others followed her around the store, even said hello to her. Charlyyk acknowledged them with a smile. Janet took lots of pictures. Charlyyk was more concerned by those who showed no interest.

Janet soon became aware, that some did not see Charlyyk, in the same way. She sought out those who glared, asking them for their views. One elderly man in particular was more than willing to respond. 'What if more come... how would we stop them? That's what worries me, and the wife...no end.

Charlyyk comes over as being nice, but what about others? They may not be so nice. That's what concerns us.'

When Janet showed Charlyyk those remarks later, asked what were her views. 'Everyone is different, that is why there is so much choice in the world. Where one person's Blue, is another person Black. It depends how they want to interpret it.' Charlyyk looked down to her hands. 'I've no choice but to accept what I have, to make the best I can, of what is on offer. Friendship is what I need most. From what I read about the history of Britain; immigration has always been at the forefront. When the first arrivals of West Indian and Asian immigrant came to Britain in the 1950's. Did they not suffer the same as I'm doing now? It was when the children of those immigrant went to school did the newcomers begin to fully integrate. That what I'm hoping going to school will achieve the same for me.'

The next morning at breakfast Bryn informs the girls he was going to the garden centre to buy the cooking utensils for the BBQ. They all agree to go with him.

Then the phone rang. Major Carter asked for some dates from Bryn to help schedule a meeting. 'We have had request from the three big major countries to talk with you. With a neutral Country their preferred venues. Interlaken Switzerland, seems to be preferred. In your report of the of your abduction, you claim to have other evidence...could you make that available when you come. I will confirm the dates when they are finalised.'

Charlyyk was explaining to Janet her life on her planet when Bryn came in. 'Nothing was expected from anybody Janet, we just tried to stay alive! There were plants and small creatures we could gather, but the nice things were dangerous to obtain. The beast that hunted us knew what we liked. would lay in wait for us. Water was our biggest challenge. There was a small trickle of water nearby where my group lived, but we had nothing to contain the water in. I would fill my mouth, then try to return, without swallowing it. Then let it out onto the leaves of the *Cruul tree* so others could drink.'

Janet kept writing. 'These *Cruul* leaves, how big were they?' Charlyyk fetched a tea towel and folded it to the size of a *Cruul* leaf. 'So, about the size of a large man's handkerchief then.'

When Janet finished writing, she looked at Charlyyk with a sincere look. 'No wonder why you are so grateful and loyal to the Collier family.'

Charlyyk was quick to respond. 'And proud, to be a part of this family.'

Bryn gave her a cuddle. 'And we are proud to have you, sweetheart.'

Charlyyk looked up at Bryn lovingly, then said 'Who was that on the phone?'

'Major Carter, trying to pin me down for a date, to meet some army bigwigs.' Bryn started to walk towards the door. 'Are you coming?'

At the garden centre, Charlyyk showed again, how well she handles herself in public. There was no more hiding behind others or covering herself. She met people head-on gracefully, allowing photos to be taken, hands to be shaken. Charlyyk was in charm mode, she must give a good impression of herself in the public's eyes.

Janet always close at hand observing everything, that showed the real person in Charlyyk. It was a young man in a wheelchair, that caught Charlyyk's attention. She was patient with him, even getting him to laugh. When Charlyyk said goodbye to him, she held his hands then kissed him on his cheek. The young man's parents thanking her, wishing her good luck.

Back at Oakleaves. Janet wanted Charlyyk to give her views of the humans she had encountered. 'Looking at how many people resent me being here. All I can do is to win their hearts and mind. This is how I see the Royal Family respond on their walkabouts. I must find the best way to counteract, any bad feelings that some people may have about me. People are very sympathetic about disabled people so for me to show an interest in that young man could help me to win them round. On the other hand, I must be careful not to overdo it, then people might say I was acting.'

Janet looked at Charlyyk cynically. 'But is that not what you are doing?'

'And if I didn't..., would you say I was not trying?'

***

Friday was manic Gwen and Harold arrived early, Harold and Bryn went into the garden to test run the new BBQ.

Charlyyk had written out the recipes for the desserts, and placed them on the kitchen table, bowls and dishes were laid out in regimental fashion. The weighing out of the ingredient, then putting them in the bowls and dishes. Gwen started on making the pastry for the apple pie. Charlyyk prepared the fruit for the trifle, then boiled the water for the jelly. Janet was peeling the apples for the pie, everyone in high spirits.

Gwen trying to emphasise that Charlyyk was in charge. Gwen was in fact gently orchestrating the procedure, always ended up saying, 'What's next Charlyyk?' It was so subtle that even Janet, had not noticed.

The Saturday morning air had a slight chill to it. The sky was clear, it was looking good for the day's event. Charlyyk was up early, excited on the prospect of meeting new friends, was well into her stride with what was on her list of jobs to be done. Taking Gwen advice, 'Don't rush, but keep a steady pace, for least mistakes, can save time.'

James arrived with the fold up tables and straw bales to act as seats, Janet could not keep herself away from meeting him. Bryn and Harold had set up the tables in garden. The cakes and pies were now cooking in the oven, the aroma from the kitchen was intoxicating.

Gwen noticed that all the time James was there, there was no chance of Janet contributing to the task that was still required to be ready for the first guest. Harold was on hand and got stuck in with Gwen and Charlyyk. There were no orders, everyone looking to see what was next to be done, then set about doing it.

The first person to arrive was the Headmistress Mrs Landon. Bryn welcomed her, gave a quick tour of the cottage. Sarah, Mace and George, arrived together on their bikes, were straight into helping out with Harold. Two teachers arrived next. They were keen to talk with their newest school member. But Charlyyk was too busy with the task she had set herself. The teachers could judge her better on her commitment.

The first of the school buses pulled into the drive at five–past-one, Sarah came out to greet them and to direct them through to the garden. One of her closest friends Julia Peters was amongst them. Julia had long dark hair with a gentle curl to it. It was allowed to grow long to cover a large birthmark that covers the left side of her face. Sarah had mentioned the birthmark to Charlyyk previously, so when Sarah took Julia to meet Charlyyk, after the introductions. Charlyyk made a point of kissing Julia on both cheeks.

A few moments later Sarah and Julia heard the distinctive high-pitched voices of the frizzy haired, Jan Freeman and her mother Alice, who always overreact on these sorts of occasions. They bounded in like a couple of over-excited puppies. 'Sarah, Julia, where is she?'

Sarah gripped Charlyyk's arm. 'She'll be fine; she can be a little excitable at times!'

Julia had stepped into the path of Jan before she knocked everyone flying. 'Settle down Jan...Charlyyk lives here, she not going to run away!'

Charlyyk greeted them. 'Hello Jan, at last...we meet face to face.' Charlyyk held out her hands and took Jan's hands in hers, Charlyyk knew this would help to settle her.

Jan soon quietens. 'I'm so very pleased to meet you Charlyyk,' Her voice, trembling with excitement.

'Likewise.'

Alice Freeman standing behind her daughter, just as excited, pushed forward to greet Charlyyk. 'I did not believe I would ever be able to meet you until the school sent us the invitation.'

Charlyyk urges them towards the garden. 'We must meet the other students, that's what this BBQ is all about?'

Bryn and Harold were busy with the BBQ. Gwen scurried about making sure there are enough paper plates, and drinking cups. Then clearing away any debris that was lying around.

To allow Charlyyk to get to meet the other students, Sarah and Julia set up small groups. Charlyyk found talking to a few people at a time, was more comfortable. She could talk at ease with them, getting a mental picture of each student. Mace and his brother had organised the music.

Mrs Landon watching how her students conducted themselves, was mighty impressed how the two girls had rallied around Charlyyk, could see that with some careful managing could use them when Charlyyk arrives at school on Monday morning.

After Charlyyk, had been introduced to all the other students, she turned her attention towards the Teachers, then made her way to the Headmistress. 'Mrs Landon I've spoken with all the students; do you think this is the right time to introduce myself to the Teachers?'

'Yes, Charlyyk. This is Mrs Butler the Maths Teacher and Deputy Head,

They shook hands, the Matronly figure of Mrs Butler came over soft and warm. 'Charlyyk if you put the same effort into schooling, as you have shown here today, not only will you do yourself proud, but also the good name of our school... welcome.'

'This is Mr Waverly he will teach you science.'

Charlyyk shook his hand. 'Sarah has told me so much about you Mr Waverly, how you make your lessons so interesting, I am looking forward to seeing it for myself.'

The rake-thin, Richard Waverly, was slightly taken by surprise. 'I'm with Mrs Butler, I also think you will do yourself proud, I look forward to Monday, your first day at school.'

'Charlyyk this is Mr Pearson he will be taking you for English.'

Tim Pearson. Had a thick set, no-nonsense appearance gave way to a gentle fatherly manner. 'I have come to admire the way you have adapted; I also welcome you to our school. Now young lady, I've been watching you, you have not eaten all day, so let us go see your father and get you fed?'

They walked together towards the BBQ area where Bryn and Harold were busy cooking. 'Hi, sweetheart what do you want to eat?' as Harold turned over a veggie burger,

Bryn selected a burger bun, putting salad, BBQ sauce, then the veggie burger into the bun. 'Now give that a try?' Bryn, placing it all on a paper plate.

Charlyyk took a small bite. 'The sauce it's a bit spicy?' Then took a bigger bite. 'But when one is hungry it tastes brilliant.'

Julia came over. 'I've never had veggie burgers before, but I'm hooked.' The two girls wander off to meet up with Sarah and Jan. At first, they all discussed about how the day was turning out. The conversation turned to the parent's reactions. Julia remarked how protective her parent's reaction was towards Charlyyk attending school. 'I told them not to be silly Charlyyk, as you have been living here for some time and have not created any problems. Though I must admit it was not easy to calm them down, considering how level headed they normally are, I was quite surprised by their opposition.'

As the girls talked and laughed, Julia seeing Charlyyk move away from them, had kept her attention on Charlyyk as she had become quiet. Charlyyk was sitting on a bale of straw looking down. She had not moved, with everyone around deep in conversation. Her attitude did not seem to fit how she had been earlier in the day. Julia left her friends, sat down with her. 'Hey, what's the matter?'

Charlyyk's cheeks were wet with tears. She could only look at Julia with a 'what do I say?' expression.

'You can do it. Start at the beginning.'

Charlyyk took a deep breath, 'It just washed over me, one minute looking at everyone enjoying themselves. The next seeing the faces of those I had left behind, pleading for help. I felt so useless as there was nothing, I could do to help them.'

Gwen also had been watching how Charlyyk was behaving, was soon there with her warmth and experience. Did not take long and had Charlyyk smiling again, the group of girls with Mace took over from Gwen, took Charlyyk away to cheer her up.

'Will this happen often?' Mrs Landon asked Gwen.

'Two years ago, when Charlyyk first arrived, we had to cuddle her, for her to go to sleep at night, she clung to my brother. He was her security. That behaviour has been sporadic, these last few months. It has been a long day... I must admit, I did expect some reaction to how she had put so much, into this day.'

Mrs Butler made the next comment. 'The girls that Charlyyk has made friends with, could be very helpful, they have been instrumental today, I believe they could be the keystone for her to settle at school?'

Mrs Landon nodded when she spoke. 'Yes... it appears that they could be our salvation, we must encourage them to look after Charlyyk to keep her in a tight group, how they organised the little groups of students so Charlyyk could communicate with them was pure genius.' She turned to Gwen. 'Can I talk with you and brother?'

They walked into the cottage, when inside Mrs Landon made it clear to the Colliers of what had taken place during the previous week. 'There were a few objections to Charlyyk attending school...not just Alderbrook, but all the other schools in this area. The letter I sent out to all the parents, we received back, were a very mixed reply. I could not take this decision on my own, consulted with the Education Authorities. We have had meetings with those parents that objected, a compromise has been reached. An area at the Academy has been designated, so Charlyyk has room to move freely. Those students that do not want to have any association with Charlyyk need not enter this area. This arrangement will not compromise the smooth running of the school. So, rest assure we will welcome Charlyyk on Monday morning with open arms.'

Bryn shook Mrs Landon's hand. 'Thank you, we thought there might be a few problems. I'm glad we gave you chance to sort out what they were. The reaction we have seen from some people, did not look promising. It will just take time to resolve itself. We just have to be patient.'

Mrs Landon sighed. 'We were lucky, Alderbrook being a new school, with how the school was designed. We were able to install screens. This gave us more room, where previously we thought we were losing. The classes we could move different Student around without affecting their grades.'

Gradually everyone left. Sarah, Mace and George stayed longer and helped to clear up. Charlyyk thanked them all for their kind efforts,

Janet appeared looking very pleased with herself. As she walked into the kitchen. 'Any takers for coffee?' She looked at Charlyyk. 'My God, you do look tired!'

Bryn also noticed Charlyyk, flagging with the enormous amount of effort she had put into the day's event. He bent down and picked her up in his arms. 'Come sweetheart. Let's get you to bed?'

***

On Sunday morning Janet was up early, not for a run. She had spent Saturday with James and was behind with her journals. She would have to remain in the bedroom to complete them.

In the kitchen for breakfast, Bryn and Charlyyk were talking about their run, when Janet entered. 'Hi good morning. Bryn, I have printed out four articles for your perusal, when you give the nod, I send them for print.'

Charlyyk felt sorry Janet's week had come to an end. 'When are you leaving?'

'About midday I'm almost packed' Janet made her way back to the bedroom to finish packing.

Twenty minutes later Charlyyk entered the guestroom. 'When are you returning Janet?'

Janet closed her case, then sat on the bed next to Charlyyk. 'I have three interviews booked for this month, so I hope to come back mid-November, we should be able to look how you have got on at school? I have left you a contact number if you need to get in touch.'

Charlyyk had felt Janet's presence a bit intense at first. As the week unfolded, she began to like having Janet around.

Later the two of them loaded up the bright red Mini with Janet's luggage. Bryn thanked Janet for the way she had handled her assignment. He was pleased how Janet had conducted herself, will be more than pleased, to see her return.

The hugs and kisses the two girls gave each other were very genuine. 'I've really enjoyed myself getting to know you Charlyyk. I hope you like, what I've written about you? See you soon.'

Waving goodbye Charlyyk and Bryn watched Janet drive off.

That evening at Gwen and Harold's for dinner, they discussed Charlyyk going to school. Gwen sitting with her. 'What are your main concerns for tomorrow?'

Charlyyk did not look concerned. 'I don't think there will be many problems, Aunty Gwen. Yesterday I met a girl who looked very shy and uncertain of herself. Her name was Sandra, she seemed to me, very cute. The way Julia spoke to her, they seemed very close. So, I'm hoping to get to know her better.' Charlyyk's face broke out into a smirk, 'Jan Freeman is funny, her

95

tongue works faster than her brain, and that moves fast enough. Mace's friend Peter, I like him also, he is like Mace very steady, you know...level headed?'

Gwen gave a little chuckle at what Charlyyk had said about Jan. 'What about Sarah and Mace?'

'No, Brother and Sister them two! Now, Sandra and Peter, that's different, the way they bounce off each other. They don't know it yet, I bet they will be an item, like Janet and James.'

Gwen was taken back. 'What do you mean, that Janet and James are an item?'

'She, had James's scent all over her when she returned last night.'

'That doesn't mean anything went on between them.'

Charlyyk pushed her face close to Gwen's. 'My nose told me that their body sweat had mixed together, like yours and Uncle Harold's before we arrived for dinner.'

Gwen's face became flushed, her eyes flashed at Harold. Gwen's realisation that Charlyyk could tell by her nose, that others have had sex, had caught her by surprise, her response, came out, louder than expected. 'You can't tell that by smelling, can you?'

Bryn and Harold could not help hearing. 'What this about smelling?' they said in unison.

'Oh nothing, girl talk!'

The men shrugged, carried on with their own conversation.

Chapter 11

Alderbrook Academy

On Monday, Charlyyk was up bright and early. Her run was a quick thirty minutes. She showered and dressed, in her brand, new school uniform. Bryn approached with a camera in his hands. 'I must take a few pictures, Janet's request. That one photo will never be enough?' Charlyyk posed in many positions, copying models, that Janet had shown her in fashion magazines. Bryn could not help laughing at her antics, when he had finished, he gave her such a big hug and a kiss. 'I'm so proud of you.'

The school bus arrived down the Lane, Sarah and Mace could not get the door open quick enough. 'Morning Mr Collier, we're are here to look after her.' They called out as they walked across the drive.

Charlyyk kissed Bryn. 'Bye dad see you after school.'

Bryn waved as the bus took off down the lane. *'Will life ever be the same.'* He thought to himself.

The twenty-minute drive to school was spent discussing Saturday's event. Charlyyk even managed to talk about Sandra. Sarah remarking. 'Sandra's father, is very ill, he is in hospital. Sandra does not know what was going to happen to him. We were hoping that Saturday might cheer her up, as you could tell Julia is Sandra's best friend, within our group.

Sarah had thought through another bit of information. 'Miss Vasey our art teacher, who you will like, because everyone else at school does. She as this uncanny knack of bringing people together. She was instrumental in forming us into a group, although at first, we did not see it as that. We were very different, always bickering, when one day my best friend, Jan, fell out with Julia. Miss Vasey spoke with us, pointing out when we start to get that bit older, it's the friends you make, that will determine how we will go through life, as most teenagers listen to their friends, more than listen to their parents. We are finding that to be true.'

When the bus arrived at the school, many of those that were at the cottage on Saturday were there to welcome Charlyyk, to their school. Mrs Butler was standing by the doors, talking to some of the other students. Jan, Julia, and Sandra were talking with Peter. Sarah, Mace and Charlyyk met them with hugs. Many other students gathered around wanting to get a glimpse of Charlyyk, the interest they showed did not result in a surge, that could have led into a crush. Mrs Butler smiled with satisfaction on how it was all turning out.

The school bell sounded, the school doors opened on cue, Mrs Landon and Mr Waverly were in attendance, overseeing the start of a new week.

Charlyyk liked what she could see of how the school was set out. The way the students gathered to greet her, gave her hope of being accepted by them. She watched Sarah mingle, set her mind to followed in Sarah's footsteps. Charlyyk greeted student's that she had met on Saturday, in the same relaxed manner, that Sarah used. This went down well, Charlyyk had made good connections.

As the students busied themselves to go to the school assembly. Each class came into the hall in an orderly manner and lined up. their form masters standing to the side. Mrs Landon welcomed them and thanked them for their smart turnout. Mrs Landon's understanding, was that this new addition to the school could have big consequence, more were plusses than negatives. 'On Saturday, the year that our newest student is joining, were invited to attend a BBQ at her home. I was also present with a few of the teachers. Now I would like to introduce her to the whole school. Charlyyk.' As Louise Landon nodded to her. 'Could you please, come and say hello.'

Charlyyk with her form master, Mr Waverly stepped forward to meet Mrs Landon on the stage. Mrs Landon received Charlyyk with a shake of her hand. Charlyyk turned and faced the whole school. She had to catch her breath, upon seeing so many faces peering back at her. 'Hello, and thank you for letting me join Alderbrook Academy, you may wonder what I'm like...Well, I'm just like you, as you were when you first came to school. I'm nervous in not knowing what is going to happen... So, please help me to enjoy what you like about Alderbrook...This will be my school, as of this day, and I want to be proud, to be a part of it.'

Gwen had prompted Charlyyk to give a good impression, so she made friends not enemies. Though Charlyyk had already allowed for that scenario, she had thanked Gwen for advice. Charlyyk knowing it would give Gwen a sense of satisfaction.

In unison, everyone said. 'Welcome Charlyyk.' Then the whole school clapped, Charlyyk could not feel happier.

The big smile was on Mrs Landon's face; the first big hurdle had turned into a stepping stone. She had watched the group of objectors. Although they did not clap, they had not made a scene. Some were still showing interested in Charlyyk.

Charlyyk had also taken notice of those that were not smiling, as well as those that had taken interest in her, taking a mental note, to work on winning them around, when the chance came.

Lunchtime saw a group surround Charlyyk. Mace was in control. His mother's policing instincts had rubbed off on him; he was like the policeman on traffic duty, in full protective mode.

At one o'clock, Bryn could hear the tractor crossing the fields at the rear of the cottage. It was towing a flatbed trailer. James gave Bryn a wave as he stopped near the gate at the end of the garden. 'How did it go Saturday, Bryn?'

Bryn shook James's hand. 'It was a long day, but a great success. Josef came up trumps with the meat, the tables and straw bales were a great idea, thank you very much.'

They loaded the tables and hay bales onto the trailer. 'I spent Saturday with Janet.' James waited for Bryn's reply. Bryn looked at him nonchalantly. 'It's not going to create a problem with Charlyyk, is it?' James continued, watching Bryn for any reaction.

'It's all OK. Charlyyk already knows about you two, so you can rest easy. The feeling I got from Charlyyk is that she likes Janet.'

At four the school bus drops Charlyyk off. She waves goodbye to those still on the bus. Bryn opens the door and greets her with a kiss and a hug. 'Did you have a good day?'

Charlyyk looked happy. 'Mr Waverly is so nice, he takes us for two subjects, as does Mrs Butler. Tomorrow I have art with Miss Vasey I'm so looking forward to that.'

Bryn served her dinner, Charlyyk kept talking; even when they were loading the dishwasher and cleaning the kitchen, she did not stop. Bryn nodded, said yes and no, all in the right places. Then grabbing her satchel. 'Homework.' Charlyyk was gone.

Bryn felt dazed, but happy with Charlyyk's first day at school. He'd had a phone conversation with Mrs Landon on how Charlyyk had adapted, with the effort she had applied to her first day.

An hour later as Bryn was watching a documentary film on BBC4. Charlyyk quietly slid beside him, cuddled up. He placed his arm around her, they both watched the program together in silence. When the program finished, Charlyyk was fast asleep.

Bryn switched the television off with the handset, sat quietly with her enjoying her company. He was transfixed with the infantile presence she now relayed to him.

With Catherine and Thomas leaving to get married then Losing Kitty, how empty the cottage had become. That bolt of light, then to return with Charlyyk. His life has not been turned upside down, it has given him a new meaning and purpose. Understanding a young girl's needs is hard at the best of times, for girls are much more complicated than boys. Girls throw many variables into the equation; they tend to confuse, what they are trying to achieve. Charlyyk was different. She debated ideas in a precise logical order. She would listen, then would repeat back to him, what she believed to be what he had said, then wait to hear him agree or disagree. There were no tantrums, no sulking. This was the joy of living with Charlyyk, a sense of being in a state of equilibrium with each other. He also remembered what his mother had told him when he informed her of Kitty; 'You know when you have found a good one; that's when something has got to be done; they roll up their sleeves, then they get on with it.' Well, he knew that saying referred to Charlyyk.

He sat there with her until she stirred. 'Do you need anything, before you go to bed?' He asked.

She looked up at him bleary-eyed. 'Mmm, just some water.' But before he could move. 'Will you carry me to bed, dad?'

He picked her up, as she placed her arms around Bryn's neck and rested her head on his shoulder. taking her to bed. He then helped her to undress, tucked her in, then a gentle kiss on her forehead she was soon fast asleep. 'Night night, little one.' He stood there for a little while watching the serenity in her face, this was so different as to when she had first arrived.

***

Charlyyk could not get home any sooner from her early morning run. The cottage door crashed as she rushed in. Bryn following behind checked to make sure no damage had been done. When Charlyyk came into the kitchen, she had showered and dressed. Her breakfast of muesli and fruit quickly disappeared. 'Slow down sweetheart... gulping your food down, could give you indigestion?'

Charlyyk looked at Bryn. 'I'm so excited to be going to school dad.'

'There is an hour before the bus arrives. How about showing me your homework?'

Charlyyk reached into her bag, retrieved her homework. She sat next to Bryn, opened the book, and they both read what she had written. 'That quite impressive, I like what you have written.'

Then Charlyyk took out another book of homework. 'Mrs Butler said she didn't need this until Wednesday, but sooner the better Auntie Gwen always says.'

Bryn finished reading. 'You did all that in an hour? Well done.'

The school bus arrived Sarah and Mace looked just as happy as Charlyyk. Bryn waved them off, he just stood there until he could not see the bus anymore. He knew she had to go, but he missed her already. The emptiness he was experiencing was similar as when Catherine and Thomas had left home. Bryn sighed a deep sigh he knew he had to get over it, at least she would soon be home, as it was only a temporary situation, not a permanent one.

Nine o'clock the phone starts ringing, Bryn picks it up. 'Bryn Collier speaking.' Bryn had been expecting this call.

'Major Carter here... Bryn, we can confirm a date for the meeting...twenty-second of this month, the venue will be The Victoria, Interlaken, Switzerland. I will collect you on the evening twenty-first at 2300hr. We are expecting it to last, about four days, will Charlyyk be OK to stay with your sister?'

Bryn accepted the arrangements. 'I'll sort out this end, see you in a week's time.'

Miss Vasey art class, Charlyyk applied acrylic paint to a landscape picture, depicting the scenes she remembered on her early morning runs. Standing beside Charlyyk, Alice Vasey was accessing how Charlyyk was adapting herself. 'That's great Charlyyk, don't worry about the paint runs. I just want to see some technique of yours, then we can progress your own personal skill levels, for art is personal, it reflects you as a person.'

Charlyyk was feeling okay with herself. The colours that she was applying, in her mind were making the picture come alive. The girls gathered around her to see how she had got on. The praises she received from them made her feel even better. Miss Vasey advised her to allow the painting time to dry. 'It won't take long. Acrylic paint is an emulsion paint which dries quite quickly.' Though the spots of paint that were splattered all around the easel, and a few other places had Miss Vasey slightly concerned.

At lunch time, Sandra needed to explain human nature to Charlyyk. 'It is, how human girls behave, when in groups. 'Watch how Jan takes centre stage, how the others gather around her. We class this as Jan, is acting as the big mother hen. Sarah is her second in command. The rest of us hang around waiting to be pecked. That what is commonly known as the pecking order.'

To Charlyyk's surprise, Sandra started flapping her arms, while clucking like the hens on the Parsons Farm. This amused Charlyyk immensely, could not hold back from her wicked laugh, this had all girls laughing with her.

As the other girls talked, Charlyyk asked Sandra how her father was doing in hospital.

'He has turned the corner, they believe they have found out what was the problem is, with his blood. The Hospital have put him on a program of chemotherapy, we just have to wait it out, but at least we know something is happening.' Sandra's face showing her concerns about her father. 'Thank you Charlyyk for asking, you are so thoughtful.'

Julia had listened in on the conversations. Her own concerns showed on her face. Julia could not let Sandra feel she was facing this on her own. With open arms, she was there for Sandra, soon the three girls had a little huddle together. A bond was forming among the three. Charlyyk was preferring their quiet relaxed manner, compared to the high-octane manner, of Jan and Sarah. Although Charlyyk had observed that Sarah did not act in the same way, when she was not influenced by Jan.

Gwen was waiting by the front door of Oakleaves. 'Auntie Gwen.' Charlyyk's eager welcoming voice showed her joy of seeing Gwen. The embrace was just as warming. As they entered the cottage the questions Gwen was asking, was how did she find school?

Harold and Bryn greeted her with as much affection as did Gwen. Charlyyk's school bag was soon opened, its contents scattered across the table. Harold reading her English exercise books, and Gwen her maths books. 'Well done, Charlyyk, this is good work.'

Bryn held the landscape painting in his hands. 'This is lovely sweetheart.'

Charlyyk pointed out the paint runs. 'I got carried away, too much paint on the brush. Miss Vasey said not to worry as it was my first time, but I loved it.' Alice Vasey wanted Charlyyk to show her father the painting, and had put the A2 size painting into a Portfolio case, so that the painting, did not get damaged.

Bryn had already told Harold and Gwen about her homework, how pleased he was how she was settling down at school.

Charlyyk did not stop talking about the Academy over dinner. Gwen had noticed how Julia and Sandra kept popping up in her conversation, much more than Sarah or Mace. Gwen inferred which teachers Charlyyk had taken to also.

Bryn let Charlyyk know about the trip in a week's time, that she will be staying with Gwen and Harold. 'They have said, about four days, sweetheart so should be back on the Sunday. I'll bring you back some Swiss chocolate.'

Charlyyk liked, any type of chocolate, Michael had told Bryn, she could only indulge in moderation.

The rest of the week fitted into a schedule of early morning runs, school runs, and homework, followed by sleep. Bryn filled his days doing the housework, trying hard to banish the feeling of the loneliness he was experiencing.

On Saturday, there was no school. The mild damp air gave the fields a light misty look. The two runners were taking the run at a gentle pace. The conversation between them was light-hearted. Charlyyk would at times turn and run backwards, facing Bryn to talk to him. At other times, she laughed and skipped. They talked about going out to lunch, then to see a film at the cinema. Charlyyk was enjoying this new freedom of movement, to go out in public, not having to worry too much, if she was seen.

As the morning past she had busied herself with the housework alongside Bryn. Cleaning and bed making did not fuss her at all, when the chores were finished, they sat down for beverages and biscuits. To discuss the rest of the day.

Charlyyk's Saturday treat was to be a visit to Pizza Hut. As they waited for their orders to be taken, Charlyyk questioned Bryn about the decision to sell his old Jensen, then to purchase a Land Rover Discovery. 'I know it is not what you are after? it's not as big as Toby's Range Rover, but do you need one as big?' Charlyyk put down the menu. 'Margarita, Chips, and a Cola.' She looked around for the waiter, she managed to catch his attention and beckoned him over. They gave him their orders, and he left. 'So, when are we going to look, you will be in Switzerland for four days. I'm going to school all week, down to one weekend only?'

Bryn nodded. 'I will look around and check out a few showrooms. If I see anything, we will both go and look.'

Charlyyk stops Bryn from talking. Two young girls had appeared by her side, Charlyyk moved her chair back, then turned to face them. Charlyyk seeing this as an opportunity to show her friendly nature, still aware that some people's feeling was still against her. 'Hello, how old are you?'

The smallest child came closer. 'I'm five.'

Charlyyk bent forward. 'My, you are a big five.'

The little girl reached up and touched Charlyyk's face, then she stroked her hair.

'Would you like to see my tail?'

The girl's eyes lit up, their mouth opened, as to say something, said nothing, just nodded. Charlyyk stood up, lifted the back of her skirt and waggled her little tail. This action delighted the two girls, who turned ran back to their parents.

Charlyyk could see in Bryn's eyes, he did not approve of her lifting her skirt in public. She could see no wrong in it, as when she lived on her planet, she had worn no clothes.

Bryn was not happy. 'Charlyyk this behaviour is not acceptable in public, many people regard this as bad taste, that lacks good morals.'

Bryn's look made Charlyyk aware it was not to be done again. Charlyyk sat back in her chair, as the pizza order arrived at the table. While eating Charlyyk contemplated what Bryn had dictated to her. When she spoke, she changed the subject. 'Dad, you check around the showrooms, it could fit in to the time frame Bill Symonds has given you for a decision on the Discovery.' She next touched on the meeting. 'Do you know what they will ask you?'

Bryn nodded. 'Oh yes, their primary concern will be to find out if the Aliens can pluck someone else or, conversely, put anything on this planet to create problems for us?'

Charlyyk left the table for some more salad from the salad bar. When she returned. 'I would have thought what Catherine had written in the circular, that we gave out to everyone...would have explained everything?'

Bryn smile had a wryly look. 'No, it doesn't work like that. These people need to cross-examine me, to make sure I have left nothing out, just the tiniest of detail, could make a massive difference, so it is of great importance, that I assist them and answer truly what I can remember?'

Charlyyk carried on eating. But Bryn knew she was thinking about what he had said. This was one of the things Bryn had like about Charlyyk, how she digested the information before she answered.

'So, as I see it, it will be the first of many meetings.' She paused. 'Probably they are going to want to speak with me also, to back up what you have told them, or add more detail.' The idea did not seem to perturb her.

'They know my military history. And I know how they operate. What they will do is to get my side of the story, analyse it. then it will be afterwards, that they will want to know your side.'

'Are you worried in what they will ask of you?'

'No, we have not committed a crime. It will simply be asking us to remember what we believe we saw. What actually happened, in logic, it should not have happened, they know that. You are the proof, that it did happen. Regardless of what we have seen, the final outcome is already known. We will not be able to mount any defence against the Alien.'

'When does the film start?' Charlyyk had heard enough, she will digest it later.

'Four-thirty. Why.' Charlyyk changing the subject, so abruptly, was not what he expected?

'Could we nip into Clarks, the shoe shop? Sandra had a nice pair of shoes; I would love to see if they would fit me?'

When the meal was over, Bryn paid at the cashier desk, while Charlyyk said goodbye to the family of the two small girls. 'I wanted to show your girls, that I had a tail. My new father said it was a rude gesture, please accept, my humblest of apologies. There was no intention of offending you in any way.'

The father of the girls smiled. 'Our girls thought it was funny. No offence taken. It was a nice gesture that the girls appreciated. But your new father is correct, it is not deemed good taste to show your underwear in public.'

Charlyyk and Bryn, walked down the High Street. As always people stopped to see her. Most waved and said hello. Others just stood where they were and watched. As the two approached Clark's shoe shop, Bryn noticed another shop, which he had been putting a lot thought into, the Apple store. 'Let's pop in here Charlyyk!'

Her eyes glistened with excitement. Charlyyk was developing a taste for digital toys. What she desired most was a mobile phone. She had not asked for one up to now, but she had seen that all the girls at school, they each had one.

A young man who looked as pale, as if he had never seen the light of day, approached them. 'How can I help you today?'

Bryn beckoned the lad, to one side. 'My daughter needs a phone, with a tablet, what deal can you do for us?'

The young lad directed them to a table, his interest was in Charlyyk's hands. 'Here are the latest models. I gather she needs them for school, not recreation?'

Charlyyk's fingers were all over the models set up on the table, she glanced at Bryn with the look of a puppy wanting a walk, her tail wagging furiously with excitement. Bryn asked for pricing details.

Ten minutes later, Bryn was trying hard to prise Charlyyk away from the tablet. They moved on to Clarks. The shoes in Sandra's style did not fit Charlyyk. She tried a few different pairs on, her long narrow feet were at best, awkward to fit. Disappointed they made their way to the Cinema.

Bryn let Charlyyk work the ticket machine, for Transformers, Age of Extinction. He put his PIN number in, two tickets unfurled from the ticket dispenser. At the sweet kiosk, Charlyyk selected popcorn and cola, then made their way to their seats.

Bryn did not want her to watch any film with animal monsters. Charlyyk still has nightmares now and again. Seeing pictures in books was OK, but not moving ones. With regards to Mechanical monsters, Bryn was keeping his fingers crossed.

Bryn had been lucky to a point, Catherine and Michel had managed to explain to Charlyyk about intimacy between males and females, Charlyyk knew what the male and female would do to make offspring. Some of the methods used, needed more explaining. He relied on Gwen to get him out of answering awkward questions. There were no awkward questions about this film. There were a couple of moments when Charlyyk gripped his arm tight but as the film went on, she relaxed. There were more giggles and fewer gasps.

Leaving the cinema, Charlyyk could not stop talking about the size of the screen, with how loud the sound had been. When they reached the Morgan. Charlyyk grabbed Bryn's arm. 'Careful it might turn into a Land Rover.' Then she could not stop laughing at what she had said.

'How did you like the film Charlyyk?'

'I had heard the girls talking about the films, with how real they make them look. it was all about the computer imagery that they use.' Charlyyk remembered an early *Star Wars* film that had been shown on Television, she had watched it with James. 'I had seen a film which showed Earth's idea of space travel and the beings, that they thought existed on other planets, James asked me how did I see it, I told him where I found you was not nice. There was beast, no kind ones.'

***

After their Sunday morning run. Bryn set up Charlyyk's new phone with her iPad. Charlyyk's first call was to Julia. They discussed what apps she needed. Bryn agreed to the girl's choice, installed them for her. 'You must be careful. Some apps have cookies that check who you are and where you are. We don't need to give out that information. So, please don't install any, unless I agree to them, that includes face book. Your e-mail address must not contain your name for the same reasons.'

'Yes dad, I promise.' Charlyyk agreed, just happy to own a phone.

At Carpenters Cottage for dinner, Gwen and Harold got the full low down on the events of Saturday. Gwen took Charlyyk to the room where she would be staying from Tuesday after school, until Bryn returns from Switzerland. Then they made a list of what she will need for the stay.

Bryn discussed with Harold about what Bill Symonds had offered him.

'It sounds a good deal Bryn, do not turn your nose up at it?' Bryn told Harold what Charlyyk had said to him about the size of the Land Rover, Harold agreed she may have a point.'

Charlyyk and Gwen entered the room at that precise moment. 'What point Uncle Harold?'

Harold remarked. 'We were discussing the size of the Discovery?'

Charlyyk and Gwen sat down together on the sofa. 'It's a little more compact than the Range Rover but just as comfortable. Actually, I think it's size is much more practical.' She reached over to the coffee table and picked up Gwen's *Vogue* magazine, when opening it. 'But Dad is going to look at other makes before he makes his mind up, buying a car he should not be blinded by the glorification of others, but by the necessity of his own needs.'

Harold shrugged. 'That told us.'

Charlyyk pointed to a page in the magazine to Gwen. 'Nobody would wear that, would they Auntie Gwen?'

'Only if they were blinded by the glorification of others.'

Chapter 12

Interlaken

On Monday, with Charlyyk at school. Bryn busied himself in his study. He went over the many things he had spoken to the family about regarding that fateful day of the abduction. Thomas, his son, had drawn pictures from Charlyyk's and his own descriptions, of some of things they had seen. Could they have missed any detail? He racked his brain. He recalled the sounds, but it was the acrid spells that still filled his nostril. A vile stench had almost turned his stomach over, apart from the perils he was facing.

He stood, reached up to the highest shelf, for the case he had placed the other evidence in. One item was the weapon he had taken from the beast. It was not a thrusting sword, more like a hacking blade-machete-like, thick and heavy. The bone spike that had broken off from the tail of the first beast, that had become embedded inside of him. Michel had to remove it.

When Charlyyk returned home. Bryn welcomed her with a big hug and kiss. 'I've been sorting out the evidence, to take with me to the meeting.' Bryn knew Charlyyk did not like to be reminded of that time, it had happened, it still needed to be explained. He gave Charlyyk another hug, just to say he was there for her.

Charlyyk liked, the human emotion that the family showed her. The soft, loving, warm sensation she got from it, made her feel wanted, made her feel valued just for being alive. She never wanted to return where she had come from. She always told herself, she would just give up and die! The memories of how she and the other *Lyyk's* would cuddle up in the warren of tunnels, that they had dug to protect them from the extreme cold of the dark periods, were not memories of love but of necessity. Each had been dependent on the others to survive.

After dinner, they both went over and over those events that had brought them together. Then they sat on the sofa and cuddled until Charlyyk fell asleep. Bryn put her to bed. He laid there with her on the bed. Charlyyk within the covers, Bryn on top. He still felt niggles that made no sense, but as hard as he tried could not resolve those things that seemed, so out of place.

***

When Bryn woke, he was still cuddling Charlyyk. she was still asleep. He kissed her on the cheek and went to slip off, to go to his own bed. Her hand reached over, took hold of his arm, pulled him back. 'Morning dad,' she said sleepily. 'Is it time to get up?'

Bryn gave her a gentle hug. 'Not quite yet sweetheart.'

'Then stay, I would like you to keep cuddling me, please?'

For the next thirty- minutes they just laid there. Charlyyk's dreams were about when she had first cuddled Bryn, keeping him warm in that forsaken hellhole of a cavern. She also remembered arriving on planet Earth, experiencing the sheer comfort of sleeping on a soft bed. She could not believe what was happening to her. Then as time went by, she had become accustom to this way of living. There was no threat of danger, all the food she wanted. It was bliss. With Bryn cuddling her, she could lay there forever.

Suddenly, she moved 'Come on lazybones...we have a run to do!'

The jog up Farm Lane, to the Parson's farm. James calls out. 'Bryn, we can do Thomas's room next week, give me a ring.' Charlyyk and James, blew kisses at each other.

This was a joy to Charlyyk, how she was getting to enjoy life on earth. She was accepted by everyone in the village. No one treated her with any ill feelings. It was only when venturing out of this safe environment, was where she needed to be on her guard.

When they arrived back at the cottage, it was a little later then they had planned. Charlyyk had to rush her breakfast while Bryn collected her bits together for school. 'I'll take your things to Gwen and Harold's then meet you there after school.' The bus arrived as she was going through the front door. She gave Bryn a quick kiss, waved as she boarded the bus.

The coffee tasted good to Bryn. It even made the buttered toast taste even better. Yet the nag of loneliness was mixed in with this new world fame of the guardian parent of Charlyyk. Bryn had appreciated the solitary living in this quite rural backwater of Hampshire. Bryn hated attention. When he received his gallantry medals, the news media were clamouring for his story. He'd managed to sneak off without anybody knowing where he was. Now he was again trying to hide, but finding it much harder,

Catherine had worked a system for him to give Charlyyk some privacy, in a way, it was helping him to share the same benefits, it was not just the nag of loneliness he had recognised, it was that Kitty was not here to help him.

At Carpenter cottage after school, dinner was a lively mix of conversations. Much about Charlyyk's day at school and Bryn's meeting with the Army Intelligent officers. Gwen spoke about Catherine and Thomas; as she had talked to them about Christmas. 'Thomas said, that he and Rachel were making plans to spend Christmas here.'

Although Charlyyk had been told the story of Christmas, she could not understand the ideology of it. She would keep saying. 'If you know, you descended from apes, so how come you believe the story that this God made you? And in his own image, surely you must be more intelligent than that, to be taken in by it?' But Charlyyk loved Christmas. The family getting together, then there was the food, it was great fun. These thoughts in her mind, with her mischievous look. 'Now I get it, you made the story up as an excuse to party.'

Harold loved this simple logic of hers, how she worked out these explanations they gave to her. It was similar to Bryn feelings about the way she digests the information, then after careful consideration, provided her answers. Though it really did upset Gwen, whose strong religious beliefs could not influence Charlyyk to see the bigger picture. 'Can't you see how it brings good values to our family way of living, teachings us the right way to behave to one another. Sets us above any other living being?'

Charlyyk shook her head. 'Auntie Gwen, do you mean like me, do I behave like a Feeng, that would stalk, and eat me. The history books tell a different story, of wars and persecution, burning people at the stake, does this sound like good family values, or have Uncle Harold given me the wrong books to read?'

Gwen knew Charlyyk meant no malice, it was just her alternative views. More to do with that Charlyyk could not believe, in something that people perceive could happen, with no proof of it actually happening, would say. 'Dad would be laughed at if he said he had been abducted without the proof to back up his story.'

Bryn's mobile phone starts to vibrate, when he answers it, it was Major Carter. 'Captain Collier, are you packed and ready to leave?'

Bryn looked at the family. 'Yes, I'm ready, I'm at my sister house.'

'Could you leave in twenty minutes?' Major Carter sounded anxious as he relayed his concerns. 'Gale force winds are forecast over central Europe tonight, if we leave early, we could miss the worst of them.'

Bryn explains the situation to the family and made himself ready. Charlyyk who had never slept away from him, since arriving, looked a little forlorn. Placing his arm around her. 'We can't hide from it. We must show that we want to cooperate. If we don't, they may believe we have something to hide. That could become an excuse to separate us.'

Charlyyk understood what Bryn was saying, but her security was about to leave her. She knew he had to go, but that did not ease the anxiety she was going through. Her gaze did not leave him, as she sucked in deep breaths, hoping that her new dad would come back. The colour change in Charlyyk's eyes and her ears projecting backwards and the little bite on her bottom lip relayed how sad she felt.

Gwen took over comforting Charlyyk. Gwen remembering waving her brother off on his army commitments, never knowing if he would come back alive or in a body bag. How she and Harold would try to help Kitty and the children through those troubled times. Gwen's comforting arm around Charlyyk's shoulders. 'It's at these times, when believing in a God, helps those who feel helpless, get through.

Charlyyk was not listening to Gwen. Her concentration aimed solely on Bryn.

Outside a helicopter had landed on the village green. Major Carter shouting at Bryn above the noise of the helicopter's engines. 'There's a plane waiting for us at Brize Norton.' As Bryn boarded the helicopter, he waved goodbye to Charlyyk, Gwen and Harold.

The helicopter rose into the air, then banked, till all Charlyyk could see was the lights of the aircraft as it faded into the distance. To Charlyyk there was nothing she could do, as her inner feelings sank to their lowest depths. She looked up at Gwen, as the well of tears in her eyes just overflowed. Charlyyk buried her face into Gwen's bosoms.

Bryn saw the military aircraft waiting for take-off. As the pilot sat the helicopter down next to it. There was no waiting in a departure lounge. As they were putting on the seat belts, the plane was taxiing up the airstrip.

Major Carter, introduce Bryn to the other personnel on board. 'Major John Stevens, Strategy Operation Officer, Lieutenant Michael Archer, Translator. Sergeant Helena Baker will be on hand, to look after us.'

Bryn shook hands with them, the blonde wig and contact lenses to change the colour of her eyes, did not fool Bryn, he recognised Helen Bennett straight away. The wink he gave her, let her know. Helen had expected that. 'I look forward to your full attention Sergeant.'

Helen smiled at him. 'I'll give it my best shot Sir.' Returning the wink, he had given her.

The flight was bumpy as the plane fought against the high winds, then struggling against the crosswinds when it touched down, with much difficulty, landed safely at the Interlaken airstrip. A Mercedes Transporter was on hand to take them to the Victoria Hotel. Built in 1865. The Hotel was a large airy building with a modern outlook. It was nicely situated, surrounded by mountains. Bryn's room was modest in size, was adequate for his needs.

He soon unpacked. Then he phoned Gwen to keep her from worrying. She informed him that Charlyyk had settled down, was sleeping, a call in the morning, it would help to calm her.

A light tap on the door took him by surprise. When he opened it, Helen quickly brushed passed him, he closed the door as fast as he could. She stood by the bed looking straight at him. 'Is there a problem here Helen?' he asked.

'No, not at all.' She stepped towards him. 'When I left you, it was to set up this meeting.' She took hold of his hand. 'There was so much I wanted to tell you, though I did not know how. I did not want to get it wrong.' Helen looked nervous, was trying hard not to say something she might regret.

Bryn's movement gave her no chance to react, as she found herself in his arms, his lips on hers. She had no way of talking, she just let it sweep over her no resistance. Her hands found their way to his back, then up towards his shoulders, with no intention of letting go.

When they eventually parted, they sat on the bed, side by side holding hands. 'I'm not used to this Bryn. I've never had a relationship with anyone before.' She sounded apologetic.

Bryn looked into her eyes. 'Then let's not rush it. Let's take it slowly, we will then be able to enjoy everything nice and easy.' She buried her head into his chest, as he placed his arm around her, Bryn with his quiet gentle manner, 'If we want a meaningful relationship, we'll need to get to know each other. We are not silly teenagers...that jump into love... to quickly falling out of love, then fall in love with somebody else.'

Helen looked at him, he could tell she wanted more. Bryn did not want to rush it. knowing there was much to do here, he needed to concentrate on that. He encouraged Helen to return to her room, telling her in about four-day time they can look how to develop their relationship.

***

After four hours of sleep, Bryn was wide-awake, getting ready for his morning jog, he slipped out of the hotel, headed towards the lake with the wind to his back, the outward run was easy, but the return run, fighting against the wind was a different story. All the time his mind was on Helen. He knew that he was struggling with Kitty's passing that made him hesitate, Charlyyk too, had something to do with it as well

Back in the hotel, Bryn showered and dressed, then went for breakfast.

At ten o'clock, they met in the reception room, designated for the meeting, a large round table had been set up so everyone could see each other. Helen had planned for everyone's possible needs. Lieutenant Archer set up a printer, which printed on A3 and A4 paper.

The first to arrive was the American contingent led by Lieutenant-Colonel Chad Smitt, Major Scot Bradley, and Captain John Hanne. Major Carter introduced Bryn, Lieu-Col Smitt shaking Bryn's hand. 'We have something in common Captain Collier, our fathers knew each other, they both served at the Imajin River Spring Offensive.'

Chad's small talk was intended to ease Bryn into trusting him. Bryn knew of his father ordeal at the hands of the Chinese, when his Regiment were overrun, when they were left as the rear-guard defensive on that dreaded hill 235, so the Americans could regroup. His father's forced imprisonment by the Chinese, was to Bryn the reason for his father early death.

Delegations from Russia, China, and the UN arrived on mass the introduction took forty-five minutes before they took their places at the table.

Helen laid out the information Bryn and Catherine had put together with numerous drawings. Major Carter, stood up and welcomed them on behalf of the British Government, but before he could continue China's Brigadier. Su Shi Ning, stood up, with well-educated English. 'Gentlemen' Then he looked at Helen. 'And Ladies, please let us make this easy for ourselves, lets drop rank. Please call me Su Shi, many of my colleges do not like my way of thinking, I believe the threat we are looking at is not of each other, but for all of us. To understand the full nature of this threat we need to trust one another and work together as a team.' As he looked around the table, he was pleased to see everyone agreeing with his suggestion. 'Thank you, now Alan Carter as you have put so much work, into achieving this, would you like to get it started?'

Major Carter smiled. 'Thank you, Su Shi. On behalf of the British Government, I welcome you all here, our thinking is the same as your own Governments, we understand the full gravity of the situation we are all facing. We have spoken with Brian Collier on the implications, how these Aliens could impose a threat towards our planet. Our respective Governments are all aware of each-others intelligence. To overcome all obstacles, we need to trust each other, to pool our resources. Now it's not me you want to hear talking, but Capt. Brian Collier.' He sat down. 'It's all yours Bryn.'

Bryn remained seated. He did not need to read from any script. He had gone over these events many times, yet he still could not explain all that had happened to him.

'We must first look at the facts. From the moment, I was taken, to being returned to Earth, it was a matter of six months. My time on that planet, in hours, equalled one day. I was not sent on a reconnaissance mission; I had been thrown into that an arena, at will, with myself trying to just stay in one piece. I did not know what was happening, I could only stay alive using the skills I had been trained to use.'

Bryn paused for a moment to collect his thoughts. 'The only thing I know, is what took place. How you can find any information that could through any light on why or how. I will be happy to be informed of it.'

'On the 14th April 2012. While hanging some clothes on my garden washing line, a bright light engulfed me. I found it hard to breathe, then nothing. The next I knew, I was gasping for air, feeling a dry warm sensation. An acrid smell, almost turning my stomach over. My eyes were trying to adjust when I was hit. A sudden pain seared through my right side...found myself sailing through the air, crashing into something solid. I did not know how long I laid there, the pain in my side is what had brought me around. As I gathered my senses, a gush of air moved over me. A dark shape landed about five meters away. It had a great mass of dark brown hair, the size of a cow, long body like a polecat. Charlyyk called it a Fuung. My eyes, now focused, I scanned the area, it seemed to me like a large Meteorite Crater. For the little attention I could apply at that time, it looked as if it been worked, to make the walls sheer and unclimbable.'

Bryn looked around to see if everyone was with him. Most of the aides were typing the story on their laptops, a few were writing on notepads. Waited for them to catch up.

'The Fuung beast before me, was eying its prey. As it stalked towards it, I saw what had attacked me.' Bryn took a sip of water. 'It was a large, prehistoric-like creature; bulbous body, long neck, roundish head. The large tail thickset with a cluster of bone spikes protruding out of the end, one of those spikes was still embedded in me. Another had cut through my side, and left a long gaping wound.'

Once again Bryn paused, as one of the Russian aides had raised his hand. The aide completed what he was writing, nodded to Bryn to carry on.

'The Fuung edged closer to its prey. With great speed, it leaped high, seized its prey...by sinking its teeth into its neck, just below the head. The tail of the prey with the same speed catching the Fuung, at its rear end, spinning it. The momentum contributed to it almost severing the head of the creature that had attacked me.'

Su Shi raised his hand. 'Brian, how did you get these drawings to look so real?' Taking a sip of water, Bryn explained how Charlyyk and himself had described the details to his son Thomas.

'Can Charlyyk draw?' Su Shi inquired.

'Not that well, for at that time, she has just managed to master holding writing equipment like pens and pencils.'

Bryn beckoned Helen over, she carried the case with the evidence inside of it, placed it in front of him. Bryn opened it, took out the bone spike, three centre metre at its widest and twenty centre metres long. He also took out a green folder.

'This is the spike from the animal that attacked me.' He said, as Helen passed it around. 'These are the first photos of myself, and Charlyyk after our return by Michel Henderson, the vet that now looks after Charlyyk.' Bryn knew he had enclosed all the information in the reports he had sent to the British Military HQ. But this review was not his call; this was for them to question him.

'As you are aware, at that time we had to be careful of who knew about her, as you can tell from the photo's that Charlyyk does not have fingernails, but claws which were fine for where she comes from, that became a problem here. Michel did a lot of research, with Charlyyk's permission, he removed one claw from each foot. As they regrew, he treated them. When Michel was satisfied that the procedure had worked to some degree, he did all of her fingers and toes. He keeps an eye on them, so they don't become a problem and revert back to long claws. It has given Charlyyk a chance to be able to use her hands more efficiently, so she is able to hold a pen. Before, she found it difficult?'

One of Su Shi aides, suggest a couple of questions. 'How wide was the arena, and how high the walls?'

Bryn shows them a drawing. 'You will find one of these in the pack.' They all shuffle through the papers in front of them till they all had one in their hands. Bryn waited before he continued. 'As you can see the arena is more oval than round, I estimated it to be about three hundred and forty metres across by four hundred metres long, the height of Fifteen metres. I did not see or hear anything on the walls to make me believe it was anything like a gladiatorial contest. Though at that time, I was just keeping myself alive, the shelter I found myself, was the carcass of something that had perished much earlier it was ice cold and stiff. The crevice between the rear legs and the under body with a little scrapping in the ground below gave me cover and just in time. The polecat looking beast was hurt, the spikes from the thing it killed had made their mark, it was in pain. It had received a direct hit to the top of its rear leg, was finding it awkward to walk.'

Once more from a sign from an aide, Bryn paused to allow him time to finish his notes. And as soon as indicated, he resumed. 'A rather large ape type, long armed sloth, with a bear-like head, about three metres tall, was making its way to the wounded beast. It circled around looking for the best way to attack, The speed of the attack with long claws, swinging with great accuracy, was frightening, it ripped it apart like a rag doll. I had no weapons, even if I had, would I have stood a chance?'

Bryn stopped to sip some more water. Several aides were making notes and discussing what they had heard. One of the Russian delegates looked at Bryn. 'What time did you think it was?'

Bryn nodded. He had been hoping for more challenging questions. 'I could not tell, there was no sun in the sky. There were five other planets near, but not as near as our moon. They gave out light like a moonlight night. I had noticed no shadows that moved to give some idea how time was running. But one thing was quite clear, was the cold. My hands were getting stiff because of it. The light was very slowly fading, the temperature was dropping. I had to make a choice stay where I was, probably freeze, or try and find some sort of shelter and warmth. As I looked around, I notice some movement of light coming from an area at the base of the wall. By moving from one object to another, which were other dead carcasses. I carefully made my way towards the light and saw an opening in the side of the rock face about Sixty-eight centimetres wide and three metres high. I slipped through the gap, into a cavern it was dark, there was some sort of fluorescent light, not electric but an organic type of light, similar to luminescence of fireflies.'

Bryn was now coming to the conclusion that they had no idea what question to ask him, he might as well just continue with his story. 'There was movement here and there. Large shapes ambled about. The stench was horrid... putrid, as my eyes became adjusted to the darkness, I could find my way around better. An enclosure with some living things sylphlike beings, huddled together, but not able to make a clear distinction as to what they were due to the poor visibility.

Then a large bear-like thing reached into the pen, grabbed one of the creatures, pulled it apart and started eating it alive. The poor thing screaming in pain. Moving cautiously, I managed to find a dark corner away from anything.'

Chad Smitt raised his hand. 'These Bear-like creatures--can you give us any other description of them?'

Bryn shuffled through the papers, then showed a drawing depicting one of the creatures. 'As you can see, the way the head is situated on its shoulders does not allow the thing to be able to talk. My guess it would only be able to growl. The slowness of movement was another thing to look at, in its inability to think fast. As to what the thing was wearing reminds me of the tabard the old knights wore over their chainmail, but of a thicker material, they stood about two-one metres high covered in hair. They moved ponderously; in a shuffling movement.'

Bryn sipped some more water and waited until they had settled. Some were writing down comments, Bryn was expecting someone to speak, but no one did.

'I attempted to treat my wounds but found it difficult, when out of the shadows, came one of the beasts carrying a creature. I noticed the beast, carried a weapon by its side. Charlyyk said it was just about to pull her apart when I threw myself at it from the side. As I flew through the air, I grabbed its head. Twisting my whole body around, I gave it one mighty yank. The neck cracked under the force of my attack. It went down, did not move. I removed the weapon but did not need to use it, as the beast was already dead.'

The thick-set Russian speaking. 'What happened to the weapon?'

Bryn pulled the case toward him. lifted out the weapon. It measured sixty centimetres long and ten centimetres wide the end was rounded more for hacking then for stabbing, it was very crudely made, and very heavy.

Helen stepped forward took up the weapon, then passed it amongst the delegates so that they could all examine it thoroughly. Su Shi moved his chair towards Chad Smitt when the exhibit reached him. 'This is not an advanced civilised people. These seem to be foot soldiers for others more capable, don't you think?' The thick-set Russian, Yuri Stanovic joined them, a light discussion took place.

Bryn welcomed the short break and talked with Alan Carter, Major Arn Sigurdsson, representing the UN. Arn and Alan had met before on UN matters.

When the group settled back to their original positions, it was Yuri who spoke. He wanted Bryn to understand that they believed his version of the story. 'Brian Collier, before we can come to any conclusion, all of us here know your reputation as an experienced soldier. That reputation is sound and trusted. We can take what you are telling us to be a truthful account of what happened. Russian Intelligence has sifted through your reports that Britain had sent us. With so little to go on, piecing together a strong theory as to what has transpired on that planet, it is like trying to find a needle in a haystack. We just need to be patient; let you go over the story until some detail triggers a new insight.

Pulling his chair closer to the table, Bryn resumed telling his story. 'The effort it took to kill the beast, caused my wounds to open. I became cautious of how much blood I was losing. My attempt at patching myself up did not work. I looked at what I had on me. In the pocket of my cargo trousers, was my wallet. I found a needle but no thread, then from my torn T-shirt, I pulled a thread of cotton, my attempt at sewing up the gash in my side were feeble. The cotton kept breaking.'

'Charlyyk who I had stopped the beast from killing and eating, took the needle from me, plucked a hair from her head, after much trouble, managed to threaded the needle. As I pulled the wound together with my fingers, Charlyyk attempted to sew me up, with great difficulty. At this point, I was exhausted'

'The next I knew Charlyyk was shaking me to wake me up. More of the beast were gathering around the carcass of their dead comrade. There were about eight of them, too many for me to encounter. I needed to find another safe position. There was none, so, I started to make my way towards the entrance. I had found earlier. I saw more beast coming from other directions towards me. I slipped back into the arena.'

Chad Smitt was looking at the photos of Charlyyk. One of his aides gave him another paper to look at. 'This young lady is a quick learner, Brian.'

Bryn agreed wholeheartedly. 'In two years, she has adapted to life here like a duck to water. The name that was given to her by the group she lived with was Charlyyk. *Char* meaning quick, and *Lyyk* meaning girl. My sister Gwen and her husband Harold are retired teachers. They could not believe someone could learn as quickly as she has. She is now attending school with other local children.'

Su Shi commented. 'Our embassy in London has followed this story very closely.' Looking at Bryn with a look of sincerity. 'They could tell from the very beginning; it had a worldwide interest. The ordinary people of China would like to know more about this young lady. But what concerns our governments more, is what could happen if these Aliens attack us. This Light Beam shows us of their capabilities, but what else could they do?'

At this point they all stopped for lunch, a buffet was set up in the reception room. As they helped themselves to food and drink, they carried on talking about what Su Shi had implied about the threat. They were also discussing how Bryn had managed to have achieved what he had done with the spike still embedded in his body. Bryn explained that to remove the spike could have meant losing, so much blood, would have been the finish of him.

Yuri asked Bryn how Charlyyk reacted to him at the beginning. 'I could not know, with the pain from the wounds, loss of blood, no food or water. I was not in the best frame of mind; a strong sense of survival was the only thing that was on my mind at that time. Charlyyk did not come into any of my options. I was taking what chances that came available, almost like I was running on the spot, trying to gain thinking time.'

Helen flitted about making herself useful, at the same time listening. When everyone had finished lunch and settled down around the table. Bryn continued with his story.

'In the arena it was light. I took great care to see what waited for me; there were still the carcases of dead beast. Charlyyk reacted seeing the dead polecat. I realised then she was still with me She had sheltered between my legs almost tripping me up.'

'I could not see any threat at that time, so I carefully made my way to where I first sheltered, Charlyyk in close attendance. I showed her the hiding space, she settled herself inside it. Then she pointed at something behind me, I quickly turned to see a creature similar to the polecat but half the size. Charlyyk called these *Feeng*. Before I could react, a bright light appeared, and another Feeng emerged from the beam of light. The first creature started to circle around me looking how to attack. It was the size of a lion, and looking just as dangerous, the size of its head looked huge, reminded me of a Chinese dragon with yellow and orange eyes that looked like fire.'

A Chinese Aide raised his finger. 'The beam of light, had it any peculiar features to it?'

Bryn thought for a moment, this question had never been asked before. The room was silent as they watched Bryn's face. 'Yes, there was a pattern. You know how the flame reacts as it leaves a jet engine, with those multiple streaks. That was how it looked.'

This set the delegate's all talking with each other. Bryn waited for them to settle, till they to bid him to continue. Eventually they nodded for him, to carry on.

'With the weapon in my hand, I felt I had a chance with defending myself. The Feeng attacked with a speed that took me by surprise. I managed a swing at it but did not get enough weight behind it. The Feeng knocked me flying.'

Bryn stopped talking, making sure everyone was keeping up with the story.

'Once again, I could feel pain, but coming from my back as I hit the floor. Twisting my body, I managed to get to my feet before the Feeng struck again. I held the blade high. I brought it crashing down in the dead centre of its head. I was ready, to receive the next attack from the other Feeng. Then in disbelief I saw two more. I had to shake my head in case I was suffering double vision.'

'Luck was on my side, the ape-like sloth was attacking them at great speed, I sought cover just in case. I found where Charlyyk was, laid there with her, watching the battle that was taking place. Charlyyk taking a firm grip on me, her eyes were moving in all directions. She knew what these beasts were capable of, her instinct of watching out for them was a natural thing for her to survive, so I was glad she was there.'

'The Sloth like ape took the attention of the Feeng away from me, as it posed the biggest threat to the Feeng, two against one was not good odds, for these Feeng work together. It was some movement from my right that took my attention for three-quarters the way up on the wall a figure appeared, it was not like I had seen before.'

'My attention returned back to the fight, for one of the creatures had been caught a slashing blow from the ape-like sloth, the strike had thrown the Feeng toward us, blood streaming down its left side. I saw my chance and moved as quickly as I could, killing it with a single blow, then realised I was out in the open, and would easily be picked off.'

Bryn took another sip of water, then waited for them to catch up.

'Charlyyk's cry sent me seeking cover. That's when the next problem arose out from nowhere. Furry alligator things, coming scuttling towards me. From the corner of my eye I saw Charlyyk had climbed onto the dead carcass she had been sheltering under, the furry alligators had turned were headed towards her.'

'Looking up at the wall I could see we were being watched. I rushed over, dropping the weapon so to be able to use both hands, taking advantage of the light gravity, as these creatures were not large, I grabbed one of them by its tail, with enormous effort, swung it around, then like a hammer thrower. I hurled it at where I had seen the movement, to my surprise I hit near the target. With that success, I had to do it again and again. The low gravity helping me to achieve that task. But the damage it was doing to me I should have just killed them.'

Bryn noticed a hand raised, stopped. One of the American aides asked. 'These new creatures, you did not mention, if they were dropped by the Light Beam?'

Bryn shook his head. 'No, I had not seen how they were introduced into the arena. Charlyyk might had seen, though did not mention when we spoke about them.' Bryn waited till they indicated to him to carry on.

'Charlyyk was quick to jump down from the dead carcass. The look in her eyes told me to turn. The sloth thing had lost the fight. The victor had turned its attention back towards us. Picking up the weapon I raised it up high and waited. Charlyyk grabbed my left leg, hung on tightly, as the Feeng charged. With every ounce of energy I could muster, brought the blade crashing down onto its head between its eyes. But it had managed to strike me a slashing blow to the chest, but then nothing. For the flash of light consumed us.'

Bryn took a moment to relate to that moment, had he missed anything. Then he remembered how the Light Beam felt, and looked when he was inside of it, before he lost consciousness. 'When the Light Beam surrounded me, I felt pressure being pushed upwards in many places, like fingers, by many light beams that twirled around me. Then nothing, when I came to my senses, realising I was still alive and I could see my cottage a mile away, it was then feeling Charlyyk tugging at me, I had a good hold on her, the realisation It had not been a dream; but as I tried to stand, the pain seared through my body, still having a hold on Charlyyk. I pointed to the cottage, Then with Charlyyk's help, and her determination, we staggered there; when inside I phoned my sister.'

The silence in the room showed how he had their attention. Chad Smitt looking at his aides. Turned to Bryn. 'What was the date?'

'It was 26th September 2012. Six months had passed, but it felt like only part of two days, that I had been away. That is just one of the many questions I have asked myself. How did I survive without food and water over that length of time?'

The looks on the delegates faces, showed the same bafflement as Bryn's was showing. How had Bryn survived the distance he must have travelled? How had he survived on no rations? It looked as though it was only Charlyyk that held the answers, would or could she be able to throw any light on the subject?

Major Carter took the floor. 'Shall we adjourn and meet same time tomorrow?'

Su Shi was still examining the weapon and the bone spike. 'Captain Collier may I see the scars.'

Bryn stood up and removed his top clothes, to exposed his body. The claw marks on his back and on his chest were clearly visible, as to the crudely sewn scars at his midriff. Su Shi took out a compact camera. 'May I?' And took three quick snaps. 'Just to satisfy our people, they look for the most minute details.'

Helen could not resist looking at Bryn's body, as she handed him his clothes. Bryn left the meeting with Helen. They entered the lift as the doors were about to close. Major Carter and Lieutenant Archer slipped in as well. 'Third floor Helen for all of us.'

Leaving the elevator, they all headed for Major Carter's room. Once inside, with the door closed, Major Carter asked. 'Helen is that what you expected?' Lieutenant Archer handed Major Carter, a briefcase, as Major Carter punches the code. 'Which one of Su Shi Aides do you think it will be?'

Helen crosses the room. 'The Major.'

Bryn looked puzzled. 'Ok Helen spill the beans what's all this about?'

Helen opens the case and retrieves a folder, removes a paper from it, passes it to Bryn, as he reads it. 'That bitch was one of ours? It was she who shot me three times in the back.' Bryn felt very angry, as he sat there still with the report in his hands.

Helen then shows him some photos. 'This picture shows the capsule she had placed in one of the bullet wounds. Bryn's memory drifted back to North Korea at that time. He had been sent in to get a colleague out, but all hell had broken out, he had flown into an ambush, found himself in the hands of the none-too-gentle Madam Ling, of North Korea's SSD. For eight days and nights, he had endured her expertise. Some of the deepest scars on him were inflicted by her. Especially that last evening, when in a fit of temper, she shot him three times in the back. The small calibre gun would not have killed him but would still create enough damage. Then she dug the bullets out of him, in not the nicest manner, even the guards could not bear to watch. She shouted and screamed, 'He is no use to me, he might as well be dead,' he was exchanged four days later, for two of theirs, he was barely alive.

Bryn was angry to be reminded of the pain of failure of being caught. This episode of his Military career was his biggest regret, had blamed himself for being careless. 'So, I was set up, hung up like a piece of meat.'

Helen pointed to another sheet of paper. 'If that's how you want to put it, yes, but look what it achieved?'

Bryn read the document. It was from MI6. Bryn recognised the signature as authentic. He then sat on the bed. Then looked at Helen, he was utterly speechless. It was proof of North Korea's intention to build nuclear armaments, those that were involved in supplying the technology to build them. Two names on the list were British Nationals, that was more reasons for the Chinese wanting to get Britain's assistance. Although China was Allied to North Korea, China was worried if North Korea became too strong, would China be able to control them. Britain was the best option to stop the flow of expertise, and the materials needed to build such a weapon. Bryn was used knowing his ability to endure long lengths of interrogation, so to make the exchange possible.

Major Carter collected up all the papers returned them to the folder, placed them in the briefcase and secured it. He looked at Bryn. 'Nobody. I mean nobody must know about this.'

Bryn nodded his head in agreement. 'So, what's this about the Major?'

Helen sat by him on the bed. 'Someone set this up from China, the code they gave then, they have used again for a meeting here.'

Bryn's mind flashed back to the time he came too after that ordeal and found himself not in the hospital but at 'Oakleaves' Kit had set up the clinic to nurse him back to health. Catherine as ever being her eager assistant, the whole family's lives, put on hold just for him. One wound was freshly opened when he had arrived home from Hospital. 'Madam Ling, had planted the information into the bullet wound in my back, that took a lot of planning Helen?'

Helen took hold of his hand. 'She was China's agent, not ours.'

Bryn stood up. 'I think we should act as normal as possible, until they make contact. I'm going to my room to get ready for dinner.'

Bryn walked to the door, Helen followed him, leaving Helen at her room, he continued to his room. He showered and dressed. He then phoned Charlyyk. He spoke with her for twenty minutes on FaceTime so she could see him. 'Sweetheart when we were on that Planet and those funny alligator things were coming at us, did you see where they were from?'

Charlyyk spent her usual think time, then said. 'No, I just spotted them. I was concerned they might have attacked you.'

At the Hotel restaurant, Bryn was shown to his table, to his surprise Su Shi was seated there, he stood up and shook Bryn's hand. 'Please forgive me for taking this opportunity, I must explain myself. My sister was responsible for the bullet wounds in your back.'

Bryn did not reply. He had been trained to give nothing away. He simply gave Su Shi a quizzical look

Su Shi took a sip of water. 'Madam Ling is my sister. Actually, she's my half-sister, different mothers, and if you are only allowed one child per family, to have more than one, have different mothers?'

'Why are you telling me this?'

Su Shi looked at Bryn. 'Eight days and nights of torture from a sadistic female needs some apology from someone.'

'My fault for getting caught, I took the risk, I lost.'

The waiter came and took their orders, when he had gone Su Shi took a photo from his wallet. 'My father, I'm standing in front of my mother, left of my father is Ling, with her mother and my other sister Li, with her mother.'

To Bryn the photo of Ling did not look like the Madam Ling he had got to know. But Li, that was a different matter. Su Shi could see in the look on

Bryn's face that was not how he saw Su Shi's sisters. 'Is there a problem here Captain Collier?'

'Seeing her face again although she looks a lot younger in the picture, brought back a few unpleasant memories.' Bryn still keeping his cards tight to his chest.

Su Shi showed Bryn another photo. 'This is my sister Li at her wedding.' This picture gave credence to Helen's theory. The man Li had married. The Major that was Su Shi's Aide.

Bryn nodded, he was seeing Su Shi was trying to justify himself, his manner was apologetic. Yet Su Shi was still in control of himself,

The waiter arrived with their orders, set them down, over dinner the conversation changed more about themselves informally, their childhood upbringing, their values that their parents had instilled in them, also about their own children, and Charlyyk. Though from different backgrounds they had generally lived with the same values.

After the dessert course, Su Shi asked for coffee and could it be served somewhere more private. The waiter directed them to a reception room that had a log fire burning, some comfortable armchairs and a small table situated close to the fire. When after the coffee was served. The mood of the conversation changed.

'I believe I should now be more honest with you Captain Collier.' He took a letter from his pocket and passed it over to Bryn. 'Please open it and read.' Bryn accepted the letter and opened it.

Dear Captain Collier,

Those bad deeds that I inflicted on you were necessary for world peace, the pain you felt, I felt too, the information your unknowing body conveyed to those that needed, that could act on that information, were invaluable, but still, the world must not know.

I, like your very lovely late wife Kitty, am not long for this world, but I could not leave it without saying, thank you for what you endured, and my most profound regret for having to inflict it upon you. My highest regards,

Li.

'When?' Bryn asked.

Su Shi chin trembled slightly. 'Three months ago, they spotted cancer too late, to save her.'

Bryn's hand reached across and touched Su Shi arm. 'I'm so sorry for your loss, convey my sympathy to your brother-in-law, he must be going through a lot of grief?'

Su Shi stood up saluted and shook Bryn's hand. 'Good night, I will see you tomorrow morning.' turned and walked away.

At Carpenters Cottage, Charlyyk is talking to Harold about her homework. 'Poems, Uncle Harold, what are they about?'

Harold walks over to his bookshelf and selects a book. 'This will excite you Charlyyk, William Wordsworth, The Daffodils.' Charlyyk took the book from him and sat down and started reading, she read the poem over and over again.

'I would not write like that uncle Harold, but it does make sense. He wanders lonely like a cloud, but the jocund company, what's that?'

'Light-hearted, cheerful, that what jocund means, so as the breeze tickles the daffodils they move gently like dancers at a party, light-hearted; now how about this one?' He selected another book. 'Edward Lear: The Owl and the Pussy-cat you will like this one Charlyyk.' He opened the book and gave it to Charlyyk; he waited to see her face light up, as she read the poem.

'This is funny.' As she looked up at Harold, her eyes twinkling with pleasure.

As Bryn walked into his hotel room, the telephone was already ringing by the side of the bed. 'Hello.'

Helen had seen Bryn dining with Su Shi and could not wait to hear, what he had to say. 'Can I come to your room?'

He agreed, she put the phone down, and in five minutes, there was a light tap on his door. She entered and did not say anything until he closed the door. On reaching the bed, they sat down together on the bed. 'What happened... What did he say?'

'Su Shi had two sisters Ling and Li; his aide the Major, who happens to be his brother-in-law, is married to Li.' He paused for a moment. 'Madam Ling was actually Li... Su Shi, half-sister... Ling's mother was Korean, and Li had used her name to get the Korean's trust, to allow her to infiltrate into The North Korean Secret Service, the SSD.'

Then he handed the letter to Helen, then waited till she had finished reading. When Helen looked at Bryn, she noted the sadness in his eyes; she took him in her arms and cuddled him. 'You still miss Kitty?' The tears welled up in his eyes. 'Do you want me to leave?'

He shook his head. 'No, stay.'

Bryn looked down to his hands. 'Helen in our line of work, we have to find the best solutions to solving situation, that could disrupt world peace. We sometimes get it wrong. Then there are the times, it just goes wrong, with the timing being the biggest factor. Then there are those moments when you sit and wish you did it differently, the regrets are knowing there would be no second chances.' Bryn's look into Helens eyes, he understood Li needing to redeem herself. 'Even I wished at some point, to apologise to those I had left behind to clear up the mess, that I had left them with. Yes, it might have been a successful operation in the eyes of those directing me, but other, innocent parties paid a price, of my actions.' The look of regret showing, the cuddle Helen was giving him was going to happen.

The reaction was simultaneous as they cuddled, they slid down laying on the bed together, fully clothed, Bryn cuddled Helen from behind, his arms wrapped around in front of her, her hands rested on his wrist. They stayed in that position, their thoughts on what Bryn had said, till they both fell asleep.

***

On Thursday morning, Helen waking up and feeling someone beside her was not what Helen had ever experienced before. Laying there enveloped in his arms, warm secure; did it give her satisfaction, was it what she wanted? What she did know, was that she did not want to move in case the embrace might end.

It was too early to do anything else. Bryn's heavy breathing meant he was still deep in sleep. She lifted his right hand and gently laid it on her breast. The excitement she felt inside her, was like a child doing something naughty, just to see if they could get away with it.

She lay there waiting... breathing heavy with excitement. Her chest moved up and down... will he feel it... much was going through her head.

His hand moved, caressing the nipple. The excitement was building inside her, as Bryn's finger moved they massaged with slow caressing strokes... Emotion rose in her as warmth, reached a part of her that he was not touching. She wished, no wanted him to touch. Dare she move his hand there? Her excitement was increasing all the time.

She felt his lips on the nape of her neck, then behind her ear. She turned her head to find his lips with hers. His arms relax their hold, she turns to meet him face to face. The embrace lingers then when they break away from the kiss. 'Help me, Bryn…I'm new to this?'

Bryn suddenly pulled back. His sense of reasoning told him it was going too fast. 'Helen we must wait, this is not the right time. Let us act with a bit of caution. We can pick this up at a much better time so we can develop this relationship with a better understanding of each other…Yes, I want your love, I also want your respect just as much.' Bryn thought for a moment. 'To be completely honest Helen, I do not know how Charlyyk will respond to us, so let see how we can win her around first of all. You see, Charlyyk has this uniquely logical way of thinking. once she has put her thought through a specific reasoning to a problem, or theory it's like it is written in stone it is impossible to change her mind.'

Helen although disappointed, saw how Bryn was thinking. He did not want to set fire to the bridge till after he had crossed it. But the words 'I want your love.' gave her great satisfaction.

Bryn was keen on Helen, The last thing he did not want, was to give her, the wrong message . Bryn was more than aware, that when they had first met at Gilmores. It was Helen's efficient manner he liked. She was not cold with it. It reminded him of Kitty's efficiency. Helen's smell that pleased him too. Yes, as Kitty's smell had pleased him. Helen was different, she was no Kitty.

He was trying to answer the nagging feeling that he had. Was he trying to replace Kitty, if so, were they for the right reasons?

Catherine's, words rang in his ears. 'Give it time Dad, you may find someone you like, you're still young at heart.'

'Helen I'm not saying no, I'm saying how?'

Helen had been patiently waiting for Bryn to explain himself. She did not want to give up at the first hurdle. She had felt his love, knew it was there, she will just have to wait, a little bit longer.

After showering and getting dressed, he arrived at the meeting at ten-to-ten Helen had laid on croissants and coffee for him, placing them where he was seated, smiled as she turned to walk away from him, but her hand gently brushed against his arm, as she passed by him.

Yuri was the first to arrive, followed by Chad, the rest drifted in. When all were seated, Major Carter opened the proceedings. 'Gentlemen… Oh and Ladies' Looking at Helen. Then towards Bryn. 'Captain Collier'

Su Shi raised his hand. 'Please let's keep it informal.'

Major Carter nodded as everyone else did. But it was Yuri who was the first to speak.

'I've had a report from Moscow, late last night a group of hunters tracking a bear, that had been terrorising a village, when they had it in their sights, a beam of light hit it, it just disappeared. It appears the Light Beam takes things at random.' Yuri replacing the report back in its folder. 'The report was sent to me by a Capt. Victor Tolmoski'

Bryn looking at Yuri while he was talking. 'I met with the captain in London, he was trying to clear up a few details on a young man, who had been placed in an asylum for his father disappearance, relating it to what has happened here.'

Yuri spoke to one of his aides, who made some notes. 'We must speak with this young man, and get a full picture of what he had seen.'

Su Shi and Chad conversed quietly. Chad nodded his approval, then turning to Bryn. 'The other Alien you saw, the one on the wall, could you describe it in any way? You were quite vague about it, in your story yesterday.'

Shifting through the folder in front of him Bryn found the picture, Thomas had drawn from his and Charlyyk's description. He held it up so all could see, then waited for them to find it from their own folders.

'As you can see gentlemen, it is vague, but it is what we believe, that we had actually thought we had seen. The ledge that stood back from the face of the rock wall hid most of what detail we would be needed to make a full description. Observation in the field of fire can distort the real facts. Thomas spoke to Charlyyk and myself separately, this was the result.' Bryn waited for them to look at the drawing. 'When I knew you wanted me to come explain, what had taken place, I contacted my son Thomas if he had made any improvements to these drawings. He mentioned a computer artist, he had contacted, Lynda Bryant. She is putting her own expertise toward the images that might help us.

Capt. Hanne, Chad's aide, spoke. 'I know of her, we have used her in some of our recruitment programmes, I'll check with my department. Capt. Hanne then left the room.

Arn, the UN ambassador, spoke next. 'With such little information, what are you all hoping to achieve here?'

Su Shi and Chad seemed to have some idea of what they thought could be accomplished. With much to discuss between themselves, while Yuri listened in on their theories. Then Chad turned to face everyone. 'All the reports of these activities have been in the northern hemisphere, So we would like all governments to check any reports no matter how small, of any unusual disappearances: Times, dates, anything, we will seek out the best mathematicians. Ccomputer analyst, astronomers, and physicist or whoever it takes to work out where that beam of light comes from?'

Chad gestures to Yuri, who nods with the agreement. Yuri turned to Su Shi 'The Russian government will put everything behind this.'

Su Shi shakes his hand, 'The Chinese government has already agreed to help in every way, whatever the situation requires?'

Alan Carter asked. 'Are we all in agreement? Is it a go then?' They all nod, then with handshakes all round, seals their agreement to work together.

Capt. Hanne returned to the meeting he caught all their attention. 'I have spoken with Miss Bryant; the finished picture should come through any moment.'

They waited for ten minutes. Then the printer burst into action, and slowly the picture appeared. Lieutenant Archer lifts up the scanner cover, laid the image in position, closed the lid and presses for six copies. As the printer feeds out each copy. He passed them out to them to check the result of Miss Bryant's art work. The printer was not finished, and another print started to appear a digital reconstruction of a full-length picture of the subject. The only image Bryn could give was head and shoulders, The surprise was it had similarities to Charlyyk.

As the group studied the pictures, all of them started to pick up on it, Su Shi turning to Bryn. 'What do you make of it, Brian?'

'If she has just used the picture that Thomas drew, it's uncanny, but if she has used Charlyyk as a guide, we must discount it.' Chad agreed with Bryn.

Yuri spoke next. 'Do not discount anything, let's get our own people to challenge it, and see what they come up with?' Su Shi, Chad, and Arn all agreed.

Chad still looking at the print. 'Brian, can you get your son Thomas to send us a better picture, than these photocopies?'

Bryn soon punched Thomas's number into his phone. In FaceTime, a bleary-eyed Thomas was on the other end.

'Hi, Dad.'

'Thomas, could you make some better drawings of the image that you did of the wall alien, head, and shoulders?'

Thomas looked more awake. 'Yes dad, I've already had made more detailed drawings so Lynda could finish her images on her computer, the first drawing was not suitable, so I had to tidy up a little; why what's happened, dad?'

'The final result ended up resembling Charlyyk, Thomas.'

The ensuing pause seemed longer than it really was. 'I'm looking at the picture now dad.' Then Thomas put the image of it on his phone. 'Can you see it?'

The group gathered around Bryn looking at the screen. 'Yes… Yes, we can.'

The group agreed nothing had changed. Chad, taking the phone, from Bryn.

'Thomas, I'm Lieu-Col Chad Smitt, could you meet me in Washington, tomorrow morning…say…eleven hundred hours at the White House, with all the pictures, I will have transport and security clearance set up for you.'

He hands the phone back to Bryn. 'Hi, Thomas can't wait to see you both, looking forward to seeing you for Christmas. Bye.'

Chad was talking on the phone to Washington, then turned to them all. 'Gentlemen this has been one enormous pleasure, let's keep in touch…not just for today, but till we can find a conclusion to this dilemma. I've enjoyed the way we have worked together. There will many more meeting, no doubt. What we have is nothing! We are no wiser than when we first started. The way Captain Collier was whisked away and then returned, has not helped us to gain any rationale to the purpose of these Aliens. The proof is the alien girl existence. The fact that Captain Collier's family has educated Charlyyk, has given us the chance, as to some idea of what kind of alien that we could be facing.

Let us not get despondent. Getting to know you has been the greatest achievement, for that will give us the ability to work together, to debate as a team. Could you get clearance from your respective Governments so we can visit each other on this. Thank you all.'

The shake of hands of farewell, were with sincere friendship. As the room cleared of the delegates. Major Carter and Lieutenant Archer gathered any debris lying about, a shredder is put into service.

Helen spent most of her time talking on her phone. 'We have clearance for six o'clock, need to be at the airport by five-thirty, so we should be out of the hotel by five is that clear?' Helen had stopped being a Sergeant, returned to being the Commander-in-Chief.

In Tim Pearson's class, Sandra and Charlyyk's hands were raised. Mr Pearson the English teacher was trying to ascertain, who had read any poetry. 'How about you Mace?' The blank look on Mace's face brought a wry chuckle, from Tim Pearson. 'How about Humpty Dumpty?'

Mace's blank face, suddenly changes. 'That's a nursery rhyme?' he blurted out.

Laughing, Tim Pearson replied. 'True Mace, but still a poem.' Then he pointed to Sandra.

'So is, the Charge of the Light Brigade, both about battles.' she said.

Tim Pearson then points to Charlyyk. 'How about Ring-a-Ring of Roses, all having a message, or depicting something happening at a certain time in history.'

The teacher wrote on the whiteboard, '*Stories that are made easy to remember, set in rhyme*'

Mace looked puzzled. 'But Sir, how can the nursery rhyme of Humpty Dumpty, be a battle.'

Tim Pearson looking pleased with himself. 'Let's look at the two nursery rhymes, Ring-a-Ring of Roses, Charlyyk you brought that one up. Can you explain?'

Charlyyk stood up. 'At the time of the plague, the Black Death meant if you grouped together like standing in a ring holding hands, you could pass on the disease to one another. 'All fall down, you would be all dead.'

Tim Pearson then asks Sandra for an explanation of Humpty Dumpty.

'During the English Civil War, the Royalist had a large canon positioned on a battlement, which inflicted heavy casualties on the Roundheads, so the Roundheads concentrated their fire on the battlement bringing the canon crashing down, the Royalist attempts of getting it back failed, and the Roundheads won the battle. Because of the round ball shape of the canon, they called the canon Humpty Dumpty.'

At the Victoria Hotel in Interlaken, Bryn was packing his bags. Checking around the room he finds the Khaki Army standard issue cardigan of Helen's. Picking up the cardigan, he took it to Helen's room. Knocking on the door, Helen called out to say the door was open, Bryn entered, Helen's laptop was open She was working.

Helen was using her computer, smiled at him seeing the cardigan. Showed Bryn the e-mailing, she had sent. '*Dad I've fallen in love.*' Her father's reply read '*Good God you are human…Keep it up old girl you might get to like it.*'

Bryn could not stop laughing; he was still sniggering on his way back to his room.

They all met in the Hotel Lobby, the Mercedes Transporter was parked outside. Lieutenant Archer loaded the bags, they were soon heading for the airport.

Bryn had bought some Swiss chocolate for the girls in the hotel reception, he had spoken with Harold that he was heading home. Harold told Bryn to go straight home to 'Oakleaves' he would bring Charlyyk back Saturday morning.

The plane trip did not take long, enough time for Helen and Bryn to explain to Major Carter, Bryn's meeting with Su Shi. 'And you accepted that apology from Li, considering what she did to you?' The Major queried.

'When we go on covert assignments Alan, if necessary, we might have to eliminate someone. Putting the wrong thoughts in my head, I cannot do my duty as expected of me, of course, we would rather save a life than to take one, but I must not lose the purpose in what I'm there for. We would expect that applies to the other sides operatives.' Bryn looked down into his hands. 'We all have to do nasty things to get the results required to settle disputes. These things can end in operatives not returning home. It is that what we must do for Queen and Country, and world peace. It is only now, that I am beginning to see the trauma, I put my own family through.'

Chapter 13

Home Comforts

When the plane landed at Brize Norton. Helen asked Bryn on what he was about to do. 'I'm going back home to the Cottage, Harold said he will bring Charlyyk home on Saturday morning.'

Helen took his hand and snuggled up to him. 'Do you want company?'

The tender kiss he placed on her lips needed no answer.

Major Carter shook his head. 'Come on your two lovebirds. I can drop you of it's on my way. Lieutenant you in the front with me.'

The Cottage was lovely and warm when they arrived. The notice board had a note from Harold. *Milk in the fridge with fresh eggs and bacon see you Saturday.* As Bryn checked the mail and answer phone messages, Helen looked around the cottage with its cosy feel to it, as if she had always lived there.

Helen noticed a Chinese takeaway menu by the telephone. As she went through it, she could see where Bryn had selected before. She had soon put the order through. The girl taking the order reckoned it will be there in forty-five minutes. Helen then followed Bryn, who was carrying the bags to the bedroom as he put down the bags Helen put her arms around him.

When the doorbell rang, Bryn grabbed his trousers put on a dressing gown. The delivery boy was pleased with the ten-pound tip Bryn had generously given him, Bryn put the meal in the oven to keep warm, afterwards he went to the lounge, to lite the log fire. Then collecting the cutlery and bowls from the kitchen, Helen came in with the duvet wrapped around her. Bryn smug smile, seeing the contented look on Helen's face.

Over the meal. Bryn put some classic jazz on the multi-CD player, just soft enough to hear it in the background. Helen did not need the warmth of the fire. Cuddling next to Bryn she was glowing in a blissful sense of freedom, nothing or nobody could take this away. A passage from the Bible kept going through her head. Enjoying Bryn's strong arms and his tenderness, the words, 'From out of the strong, came forth sweetness.' These words could not have rung truer to her.

Charlyyk was enjoying her stay with Gwen and Harold, but she was missing Bryn big time, Gwen and Harold could tell every time she was talking with them every other thing she would say, 'Saturday when I see Dad.' Over breakfast, Charlyyk spoke about the English lesson, and the poem Mike had recited. Harold talked with her about the life of Thomas Hardy.

Gwen was more interested in Charlyyk's maths homework the answers were correct, there was something Charlyyk had missed. 'If you don't show your workings out you can't correct yourself. It looks though you have plucked the answers from the air.'

Charlyyk did not get angry or sulk, she just said. 'I will remember that Auntie Gwen.' Charlyyk's mind had been her dad. She had forgot about acting the ages of those around her at school, she quickly altered her homework.

***

Helen cooked breakfast. She had never been this hungry in the morning before. Everything seemed different. She acted like she was much younger. When she was near Bryn, she wanted so much to touch him. She knew if he continually touching her in the same way, she would soon get annoyed, still found it was hard to restrain herself.

Bryn could still sense some nervousness in Helen, took her by the hands. 'We have so much to learn about each other. We will make mistakes, but we must learn from them, not harp on them. The first time I met you at Gilmores I felt something inside, and every time after that. It was not a lustful feeling, just a desire to get to know you. Then on that Saturday here, I saw you blow that kiss at me. It felt like that a carrot was being dangled. After the kiss in the evening. I knew...there were no more doubts.'

Helen leaned forward and kissed him. 'I had been observing you for some time. When the Home Office informed me of the strange request for assistance you had sent in, you intrigued me. Toby gave me the best insight of you. I had to find out if meeting you would confirm the interest that festered inside of me, was not professional, that it was personal.

Bryn cuddled her gently. 'Yes. Toby would have given you the full low down on Kitty and myself. The amount of time we had served together. then with Toby coming to the cottage. He knew more about me and my family, than any other person.'

Helen loving the attention she was receiving from Bryn's lips. 'I did not know what I was looking for, but found myself looking all the same. Somewhere deep inside of me, a teenager was trying hard to escape. So many emotions were breaking out all at once. Then running away, panicking like a silly schoolgirl. I tried to bury myself in work. Bryn, I was a mess. My brain was scrambled. I had never been in a position like that, it did concern me.'

Helen paused for a moment, she reflected back on how she was looking at the situation given to her by the Home Secretary. 'Bryn, when I dug out all the files on a Capt. Brian Collier. as I sorted through the information it was becoming apparent that you were not a man that would make up stories. The name Toby Scalon kept appearing in the files. I confided with Toby, he told me stories about you, and about Kitty and the children. It confirmed the feeling I had when I shook your hand, I just did not admire you, it was much stronger than that!'

Helen was blushing with a coy look, as Bryn smiled at her. 'Bryn, that was not me I did not do fairy tale, love at first sight, or silly schoolgirl emotions. I'm the hard-nose cold-hearted ice maiden bitch that everyone sniggered about behind my back person. But it did happen, I had planned to tell you when all this business was over. But the other evening lying there with you, that naughty little girl inside me appeared, I am so glad she did.'

Bryn took her in his arms. Their kiss just lingered and lingered. Tears of sheer happiness were streaming down Helen's face. She buried her head into his chest and trembled with joy, overcome with the emotion of truth, that the Ice Maiden had finally melted.

Helen then drew away from Bryn. 'You mentioned about your concerns about Charlyyk, have you worked out a way for us to handle it?'

'Yes, I realised last night when we were cuddled up, that we must just act as normal. Knowing Charlyyk, she will tell us.' The look Helen gave Bryn was inquisitive. 'It's Charlyyk's nose Helen, it will tell her before we get the chance to. By playing it casually, I'm calculating she will accept it in the same way.'

At the Academy, Charlyyk was not her usual calm collective self. Mrs Butler was the first to notice her odd behaviour. Mrs Landon, should be notified? The grapevine was in full swing, at lunchtime, a very casual Mrs Landon sat next to Charlyyk, trying not show she was concerned. 'Hello, Charlyyk how are you today?'

She did not expect the barrage of conversation, Or the speed in the way it was delivered; if this were an animated scene from a comic strip, Mrs Landon would have been depicted leaning back, mouth opened, hair flying backwards.

It was Sandra that came to Mrs Landon rescue. Seating herself next to Charlyyk putting her arm around her shoulders, then kissing her on the cheek. 'Hi, kid.' Charlyyk calmed down. 'Her dad has been away Mrs Landon, and he will be home tomorrow. Charlyyk has been getting more excited as the weekend approaches. We have kept her away from the topic as much as possible. But a direct question as you have just asked was bound to set her off.'

Mrs Landon nodded. As she stood up, she placed her hand on Sandra's shoulder, and with a sigh of relief said. 'Thank you, Sandra...Thank you.' Then stroking Charlyyk's hair. 'Have a lovely weekend with your father, Charlyyk.'

At the cottage Bryn, had been sorting through the yellow pages to find Car showrooms. He explaining to Helen the timescale he had given by Bill Symonds on the Discovery. He found a trading estate that had car showrooms with franchise for four popular makes of cars. He looked for a Land Rover Dealership, near to those garages, there were two dealerships.

Helen had changed into civilian clothes and was feeling more comfortable with these surroundings. Though she had lived mainly in London. She was now finding the Country side to her liking.

'Well lets us go there first said Helen, we could go now, then to the others on Saturday?'

Helen liked the drive in the Morgan, with her hair flying in the wind, it endorsed that young girl feeling she was now experiencing. They parked up outside the Land Rover Garage, where they casually browsed, looking at all the different models. Picking up the details on each of them and their prices.

Then they walked to the showrooms of the Mercedes garage. Helen liked an SLK sports model in bright red with cream leather upholstery. She didn't need to know the engine size, or how fast from zero to sixty Her attraction towards the car was how it looked. As they walked from the showrooms, she grabbed his arm. 'Do you know Bryn; I do believe I might be able to afford it?

At Carpenters Cottage, Charlyyk was helping Gwen lay the dinner table. She was very excited about tomorrow, but the attention she gave to what she was doing, Gwen could not find fault. After dinner, she sat on the sofa with Harold looking at her homework, he suggested a couple of ways to tackle the subject and gave her a couple of books to study, with that she gave them both a kiss and said goodnight. Later when Gwen looked into her, she was still studying quite hard. 'Not too late sweetheart.'

Chapter 14

Picking into her Memory

The dark mornings did not bother Bryn, the heavy breathing of Helen in a deep sleep, allows Bryn to slip out of bed without waking her, He then dressed for his early morning run.

Out in the garden, he goes through his stretching routine. Then headed out through the gate onto the fields, picking up the dirt track that the tractors used. He skips over the style steps at the field gate, and onto the lane that leads up to the Farm that also leads down to the village. From the corner of his eye, he caught sight of a familiar lone runner; he slowed to allow Charlyyk to catch up.

Seeing Bryn her pace quickened. He anticipated the beaming smile on her face. His smile was just as broad. What he did not expect was the leap Charlyyk made. He caught her in mid-air as her arms wrapped around his neck. The force caught Bryn entirely by surprise, they found themselves sprawled on the ground. The hugs and kisses showed Bryn how much she had missed him.

She suddenly stopped, her nose had picked up something, that was on him, the look on her face had changed for a moment. Then the smile came back, the colour of her eyes turned to a golden hue. Charlyyk's ears twitched as they honed in on her dad, as though they were listening to his inner thought. 'Have you something to tell me?'

'What do you mean?' He said with a smile.

'You have someone's sweat mixed with yours?'

Bryn did not answer, but the coy look on his face made Charlyyk look at him more closely.

They got to their feet and began to jog. but they had not gotten too far before she playfully punched him. 'Yes, but whose?' She was silent for a moment then with a squeal.

'Miss Helen Bennett.'

Once again Bryn is amazed at the power of her nose, the rest of the run she peppered him with questions.

Arriving back at the cottage. Bryn instantly phones Gwen. 'Charlyyk is here with me?' Gwen told him how she had missed him and she would bring Charlyyk's things over later.

Bryn hung up, looked around. Charlyyk had gone. He heard laughter. As Helen and Charlyyk walked in holding hands. 'She was trying to hide?' The mischievous smile on Charlyyk's face and the way she was holding hands with Helen eased Bryn's worry, about how she was going to except Helen. 'No chance, no one can hide their scent from me.'

Helen could only agree with her. 'I had showered, made the bed, put everything away. Then I hid in the wardrobe. Charlyyk just walked in opened the wardrobe doors, said, pleased to meet you again Helen. I thought you must have told her, she said she smelt me on you when you met down the lane?'

Bryn shrugged his shoulders, while nodding. 'I told you she would.'

After Bryn and Charlyyk had showered and changed clothes. At breakfast, Charlyyk asked some poignant questions to them both, Helen answered most of the issues.

'As neither of you are teenagers, do you know where you want to go with this relationship? And how do you feel I might be a problem with it?'

Helen's answer was just as direct. 'No problem with you, Charlyyk. If there could be a problem it would probably be from me, with the work I do. I don't intend to keep going on working forever. It is when can I stop...that will be the problem?'

They talked about the meeting at Interlaken and what they were trying to achieve when Bryn showed Charlyyk the 3D picture that Lynda Bryant had made on her computer. Charlyyk looked confused. 'Can this be real?' Bryn explains to her that they were going to find out the best way they can.

Helen could see the worried look on her face. 'Have you seen them before Charlyyk?'

Charlyyk stood up and left the room, and in five minutes she was back holding her pencil case. She selected a soft pencil. gently shaded in a couple of areas, then shows the picture to Helen, the image had changed, not dramatically but enough to give it another new dimension.

'Where have you seen them, sweetheart?'

Bryn placed his hand on Helen's shoulder. 'Leave her, she is thinking, she won't let it go until she remembers.'

Bryn took the picture Charlyyk had altered and faxed it to Thomas with a forwarding note telling him what had happened for the changes that Charlyyk had made.

Forty-five minutes later Thomas makes contact. 'Dad I spoke with Lynda she has put the new information into the computer the new Image will be with you soon. Have a lot to tell when we meet... love you.'

Charlyyk knew what she was looking at, could not place where she had seen it before. It was a vague image in the back of mind, feeling something was blocking her memory. When the printer sprung into life. Charlyyk could not get to it any quicker: She looked at the image appearing, Then taking the image, her eyes transfixed, at what she could see.

Turning the picture, twisting it about, Then back to the table, drawing onto two separate pieces of paper then moving the paper about, when it came to her, Now knowing where it was, she relaxed and sunk down. Her head into her arms leaning on the table. The mental strain of searching her mind, had put pressure on herself.

Bryn sat beside her and put his arm around her. Charlyyk turned towards him, burying her head in his chest. Bryn could feel her whole-body tremble as she gripped him tightly. He knew Charlyyk was reliving that traumatic moment.

Helen was feeling the strain also. She stood and watched as the two of them went through the drama. She was way out of her comfort zone and struggled with what she should do. Bryn beckoned her to come over to them. Helen came up to them put her arms around them both, kissed Charlyyk on top of her head.

Charlyyk settled herself she explained the drawings. 'The glimpse I remembered were vague misty images, it was like a flashback from the back of my mind, those images were not clear. Then there was another image, I drew the other image separately, then placed them in different positions, then there it was.'

Helen was looking at the two other drawings Charlyyk had made, putting them together she could make out a sort of an ally or a corridor. Then it dawned on her, Charlyyk had been in a craft of some type, she had been transported, not taken by a beam of light, the drawing of the alien, was the image of how it looked to Charlyyk, as it piloted the spacecraft.

Helen needed thinking time, made coffee for Bryn and mint tea for Charlyyk and herself, all that time she had put her thoughts into the drawings.

Charlyyk fetched some more A3 piece of paper, then using the previous pictures, she dug deep into the deepest depths of her mind, as she concentrated hard the image started to appear not of the alien...but the inside of the craft.

Helen made some phone calls, then putting her arm into Bryn's arm. 'Do you mind if we don't go out, I've called Major Carter he is collecting together some plane designers, they are coming here, now. They are dropping everything to be a part of this. Charlyyk's memories must be captured while they are fresh in her mind.'

Not even Helen expected twelve people turning up with; servers, computers and large monitors. In minutes they were working. They put Charlyyk's picture in a scanner, and it was projected on the large monitor. They manipulated it with some hi-tech software, with a lot of help by Charlyyk. They pinpointed a part of the drawing, asked how big did she believe it was. Charlyyk looked around the cottage then found an old dinner plate, when they keyed the information into the software then did the whole thing come to life.

A Sister-and-brother team Sam and Philip worked with Charlyyk trying to squeeze as much information they could get out of her. Digging into her memory bank like lock pickers. Each tiny fragment fed into the software changing the construction design, bit by bit, then the computer operator pressed the right keys, a digital 3D animated version came to life on the large screen.

Charlyyk's mouth dropped open; it looked so real. Philip puts the details of the alien into the mix, and places them in the positions as shown in Charlyyk's drawings. It frightened the life out of her, her mind was inside the craft the smells the noises all smacking at her memory cells, she rushes to Bryn for protection.

Harold and Gwen who had arrived earlier, had stood with Bryn and Helen spellbound at what was being played out in front of them. Two of the aircraft designers spoke with Helen, giving her a disc of what they had made, then as quick as they had come, they left.

Harold asked how it happened? 'We were telling Charlyyk about the meeting in Interlaken.' Bryn showed the computer image that had developed from Thomas's drawings. 'When Charlyyk reacted to them, we asked where she had seen the Alien before.' Helen then shows them the next drawings, Charlyyk had drawn.

Gwen puts her arm around Charlyyk. 'Poor thing it must have been so frightening for you?' And gently guided the conversation away from what was her ordeal.

Harold was still interested in what they had found. Helen collected her laptop, opened it up. She put in the disc, that the aircraft designers had left her, it up was now on the screen. The images looked so real even Harold remarked. 'I can now see why she was so frightened. It must have felt like she was back on board that ship.'

Because they had the detail of the inside of the craft, the aircraft designers could get an estimated idea how the outside of the ship might look like? In 3D mode it was impressive. Harold played around with the program, totally engrossed in the fine details it delivered.

Bryn suggested that they all gave Charlyyk some quality time by going out to lunch. When this was put to Charlyyk the smile they received convinced them that it was a good idea. They expected she would like to go to the Pizza parlour, but instead she suggested a fish and chip restaurant the other side of town.

Sandra had told Charlyyk. 'Because it situated out of town it has adequate parking outside. The interior is modest, but the fish which is freshly caught, taste great.'

At the restaurant, Bryn and Helen told Gwen of the relationship they were having. Gwen took Helen in her arms, welcomed her into the Collier Clan. 'I'm so pleased for you both this need celebrating properly.'

Gwen, could see the role that Helen could take on as a mother figure. Charlyyk was getting older she was beginning to get more and more demanding for views on earthly values. Gwen was okay for now but the strain for finding the right answers were becoming more awkward for her.

Harold ordered a bottle of Prosecco. Charlyyk got a sip to toast them. Charlyyk sitting between Helen and Gwen with Bryn and Harold facing her. Happy talk and laughter surrounded her. All Charlyyk could do was to soak in the joyous atmosphere; to her it was sheer bliss. Since going to school there had been something the other students had, that she did not. This could be the answer that would resolve what was absent in her life.

Later the conversation had turned to cars Bryn telling Harold about Friday. Helen talking about the lipstick red sports model with cream leather upholstery. The boys ribbing the girls on how they looked at cars. Harold pushes Bryn on his choice of the car.

Then Charlyyk spoke. 'It will be the Discovery the deal is too good to let go. We are not far from Bill's garage we should accept his offer today.'

For a moment, it went quite, then Bryn broke the silence. 'To be honest, you are right Charlyyk. Where's money is concerned I hate snap decisions. I already know it's a great deal, on a very nice motor.'

The satisfactory look on her face, was not a smug. From under the table, both Helen and Gwen's hands each grasped at Charlyyk knees, a touch of approval, of girl power.

At the garage Bryn concludes the deal with Bill Symonds, while the others admired the classic cars parked outside. Helen, and Gwen gently discussed the car with Charlyyk. 'So why were you so keen on this one Charlyyk?' Helen enquired.

'Any type of car of this range would be ideal for us, when it snowed, we found ourselves a little inconvenienced, the Morgan slipped about on the hills. Dad might be a good driver, but in those adverse conditions, it could easily catch him out, where the Discovery would cope, in all adverse weather conditions.

Quietly Gwen said to Helen. 'That sounds more like Harold talking?'

Helen nods in agreement. Then asked Charlyyk 'Would that worry you?'

'It should worry us both.'

Bryn checked his phone as the ping usually meant a message. It was from Thomas. 'Dad, I have given Chad Smitt your e-mail address and phone details, he needs to get in touch?'

Bryn relays the message to Helen. 'We'll know what he wants, when he makes contact?' She remarks.

Back at Oakleaves, Charlyyk went to her room to unpack her bag.

Bryn and Helen snuggled up together on the sofa. Their eyes closed till the ring of the phone, makes them move. Lieu-Col Chad Smitt had made contact.

'Brian, with these new developments, I'm pulling together everyone that I can. NASA's Johnson Space Centre at Houston will be the venue as it can accommodate a large contingent of visitors, let's say around the first weeks of November, I will confirm dates when the time is known?'

Bryn wrote everything down, as Helen listened in with the conversation, her ear as close to the phone as she could get it.

Helen looked at what Bryn had written. 'Come on, let's go to bed, we'll start on this in the morning.' They look in on Charlyyk; she was sitting up in bed reading.

'What are you reading sweetheart.' As Bryn bent down and kissed Charlyyk

'Poems.'

'We are off to bed, sleep well.' They both gave her a kiss, with little hug.

***

Next morning, during the run. Bryn updates Charlyyk on the trip to America. At first Charlyyk said nothing just mauled the information. This was what she expected to happen, she needed to evaluate how she was going to portray herself. The more she thought about her predicament, noting how the other people around her and their feelings, that she could be a threat. The changes that were happening to her, were making her realise, just how important that was becoming.

At the Cottage, Helen had already set wheels in motion. Major Carter was her first call to work out schedules. She called the Home Office to give them all fair warning on what was taking place. When Bryn and Charlyyk returned, she was ready to give Bryn an update of the progress she had made. 'I've managed to contact Major Carter he will make the arrangement for transport, and the Home Secretary will get back to us, on the security for Charlyyk. I don't think Gwen will be too happy her going, but it will all depend if we can satisfy her requirement for Charlyyk's security arrangements in America... You know I cannot go?'

'Not as Sergeant Baker?'

Helen looked at him sternly. 'No Bryn, I have still commitments here to take care of...Major Carter is the only official person that has been assigned to Charlyyk's security, so he will be with you.'

At dinner at Carpenter's Cottage. Helen consulted with Gwen about the visit to America. 'You will have to go with Charlyyk, as her chaperone. I have spoken with Thomas and Rachael this afternoon, and they will be there to help you. If you have any concerns with this, let me know and I will get them resolved before you leave. That's a promise Gwen.'

Charlyyk sounded excited at the prospect of going to another country, meeting Thomas and Rachael again. Then kept asking about what it was like in America, she had seen pictures that made it look idyllic. Though some of the news footage showed an entirely different story. It was the latter that worried poor Gwen, her look of anguish indicated this is not what she wanted.

***

Monday morning, Bryn waved Charlyyk of to school, waited till the bus was out of sight, there was much to be accomplished before the week was through. Helen was making progress with the schedules. Her clipboard held a folder case, so as she confirmed each task was completed, they were ticked off, then instantly filed. She used Bryn study as her office, it was well equipped. An old fashion desktop computer that Bryn and Harold built themselves, with two large hard drives installed, so plenty of storage, sat majestically to one side. There was no password set, so she soon had created a filing system with her own password; It was operating on 'Windows 7' that had not been updated. She was quickly shredding paper, an old security habit she had maintained.

Helen knew she was using the cottage like a hermit crab, inhabiting somebody's else's shell, Was it to protect her from predators, or just to be near

Bryn? Bryn affected her like a magnet; she kept on being dragged towards him. From that moment, shaking hands with him, although she had tried to run away, her thoughts kept her thinking of him and the pull just got stronger.

Bryn sorted through Charlyyk's clothes; when he had a good mental idea of her wardrobe, he then consulted with Helen. 'How cold will it be there?'

Helen texted Major Carter, for that information, then sitting down over a cup tea, they went through the schedule together, so if Charlyyk was in need of any new clothes they still had time to purchase them. Bryn was anxious, 'We will only have Saturday to shop, it's the shoes that are the hardest to get for her because of how narrow her feet are?'

Helen took hold of his hand. 'Do you know how much I am enjoying this? I've never had to think of others before, well not in this way. Bryn I'm becoming addicted to you and Charlyyk, thank you for letting me into your lives.' The smile he gave her as he squeezed her hand, confirmed he felt the same.

At dinner, that evening, a very excited Charlyyk was keen to tell them about the comment made by her schoolmates about the trip to America. All of them had their personal likes, with dislikes. Pop, TV and Movie Stars, were the usual likes.

***

Saturday had arrived, Charlyyk woke up with a determination to do a longer, harder workout, Bryn found it hard to keep up with her, allowed Charlyyk to push on without him. He returned back to the cottage. Helen looked surprised when he came back on his own. 'Is this what they mean, when they say girls weaken legs?' Bryn threw a towel at her.

When Charlyyk arrived back. Bryn had showered and dressed. She showered straight away her hair still wet when she came for breakfast. Helen soon had a towel wrapped around it. 'This will stop you from catching a chill!' Charlyyk saw Helen cared about her, just like Catherine did; just a little amount of authority, but mainly with love. Sandra and Julia had remarked on how their mothers reacted to situations, in the same way.

The girls planned to go with Gwen to the shops. Bryn was waiting for Bill Symonds, who was delivering the Discovery. When the doorbell rang Bryn was expecting Bill. Instead, it was Janet Stokes. 'Hello Mr Collier I'm spending the weekend with James it would be rather rude of myself, not to stop in and say hello!'

Bryn welcomed her in. 'Charlyyk is in her room; she would love to see you.'

Janet gives Bryn a large folder. 'These are some of the articles that are ready for your approval. You will see I've noted the Magazines they are intended for, with the photo's that will go with them.' Then she went to find Charlyyk. She was laughing with Helen, when Janet came through the bedroom door.

'Janet!' Charlyyk yelped, showing the pleasure seeing Janet.

They hugged, the joy on their faces of seeing each other, could not be mistaken. 'I'm spending the weekend with James.'

Charlyyk introduced Helen. 'Janet is writing my story for the press.'

Helen shook Janet's hand. 'Yes, I know! I vetted you... oh by the way, what are you doing next week?'

'Why?'

'Would you like to go to America with Charlyyk?'

Janet's face lit up. She knew full well this is going to develop into something more significant, that she will be right in the middle of it. 'Oh yes, count me in.' Then Helen gave Janet all the details. 'Then I better go home and pack a different bag. But before I do that, there's someone who should know. I must explain to him what is going on?'

With slight trepidation, Janet phoned James, who surprised her. 'That okay darling. How about we drive to your place together. When you are ready, come and pick me up.'

James really did not mind. He knew he would have never met Janet if it was not for Charlyyk. Sharing Janet with Charlyyk, was a small price to pay.

When Helen had worked out the finer detail to Janet. Janet left to pick up James. As her red Mini turned left and headed for Parsons Farm, the Discovery with Bill driving pulled in with his wife close behind him, in a silver Mercedes Sports SLK.

Ted had fitted the accessories, and Bill was willing to show them how they worked, The Stereo player was the most essential piece of equipment for Charlyyk, adapters to operate the Radio and CD Player, with plugs for earphones so Charlyyk could listen to her music, and he did not. 'Showing your age Bryn?' said Harold with a laugh.

Bryn could only chuckle. After all, Charlyyk would sing at the top of her high-pitched voice, with what she would be listening to.

Bill and Tina made their way to the Mercedes. 'Bryn when you have time come and see us with Helen and Charlyyk?' Then the Symonds left.

Back in the cottage, Helen put her ideas to Gwen. 'Janet could use this opportunity to write about Charlyyk, but this does not mean you cannot go. Janet presence will free you and Harold to exercise more supervision over any situation that may transpire there.'

Gwen thought through what had been said. 'So, I have the final word?'

Helen smiled. 'Gwen? You have all the say, where Charlyyk is concerned. I'm trying to give you help to make the right decisions, for all of the right reasons. You looked very concerned when this meeting was put upon you, the last thing that Bryn would like is for you to be under any stress. He loves you, but most of all he relies on you and Harold. When I see Charlyyk's love for you, that's when I know no one could take your place.'

Gwen's face showed she had settled her fears of going to America. Helen felt relieved, inviting Janet was the key to settling Gwen.

The women soon were ready to engage in retail therapy, were on their way, in Gwen's car. The men had a new toy, so for them it was playtime. They headed for Parson's farm.

Edward and Jane were delighted to see Bryn and Harold. Edward Parsons owned an earlier version of the Discovery. Bonnets went up as the men compared engines and improvements. It was not long before Edward was in the driver's seat of the newer model, Harold by his side. They were off over the tractor tracks around the farm. Bryn stayed with Jane talking about what she had in mind for Thomas's room. 'Rachel and Thomas are coming for Christmas, so more like a guest room than a boy's room.'

When the Discovery returned to the farm house. Edward was liking the improvement in the Discovery. Over mugs of strong coffee, the four of them were talking about old times, and of Helen.

Bryn's late wife Kitty, use to be great friends with Jane. Kit's untimely death had a terrible effect on her, Edward had said once to Bryn. 'It is like Jane had lost a big sister. she would just mope around lost.'

Jane listened to Bryn and his views on Helen. 'From what I hear, you describing this Helen you have taken to, has brought some fresh air around here. She is no Kitty, but my, she's sure is something else.'

Edward patted Bryn on the back. 'This family wants to see you happy. It sounds like Helen will certainly achieve that. So, put a ring on her finger and bring her home, the sooner, the better.'

Mugs were raised in mutual agreement. Harold knowing Bryn, could see something was at the back of Bryn's mind. 'Are you concerned about Charlyyk, Bryn?'

'So much is happening so quickly. I would like to be sure it won't hurt her?'

Jane put a big comforting arm around his shoulders. 'That girl is the most level-headed girl I've ever met, take my word on it, she would love having a Mum and Dad. I suggest you talk to her about it?'

Harold patted his arm. 'Jane's right. You should talk to Charlyyk.'

Chapter 15

The Proposal

Bryn used the Sunday morning run, to speak with Charlyyk. As they turned down Bishops Lane he asked casually, 'What do you think of Helen?'

Charlyyk did not say anything at first, nor did she falter in her stride. Bryn for a moment thought she had ignored him. Finally, she said 'She's nice, I like her, so different then Auntie Gwen, but yet so similar. Care shows in what she doe's and says.' There was a pause... 'She will stay, won't she?'

Bryn, at ease with himself, started to slow down.

'You ok, dad?'

Bryn stopped running.

Charlyyk turned back. 'Is there a problem?'

Bryn took a deep breath. 'Would you like Helen to stay here for always?'

Charlyyk leaned her head to one side, as though she was trying to read Bryn's eyes. 'That would be nice... But is there more. Dad. You seem to be hedging around, as though you need to tell me something, so come on spit it out.'

Bryn smiled at her. 'If I asked Helen to marry me?' He did not get a chance to say much more.

'Sarah said if you met someone, then got married, I would have a mum just like she has. Is that right?'

'Would you like that; would you accept Helen as your mum?'

Charlyyk showing her excitement. 'Then we would be a proper family, of course, I would.'

Bryn took her hand in his. He wanted to put the right meaning to her about what marriage meant. 'Charlyyk if I marry Helen, it will be forever. It won't be a game we are playing, and if you are tired of it, you cannot just walk away...Marriage and family...is not like that. You have to take the good with the bad.'

'I have watched you both, it is my nose that tells me this is right. Helen fits you like your T-shirt... snug... Yes... do us both proud... Marry Helen, make her my mum.'

He hugged her and kissed her. 'Now all I have to do is propose to Helen, please don't say anything until then?'

The rest of the run was light-hearted Charlyyk skipped and jumped about like a spring lamb. Yes, she had listened to all of her friends, each one spoke, how largely their parents figured in their lives.

In the cottage, Helen was sorting out her clothes, what to take back to her place, what could she leave at Oakleaves. Sitting on the end of the bed with thoughts running through her head. Was she taking things for granted, was it going too fast? She looked around the bedroom, taking it all in?

She found herself fondling Bryn's T-shirt, putting it to her nose, taking in his smell of sweat and the aroma from his aftershave, the doubts started to ebb away, as a soft gooey feeling started moving inside of her. When she heard the garden door close; the wanting became stronger. The sound of them laughing made her laugh, the little girl in her was taking over. Her heart trembled like a tuning fork that had just been struck, just feeling his presence, she knew she loved him if only she knew, that he loved her as much.

Bryn entered the bedroom, stepping towards her. He swept her into him, then kissed her. 'Helen Bennett with the authority of Charlyyk I have permission to ask you?'

Helen's heart nearly stopped.

'Will you marry me?'

She threw her arms around his neck, kissed him so hard, then without any hesitation. 'Yes, yes, yes I will...Yes I will. And kissed him again and again, then her eyes glimpsed a very excited Charlyyk standing by the bedroom door. She broke away from Bryn, held her hands out to Charlyyk.

They all embraced each other. Charlyyk looking directly into Helen's eyes. 'Will you be my Mum?' Charlyyk's ears swivelled forward, her eyes changing colour as she spoke.

The smile Helen produced needed no words for Charlyyk, the vibes Helen gave, said everything. 'Yes, sweetheart...if you want me...forever and ever I will be your, Mum.'

Charlyyk was experiencing utter joy at the thought that she now was a part of a whole family. Since going to school and hearing about the other girls talking about their parents, how they shared their lives. She never felt envious, she just felt that with only her and her new dad, it seemed incomplete? And since Bryn and Helen had joined sweat with one another, he looked so happy. Sandra had confided in her about her father, when he became ill, her mother gave her so much strength to tackle the problem together. Mace told her how strong his mother was and how soft his dad was, each needed the other. Now Charlyyk's family would be complete.

Charlyyk, then remembered what Catherine once said, 'If you think it's a dream, pinch yourself and if it hurts it's not a dream.' Charlyyk pinched herself really hard, and it hurt, Bryn and Helen watched her flinch, looking at them, with a silly smile on her face. 'It's not a dream, it's real.'

Helen was going through the same experience; she did not pinch herself she was going to live the dream.

At four thirty the red mini pulled up in the drive Janet and James were in a happy carnival mood. They unloaded Janet's bags and placed them by the front door. When Helen opened the door, their tongues were down each other's throats. Helen left the door open, she knew what it meant to them, to feel that way.

Helen's bags were already in the Discovery, Bryn had given her the keys, she had phoned her parents and told them she had something to tell to them. When she had completed her business at her apartment, she would be coming to see them.

Harold and Gwen arrived ten minutes later, As Harold loaded the bags into his car, Bryn and Helen broke the good news to them of their engagement, the happy look on their faces, looked as though they had won something. Helen kissed them both, then with a big hug for Charlyyk and Bryn, she drove the Discovery out of the drive, driving off, waved her goodbyes.

The Hobart's car arrived at Brize Norton the duty Officer directed them to where the plane was waiting. A young Flight Sergeant, arranged the loading of their luggage, stored the Vauxhall Insignia inside the hanger.

Major Carter showed them to their seats. 'We're still waiting for four more, then we are ready to go. They have entered the airport, ten minutes at the most.'

As they looked around the plane some familiar faces, some of the team that came on that Saturday when Charlyyk remembered about the other Alien, also there was Philip and Sam, the brother-and-sister team, who asked Charlyyk and Janet to sit with them on the long flight.

When Helen arrived at Charlton Court, the block of flats where she lived in Chelsea, Charlie the janitor welcomed her back, she gave him the keys to the Discovery for him to park it in the garage. 'Miss Bennett, I put some boxes in your store cupboard, they arrived Thursday, there were no messages.'

Helen took the lift to the top floor, entering the flat, it had a musty smell to it, this was the first time she noticed the emptiness, that cold and alone feel it had. She was missing the cottage already, with its cosy warm lived-in feel. She put the heating on and opened some windows. She opened the large cupboard where her safe was enclosed, including the servers that contained all the encrypted messages from her agents. Checking through the system she could see how Toby had kept control, while she had been with Bryn.

Helen had no reason to worry, Toby was there from the start when she had set up the operation of MI9. Toby knew everything that needed to be known to run the operation, when she steps down. Helen had been contemplating this scenario before Bryn and Charlyyk had entered her life. There had been times when loneliness had crept into her life, on more than one occasion, it had concerned her

Chapter 16

Houston

The plane carrying the Colliers, landed at Houston, as the early morning sun gave America a golden glow. Charlyyk was looking through the port window. '*The land of Walt Disney*' she thought. How she loved those films. Conveying with the other girls, everyone had their own favourites. Now here she was, where they were created.

Among the excitement, there was something else she was feeling, the changes in her had started to happen. Not knowing how they would manifest, Charlyyk felt she should compose herself, to still appear to be the same little girl.

During the flight, remembering the trip she had been taken on when she had been abducted from her own home planet. She spoke with Philip and Sam about what she remembered, with their excellent communication skills, managed to extract the most minute information from her, even Janet was amazed at their technique. Under their consistent pressure, she had managed to give them extra information. They knew that deep inside Charlyyk's brain there was more knowledge of what took place aboard that alien spacecraft. They felt that there was something blocking them out, it was not Charlyyk, she was trying hard to help in every way

A team of aviation experts all waiting to digest any information that was given to them, laptops were being upgraded with new findings. They too were getting excited; the best aviation engineers will be there at Houston and would be working together to combat this global threat. NASA already employs some of the top Science Specialist. With more coming together, what could be achieved?

The touchdown was so smooth, only a few of them realised they had landed. The plane taxied towards a large hanger then stopped. Gwen and Janet helped to assist Charlyyk, she seemed over excited and not entirely in control of herself, Janet made her sit and take deep breaths to settle her, only when she was calm did Gwen allow her to leave the plane with Bryn.

Charlyyk knew the media attention she would have to overcome if she wanted to project herself as a young girl. She used Sandra as the key subject into her mind-set, that she needed to imitate, then with a deep breath she was ready.

A large crowd had assembled inside the hanger. TV crews, and reporters, cameras flashing. Charlyyk strolled down the steps a little wave here and there, with soft smiles. Sam said to Janet. 'You would think she was the Queen.'

Charlyyk found going with it, was better than hiding from it. A little wave was better than a big wave. The news coverage was inclined to be more with her, than against her. Well, that what Sandra and Julia had said, about the big celebs. The George Clooney's, Adele's the Beckham's didn't fight it; they rolled with it.

Janet said to Gwen. 'I would say, she has it well covered, not too little, just enough to keep them at bay. Clever girl!'

But Gwen was getting anxious. The waiting crowd worried her. A sense of foreboding was building up inside of her. Seeing the crowd surge forward did not make matters any better.

At the bottom of the stairs leading from the plane, Lieutenant-Colonel Chad Smitt greeted them. Bryn introduced his family. Taking hold of Charlyyk's hand. Chad was all smiles 'It's my pleasure to welcome you to America young lady. You have sure set tongues wagging. We have been overwhelmed by the media coverage this visit of yours has created.'

Gwen with hurried steps, with an angry look, that was glaring. 'We came here to share what Charlyyk has remembered, to see if it can shed any more information on these Aliens. We now find ourselves at a circus!' Gwen terse sounding voice, carried across the hanger. To the Lieu-Col it seemed to vibrate off every wall, like an echo chamber.

Chad was taken back by Gwen remarks. 'Sorry, ma'am... please accept our apologies?'

Gwen's anger had boiled up, she was furious. Her words had a vicious bite. 'That's like kicking a hornet's nest and saying, Oops. Where is the chance of security with this damn amount, of people around?'

Chad quickly looked around for some help, but it was a forlorn plea, for Gwen had not finished.

Bryn made a move towards his sister, seeking to ease the situation. 'So, who is going to stick the target sign on her head, you or one of your lackeys?'

Major Alan Carter was quick to respond. 'Please this way we have transport waiting.'

A white bus with the NASA emblem painted on it was on the tarmac. Janet and the Collier family had surrounded Charlyyk, guided her to the bus. Close behind them Philip and Sam with the rest of the passengers straggle out behind them in slight confusion. With Gwen still fuming,

As soon as they were settled, the bus took them to the Johnson Building.

They were soon walking through the concourse. Inside an official tour guide; a good-looking, fresh-faced man in his thirties, introduced himself as Marlon. 'Please if you would follow me, I will explain the setup of these facilities.'

Gwen's outburst had taken the welcoming committee by surprise, they were still in the hanger looking utterly bewildered as to what had happened.

Major Alan Carter had stayed on the bus, which was now on its way back to the hanger. He could see at the entrance of the hanger, there two more buses, being loaded with dignitaries. Lieutenant- Colonel Chad Smitt had various people around him.

Chad certainly did not like the snub that Gwen had given him. He seemed like a boxer who had walked onto a sucker punch, was still trying to clear his head.

When he saw, Major Carter approaching he vented his feelings straight at him. 'I want an explanation for what took place here Major. I do not like the way I've been humiliated, in front of the nation.'

Major Carter, looked straight at him, then calmly, yet sternly. 'I suggest we find somewhere more private to continue this conversation, Sir.'

Lieu-Col Smitt headed towards the bus that Major Carter arrived in, once onboard the bus, the Major closes and secures the door, and then without any ceremony, he confronts the Lieu-Col. 'I personally sent you all the details expressing the need for diplomacy, including with regards to the video recording, referencing the way Mrs Gwen Hobart, reacted at the Press Meeting at Gilmore's, where a NASA employee posing as a news correspondent for CN news. Had you not taken heed of Mrs Hobert feelings for Charlyyk. Did you not read it or try to understand the meaning of it? This family has done their utmost to help us, you have turned this into a tacky sideshow attraction. I suggest you had better get your house in order, so you can explain yourself to the British Government, they will want to know how this was allowed to happen, for now, we had better rebuild the bridges you have just destroyed.'

This was not what the Lieu-Col had expected to happen. He stood there frozen to the spot. As a Lieu-Col it was he who gave out the reprimands, now he was on the end of receiving one. Actually two, and in a short time span, he was speechless. He stood there trying hard to understand what had gone wrong.

It was Capt. Hanne, who standing outside the bus, had overheard what was said. When the Major left the bus, the captain approached the Lieu-Col. 'May I make a suggestion Sir?'

The Lieu-Col looked at his Capt. 'It had better be good John?'

The Capt. could sense the anxiety in his Commander's voice. 'Let me work with Major Carter and try and pour oil on these troubled waters. I may be able to smooth this out?'

The Lieu-Col thought for a moment. 'If I kept away from the Colliers, that could calm the situation.' 'Well done. I like it.'

At the Johnson Space Centre, Charlyyk was enjoying Marlon's guided tour. Gwen and Janet worked hard to stop her pressing buttons, she should not press. This allowed Gwen to forget what had happened earlier. Bryn and Harold had noticed how Gwen was beginning to enjoy the tour.

When Capt. Hanne arrived, he quickly joined in with Marlon helping to explain the workings of various equipment used on the space shuttle. Paying a lot of attention to Major Carter, soon the two Officers were becoming friends, the group were more relaxed.

Then after a while the Capt. suggest some refreshment. 'We have an excellent array of different cuisines here. May I recommend the Mexican food?'

The mention of food brought a bigger smile to Charlyyk's face. Food was always her idea of sheer joy. Janet noticed the excitement in her, she pulled on Gwen sleeve. 'How is she with Chilli?'

Gwen's expression as she turned to face Janet was vague, 'I don't know, we don't eat it ourselves.'

At the Mexican restaurant, they selected a table, that was a bit sheltered from most of the other diners. The attention, mainly of curiosity, was no different from home. Captain Hanne described the menu to them.

Charlyyk's facial expressions were of a child in Santa's Grotto trying hard to see everything, and miss nothing, with that look of wonderment that only children possess. Her hands clenched with the excitement of it all, just not the food, that Walt Disney effect the Americans seem to sprinkle on these occasions.

Janet recording as much as she could on a new mini camcorder. She had purchased just so she could capture the changes in Charlyyk, in different environmental circumstances. Janet sat across from Charlyyk, who was sitting between Bryn and Gwen with Harold and the Major.

Capt. Hanne ordered a chef's special selection, for eight persons, everyone ordered what they wanted to drink.

Capt. Hanne was slowly and gently gaining their trust. He understood they wanted no more, than to be as a family with Charlyyk. When he had met Bryn in person at Interlaken, he had studied him carefully. This quiet man who did not fluster when under pressure. He was always calm, his eyes taking in what was around him. He only spoke when something had to be said. Bryn was what was written in his records and Capt. Hanne had studied those carefully.

The threat from outer space was not to be taken lightly. He felt the pressure to gain precious information to booster America's Space programme. That was America's biggest incentive. Yet, they definitely did not want to upset Britain, who had Charlyyk under their wing. Many of the US Military would like that reversed, it would give them the upper hand in the extracting valuable information to suit their own ambitions.

The waiters arrived. Trays of food were set on the table with the drinks, Nachos, Tortilla chips with guacamole dips, Chillies en Nogada, Corn on the Cob, Chilli con Carne, Grilled Tuna with tomato salsa. Charlyyk's nose twitched and sniffed the spicy aromas that were drifting around the table overpowering the massive Old Spice aftershave, that Major Carter used unsparingly.

Taking a small piece of soft nacho coated in cheese. First, she sniffed around it. Then her purple tongue touched it very gently. Finally, placing it in her mouth, chewing it slowly. The pause she took to allow the food to settle, closing her eyes tightly her throat moving swallowing the last bit. When she opened her eyes, they were wet and glassy.

Charlyyk looked straight at Janet, then grabbed her glass of orange juice, gulping at it. With a little laugh, she looked around the table, she could see they were all watching her with big smiles on their faces.

Janet with an inquisitive smile asked. 'Well?'

Charlyyk reached over and took another small helping of the Nachos placed it on her plate then dissected it. She removed the green and red bits, and discarding them to a side plate. Charlyyk looked at Janet. 'The taste was okay... but why put those bits in?'

She liked the Tuna and the tomato salsa and finished with ice cream; Janet recorded the whole mealtime.

The conversation returned to the space station, Marlon was keen to take them on another journey, a mystical story of space and new planets. 'Each year, we find something new about the solar system, it never stops changing, it so exciting.' The sheer joy in his voice confirmed he meant every word he had said.

The Major's phone vibrated. Bryn noticed it was the same model that Toby had shown him at the Cottage. He watched the major punch some text into it, then turn it off. As they followed Marlon on the next tour. Bryn asked quietly. 'What's next?'

Alan did not look at Bryn. 'Toby has checked the Hotel, all rooms are clear so when you are ready, we can go?'

The tour held everyone's interest. that meant most to Charlyyk and Bryn. They studied the planets, with their different reflective glows, that they gave out, yet could not identify, any they had seen from the battlefield he had been thrown into.

Charlyyk stood by some large photos recently taken by the probe satellite Voyager 2, They were very grainy, but a computer operator was cleaning the images. In a far corner of the photo were some tiny dots that she had noticed and the concentration she was given it, caught the attention of the computer technician that was handling the program. 'Is there something you recognise?' He asked her.

'I'm not sure, but in that corner, that particular pattern looks familiar.' She pointed out the corner to him.

He then punches some keys on the keypad, an A3 size print starts to appear from a printer close by. Taking the copy and laying it on a table he pulled down a large magnifier with built-in lights and explains to Charlyyk how it operates. He gave her a pencil scanner to trace over the area, she had shown interest in. 'You can move the print, so the pattern represents how you think you remembered it?'

After fifteen minutes, moving it one way and another, she said, 'It's as near, to it as I can recollect but I'm still not certain?'

He pushed some more keys on his pad. 'That's Ok, let's let the computer work it out, it might take an hour or two or eight hours, but at least we have given it something to work on?'

Captain Hanne and the Major had called in the station controller. A portly woman, who reminded Charlyyk of Mrs Butler, but with blonde hair, thick purple-tinted glasses. She spoke with a foreign accent. Two other personnel were with her, were soon talking with the computer operator, that Charlyyk had spoken to earlier.

Charlyyk started to feel drained, the long flight and all the excitement had caught up with her. 'Dad, can I go to bed, I'm so tired.'

Major Carter had already spoken with Harold and Gwen, had already arranged transport to take them to the hotel. No sooner had they arrived, and been shown to their rooms, then Charlyyk was in bed, asleep. Gwen and Janet undressed her, while she slept.

Charlyyk's eyes opened to the strange room, lifting herself to a sitting position, she took a long, hard look at where she was. As she listened to Janet's slow breathing pattern, with her mouth open. Charlyyk notices how dry her mouth was. Her nose sniffed the air, it tasted different from the cottage, where the moist air, had the taste of the farm. Here the air was dry, the smells were of urban living; petrol, and fumes from the Hotel kitchens, pollution with dust, she could taste it in her mouth, most clearly of all, was the vegetation, that was different.

She remembered when she had gone to London for the first time. How strange it made her feel. The pollution in the air tasted like grit in her mouth. The carafe of water with a tumbler sitting upside down on top of it, that stood on the bedside table, looked welcoming. She had soon poured herself a drink, but even that tasted different, more clinically clean, than the water from home. It still refreshed her.

She slipped out of bed and went to the window. Looking straight out at the flat landscape she could see a large mass of water on the far horizon. Movement caught her eye looking down, she quickly stepped backwards, the height had caught her by surprise. 'Wow.'

Her shriek woke Janet. 'What's the matter Charlyyk?' and jumped out of bed and was quickly by her side.

'Don't go to close you might fall!' She beckoned at Janet.

Taking a good grip on Charlyyk's arm, Janet guided her back to the bed where they both sat down. 'It's Ok, sweetheart, you won't fall.'

Then Janet went back to the window and opened it; strange noises came into the room, on the breeze. The buzz of the traffic, the sound of people that drifting up from below. Charlyyk joined Janet and marvelled at all these new wondrous things.

Bryn knocked on their door, called in. 'Are you decent?' Janet opened the door for him, let him enter. 'No run today outside, they have a gym here. So, if you like we could go there for a workout?' The girls agreed. 'Give us five, we will be ready.'

Bryn waited for them in the corridor, then they walked to the gym. Afterwards, they met Harold and Gwen for breakfast, at the buffet table Charlyyk sniffed the food carefully, Bryn smiled at what she was doing. 'It's Ok, no chilli.' She informed Bryn. Though she prodded the food with her fork just to be sure.

At nine-o'clock they were met by Major Carter in the reception lounge, the NASA bus was waiting for them outside. A short drive to the Space Centre, where they were met by Captain Hanne, who took it on himself, to be extra nice to Gwen.

Inside the centre, they were introduced to the mass of people. The Station Controller present herself as Mrs Lomax. 'As you have been well informed of the task, I suggest we get on with it?'

It was the friendly computer guy that got up to speak. 'Hello my name is Bruce Foster, yesterday Charlyyk and I did some studying together.' He turned and pressed some keys on his keypad. Then on a great big screen, the image that Charlyyk had pointed out to him was there, in a 3D image. It showed dots in a pattern, He took Charlyyk by her hand and led her to where he controlled the image. On a smaller monitor, next to the keypad, Bruce moved the cursor to the area and started to enlarge it.

Bryn walked over to them. He could see what Charlyyk had noticed, And for a couple of minutes, they spoke to each other about the pattern. It was not what Bryn remembered, It was what Charlyyk had seen from her own home planet. She had talked to Bryn about what it was like in her own world, how the planet that she saw, looked like. These were similar to how she described them. Speakers set up around the Centre allowed everyone to hear what was being said.

Charlyyk asked Bruce if he could alter the angle. Bruce had a gaming console stick attached to the computer, preceded to show Charlyyk how to operate it. At first, she found the stick moved the objects too fast. Then gradually managed to slow down her impulse to achieve things too quickly. Then applied a gentle touch, the planets started to move around at a measured pace. She stopped. 'That it, that what I saw, when I emerged out of the burrow in search of food and water.'

A snapshot was taken, then people start pushing buttons, all the screens came into life, different images in different formats, all working on various theories. Bruce, then asked Bryn, had he seen anything, that resembled what he had seen, he could not.

Philip and Sam stepped up. 'Can we help you?' Remembering what they achieved before. He agreed, they pulled some chairs up and sat in a circle.

Sam had a drawing board, and sitting close to Bryn, she asked him to draw what he thought he had seen. This he did. But Bryn, was not an artist, he struggled at first. The team did not criticise him. Philip sat at the same computer controls as did Charlyyk, moving the stick. Charlyyk stopped him, leaned in. She rotated the stick and turned the whole thing around.

Bryn could not believe his eyes; now it looked, just as he remembered it.

Though there were so many people working, it seemed to go very quiet, as the screens changed, new images started to appear. It was the colour of the planets that Bryn attached his thinking to. He only had brief moments to take in what was happening at that time, for his concern was on survival.

As they all concentrated, a familiar voice spoke. 'Ha Captain Collier, it is a pleasure to meet you again.' Brigadier Su Shi jovial mood was as big as his handshake.

'Likewise, Brigadier, this is Charlyyk.'

Su Shi took her hand and kissed it gently. Charlyyk smiled and accepted his welcome. 'Nice to meet you, Brigadier.'

He looked at the screens. 'You've come a long way, to prove to your new father, this was not a dream.'

The scientist was working out how far away these planets were from Earth, with the speed a craft would have had to travel, to bridge that distance, the cluster that they had concentrated on was in the Draco Constellation and near to HIP 56948 which was recognised as the Sun's Twin, it was two hundred and ten light years away, there was no way it could have happened, but it had. They checked and double checked, no way could they solve the problem, it defied the rules of Logic let alone astrophysics, Earth's best rockets would take hundred years or more to travel one light-year. Taking that it takes only eight minutes for our own sun rays to be seen, thinking how long it would take a rocket to reach the sun, a single light year would be 65700 times that distance.

The eminent Russian mathematician Leonard Tamorov remarked. 'We must look at this, in a much different way, our methods fit our system of thinking, they must have another system. We must input what we have discovered and revaluate it. Ladies and gentlemen, it seems we must reinvent the wheel?' The Russian looked around at all the eminent scholars. 'We must take everything into account, for this light beam to take object it must generate light mass energy. Einstein's theory in everything apart from light has mass... this throws his theory in to reverse. Good luck everybody.'

Everyone, scratched their heads, wondering where to start. A group was looking at images of the spacecraft Charlyyk was taken aboard, when she was abducted. That the plane designers had put together at Saturday also the picture that Lynda Bryant had produced. They added the new information Charlyyk had given, with the help of Philip and Sam. Could these images give them clues to how these Alien's, could have travelled.

While all this was going on. Su Shi wanted to know more about Charlyyk. He was interested in the life Charlyyk had led, to exist on her home planet, the beast that roamed and hunted her group, did she know of any other creatures existing on that world. Where Charlyyk had compared her group to Meerkats

'We did not travel far from our tunnels the Fuung was a solitary beast, that hunted on their own. The Feeng hunted in packs, they were more dangerous, more cunning. When we could, we replanted the *Naamnaam* plant close to our tunnels, as its odour hid ours. We chewed the leaves then spit the saliva into our hand and rub it all over our bodies to disguise our scent. Our only protection from them if caught in the open was try and get to the shrub and hide within it, hoping it would save us. The Fuung yes, sometimes. The Feeng no, there must have been other prey for them to exist, but we did not see any.'

'I find you very fascinating, and I could listen to you all day. The way in which you describe how you existed, but how do you find living in our world?'

At her big smile; Su Shi laughed. 'Such a silly question to ask, after what you have already told me.'

She laughed with him, then she became serious. 'Some things confuse me, why people believe in things they can't see, the tribal way of living, the attitude that our way is better than your way.

'It's to make people feel better about themselves probably.'

It was Charlyyk turn to stop and think. 'Like living a lie, believing they are better than everyone else. More likely they are hiding their own inadequacies?'

'Have you studied Earth's history, how nations evolved. Empires how they were created?'

She looked up at Su Shi, with a mischievous smile on her face. 'Like beast crawling out of the water, turning into man, then turning back into a beast?'

'That's a simplistically, harsh theory.'

'One nation wants what a smaller nation has, attacks it, becomes a bigger nation. Not intent on that, it then attacks another smaller nation, becomes even greater. Another nation seeing a threat, decides to do the same; soon two large nations stand toe to toe, then a big war happens. The winner takes all. The losers on both sides, the mothers who lose their sons, the wives that lose their men, the children and the grandparents. The beast, the leaders?'

Su Shi chuckled. 'So, all the big nations are the bad guys?'

Charlyyk gave a snigger. 'No not necessarily, but big does not always mean best, does it? It only means a bigger stick to beat others with, like school bullies in the playground.'

Su Shi stood up from his chair. 'Let's get something to drink?'

Gwen and Janet had been listening to the conversation with great interest and watched as the two of them walked towards a water station, that was set up at the back of the room. Janet checked the camcorder and replayed it back. The two of them laughing at what had been recorded on it. 'Did you, or Harold teach her that?' Janet asked.

'No, well not like that, we gave her books on history to read, then we discussed the writing and the meaning of the writing and then asked her how they related with the same passage of history, to each other's history books. Teaching her how to cross-reference and not to take just one book as factual truth.'

Janet took a hard look at Gwen. 'Wow, Gwen that's heavy.'

'When we first looked after Charlyyk, Bryn was very sick and needed time to rest, Harold and I moved in with Bryn and Charlyyk, it took only six weeks to teach her basic pigeon English, so she could at least understand us, and we could with her. Like a sponge, Charlyyk soaked up everything we threw at her. She could not get enough education, it was one to one, eighteen hours a day. It was not us pushing, but her demanding. I would do two hours, then Harold would do two hours, and so on. Then when Bryn got stronger, he helped. The morning runs, was Bryn's idea. To slow down her consumption of learning, a healthier way for her to live. That first year was so hard on Harold and myself, but then it got easier. That last year was so nice, we were looking at an entirely different person. She would sit for four hours on her own studying.'

Janet closed the screen on the camcorder. 'I've watched her closely, she always surprises me of the honest way she looks at life, the way her nose lets her know things we could never realise has happened. To say I love my job, underestimates my real feelings of getting to know her. When we talk girl talk, it so different to when I would talk with my other girlfriends. For Charlyyk hold nothing back, she says how she thinks. My friends will only tell me, what they wanted me to know.'

But before she could say anything else, Major Carter interrupts her, I've arranged transport back to the hotel, so when you are ready, make your way to the exit.

Bryn and Harold had met up with Charlyyk, who was still talking with Su Shi.

Su Shi asking many questions to Harold on how he managed to bring the best out of Charlyyk. Harold did not want to take full credit. 'Charlyyk, in the end, had taught us more, for she opened our eyes to the paradoxical way we look at life.'

'In which way do we do that?'

Harold paused to think. 'Charlyyk was watching a documentary, about the aging population. When it finished, she said. 'With age comes the problems of aging, so why do you want to keep people alive for longer knowing the effects it will bring with it, though you are not prepared to look after them properly when they become older? Is that not a cruel way to behave? I had no answer to give her.'

The director of the space centre approached them. 'There is still so much to be work out, so I suggested to the Major it might be a good idea that you return to the hotel. Come back here again tomorrow.'

Philip and Sam joined them. 'You are returning to the hotel can we go back with you. We have some ideas of our own. Sam has some drawings which we had dismissed, but with the new information you and Charlyyk have provided, we think now has relevance, which we hope you may confirm or reject.'

Su Shi was genuinely upset that Charlyyk was leaving. 'We must continue tomorrow Charlyyk I've so enjoyed meeting you.'

On the bus, Bryn sat with the Major talking about the progress being made. Philip, Harold, and Gwen sat in a tight group, their interest was mainly about Philips courses he had taken, first at Sheffield University, Engineering, and Physics; Then when Sam went to Sussex University, to read Law and philosophy. Philip enrolled in a course at Brighton University in Computers Studies. Sam, the same age as Janet sat with her and Charlyyk; talking Girl Talk: makeup, fashion, music, and generally making a lot of noise.

When they disembarked at the Hotel, they all agreed to meet in the sun lounge at about five o'clock. Bryn wanted to go to the gym; hanging about doing nothing was not his thing. The three girls had arranged to shower and then visit the hotel's beauty parlour together. Harold and Gwen wanted a nice glass of iced tea. Philip went straight to his room.

At five they started to meet in the sun lounge, the three girls were the last to arrive, Philip had brought Sam's portfolio case, with the drawings that had been drawn on the Saturday. Sam took out six pictures from the case and placed them in front of Charlyyk. Charlyyk sat there pulling the three drawing about looking at each one with high concentration. When Sam tried to introduce the fourth drawing, Charlyyk stopped her. There was something in the first three but could not put her finger to it.

Charlyyk sat back in her chair, paused for a moment, then allowed the fourth drawing to be placed in front of her. For ten whole minutes, Charlyyk just sat there, staring at it. Janet thought she had gone to sleep, when Charlyyk had closed her eyes, for a few seconds. Then Charlyyk asked for a pencil.

Sam reached into the case and produced a pouch with all various types of pencils inside of it, selecting a soft B4 pencil Charlyyk added a couple of subtle additions. Sam looking on, then brought forward the fifth drawing, again there was intense concentration in Charlyyk's face. She made some small changes.

Sam went to bring in the last drawing, but Charlyyk again stopped her.

started looking at the third drawing again, there was still something, it niggled at her. Sam was convinced something was stopping her to remember.

Bryn whispered to Gwen and Harold, then to Janet, they all left the table. The Major followed the others to another table. Leaving Charlyyk alone with Philip and Sam, Bryn then told them she would not stop till she has found what the issue was.

Harold agreed. 'Even if she was there all night. When something bugs, her she does not let go.'

The Major remarks that he had booked a table for dinner at seven-thirty. Janet started to enter some information into her laptop, when they heard Sam congratulate Charlyyk, looking over at them, Sam was hugging Charlyyk. The Major and Bryn were soon there, inspecting what Charlyyk had found. The Major was soon on his mobile, and rapid instruction was being issued.

Bryn staring down at the drawings could make out clearly, a new alien. Different from the first, sitting in an alcove that had not been depicted on the spacecraft before. Sam explained to Bryn, that two marks in the spaceship had not made sense. There just had to be something else there. This new being was thin, the face longer, eyes smaller slit-like, the nostrils were like flaps on either side of the long nose, the chin, was also thin and long. But the hands were the same as Charlyyk's.

Gwen cuddled Charlyyk she looked exhausted. Janet, was recording it all. Bryn texted Helen, on the new findings they had uncovered.

Philip and Sam, were rushed back to the Space Centre by the Major, when they arrived, there was a buzz of anticipation like the sound of bees in a hive, ready to harvest a new field of pollen. The night was going to be long, but these dedicated people, were used to this type of environment, they thrived on it like a shot of caffeine.

Chapter 17

Bay Lake

Wednesday morning, Janet woke to the sound of cars from the motorway. Looking over to the window Charlyyk was leaning against the opened window taking in the smells, the soft sweet salty smell coming through the window, the wind direction had changed, sea air was being carried in on the breeze. With it, the scent of seabirds.

'Morning Charlyyk.' Janet sat up in bed and stretched her arms out.

Charlyyk went to her, sat on her bed. 'It's lovely out, the sun is shining, birds singing.' She stood up. 'Come on, let's meet a new day.'

They all met for breakfast. Philip and Sam slightly red-eyed. They described, how exciting the previous night had been, even the Major was in a somewhat overtired condition. 'I could not leave until all the computer guys had done their work. You will not believe the finished picture that they came up with absolutely marvellous.' Then turning to the brother and Sister team. 'What Philip, Sam and Bruce Jenner achieved last night was just outstanding, it was as though you three had been working together for years. Bloody marvellous.'

Before they had finished breakfast, Captain John Hanne arrived with three other people. Bryn's smile, lit up the room. The mop of wavy chestnut hair belonged to his son Thomas, and the American film star looks, big hair and sparkling teeth, belonged to Thomas's wife Rachel. With them, a woman in her late thirties was walking behind them. They all met in a big family huddle. 'We flew down this morning. All flights were cancelled yesterday because of the storm. Dad this is our good friend Lynda Bryant.'

Charlyyk made a beeline towards Rachel, Charlyyk's enthusiasm had just taken over. Her nose had picked up the little secret that Rachel was carrying. Charlyyk took Rachel's hands and holding them wide apart wanting to see the baby bump that was just visible. Thomas joining in watching the joy Charlyyk was showing. Thomas was special to Charlyyk, for he had shown her the first human kindness, had given Charlyyk, her first kiss. So, grateful that Charlyyk had helped his dad to stay alive.

Rachel looking into Charlyyk's eyes wanting to see them change colour, this little wonder of Charlyyk always fascinated Rachel.

Philip and Sam were soon talking shop with Lynda. The Major and the Captain went off together to arrange transport.

Thomas and Rachel could not believe how Charlyyk had changed. They made quite a fuzz of her, then were quick to pull Janet into the mix as well. They had kept up with the news on Charlyyk through Janet's articles in the news media, apart from seeing each other on skype.

Thomas and Bryn had a lot to catch up on. They started to walk to the Hotel entrance, the rest followed.

Harold brought up the rear, smiling at the menagerie of noise the girls were making.

At the Johnson Space Centre, the applause given out when they entered was quite warming. Thomas and Rachel laughed when Charlyyk curtsied to the crowd.

Sam put her arm around Charlyyk's shoulder and led her to where Bruce Jenner was sitting at his computer. He stood up and gave her a hug. 'Charlyyk, you have given us a time to remember for the rest of our lives. On behalf of everyone here, thank you.' He pressed some keys on his keyboard, and the big screen came into life as the images were shown, this was frightening for Charlyyk it threw her back in time, to that terrible day. Janet was quick to react, managed to seat Charlyyk in Bruce Jenner's chair.

Now, the spacecraft was precisely like the one that had taken Charlyyk and her group to be eaten as food. Charlyyk knew she was the sole survivor. Everyone in the Space Centre could see what the effect it had on her. The Collier family were soon consoling. The drawings last night were just drawing, now the computer has given the images life. Charlyyk looking up seeing Bryn, dived into his arms, holding him as close as she possibly could.

Bryn owed Charlyyk so much, he could not play down the importance of what Charlyyk meant to him or the part she played in his survival, when he was fighting for his life. Now Charlyyk was fighting just as hard to stay alive. Yes, it was a different situation, but with the same sense of meaning, survival. Bryn carried Charlyyk out of the Centre. Mrs Lomax opened her office for them.

Meanwhile Lynda Bryant set up her laptop, was soon entering the image of the second alien into it. Just over an hour later on the big screen, the 3D image was showing this new Alien, Linda even had it walking. Then to everyone's amazement a new image came up. Linda had put the three aliens together. This gave everyone an idea of their proportions, especially when the image of Charlyyk, and the size she would have been when on the spacecraft. Thomas explained what Michel the vet had said, that the diet Charlyyk was on when she lived on her own planet, Charlyyk would have stayed relatively small. The diet and exercise she had become accustom to, she has put on body size, height, with muscle. He describes the other Aliens. The minimum height two metres ten centimetres, or seven feet tall, it was with these measurements they could estimate the size of the spacecraft.

Leonard Tamorov had worked out the weight of gravity of the planet Bryn had visited and therefore the driving force the ship would have to have to be able to take off. if they were using the same type of propulsion engines that us humans make and use.

Philip spoke up, 'If that were the case would not Charlyyk had noticed the vibrations?'

Mrs Lomax then stepped up. 'So, we must work on the theory they had another power system?'

The buzz suddenly got louder. People suddenly were pushing buttons on their keyboards. The work was not finished. Little groups debating theories then working out those theories on the computers. Then worked out, their probabilities. Nothing was taken for granted or underestimated. Silly could indeed be sensible.

Leonard Tamorov, wrote on the big screen 'LIGHT HAS MASS???'

Thomas went in search of his father; he found them in the station controller's office. 'How is she?'

With Charlyyk's eye's wet with crying, Rachel looked so sad, and said with a sniff. 'Oh Thomas, she was so upset.' Thomas cradled Rachel to him.

Bryn looked up at his son and smiled. 'She will be Ok, with all this love around her, she will be all right.'

Charlyyk's head moved, looked around at her new family, all feeling for her. 'Sorry, Dad.'

Gwen knelt down beside her and cuddled her. 'Feeling better sweetheart?'

Charlyyk released her grip on Bryn, then hugged Gwen, which gave permission for everyone to come and give her a hug. Thomas and Harold took Rachel and Janet back into the Centre.

Gwen, with a soft, comforting looks on her face. 'How about some comfort food?'

Charlyyk's eyes widened. 'Yeah, that sounds good.' She slipped off Bryn's lap.

They head for the entrance, where they found Marlon sitting his inquiry desk. 'Hello, how can I help you?'

Gwen, with her happy face. 'We are in search of comfort food Marlon, any ideas?'

Marlon came away from the desk. 'Follow Me, I have the perfect place for you.' Then speaking into a walkie-talkie. 'Simon, entrance door please.'

They walked out of the main building. A golf buggy pulled up. Marlon invites them to join Simon, and himself, they were soon heading for a diner. It was one of those 1950s diners that looked like a disused rail carriage, like something out of an American film. It was a short drive Marlon was soon showing them to a table. Classic 45's records played on an old fashion jukebox gave the diner a nostalgic feel. With tunes, like Blueberry Hill, and That will be the day, and Chantilly Lace.

A very young girl, with big hair and an even bigger smile. 'How can I help you today?'

Marlon introduced his charges. 'Tandy, these are the extraordinary VIP guest of the Johnson Space Centre, and Charlyyk requires a very special Ice Cream.'

The waitress shouts out the order. Another clean-shaven young man behind the counter, puts the ingredients into the machine, whistling as he works. He scoops the mixture into the sundae beaker. It got bigger and bigger as different layers were added. Charlyyk's eyes got bigger and bigger, with every scoopful. He finished the concoction with fresh fruit, nuts and candy, with three sparklers perched on top, which he set alight. By this time Charlyyk's sad moment, had totally evaporated.

Tandy put the sundae on a server, brought it to the table. Charlyyk, wielding a long spoon was soon diving into this wondrous looking confection. Even Marlon was swooning over Charlyyk's show of sheer joy. Bryn and Gwen enjoyed their Iced tea, Marlon had a coffee.

Gwen was worried that Marlon would get into trouble spending so much time with them. 'Not at all, this is my job, this is what I'm employed to do, that is to make everyone stay here, memorable.'

When Charlyyk had finished, Marlon and Simon the buggy driver, gave them a guided tour of the surrounding Johnson Space Centre buildings, and then returned them to their hotel.

When everyone had met up. Thomas and Harold, brought Bryn up to date, as to what had been going on at the Centre, since he and Gwen had left. How Lynda's graphics had shown them, what the aliens would be like if the information given, was accurate. Also, with the added information provided by the spacecraft, there was as much confusion, as there was clarity.

At seven-thirty they began to sit for dinner, Su Shi joined them he was genuinely concerned about Charlyyk, wanted to make sure she was Ok. She had touched his heart. He had spent much time telling his wife what importance Charlyyk was, for Earth existence.

Charlyyk did not eat much; as the Ice cream had filled her up, joined in with all the conversation, putting her own ideas forward.

Major Carter told some strange, funny stories when he was at school, Su Shi described his home and talked about his family. Bryn was quiet, his thoughts were about Helen when he had spoken to her last, she was going to tell her parents about them getting married. Although she did not need their permission, still felt nervous. Rachel noticed Bryn, in deep thought asked him if he was Ok.

'Yes, I am. I was just thinking of Helen. She is going to tell her parents that we are going to marry.'

His thoughts just slipped out. Thomas and Rachel's mouths dropped. Gwen looked at them both. 'He has not told you?'

In unison, they both replied. 'No!' Thomas continued, 'Congratulations Dad. This is great news...when are we going to meet the bride to be?'

Su Shi reached over the table and shook his hand. 'Of course, I and my good wife, we be delighted to attend, Charlyyk you will be a bridesmaid! How wonderful.'

But the look on Charlyyk face was blank, the look of not knowing what it implied.

Janet and Rachel explained the joys of being a bridesmaid. Sam felt envious. She had never been a bridesmaid, and the feeling, of never being asked, had made her want it more than ever.

Charlyyk was confused. All these emotions just for putting on a dress? 'Sam, why all the fuss?'

Sam looked at Charlyyk. 'It's the nearest thing to being a princess, Charlyyk.' Sam's, face scrunched up in the agony. 'I vowed, not to marry until I've been one.'

Philip laughed at her. 'Is that why you turned down all those guys, trying so hard to take you out, because you haven't been a bridesmaid?'

Her mouth twisted. 'Well, not exactly.'

He took a hard look at her. 'So why then?'

Again, her mouth scrunched up. 'Most of them are your mates. Be honest. They are all dickheads, to say the least.'

Major Carter taps Sam on the shoulder, then shows her a video recording from his phone. The man in the video was playing the piano and singing. Sam watched it right through to the end. 'Who is he?'

Major Carter smiled. 'He is my kid brother, Chance.'

Philip took a look at the video picture. 'Why Chance?'

The Major gave a little snigger. 'It was Mum and Dad's last chance to have a daughter. They had banked on it so much they only choose girls names. So, when it turned out to be another son, Dad wanted to call him Last Chance Carter.'

Then he showed Sam a short video of herself, he had taken. 'I sent this to Chance.' He scrolled through his messages, then showed her what Chance had to say about her.

'Alan, she lovely, find out more, and keep me informed Xx.'

Sam looked straight at the Major. She was a level-headed girl generally, but these revelations from Alan Carter had her feeling a little uneasy, though not entirely unhappy. She pulled her phone from her pocket, showing the Major her phone details. 'Can you send it to me?'

Thomas repeated his question. 'So, dad when are we going to meet the elusive Helen, destined to be my new mum?'

'On your, say so. You hinted coming for Christmas, is that still on?'

Thomas with a bit of hesitation. 'Actually, Rachel and I will be coming to stay for a year, and a bit.'

Charlyyk could not help hearing; she had one ear turned in their direction. Janet had noticed many times, how her ears could operate separately to each other. Charlyyk could not disguise her delight. 'Then we will see the baby born. Wow.'

Then Bryn looked at Rachel with concern. 'What about your mother? She would want to be by your side, when that happens?'

Rachel gave him a warm smile. 'Mummy is coming too. We did a big project, which was a great success, we have been asked to take it to England.'

Janet pricked her ears up, always looking for good news stories. 'When you come, let me do an interview. With my contacts, it will reach out all over Britain even into Europe.' Then asking 'What is it you do, Thomas?'

'I'm a watercolour artist. Rachel and her mother promote art and artist. They have brought together the top watercolour artist to exhibit their work. Four brilliant Chinese artists, and one of the new exciting women from Poland. And many other great artists from around the world.'

Later as Charlyyk, and Janet were getting ready for bed, Janet casually asked 'Do you have dreams Charlyyk?'

Charlyyk slipped between the sheets, reposition, the pillow. 'Of course, I do. Some are nice, others very painful. Like sometime I'm on the top of that hill, wondering whether I will slip down into a valley of nightmares, or into a meadow of sweet dreams?'

Janet settles herself in bed. 'What language do you speak in your dreams?'

Charlyyk just laid there, thinking. 'Mostly in English, I sometimes hear one of my groups, calling for me. The screams frighten me, but when I dream that the Feeng are chasing me, I get in a terrible state. Sometimes, I see dad killing the beast, then collapsing with exhaustion. He had to drag himself to check if it was dead, to remove the weapon. He did not once look at me, not at any time. I watched him trying so hard, to repair himself. When I had worked out what he was trying to do. I decided to assist him. Pushing the needle through his skin was so hard... My fingers were not the right type. They kept slipping down the needle. Michel told me if I had not succeeded Bryn would have died that night.' She looked at Janet, sadly. 'And that would have meant, I would have died a terrible, terrible death.'

Janet got out of bed and went to her; seeing the tears streaming down Charlyyk's face. They lay there cuddled together when they woke in the morning, they were still nestled together.

***

At breakfast, the Major filled them in on the progress at the Centre. 'There is no need for us to attend there today. Lieu-Col Smitt has arranged a visit to the other side of the bay for you, if we can hurry the breakfast, for a quick getaway.'

The rush that ensued, even took the Major by surprise, he had not told them where they were heading for. It was the thought of different scenery, that was a great incentive for them.

The bus took them to a waiting plane, which flew near the Gulf of Mexico. The Caribbean stretched out underneath them. Charlyyk liked this way of travelling. She sat by a window, looking out. One air hostess in particular was fascinated by her and every chance the air hostess could, she would take photos of Charlyyk. Then Charlyyk asked the woman to sit with her. Bryn took pictures of them, with the air hostess own mobile. She could not stop showing the other crew members the pictures. It gave Charlyyk a little rest bite from all the attention she had been receiving from her.

The plane started to descend, Orlando Airport could be seen, as the seatbelt light, lit up, Charlyyk even enjoyed the landing part, like a ride at the fairground. Another bus was waiting, soon was heading for Bay Lake, to the magic of Disney World, that was now rolled out in front of them. Charlyyk could not contain herself. Gwen and Harold trying hard to restrain her. The Major who had already been there before and had seen how excited children, had wet themselves with the excitement. Gave Charlyyk a toffee to chew on, in a few moments it had the desired effect, she soon settled.

Captain Hanne, with the Major had arranged for an exclusive guided tour, where they met many of the Disney characters' that make the magic work.

Captain Hanne had made a great effort to get security right, he did not want another issue like they had in Houston, so he kept close to Gwen and made sure she had a good time. Harold and Bryn, following behind aware of what the captain was attempting to achieve. Janet was just as excited as Charlyyk, and the Major made sure he was at hand to smooth any ripples, with candy floss, popcorn, ice cream. Charlyyk and Janet just loved it.

Then it happened. Elsa from *Frozen* caught Charlyyk's eye. Was she smitten? Oh yes, Janet's camera, captured every mouth drawling, hands-on heart moment? Janet could see how Charlyyk was melting into the glow of the wonder of dreams coming true. Tinkerbelle's magic wand had sprinkled stardust all over her, where she now had drifted into Neverland.

Then Olaf came to cap it all. Now Charlyyk was bouncing about, she could not stop squealing in joyous laughter. No one, could not resist joining in with her, young children, who stopped in their tracks for seeing this girl, who looked not so different to those Walt Disney Characters.

Rachel who was walking arm in arm with Gwen and Thomas. 'Oh my god, Charlyyk is in meltdown.'

On the return flight, back to Houston. Charlyyk sat in her seat watching the videos, that people had taken of her, that they had placed them on Facebook. Was she embarrassed? Not at all, she even laughed at herself. Charlyyk pointing to the scenes where she had lost control.

Bryn with a laugh 'I gather you enjoyed yourself Charlyyk?'

'You bet, Dad.'

On Friday morning, at breakfast, it was quiet. Nothing would compare to the day before, here they were, not knowing how long they will stay. Major Alan Carter had been in touch with the Centre. Although lots of new information had been given, no real headway had been achieved.

Gwen and Harold, had decided to go into Houston with Thomas and Rachel. Janet was given a chance to go with them, but chose to stay with Charlyyk. The sister relationship she had built up with Charlyyk was holding firm; as Janet enjoyed her companionship.

As they walked into the Space Centre. There was an atmosphere of despondency, a 'why are we here.' feeling. After the Lord Mayor's show comes the clean-up.

Mrs Lomax invited them into her office. 'I'm Sorry to say we are going nowhere." She started to give them the lowdown on the progress made. 'We have established where Charlyyk's home planet, could be situated in the solar system. The planet you were on, but given the distance and the speed of light years. How they could achieve it is beyond our expertise. There was a knock on the door. 'Come in Sam, what can we do for you?'

Sam entered and sat next to Charlyyk. 'Philip and I spent yesterday, with most of last night, going over what you have told us, We have been so intent on what you had to say, we have forgotten to ask the simple things. So, we have set up a team of aircraft engineers, to ask you those questions.'

Philip, standing in the hall, beckoned them back to the centre. The working group were assembled in a circle. The four of them sat down, and Philip explained how they hoped to conduct the meeting. 'When you were in the spacecraft how were you positioned, seated or standing?'

Charlyyk thought for a moment, then squatted down.

Philip instructed. 'For what I'm about to ask you, I need you to close your eyes?' This she did. 'Not too tightly...These questions, are on what you heard, not what you saw. When you were taken on board, it's about noises, can you recollect if there were any sounds?'

Minutes passed. All eyes were on her. Then Charlyyk moved. Her left hand, it rose up to her shoulder, her left ear twitched. 'A hum to the left of me, like a fridge.' Then her hand dropped to waist height. 'There was a vibration coming from that direction.' Her finger on her left hand, pointed outwards, Sam was marking it on a pad, one of those electronic pads that worked with a stylist pen, all connected to a computer.

'Where were you at that time Charlyyk?'

Philip was checking if they had her in the correct position on their computer screen.

Once again, it was clear from the concentration on her face that she was reliving the moment, second by second. 'The entrance to the craft would be on my right, so the sound and vibration were coming from the rear of the Craft.' She raised her right hand up, and then she moved it forward. 'There was a clicking noise, six different ones from that direction.' Again, the finger pointing in the direction the sounds came from.

One of the engineers had noticed her finger had moved six times and ask to delay the meeting for a moment. The group huddled in a small circle. Bryn fetched Charlyyk and Janet some water.

Soon four men arrived with some new equipment. They connected electrodes to Charlyyk's fingers and taped the wires to her arms, then asked her to move her hands and fingers about while they configured the program. One of the men produced a blindfold, then asked Bryn to put it on Charlyyk. When they were ready, which took them another thirty minutes, to be satisfied it was working correctly. They started again from the very beginning.

Charlyyk came to the place where she pointed her finger six times, the computer showed them where her finger had been directed too, with the computer image of the inside of the craft would register, where a control panel was situated. The questioning went on for hours, but nobody noticed, they had become so engrossed, frightened that they would lose the momentum if they stopped. Bryn and Janet fetching refreshments for her to keep her going.

Major Carter watching it all happen with Captain Hanne, Thought it looks like they were whipping the horse over the finishing line.

Charlyyk would stop now and again to make sure she had got it right; Philip keeping the pace just right, allowing her to control it. He could tell she knew this to be important, he did not want to rush her into missing something, no matter how small or insignificant that they may believe it was.

After a while Charlyyk came to the conclusion that she could not carry on anymore, she had been going over, and over the same things, again and again; She removed the blindfold and blinked with the brightness of the lights.

Bryn placing his arm across her shoulders. 'Do you need anything sweetheart?'

The warm smile she gave him, with affection. 'Food! I'm starving?'

Janet responded. 'Leave that with me.' And rushed off to the café.

Philip and Sam came to Charlyyk, removing the gadgets that were strapped to her, then took her hands in theirs. 'Thank you Charlyyk. We do not know what this will gain, but we had to give it a go?' Philip's tired eyes showed how much he had given to this task, Sam's eyes looked no different than her brothers. The rest of the group of highly skilled engineers, remained huddled around a computer, trying to see if they had learnt anything.

Janet returned, with Pizza's, colas and coffees. Although Bryn at first did not want anything, found himself eating and drinking, especially the coffee. His thoughts drifted to how Helen at a spur of the moment had invited Janet to come. He could not thank Helen enough. Janet had proved her worth over and over again.

The Military officers, had met together, were now discussing the pro and cons of the time spent, working out the next course to follow. Mrs Lomax had joined the group. They all headed for her Office, Sam stayed with the girls. Philip joined the aircraft engineers.

Charlyyk did not want to move from where she was sitting. The refreshment was starting to work, her energy levels were increasing slowly. Bryn was feeling like the wallflower at the local dance. Everyone doing something, while he watched and did nothing.

Mrs Lomax approached Janet, and the pair walked off in the direction of Mrs Lomax Office. Later Janet returned and spoke with Bryn. 'The News media has requested that you and Charlyyk do a TV Show in Houston on Saturday Evening. It will have a Nationwide Broadcast. They feel it fits into the agreement they made with your Family?'

Bryn was not surprised by this request. He had been ready for such an ultimatum. Then to Janet's surprise, Bryn asked for her advice. 'How do you think we should respond to their request Janet?'

Janet felt a nice warm feeling that he respected her, for what she was doing for them. 'Yes, I think we should, the American People know we are here, the trip to Orlando confirmed that, many people have sent in videos of sightings of her, which have been widely broadcast on most of the networks. We refuse, then you won't be able to move from the pressure the press will put on you, I won't be allowed to carry on doing what I've been doing?'

Bryn walked with her to the Station Controllers Office. The press officer was sitting with a large carton of coffee. As soon as he saw them approaching, he shot to his feet, his hand ready to shake Bryn's hand. 'Sure, is a pleasure to meet you, Mr Collier, I hope you and your family are enjoying your stay in this great country?' The grin on his face was so wide you could drive a bus through it.

Bryn shook his hand. 'And your name is?'

The press office blushed with embarrassment. He had not introduced himself properly. 'I'm so sorry, Bill Braddock, Press Officer for the Johnson Space Centre.'

Bryn felt good, one of the primary training techniques is to take control of negotiations. 'Janet said you would like us to appear on a TV interview. What had you in mind? How this would be organised, at such short notice?' Bill Braddock produced a paper with the detail of the set layout, with the product sponsors. 'I'm sorry to inform you we do not endorse commercial products, so no commercial breaks?'

Bill Braddock looked shocked. 'Are you rejecting this offer, Mr Collier?'

Bryn looked at him sternly. 'Indeed no. Just the Commercial Breaks.' He turning to Janet and winked. 'They will soon turn out dollar bills, with advertising on them. Whatever next will they stoop, to make a fast buck?' Then he went to walk out the office, stopping at the doorway. 'Janet, the press council, put you in charge of Charlyyk's news coverage, could you get this sorted.' Then he carried on walking out of the Office. 'Good day Mr Braddock.'

The Press Officer was shell-shocked. He had always held the view, that everyone wanted to be on television. They all wanted fame. To hear, someone make stipulation in this manner, left him in a state of confusion.

Janet sat down. 'Well, you heard the man. Let's get started?'

These decisions could not be taken on Bill's say-so, he was soon on the phone to the studios for help. He passed the phone to Janet who confirmed what had been discussed, those of the Collier family.

Janet waited for their reply, her last words to them. 'What you show before and after is up to you, but no commercial breaks during the interview, they have not asked for anything but that, they will not endorse any product at all, they do require the network to state it before they broadcast. Is that clear?' Janet was enjoying her new status, she felt so in control, instead of towing the line and being told what to do, she now felt a bit of power. Then thinking to herself. No, not power, she had been given some control 'There Mr Braddock it's been sorted.'

At the Hotel, during dinner, Bryn informs them of the interview they would be doing on Saturday evening. Gwen seemed quite happy with how Janet had responded to Bryn's directions and agreed it was something that was going to happen at some time...just one of those inevitable things that had to happen.

Charlyyk was not fussed by it at all, was keen to buy a new outfit for the occasion. The girls started to plan the retail therapy expedition in search for the elusive, but right-for-the-occasion dress. No shop must me neglected or passed by, without close examination of its contents. Rachel led the planning committee, with Janet as her second in command. Gwen and Charlyyk stood to attention and saluted. Major Carter joined in with the fun, promised Rachel the use of his own personal swagger stick. This was when, Thomas started to sing the song of the Dawn Patrol from Walt Disney's *Jungle Book*.

Charlyyk went and sat on Bryn's knee, enjoying all the fun and laughter that was being had by all, including the other diners, and the Hotel staff.

Major Carter sat there remembering something that Helen and Toby were saying about the Collier family. 'Here is a family you can sink into, and hope you are never rescued from.' Looking at Gwen and Harold then at Thomas and Rachel, a perfect pairing, their personality blending so well together.

Bryn the quiet man, but a leader, you don't hear orders, they just follow him, Then watching Charlyyk, how she is listened to, helps her to understand how to grow and express herself. He thoroughly understands Helen falling in love not just with Bryn, but the whole family.

Chapter 18

The TV Interview

On Saturday Morning, the hotel lobby was busy with a bevvy of hand-picked female security guards in plain clothes, the early morning staff were not accustomed to this amount of activity so early in the morning, it did not affect their routine in any way what so ever. Captain Hanne and Major Carter had coordinated with Washington on this, nothing was overlooked. Lieu-Col Smitt had sought the imprimatur of the highest person possible. He and the First lady were attending the interview themselves, as spectators, as with most of the notable individuals in the vicinity of Houston.

At breakfast, the planning committee checked that all credit and debit cards were present and correct and were ready for duty. They all headed for the lobby, and the waiting stretched limo, with security falling in around them discretely, with leading cars and trailing cars. Rachel with a heavy southern drawl. 'Gawd, I feel like the First Lady.'

The Captain and the Major had organised a trip for the boys, to a practice game of the Houston Texans Football Team.

In one shop's fitting rooms, Charlyyk and Janet took a considerable interest in Rachel's little baby bump, Charlyyk conferring with Catherine's baby bump. In another shop, they met up with Sam. They pulled her into their group, would not let her go on her own. There was no talk about the Space Centre, just buying clothes. They returned back to the hotel for dinner, and their appointments at the Hotel's beauty parlour.

Philip and Sam joined them for dinner. The jovial mood had not changed, Major Carter related a story when he had been Stationed in Germany. He had been on manoeuvres in an old abandoned village. He was invited to drive a tank. The tank commander explained. 'This Centurion Tank, could drive straight through a house,' The major turned, the tank into this house, but did not know it had a basement and found themselves upside down in the cellar. The house tumbling all around them burying them for the rest of the day.

This story helping to take off the excitement that was building up within them, for in a way the press officer was right, that people did want to be on television.

A flotilla of cars brought the Collier family to the TV Station. Every person looked smart in their new clothes. As the cars pulled up outside the Studio's Charlyyk tugged on Bryn's sleeve. She had seen the banners held by protestors. Charlyyk's eyes scanned the area, the police were there and were making sure all protester were contained, yet could still protest. Charlyyk singled out two groups of families, one young, the other older. These she will talk to. Where those close by, joined in asking questions. TV camera's catching the mood of the spectators.

Entering the studio, the applause they received was very warm. The interviewer was a veteran with many years' experiences, he had been advised to be down to earth, not to be too slick, He had studied the footage of the Colliers previous Press Conferences. He was concerned how Gwen could quickly change from timid mouse to vampire bat. To top it all, the President and the First Lady will be sitting in the audience. As they sat in their seats, the floor manager counted down the seconds, three, two, one. The introduction music played.

'Good evening, my name is Stem Little. Our guest tonight is the Collier family. Tonight, is something special, because tonight there will be no interruptions. For the Collier family, do not want to endorse any commercial products. It is all BBC TV...So I'm pleased to introduce this very particular family, because one would not be here, without the other.'

After the introductions, he then turned his attention towards Charlyyk. 'We have read with much interest, how Janet Stokes has written about you, it has given us a real insight, to who you are. So, in your own words how do you find America?'

Charlyyk turned towards the audience. 'Hello everyone, it's lovely being here, although I have spent most of the time at the Johnson Space Centre, we did manage a tour, with everyone sending in their videos of me losing it at Disney World, I can only say, I just loved it. We hit the shops in town today, and everyone we met were fantastic, so friendly, I can only say, for your warm welcome, that helped make me feel, so at home. Thank you.'

Stem then spoke, to Bryn. 'Your first name is Brian, but you answer to Bryn?' These easy questions were meant to make them feel comfortable.

'Yes, there were many Brian's at my school, because my father was Welsh, I was nicknamed Bryn.'

'You were taken in a flash of light, then returned the same way, did you expect to find Charlyyk with you?'

'No, but I was so glad she was.'

'Why was that?'

'How would I explain the condition I was in; would you not have laughed at such a silly story? Like Betty and Barny Hill who said they had been abducted by aliens, you interviewed in 1961?'

Stem, nodded, slightly embarrassed, but he soon smiled it off. 'How as it changed your life?'

'Considering I had lost my wife four years earlier with breast cancer, Charlyyk gave me a new purpose to live, but don't get the wrong idea I wasn't suicidal, I was just drifting about, like a yacht that had lost its rudder. My sister Gwen and her husband gave me a crutch to lean on and stability. But Charlyyk not only changed my world, but theirs as well.'

Stem turned his question to Gwen. 'When Bryn disappeared, what did you think, had happened to him?'

Gwen looked towards her brother; the flash of memories rushed through her mind. 'Harold and I live very close to Bryn. We would pop into him as often as we could, on that day in April 2012, we had called in with some shopping Bryn had asked to get for him, as we entered the cottage the radio was playing, there was no sign of Bryn. Harold went to his study but still no sign of him. The kettle was still hot, and there was a half-drunk cup of warm coffee on the kitchen table. The garden door was open; there were clothes on the line, some lying on the ground, clothes pegs scattered about. The grass on the lawn was long, we could see footmarks going to the line but no footmarks coming back from the line nor anywhere else. I phoned our local police, our friend Sgt Wendy Bailey with many of villagers, searched for him. Then six months later, the phone call that changed our lives.'

Harold looked at Charlyyk. 'And how? If Bryn had found a new purpose in life, so had we.'

Thomas was next to speak. 'When I received the call, that Dad had returned, I left Rachel with her mother in New York. took the first flight available to London. They had finished their quarantine period, but Dad was still in a terrible condition, it frighten me to see the wounds still had infections. Michel the vet, who was treating him, had reopened them to clean them, dad had become delirious. I stayed, till he pulled through.'

Rachel shook her head. 'When Thomas returned home to our apartment in New York, told me the story I called him a liar, till he showed me the video of Charlyyk on his phone. I had to play it over and over. Then we caught a plane to London. I still had to see it with my own eyes before I could trust him.'

Stem turned to Charlyyk. 'How did you react, when you found yourself on a different planet, with many strange people.'

'Not strange...different.'

Stem looked at her quizzically.

'This man saved me from a terrible death, he was not strange. He was different. Everyone here has been so kind to me, they did not want to eat me. I felt good about where I have found myself, then there is the food... Now Stem, how would you feel if wanting something to eat, it could cost you your life... every day?'

Stem, shook his head while giving a gentle chuckle. 'I don't think I would be happy Charlyyk?' Pausing for a brief moment looking at the notes he had written. 'So' how are you enjoying, going to School?'

The smile that beamed from her left no one with any doubts that she loved School. 'It's great, for two years, Auntie Gwen and Uncle Harold had taught me to speak English. To read and write, they made it a pleasure to learn. To be able to achieve this, they managed to do it with a tight group of friends, that kept my existence secret... So, all the people I knew were older people... Now I mix with people of my own age group... hear their feeling, share their thoughts... able to join in, with their fun... see their sadness... learning about life, through their eyes.'

Stem now turned his attention to Bryn. 'You made a deal with the press that you would have one person to cover this story; Janet Stokes has been supplying us with some fantastic personal stories about Charlyyk, how much room do you allow her to get those stories?'

Bryn pointed to the wings of the studio. 'Why don't you ask her personally, she standing right there?'

Stem beckoned Janet to come and join them, as someone quickly produced a chair for her to sit on. 'Ladies and Gentlemen, Miss Janet Stokes.' There was a slight pause as Janet settled herself. 'Well, Janet you heard the question, how much room are you allowed?'

Janet was all smiles; once again Bryn had shown his trust in her. 'No room, the whole house, to be able to see Charlyyk through her eyes I would have to live with her, and that is what the family allow me to do, just that. I have even slept in the same bedroom with Charlyyk, in separate beds of course.'

Charlyyk laughing. 'No, she does not snore.'

The audience had been silent up till then, intent on what was being said; now they were laughing.

Janet carried on. 'We then can talk girl to girl... when one night, she was looking out of the window looking at the stars, I asked did she think about what she has left behind her...she replied, my old life. A few words, meaning so much.'

Then Stem produced a photo of Charlyyk looking out of a window. 'Was this the picture you took, taken on that same night?'

Janet making sure it was. 'Yes.'

Stem noticed the wave the President gave. 'Yes, Mr President?' The President stood up. 'Charlyyk, you call Bryn dad, have you always called him dad?'

'No Sir, I called him Bryn, the family said I should have a secure identity... a passport would give me just that. That was to adopt me as their own and give me the name Charlyyk Collier. Now I have a real family...now I can call Bryn, Dad.'

The First Lady now wanted to ask a question. 'Do you know what you would like to do after school?'

Charlyyk's impish smile broadened. 'Mrs First Lady, I do not think you mean, playing with my friends and listening to music or reading a good book. But, maybe a career; I have much to learn, in many ways, I have a lot to catch up with, considering the short time I've had. But with the guidance, I have already received from the family, it should be something meaningful.'

Harold approved of Charlyyk's answer to the First Lady. 'Knowing Charlyyk, it will be something she will want to do, whatever it is, she will put her heart and soul into it!'

The Mayor of Houston stood up. 'Will you come and see us again?'

Charlyyk was genuinely happy to reply to his request. Her ears were forward, and the colour of her eyes was a bright bluey, green. 'I don't think the Space Centre will have finished with us, so there will be a great chance of coming back, the welcome you have given us and the warmth of the people we have met, I would love to return to this lovely city of yours.' Charlyyk had chosen her words well, she needed to win the hearts and minds of the people if she wanted to move around freely.

The one-hour slot the TV Company had been allocated finished. Stem closed the program; the questions from the audience, did not stop, with the President and the First Lady joining them on stage, the talking continues for another hour.

Everyone was pleased how it had gone without any hitches. The feedback the TV company received, gave a positive reflection of how the American People were accepting Charlyyk, as only a few threats were aimed towards them for giving an Alien, air time. Many Channels were showing repeats of the program. News Channels reported, there had been protest, showing some ugly scenes outside the White House.

One commentator relating how they compared to other protest. 'Banner waving protesters were out in front of the White House today. These protesters were up in arms that an Alien being was allowed entry, into this Country.

This reminds me of the anti-abortion protest that had taken place here on previous occasions, with the different religious bodies voicing their strong feelings as well.'

The White House spoke-person gave out a statement earlier, that the Alien, Charlyyk is here to help find a solution to the potential threat from an alien invasion. Similarly, America with help from the other Major Powers. With leading Scientist from all other countries, have gathered at Houston's, Johnson Space Centre.

Many of the hotel staff had watched them on the TV. As they entered, the staff on duty applauded. To them it had been a very successful day.

Janet was quick to open her laptop, soon as they enter their room, the messages she was getting and the feedback, just kept downloading, she quickly got in touch with somebody called her virtual assistant, from her phone, to sort them out.

Charlyyk had put on the TV, then scrolled up and down looking at all the different News channels. The amount of coverage and the comments she noted, she needed to see what were the concerns these protesters had about her living amongst them. The folder Charlyyk retrieved from her case, had her comments on what was needed, for her to adjust herself to be able to achieve acceptance. She entered further details on its pages.

'So, how will you use all this information Charlyyk?' Janet enquired.

'Sandra and Julia will sit with me; we will debate all the details that these protesters have aimed towards me. Then we work out a way of answering those comments, Sandra wants to open an Instagram account to try and put over our message, Julia believes it to early, that it could be open to abuse. We all agree we must continue to work on a strategy.'

Charlyyk and Janet, sat in their beds talking about the day, till they both fell fast asleep.

***

Janet woke to movement in the room, Charlyyk was sorting through her clothes

'What time is it?'

'Ten pasts five.'

'Oh, Bloody Hell, Charlyyk it's still night time.'

'Then go back to sleep.'

Charlyyk had not stopped busying herself, she had woken by the sound of the refuge truck removing the waste bins from the hotel, had decided it was a good time to tidy her clothes, she had used that week. She had put her soiled underwear in one bag, now she was checking her outer garments; T-shirts, blouses, shorts, skirts and tights, to see what could be worn again, or any garment, need washing.

Janet had resigned herself, that morning had indeed arrived. Sat up in bed; watching Charlyyk sorting her clothes, she sat there admiring her resolve. Her camera was now in use, as the facial expression were showing a different Charlyyk.

Chapter 19

A New Helen

In Helen's apartment, she was getting ready to meet her parents, she had spoken to them on Friday, and they had insisted she came to dinner, at midday Sunday. It was twelve, and she had ordered a taxi, for the ten-minute drive to Kensington. But a thirty-five-minute journey by bus.

She had purchased a new dress on Saturday and had her hair restyled. As she looked at herself in the long mirror, she felt pleased with how she looked. It had the desired soft look she had asked the stylist to create; the assistant at the clothing boutique had said to her, gently. 'Madam needs to dress, to impress, the style she wears at this moment makes her older than she really is, if her hair was slightly different, she could wear, dresses to compliment her figure.' The assistant gave her a card. 'This girl could advise you. If you like I could speak to her now?' Upon a nod from Helen, the girl promptly phoned her. 'She could fit you in at two.'

Now Helen felt great, but nervous. Was it being too big a change? Her phone ringtone sounded that the taxi was waiting. When the cab arrived outside her parent's house. Anna, her mother's housekeeper, answered the door. 'Yes, madam?'

'I'm expected, Anna.'

'Is that you Miss Helen? Your parents will be surprised.'

Helen following Anna into the drawing room. 'Good God Lizzy, look who we have here!' her father exclaimed.

His reaction startled Helen's mother, who looked up.

'Helen, you look fantastic, at last, I have a daughter, not a sister.' She quickly rose from where she sat, gave her daughter a huge hug.

Standing behind Helen, Anna remarked. 'Lady Elisabeth dinner will be ready at one-thirty.'

'Thank you, Anna...Come sit down Helen you must have much to tell us?'

Anna took Helen's coat, Helen sat with her mother on the sofa. Helen glanced around the room nothing had changed, the old furniture, the curtains, even to the carpet had been there when she had been born. The furnishings were a mixture, nothing matched.

Father's chair a relic from his days at Oxford. He had bought at an auction. In the catalogue, it was described as a Victorian button backed, leather, smoking chair. He did not care what it was called, he just loved the feel of it, purchased it for five pounds. Where ever he went, the chair went with him.

The rest of the furniture fitted their lifestyle, the large table had been cut down in height, again not for its looks or style, for its practicability, the curtains came with the house, this room was suited for living and working in, the other rooms for showing off.

Helen's Mother still trying to accept the changes her daughter has made. 'Now tell me the reason for this dramatic change in you, like a butterfly emerging from its chrysalis. A girl makes these changes for only one thing, a new man in her life, am I, right?'

Helen's father looked straight at her. 'I bloody well hope so!'

Helen, let it sink in. She could see her parent now as she had not known them before, and the realisation that it might have been her own fault that she could not relate to them, not them to her. 'You are right mother. I've have met someone. I have fallen in love with him and his family.'

Her father reached over to her. 'That is great news Helen whoever he is, we will get to like him too, it is about time you found some love in your life, we can only wish you the very best of happiness.'

Her mother took her arm. 'Come let's have dinner, and you can tell us all about him.'

Anna had laid the table for four persons, she had become almost one of the family, and dined with them, as they ate.

Helen was asked many questions. Her father had begun the cross-examination. 'Do we know this man you are seeing by any chance?'

Helen responded. 'Well, you have met him.'

Helen's mother did not look at her, but as she cut off a piece of chicken. 'We have dear?'

'Yes mother, you came to his house a few weeks ago, with father.'

'The Collier family with the alien girl?' her father replied. 'Nice I liked the chap... Catherine, his daughter, damn fine cricketer...pity, not a fellow... we could have done with her likes in the men's team, those hapless wonders, could not catch a cold.' Then moved some of his dinner on his plate. 'Anna any more of that lovely gravy?'

Helen's mother passes the gravy boat to him. Looking at Helen. 'How far have you gone with Brian Collier, have you warmed his bed yet?'

Helen did not answer.

Her father commented. 'You don't need our permission. You are a big girl now with grown-up needs.' Then placing his knife and fork neatly on the plate. 'That was lovely Anna thank you.' Wiping his mouth, with a napkin. 'Have you made any plans?'

Helen finishing her dinner and placing her knife and fork on her plate. 'I've already accepted his proposal, only need to settle time and place.'

Her mother looks at her, a warm smile on her face. 'Damn good show darling, nice catch.' Then, with a tittering laugh. 'It will take some explaining, that we have an alien grandchild, to some of our friends though.'

After the dessert, they all retired to the drawing room for coffees. 'What are you working on dad?'

'On the reform of the House of Lords, there are just too many of them, we need to reduce the size of the house, many of them do not have a clue, why they are there. They have brought party politics with them when they should be looking whether the acts the incumbent government is trying to introduce are right for all the people of this Country: The Hereditary Lords, for their tenants, the Law Lords, is it legal, and the bishops, is it moral... Politics is for the House of Commons, one man one vote, but as soon as they brought whips into the House, Democracy went right out the window.' Then he changed the subject. 'What do we know about this Brian Collier chappie, is he sound?'

Helen's mother scoffed. 'Darling, you met him that Saturday, your comments were, He's nice, like him a lot.' He looked up at her sternly. I know what I said, just want to know what Helen has to say, it won't make a blind bit of difference to the outcome, but I do care about her feelings.'

'Daddy, I read his military history. One of my colleagues is a personal friend of his, and his family. He told me stories about him, by the time I came to meet him personally, to shake his hand. I knew I had met someone...I could have feelings for. Then that day at his home, I just knew, I was in love with him. But I ran away, it scared the living daylight out of me.' Helen looked at the faces of her parent, they looked so concerned at what she was saying, all she could remember them saying before was. 'Hi Dear, Bye Dear.' Now it's a deep conversation, they were actually listening to her.

Her mother, with a searching look in her eyes, reached over and placed her hand on hers. 'So, who made the first move?'

Helen's thoughts went to that evening in Interlaken. 'In a way, it was I that made the first move.' She paused for thought. 'He is still in love with Kitty, his late wife, her death still pains him.'

Helen's father looks out over his reading glasses at her. 'Big shoes to step into my girl, the mother of his children, do you feel you can do that?'

'No, not right away, but with time and patience, I could.' With that Helen rose from her chair. 'Tomorrow I hand in my resignation and advise them of my idea, as who I think should be my successor.' Helen needed to prepare for her meeting with the PM and made an effort to leave. 'It's been lovely... Anna thank you for such a lovely meal, we really must keep this up.' With that, she embraces them all and bade them goodbye.

Back at Houston Harold, Gwen, Thomas, and Rachel went to church. Janet caught up with Charlyyk on her views how the week had gone.

Bryn looked as though he was reading. Yes, he had a book open in front of him, but the thoughts in his head, were not permitting him to read. He was not too worried about the marriage proposal he gave Helen, nor with the facts of the timing with Catherine and Rachel being pregnant, with careful planning it should work out Ok, but since returning back to this planet with Charlyyk. A constant flashback had kept recurring, It always seems to relate to the first day in that bear pit of a battlefield, he had found himself in, at about the time the beast that Charlyyk had called a Fuung, was preparing to engage with the thing that had left its bony spike embedded in him. It was just a flash, and as hard as he could try and concentrate on it, he could not seem to be able to put a reasonable explanation to it.

Monday morning in London, Helen's Taxi arrived outside No10, the door opened, and she was shown into the cabinet office, the Prime Minister, Home Secretary, and the Director of MI6, were all waiting to receive her. 'Helen, is there any way we could make you change your mind?'

Helen shook their hands. 'I've put myself in a very compromising position.'

The Home Secretary's concerned look. 'How Helen?'

'Capt. Brian Collier, do you remember him?'

The Home Secretary nodded. 'Charlyyk.'

Helen was sitting opposite across the Cabinet Office table. 'I've fallen in love with him and have accepted his proposal to marry him, with the media coverage attached to this, it could leave me exposed to some scrutiny, the new MI9 department must not be jeopardised.'

The Head of MI6 agreed with her. 'Congratulations Helen, I believe you have made a wise choice, Capt. Brian Collier has been a great asset to his country, and everyone who has served with him, hold him in high esteem. What I personally admired about him, was he was not ambitious; he did what he thought was right and just, turning down four commissions, just so he could remain one of his team.'

The Prime Minister looked disappointed. 'Knowing you Helen you must have put a lot of thought into your decision on this matter, so advise us on your successor?'

Helen passed a folder, over the table. 'Major Toby Scalon, before you are his credentials. He has been my second in command since I set up this department. He has been instrumental in promoting and training all of our teams, so he knows the setup?'

The three of them discussed what Helen had presented them, and made their decision, there and then. 'We accept with regrets, your decision to stand down, when will you let Major Scalon know?'

Thanking them Helen preceded in informing them. 'He arrives back tomorrow, I will tell him then, and if he agrees, I will give him some time to adjust to the transition?'

At the George Bush Airport, notorious for its delays, the Collier family were saying their farewells, Rachel after hugging them all, took Charlyyk to one side 'Now remember it won't be long, we will see you for Christmas. Could you let us know what should we buy for dad?'

Charlyyk gave Rachel a kiss. 'I'll text you when I find out?'

Two security guards kept close to them at all times throughout the trip. Major Carter informed Bryn on the week's progress, although it seemed at the end, to have hit a brick wall, much was achieved, and there were still problems to be solved. Sam, Janet, and Charlyyk, carried on with their discussion on make-up, fashion, and music; where Harold Gwen and Philip crashed and slept right through the whole flight.

***

The cottage felt so much cosier as soon as Bryn warmed it up. Sitting down to a cup of tea, Charlyyk cuddled up to him. 'Nice to be home dad, all though I liked the Hotel, and everything was done for you, it's still not home, is it?'

Bryn squeezed her to him and kissed her forehead. 'What part of it did you like best?'

'Disney World that was magic, I know they were people dressed in costumes, it just made it feel right.'

An hour later Charlyyk had her homework spread out, checking that it was ready for the next day for school, the text messages from Julia and Sandra pleased her most, *'Missed you, cannot wait till tomorrow* Xxxx.'

***

As Bryn looked in on Charlyyk, her bed was made, and her school uniform was set out ready for her return to Academy. But she was not in her bedroom.

He found her in the Kitchen drinking water, she passed him a glass of water, he could see the change in her, she was growing up, The tracksuit was starting to get tighter, and more of her socks were showing, the sleeves were creeping up her arms.

Out in the garden, the frost gave it a silvery look. After doing stretching exercises, they were off running across the fields towards the farm. They could see James guiding the cattle towards the milking sheds, to their surprise Janet was with him, trying to help, without much success, The cows were more guiding her.

Charlyyk shouted out to her, punching her arm into the air. 'Go get em, Janet!'

Janet raised her hand and waved. The low morning sun catching her copper-coloured hair, making it glow like a burning beacon. The big broad grin Janet had, spread across her face, showed Charlyyk how happy Janet was mucking in with James. Janet looked resplendent, in the olive-green boiler suit with matching green hunter wellies, she had borrowed from Jane.

Then Janet was nudged in the back by one of the cows, pushing her toward into the backend of another, grabbing its tail to stop her from falling, the cow in front pooed, all down the front of her, James could only lean on another cow to prevent falling over with laughter. Janet joining in with the laughter. Yes, she loved getting mucky with James; it was the complete opposite of what she normally would do.

As the school bus arrived at Oakleaves, Charlyyk was waiting, she looked smarter than before, now she was filling out, her school uniform was beginning to fit her better. Sarah and Mace jumped down from the bus to welcome her back to school.

Bryn watched her go, although he felt so proud of her, he still felt so lonely and wished she could always be here with him.

At dead on two. Helen pulled into the drive, the Discovery stopped by the garage where Bryn was working. Getting out of the car and jumping into his arms, could not help but smothering him with kisses. This behaviour was nothing like the usual Helen, she could not stop herself. tried to drag him towards the cottage, and towards the bedroom, despite the work going on inside the cottage.

Bryn scooped her up in his arms. He pushed through the side door to the garage. She wrapped her arms around his neck, her over-enthusiastic embrace telling Bryn she was glad to be back. Helen soon found herself on her back over the bonnet of the Morgan, with her legs wrapped around him.

Mrs Landon managed to speak to Charlyyk at the end of the lessons, about her trip to America. 'Charlyyk it would be nice for the school to hear what happened in Houston, would you put some thought towards it, maybe a little talk to what took place and why?'

Charlyyk liked the idea, for it could win around some of the doubters that were still amongst some of the students. Charlyyk nodded. 'Yes, Mrs Landon I would love too.'

Miss Vasey had mentioned to Julia and Sandra how hard it would be for Charlyyk to maintain a healthy lifestyle with what was happening to her. 'We must form a group of your friends together and work out a way to help Charlyyk to be able to adapt. You know, like a sheriff's posse.'

The school bus arrived at the entrance to the drive. Charlyyk said her goodbyes. Helen and Bryn were waiting for her, and the hugs she gave them both, pleased Helen immensely it was her way of knowing Charlyyk had accepted her, knowing if she could not get her trust, there would be no future with Bryn.

Later Helen and Charlyyk, were cooking the dinner together. 'I've given in my notice of resignation. This is to say that my commitment to you and your dad start from now.'

Charlyyk did not smile. She was happy... but she had her serious face on. 'Helen, I feel that this is how it should be. Dad has changed since you have been around, the way he has relaxed was not what I thought how he would react. It is though, a weight has been lifted of him; The vibes he gives, fit how he is. He is where he wants to be, that makes me happy. The vibes you give, tells me you to are happy where you are. We are a family.'

Helen had stopped what she was doing, this serious side of Charlyyk was portraying a very mature person, not the young girl she had previously seen. 'Yes Charlyyk, you are right. We are a family.'

During dinner, Bryn and Charlyyk relating to the visit to Houston and Disney World, showed Helen, some of the video footage that had been taken. Especially the part where Charlyyk met Olaf. Helen could not stop laughing, the cuddles that they gave each other, told Bryn that his proposal to Helen was right.

When Charlyyk and Helen had cleared up after dinner, Charlyyk said goodnight, and went to her room, to finish her homework. This gave Helen a chance for her to talk to Bryn. He listened intently to her decision to retire, and the reason why. 'Bryn, I'm marrying you because of the love I feel for you, but I still will have to accept, to take on the responsibility, of helping you to bring up Charlyyk. I could never achieve what Harold and Gwen have. Though I can join in with the family, and build my trust with you all, with your help...Bryn, I have put my apartment on the market; when returning to it last week; I had never felt so lonely, as I did that day. Then meeting with my parents, it was so different I really enjoyed being with them.'

'We must invite them here. I liked your parents when we met here that Saturday. But I did not get a chance to get to know them properly. Should we invite Anna as well?'

Helen's expression was of guilt. 'That would be nice Bryn, I've been, so out of touch with them, meeting them again after experiencing this environment, I have started to realise they are not totally all to blame for how we have been so distant from each other.'

***

Charlyyk returned from her morning run, Helen's had to laugh when she saw how ill-fitting Charlyyk's tracksuit had become. When Charlyyk saw herself in the tall mirrors of her bedroom she could not help laughing too. Her hands stood out, they looked long and un-gamely. These differences from human hands did not worry her but made her aware of how others saw her. The claws were getting longer and they showed. Michel had said he will try and keep them in check.

Charlyyk collect the special nail-file that Michel had given her, thinking, '*Sarah will do them for me*' placed the nail-file in her bag.

At ten, Toby arrived at the Cottage. He never knocks, he just walked in. Finding them both doing their domestic duties. They did not notice him, as he leant against the door. 'Bloody hell Toby, how long have you been standing there?'

'Long enough, to see that you two are like an old married couple.'

Helen threw a wet dishcloth at him.

Over Coffee, Helen confirms to Toby, of her resignation. 'Meeting Bryn I feel young again, I want to enjoy the new me. This department, that we have built up together, will run just as smoothly with you at the helm. That is why it is time for me to step down, and hand the reigns over to you.'

Toby's look was wistful, he knew he could run the operations, but the respect he had for Helen he was just as happy to work for her. 'I'm glad it was this way, you leaving like this, I would have felt bad if it seemed I was pushing you out. You two have been the most influential people in my life. That I owe so much. Thank you.' He kisses Helen, then hugs Bryn.

Helen then fills him in on the details, he needed to know. 'When you are ready, we will go, and confirm it with the PM.'

With a broad grin, Toby comments. 'Cos, you know marrying Bryn, is going to age you? You will become a grandmother overnight.'

Helen gave him a playful slap. Bryn just laughed.

With Bryn's permission, Toby spent the rest of the afternoon, locked in his study, while Bryn and Helen, tried to work out when her parents could come for a visit, to get know each other. Eventually, they found five possible dates, so her parents could choose at their convenience. Helen spoke with them, and they promised they would ring back as soon as a slot opened, an alternative option was to stay for a few days if they preferred.

The morning hoarfrost gave the fields a thick white blanket. Hedgerows and trees covered in a white candy floss. Climbing over the Bishops Lane style, Bryn slips and finds himself lying flat on his back. Charlyyk helps him up. They set off again, but she noticed the limp in his stride. 'Let's take it easy dad, you are not so young to be able to just run it off, you will probably do more harm than good.' They take a shorter way back to the cottage.

Helen seeing him limping gave him a sympathetic smile. 'Oh, my poor wounded soldier.' She was quick to provide him with an arm to lean on, taking Bryn straight to Kitty's Clinic for some therapy.

Chapter 20

Meeting Helen's Parents

Bryn's hip gave him, an uncomfortable night, and did not go on his usual morning run, Charlyyk went on her own. Helen, checked his hip, it had extensive bruising, and was very tender, to the touch. She applied some more arnica cream to it, to reduce the bruising. Charlyyk was soon back, telling Bryn with a mischievous smile, that she had no one holding her back. But giving him a hug and a kiss, remarked she had missed him.

Helen worked hard getting ready for the visit of her parents up till lunchtime. When Harold and Gwen arrived and joined them for lunch. Harold had brought Charlyyk many books from his library, to help her with a school project 'The changing face of Britain since the war'.

Helen looked at Gwen. 'Well, that one bucketful of worms, to get your hands into.'

Bryn turned to Helen. 'Well that something we have not discussed, Politics, Red, Blue, Yellow or Green?'

Gwen chirped in. 'Don't forget Purple?'

Harold sat back. 'I'm not liking this multi-party thing we are getting ourselves into... look at the mess European politics is in, too many parties, like a pack of Hyenas squabbling over any tit-bit they can sink they're missed guided views into... the result, nothing of solid substance coming from it, more a compromised, complicated mess. Then the more I hear of our politicians... makes '*Yes Minister*' more a reality, than a sitcom TV show?'

Helen had made fresh tea, placing it on the coffee table. 'I don't know if that makes you red, blue or just plain angry Harold?'

Gwen reached over taking her cup of tea. 'That the problem Helen. When the people get angry, they tend to give a protest vote and in a way, that how minority parties can affect elections. We have too many politicians who are Dinosaurs, stuck in a time warp, spouting out what the people only want to hear.

Helen had never been interested in politics her roll in the army meant she had to remain nutral.

Gwen smiled. 'My Welsh grandfather who was a Liberal, he was a great admirer of David Lloyd George, would always say. 'The poor don't like the rich, but they like to have their money, then they would be rich, then the poor would not like them. Until we've taken the blinkers of the poor, will we get better politics? You see the rich, make work for the poor, not the poor, for the poor, so you see we need the rich, though it's going to be the poor, who are going to do the bloody work, not the bloody rich!'

Bryn reached for his sister's hand, both remembering their grandfather with great fondness, his stories always rich in colourful detail, always a source of laughter. Gwen told them of the day he had met his future Daughter-in-law for the first time, as told to her, by her grandmother. 'Bloody hell, our boyo, is going to be a snob, but he will make a good snob.'

Bryn looked at the joy, those memories had given his sister. He had many of his own. During his second game of rugby, he had taken some big hits from two lads. As he came off the pitch his grandfather said to him. 'Remember where it hurts you the most, that's where you hit them next... the family is from the valley, we take our knocks, then return them harder.'

Helen had met Charlyyk from the bus. Walking in together. 'Hi everyone.' Charlyyk kissed them all, looking at Bryn laying on the sofa. 'You have not been there all day, have you?'

Bryn looked at Helen for support. She shook her head. 'Don't look at me, I only said you can stay there, it was up to you, what you did?'

Bryn, with that look off. 'But.' Then Charlyyk threw her arms around his neck and kissed him. 'You poor dear, did we tease you?'

All the girls went to the kitchen to start the evening meal, Bryn and Harold discussed Helen's parents coming for the weekend. 'It will be a full house, with Janet coming back tomorrow, Bryn.'

Bryn corrected Harold. 'Jane said that Janet is coming here with some articles she has written and needs our approval, then she is spending the weekend with James. So, it should be alright.'

***

Saturday morning, Helen was busy with febrile excitement, wanting to impress her parents. Charlyyk took her hand and made her sit down, she had made Helen a mug of coffee. 'The cottage looks lovely, they won't even notice it, they will only be interested in you, and your happiness.'

Helen took a deep breath. 'Thanks, sweetheart...I have just got to get used to my new life, it seems I am not sure of myself... if I am getting it right...as I have never had to do this before, for this is the very first time, I have asked my parent to stay with me...ever.'

Charlyyk gentle smile, then giving Helen a hug. 'Same for me, everything is a first.'

Helen nodded. 'Sorry sweetheart, I didn't think.'

Charlyyk taking Helen's hand in her. 'That's why I understand how you are feeling right now.'

Helen's parents arrived at five minutes to ten. Anna was soon with the help of Bryn and Harold, taking the various bags to their designated rooms, once the activity died down, they introduced themselves, in a more relaxed manner. It was Lord Edward, being introduced to Bryn. 'It's Edward we are family now Bryn, let's not stand on ceremony, in court it gives me standing, in real life, it's a pain in the arse.'

Elizabeth kissed Bryn. 'You have given me a daughter Bryn, I never thought existed. which I am truly grateful, from the bottom of my heart.' Helen then introduced, Harold and Gwen, Helen's parent, gave them much praise for how they had helped Bryn with Charlyyk.

Charlyyk stood patiently to be introduced. The warm smile, with a long tender cuddle, she received from Helen's Parents, gave her a special feeling, she had received many welcomes before, but this was so different, the tingling excitement she could feel as Elizabeth taking her hands in hers.

Elisabeth spoke softly. 'When people get to a certain age Charlyyk, the thing they like doing the most, is to talk about their grandchildren...at last, we will have that special moment, and what a unique granddaughter we have to be able to speak about. We don't have to be a Lord and Lady to make us special, just being grandparents will do nicely.'

Charlyyk felt the vibes that Elisabeth gave out, was those same vibes that she felt from Helen. This was how |Charlyyk sensed who she could trust, then when she touched hands with that person will confirm to her the full extent of their sincerity.

Helen's mother then introduced Anna to the family. 'Anna is another special person in our lives, for she looks after us, caters for us, keeps us organised, keeps us grounded. Our work, can take over our ability to be able to care for ourselves, if it was not for Anna, who knows what would happen to us?'

Helen gave her father a nudge, 'You would survive dad, but only just.'

Helen's father sitting next to Charlyyk. 'Tell me, young lady, how do you find school?'

Charlyyk slipped her arm into his and gave him a little tug. 'Love it.' Her body movement, of her shoulders squeezing together, reflected her excitement. 'Meeting people of my same age group, hearing and seeing how they look at their world, music, fashion and the way they look at themselves; then there are the teachers, how their own personality controls the way they teach.'

Helen's, mother looking just as excited as Charlyyk. 'Who's your best friend, Charlyyk?'

I have two. 'Julia and Sandra, really steady girls. Their feet are firmly on the floor. I'm also friends with Sarah and Jan, who are arty, though more eccentric. Mace and his brother George, nicely well behaved and steady. Miss Vasey, the art teacher, calls them the posse. It's the way they surround me and make sure that not too many people are with me at any one time, but it still allows me to be able to talk to everyone in turn.'

Helen's mother was enjoying listening to Charlyyk, the enthusiasm in her voice, depicting how she saw school life. 'So, what's your favourite subject?'

Charlyyk looked up, thought for a moment. 'I like all the lesson, but enjoy art the most.'

Elizabeth could tell that Charlyyk liked art, her eyes changed colour and her ears moved forward. 'Are you good at art?'

Charlyyk again paused for thought. 'I don't know, whether that matters, as long as you enjoy it, I just love the way the colours, bring things to life.'

During dinner, the conversation began with Janet Stokes. Then Anna, asked Charlyyk, her likes, and dislikes in food, books and music, when Charlyyk began to talk about X Factor it started to get noisy. Gwen and Harold hated it, Anna loved it, Helen and Bryn accepted it, Charlyyk sat there enjoying the interesting differences being put forward, from all quarters. Elizabeth reached over and touched Charlyyk's arm. 'This is fun.'

Charlyyk was smiling at what was being said. 'It's the same as being at school.'

Anna asked Charlyyk. 'Who do you want to win?'

'Fleur, who do you want to win?'

Anna with, a twinkle in her eye answered. 'Ben.'

***

On Sunday morning the hard frost did not deter Bryn and Charlyyk's run. Bryn still felt a slight pain because of the bruising, but soldiered through it.

At breakfast, the Bennett's looked relaxed, asked if they could all walk to the village? As they walked down the lane towards the village. Bryn pointed to the wooded copse on the hill, where he and Charlyyk had landed back on Earth. Edward wanted to know how Charlyyk felt. 'Anything here, you like in particular Charlyyk?'

Charlyyk's smile, was soft as she remembered those earlier days. 'The birds, we did not have anything like them, Dad and I laid in the grass one summers day, just listening to them chirping away it was so nice. Dad pointed out one bird, a skylark, it just hovered in the sky above, singing away, it was so beautiful; then there are the insects: bees, butterflies, dragonflies and the crickets, just fantastic.'

Elisabeth watched the changing colours in Charlyyk's eyes, as she reflected on those idyllic moments. Holding onto her husband arm, Elizabeth asked. 'What else do you like Charlyyk?'

Charlyyk thought for a moment. 'When dad mentioned going for an early morning run, I thought he was going mad...who would want to run when you don't need to... but when we put the tracksuits on and started running, it was like freedom... before we had to be so careful who saw us, I was sneaked in, and out of the house, so no one would see me... now I was running freely without a care.'

Helen's mother could now see the girl, more than an Alien. The feelings Charlyyk was expressing would be no different than her own feelings. 'Were the differences from your planet to this planet so different Charlyyk?'

Charlyyk scrunched her face, as the thoughts were going through her mind. 'We could not travel far from our burrows so it is hard to give overall idea. of all the planet where I had come from. But here, the buds forming and the new leaves appearing, rabbits with their young, the intoxicating smell of the land, as the days got shorter, with cold breezes that came, the changing colours on the trees, with their leaves falling. The frost, then snow, so... So, beautiful.' Charlyyk did a couple of twirls, she was so happy within her thoughts.

As they enter the village, they could see the families walking towards the 13c Norman built, village church. St Pancras. The Bailey's were just leaving their house. The Martin family were talking to Father Stevens at the church gates.

Harold and Gwen, looked up, as they walked towards the church, and seeing them, stopped to allow them to catch up. Gwen giving Charlyyk a big hug when they met.

Father Stevens greeted them. It was his first time seeing Charlyyk. He shook her hand, and would not let go, asking many questions. It was Sarah and Mace that came to her rescue, managing to get her away from Father Stevens clutches. James, hands grabbed Charlyyk from behind lifting her up and placing a big kiss on her cheek. When he put her down, it was Janet's turn to hug her and kiss her too.

Charlyyk felt apprehensively awkward, this was not where she wanted to be. She had been caught off guard, now she had no escape route. Nobody could see the dilemma Charlyyk was in. Decided, she would take whatever emerges.

After a quick survey, the church did not look so bad as there were many on hand to protect her. Bryn her dad was her security...Helen her comfort. With these thoughts, Charlyyk pulled together Helen and Bryn, so she was sandwiched between them. Now she felt much more secure.

The Church Service was running a little late. Old Mrs Lilly Evans, the church organist, was trying to hurry it up by playing some loud organ music, but no one took any notice. So, it became louder and loud

Father Stevens welcomed the Collier family. 'It's been a long-time, but we...and I mean the whole village...are so pleased to see you here today, with that charming little girl.'

Father Stevens and Gwen had talked about Charlyyk, her views of religion, Father Stevens was looking at it as a mission to show Charlyyk his God was a good God. Someone Charlyyk could use to help her live here on Earth.

Inside the church felt so cold to Charlyyk. Once the congregation were settled, they were soon in fine voice singing the first hymn. Positioned between Helen and Bryn, she felt safe. She did not know what was going to happen. Was this God of Gwen's going to show his face or what? She had no idea. She waited for something to materialise.

The sermon was long, and monotone. Bored expressions, were apparent. There were those that had stifled yawns, where others looked down at their feet, some with their eyes closed, could they be asleep? Reminding her of some of the lessons at school, where some of the students, found it hard to concentrate. As a plate was passed around. Charlyyk, looked at it and observed the amount of money. After, the service had finished and everyone was leaving. She looked around to see if she had missed something. No, nothing had changed--still clutching tightly to her dad just in case, she followed as close as she could behind him, with Helen's comforting hand on Charlyyk's back as if Helen was guarding her from behind.

The mild Autumn sun felt warm, she turned to face it, closed her eyes. The light smile on her face, showing the good feel factor it had on her, or perhaps it was, that she just felt safe.

Gwen seeing Charlyyk's face. 'Did you like that Charlyyk?'

Charlyyk opened her eyes. Seeing Helen standing behind Gwen, nodding her head and mouthing 'YES' She looked at Gwen. 'The singing was lovely Auntie Gwen.' Helen closed her eyes and shook her head.

Helen's mother had been watching all this, quickly took Gwen's elbow. 'What a lovely church, Gwen how old is it?' Led her away gently.

Helen stepped forward, putting her arms around Charlyyk, pulled her towards herself, kissed her on top of her head. 'That was so close sweetheart,' Helen remarked.

Charlyyk's face showed that she was not sure what Helen had implied. For her response to Gwen Had been sincere, so why was Helen so concerned. Then seeing Helen's mother nodding to Helen, it became clear. Charlyyk smiled at Helen. 'Yes, mum I was not thinking properly, my thoughts had me at a disadvantage. I was so enjoying the warm sun on my face.'

Bryn had lingered behind, spoke with Father Stevens, to stop him from talking to Charlyyk. Helen quickly took hold of her father's arm, beckoned to Charlyyk to follow them. They crossed the village green to Carpenters Cottage, for coffees, then later for dinner.

Harold had put the meat in the oven, on a slow cook, and the smell as they entered the cottage, was very welcoming. Helen had to work hard to stop Anna from stepping into the kitchen, trying to take over. 'This is Harold's sacred place, you are allowed to sit, and watch, but Harold does the cooking.'

Edward, to his wife's dismay, started to ask Charlyyk about the Church service, she quickly tapped his knee and told him. 'No.' She changed the conversation, till she managed to get Gwen to show her the house. Elizabeth had observed Charlyyk during the Church service, had noticed how uncomfortable Charlyyk looked, was helping to try and reduce the pressure that Gwen was putting on Charlyyk to go to Church.

Dinner was a slow affair. Harold had made an apple pie beforehand. After the main course, Harold made a large jug of custard. Edward was keen to get as large of a helping as he could, but first, he had to allow the main course to settle. Bryn poured him another glass of wine, to help him settle his stomach. The afternoon, drifted by. The women talked about the house and its history. The men talked about rugby and cars.

Elizabeth had got the measure of everyone there. Was now showing why she held the position of Chief Justice. How she listened, yet still held control, of the conversation. Charlyyk sat and admired Elisabeth technique. She saw that Helen had similar qualities.

***

When Charlyyk returned from her run she quickly showered, and changed into her school uniform. Checking that she looked OK, she knocked on the door where Edward and Elizabeth were sleeping. 'Come in.' Elizabeth called.

She slipped into the room. 'Hi, I wanted to say goodbye, and to tell you I so enjoyed you being here.'

Elizabeth held out her arms. 'Come here.' She opened her arms, gave Charlyyk a very warm cuddle. 'We have learned so much about you Charlyyk, also about ourselves.'

Charlyyk's quizzical look. 'About yourselves?'

Elizabeth nodded. 'Yes, we had wrapped ourselves up in our careers, we forgot we were a family. Helen missed out on a lot of things. We should have given her more of ourselves...We should have been there for her.'

Edward reached across the bed. 'We will always be there for you if you need us?' They exchanged hugs and kisses.

When the school bus arrived, everyone was there to see Charlyyk off. She rushed to the back of the bus to wave them goodbye. Sarah and Mace joined her. Helen sat down with a mug of coffee, next to Bryn. 'What a lovely weekend, mum and dad really enjoyed themselves.' Bryn gave her a hug. Helen looking very pleased with herself. 'They really hit it off with Charlyyk. She went and said goodbye to them in their room this morning...it really touched them, and I've never seen Anna talk so much either.'

Bryn and Helen said goodbye to her parents and Anna as they waved them off at ten.

Bryn helping Helen to tidy up. 'We've to go into town. Gwen has given me the name and colour of the tracksuit that Charlyyk likes, while we are there, I do think we need to get you one. I've noticed you could do with a little toning, maybe Pilates to start with, then some jogging not too heavy, something light.'

Helen looked at him, her stance gave Bryn the feeling that she was questioning him. Bryn raised his finger. 'Come with me.' He led her to the clinic, took a book from the shelf. 'This will tell us the correct body weight for your body size, but more important you bone structure. With a tape measure; he measured her waist, wrist and ankles, and her height, then checked the chart. 'Give and take a pound, that should be your weight.'

Helen stripped down to her knickers and stepped onto the scales.

Bryn checking the scales. 'There you are seven pounds over?'

Helen taken aback. 'Are you a control freak?'

'No, but honestly. How do you want to look, at our wedding?' Raising his eyebrows at her. 'Well.'

She cocked her head, contemplated the reading on the scales. 'Would more sex, do it?'

He laughed. 'It could help, but it's not the complete answer to it.' Bryn cuddled up to Helen, with his arms, wrapped around her. 'I promise it won't be an assault course, we are not in the army and have no battles to fight. We'll start off lightly, then gently build it up.'

Helen, with a coy look on her face. 'Are you talking about the sex?'

'No, the Pilates are not supposed to be painful.' Reaching down, taking a firm hold of the cheeks of her bottom. 'This could become firmer.'

Helen lifted her head up, the kissed him, she had thought of what changes she would like in herself, and this was one of them. 'Then let's do it, let's give it a try?'

When Charlyyk arrived home, she checked the tracksuit and tried it on, bending and stretching to see if it felt comfortable. 'It's great, thanks.' Then she spotted another package. 'What's this then?'

Helen explained what they had in mind. Charlyyk's full attention on what Helen was saying, she could sense that Helen was keen to give it a go. 'That's great, you will feel much better for it.' Charlyyk looked at Bryn. 'When you going to start, Dad?'

In a matter-of-fact manner, he replied. 'Tomorrow, we will start with stretching exercises, then build it up.'

***

After four day of Pilates; Helen soon began to enjoy it. She found Bryn to be a good teacher, he did not push her hard but allowed her, to find her own limits. Making sure she drank lots of water, but most of all the slow deep breathing through the nose and out of the mouth, Bryn explaining all the time, the exercise, and its benefits.

Janet arrived for another stay with Charlyyk. She used Bryn's study, to work in, and applied to Mrs Landon for permission to attend school with Charlyyk. This was one of the conditions the press had made.

Janet spent Friday afternoon, with Mrs Landon, to see how it could work. They agreed that Janet could begin on the Monday.

***

Four runners, were jogging carefully over the icy tractor tracks. It was Helens first run; she was coping well and keeping up. Janet and Charlyyk had already waved and shouted at James. 'Up to the top of the hill, then the homeward run down the hill.' Bryn had set an easy pace. What Helen had not told them; she had run for her college at cross-country. Bryn would have known; she would have done training with the army.

That had been some years back. But it was all coming back to Helen, as she settled into a smooth running pattern. Talking while running, was hard at first, soon it became easier. She joined the banter of the two younger women.

Harold and Gwen arrived at ten, then they all went to town, to shop and have lunch at Pizza Express. People had started to accept Charlyyk, some would turn and take a second look, or point her out. The occasional fellow student, said hello or introduce Charlyyk to a member of their family or friend. Now and again the odd doubter would be there, how they would react depended how angry they felt. Charlyyk's passive response usually calmed the situation.

The discussions Charlyyk had with Sandra and Julia about how to handle these situations were beginning to bear fruit. Sandra's mother had a saying, 'Your probably right. For you have not agreed or disagreed.' And this was basis of how they would look at any confrontation

Janet brought clothes to wear on Monday; nothing too fancy, so she could blend in.

Charlyyk managed to find out what her dad would like for Christmas, immediately texted Rachel, ten minutes later, a reply came back. *'Thanks, sweetheart, see you all soon, love R&T'*

As she went to turn off the phone another text came through. *'Miss, you already. Love Liza.'* Looking over her shoulder, Helen remarked. 'That my mother.' And showed her the same message on her phone.

When they returned to the cottage, Charlyyk pushed Janet to help her finish the presentation, she had promised Mrs Landon. Janet liked what Charlyyk had laid out, pointed to some small alteration. Then went through some of the photographs she had taken, with one video clip, a DVD promotional video of the space centre. Then Janet showed Charlyyk how to put the whole sequence together. then entered it into Charlyyk's Laptop. 'Tomorrow we will have a run through, to see how long it takes. Have they a large TV screen in the Assembly Hall, we could show it on?' Charlyyk nodded.

Janet helped Charlyyk to tidy up. 'How you getting on with that project, the changing face of Britain' Charlyyk took a folder from her satchel and gave it to Janet. They sat on the bed together, while Janet read through what Charlyyk had written. 'It a bit patchy?' Janet made some suggestions, stuck sticky notes where she thought they should go. Charlyyk did not seemed concerned, as it was only a draft paper.

Chapter 21

Dippers Meadow

Dippers Meadow, had a little Brock that babbled at one end. Weeping willows drooped down into the small chalk stream. Bryn had taken her there, one spring morning. She stopped and stood there in sheer wonderment, taken back by its pure beauty. She sniffed the air and smelt the blossom of the flowers scattered about the meadow, intoxicated by their scent, and the busy sound of insects that hurried about working with nature to keep this environment going.

Even at that stage of late autumn, it still held its beauty. It sat between two small hills with many species of trees scattered about them, some still with their autumn leaves, of brown, red and gold, with a sprinkle of dark evergreen of spruce and pine with their emerald green pine needles. It always felt special to Charlyyk. That why they were there. Charlyyk wanted to share it with Helen

Helen stood beside Charlyyk, feeling her emotions, as they viewed the scenery. Helen hearing Charlyyk keep mentioning her favourite place in their conversations, felt honoured to be there. 'Its lovely sweetheart.' As she reached down and took Charlyyk's hand in hers. 'Thank you so very much for sharing it with me.'

After they had returned to the cottage, Janet and Charlyyk ran through the presentation. They fine-tuned it, to run for an hour and a half, to Charlyyk's satisfaction. Janet then left, to spend the rest of the day with James.

Sunday dinner at Carpenters Cottage was always, special to Charlyyk, it was a second home from home, as she had spent so much time there in those early days on earth. Michel had come for dinner, it made it even better. She found him in the kitchen with Harold. In one corner of the kitchen, was a special chair, that Michel loved to sit in, this enabled him talk to Harold while he cooked.

Charlyyk liked to sit on Michel's lap, to listen to the stories they told of their youth. Today Bryn had joined them, as the stories of them, began to unfold. Charlyyk sat there spellbound by their interpretation of the events, how they remembered what they thought had incurred. Then as the wine flowed the stories became less lucid, the laughter became more raucous. This behaviour from them, at first she could not understand, as time passed by, she started to understand the stories better, for each time the stories would change, little by little the truth of the stories emerged. Gwen would tell Charlyyk. 'Boy's love to brag in these situations, though when they drink their tongues get loose, the brain loses control, then the real story flows out unabashed.'

***

Charlyyk and Janet, sitting at the breakfast table, discussing her school assignment. 'You could go down the path, of discussing social changes, the way people lived. Today we can get into our cars and buy a week's shop all at once, at the supermarket. We have fridges and freezers. We can buy all types of food all year-round. When in my grandmother's time, the women would have to shop on a regular two day's shop. The choice was what was in season.

Bryn and Helen listened carefully. Janet did not tell her what to write, more how to look at all the different elements that caused the changes.

When Mrs Landon met Janet in her office before Monday classes started, she was pleasantly surprised at how Janet had dressed. The clothes were plain and simple but yet stylish. She wore no makeup, yet still looked good. Charlyyk gave Mrs Landon her iPad to review her presentation about her trip to America.

Janet had agreed to Mrs Landon's with the school governor's terms on how she should behave, observing Charlyyk at school

At the end of the day when lessons were over, all the masters and Janet, met in Mrs Landon's office, to discuss the events of the day. Mr Waverley agreed that at the start of the day there could have been a little disturbance, but it soon evaporated, Mr Pearson reckoned that it improved his class 'They were more attentive.'

Mrs Thompson agreed. 'My class definitely behaved better than before.'

Janet was pleased with their comments, as was Mrs Landon. 'Well, Janet it looks as if this could be the way forward.'

'This was just the first day, let's not get carried away, that it will be the same every day. I will try and conduct myself professionally at all times. This is as important to the school, as it is to the News media. In my capacity as a reporter. I've become good friends with Charlyyk, I therefore must do what is right for her. So, if there develops any need for change, we must find the right ways to make those changes.'

Mrs Landon then spoke about Charlyyk's presentation about America. 'I can see your input in the photos, and the video clip. It is well thought out, being very informative, I'm looking at Wednesday afternoon to show it. That is the least disruptive period. Does anyone have any comments on this?' When no one objected. 'Great that settles it. Than you all for your valuable time.'

Janet and Charlyyk returned to the cottage. Janet had noticed how different Charlyyk was. She had always had an air of confidence about her. Now it felt as though she had grown another year older. She seemed more mature. When she needed explaining something, her comments and movements were more confident and persuasive.

Sitting at the kitchen table, Charlyyk talking about the events of the day. Even Bryn noticed the hand movements, the shrug of the shoulders the toss of the head. Janet looked at Bryn and gestured as if to say, 'What you thinking?' He shrugged.'

After dinner, Charlyyk went to her room to do her homework. Janet sat with Bryn and Helen in the lounge. 'I don't know if you have noticed, but Charlyyk has matured overnight.' Bryn agreed that since she went to school in the morning, till she returned home late in the afternoon, there has been a change in her. Helen said, she had seen girls at her school. change in a single week, but not in a day. They all agreed to keep their eyes open to see, where it would lead to.

The mornings were feeling colder. Charlyyk wore her winter's coat, with a long multi-striped scarf, wrapped around her neck. Her bag was bulging with books; Harold's books, all concerning post-war Britain. It had been a bankrupt country, trying hard to get back on its feet. Rationing had been enforced for almost a decade after the war.

Charlyyk had burned the midnight oil reading about the problems, faced by various governments after the war, the different solutions each one took to solving those challenges of trying to get Britains ecomony back on track. Taking on board what Janet had mentioned, she had only looked briefly at the political element of it. Lack of proper finances at the beginning, then the inventions of household appliances seem to be the prominent factor for the changes that have turned life around for so many.

At the Academy, Janet went off to set herself up in the first Classroom. Charlyyk went in search of the Posse. Sandra and Julia, seeing her waved her to them. 'Crikey, how many books have you bought?' They were soon opening them, to see what they were about. Mace and Sarah found a book about the Rag Trade and British fashion.

The school bell rang to beckon them to class. The posse made their way to Mr Pearson's classroom, He was talking with Janet. 'Ok settled down, has anyone, anything on the project?'

Julia stood up. 'I spoke with my grandfather, lived in the Midlands, He worked as an apprentice machinist in a large factory. The company found it hard to recruit workers. They had so much work, they worked long hours on bonus schemes, to keep up with the demand.'

Paul Gunn, a thin, pasty looking lad, who had lots of spots on his face, spoke up. 'That makes sense to what my grandfather was talking about, He worked in the building trade, he reckoned that the Wilson Government, put a Selective Employment Tax on the building companies to get workers out of the building trades, into the factories. He said, what it achieved, was to stop firms employing apprentices, then has many retired from the building Companies, they were not replaced, so when the country wanted more houses, we did not have the tradesmen to build them.

Jan raised her hand. 'But other things changed Britain; like music and fashion?'

Mace made the next suggestion. 'Mass immigration in the 50's, how did that change Britain was that a good policy, or was it a mistake? Did they keep up the pretext that it was a good thing, just to justify their error?'

Mr Pearson looked at Mace. 'What made you say that Mace?'

'Well, I read, that the more people you let in, the more work it creates. Then you need more people to do the jobs. So, it does not solve a problem it creates a problem. It's like telling a lie, that you have to tell more lies, to cover the first lie.'

Tim Pearson, reaction to this was to nod his head in that way people have when a comment makes them look at themselves or at an alternative view. 'Interesting Mace, I can see what you are trying to say, who was it who wrote it, was it a politician?'

Mace gently shook his head, 'No sir, she was an economist. Her views were based on efficiency in the workplace, where more workers meant less output.'

Mike spoke next. 'When I spoke to my parents, about this project, it ended up them not speaking to each other.' Mikes facial expression looked like he had eaten something and was not quite sure what. 'Mum calling dad, a racial bigot, he said immigration can be beneficial, to large businesses, it allows them to bring in more workers at a cheap rate, but it throws the country into chaos to accommodate at short notice. The strain it puts on the internal infrastructure of the country. Like Hospitals, Housing and schools. Should only be allowed if these had been built before immigration was allowed to happen. Mum shouted at him that these starving people, came here to work, to provide food for their families.'

Mr Pearson raised his hand, 'Can we not be too political... Please.'

Peter Elliott, 'My parents reckon, that the swinging sixties was the changing face of Britain. Winning the world cup, James Bond the Rolling Stones, the Beatles, the Who, Carnaby Street, Mary Quant were some of the good things. The bad stuff was the way the Trade Unions behaved. They reckon if Margret Thatcher had not stood up against them. We were heading in the direction of not a Labour Party. But a Trade Union Party and could have us ending up as a satellite state of Russia.'

Tim Pearson held his hand up. 'We seem to be going too political here.' Turning to the Smartboard. 'Peter mentioned, winning the World Cup, Music Icons and Fashion. Can anyone tell us what that did for Britain?'

Charlyyk, who was as usual been quiet, raised her hand. She had been listening to what was being said, but it was not the Political side of the subject that she had concentrated on. 'Foreign money, the world saw Britain as an innovator, wanted to buy our goods, this brought in a vast amount of foreign money into Britain. Where before the world wanted to speak English to listen to American films, and music, were now listening to British movies and music. Buying into British fashion.'

Doubt had made Charlyyk blurt out her points. She made a mental note of the political side of the debate to look at it later.

Tim Pearson wrote down Charlyyk's comments on the whiteboard. 'Ok, we have to leave it there. Can we not be too political, please?'

During the lunch period, Janet spoke to Charlyyk's classmates, on how they saw Charlyyk now, as to when she first entered school. Peter Elliott was keen to respond. 'I believed Charlyyk was going to do some strange things. She is just like us, but cooler; apart from her encounter with Olaf at Disney World, where she just flipped. Charlyyk is no different than us, and great to be around. Just don't get to hear her sing. For what comes out is like a wolf, howling at the moon.'

Jan Freeman pushed forward. 'What I like about Charlyyk is she actually listens to you. No matter what rubbish come out of your mouth, she still listens to you. Then thinks it through, what you have said then gives you a straight answer.'

Sandra, speaking for Julia as well as herself. 'We like Charlyyk, she senses when you are troubled in yourself, and has that knack of making you talk about it. It takes so much off yourself, to know someone has listened, to your problems.'

Sarah puckered her mouth, thinking carefully about what she was going to say. 'She appreciates friendship. It's as if she wears it like a cloak...If you need her... she wraps it around you, like a comfort blanket.'

Mace nodding. 'She like an all-knowing big sister, you go to for advice. Janet when I first met Charlyyk, her appearance did not seem that strange, it was her hands that at first took a little time to adjust to. But now they seem normal, looking into her eyes... now that is different. You can never get enough of them. But don't try to see both eyes at the same time. That can freak you out how they move independently from each other.'

At dinner, Charlyyk explains her day to Bryn and Helen.' I was going to say so much, about the changes in Britain, but listening to the rest of the class I felt I had missed something. I needed to re-examine what I had actually read about?'

Janet looked at her. 'I thought what you said was quite good.'

Charlyyk shrugged her shoulders. 'It's what I know, as fact, and it was not political at all.'

Bryn quired. 'Was the project, meant to be political?'

Charlyyk looked more interested, with what she was eating then the question being asked. 'The project was about the Changing Face of Britain, not the Political Face of Britain?' Placing her knife and fork neatly on her finished plate. 'That why I said, I needed to re-examine what I had studied on this subject?'

Helen began clearing the dirty dishes into the dishwasher. 'So, does that mean you will look at the political consequences, of the changing face of Britain?'

'Mr Pearson picked up on the value of the World Cup: Music, Films and Fashion. He purposely ignored the influence of the trade unions, that Peter had mentioned. I took that as he did not like the political element being discussed. But to debate the question fully, we must look at all the fractions that took place at that time?' She kissed Bryn and Helen. 'I'm going to get myself ready for bed, then sit in bed and revise, so I say good night. See you in the morning...love you.' She, high fives, Janet. 'See you later.'

Sitting in the lounge drinking coffee. Bryn, Helen and Janet talk about how Charlyyk had changed in such a short time.

'Basically, she is still the same. She has always been able to adjust to what is needed of her,' Helen said. 'In the brief period, I have known her. It seems she has grown in stature, like she has changed from a sapling into a young tree.'

***

The posse gathered together, discussing the events of the day before, when

Charlyyk arrived. Sandra and Julia quickly gained her attention. 'Did you work out the problem, Mr Waverley set on his homework page?'

Charlyyk put her satchel down and opened it, taking out the relevant book. 'I was not too sure what he really wanted, then I looked it up in one of Harold's books. It explains that the Ethylene gases avocados give off, effects bananas. If you put them together they both deteriorate quickly and that's why you must keep them separated.

As they all made notes. Sandra remarked. 'Does that mean they both give off gases if it affects them both?'

Charlyyk nodded. 'It seems that all fruit and vegetables give off some sort of Ethylene gas. It could be what we smell, is to be able to recognise what is.'

The rest of the posse then quickly finish their homework and congratulate Charlyyk, with smiles all around.

Mace sitting down with Charlyyk. 'Are you nervous about this afternoon, doing the presentation?'

She touched his arm. 'Not at all, actually I'm looking forward to it. There was so much to see there, I'm hoping to go back and see it again.'

He gave Charlyyk a concerned look. 'Mum said that your Auntie Gwen had told her, that you got upset, at some of the things they asked you to do.'

Charlyyk gave him a comforting smile. 'Those types of questions had to be asked. Some of the memories are still quite painful, remembering those friends I lost, and how I lost them. Their cries of pain will always be with me.' Now she was talking about her experiences, the guilt was not that painful as before. Yes, the pain was still there, but Charlyyk knew she was beginning to control it, with time she will be able to put it behind her.

The bell for lessons began to ring, they made the way to the appropriate classroom. Mr Waverley had already set up the work on the smart board. They placed their homework on his desk and sat down. 'In our last class, we touched on the needs of four persons and their recommended daily intake of Protein, Iron and Calcium, and energy.'

When the lesson was over, they moved to Mrs Thompson's classroom to study the works of Shakespeare, when lunchtime came, Mrs Landon approached Charlyyk and Janet, about the presentation, sat with them talking, until the lunch period was over. It was time for the presentation.

Charlyyk and Janet connected the computer to the system, with a couple of tests, they were ready. The whole experience lasted two hours, including half-an-hour, for questions. Mr Waverley stood with Charlyyk, to help with any of the issues of science that might arise.

When it was over, Charlyyk asked the school to raise a big hand to

Janet Stokes on her enormous contribution to the presentation. Afterwards, Charlyyk was delighted to see that standing with Mrs Landon, were Bryn, Helen, Harold and Gwen.

At dinner that evening Janet had waited for the right time, to ask their permission to set up an interview from the BBC producers of. '*The Sky at Night,* that wants to do a special programme on Charlyyk.'

There were no concerns mentioned, they all agreed it should go ahead. Janet and Bryn went to his study to inform the producers and set up a time frame for the event to take place.

During their early morning run, the weather was mild, with a damp feel to it. Bryn and Charlyyk were at the lead of the group, some three metres in front of Helen and Janet. They were discussing the men in their lives, then after the usual waves, and blown kisses between James and Janet 'Do you have separate rooms when you stay at the farm, Janet?' Helen enquired.

Janet laughed. 'Oh no, Edward and Jane spoke to us. They said that we were old enough and ugly enough to make those decisions, as long as we played safe, showing respect to each other? How are you finding life, with Bryn?'

Showing a little blush on her cheeks. 'What after living life as Nun. I've turned into a slut. I just can't say no, can't help myself. My hands keep wanting to tear his clothes off, no matter what I do to resist the temptation?'

With a glazed, look on her face, Janet, with deep sighs. 'Yes, I know just how you feel, Helen.' There was a short pause while they thought about their conversation. 'I bet Bryn does not complain though?' With smirks on their faces, then with a quick spurt, they caught up, with the leading pair.

Charlyyk seeing the smirks on Helen and Janet's faces, was well aware, what they had been discussing. Did it cause her concern? Not on your life. Charlyyk knew these two people, were needed to secure her life on Earth. The influence Janet was now giving her younger readers, will make that happen.

Chapter 22

The Change in Charlyyk

In Miss Vasey's art class, Janet soon was asking permission to video Charlyyk's reactions, on her attempts to paint. Charlyyk was no artist, and did not pretend she was, but the sheer pleasure of splashing acrylic paint onto a cheap paper was her idea of heaven. She was always the lesson was over too quickly.

Mrs Landon would now and again sneak a view of her while she was painting, to capture the look Charlyyk gave; thinking, if only all her students enjoyed their days at school, as much as Charlyyk enjoyed art class.

Alice Vasey explains to Janet. 'I dress Charlyyk in a smock to save her clothes, from the drips and splashes she always creates when she paints. I also keep her well away from the other students otherwise their work, would be covered by her over-enthusiastic endeavours. I encourage her as much as I can. Art is not how well you can draw or paint, but what you achieve from it. The portfolio of Charlyyk's work, proves just that. You can see what she is trying to paint, with her choice of colours, in itself is specially imaginative. There is so much you can see in Charlyyk's paintings.'

Alice Vasey showed Janet some of Charlyyk's paintings, Janet remarked. 'Change the Acrylic to Oil and the paper to canvas, these could be worth a small fortune?'

One picture stuck out more than all the others. Charlyyk had painted Dippers Meadow from memory. She had seen the sun's rays hitting the trees and how it caught the water in the babbling brook. There were butterflies, rabbits and birds on the wing, that were using the warm thermals to keep them afloat, drifting about in a sea of air.

Alice, interested in Janet's reaction, to that particular, painting. 'Does that picture ring-a-bell?'

Janet nodded. 'It's her favourite place, she took me there one morning when we jogging. It's called Dippers Meadow. Those splodges are Weeping Willows, that streak there is the babbling brook. The flicks of paint here and there are the sun rays through the trees. I can see it because I've been there and seen it.' Janet shows Alice the picture she took with her phone.

Alice Vasey had always wanted to see through Charlyyk's eyes. Here was the key to help her interpret how Charlyyk expressed herself. Previously it had seemed that Charlyyk was simply slapping paint to paper, now Alice knew she was actually painting a scene from her mind.

Alice spread other paintings over the table. It was easy to see which way they should be oriented, because of the paint runs. Alice now looking at them, with a real artist's eye. The more she looked, the more she saw. Soon making notes and attaching them to each painting. She was so engrossed in what she was doing, did not realise the lesson had ended.

Later at the cottage. Charlyyk and Janet helping to prepare for dinner, were telling Helen about the day at school. Helen knew how Charlyyk liked art. 'So, you liked watching Charlyyk paint then, Janet?'

. Giving Charlyyk a playful nudge. 'She really gives it her all, for there is no holding back. She wields her brush like Joan of Arc going into battle carrying a sword, taking no prisoners. But it's the joy in her face that tells the real story.'

Holding a wooden spoon in her hand, Charlyyk spun around waving it about. In a mock French accent. 'On guard, or I shall cover you in paint.'

The three of them could not stop laughing, when Janet said. 'You should tell the class that, when you go into your art lessons.'

Janet left the cottage, to go and stay for the weekend with James at the farm. While the three of them, settled in to watch '*Dirty Dancing*'. Helen would not watch it before she met Bryn. For romance was not on her 'to do list' Wendy Bailey had given it to Mace, who gave it to Charlyyk to give to Helen. Bryn was a little wary, how Charlyyk would respond to the film, with its innuedo to 'dirty' dancing, but Helen reckoned it would be Ok.

Charlyyk began by sitting between them. Then on Helens Lap. Then between them. Then on to Bryn lap. And so, it went on until the film ended. Charlyyk was now sitting on Helen's lap. Helen with her arms wrapped around Charlyyk. 'Well did you like that Charlyyk?'

She looked at Helen. 'I thought he was going to drop her, but I'm glad he didn't, they are like Janet and James. She was bigger than Janet, well she looked bigger than Janet, and James is bigger than Patrick Swayze. Julia said it was her favourite film, it's all about girl meets boy. I'm trying to understand, why it's called Dirty Dancing?'

Helen slightly biting her bottom lip. 'It's…more to do in how they are dancing, the sexual orientation it implies.'

Charlyyk nodded, remembering what Julie had said. 'This type of dancing is like sexual foreplay.'

Helen thoughts, that near enough' quickly changed the subject. 'What homework have you sweetheart?'

Charlyyk, reached for her satchel, pulled a paper from it. 'Shakespeare's Romeo and Juliet. Mrs Thompson wants a four-hundred-word, synopsis of it for Tuesday. Mr Waverley, needs the difference between farm workers, office workers, and fifteen-year-old, boys and girls, there their needs for nutrients and energy?'

***

The cold air Helen had been breathing in, hurt her throat, it made her cough during the run. She was pleased to be back at the cottage, to be given a little extra attention from Bryn. Charlyyk laid in a hot bath; she enjoyed the relaxing feeling.

As Bryn and Helen prepared breakfast, a worried looking Charlyyk, arrived still wet in a bathrobe Helen had giving her. 'What's the problem darling?' Charlyyk showed her the towel, it had blood on it, then opening her legs showing Helen where it had come from. Helen wrapped her in a big cuddle. 'It's what we have been expecting sweetheart, it's a part of what Michel was saying about you changing, from a girl to a woman?'

Bryn placed his arms around her. 'It's a regular thing that girls go through darling. Women on this planet of a certain age, endure it on a monthly cycle. We do not know how you will respond to it. Would you like to talk to Michel about it? I could phone him now, if you want me too?'

'Yes Please, dad.' Charlyyk looked at Helen, her face still showing concern.

Helen again pulled her in, cuddled her. Feeling more and more a mother towards her, placing soft maternal kisses on Charlyyk's forehead. 'There, there, sweetheart, don't fret. You will see, there's nothing to worry about.'

When Bryn phoned Michel. automatically passed the phone to Charlyyk. 'Michel I'm worried.'

Michel's voice was calm and collective. 'That's Ok Charlyyk. We do understand. Ask Helen to get you some pads to wear. She will know what I mean. But don't discard them, keep them so I can test them. Do you understand?'

'Yes. Thank you,'

Charlyyk explained to Helen what Michel had said.

Helen with a reassuring voice. 'We had expected it darling; I have already purchased them. Let's go, and get you sorted.'

When Helen and Charlyyk returned, Charlyyk was in a better place. Her smiling face showed Bryn she had got over her fears. She wrapped her arms around his neck, gave him one enormous squeeze. 'Love you, Dad. I'll talk to Catherine about it. She would want to know?'

Bryn was proud, seeing how she had grown in these two years. He was not involved when Catherine went through her menses; once again the Army had other duties he had to attend too. He had returned, to find his daughter, had matured at that time, he was away from her, had to make do with Kit's explanations. Kisses from Catherine were different. She would close doors on him, became more exclusive and bossier. He could not tickle her like he uses to... as she would turn on him. 'No dad, I'm a big girl now.' How will this change Charlyyk?

Helen watched the reactions across Bryn's face. 'Let's wait and see how she changes. Let's take it one day at a time.' She spoke quietly in an assuring way. Helen then sat down with Charlyyk, talked about her own experiences when she began her periods, she had been at boarding school at that time. The Nurse of the college, had been informed, had sat with Helen. Now she could explain the same procedure with Charlyyk.

Bryn watching, his memory wandered back to the day, when Catherine was chosen to play for England, how she clasped his face in her hands, kissed him on the lips. 'Love you, daddy.' He had not lost his daughter, she was still there, just bigger. With this thought, a smile beamed on his face, which brought smiles to the girl's faces. The sun was shining inside the cottage, with a warmth of happiness.

At Carpenters Cottage for Sunday dinner, the conversation was mainly about Charlyyk. Michel had been in touch with Prof Taylor, agreed to share the study with him, and his team. Helen and Charlyyk Had been labelling the used pads, with the date.

Gwen gave Charlyyk a big hug, congratulated her on becoming a woman, presented her with a small gift. The unexpected but pleasing look Charlyyk gave Gwen, as she gently unwrapped the neatly wrapped package. Turned into a whimsical smile. Her eyes sparkled, for Gwen had given her a Pandora bracelet with a unique charm, indicating Charlyyk was female.

The bracelet was lovely. It felt nice, and it looked good on her wrist. She knew Gwen would not give her something like this, unless there was a meaning attached to it. Charlyyk's brain did not take long to register the meaning of the charm. 'It's lovely Auntie Gwen...Love the charm.'

Later in the afternoon, Charlyyk was telling Michel about her homework, Michel explained the difference between 15-year-old boys and girls. 'When girls go through what you are experiencing, they need more iron in their diet than boys do, boys require more protein and calcium.' He went on to explain. 'When we talk about the average age of this and that, some teenagers, develop early and some later. You could say, we go through a seven-year cycle of life, from birth to seven the growth rate is fast, even up to fourteen years old, where some teenagers develop a lot of spots, this could be down to how the blood changes, or poor diet. From there to twenty-one we grow more to our actual height, have fill out more, develop, get stronger, then twenty-eight to thirty-five years old. We are what they say, in our prime. Forty-two, forty-five, now that's when we should be more aware of ourselves. That's when our body cells immunities, start breaking down. Then it's more about your diet or unhealthy lifestyle, that could catch you out. After that, it's potluck.'

Charlyyk looked at him. 'And me?'

Michel smiled apologetically. 'We don't know. That why we study you, to find out?' Drinking from his teacup and placing it back on the saucer. 'We humans are aware, that we experience a lot of hereditary disorders. Cancer is one of them. That why we ask people to keep a check on themselves, to inform their doctors early, when any symptoms develop. We have more chance to act and reduce unnecessary deaths that way. With you Charlyyk we need to obtain as much information as we can, so we can give you the best care as we can.'

Helen gave Charlyyk's arm a little squeeze. 'As you can tell sweetheart... as we find out more about you...You, find out more about us. We are all different from one another in our chemical build up... where one person has more of one thing, another person may have less, each one different, each person has to find out about themselves, their own personal needs, what suits them best, to be able to lead a healthy lifestyle.'

Charlyyk thought through her own experience of how her friends had a different problem with themselves. With what Michel and Helen had said; she started to understand why Mr Waverly had given them the homework... to make them more aware of themselves.

Janet was staying at the cottage, she had ten consignments to finish. Bryn had given her, his study to use.

Charlyyk was taking the school bus. The differences she was experiencing, was being more assertive...much in control of herself. The walk towards the bus, the way her hips moved. Sarah saw it, her expression on her face said, 'Wow.'

Helen leaning towards Bryn whispered in his ear. 'Has she hitched her skirt up?'

Bryn turned his head to face her. 'I don't know whether she has or not, but bloody hell, she has done something, but I can't tell you what?' It could be seen clearly as she went to board the bus. She turned, put two fingers to her lips, blows them a kiss. Bryn returning the gesture said to Helen. 'What's happened to the whole hand to the mouth, when blowing a kiss, where does this two-finger kiss come from?'

They wave the bus off and head indoors. Bryn, was utterly perplexed as to what has just occurred. Went in search of a task to take his mind off it. He opened the garage doors and started to grease the rollers he could not stop thinking. Kit's voice was in his head, complaining about the attitude of Catherine. 'Bryn it's Ok for you, you don't have to live, with a girl of fourteen who bloody well thinks she eighteen?'

No, he had not seen it. All he saw was his sweet little girl growing bigger. In a week's time from then, he would be in some dirt pit of a country, blowing up some secret rocket launch pad, which was a threat to world peace. Could he see the wrong, in his little girl... did he want to see if there was something wrong?

He shook his head. He had missed, so much of his children growing-up? What did Catherine say, 'Still playing toy soldiers Dad'. These thoughts kept going around and around, he was feeling very uncomfortable about it all. *'Was I really that selfish. Living the Boy's Own Storybook Life. The ones my father read to me at bedtime? If that was the case no wonder the kids of today, grow up with the attitude of 'Grand Theft Auto'.'* Bryn thoughts kept on bringing up little niggles that he was feeling of that time.

Helen's call, took him away from his thoughts. 'Bryn I've made lunch, love.' The cheery way she said it, calmed him. Wiping his hands, with an old cloth he was soon back in the cottage. The feel of the heating making the cottage homely helped him also to relax.

Sitting down with Helen and Janet, the conversation was soon about Charlyyk. Bryn told them of the thoughts he had on how he felt, that he had been so selfish. The fact that his career serving in the army, he had missed the best part of his children growing up.

Helen reached over and took his hand in hers. 'Oh, come on sweetheart, you are too hard on yourself.'

Janet looked startled. 'Most men would not be so honest with themselves. They would have said nothing, for fear it would deem themselves weak. My father, in particular, would have made up something, to justify himself. An out and out coward, that's my dad... but I still love him.'

Helen knew what Army life was all about. One was given a number, and when they say jump, one jumped. But she also knew that some men's names were always put on the top, time after time. They knew what to expect from them, the army demanded just that. It was not a written law, just the rule of the jungle…the peckin order of army life.'

Sarah could not get over the change in Charlyyk. At lunchtime, expressing to Sandra and Julia. 'Come on! The way she's walking, even the way she talks, it's so…you know different! I'm not saying it's bad… it's just different.'

Julia was staring at Charlyyk. 'I think you are right, there is a different air about her, look how she is talking, to Peter and Mike.'

Sandra leaned back in her chair. 'I'm not looking at Charlyyk, but Peter, look at him he's mesmerised by her. He's gone all gooey eyed. Look at the way Charlyyk is using her hands. She has Peter in a trance.' Mike was no different. As Charlyyk moved her hand, Mike and Peter's heads moved, in the same direction. The three girls could not help laughing.

Charlyyk hearing the laughter turned to look at them, with a smile so big, that anyone looking at her would have smiled with her. Moved her hand, just for affect. The three girls now knew that she had been listening to them all the time.

Charlyyk joined the girls. 'Yes, a lot happened this weekend, I had my first period. After the morning run on Saturday. I took a bath, and then when I dried myself, I found blood on the towel.' She went on to discuss with the girls, the advice Michel had given her, and how it fitted into the homework for Mr Waverley. Sandra was quick to gather the rest of the class where they informed them of what Charlyyk was told by Michel. The posse did not just look after Charlyyk, but the rest of the class as well.

Janet had worked hard all morning, achieved a great deal. So, when the producer of *The Sky at Night* phoned, she was not upset about being disturbed. Walking to the lounge talking with the Producer. Janet attracted Bryn's attention. He picked up the other phone and joined in on the call. They all agreed to do an interview, at the next weekend. The producer will, send a team down to do a survey on Wednesday.

Janet looked very pleased with herself. 'Thank you, Bryn. The exposure I'm getting from this, has been enormous. It is all down to you giving me your trust. Do you know the bit I love the most, it is the way you have brought me in as one of the family? Charlyyk has made me her friend, making myself feel at home here, just as I do in my parent's home.'

Charlyyk exited gracfully from the bus. Bryn was there waiting for the buoyant Charlyyk, who could not be happier to see him. She flung her arms around him, hugged him tightly. As they walked into the cottage, she bubbled with excitement telling him what her friends were saying about the changes in her. 'A lot of what they said, was good. I had been so worried about how I was going to change? More so into what. Now I understand when you said, to give me space to be the person I want to be. I realise now that the change is in my perspective of life not of other people's views. It's a mental attitude, not all about the physical changes. When I talked about it to Julia and Sandra, they said I've got girl power... I'm still not sure in what that means, but it sounds good!'

Helen and Janet could not help to overhear what Charlyyk had said. Her excitement made her talk loudly. Janet slid her arm into Charlyyk's arm. 'For so many decades, men have controlled women for their own self-satisfaction. Now women have emerged from their shackles, are taking control of themselves. Now that's girl power.'

Charlyyk's, face changed. The smile had gone. 'But Dad, has never shackled me. He has always asked me what I would like to do, never demanded'

Helen quickly answered. 'Janet is right. 'Shackled' is a metaphor for male behaviour as a whole...something in general, not individual, more them... than him.'

Janet squeezed Charlyyk's arm. 'I like your dad too. He is something special.'

Helen gave Janet a playful tap. 'You concentrate on James. Bryn is mine.'

Bryn could only admire his two women. Not only Charlyyk, had changed; so too had, Helen. When they had first met, he had seen the girl in her, she needed someone, to allow her to come out of her shell, now she is out...she will never revert back to her old self.

Chapter 23

The Sky at Night

Bryn and Helen made sure the house was clean and tidy. The team from *The Sky at Night* were expected at two. Janet stayed in Bryn's study going over various materials to assist the survey team if needed.

The team arrived at ten minutes to two. Introduction and general talk, occupied the time to three. They measured the lounge and set up a camera, making various notes, on how the shooting could be done. Were still there when Charlyyk arrived home.

The cameramen showed Charlyyk how the camera worked and demonstrated it through their own Monitor. They set up another camera in the garden, so it could tell if the sky was clear enough and there was no light damage. They left at six, completely satisfied with what they could achieve on Saturday.

After dinner, Janet produced material that could be used for the interview on Saturday. Helen's interest was growing stronger with the more she learned about the early days when Charlyyk first arrived. Harold had made three monthly assessments of her changes. Gwen had kept a diary of those first days. With photos, and Michel's notes. Helen was soon getting the full picture of Charlyyk's progression.

Janet remarked on her understanding why Charlyyk responded in the way she did. 'Helen its the careful way she listened, then values what had been said. She had been copying Harold and Bryn, in the way they listen. So, not to offend anyone, more earning their trust...just like them. Her hard-working matter-of-fact manner, that's Gwen and Catherine.' With a reflective pause 'Helen, Charlyyk is a survivor, she adapts to survive. Her motto of don't make enemies, but friends. That's Charlyyk being a very clever girl'. Helen agreed.

***

Friday, After Charlyyk had left for school, Helen and Bryn check to see what shopping was required, as there would be no chance to collect shopping on Saturday. The trip to the supermarket went without a hitch. Bryn was becoming used to Helen being with him, he liked how she got on with the everyday task without continually asking him what he thought. Helen had accepted the responsibilities, as if she had been there for years.

During the afternoon, Janet was showing them some of the articles she had finished, the phone rang. Helen picked it up. 'Hello...Rachel how are you... let me call Bryn.'

Bryn took the phone. 'Hi, sweetheart... Wednesday, 19.00 p.m. Heathrow, Terminal 5. OK, love, see you then.' He beamed.

Helen slipped her arm into his. 'I'm going to meet them at last. I'm so looking forward to it.'

Janet looked pleased, remembering how well she got on with them in Houston, especially Rachel.

When Charlyyk arrived home. Helen told her that Thomas, Rachel and her mother were coming on Wednesday. The pleasure they both reacted to it pleased Bryn. Seeing the bond building between them.

Bryn could not be happier, his association with Janet, to how she interacted with Helen was another relief to him.

When Janet set the meeting up, for '*The Stars at Night*' Bryn knew Janet was keen to meet Maggie Aderin-Pocock. Janet's excited view, that she is one of the most exciting Nigerian-British female space scientists. 'She should be called Peacock, not Pocock, for she is so colourful.' Bit it relayed to Bryn the ambitious side of Janet.

***

Charlyyk had a reckless night, could not sleep, she had gone down into the lounge at three and read a book on Post-War Britain. When Bryn found her there, he made her a cup of tea, then sat with her to talk her through what had troubled her. 'Over these last few months, so much has happened. I've missed Catherine...I know I have Janet and Helen and the new friends at school. With school and the trip to America...my head was full of lots of things going around and around. Not frightening things, nice things... Cinderella things, it's like a fairy godmother has not just waved, her magic wand... but tipped a whole sack full of magic dust over me.'

He held her in his arms, just like any dad would do, and gave her a gentle squeeze.

Charlyyk loving this emotional thing these earthlings did. 'Come on dad, let's go for a run, then I'll have a kip in the bath.'

She was in the bath for about an hour when Bryn and Helen started to worry about her getting cold, and went to hurry her along, they found her fast asleep. Bryn lifted her out of the bath, Helen dried her and put her to bed.

The Television Crew arrived while Charlyyk was in the bath, and had quickly set up, were testing by twelve. That's when Charlyyk came down. She was wearing the Laura Ashley dress that Gwen liked her wearing. She knew it would portray her as a young girl. As this program will probably be shown in many Countries. She wanted to set the right image.

The floor manager was a little worried; they were short of a make-up artist. Bryn mentioned Liza Martin and gave him the Martins Phone Number. The Presenters arrived at two.

The Martins ten minutes later. Charlyyk was so pleased to see Sarah had come as well. 'My mum was so excited when they called her, she kept turning around in circles. Dad had to get her things together. Otherwise, we would still be waiting for her.'

Chris Lintott, Maggie Aderin-Pocock and Pete Lawrence, sat down with Bryn, Charlyyk and Janet to work out what they wanted to discuss. Pete Lawrence had some great images of the Draco Constellation where Charlyyk's Home Planet is thought to be situated. He was at the Johnson Space Centre, as one of the astronomers, had brought back much of the material they had produced there.

Bryn and Janet helped Maggie to ease Charlyyk's over-excited enthusiasm. Maggie soon had Charlyyk laughing, as they did a test, in front of the cameras. Chris Lintott did a test run with Bryn and Janet. Liza Martin was kept very busy, did not falter with the demanding challenges. Sarah was proud of her mum, she sat with her dad, and the Hobart's and Helen, well out of the way. The camera set up in the garden promised a clear sky.

Then the shoot began. Pete Lawrence explained to the TV audience where they believe Charlyyk originated from. 'The Draco Constellation circles, the northern hemisphere. The Polar Star is situated within it. All the abductions from the light beam occurred in the northern hemisphere. This fact gives credence to the hypothesis that Charlyyk's planet must look to be in the northern hemisphere A sun like our own, also is situated in the Draco Constellation, with the similar levels of lithium depletion. This points us to the presence of planets, with the possibility that small Earth-like planets could be in its orbit. Still, it is 210 light years from the Earth.'

He points to a graph on how long it would take to reach Mars then showing the distance difference of where Charlyyk's Planet was presumed to be. The notion that Bryn and Charlyyk, had experienced six months travelling time had to be thrown right out of the window. It was just not logical.

Charlyyk's views of her life, and how she lived to survive, then the reality of other planets with different life forms, made the program fascinating. The presenters giving every known detail they had gained through Charlyyk and Bryn's observations of their experiences.

During the show, Maggie was keen to talk to Janet about encouraging girls into taking up science as a career. She named some of the female scientists that inspired her, 'So many good women have taken up the challenge of space. Did you get the chance to meet, Amy Ross at NASA? She helped to design the Z-series spacesuit. One of the biggest challenges in space is every aspect, is of mobility, she led her team to achieve that in the Z-series.' Janet was so enthralled with everything Maggie was saying. 'Janet there are so many avenues' girls could take up that connected with space, as it does not mean only one thing.'

Charlyyk was well aware to portray herself in the right passive manner, encouraged question to be asked of her. When asked what, she ate on her planet, she purposely did not mention eating small animals, and just mentioned vegetation, fruit, nuts and insects. She did not want to upset even the timidness of viewers.

***

Janet spent Sunday at the Parsons Farm. There were only three, on the early morning jog, the conversation was mainly about the eagerly awaited arrival of Thomas, Rachel and her mother. Helen was keen to find out as much as she could about them, mainly what their needs were, if anything she should be wary of.

Charlyyk had kept quiet to allow Bryn to make his comments. then when he finally finished she corrected him, where she had thought he had made mistakes. She reminded him, that Helen was trying hard to make a good impression on them, it would be good for him to help her the best way he could. 'I am trying.' He blurted.

The glare Charlyyk gave him, made him think again. 'Ok, I might have been a little flippant, about Rachel's mother.'

Charlyyk again looked sternly at him. 'We will be sharing our home with them, for over a year. Let us try and get it right, from the first day, if it is not too much to ask?'

Later, when Bryn and Helen were showering together, Helen asked him to explain Charlyyk's attitude. He did not want to talk about it at first...did not like getting another stern look from Helen.

222

'OK...When Thomas was here before, I wanted him to stay longer. But he said he had to go; he had commitments in America. I accused him of slinking back, because of Rachel's overpowering mother. Don't forget, I was not in a good place, at that time. So, when I mentioned that Rachel's mum, could be a little bit overpowering...That why Charlyyk was so curt towards me.'

They dried each other with large, warm bath towels. Helen had been thinking, on what had been said. 'I've not heard Charlyyk speak so angrily before. But it was a controlled anger, which did not have any malice to it.' She started to get dressed. 'Has she ever, spoken like that before?'

Bryn shook his head. 'No, not like that.'

Helen was quiet. She finished dressing, then putting things away in their appropriate places. 'Then she is changing?'

Bryn sat on the end of the bed, looking out towards the window. His mind drifting back, to something that Harold had mentioned. Harold had been reading one of Dickens novels, *Oliver Twist*, to Charlyyk. In it the orphan Oliver asked for more. 'Why should he have asked for more? Was he not satisfied with what he had?' When Harold tried to explain, she looked angry. 'He should have tried to live, how I had to, he would have not complained then.' Bryn related to Helen.

Helen nodded. 'She sensed some form of injustice. There is another side of Charlyyk we've yet to discover. Interesting?'

At breakfast, Charlyyk did not mention, anything relating to the morning run. She laughed about Gwen and her experience in the Church. 'I waited for something to happen, but nothing happened, then everyone got up and left, I looked around to see if I had missed something, but no. The place was empty, it was no different, to as we found it!!'

Helen felt she needed to explain. 'Charlyyk, Gwen has always believed in God. Her belief gives her a form of inner strength, and helps her to accept the injustice, that man does to a man, like any kind of violence that exists today.'

Charlyyk looked into her empty cereal bowl. 'So, Gwen, believes that praying will solve the problem?'

Helen could sense, that she was being set up. 'Well, yes!'

Charlyyk cocked her head to one side, a smirk of a smile, on her face. 'So, a big Fuung is attacking me, I kneel down and pray, it would not eat me?'

Helen had fallen into the hole. Charlyyk's face now had a smile. 'It would eat me! maybe because it doesn't believe in God?' Then Charlyyk burst out into laughter, she went to Helen and put her arms around her. 'I was joking with you Helen, I know Gwen, is very serious about her faith, I do respect her for it.'

Helen shook her head. 'You, little bugger!' They laughed with each other.

Bryn already knew this side of Charlyyk. She only joked with those she loved. That would not get upset easily and specially not Gwen. Charlyyk had already upset Gwen once, did not want to make her cry again.

At Carpenter Cottage, Michel was explaining to Charlyyk, the reason for the test he and Prof Taylor were doing. 'When a woman has a period, it is to flush away the old eggs. But in other living beings on this planet, a process like a period has other functions. We are trying to find out, what form of function your period is for. There may be other things we can evaluate by doing these tests...We are not looking for problems, just trying to get an understanding of how you will respond.'

To Charlyyk's surprise, Michel pulled up his shirt to reveal his stomach. 'As you can see, I have a navel, where you do not. But then there are life forms on this planet, that don't have navels but still give birth. One particular lifeform is the Duck-bill Platimus which lays eggs and excretes milk. that only goes to show, we have much to learn. So these tests are just to satisfy our curiosity also could provide us with a chance to give you... the best health care we can.'

Charlyyk accepted Michel explanation without fuzz or concern. She had come to trust Michel explicitly. whenever he examined her, he always explained the whys and the wherefores.

Chapter 24

The Arrival

Charlyyk had already left for school. Bryn had a few repairs to do. Helen sorted the laundry. Then Toby arrived, and as usual just walked into the kitchen and put the kettle on. 'I must have a cup of Coffee, I've a throat that's as dry as the bottom of a birdcage.'

Helen laid out mugs and a jar of instant coffee. 'Are you in need of feeding?'

The look he gave her did not need a reply, she soon was rustling up bacon and eggs, with a large round of toast.

Bryn entered the kitchen. 'Cor, that smells good.' Helen did not hesitate, soon, egg, bacon, between slices of toast, was in Bryn's hands.

'To what do we owe the pleasure of your company, Toby.' Helen knew Toby, would not be there unless he had a problem.

'There's no problems Helen, but when you are ready to wipe your records from the data bank, type in your password, followed with 'final exit' in all caps. Then you will be free, to marry Bryn.'

The smile on Helen's face, relayed to Bryn that she was ready to relinquish her past, and to start her new life with him. She kissed Bryn, then leaned back with the look of a cat that had licked the cream. 'Well, that's found the four corners of the jigsaw. Now we just have to fill it in.'

Toby related. 'Your military records are intact. We have placed a military history for a Sergeant Helena Baker. You have cover from any fall out from Interlaken. we have given you a stellar civil service record, which allows, the Government room, to honour you, if they deemed, to do so? That leaves me, to suggest the New Year, for your resignation. I've already taken up the reigns. You may press the button when you are ready.'

Janet's red Mini, pulled up in the driveway. Helen went to help to unload it. The coming and going between car and Charlyyk's room lasted ten minutes. Janet, showed Helen, her latest articles, ready for publication. One was destined for the *Sky at Night Magazine*. The one for a girl's magazine caught Helen eye. It was mainly about Charlyyk going to school. It was witty, that showed the funny side of Charlyyk. The in-depth comments, from her fellow students gave the younger reader a real vision of a girl facing the same difficulties, as every young girl has to experience, the onset of puberty.

When Charlyyk came home and read the article, she looked at Janet with curiosity, 'Did they really say that about me?' Janet showed her the notes she had taken. 'Like a comfort blanket?' Then reading a bit more. 'Like a big, all-knowing sister?' Charlyyk was not upset. She looked humbled.

Helen placed her arms around her. 'Well, what do you think?'

Charlyyk re-read the notes. 'I like what they have said. It shows that they respect me as a friend.'

Bryn ventured in the conversation. Helen gave him what Janet had written. He read it and then re-read it. 'Janet this is so Charlyyk.' Then putting his arm around Charlyyk's shoulders. 'What do you think about its sweetheart?'

Her shoulders rose and her head dropped to one side. 'I cannot but like it. It is what Janet has seen. I remember being there. I did not realise that was how they felt about me!'

Then showed Bryn the pictures she had painted. 'They are not as good as the paintings Jan and Sarah have painted, but I like them.'

'So, do I, sweetheart. I can see what you have painted, with how you have used the colours. With time and practise everyone can improve. The main thing, is you enjoyed doing them!'

***

Excitement was building up in the Collier family for the arrival of Thomas, Rachel and Rachel's mother. Helen emptied cupboards, washing them, then placing back their contents in an orderly manner. Bryn was called upon to agree what could be thrown away. Janet taking all the books from the bookshelves, cleaning then rearranging the books back on the shelves. Furniture moved to allow vacuuming under, or into areas, that generally were inaccessible. Black plastic waste bags, filled up with various things deemed as rubbish.

When Charlyyk arrived home, she walked around the cottage, inspecting, the enormous effort the three of them had achieved. Janet was still cleaning out an old cupboard under the stairs, at the base of the stairs Janet had found an old wooden box which had been hidden in the darkness. Their heads turned towards her when she called Bryn's name. 'There is a large wooden chest in here?'

Bryn pulled it out. It was an old blanket chest. It had been hidden down at the base of the staircase. The catch was stiff with age. Bryn soon had it open. Inside were old cotton sheets, and curtains. Among them wrapped in a waxed linen cloth, lay an ancient leather-bound family Bible.

Janet opened it very carefully. On the inside of the cover was written with a quill pen. *This is the Allcott Family Bible 1557.* The first entry was, *John Edward Allcott, Born 29th May 1557, To Edward James, and Mary Anne Allcott, Nee Parsons.*

The Bible became the talking point of the evening. As they turned the pages, many entries were written, on the history of the Allcott family. It was a Coverdale Bible, printed in English. Janet was soon explaining to Charlyyk about how the Roman Catholic Church had ordered the death sentence on those who had tried to translate the Bible into the English Language.

Charlyyk cocked her head to one side, her impish look saying *I told you so.* Helen looked at her sternly, her face saying *Don't you dare.* Bryn nodded. 'Charlyyk, Gwen has strong feelings. Don't upset her.'

Charlyyk shook her head. 'I would not do that. Gwen means a lot to me. But when she is not here...well, my feelings are my feelings.'

Janet seemed a bit upset with what Charlyyk had said. 'Why do you feel that way?'

'Aunty Gwen's belief, is not logical. It is a form of Brainwashing. It's telling people to believe that praying is going to solve all their problems. But it does not. Only action solves problems. Gwen's belief tells people not to face reality, only to roll over, cover their heads, and hope the problem will go away. Religious leaders should be encouraging people to face reality, work through problems with logical thinking and rugged endeavour.'

Charlyyk's succinct way of talking made Janet realise Charlyyk had strong feelings about how she saw certain forms of injustice. To Charlyyk, faith was an injustice.

Janet had spoken to Gwen how Charlyyk handled Bryn going to Switzerland for the meeting and leaving her there with Harold and herself. Gwen reply was. 'Charlyyk did not want Bryn to go. But once he had left, she just accepted it. At first it concerned me, so I asked her how she felt. Charlyyk said she will miss him while he is away, she knows he will return. Then Charlyyk just carried on as if Bryn had not gone away.'

***

Wednesday, for once Charlyyk did not want to go to school. Bryn and Helen had to work hard, to push her onto the bus. Sarah could tell Charlyyk wanted to be somewhere else. 'You don't want to stay at home, the time would just drag.'

Charlyyk said dejectedly. 'I know you, right? I don't want to miss meeting Thomas and Rachel. It's going to a different place, seeing something different.'

'But you went to Heathrow to see Catherine off?'

'Yes, but that was Terminal 2... this will be Terminal 5.'

Once Charlyyk had met up with the rest of the posse, however, she quietens down, promptly forgot her anxiety.

Helen and Janet had made a list of needs, had headed for the town in the Discovery. It was going to be a long day. As the hours drifted by, the tempo quickened. Then all at once Charlyyk was home, it was as if there was an electrical storm brewing. Everyone was getting ready to head for Terminal 5, Heathrow Airport.

Bryn had hired a mini bus taxi with enough room for the luggage. Charlyyk was the first one in the Taxi, urging them all to hurry. Helen and Janet sitting with her, trying hard to settle her down.

Standing in the arrival lounge, Charlyyk paced about. She could not keep still. Bryn had to take a grip on her to slow her down; she was oblivious to what was happening around her. Charlyyk just kept looking, as so many people strolled through the arrival gates. The minutes seemed like hours to her. Then the first sight of Rachel, with Thomas struggling with the overloaded trolley, trailing close behind.

Charlyyk slipped Bryn's clutches, diving under the barrier and into Rachel's arms. Thomas had expected that to happen, had urged Rachel to go ahead of them. Rachel's Mother grabbed Thomas's arm; afraid she might get knocked over.

Bryn was soon helping to get them to a place, so they could greet one another without obstructing the other passengers. The introductions were warm and sincere. Bryn collecting another trolley, as the one Thomas was pushing was well overloaded.

Rachel's mother was at first very wary of Charlyyk, kept a slight distance from her. Charlyyk did not seem to concern herself. Other passengers and their relatives, looked on at Charlyyk with amusement, at her excitement. As at Disney World. Charlyyk was in no way able, to control her emotions when she became excited. Janet, as usual took video footage, for her own advantage. She would be able to use this material, mainly for the teen girl audience.

Helen soon had Rachel's mother Margret, settled. She walked her arm in arm, towards the waiting taxi. Thomas and Rachel taking control of Charlyyk, with Bryn and Janet close behind

Then something was thrown at Charlyyk, which missed. Bryn was quick to react and directed Rachel away towards Helen. Thomas closed rank with Bryn to shield Charlyyk. Airport security was soon in attendance. A man was being escorted from the area. Two-Armed officer then stood by to protect

Charlyyk, but Charlyyk did not agree with that. 'Please, no one was hurt, I would like to speak with the man if I may.'

Helen stepped forward and spoke with the two Officers, who agreed to Charlyyk wishes. A meeting in the detention room was set up.

The man looked angry when Charlyyk entered the room. She sat down opposite him. Charlyyk then spoke. 'I did not ask to come here, or have any say about living with you. I can only hope to live in peace with you. I promise that I will respect all your customs and traditions, and behave with respect to how you would want me to behave as citizen. So please if you have any grudges against me this is your chance to voice them.'

The man just glared at Charlyyk. Then slowly he relaxed. 'You are not one us, you could bring us trouble if your people come and invade.'

Charlyyk smiled warmly. 'I lived in fear every day of my life. Where I came from, my people and I were the food for many beasts. My new father had rescued me from that. Now I am here and finding my life living amongst you, so nice. My friends treat me with respect. I would like to treat you with respect and not press charges. Could we leave as friend? When my friends agree on something, they like to shake hands. Will you shake hands with me?'

Slowly, the man's expression changed. He nodded and offered his hand to Charlyyk. 'Sorry, I should have had, controlled myself better. It was a rash moment. Accept my apologies.'

Charlyyk accepted his hand and gently shook it 'Thank you, I appreciate your friendship, and I wish you well.'

The drive back to the cottage was noisy as Charlyyk was now back to her old self. Margret, not being sure of Charlyyk, continued to distance herself from her. Helen assured her that Charlyyk would settle down.

At the cottage, Thomas soon took control and showed Margret where everything was. Helen had a surprise for them all. While they were at the airport, Helen had asked Harold to hang one of the drawings Thomas had done of Kitty and Catherine. Helen, had it framed, Harold and Gwen had collected it in the morning.

Helen stood there admiring the looks of satisfaction on their faces, 'I thought it was fitting as Kitty was, so much the influential part of this family.

Bryn was taken back by the gesture and gave Helen an appreciated hug. She received the same from Thomas and Rachel. Giving Bryn, a warm cuddle also.

Helen was implying she was not competing with Kitty. Taking za leaf out of Charlyyk's book, needed Bryn's family to recognise her.

Gwen confided with Thomas. 'When Helen asked Harold to collect a package from Taylor's Frame Shop, and hang it here on the wall. I did not realise it would be a picture of Kitty. Harold unwrapped it, I must admit, I became a little emotional about it, I think it is such a lovely gesture. Harold knew that Helen was telling us that we should not forget your mother.'

Rachel was nearest to Helen when Gwen was speaking, Rachel placed her hand in Helen's hand and congratulated her.

Thomas put his arm around his father's shoulders. 'Where did you find it, Dad?'

Bryn then explained about clearing his old room, how they had come across it at the back of the wardrobe.

Rachel and her mother examined the pen and ink drawing very carefully. 'How old were you when you did this?' Margret asked.

Thomas stepped forward and looked at the picture. 'I was eighteen, it was one of the drawings, I submitted for my First Year at the art college.'

Harold had cooked the dinner. As they enjoyed the fruits of his labour, Margret saw a different Charlyyk. She was more subdued and coherent. A conversation sprang up between them, with Rachel prompting Charlyyk about her art. The laughter that Janet provoked, when telling them about Charlyyk's art class, but when Charlyyk said. 'My duel with a brush against the paper can be a messy ordeal, can leave many victims, splashed with spots of colourful mementoes of those encounters.' With a spoon in her hand and waving it about. 'En Garde, or I will cover you in paint!!'

After the evening meal, Charlyyk showed them, her artwork. Margret perused the pictures, as she would do professionally. 'Your use of colour is splendid.'

'I get a little carried away with the amount of paint I load my brushes with. I'm much too enthusiastic to get the paint onto the paper. I end up with runs.'

Margret's smiled. 'That not what matters, but the vibrant way you administered the brush strokes. That shows how you enjoy your art. Those who look upon your work will feel the same way. With many famous artist, you must not stand to close to view, otherwise, you would not know what they were trying to achieve. But looking at what you have painted. I can see open spaces, with trees, the sun's rays shining through the branches. The butterfly is extra-large, but that is how you saw it. With time and practise you will challenge yourself, and become more aware of perspective with technique. Thomas will no doubt give you a few tips.'

Rachel tugged on Thomas's arm and whispered in his ear. 'Mums warming to her, look how she has moved closer to her.'

Torrential rain made the run difficult, though did not deter them. Soaking wet and muddy, they returned in high spirits. This was Janet's last day. She had two interviews booked in before the Christmas break. She had cleared with the Colliers her latest issues. Giving Charlyyk a cuddle. 'I'm staying with the Parsons for Christmas, so I will see you then.'

Rachel, Janet and Helen waved goodbye to Charlyyk as she left for school. Inside the cottage, Bryn was sorting out a couple of issues that Margret had spoken off. 'The mattress is too soft, and the pillows are too firm. I struggled all night to get a good night sleep.'

Bryn accepted her concerns. 'I will sort it immediately. We will go to the store today, so you can choose whatever mattress that suits you.'

Thomas felt a little awkward, but his father just smiled at him. His father's casual manner, allowed him to relax. But Thomas knew what his mother-in-law really wanted was a new mattress. She was not prepared to sleep on a mattress that she deemed old, which others had slept on before.

They met the girls in the kitchen. Bryn, indicated a trip to the Furniture Store, then a stop at Bill Symonds. 'I spoke to Bill the other day about a runabout for Thomas. He has a choice of three, so that you don't feel that you have to rely on us. You will have the freedom to go as you please.'

At the academy, Mr Pearson raised his voice, that was to get his charges, their full attention. 'Come on, let calm it! OK, we touched, on the elements of the social changes, that Britain was going through, can anyone add, anything more towards it?'

Charlyyk puts her hand up. 'Mr Pearson, you did not want us to bring politics into this, but politics created some of the changes.'

Tim Pearson looked at Charlyyk. He had thought, she would be the last person, to have brought this up. 'Have you, any views about this, that you think relevant.'

Charlyyk sat forward in her chair. 'Women were given a bit of a raw deal, in the law courts. They were treated differently to men in the workplace. Even if they did the same work as men, they received only half the wages. This could only have changed through politics?'

'Yes, Charlyyk I must concede you are right.' Turning to the smart board, he entered onto it what Charlyyk had mentioned. 'Right. We can see here the fundamental changes that have happened to Britain, and the time span that these changes took place. Are there any other noticeable changes that you can see here, and why?' Peter Elliott, shot his hand up. 'Yes, Peter?'

'The National Health, sir. My gran and granddad said it would cost ten shillings a week to stay in hospital, with my granddad's wages of Four pounds and seventeen shillings a week they found it quite hard to pay.'

Julia made the next move. 'New medicines have made the most of changes to the NHS, this has made it a job to keep up with the changes, with the rising population, unless new hospitals are built, the old, out-of-date hospital struggle to keep up.'

Paul Allen gave out a chuckle. 'A bit like my hamster in its wheel, the faster it goes, the wheel goes faster, then it stops with fatigue, the wheel spins it around as though it in a tumble dryer and has no control.'

Jan commented. 'My nanny Scott reckons the NHS, is like a furnace, and whatever government is in; they have to stoke the furnace with more and more money.'

Tim Pearson, was now getting annoyed with the comments about the NHS. 'The National Health Service was set up to give every person a chance to have good medical care at the point of need, not if you could only afford it. Although there was a cross Party acceptance that this country was in need of a National Health care, it was Aneurin Bevin that eventually got it through Parliament. And in 1948 opened the first NHS Hospital in Manchester.' Turning to enter more detail to the smart board. 'Right make some notes on where we are and try if you cannot be too political. What are we trying to achieve here? Is that in the Scottish referendum the voting age was lowered to 16. You may one day be given that opportunity. How would you know what to take into consideration when casting your vote? I as a teacher should not politically influence you in anyway. For you must evaluate what you see is best for yourself and the country. That's why this is a debate, so you can voice your opinion and to listen to others' opinions. The changes made could make a big difference in all our life's.'

During the lunch break. Charlyyk felt the low vibes Sandra was giving out. She knew that Sandra's father was not well, sat down beside Sandra to give her comfort.

Mrs Landon was keeping a close eye on Sandra. She had made her way to where she was sitting and joined them.

Sandra started to talk about her father. 'The trouble with chemotherapy it affects the patient's immunity, and the patient is prone to infection. My father was rushed to hospital last night, in a very critical condition. I was all right this morning coming to school, but then I started to think about him, it just became unbearable.'

Mrs Landon asked if she should call for her mother. Sandra, with a worried look on her face. 'Please don't. Mum, is suffering inside, I don't want to be another worry for her. She should be with my dad, helping him.'

Charlyyk put her arm around her shoulders. 'As your mother needs to give your dad strength at this moment, you also need someone to give you strength, I have a spare bed at home. If you ever think it would help, please don't hesitate to use it.'

Mrs Landon phoned Sandra Mother. After, she spoke to Sandra. 'Your mother is at the hospital and agreed that if you would like to stay with Charlyyk tonight, you could. She also said that your father is in a stable condition, but not out of danger. She intends to stay by his side.'

Charlyyk, then phoned home, Margret answered. 'They are all out at this moment, Charlyyk. I will relay your message to them.'

At Bill Symonds Garage, Thomas received the call from Margret. Passing his phone to Helen, he left her to resolve the situation.

Bryn was sitting in a silver 2012 Citroen Picasso C3 MPV 1.4 VTi. 'It's not what I like Bill. But it's not for me.'

Ted lifted the bonnet. 'As you can see, it spotless and the service record, I have cleared with the Citroen service department. It is genuine.'

Rachel had fallen in love with the car the moment she saw it. When she came back from the test drive, she had not changed her mind. Bryn saw that Rachel was set on this car. 'Ok Bill let's do the figures.' Bryn headed for Bill's office.

Helen helped Thomas to sort out the road Tax, and Insurance. 'There you have wheels.'

When Bryn returned, he gave Thomas the documents to the car. 'It's all yours, son.'

'Thanks, dad.'

Thomas and Rachel waved as they drove off the Forecourt. Bryn shook Bill and Ted's hands and thanked them, then headed to the academy to pick up Charlyyk and Sandra.

At the school, Mrs Landon welcomed them. 'Thank you, Mr Collier,' Then told them what Sandra's mother had told her. Helen was soon comforting Sandra. 'Come, let's take you home, and pick up a few things you will need.'

When they arrived at Oakleaves, Charlyyk showed Sandra around the cottage. The tour ended in Charlyyk's bedroom. Helen put fresh bed linen on the bed. 'Any likes or dislikes Sandra?'

'May I have a hot water bottle? I hate a cold bed.' Then with a sheepish look, she added. 'May I also have some warm milk when I come to bed, please?'

Helen placed her hand on her shoulder. 'Of course, you can. Dinner will be about twenty minutes.' She smiled at Sandra. 'Don't forget to phone your mother, she will be concerned, would like to know that you are OK.'

Charlyyk looked at Helen with great respect. She saw the sweet side of Helen, sensed that she could be very strict if needed to be. It was evident in the efficient way she handled situations with cool, calm control. she did not fluster, nor did she shirk from responsibility.

What had Charlyyk more interested, was her own ability to understand the medical conditions Sandra had referred to about her father. For her to have lived the life she had on her home planet, how was this possible. Michel had talked to her about Bryn and the infections that he had suffered due to the injuries to the wounds on his return. She had understood the implications and the threat it imposed on him. The reference books Charlyyk had studied were nothing to do medically, so why could she understand all the right technical terms, and their meanings.

After dinner, in Charlyyk's bedroom, The two girls were busying themselves with homework. Charlyyk had encouraged Sandra to keep busy, to keep her mind from her troubles. Rachel entered the bedroom with the hot water bottle, with a mug of warm milk. Stayed for a while discussing their homework. Then tucking them up in bed. Sandra's traumatic day, had taken a lot out of her, she was soon fast asleep.

Chapter 25

Charlyyk's House Guest

Next morning, when Sandra woke. Charlyyk's bed was empty. Sandra tossed the duvet to one side and slipped out of bed, went over to the window. It was dark outside, she could see the fields, with the three runners, that were heading for Parsons Farm.

Sandra stayed at the window looking out, this was so new to her. Her own bedroom window looked out onto more houses. The gardens were small with so many houses built close together. She felt that if she spread her arms out, she could touch them. At least she had a home to live in. Many families struggled to be able to afford buying a house, only able renting tiny flats in the middle of town. She would not like to live there.

She thought how lucky Charlyyk had become. She realised how Charlyyk had suffered also. Sandra wonders to herself, how she would have coped with that constant threat of a beast wanting to tear you to pieces. Sandra shuddered at that thought.

Moving away from the window, she saw a folder lying on Charlyyk's dressing table. Written on the front *'Charlyyk's fears'*, the writing was in Charlyyk's distinctive handwriting. Picking the folder up, she sat on the bed, then began to read.

The writing at first was hard to read. It dated from period when Charlyyk had first learnt to write.

> *'I am putting down in writing, my fears so that I can appreciate what I have, to accept it is as normal. My biggest fear is to wake up, to find it was all a dream, that I will have to find food and water again. My second fear is to lose my Bryn, my saviour, and my security. Gwen and Harold, my teachers, but most of all my comfort, they make me calm. To lose them, would really upset my balance'.*

Once she had adjusted to the crabbed script of Charlyyk, Sandra went back to the start, then read it over again. She saw the influences that had changed

Charlyyk's perceptions of life. The folder held a jumble of writings. Little notes appeared in the margins, these were Charlyyk's, trying to understand herself. She did not write about other people, only about herself. Sandra closed up the folder, replaced it as she had found it.

The sound of Charlyyk's voice took her away from her thoughts. Charlyyk came bounding into the room. 'Hi, you are awake, do you need anything?'

Charlyyk then started to undress, then headed for the shower. Sandra watched with amusement as Charlyyk's little tail flicked about. It did not wag, but now and again would just give a little swish. Sandra followed her into the bathroom, sat on the toilet, watching Charlyyk shower. She could see Charlyyk was similar to herself, apart from some aspects of her bone structure.

When Charlyyk stepped out from the shower, she grabbed a towel to dry herself, Sandra found herself looking at Charlyyk's female frame, the breast was developing, noticed she had no pubic hair.

Charlyyk sensed Sandra's curiosity. 'Do you find me different?'

Sandra gave an awkward smile. 'I think you're fascinating? I was looking to see how different you could be, then of myself.'

Charlyyk finished drying herself. She led Sandra back into the bedroom. Charlyyk took Sandra's nightie off then beckoned her to stand side by side in front of the long mirrors, so, Sandra could see them side by side. 'Well, what do you think.'

Sandra admired the comparisons. 'Apart from your height, facial features, your hands and feet, not a lot of difference.'

Charlyyk laughed. 'I'm almost human?'

Sandra laughed with her; they both gave each other a hug. 'Come on, let's get ready for school.'

At breakfast, they could not stop talking. Helen again reminded Sandra to speak to her mother, before the bus arrived. Sandra made the call, right there and then.

Charlyyk looked on nervously, hoping that it was going to be good news. Sandra's approach was calm; holding the phone like a delicate flower, the tip of her tongue, just showing through her lips as she listened. A smile broke across her face. 'Yes mum...that's great... love you too.' Putting the phone down, still smiling but tears trickling, down her face. 'Dad has pulled through, mum sat there all night holding his hand.'

A delighted Charlyyk 'That great news, Sandra.'

Helen was on hand with plenty of tissues.

When the bus arrived Sarah and Mace stepped off, the look of hope for good news written all over their faces. Mace picking up Sandra's bags, as the girl's usher Sandra onto the bus.

Helen had phoned Mrs Landon, to inform her that Sandra, had good news. Bryn and herself, would be on hand if there were any need. Mrs Landon waited at the school gate, with Mrs Butler, they watched as the bus arrived.

The posse was soon in attendance. Julia could not wait for Sandra to get off the bus. Rushed to the bus to greet her friend. Mrs Landon nods to Mrs Butler with a pleased look. 'She is in good company, let's keep an eye on her, just in case.

Bryn and Thomas were making a few adjustments to the guestroom for Margret. She had mentioned that a mark on the wall opposite the window, was giving her cause for concern. 'I'm sorry to bring this matter up Rachel, the shape of it, looks similar to a skull, it gave myself a sleepless night.'

Thomas felt a little guilty about it all, offered his help, to ease his conscience. Bryn just said to him. 'These are teething problems. Let's not make an issue out of them, let's try and resolve them. We have to remember if she was not here, nor would you and Rachel be here. To me, it is well worth keeping Margret happy.'

The smile on his father's face eased Thomas's worries. The delivery of the new mattress will also alleviate his concerns about his mother-in-law.

At the back of the garage, Bryn found the tin of paint that had *Guest Room* written on it. There was sufficient paint to complete the task. So, with a small brush, he painted a small area to test the colour. And while it dried, he joined Helen, with the others for coffee in the lounge. The conversation was about Charlyyk with Sandra.

Rachel was talking as Bryn entered. 'I must admit comparing the Charlyyk I saw in Houston, to the one I see now, she has changed dramatically. She is much more mature. though still there remains a part of her that has not changed. The way she mothered Sandra was very touching, then she wanted the loving touch of Helen. It felt as though she needs Helen's sense of direction, or could I say trust Helen's direction?'

Bryn sat down next to Helen. 'Don't be fooled. Charlyyk has learnt to survive the best way she can. She uses everything to keep the balance. Charlyyk has worked out that without us she has nothing, so she bends like a tall blade of grass with the wind, so not to break.'

Thomas looked at his father quizzically. 'Do you mean she using us, to gain her own advantage?'

Bryn smiled at his son. 'Don't we all use each other, to gain our own advantage?'

Margret looked at Bryn, pursed her lips. 'You know this, still allow her to use you?'

Helen left them talking in the lounge, headed for Charlyyk's room. When she returned, Helen held the folder that Sandra had read that morning. Helen passed it to Thomas, Rachel moved closer to Thomas, so she could also have the chance to read.

After a while, it was Rachel that spoke. 'I see what you mean. This is her understanding our ways of living, by moulding herself, so she can live. She's a very talented girl.'

Thomas passes the folder to Margret. Putting her reading glasses on, then sitting back in the armchair she began to read. Now and again, she stopped and goes back a page or two, then with a lump in her throat. 'Poor girl, it must have been a very worrying time for her. I can feel the anxiety in some of her writing, telling herself, what she must do to earn your trust. There are no nasty words about anyone, just discussions with herself, how she must adapt if she is to survive?' As Margret removes her glasses, she wipes a single tear from her eye with a tissue.

Thomas speaks up. 'Should we not put this back where she hides it?

Helen glanced at him. 'She does not hide anything; it is left out in the open, Charlyyk will talk to you openly about it. Charlyyk feels, the more she knows about us, the least mistakes she will make.'

Twenty minutes later, when Harold and Gwen arrived. Margret mentions Charlyyk's folder. Harold replied. 'Yes Margret, Charlyyk knew that Bryn needed help when finding himself stranded on a planet that was way beyond his knowledge. She smelled his uncertainty. She knew it was not fear, but a strong determination to find a way out of his predicament. This is the same example she has taken, to help herself to survive. When she started to be able to write, these were her scribbles to keep herself in line with those that lived on this planet. It's like the old saying, 'When in Rome do like the Romans.' Charlyyk and I would sit and debate what she had written, Charlyyk would ask if I agreed with her understanding on the way we live. She needed to be sure, she had not misinterpreted any off her findings.'

During lunchtime. Mrs Landon had spoken with Sandra's mother. Now was sitting with Sandra. 'Your father is responding very well, but it still needs time. Charlyyk's parents assured me that you could stay with them as long as you want to? They also said they would take you to the Hospital to see your parents.' Sandra thanked her for the care she was giving her. Louise Landon gave her hand, a gentle squeeze with a warm assuring smile.

Bryn and Helen arrived at the school, after lessons had finished, to pick them both up, waited patiently while they all said their goodbyes. When they got into the car, Helen gave Sandra a carrier bag with a few items inside. 'I've spoken to your mother. She needed some bits, which I've placed in the bag. We can go to the Hospital now, so you can see her.'

When Bryn had dropped Helen and Sandra, at the Hospital entrance, he drove to a just vacant parking space close at hand. Once he had parked properly, he turned to face Charlyyk. 'How did it go at school today?'

Charlyyk climbed into the front seat next to him. 'Sarah and Jan gathered the class together and organised a routine, so Sandra had someone to talk to. So, she could not mope about, and get despondent. Mrs Landon spoke to her at lunchtime, the teachers did not bother her, but made sure they involved her in the lessons. My classmates asked that I should just be myself. At first, I did not understand, what they were asking. Mike explained, that with moments like these some people will overthink, what is happening. That could easily lead to making things worse. He is so nice, when you get to know him?'

Bryn gave her a smile. 'You said, he does not look after himself properly, that he smelt of yesterday's dinner!'

Charlyyk laughed. 'I did, didn't I...that's because he is always inside his own head, not outside it. He is thinking all the time, like daydreaming. It turns out, he is trying to solve different problems?' Then she laughed. 'Mostly the one he causes himself!'

Sandra, upon meeting her mother, ran into her arms. She buried her head in her mother's breast. Her mother allowed her to let her emotion out before she said anything to her. Outside the ward, some bucket chair was situated. her mother took Sandra to them, sitting down, Sandra sat on her mother lap. Helen sat beside them, as they discussed the condition of Sandra's father.

'He is frail, but has responded well to the treatment. I will stay tonight with him. The doctor said, if he is Ok by the morning, he should be able to come home on Sunday.' This perked up Sandra. Helen remained seated, while Sandra went to see her father.

When Bryn noticed, them coming through the entrance, he started the engine, then cruised gently towards them. When he pulled up, Charlyyk hopped out of the vehicle, allowing Helen to sit up front with Bryn.

***

It was a cold frosty Saturday morning. It gave a silvery glow to the countryside, although still dark it was still easy to see where one was going. Thomas had joined them on the morning jog, he had been a regular jogger, around New York's, Central Park. He took the lead with his dad, with Helen and Charlyyk trailed behind; as they passed the cow sheds, the familiar figures of James and his father Edward were seen bringing the cows that had been milked. James seeing Thomas, shouted out to him. 'Come up for a coffee, bring Rachel.' Thomas replied that he would.

Charlyyk was telling Helen, about Sandra, although she was asleep, she tossed and turned all night. 'I stroked her head, it settled her for a little while. Then she went back to tossing and turning.'

When they returned back to the cottage, Rachel had already started getting breakfast. Sandra sitting there watching and talking to Rachel. Sandra looked happy.

While everyone ate breakfast, Sandra sat next to Helen and Rachel. 'It's nice here. I love the atmosphere it makes you feel warm inside...you know that cosy feeling you get when you are contented. It makes me feel like my cat Bonny after he has had his favourite meal, he curls up and purr's, that how I'm feeling at this moment.'

Rachel put her arm around her and gave her a gentle squeeze. 'I know what you mean, I feel it when I come here. It feels... this is home.'

Margret, her mother, gave Rachel a frosty look. 'Your apartment is so lovely, the modern furniture, the stylish paintings. You are saying, it's not homely?'

Thomas could not allow Margret to dominate Rachel. 'The apartment is for show. It is there for our clients. We will be changing it, to bring up our family. Rachel will tell me where, and how she thinks the changes should be made.'

Rachel smiled. She often said to her friends that although Thomas resembles his mother, he had inherited his father's hidden strengths.

Helen seeing Margret's hurt expression, decided to change the conversation. 'What are your plans, Margret?'

Margret face brightened up, 'We have a delivery of paintings arriving early January, have yet to finalise Manchester and Liverpool, so I have to go there to confirm the arrangement we made over the phone. All the artist, have confirmed the dates they can attend, there are some artists that can visit all the exhibits; Janet has asked to write up an article, which we will take up on her offer.'

Helen turned her attention to Thomas. She was keen to take the friction out of the situation. 'So, when will I be able to see some of your work?'

He looked up at the picture hanging on the wall. 'That's an early drawing of mine. My latest works have all been sold, I promised Charlyyk I would give her lessons. I will do a couple more paintings then.

The sun was warm in shaded areas away from the cold breeze, that persisted in blowing. Bryn was washing the Discovery. Helen sorting out the dirty laundry with Rachel. The morning drifted by.

At twelve-thirty, a text message came. Sandra could not contain herself, 'Dad will be coming home. Mum is going home now to make things ready for him.' The girls rush to Helen to relay the news.

Helen had Sandra's mother's phone number just in case of an emergency. She dialled. 'Hi, Rebecca... Helen, do you need any help?' They agreed for Sandra to stay till four, then she could go home.

Charlyyk watching Helen how she handled situation, arranged her thoughts in her mind. Would she need this way of handling situation as she grows older?

At four thirty they arrived at Sandra's House. The reunion between mother and daughter was very touching. Rebecca thanked them warmly for looking after Sandra. As Helen and Charlyyk drove off, they could be seen, still standing at their front door still cuddling each other and waving their goodbyes.

Chapter 26

Christmas Invite

The sun had just started to make an entrance to the day as the four runners returned to the cottage. Thomas had been asking Charlyyk if she would go with them to church that morning. Charlyyk looked hesitant, did not want to go, 'I know Aunty Gwen goes every Sunday, but Uncle Harold only sometimes.'

Thomas put on a, 'please; please me' face.

'I don't know' was her reply, quickly rushed off to shower.

Thomas looked up at his father, who was smiling at him. Bryn putting his arm around his son's shoulders. 'She just cannot see what other people think they see, like you and Gwen.'

Thomas sank down into the nearest chair, 'Well at least I tried.'

Rachel and Margret, walked into the room, 'What that's, what were you trying to do?'

Thomas shook his head; 'I asked Charlyyk if she would go to Church this morning.'

Rachel sniggered. Her mother gave her a quizzical look. 'Why are you sniggering.'

Rachel did not back down. 'I had spoken to Harold. He said, she can't be brainwashed. She has been to church once. She informed him, the only thing that happened is that. A man with a dress on, bored everyone and expected people to pay him.'

Helen and Bryn quietly left the room, trying hard not to laugh, 'Come sweetheart, I need your personal attention in the shower.' Bryn said to her, as he gave her arse a slap.

'Oh, Sir Jasper. Do not harm me?' Helen took hold of his hand, dragging him towards their bedroom.

At breakfast, Margret intended to raise the issue of the church with Charlyyk. Ignoring what Rachel had said, she was puzzled to pick the right words to say, 'How was the run this morning Charlyyk?'

Charlyyk finished eating her muesli, 'It was nice, it refreshes you for the day.'

Margret could now open her gambit. 'I go to church, to refresh my inner self!'

Charlyyk did not respond. Helen and Bryn looked down, making sure that no one could notice the silly smirks they had.

'Oh yes, the tranquillity it gives me is so rewarding.' Margret continued.

'That must be nice for you?' Then Charlyyk took a sip of water. 'You must go with Auntie Gwen she gets the same feeling as you do, she would appreciate your company, as Uncle Harold does not always go to Church.'

Helen got up from the table, quickly gathered up dirty dishes, then took them to the dishwasher, if she had not, she would have definitely had not been able to control herself.

'So, would you like to come to church today?'

Charlyyk made no attempt to fudge her, 'No. but thank you for asking.'

Margret was not someone who gave up easily. 'I think it will please Gwen that you give it a try.'

Charlyyk finished her water. 'I have been to church. I found it so cold that it made me shiver. Whatever the effect it had on Auntie Gwen. I had missed it. Looking at everyone afterwards, it seemed they had missed it too.'

Rachel had been watching Helen. Though she could only see her back, the tell-tale signs of the trembling of her body, said Helen was either crying or laughing. Rachel accepted the latter.

Thomas, Rachel and her mother, left for church. Bryn, Helen and Charlyyk left later for Carpenters Cottage. Harold was in the kitchen when they arrived. He was in fine form. Michel was in the chair, which sat in the kitchen corner. Charlyyk kissed Harold, then jumped on Michel's lap. He always liked the way she cuddled into him. 'Hello you, how are we?'

Charlyyk threw her head back, 'I'm fine Michel.'

He put his arms right around her, gave her a squeeze. 'The test we've been doing on your menstrual cycle, has not proved anything different or anything to worry about, we are still going ahead.' Your occasional dropping off to sleep, we can put down to you, losing iron in your blood, due to your menstrual period. Which I am glad to say you soon replaced. We will no doubt understand more about it, at or when you have your next period.'

Helen who had been listening in on their conversation, 'Could we give her something to counteract the loss of iron?'

'I don't like to give her chemicals unless I really have to.' He paused, 'We could do a menu test, work out a month's food according to one diet, then a second month according to another. I can compare their effects with blood samples.'

Harold whisking the batter for the Yorkshire puddings, 'We should feed her on beef, that would put some metal into her.'

Charlyyk looked sternly at Harold. 'Uncle Harold you know I cannot eat course red meat like beef. My stomach cannot digest it. Even turkey I find hard to digest.'

The sound of Gwen's voice was the cue to put the Yorkshire batter in the oven; Harold kept to his mother's way of putting the batter in the roasting tin, with the Beef on a rack cooking over it. Then making the onion gravy, which was always a favourite of Thomas's. Bryn and Helen had laid the table, Gwen showed Margret some of her magazines, Thomas and Rachel had drifted into the kitchen, pulled in by the intoxicating aromas that Harold had conjured up.

'Uncle Harold, you haven't?' Thomas's eyes closed, his nose sniffing the memories of his youth, those wonderful days when Harold would reward him for achieving good marks in his exams. Thick onion gravy, poured onto a Yorkshire pudding.

Harold carved the roast beef; the first slices, for Gwen and Margret; they did not want pink meat. Charlyyk and Rachel were having fish pie. During dinner, Thomas's recalled memories of other family coming together. He suddenly remembered that Helen had not been there.

'I'm so sorry Helen.'

Helen just smiled, 'Don't be. Those memories should never be forgotten. They should be remembered, and retold over and over again. For what I have been told about your mother Kitty, she was an exceptional woman, that should always be remembered.'

Gwen took Helen hand in hers, 'Thank you, Helen, you don't know how much we appreciate what you have just said.'

Thomas agreed. 'Not only does Charlyyk gives you her blessings, so do the rest of the family.

Michel raised his glass, 'Here's to Helen, you are staying whether you like it or not!'

Helen buried her chin in her chest, 'Oh yes I like it, I like it a lot.'

Charlyyk picked up Michel's glass, lifted it aloft. 'To my new mum Helen.' She took a sip. Her face screwed up, her eyes closed, and her body trembled, 'Yuck, how can you drink that! It is horrible! Michel,' Charlyyk's first taste of red wine, will definitely be her last. Though it did give, the rest of them something to laugh about.

Margret was seeing Charlyyk, as a person, the realisation that this alien, was not at first what she had thought, that of being a family-pet. Seeing Charlyyk was someone that thought things through, and showed feelings. Her helping her friend through troubled times. Margret started to think of Charlyyk as any other young girl.

Rachel touched her mother's hand, 'You Ok mum?'

Margret smiled at her daughter, 'Yes I'm all right, I now see what you have been telling me, all this time about Charlyyk. It is true, she just a little girl growing up.' With a sigh, 'She may look different, but she is no different to any other young girl.'

Gwen overheard her. 'Margret I was no different than you, but when you come to know Charlyyk, as we do, you can't but just love her.' Gwen paused for a moment looking at her brother, 'What she has given Bryn, has been remarkable, he was a lost soul after Kitty died, yes he had Catherine and Thomas, but no Kitty. Charlyyk has been his salvation, just look at him, it tells you what she has done for him.'

Margret watching Bryn and Helen lost in each other company, 'Without Charlyyk, they would never have met.'

Charlyyk listened as they spoke about her. She was pleased to be able to judge each person's eyes for false feelings. Margret was Charlyyk main concern, as like Gwen held her believes longer than others. The remarks Thomas and Rachel were saying to Margret were becoming more and more harsh. Thomas was home, it influenced him by its presence.

Harold asked, 'What plans for Christmas have you, Michel?'

Michel responded, 'Ah yes, have you not spoken to the Parsons? They want us all there for Christmas. So, I will let them talk to you first.'

***

Monday, with Charlyyk at school, Helen was sorting out what was required to be ready for Christmas. She was so involved in what she was doing, did not know she was being watched. 'Well, what a busy bee we have here.'

Helen spun around Jane Parsons was standing there, 'Jane you frighten the life out of me.' With her hand on her chest, Helen took a deep breath. 'Coffee?'

'Why not.' Walking into the kitchen, Jane picked the kettle up and filled it with fresh water.

Sitting down with mugs of coffee, 'This is nice Jane.'

Jane smiled, 'We are having a big Christmas do on Christmas Day for all the farmworkers and their families. We wondered if you all would like to come. We have come through a tight financial period, and we would not have been able to without the help of everyone. This is our big thank you to them. We have cleared out the old barn and made an area to park.'

'Can we help in any way?'

Jane paused, 'You know Kit and I were very close. When she died, a bit of me died with her. I must admit, at first I became a bit wary of you, I thought that you would not live up to her. I was wrong, in your own way, you are so much like her, not in looks, but the same type of character. I would love it if we could be friends?'

Helen gave her squeeze, 'I would love to have you as a friend, it would please me no end.'

Sipping coffee Helen mentioned to Jane 'We found an old family Bible, belonging to the Allcott Family dated 1557.' Helen went and delved into the cupboard, retrieved the Bible. Sitting next to Jane, Helen unwrapped it, turning the cover to open it. She placed it in front of Jane.

Jane's finger followed the text, 'Wow Edward is going to love this. This answers lots of questions. May I take this to show Edward?'

'Of course, you can. We can see there are mentions of Parsons, marrying Allcott's.'

Jane turned a few more pages then turned it over to see the back page, 'Oh my, this is getting better all the time.'

Helen strained to see what Jane was reading. 'Come on put me out of my misery, what can you see.'

Jane pointed to writing in red ink, '*On this day August the 10th 1898, a boy is born out of wedlock, To Alice Allcott. The father, Edward Parsons, may he rot in Hell*'

Helen looked at Jane, 'Oh such scandal.'

'It would have been enough for pistols at dawn, in those days.' Jane said with a little twinkle in her eye, 'There was a rumour in the family, that the Allcott's ended up as head herdsmen after being the real owners of the farm. The last Allcott was why Ned had re-built this Cottage for them, they were as good as family, the dates tally up. Arthur Allcott was Ned's elder half-brother!'

There were no more entries of births in the Bible only the marriage. Arthur to Christine Bishop in 1913, who died in childbirth 1915, the child was stillborn. That was end of the Allcott Family.

Bryn was in a happy mood, a nippy little tune, he had heard on the car radio was playing in his head, that he was whistling along to the song as he entered. 'Hi, Jane, Hello sweetheart.' Then he saw the Bible, laid out on the table, 'Ah you've seen it, what you reckon Jane?'

Jane sniggered, 'Some interesting bedtime reading probably.'

Bryn sitting down with them, 'We noticed the Parsons name, crops up now and again.' Jane showed him the last page, turning to Helen. 'Wow, that should keep Edward interested?'

Jane closed the Bible and wrapped it in the cloth it came in. 'I've come to invite you all to have Christmas Day with us, Bryn.'

He kissed her on the cheek, 'Thank you, that sounds great Jane, we accept wholeheartedly.' Jane left twenty minutes later, holding the Bible very close to her.

Bryn helped Helen to finish cleaning the cupboards, then deciding on what should stay and what should go, while he discussed how they should do the Christmas shopping, 'Rachel and your good self should take Charlyyk one day, Thomas and I will take her another day...I have been to the bank and have drawn some money out for her to spend. I have opened an account in her name, and ordered a debit card for her.'

Helen gave him a stern look, 'But you give her pocket money. Is this a wise move?'

'I did the same for Catherine and Thomas when they were this age, I gave them an allowance, to teach them about how to handle their own finances.'

Bryn took some of the boxes to be stored, in the garage. While Helen dumped the black bags in the rubbish green wheelie bins. Back in the kitchen, Bryn answered Helen. 'I give her pocket money, so she has something to spend at school, I want to teach her how to manage, buying her own clothes, and entertainment on a set allowance!'

The day had gone quicker than they had expected. Charlyyk had returned home, removing her coat, she soon was asking Helen, about Christmas. 'Everyone at school is talking about what they were getting their parents for Christmas. I was lost to say anything. I did not know what was expected from me?'

Helen guided her to the sofa, sat down with her, 'Your father, has said today, that you should go with Rachel and myself one day, then to go with him and Thomas another day. He has drawn out some money for you to spend.' The look of excitement on Charlyyk's face, with the hug she gave Helen. Left no doubt, that is what she wanted to hear.

When Bryn entered the lounge, she threw herself at him, wrapping her arms around his neck, and kept kissing him.

'OK enough!' He laughed. 'I gather you heard about you going shopping.'

Charlyyk leant back and with the most enormous smile on her face, 'Yeah, and with my own money.' Hugging him once more.

'I get the picture. You just want me for my money.'

Helen came up to from behind and tickled her. 'You old, gold-digger.'

With shrieks of laughter, 'Less of the old! if you haven't noticed, I'm quite young.'

Helen tickled her some more, 'OK, you young, gold-digger.'

Over orange juice and biscuits. Bryn explains to her his intentions. Charlyyk's wide-eyed look with a smiley face, 'So then I can buy my own clothes?'

'Remember when Michel told you, that there was going to be a change in you? Well, this is a part of that change. Growing up, it takes on responsibility for yourself. We should not think it is going to happen overnight. We must allow time for adjustments, learning what to do and how to do it. The most important thing, is to get it right.'

Charlyyk now had a serious face on, 'Thank you both for having trust in me. I promise not to let you down.'

Thomas, Rachel and Margret arrived later. They had been to an art gallery in London to finalise the shipment of paintings. Over dinner Bryn explains his ideas on shopping for Christmas. Rachel was the first, to think it was a great idea. She loved the thought of taking Charlyyk to the stores. 'It will be like Houston all over again.' With that thought in mind, Charlyyk's face was full with excitement.

***

At school the next day, Charlyyk talked excitedly to the posse, about going Christmas shopping. 'I've never had a lot of money before, but then I never needed it. I'm going to have an allowance, to buy my own clothes, of course, I can purchase other things I need.'

Sandra touched her bottom lip with one finger, then sighed. 'My parents could not afford that for me. Since my dad has been ill, money has been very tight.'

Charlyyk looked very solemn. 'I mustn't allow this to go to my head, or take things for granted... I feel, so awful.'

Julia touched Charlyyk's hand. 'Don't be silly. Sandra is not trying to put you down. Everyone here has a different family situation. I get an allowance and have to budget, how I use it.' Julia had never mentioned this to anyone before. 'It's a modest contribution, it makes me understand the cost of things. Dad said, the price of those shoes, he worked hard for three hours. The value of money? It's what's it incurs, to earn it.'

Peter sighed, 'I have to do a Saturday job if I want anything, I give my mum some of it. She doesn't ask, but I know she appreciates it.'

At home in Oakleaves. Charlyyk talked with Helen, Rachel and Margret, relating to what the posse was discussing about her allowance. 'Gwen has told me about the different circumstances, that families find themselves in. I should not think that everyone lives the same way as we live. I forgot, and I felt so bad. It made me feel I had been gloating.'

Margret asked her why she had that impression. 'It was when Julia said her dad had to work three hours to get the money for her shoes, I have never seen dad go out to work, so I did not understand the value of money, I knew thing cost money, but the value, that's different.'

Margret touched her hand, 'My father uses to say, no matter what's the inflation, a day's money buys a pair of shoes, and a week's money buys a suit.'

'Peter told us that he works all day on Saturday's, gives his mother some of it. That made me feel guilty.'

Helen gave a little laugh, 'But sweetheart you do give something. When you help with the housework, you are giving something back.'

Charlyyk's face perked up, 'Do I... Oh yes I see what you mean. Peter does not help indoors, so giving his mother some of his wages, compensate her for not doing housework, at home?'

Helen nodded, 'Yes, sort of, he might still do a few things for his mother though.'

Charlyyk became quiet. She was going through what had been said, in her mind. 'Yes, as Harold would say, when help is needed, we must roll up our sleeves, and put our noses to the grindstone.'

'That right.' Rachel remarked. 'In the hour of need, one must do one's duty.'

Charlyyk looked around, then biting her bottom lip, 'This is telling me, it is not what I spend, but what I can save.'

Margret smiled at her, 'You could look at it differently, ask yourself do I really need it? If you do, then buy it.'

Charlyyk's beamed, 'I could give myself many reasons to spend money.'

Helen gave out a chuckle, 'Saving is a virtue we should all adopt, but saving for the sake of saving, and not acquiring the essentials of life, is downright silly. Moderation is what's required.'

'I was only kidding Helen, I do understand. Dad has put his trust in me, I should repay it, by treating it with respect.'

Helen gave her a hug and a kiss. 'That's my girl.'

***

Wednesday, sitting down at the kitchen table for a mid-morning coffee. Margret was remarking on the previous day's debate, on Charlyyk's allowance. Bryn listening intently on what was being discussed. 'I'm sure that in a year's time you will definitely see a different Charlyyk. She has changed so much, just in these last three months.'

'Taking into account the length of time between the three times that I had seen her, the changes have been immense.' Thomas observed. 'She has grown so much, seeing her in Houston...to now. She has so matured, almost a different girl.'

Rachel did not agree, 'She is the same girl, what I have noticed, is how she imitates the people around her who she admires.'

Helen agreed, 'Oh definitely, she certainly does that.'

Margret now seems more relaxed talking about Charlyyk, 'Is this how she handles adapting to living with us.'

Bryn remarked 'I think if I were in her shoes, I'd probably do the same.'

'I'm with you, on that.' Margret thinking aloud. 'She certainly is, a remarkably adaptable young girl.'

Thomas dunking a digestive biscuit in his coffee, 'I just love her, she so refreshing. You always get an honest reply from her.'

'Like at Disney World.' Rachel mused. 'She was so excited. Knowing she made a fool of herself, but it did not embarrass her, she just excepted it. Even laughed at herself, it was so funny...I wish I could be able to be like that. Make a mistake and not be concerned about it, not worrying how others are think of me.'

Margret had not listened to Rachel her mind was elsewhere. 'The TV show you all did, I just loved it. I watched it with my neighbours, Bill and Brenda O'Brien. Bill thought Charlyyk was sweet, Brenda liked the bright coloured clothes Charlyyk wore. Why were you not there Helen?'

'Work I'm afraid, could not get away from it.'

Margret had a quizzical look on her face. 'You're not working now I, see?'

'No. I've retired, it was what I was doing at that time making way for my successor. I can spend my time here.' Looking at Bryn, with a soft loving smile. 'And I just love it...It's been like living in another world. I now know how Charlyyk feels.'

Rachel looked between them. She saw the chemistry, 'Good for you, you enjoy every minute of it, you both deserve what you have here. Thomas and I think the same...we can't wait for the wedding.'

Margret chirped, 'Well they haven't... have they?'

The laughter took a little time to subdue. Margret took the longest time to settle once she realised what she had said. Helen's smirk did not hide how she felt. 'That's the beauty of being the age we are Margret we can live the rest of our life without any regrets...you could say we can go for its big time. For in a way we have nothing to lose.'

When Charlyyk arrived home, she spoke with Helen about Sandra, 'She is struggling to cope with her father illness. Her mother is working hard, trying to put a brave face on...but she knows her mother is struggling too. That's what's upsetting her.'

Helen picked the phone up, dials Sandra's mother number. 'Hello, Rebecca... Helen... how's it going?' The sigh Helen heard, was more relief than stress, 'Is there anything I can do for you, Rebecca?'

There was a slight pause. 'I could do with a little company Helen if you could spare me your time?'

Helen said she could. They agreed, they would see each other at ten the next morning.

***

Thursday morning Helen arrived outside of Sandra house. She needed an umbrella for the drizzling rain. At the door, Rebecca was already waiting. Helen gave her some flowers; she had stopped at Marks & Spencer's which was close by, to pick up some bits and pieces. They both kissed each other's cheeks and went inside.

Rebecca's husband Len was sitting in an armchair by the window, a duvet covered him. Helen placed a hand on his shoulder, 'You are looking a lot better, then when I last saw you, Len.'

He replied with a weak smile. 'Thank you, I'm feeling much better.'

'That's good to hear Len.' Helen placed a box of mixed pastries on the table, 'I thought these would go down nicely, with tea or coffee.'

Rebecca started to relax, to have someone different to talk too, was to her like having a weight taken off her shoulders. Helen kept the conversation light and cheerful, trying to distract Rebecca's mind of the constant strain she found herself in. Helen left at one so that Len could rest.

At the door, Rebecca instead of shaking Helen's hand, she gave Helen a big hug. 'You don't know how much I enjoyed your company, thank you.'

Helen promised they would do it again, 'Rebecca if you need me, just call.'

Chapter 27

Getting ready for Christmas

Friday, was the last day at school. The Christmas break had come. The posse had given each other cards and keepsakes for Christmas, the excitement at school was tingling with expectation.

Peter had brought in a twig of mistletoe, he had eyes on one person to try it out on. Mace had a good idea, that was Peter's intention of getting a kiss, from Sandra. Only a few of the posse knew that Peter had a crush on her, but as yet he had not made a move. Could today, be the day?

Charlyyk had spoken to Julia about Peter before, telling her how she had sensed the vibes they gave out. Julia had dismissed the idea as pure speculation as Sandra had never mentioned Peter in that way, now she was not so sure, seeing Peter trying to build his courage up. Mike was reacting a little nonplus on it. He could not understand why Peter was behaving the way he was.

As Sandra was collecting her things from her locker. Peter made his move. Those of the posse that knew, had positioned themselves, with the clearest view they could obtain without giving the game away, as Peter made his way towards her, mistletoe in his hand, held behind him. 'Sandra, can I wish you a Merry Christmas?'

Sandra looked at him and smiled, 'Of course you can Peter.'

He held the mistletoe up above her head, then leant his head forward. Sandra reached up, cupping his face in her hands, she kissed him on the lips, 'Merry Christmas Peter.'

Julia's look of disbelief aimed at Charlyyk, 'How did you know?'

Charlyyk smiled, 'When they got close to each other, their smell changed, not one of them, but both of them, my nose does not lie, it tells me everything.'

The posse started clapping, then burst into song. 'We wish you a Merry Christmas, and seal it with a kiss' They converged, congratulating Peter and Sandra.

Julia still could not see, how Charlyyk could have known about them, 'Are there any other surprises, that you know about?'

Charlyyk stepped back, 'Yes, but I must not tell you.'

'Why?'

Charlyyk took a good look at Julia, 'It is much too early, at this moment to reveal who likes whom. When the vibes grow strong enough, I might tell you.'

Julia tugs on her arm. 'Oh, come Charlyyk, you can't leave me in suspense, it not fair.'

Charlyyk takes her arm in hers, 'You are not ready to know.' Then kisses Julia on the cheek.

Sandra seeing her two friends, made her way to meet with them. 'I've been waiting for Peter to make the first move, if he was big enough to do it, it meant it was the right time to accept him.'

Julia looked at Sandra, more in annoyance of not being let into Sandra's secret, 'You're saying you knew all along how he felt, with you feeling the same way, yet did nothing to push it forward, why not?'

Sandra smiled at Julia, 'It was too soon, I did not want to, unsettle him, or make him feel too big and important. He has to come to me...on my terms, but thinking it was his terms. If I had confided with you and you let it slip out... that might have scuppered my control of the situation.

Sandra pulled Charlyyk closer, 'I have so much to thank you for Charlyyk. Your mum visited my mum and dad yesterday, mum was so happy when I got home, as it picked my dad spirit's up as well, the smile on dad's face. When he heard mum whistling when she cleared up after dinner, that was the best Christmas present we could ever have wished for.'

Julia joined in with the cuddle, to wish each other a Merry Christmas. Julia casually asked what Charlyyk was doing for Christmas. 'Christmas shopping in London with the girls, on Saturday. Monday, I shop with the boys in Winchester.'

Julia gave Charlyyk a playful punch, 'For someone that don't believe in God, you certainly like the trappings of Christmas.'

Charlyyk, did not need to time to think, she had fielded the same question before. 'You bet Julia. We know that Jesus lived. The bible tells us of so many mysterious stories about his miracles. Then did not the Romans write clearly in their records, that Jesus lived. So, are you not celebrating the birth of Jesus? That's still not saying, that praying to your so-called God, will change anything.'

Julia just shook her head, thinking to herself. *Charlyyk has just been living with us for a couple of years and know more about us, that have lived all our life here'.*

Charlyyk walked with Mace and Sarah to catch the bus home. They stopped to watch Peter walking arm in arm with Sandra, then he held out his other arm for Julia to join them. That day Peter grew extra inches. As they started to walk out of the school gates. Sandra turned, then blew them all a kiss.

On the school bus, Sarah sat with Charlyyk. 'Mace said you knew about Peter and Sandra, for some time, we knew about Peter...that was so obvious... but Sandra she never gave a hint she liked Peter.'

'There are others who, at this moment don't know their true feelings, but will find them later. There are those who have feelings for someone, but the other person doesn't reciprocate. Time can change matters.'

Sarah looked long at Charlyyk. 'Well?'

Charlyyk pulled her closer, 'Do you have feelings about someone?'

Sarah with a puzzled look on her, 'I thought you could tell me?'

Charlyyk gave a chuckle. 'What's this wishful thinking? No, it doesn't work like that. You get feelings for someone; your body responds to those feeling by giving out signals. My nose then picks up on those signals. No, I can't pick up anything; you are safe.'

Sarah looked disappointed. Charlyyk put her arms around her. 'Look, it is early days. You have time on your side.' Sarah's look did not change. 'Look at it from my side... I've no chance... if I liked somebody, people would say it would be wrong. Friends yes, relationships no.'

Sarah face changed, she had not looked at that situation, she had always looked at Charlyyk just being one of the girls. She returned Charlyyk's hug. 'Sorry Charlyyk I was acting selfishly.'

The colour of Charlyyk's eyes changed to a soft blue. 'No don't say that, you will meet someone. Your body will respond to them, at this moment it has not happened, but it doesn't mean it won't happen. Take Mace, when he gets near Julia, his body responds. But Julia's doesn't, but it is not to say it won't but at this time nothing.'

Sarah looked at Mace. 'He likes Julia?'

Charlyyk chuckled, 'His body is reacting, but he does not know it. If Julia's body responds, to those vibes, hers will accelerate. Mace's will sense those vibes, that would tell him he likes Julia.'

Sarah mused. 'That makes sense, so if Julia's body doesn't respond, they won't want each other. He could meet someone else; their vibes could respond to one another; he would never think of Julia... Gotcha.'

Charlyyk could sense, Sarah's despondency. Her love for Mace was a sister's love. But Sarah could not distinguish between the different types of love, she did not want to lose him to someone else.

When Charlyyk arrived home, she gave Helen an extra hug. 'What was that for.' Helen asked.

'That was from Sandra, for what you achieved with her mum and dad.

She said her mum was whistling, while she was clearing up, it made her dad so happy.'

Helen returned the hug. 'Then that makes me happy too, see if we can see them over the Christmas.'

Charlyyk could not be happier herself. 'We could get something nice, so they could share together.'

At dinner, the discussion, was the girls Christmas shopping to London, 'We will go by train, then underground.' Said Helen.

Charlyyk looked at her hands.

Rachel laughed, 'No Charlyyk, we have not to dig our way into London. The Underground is another train that travels underground.'

Helen carried on, 'I booked a table at the 'La Brasserie' for one-thirty. You'll love it, Margret. Also, you will meet my parents. I've invited them to lunch.'

Bryn put his arm around Charlyyk, 'And its baked beans for me.'

Charlyyk cuddled up to him, 'I tell you what the meal tasted like when I get home...but hey, what's wrong with baked beans?'

Bryn tickled her, 'Thanks for nothing.' And tickled her some more.

**

Saturday Christmas shopping day. Charlyyk could not get dressed any quicker than she did. Rachel came to her rescue. 'There's a saying 'more haste less speed'... Now, slow down... Deep breathes... Relax.'

Charlyyk, began to settled the febrile excitement that had built up inside her. With Rachel's help, she felt much better. By the time they were ready to leave, Charlyyk was looking resplendent. Helen had brought her a Burberry Camel coat, which she wore over the Laura Ashley Dress. She also wore cherry-red, tights and brown leather court shoes. Helen had put foam padding inside to fit Charlyyk's narrow feet. Not only did she looked good, but more important she felt good.

Bryn took many photos of them. He was proud of how they looked. Then he drove them to the station.

Standing openly, on the platform was another first. Though Charlyyk could not stop herself, thinking about her home planet, and all the terrors that came with it. 'Now look at me' trying hard to push though thoughts back. She looked around her, she could see everyone was watching her. She nodded to them, acknowledging them with a warm smile,

Margret watched her, she could tell the more Charlyyk met people, the more she looked in control.

The train pulled into the station. As the doors opened, Helen stopped Charlyyk from getting too near to the train. The surge of passengers getting off, could have knocked her flying. As they boarded the train, the other passengers were straining to see Charlyyk, trying to get photos of her.

Margret could feel the stress of it, wondered how Charlyyk could cope with that constant pressure.

Helen had it all under control. Even when the train pulled into Paddington Train Station, although the platform was crowded, they seemed free to walk. But when Margret saw the crowds heading for the underground that's when she put her foot down, 'No we don't. Taxi.'

They walked outside where many taxis were waiting. They were soon heading, for the very short ride to Regent Street's shops.

Charlyyk, looking around she could not believe how many people there were, all rushing about with their own agendas. She was amazed when she saw what was there waiting for her. The shops were decked out for Christmas, a mass of twinkling lights, that strung out across the streets, with the displays in shop windows it was taking breath away. Charlyyk found herself, looking at the decorations, more than the items for sale. Other people found themselves looking at Charlyyk.

Though she was still carrying many bags. Her amazement had not stopped her buying. Rachel watched Helen take control of Charlyyk. Helen's hand would gently put Charlyyk on course in the direction they were heading for. Helen kept the conversation going smoothly, she knew that Charlyyk mind could go floating on a sea off clouds, eyes and ears moving about in so many directions like a ships radar scanner. Charlyyk's mind was bamboozled by everything that was happening, making sure she had not missed a single thing.

At La Brasserie, the staff were soon fussing around her making her comfortable, Helen's Mother was already seated, when she saw Charlyyk she was up out of her seat, her arms stretched out, 'Sweetheart comes here, let me see you... My you do look grand.'

Edward was soon with them, 'Come Charlyyk, give this old man a big kiss.'

Helen introduced Margret and Rachel to her parents, Elizabeth was quick to drop the Lord and Lady tag that Margret eagerly wanted to use, 'Please, it gives us credence in our work, but we are going to be family. Let's drop the pomp and ceremony. It gives us indigestion.'

Charlyyk sat between Elizabeth and Edward. Their constant banter amused her.

The maître d' was soon at their beck and call, with waiters serving the drinks, hurrying about to make sure their needs were met. A young Chinese waitress looked after Charlyyk, stood close behind her, she was under strict orders, to be on hand at all times. Anna, arrived later. Elizabeth had pre-ordered for her. Much was spoken about how Charlyyk liked the decorations, how did she feel spending her own money. The lunch took an hour and a bit, with an extra half hour, that was required for their goodbyes.

Helen had a few favourite stores. Margret wanted to go to Liberty's and Harrods. Rachel wanted to visit Harvey Nicholl's. By the time they had finished, poor Charlyyk was finished too. She flopped into the seat on the train, her leg spread out, and her arms draped down each side. Helen and Rachel taking lots of shots of her on their phones. Helen sending her photos to Bryn.

Rachel, after taking the content out of one of the bags, used it as a fan.

Margret magically pulled a water bottle from another bag and gave it to Charlyyk. 'This might make you feel better.'

As Charlyyk finished drinking, 'Thanks, Margret. You are a lifesaver.'

Margret sat beside her and held her hand. 'My dear girl, it was a pleasure.'

Helen smiled a victory smile; it was a roaring success. Margret has entered the human race at last.

Rachel grasped Helen's hand and gave it a squeeze, 'Thanks for a fabulous day, Helen.'

Margret reached over and touched Helen's knee, 'Yes a great day, my appreciation also.'

Charlyyk raised a hand then flopped it down again, 'I'm shattered.'

Bryn met them at the station Rachel trying hard to help Charlyyk, who's legs were sagging under her own weight. Bryn scooped her up, carried her towards the car, 'I just want to go to bed.' Charlyyk groaned.

***

Bryn was busy in the kitchen when Charlyyk arrived, dragging her feet. Her eyes like slits, her mouth ajar, her little purple tongue trying hard to moisten her lips. 'Fluid... Any type of fluid?'

Bryn filled a glass with water, then with his arm gently around her shoulders guides her to a seat, 'Morning sweetheart.' The sagging shoulders of Charlyyk and the feeble attempt to get the glass to her lips, 'I do believe you should go back to bed?'

She looked at him and gave a deep sigh, 'Yes, you are right.'

Bryn took the glass of water from her, then gently helped her back to bed, then he went back to the kitchen and collected the tea tray.

Helen looked directly at the tea that was on tea tray, not at Bryn, as he entered the bedroom, 'Oh yes, there is a God.'

He placed the teacup and saucer on the nightstand. While Helen tried to get herself sorted. Bryn took the tray to Thomas and Rachel, he tapped on their door. 'Are you decent? I have some tea.'

Thomas answered, 'Yes dad, come in.'

Bryn placed the tray on the side, 'I have not poured it.' Thomas could see the cosy on the teapot, 'There's a cup there for Margret. It's pouring with rain outside, the forecast said it will be dry later.'

'Cheers, Dad.'

Bryn made his way back to Helen: She pulled the duvet so he could get back into bed, Bryn getting back into bed 'Charlyyk looked like a walking zombie.'

'London can be quite tiring for non-city folk.' Helen had just spoken, when the bedroom door opened and Charlyyk's head appeared. 'Can I?'

Helen and Bryn opened their arms. Charlyyk soon had nestled in between them.

Helen would have given anything to have been allowed this, when she had been a little girl, now she wished she could have been a real mother and given birth, to her own little girl, then looking at Charlyyk. Helen thoughts? *'You will do'* and gave Charlyyk a big hug.

Charlyyk returned the hug, 'Helen, when can I call you mum?'

This unexpected revelation from Charlyyk, brought tears welling up in Helens eyes. For a moment Helen found it hard to answer. 'Whenever sweetheart, when you think, I've deserved it.' Helen's bottom lip wavered, a single tear trickled down her cheek, she pulled Charlyyk towards her and hugged her. Now the tears were flowing. Those thoughts of wanting to be a mum, then Charlyyk wanting her as a mum, was a little nudge in the right direction, she had been wanting this to happen. It sealed the affection with them, this was to Helen the making of a family.

Bryn grabbed some tissues and joined in with the bonding, wiping Helen's eyes, then kissing them both. Charlyyk looked at them, 'I've got the best Mum and Dad in the world.'

Breakfast was a lazy unhurried affair, much talk of London over many cups of tea. They shared photos of themselves in the shops, the restaurant and on the train. After Helen and Charlyyk cleared away, they moved to the lounge.

At eleven, Janet and James arrived. They behaved like an old married couple. Loving but controlled. After hearing of the exploits in London. Janet tickled Charlyyk 'You did that without me, how dare you?'

Rachel showed Janet, some video of the trip, she had not shown the others. Where Charlyyk just kept turning around and around amazed at the colourful illuminations. The look of wonderment on her face was a treat to watch. 'Rachel this is fantastic' Janet, then exclaimed to James, 'Work hun, keep yourself amused.' The girls, trooped off to Bryn's study.

Janet soon had downloaded the video and the photos. With the help of a voice recorder, she took the statements on how the shopping exhibition had gone. She gave Charlyyk little nudges, their friendship blossoming, 'Are you coming to the party at the Farm on Christmas day Charlyyk.'

'Will there be a lot of people there Janet?'

Janet thought for a moment, 'About the same as you have at your year in school. Then there would probably be some of your school friends there, of course I will be there.'

'That's true, James as well.'

When they returned back to the lounge, Janet said. 'Bryn a man's mag, wants me to do an article on you. Could that present a problem for you?'

Helen's head, shoot up, 'It could, I will get onto it tomorrow.'

Janet collected up her possessions, including James, then with kisses all-round they left.

Margret was looking at Helen with a bemused look. Rachel saw the look on her mother, 'Is there a problem mum?'

Margret hesitates. 'Why would Helen, sort that for Bryn?'

Helen was quick to respond. 'I met Bryn, through my capacity as the intelligence officer in charge of Charlyyk's protection. Although I have resigned from that position, my successor has not yet taken over, so I'm still technically in charge?'

'But everyone knows who Bryn is?'

Thomas sat next to his Mother-in-law, 'You asked me once, why I did not talk about my father very much. The reasons are that dad's military commitments, prevents him, from talking about his involvement in the operations he has served on.'

Margret still looked puzzled. 'But Bryn, doesn't look that type of person?'

'My father has served many years in the military. He did some very dangerous things that were connected to our homeland security.' Thomas went on to explain. 'Those operations need to be kept secret. Not to be known to the whole wide World. So, any publications, are needed to be cleared first by those in a higher position.'

When they were at Carpenters Cottage for dinner. Margret asked Gwen about her brother. Gwen showed her the family photo album. 'Margret this is my good album, all the pictures in this one is to make me feel good. It has Bryn and Kits wedding, the baby photos, the children growing up, their wedding photos, these make me happy.'

Then she went to the sideboard, and collected a black covered album, 'This is my sad album.' It contained pictures of Bryn's battle injuries, and his condition when he returned from the abduction. 'During the many trips he did, I sat here shaking in fear, of how he would return, or if he would return. I tried to give strength to Kit and the Children, all the time fearing the worst. I feel for all the service families when their loved ones, march off to war... I really do because I know what they are going through.'

Harold took the album from Margret, 'Bryn has retired from that life so we won't need to get this out anymore, we can now relax and enjoy life.'

Margret looked at Gwen's anguished face, with all the pent-up emotions, that were still flowing through her. She was still living those moments, the trembling around her shoulders, trying hard to control those feelings, that the black album provoked. Margret could understand why Harold did not want Gwen to open it again.

Bryn, Helen and Thomas were in the kitchen, talking with Michel with Charlyyk on his knee. She loved the way they all talked about so many things, telling stories that had happened to each other, each with their own take on it. They laughed at each other, on the little silly mistake, without getting angry, or sulking, as she had seen students at school do.

Her thoughts. *'She must observe those around her. How was she going to survive living amongst them, unless getting to know their ways?'* Yet what fun they were, all so different from one another, yet their vulnerabilities were the same. The wanting or not wanting, being big or small, pretty or ugly, rich or poor, good or bad; when being on their own, they can pretend to be whatever they want to be.

Charlyyk then started to look at herself. *'Can't hide from who I am, even if I wear makeup, to try and hide from the world, I'm different, and it is so obvious... must just make the best out of it as I can.'*

She realised Michel was talking to her. 'Charlyyk, I'm going to turn you into a guinea pig. I'm setting up a program of diets, so we know what is right for you. Auntie Gwen feels the stodgy food you've been eating, may be bad for your long-term health. So, I'm asking the family, to list your favourite foods, and in the order that you eat them. Then I will look at their nutritional benefits, as we see them, then try and balance them up, to suit your taste. This will mean more blood test to assimilate how the diets are working.'

'Not right on Christmas, please! That's when the nice food is put on show.'

Thomas could not help, laughing out loud.

'It's OK for you Thomas.' Charlyyk retorted. 'You will be able to eat all the goodies while I can only stand there in envy.'

'Sorry for laughing, but what an image! You standing there, looking at the food, with your little purple tongue licking your lips, with saliva running down your chin...'

Charlyyk's body went stiff, 'Go on rub it in.'

Michel cuddles her. 'I love you too much to do that to you, Charlyyk.'

'So, when?'

'Mid-January, let's get Christmas over and then sort out a routine to suit you.'

She liked what she ate, did not like the idea of changing, but Michel always looked after her, he would not suggest something, unless it meant her best welfare was at stake, 'Thank you, Michel.'

Helen beckoned. 'Come, let's go to the table.' Sitting at the table in between Gwen and Helen. A large dish of roast potatoes, cooked in duck's fat with sprigs of Rosemary, sprinkled with sea salt, sat majestically, right in front of her. Her little purple tongue, licked her lip, Helen whispered in her ear. 'You've got to mid-January, so enjoy.'

Charlyyk looked up at Helen, 'I have, haven't I?' Her shoulders scrunched up, her fist clenched, and the wickedest look on her face appeared, and the voice in her head said, *'You bet I will.'*

Chapter 28

Winchester

On Monday morning, Charlyyk was feeling impatient. 'Come on Thomas. You are losing me shopping time.'

Charlyyk was bound for Winchester. Bryn had promised Thomas, that's where they would do their Christmas Shopping. As a young boy Thomas loved the atmosphere, of the antiquated Cathedral City, especially at Christmas time, when it holds it German-style Christmas Market. Thomas liked to sit in the café opposite the Cathedral and imagine the Gentleman in their tricorne hats, the ladies in their crinoline dresses, that walked those same cobbled streets in bygone days. Some of those current shops dated from that era, which added to the nostalgia of the world-famous Hampshire city.

Bryn gave Helen a nice cuddle, caressing her face with his hands as they were waiting for Thomas by the car. Thomas no doubt was being given his instructions, or other things, as Bryn thought, seeing the red face on Thomas. Charlyyk was sniffing him and giving him a knowing look, this made Thomas feel even more awkward. Charlyyk look of disappointment, told Bryn, it was nothing.

Charlyyk had set her budget on presents, if she was diligent, she might be able to buy a new dress for the party. With this thought in her head, she was not keen on Thomas keeping her waiting.

Finally, Winchester looms up in front of them. She had not expected the enormous effect its presence would have on her. She knew it was a religious building, had not expect it to be gigantic, compared to the little church in the village. Once again, her eyes could not take it all in, as to what she was seeing.

The Tower rose to a height of over forty-five metres, the building has the greatest overall length of all Gothic Cathedrals. Charlyyk had googled for the details, but seeing, took some believing.

Bryn parked the car and as they walked to the shops. 'Well, Charlyyk, what do you say about this then?'

She just kept looking, around and around, the decoration, the shop windows, with their displays, then she saw it, then being drawn to it as a magnet to metal, it was a girl to dress. Charlyyk was looking into that shop window display like a moth to lamplight.

Bryn took her hand, 'Come, let's walk around, and make some notes. Then we will eat lunch to plan, how to spend the afternoon.

Helen had been in touch with Toby, he was soon in contact with Thames House, and the Ministry of Defence departmental Offices. Toby was to relay to them, that there was a possible publication being planned on Bryn's life-story. 'Helen, the Ministry for Security had been expecting, that this could lead to questions being asked of him. Especially since Bryn had introduced Charlyyk to the world. They have had many meetings to sort out what could be exposed, they will inform you.'

Margret and Rachel went off to the town together leaving Helen on her own. At one, Gwen and Harold arrived, they wanted Helen's advice on their choice of present for Margret, 'We were not quite sure, she can run hot or cold at any time?'

Helen agreed with them, 'Sometimes, I do believe she has a dislike of men, maybe, she still hasn't got over her husband's infidelity, or just won't?'

They made cheese on toast with some baked beans, and a large mug of tea, and sat at the kitchen table, talking.

At Thomas's favourite café, they ordered a light meal. Charlyyk eating a baguette with a creamy Brie cheese, salad and Cranberry sauce.

She had made her list, and the order to buy them in, And if everything goes to plan, that should leave her standing outside the shop with money in her purse to fulfil her dreams. But what was making her more pleased? Hardly anyone had taken much notice of her. The waitress in the café, had said, 'Yes madam, what can I get you today?' That was when she came to their table taking the order down...then to placing her plate, in front of her, saying, 'And the baguette is for Charlyyk.' It was that simple, as though she had known Charlyyk all of her life.

When they were ready to leave, Bryn indicated he wanted to go in one direction. Thomas and Charlyyk in the opposite direction. 'See you both at WH Smiths.' Bryn remarked. They went in their different directions, Charlyyk arm in arm with Thomas, she was in heaven, she had never felt so in control of herself.

After they had finished shopping for presents, she was stood outside the Boutique. 'Well, are you, or are you not?' Thomas inquired.

'Thomas! This is something you have to savour...you must not rush it...

you must realise, this is the very first time, I have bought a dress of my very own. This moment being so special, and you are here sharing it with me.' As Charlyyk looked, admiring dress, from outside of the shop.

The door opened, one of the shop assistants was standing there. 'You will have to try it on, we have fitting rooms.'

Charlyyk bounded into the shop, was soon being given the full treatment. Two girls fussed around her, showing her many dresses, they had in her size. She felt dizzy for choice, kept going back to the original dress in the window. The girls pampered and fussed, to make sure she was happy. Even the shop owner getting needle and cotton to make a slight adjustment to the dress, so that it would fit her slight frame. Charlyyk spun around. For in her head, she was Elle in frozen. When the girls ask if she was happy, all she could do...was nod her head, for she was speechless.

Thomas took a video of the whole thing and was showing Rachel, while it was happening. This was what Rachel had told him to do that morning, 'Oh yes' he needed buttering up to comply, of course, but to Rachel, what man didn't?

Bryn had tired of waiting at WH Smith's. He went in search of them. It wasn't hard to find them; he remembered the look on her face when they first arrived. When he walked into the shop, Charlyyk still had the dress on. She swirled around in it, showing it off. It had a light green, blue and pink large flower print, with a tight bodice, three quarter length sleeves and knee-length full skirt. Bryn nodded his approval. The two girls went with Charlyyk back to the fitting room to change. Bryn could hear the laughter coming from them.

One of the girls came back with the dress to be wrapped. When Charlyyk appeared. She again, had grown tall in stature, another big step taken. The feeling of being somewhat independent, and becoming her own woman, just has her dad had said she would.

Bryn did not expect the amount of love in the kiss she gave him, though he sure appreciated it. How proud she looked leaving the shop carrying her prized purchase. How proud did he feel, seeing how she was handling her new life, he was fully aware, he was still going to need Helen's help and guidance, with Charlyyk all the same?

At Oakleaves, Margret and Rachel had returned, and Rachel could not wait to show Helen and Gwen the video that Thomas had sent her. Gwen wanted to see it again because her phone did not receive videos, 'If I changed my phone could you send it to me?'

Rachel gave Gwen a big hug, 'Course I will.'

Helen loved it, 'Just look at her face! If she tried to smile anymore, her face would simply explode.'

Harold melted, to see this girl growing into a woman. A little waif of a thing, who two years ago, did not know where she was, that struggled to communicate. Now she was turning people heads, turning into a woman. The emotions inside him took over. He found he had to sit down.

Gwen sat down beside him, 'Can you believe this is happening?' He said to her.

Gwen took hold of his hand. 'It was going to happen one day.' Her hands cradled his face. 'She was bound to grow up. They never stay the same. Think of all the student we have nurtured over the years. They have grown, now some of them, have children of their own.'

Helen watched these two helping each other to grasp, the reality of life. Charlyyk was not simply another student. It was like bringing a little ball of fluff home, be it a puppy or a kitten, and living with it constantly. No matter how it looked or what size it becomes. It grows up to be a big part of you. Charlyyk is no pet and to many would appear to be one. But Helen knew to Harold and Gwen she was so much more.

Suddenly the door opened and Charlyyk storms into the cottage. All heads turn towards her. Who would she run to first? She didn't run. She put the package on the table, dove inside of it, and gently took out the dress from the bag. Slipping her coat off, she undoes the button on her dress she was wearing and dropped it to the floor.

Gwen was so startled, 'Charlyyk! A lady does not disrobe in front of everyone.'

Charlyyk totally ignored Gwen. Her new dress, was soon hanging on her.

Rachel, was quickly by her side, 'It's lovely Charlyyk, the gentle pink, blue and green, and the style, really suits you, it fits your complexion beautifully.'

'Thank you, Rachel I fell in love the moment I saw it.'

Charlyyk looked at Helen. Helen raised her arms, Charlyyk rushed into them. Helen beamed with pride. Charlyyk buried her head into Helen's breast. For a few moments, they stood there cuddling each other, 'Do you like it, mum?'

Helen could not hold back the tears, all Helen could do was to kiss her on top of her head, 'I love it sweetheart, and you too.'

Gwen was not envious but pleased. She had been hoping that Charlyyk and Helen, would bond as mother and daughter. And waited for them to ease the emotions down. When she thought, the time was right, she was just going to say something.

Charlyyk turned towards her, 'Auntie Gwen.' No further words were needed. The love between them just oozed from them both. Charlyyk sat on Gwen's lap, Harold leaned over and joined in the embrace.

Margret just stood there she was feeling out of the equation. Helen sidled up to her and placing her arm on hers. 'Give a little time. You have only been here a couple of days. Rachel has known Charlyyk for some time. I was the outsider once. You will see...she will pull you in, but only if you want her too? Once you show her, that you do, she will do the rest.

***

After the morning run and breakfast. Charlyyk locked herself away in her room. After an hour, she made a phone call. Twenty minutes later, Sarah was there with a large carrier bag. She walked straight in, 'Hi everyone, the cavalry is here.' She disappeared to Charlyyk's room. Within the hour the music was loud, and the singing was melodious...more like meltdown, they were enjoying themselves. Everyone was relieved when Sarah went home. Across Charlyyk's bedroom was the most decorative parcels, you could imagine.

Rachel could not help, but stick her head through Charlyyk's bedroom door, 'Wow Charlyyk that was not the cavalry...that was a fairy godmother.'

Charlyyk could not hide from the reality that parcel wrapping was not her thing. 'I tried but it did not happen, so I phoned Sarah, I showed her my attempts on the phone, and she said, 'Hold on tiger, I'll be there in a tick.' She is so... so, vibrant.'

Rachel smiled, 'And loud.' Rachel then sat on the bed, 'Have you anything to do this afternoon?'

'Yes, Helen is taking me to Sandra's. We have brought them a hamper. Why don't you come?'

When they arrived at Sandra's, the Fortnum & Mason Hamper that Helen and Charlyyk had brought was most welcomed. 'We were going to buy you some flowers,' said Helen. 'But we thought that Christmas was for giving...spreading good cheer. Each of you will find something in the hamper to brighten your Christmas.'

Sandra's mother looked a little wistful, 'I cannot afford to buy you anything in return Helen.'

It was Charlyyk who spoke next, 'But you already have, you have given the trust of your friendship, and that's worth more than money can buy. So, please accept with our thanks, our small show of friendship, not charity.'

Sandra could not help but give Charlyyk a hug. 'We as a family accept, dad getting well, would be our greatest present ever. This is a pleasant surprise that was not expected, but most appreciated. Even dad will find something to like from that Aladdin's box. Thank you, thank you very much.'

Helen giving them hugs and wishing them a Merry Christmas,' After you get on your feet, we must have a get-together and celebrate your husband recovery.

When the three returned to Oakleaves, the cottage was lovely and warm. A flickering log fire was burning in the grate. Gwen and Margret were looking at some of Thomas's old sketches. he had done as a lad, depicting the family as he and his sister had grown. With the different styles of clothes, the best indication of change, was the hairstyles. A rough drawing of Bryn after a tour in an African Jungle conflict, his hair long, Margret replied, 'All he needed was a bandana tied around his forehead, he would have made a fine Rambo.'

Rachel seeing how Thomas honed his early drawing skills, was soon asking questions. Thomas could not keep out of the debate that was directed at him. 'Man, before he could talk, used drawings to teach his children what to hunt. With the more you draw, the better you can express yourself. Because charcoal the earliest writing tool rubbed off easily, man then used water and even egg white, mixed with the charcoal, to make it more permanent. That was discovered in some of the early cave drawings...the start of art as we know it.'

Charlyyk had sat between Bryn and Harold, but one of her ears, had turned towards Gwen, the others were directed at Thomas, Harold gave her a gentle nudge, 'You are earwigging Charlyyk!'

Charlyyk's mouth dropped, 'Who me?'

Harold gave Charlyyk a stern look, 'Yes you, and it's rude.'

Her head bent down, but her eyes looked up, 'How am I to learn if I don't keep my eyes and ears open?'

Harold's look, still stern, 'Then join them in the discussion, that way you are not being rude.'

Helen brandished the local paper, 'Anyone interested in going to midnight mass at the cathedral?'

Margret's head shot up, 'That sound good Helen, I would love to go.' Gwen and Rachel nodded in occurrence. Margret turned and look at Charlyyk, 'How about you Charlyyk? Would you come and give me moral support?'

Charlyyk looked concerned, 'Why Margret! Is it a bigger god that lurks there?'

Gwen thoughts that's how Charlyyk would see it. *'Small church little god, big church, big God, if the little god concerned her, what would a big God do to her.'* Gwen smiling, 'No Charlyyk same God, more singing though.'

Harold touched Charlyyk's hand, 'Give Margret a chance she wants to make friends, but don't know how.'

Bryn had been silent but was listening to what was being said, he touched Charlyyk's hand, 'You don't have to, but it would be a nice gesture.'

His quiet, controlled voice and gentle manner soften Charlyyk, 'OK, I will go with you, Margret.'

Margret smiled softly towards her. 'Would you wear your new dress? You looked so lovely in it earlier'

A smile shot across Charlyyk's face, upon the realisation, she had a reason to wear her new dress. 'Margret, that gives me an excellent reason why I should go.'

Gwen, Helen and Rachel start to prepare dinner. Charlyyk could not resist the temptation to join them. For she loved the banter, that the women talked about, when they were cooking. Margret had noticed how Charlyyk joined in with all the cores, always willing, the effort she gave was full on; she never held back.

Margret remained in the lounge with the men. She asked more questions about Charlyyk. Harold explained the rudiments of their first encounters and the effort to adapt to human ways. 'It was never going to be easy, Margret. That girl gave us 100% effort; we could only try and return it. The nightmares she had, took some getting over. We must remember she was just a slip of a girl, now we see her growing into a lady it makes us want to cry...that how proud we are of her.'

Bryn sat in a semi-prone position that made him comfortable. 'What happened on that planet Margret, frightened me. What it did to her, I don't think anyone could fathom. Without her help?... I would have surely died that night, with the loss of blood, and the freezing cold. I love that girl so much. She is as much to me, as Catherine and Thomas are.'

Margret now understood Charlyyk's position in the family circle. She remembered Thomas when he returned back to New York, saying, 'That girl is Dad's saviour,' Made her realise, why they all felt so strongly about her.

Harold smiling, 'Wait until you hear her singing. That is something else.'

Margret thought back to the morning, when Sarah was there, 'Was that Charlyyk this morning?'

Bryn laughed, 'Oh, yes, did you like it, Margret?'

Margret's hand went to her mouth.

Harold nudged her, 'You will be alright tonight. She will be more worried about Gwen's God appearing, then trying to sing.'

Margret let out a loud laugh. She imagined Charlyyk peering around the Cathedral looking for anything resembling a god.

When dinner was ready. Margret sat opposite Charlyyk, 'How was your friend today Charlyyk?'

Charlyyk gave Margret, her serious look. 'Margret, we feel for Sandra at this time with their concerns of her father. Sandra had said, that although her father's improvement was encouraging, it didn't mean he was out of the woods.'

Rachel explained to her mother about the hamper. 'It was a lovely gesture for the whole family, each one could find something to enjoy.'

'I wanted to buy some flowers. Helen suggested the hamper, when we were on the train going to London. So, when we went to Fortnum & Mason's for mid-afternoon tea, we selected what would be in it, had delivered here for today.'

Helen smiled, nodded her approval, 'I advised Charlyyk, to give them something that was useful and would cheer them all up. After many suggestions, this proved the best idea. The input Charlyyk put into it, led to the final result.'

Gwen looked towards Charlyyk, and winked at her, 'I would have loved to have gone with you, but I hate London. The pollution in the air, the constant noise it is not for me.'

The ride to Winchester took two cars. They managed to find parking places in Colebrook Street, then joined the congregation in the cathedral.

Charlyyk had not prepared herself for the interior of the massive structure. It looked huge from the outside when she went Christmas shopping, inside it seemed enormous. She was still uncertain what was going to happen. Using Bryn and Helen as shields, she felt protected. As she sat down pushing herself closer to Bryn, then pulling Helen closer to her, she was ready for anything to happen.

The service started with singing. It was so different than the church in the village. The service flowed at a gentle pace. Charlyyk settled into the relaxed rhythm. She did not look worried at what could happen, found herself more interested in the Cathedral itself. Her thoughts started to drift. The holes in the ground she once lived in, her thoughts then would be what would she be able to find to eat, in the next light period. What could be waiting for her when she left the tunnel. A cold shiver converged over her, taking a tight grip on Bryn's arm, she buried her head into him.

Helen seeing her struggling, put her arm around her. 'We are here sweetheart. You are not alone,' When the service was over, Charlyyk had settled down, was more herself.

As they were leaving their seats an elderly couple, came to them, The woman held out her hand to Charlyyk. 'May we wish you a Merry Christmas? It gives us so much pleasure to see you have joined us tonight, it must be very bizarre for you. The fact you have made such a big effort to be here warms our hearts. May our God look over you, and protect you from harm.'

Charlyyk taking the woman's hand, 'Thank you for your kind words, let my new family and I, return your compliments. We wish you and your family a very Merry Christmas.'

Sandra and Julia had emphasised the importance of returning compliments, 'Being in the spotlight, to say the wrong replies, leads to so many problems for famous celeb's, as the Press and Twitters love to make more of it, than it usually deserves.'

A small group of worshippers had lingered outside of the cathedral just to get an extra glimpse of Charlyyk. She acknowledges them, pausing just enough to allow them, to take photos of her.

Margret walking with Gwen, 'Charlyyk certainly know how to handle the situation.'

'We did not teach her how to behave, because we did not know, what was to be required. It seems she has grown into it.'

They collected the cars, Margret went in Gwen's car, continued asking Gwen, about Charlyyk, 'How did she adapt to school life?'

'Like a duck to water.'

Harold said with a smug look, 'She had a two-years education from us. It was like moving on to the next year for her.'

Margret could see that the gradual procession, had allowed Charlyyk to adjust regularly, 'You make it sound that it was like a walk in the park. Hearing the whole story, I can only marvel what you have all achieved with her.'

Gwen quickly responded, 'We were only allowed to achieve what we did because Charlyyk wanted that for herself.'

Harold chirped, 'You can lead a horse to water, but you can't make it drink.'

Chapter 29

Christmas Day

Bryn and Charlyyk were the only ones that had ventured out that morning. It was dark. Only the gradual rise of red in the distant shy, looming up in the east indicated it was morning. Side by side they strode, as they reached the top of Bishops Lane, did they pause to looked over the surrounding countryside, the early morning sun had risen just enough, anointed the top of the trees with its golden crown of glory.

Charlyyk held her head up high, her eyes closed, feeling the first glow of the sun on her face, it was not hot, just warm. It felt so lovely. Janet had asked Bryn to take as many pictures as he could, whenever opportunities arose. Bryn had put the camera into burst mode, just clicked away. The backdrop of the trees, some still had the remnants of autumn, and with the drifting wisp of mist between them made it look magical.

The women getting breakfast were singing Christmas carols when Bryn and Charlyyk returned back to the cottage, with that special Christmas morning feel, radiated amongst them. Helen grabbing Charlyyk and smothered her with kisses. 'Our very first Christmas Charlyyk, Merry Christmas.'

Charlyyk's response. 'With many more to come.'

Rachel, Thomas and Margret quick to join in with the well-wishing. Bryn also receiving many kisses. After a quick shower, and getting dressed, They were at breakfast. Margret had made waffles smothered with maple syrup. Charlyyk could not get enough of them. Helen had to put a stop to her. 'You will not have room for Christmas dinner.'

After clearing the table, Helen and Bryn handed out their present to Charlyyk. The little parcel lovingly wrapped, for a moment Charlyyk did not want to harm it. She gently used her long fingers to unpick it, removing each piece so carefully to reveal a small leather-bound case. She gently opened it, a glistening gold wristwatch, sparkled within. Helen had especially had it made to fit Charlyyk wrist. Bryn helped her to put it on, the kisses she smothered them in told them she loved it. She shot off to collect her presents to give them all.

When Helen and Bryn opened theirs from Charlyyk, it was a silver picture frame, embossed with flowers, 'It's for your wedding photo.' The look of pleasure on her face, told them how she felt about them getting married.

Rachel gave Charlyyk, her and Thomas's present. The beautiful wrapping and ribbons, excited Charlyyk. She did not know where to start to unwrap it. Just kept looking up at them eagerly. Then finally with a flourish she pulled the ribbon, gently lifting the wrapping paper not to tear it, then lifting the lid of the box. The look on her face, as her finger felt the soft silk lingerie, let it slide through her fingers, then held it gently to her face. Charlyyk reached out to Rachel collecting her in towards her, thanking her with hugs and kisses, then smothering Thomas equally.

Margret waited till she had settled before she gave Charlyyk, her present. Again delicately wrapped, when opened, it revealed a rose-pink leather-bound diary with a clasp that could be locked. Down the spine a pen nestled, ready to be used at any time. Charlyyk held it in her hands, gently. 'Thank you, Margret, it's so me, I love it.' Then carefully placing her arms around Margret's neck, kissed her sweetly.

Margret responded, by putting her arms around Charlyyk's waist, 'My dear child, getting to know you... the real you. Is becoming a pleasure, you are many surprises all wrapped up in one big beautiful person, Merry Christmas.'

After the giving of presents, Helen set up the computer for the video link to Auckland.

The Leany family were ready. Little Amy waving the doll that Charlyyk had sent her for Christmas. Lots of laughing and gaiety was being shown all around. Then Catherine held up a present. 'Dad, can you give this to my sister?' Bryn leant forward, and a well-rehearsed, sleight of hand, it looked as though he had pulled it out of the screen. The present was in his hands, even Margret was taken in with the trick, Bryn turned and offered it to Charlyyk who's mouth was gaping.

Catherine and Brent watching intently to her reaction's, as Charlyyk opened it, a new set of silk bed sheets and pillow cases were inside. 'Sweet Christmas dreams, little sister.' As Catherine and Brent blew her kisses. Charlyyk returned the blown kisses. The feel of silk to Charlyyk was her treasured luxury. She could not explain why it just felt right to her.

The drive to Parsons Farm for dinner did not take long, Harold and Gwen greet them alongside Janet and James. Inside the old timbered barn, had two long rows of tables decked out with Christmas fare. A giant Christmas tree stood proudly at one side of the entrance. Decorations adorned the interior.

Edward and Jane Parsons were overseeing the arrangements. The atmosphere was chaotic as many of the farm employees and their families were enjoying the get-together. A group of musicians were tuning their instrument, catering staff were setting out the tables. Some of the farm workers children that attended Charlyyk's school, were soon surrounding her, wishing her Merry Christmas.

Janet and James organises games for the younger ones, soon had Thomas and Rachel roped in helping, as more of the employees arrived. Margret looked on with amazement, at such an enormous undertaking the Parsons had taken on. Bryn and Helen lending a hand with the procedures. Harold and Gwen were talking to the older children, and some of their parents. Comfortable chairs were laid on for some of the more elderly people. A form of order was gradually being reached, considering how many were there.

The sound of sleigh bells from outside could be heard. The children flocked to the barn's entrance to welcome Father Christmas. A horse-drawn carriage appeared. A sizeable jolly man with an authentic long white curly beard, with a thick guttural. 'Ho, Ho, Ho, had the children running around him in glee. He gave out presents all around, spent much time with the younger children.

By the time he left, they were starting to sit down for the meal. Centre tables had been set up, where the choice of meats was placed there for carving. Vegetarians also catered for. Barrels of real ale, and various red and white wines were situated around the barn for easy access. After a big thank you from the Parsons Family, the feasting began.

An area was cleared after dinner, and entertainment was laid on. Buffet tables were set out, later barn dancing was the order of the evening. By ten that night, Bryn had an exhausted Charlyyk cuddled up on his lap. Having joined in with everything, with the younger children following her around as if she were the Pied Piper.

Janet thought this was a good time to ask Charlyyk her recollection on previous Christmases. 'At my first Christmas, we had just finished being in quarantine. There was a living Christmas tree from a previous year that Thomas had planted in the garden. Bryn decorated it while Gwen and Harold decked out the lounge. There were no presents but the games we played were silly but much fun.

When the next year came around, I had a more robust idea what Christmas was about, and was instrumental in contributing much towards it, giving it all my enthusiasm. I had learned the meaning, of being a Party Girl.'

Janet was careful what question she asked, knowing Charlyyk's view about religion. 'So, you know what Christmas represents?'

'The followers of Jesus Christ, celebrating his birth.' Charlyyk to was being careful, the times she had upset Gwen were still vivid in her mind. 'The banqueting was more to do about the approach of winter and the food that would soon degrade needed to be consumed and not wasted.

The morning run on Boxing Day was meant to clear previous day's excesses from their bodies, also the cobwebs from their minds. Their pace was a steady jog, allowing them the chance to talk more directly.

Thomas, Rachel and Margret, were heading for the Forest of Dean, to catch up on an old college chum of Thomas's. He had promised to visit next time he was in England. They would return back on Wednesday.

A phone call from Helen's father, gave Helen a chance to set a date to see her parents over the Christmas period. 'Yes, we would love to see you on Monday. It will be just us three. Love, you all. See you Monday. Bye.'

Charlyyk at the same time was speaking to Sandra, who informed her that Julia will spend the day with her. She loved the hamper idea, saying what a great gift it was. Her father had perked up, and the doctor was pleased with his progress. Her mother had managed to relax, and she was looking a lot better for it. This made Charlyyk happy and could not wait to tell Helen the excellent news.

Helen and Charlyyk spent most of the day together. Nothing special they talked, looked at photos, and just ambled through the day. They loved being together, and talking about girly things. For Charlyyk was not the only one adjusting to a new way of life, so was Helen.

Bryn had spent the day catching up with paperwork, going through some of the issues that Janet touched on those that needed answers. The bottle of single malt whisky, helped him to get into the right mood for it.

***

Three of them enjoyed a brisk jog on Saturday morning. The chit chat between them had made the run seem quicker than usual. Over breakfast, a shopping trip was discussed, and Bryn suggested Southampton, for a change of scenery. Any new destination would suit Charlyyk, having previously said to Helen, that on her planet they kept close to where they knew was safe, so she only got to know about her world, was in the confines to where they lived.

Now with a purse full of Christmas gift vouchers, then with money people had given her, was keen for some retail therapy. One of the girls she had met at the Christmas dinner had shown her the skinny jeans that she had been given for Christmas. Now they were on top of her list of must-buys.

The drive to Southampton was on congested roads. Many other people had the same intentions as themselves. Finding a parking place was just as frustrating. Charlyyk found herself being jostled for the first time, did not find it pleasant. Helen was becoming more, and more concerned. Bryn agreed to call it a day, to return home. Helen still needed a couple of things, they called into a Tesco supermarket on the way to pick up some essentials.

In the same retail shopping centre, Charlyyk saw the store that the girl had mentioned, to where the jeans could be purchased. She dragged Helen into the store. She was determined to salvage at least something from that day. Helen and Bryn sat back and let Charlyyk fend for herself. She left the store a happy girl, with many items of clothing she had purchased for herself.

Home in her room at Oakleaves, she immediately tried the garments on. She matched them with her other clothes, explaining to Helen, the reasoning behind each purchase. Most reasons had to do with how clothes would change her appearance and lift her moods. 'I sometimes feel down on myself, needing to lift myself up... it is the way I query why I'm here, and not another member of the group. Sometimes the guilt of it really makes me sad.'

Helen placed her arm around her, 'Sweetheart, if you had not come here, you would have died on that terrible planet.'

Charlyyk wrapped her arms around Helen and squeezed her tight.

'And I would not have met you and your dad, now, would I?'

Charlyyk looking up into Helen's face. The wistful look, made Helen kiss her, 'both of us have to thank each other for the position we now find ourselves in.'

Charlyyk replied. 'For, without one, there would be no other.'

Helen gave her a little extra hug, 'Without your dad, where would we both be?'

Charlyyk's morale had lifted, she started to be more assertive. 'Not here definitely. I still wake up in the night, worried that it is all a dream. I have to tell myself, that if I were not living through it, I would not have known about this sort of life existed, so it cannot be a dream. Though it still feels too good to be true.'

Helen nodded. 'So, what does that make us?'

Charlyyk's eyes sparkled, 'The lucky girls.'

Helen gave her a hug and big kiss. 'Here's to the lucky girls.' Helen taking her by the hand, 'How about a takeaway?'

'You bet...Michel hasn't set my new diet as yet, so I'm free to indulge in any fancy I like.'

Bryn found them discussing the menu, that was laid out in front of them, peering over their shoulders. 'Don't forget my spring rolls and dumplings. What were you plotting in your room?' Digging his finger into Charlyyk's ribs, with a squeal she turned around wrapping her arms around his neck.

'How we were going to get you to pay for the meal dad.'

Bryn gave her another dig, 'So you are a little gold digger!'

Kissing him. 'You bet.'

***

Sunday at Carpenters Cottage, Charlyyk was explaining to Gwen the events of Saturday, 'It was so crowded I was being pushed around like a ragdoll. But it had a plus to it...we stopped at a retail centre. The store that Charlotte's jeans had come from, was there.'

Gwen had admired what Charlyyk was wearing. The pair of skinny grey jeans, black pointed toe, ankle boots with three-inch-high heels. A white long-sleeved shirt blouse, with a black cashmere, deep V-neck jumper three quarter sleeves. Her rose gold colour hair matching her new gold wristwatch, just showing under the cuff of her blouse. The outfit was simple but stylish. Helen sitting there as proud as punch. She was admiring the way Charlyyk was associating with Gwen. The little girl was definitely growing up.

Michel teased Charlyyk during the dinner. He had finalised the diet sheets for her, though not as yet shown her... kept hinting...but not confirming. 'You are rotten, don't torment me. Otherwise, I will ignore you.'

After dinner Harold prompted Gwen. 'Shall we?'

Gwen rose from where she was sitting and walking to the sideboard, collected an ornament case. Sitting down with Charlyyk. She opened the case. 'This neckless belonged to my grandmother.' As Gwen allowed the neckless to fall between her fingers, a beautiful gold pendant on a square chain, dangled, it sparkled as the lights caught it. 'It is made from Welsh gold...as our Queen's wedding ring is made from. Taken from Clogau, St David's mine.' The pennant oval in shape, depicting, the mother and child.

Charlyyk reached for it, and let it dangle between her fingers. 'It's lovely Auntie Gwen.'

Gwen placed it around Charlyyk neck. 'I spoke with Catherine, she wanted you to share our family history. Both you and Helen.' Then Gwen's hand delved back into the case, removed a little leather pouch, opening it she took out a wide plain gold wedding ring, this was also my grandmothers, passing it to Helen.

The ring slipped onto her finger. Helen showed Bryn how it looked. 'It's fit's you well, it looks very elegant. Are you sure, Gwen?'

Gwen retrieved one more item...an old tattered photo. 'This was my granny, Gwyneth on her wedding day. Who I am named after' As the photo was passed around the resemblance was noticeable? The pennant could be seen hanging around the neck of the young bride, 'She was just sixteen when she married my grandfather.' The ring and the pennant belonged to Gwyneth's mother.

Gwen showed them some papers. 'These papers are the history of her family, and how she ended up being an orphan, at the age of twelve. Her ageing aunt looked after her till she died. My grandfather married her to stop her from going to the poorhouse, or the convent.' They all had a chance to read the papers, although the handwriting had faded a bit, but could still be read, 'They were together sixty-five wonderful years.'

Bryn in recollection, 'She was pretty until the day she died. Granddad dotted on her, she only had to smile at him, he would melt.'

Charlyyk looked at Bryn, with a quizzical look, 'He would melt?'

Harold laughed, 'No Charlyyk not like that, he would give into her, do as she bid him.'

Charlyyk thought for a moment. 'Yeah...Julia said, she has her father wrapped around her finger, she only has to say 'daddy' seductively, and he gives into her.' Then facing down into her lap then flashing her eyes up towards Bryn, 'Daddy...' she said.

Michel slumps back in his chair. 'Careful Bryn, she learning fast.'

Helen slipped the ring off her finger, handed it back to Gwen, 'It is a lovely gesture Gwen, I would love Bryn to slip it back on my finger when that day arrives.'

Charlyyk looked at Gwen, her eyes full of doubt.

'The pennant is for you to keep Charlyyk.'

The smile on Charlyyk face as she fingered the neckless.

Michel reached over and touched her on her shoulder, 'Now you are worth knocking off, with all that wealth on you.'

'Don't scare her Michel.' Helen chided

Charlyyk respond, 'I'm not going to wear the neckless to school.'

***

The drive to London fascinated Charlyyk. She gazed with wonder at the crowded streets. There were so many cars, then the tall buildings, let alone people. Outside Helens parent's residence, Anna was there to park their car. Edward welcomed them into the property. 'How was the drive up?'

Bryn cocked his head to one side, 'Fair till we hit London.'

Elizabeth had made a beeline to Charlyyk and Helen. 'Hello, my girls, at last.' She gave them both a hug. 'Come, let's get a drink.'

Sitting in the kitchen, Helen was surprised her mother knew where things were kept, let alone be able to boil a kettle. Anna strolled in, within a few seconds was in charge, she started up a conversation with Charlyyk. 'How was Christmas?'

Helen and her mother, left them to talk and went to the drawing room to meet up with Edward and Bryn. When Anna carried in the tea things, Charlyyk was helping her.

Over tea, Anna recounted her version of Charlyyk's visit to Winchester Cathedral for midnight mass. 'Charlyyk was concerned that, because it was a Cathedral she was afraid it might contain a bigger God.'

Edward laughed, but Elizabeth was not happy with him. 'No Ed, it was a serious worry for the poor dear, not understanding the meaning of our complicated religious fervour. She was waiting for some sort of sign, of what we were praying for. When nothing materialises from it, it must be very confusing for her.'

Edward gave a sideways glance at Charlyyk. 'Forgive my rude behaviour Charlyyk. I could see you in the Church hiding behind your father, waiting for a second coming of the Lord.' He could help but chuckle at thought.

Anna stifled a laugh. Elizabeth gave her a stern look.

Helen tried to change the conversation. 'Shall we go for a walk later?'

Anna chirped in. 'I've arranged a special lunch for today, something light, not too heavy, it will be better to have a walk after, than after something heavy.'

Charlyyk was curious the way the room was laid out. It was a mixed bag of odds and sods, none of the furniture matched, the coffee table, or whatever it was, was covered in reams of paper, in disarray. Some of the piles had paperweights on them. Anna touched her arm. 'On-going paperwork Charlyyk, the piles with paperweights, are waiting for confirmation, the ones without, are being read at this moment.' Charlyyk was amazed, 'They have read all that?' Elizabeth looking at her. 'Most of it is about points of law, mostly International. Where the government needs advising, some of it is for companies that need advice on particular parts of EU Law.'

Edward made a gesture with his hand. 'I'm looking into reforming the House of Lords, it needs change. Some want it more democratic; some want it reduced in size. What I must do, is to look at all its possibilities... So, that it meets our democratic constitutional duties, and what is best for the UK. Not like political parties, who only have set agendas, have set tendentious objectives, and forget about the chaos they cause implementing them.

Anna set the lunch. Savoury pancakes, filled with asparagus, and a light cream cheese and ham sauce, with a mixed bean salad. Bryn and Edward picked it at first but ultimately cleared their plates.

After lunch, they took a stroll around the area. The pavements were busy, not like Southampton. As people started to recognise Charlyyk, little pockets of them began to congregate to get nearer to her. Charlyyk walked between Helen's parents, with Bryn behind her, between Helen and Anna. She felt comfortable and acknowledge anyone that showed interest in her.

When Elizabeth met some old friends, she could not wait to introduce Charlyyk, as their future granddaughter. Anna commented, 'She sure is strutting the strut.' But Helen had noticed her father had grown an inch or two, he too was milking the occasion. Waving to all and sundry, no matter who they were. It really did not matter he was as proud as any grandfather with a new grandchild.

***

On Tuesday, the unexpected arrival of Toby at breakfast was greeted with suspicion. 'Hello what are you doing here,' Bryn remarked.

Toby pulling a chair up, 'I've come to see the New Year in with you. If that's OK?'

Helen poured some coffee for him, 'Breakfast?'

The broad grin flashing across his face, 'Yeah, I'm famished. Full English would be nice?'

Bryn, asked suspiciously, 'So?'

Toby could not hide behind a false smile. 'That's always been the trouble with you Bryn...you don't trust me.'

Bryn took a sip of coffee, 'No, I trust you to try any way you can, to get your own way. Why are you here?'

Helen preparing his breakfast. 'You've made up your mind, that it time to take over Toby?' He pulled a paper from his inside pocket. 'This came to me late last night.' He placed it in front of Bryn when he had finished reading it, he took it over to where Helen was cooking and changed places with her, so she too could read the note. It was a request for the Collier family to visit Russia, and China. It would coincide with Charlyyk's Summer School Holiday's.

Helen turned and looked at Toby, 'You could have shown us this at any time. Spit it out...why now?'

Toby gave her a sheepish look. 'Ok I was lonely, I thought of you.'

Bryn touched Charlyyk's hand. 'He has upset Wendy.'

Helen placed the breakfast in front of Toby. Then picked her phone up. She texts, *'What has Toby done?'*

Toby an old childhood friend of Wendy and Brian Bailey. They all originated from Manchester. He had been staying with them during his duties while protecting Charlyyk.

Helen received the reply ten minutes later, *'That freeloader! He walks in, expects to be fed, then sits there waiting for everyone to fan him. Then he goes off without a bye or leave, then drift back in as though he had never left. Bloody sponger.'*

Helen placed her phone in front of him, 'You earn good money Toby, so why?'

Charlyyk leaving the table. 'He is lazy, not lonely.'

Toby's mouth dropped. 'How can you say that?'

Charlyyk putting the dirty crockery in the dishwasher. 'When the truth smacks you in the face, how can you ignore it?' Without losing her momentum. 'You don't need a wife; you need another mother.' And as she closed the door to the dishwasher. 'Or a slave.'

Bryn could not help but nod his acceptance of what Charlyyk had said. 'Looks like you have got to sort your life out before you get thrown out of all your friends' houses.'

Toby thought for a moment. 'How did you cope with living on your own, Helen?'

Filling the kettle and putting it on the hob. 'I bought my apartment. It was not too close to anybody or anything. It had parking under, and a janitor, who looked after the flat when I was not there. An excellent restaurant just around the corner, with a great fish and chip shop around the other corner. But the pub was the real God saver. Many times, finding a nice quiet corner there with a pint of ale, pie and mash. Very fattening but a lifesaver.'

Toby reflected on what Helen had said. 'Is it still for sale?' Helen left the kitchen. When she returned, she gave him the Estate Agents Brochure. As Toby read through it. Helen pointed out some of the additions she had added. The built-in safe was a big plus. He was soon on the phone, setting up an appointment for a view.

Chapter 30

Ringing in a New Year

Thomas and his charges arrived at one-fifteen. Rachel was first to enter followed by her mother. Bryn, saying his hello's, went to help Thomas with the bags.

Helen and Charlyyk over cups of teas, with Rachel telling them how the trip went. 'Mum loved Thomas's friend Jim. She wants to show some of his paintings at the exhibition. They will compliment some of the other exhibits.'

Margret opened a portfolio case, revealing five paintings of local scenes from where Thomas's friend lived, around the Cotswolds. Charlyyk was amazed at the beautiful paintings. 'These are paintings?' She exclaimed, thinking of the attempts at paintings she had done. 'Wow!'

Margret smiled at her, 'These are the results, of many years of studying art, the same as Thomas has had to do. Through much practice, Jim has achieved this very high standard of workmanship.'

Charlyyk greeted Gwen and Harold, when they arrived at two. Charlyyk could not stop talking to Janet about London, when she arrived. As the two girls laid the table, the laughing and gossip did not stop.

While Helen, Gwen and Jane prepared the meal. Bryn, Edward and James Parsons, talked about the family bible that Janet had uncovered. Michel and Harold soon were involved in the story of the Allcott Family. Edward relaying to them that the Parsons was actually the head herdsmen to the Allcott's and not the other way around, but a John Parsons left the farm life, and became a Mercenary Soldier. On his return home, he found the farm in neglect, then promptly bought the farm from the Allcott's. that reversed their roles. But over the years, the Parsons and the Allcott's intermarried, and the last Allcott was Ned Parson's half-brother.

Michel had a response to the story. 'As you walk into the Fords farmhouse, there is a family tree hanging on the wall it was compiled by Burkes Heritage, in 1965, it goes right back to 1678, the marriage of a Ford to an Allcott.'

The conversation carried on through dinner. With Janet admitting, that she and James had researched the family on the Internet. James laughed, 'We stopped when we got to 1774. There we found an Agnes Parsons, who gave birth to seven children, never married and none of the fathers were named.

Janet took the first names of the children and the name of all the males living at that time. It was speculative but came up with some interesting results.'

Gwen could not resist saying. 'That's what a good journalist does...speculate. Hoping by turning over a few rocks a snake might appear.'

Janet smiled at her. 'Sometimes bones rattle about. With a little digging you can find a trace of flesh, when you dig some more, blood can flow. That what my first Editor told me, all you got to do, is keep digging.'

Helen chirped, 'Remember Watergate?'

Janet was quick to respond. 'Exactly. Isn't the truth worth digging for?'

They all helped to clear up. Gwen put the television on. 'BBC 1, the fireworks display at the London Eye, I don't want to miss it.'

Bryn giving Charlyyk a little hug. 'Did you text Catherine?'

Charlyyk showed him what she had texted her with, *'Happy New Year Sis, how's your resolution going,'* The reply Catherine had sent, *'Failed, I'm getting bigger'.*

Bryn opened a couple of bottles of Champagne, ready to greet in the New Year, with glasses raised, to chimes of Big Ben, the cheers and celebrations, was in full swing, the fireworks, looked spectacular. With kisses and hugs, Charlyyk was getting to like all the funny things these earth people would do, just to party, knowing she was just as guilty. Because deep down she just loved it too. It was also these pleasures that made her more aware of the two different lives she had lived.

***

At three o'clock the following afternoon. Janet returned with a few articles she had been working on. She had spoken to Bryn the night before about them. Working in his study to finish them. Bryn went through with her with the number of photos they had taken of Charlyyk. Janet was as pleased as punch about the information he had given her, with the pictures. Bryn had also shot some video footage, which she downloaded to her computer. The shopping exhibition in London and Winchester gave her much material to work with.

'The feedback I'm getting has been very encouraging. Bryn, I want to set up a trust for her. Charlyyk should get something out of all this. I've spoken to my Accountant, who will arrange the legal set up, he will be in touch with the HMIR, to make sure it's straight and above board... My Accountant recommended a percentage amount, to be agreed with by all parties. I hope you are happy with what I'm trying to achieve.'

Janet searched in her big shoulder bag and retrieved an envelope. 'This is a letter you will need to pass to your Accountant.'

Bryn looked a bit concerned, 'Janet we are not doing this to make money.'

Janet smiled, 'I did not know, where this would go, Bryn, when it all started. Now the cheques are coming in. 'Wow,' my Accountant advised me, that some should go to Charlyyk, it would offset some of the Tax I would have to pay. Then Charlyyk has something to fullback on later, a Trust, would be the best way forward for her.'

Helen knocked the door and entered with two mugs of tea, 'I thought you might like these?' Bryn was quick to involve Helen in on the conversation he was having with Janet. 'That sound a good idea, I like it, Janet.'

Janet quickly gave a breakdown of how she operates. 'I have a VA, she is disabled, but can work a computer, she works from home. Since this has taken off, she now employs two other girls like herself. The press media gets in touch with her, she sorts out what my schedules should be. All my paycheques go to my Accountant, who settles who is to get paid. All I have to do is the fun side, write about my friend Charlyyk, life could not be sweeter.'

Helen put her arm around Janet's shoulders and giving her a squeeze, 'You make it sound like a life of Riley.'

Janet laughed. 'James reckons, its sound as easy as rolling in pig shit.'

Then Janet got serious, 'Now how about your story, Bryn?'

Helen was the one to reply. 'Many operations that Bryn was involved in are still classified, and cannot be discussed. But Bryn has made some outlined information, on what he can disclose. We feel if you read through them, you might be able to form some sort of story, that would fit into the type of publication you would be writing for.'

Janet thought for a moment. 'Yes, I could then be able to aim my questions, in the right directions, that could work Bryn.'

Bryn opened his filing cabinet, and pulled out a folder 'This is it Janet, my life story, the good, the bad, and the downright ugly.'

Janet quickly shuffled through it. 'This will make some good night reading. Thank you, Bryn.'

At Parsons Farm, the Parsons were discussing Bryn. Jane went to the shelf on the antique Welsh dresser and removing a large biscuit tin. She showed Janet, letters she had from Kitty. Bryn's late wife. They spoke, of the empty anguish she went through when Bryn went on what he would call one of his jollies. The dates tied up to the years in Bryn's document, but the things Janet was picking up on was, the times he returned home, found herself making many notes about those times. Jane related to some of those days he came back in not a too good condition, how the children would rally around Kit, pulling him through the pain he tried not to show, though they knew he was suffering with.

Edward showed Janet some of the photos of Bryn in those days. 'It's when you see the scars that you realise what he has endured for Queen and Country. Janet, on one occasion, the team he was leading, got caught in a mortar attack, with much shrapnel damage to himself dragged two of his men to safety, saving their lives. Bryn is a born leader; when he first arrived in the village Kit and the children had already lived here for six months. Kit had rented the Taylors, old cottage. He was so quiet, nobody realises who he was, they thought he was just Gwen brother.'

Sitting up in bed cuddled together, Janet and James, read Bryn's account of his life. They would come to parts of it with brackets in-between blanked out pieces, written in the brackets 'Classified' and there were many such brackets.

Janet had already the profile of Bryn, in her head, it had not changed, she knew this quiet man, had inner strength, that was already born in him, he did not need to work on it, but just let it mature, like the scotch whisky he drank.

***

On Friday, Janet spent much time going over and over Bryn's story, and how would he like it to be told. She knew this type of man, and their characteristics, who did not like bringing attention to themselves, and would instead want the focus to go on others. But this spotlight was something he could not hide from. It was Janet's duty to portray him in the right light... not try and hold him too high, so other could try and knock him down, but rather to describe him as the loving dad that he was.

The fact that Bryn had already seen that he could not hide from it. The detail he had given was so intensive...in a way, he had given her too much. She started to break each section down, bit by bit intent not to lose the full meaning of why she was doing this in first the place.

By the afternoon, she had three stories, that still related to the man, yet did not make him an alpha man, well not quiet. From the first day the Collier Family introduced Charlyyk to the world, the press media had delved into Bryn past. The researchers soon found evidence of the military life he had been living and much interest had been shown on the snippets published already. The scars Bryn had shown to prove he had been in conflict with strange beast, all so showed other scars as well.

Janet's phone call to Harold and Gwen to speak with them, was in her Mini heading for Carpenters Cottage. When the Hobart's had read what, Janet had written, Harold could not say very much he could see the Bryn he knew in each profile, but which one he preferred was hard to say.

Gwen was different, she took a couple of things from one, and added it to another, 'That is my brother.'

Harold read how Gwen had made the changes, 'Yes I agree, that puts it in perspective.'

Gwen and Harold would not let Janet go so quickly and discussed many things. How Janet felt about how long would she be following Charlyyk story. 'That depends on the interest the general public thinks about her, no interest no story.'

'Then what would you do?' asked Gwen.

'I would carry on doing what I'm doing here, but about other people. Being a freelance writer, this project has given me such a huge profile, I do not envisage to be ever out of work, unless I get too cocky and blow it.' Then thinking out of the box. 'Then James could make me an honest woman, and turn me into a mother, now that could change my life and how?'

**

A light drizzly rain swept over the county, the weather front had slowly moved up the English Channel from the Atlantic, affected the southern coastal regions. But did not deter the effort being shown by the four runners, as they skipped over the slippery ground, and the many puddles. The chatter between them was lively.

Helens Pilates was paying off; she was more light-footed. Age had limited her, but was aware that she felt better for the efforts.

Thomas only ran when he thought he needed to, but these runs were making him feel he should try harder.

Bryn's initial idea behind the runs had been to decrease the amount of studying Charlyyk was doing. The brainstorm had turned out better than he had first thought. When Kitty became ill, Bryn had stopped training to look after her. After Kitty's death, he just imploded. He could not find any incentive to do anything. Then when he was abducted, it showed he still needed to be fit to survive. He was now more determined to be ready to face whatever will come next, for he knew this had not finished. There were to many unexplainable issues.

He had a talk with Michel on what was the effects, Charlyyk of eating food she had not eaten before. Could it change the way she grew? He had Michel's full attention. Michel had noticed how the effect of the different food, and the exercise was increasing Charlyyk physical size. Harold also had spoken about it when at Houston. The detail that Lynda Bryant had put into her illustrations of the aliens had given Michel concerns. If Charlyyk achieved such heights, that could make people wary of her.

The cottage was warm and welcoming it gave them when they returned. Rachel was in a loving mood and snuggling up to Thomas, was making him feel good inside, were soon heading for their room, under the stern eye of Margret.

After breakfast, Thomas planned to take his charges to Portsmouth to visit the Mary Rose exhibition.

Janet arrived at ten. 'I've come to see you, Helen.' And they headed for the study. 'Helen I've gone over the information that Bryn gave me. This is what I've come up with, I could not show Bryn until I had spoken with those special people, that are very close to him.' Helen sat down, started to read what Janet had placed in front of her.

When Helen finished reading, 'Just a minute Janet.' Then she left the study. She returned with Charlyyk. Janet explained to her what it was about. Then allowed Charlyyk to read what she had written. It was the original version, without the changes Gwen had suggested.

When Charlyyk had finished. She laid out the papers, bracketing individual sentences in pencil. 'Move that to there, that to there.' She sat back.

Helen agreed with her. 'Yes, you are right darling,'

Janet then put what Gwen had edited next to the other papers. Charlyyk read Gwen's version, 'Yes, that my dad.' There, was pride in her voice. Helen could only put her hand on her shoulder and squeeze. Janet then explained, what Gwen had said.

Charlyyk looking straight into Janet's eyes, 'You would have had to live with a person like my dad, to really believe that people like him existed. He's not the only one, but how does a girl like me, deserve a man like him as a father?'

Janet wrote what she had say, down on paper, 'That's the ending, I was looking for.'

Helen cuddled Charlyyk, 'I could not have said anything, that summed up the true feelings of us all better than what you have just stated.'

Janet proof read the main article, then pressed print. Watched as the paper unfolded from the printer. Janet, ask Helen to get Bryn, 'Let's see what he thinks?'

Bryn came into the study. Janet had removed the finished article, so he did not see it. He sat down and started to read when he finished. 'That's three ways of seeing me, but do we really see ourselves as others do?'

Then Janet showed him the finished article, he was not sure. 'I know that is not how you saw me, Janet?' Janet asked him to explain, 'The first three is how you saw me, the last one, you have asked those close to me to comment, and this is the final piece.' Janet relates what she did these last three days. Bryn then agreed to the publication of the final article.

'I want a particular photo to go with it. Could you dress in something casual, but classy?' Janet asked. 'Could you help him to choose Helen. Charlyyk, I need you to wear something similar.'

The photo shoot was set up. A white sheet was draped on one wall, with folds to give it some features, a wing chair from the lounge, for them to sit in, individual lamps and reflectors, set up to prevent shadows. The photo shoot lasted about an hour. Janet had used her three cameras, for different effects.

When she checked the results on the computer, the picture that stood out the most. Bryn with Charlyyk sitting on his right leg. His right arm behind her, with the right hand cradling her right elbow. Her right hand was draped over the end of the arm of the wing chair. Their left hands were together. They looked into each other's eyes, pride radiating from them.

Charlyyk put some A4 photo paper into her printer, then they printed out four copies. On the back of one of the photographs, Janet wrote the number of the photo, to save time when she needed copies. 'This will be in next month's issue. I will get the mag to send you a copy.' Janet informed him, as they were clearing away the equipment.

Helen had prepared lunch, and they sat around talking about how the Christmas that had gone. Janet was full of herself as James, had mentioned casually, that they were to marry. The tingling excitement she was expressing, was pulsating. Helen could tell by the body language, that the idea of marrying James excited her.

Charlyyk's nose twitched. Bryn could tell she was seeking the smell of Janet. Then she stopped. Bryn raised his eyebrows. Charlyyk shook her head, with a look of disappointment.

Helen could not help following the unspoken conversation, transcending between them two. More and more, she understood how Charlyyk started to respond to situations. Ear movement was the first. How her ears would move in specific patterns, even to how they would twitch when she became excited. Then the eyes, with their colour changes, mix the ears and the eyes, that told her when she was happy or agitated, or she felt threatened. The nostrils were harder to detect, but she was learning. She had time on her side.

When Janet had left the cottage, the photos still laid on the table. Bryn put two more pictures of Charlyyk with them. One when she had first arrived on this planet, the second a year later. Even Charlyyk saw the changes. She had filled out and was eight-inches taller. She stood more upright, straighter in the back. Her face softer and her hair, not straw like. She could see the confidence oozing from herself. She was different. Just as Michel predicted. Yet she still felt the same.

Charlyyk looking at Helen, then at Bryn. She felt secure, like a Feeng cub lying next to its parents, enjoying the warmth of the sun, without a care in the world. With what's for dinner being the only thing, would the young cub have to think about? As she dwelt on that last thought. That summed up what her life has been with Bryn her new dad. He had always been there supplying her the needs to help live on this planet.

Bryn had been watching her, 'What are you thinking sweetheart?'

She sidled up to him, and nestled into him, as though he was a duvet. Slipping an arm around him to get even closer, looking up into his eyes, showing the affection, only a daughter can demonstrate.

'Love you, daddy.'

Helen saw Bryn, melt before her eyes, he could say no words, just a soft gooey smile, and the eyes, spoke volumes, even she felt emotional watching them.

When Thomas, Rachel and her mother returned from their visit to the Mary Rose, the smiles told them, that the day had gone well. Margret was taken back with the whole history of it all, 'Placing the history, with the artefact, gave the exhibit, so much meaning.' she commented, when sitting down with Charlyyk to describe the day.

Rachel helping Helen with the evening meal. She said her mother did not moan or criticise once...well, only when she was tired and wanted to leave. It made for such a lovely day.

Over dinner, Helen told Thomas about Janet's visit and the photo shoot. Thomas reading the article and perusing the photos. 'She is such a talented girl. She certainly has a way of showing the best, out of people.'

Margret wished she had been there, 'We must go and see her, to set up a time for an interview. Rachel, we need to get the advertising sorted?'

Rachel stopped eating, 'Can't we use the Catalogue from the Exhibition of Chicago? It would fit the Artist who are exhibiting their works.'

Thomas looked at Margret, 'Just change the cover, and the introduction... it could work.'

Margret went silent, but all could see her brain cells working. Then she spoke. 'I hate to admit it, but I think you are right.' Rachel had a smug look. Looking down at what she was eating so her mother could not see her, her eyes flashed up, to see Thomas doing the same as her. The little nod they gave each, said the plan had worked.

Helen who had been observing them could see what Bryn had said, about Margret bore a lot of truth. Margret was very domineering, as she saw how Thomas and Rachel could controlled her to a point. Helen wished she could be a fly on their bedroom wall, to see how they managed their plots, for they seem to be able to do it so subtlety.

Some idle chatter was banded around for a little while. Helen sensed it was to take them away from the subject. They had furthered their course, and to move away from it, was to cement it in, don't rub her nose in it. Otherwise, Margret will change her mind deliberately.

***

Sunday saw a light flurry of snow, but it was wet, so it would not last long. Charlyyk did not like the damp cold. On her planet, it was dry and arid, with so little clouds. There was hardly any rain. The moist atmosphere of England, made the cold feel colder, but the run warmed her. Then after the shower and fresh clothes. the pleasant feeling it gave her, made the efforts well worthwhile.

It was during breakfast, at the Parson's Farm when Janet's phone started to vibrate. The Editor of the men's mag wanted a photo of Bryn in a different pose, without Charlyyk.

Janet turned up at Oakleaves around about ten with James in Edwards Discovery, towing a trailer. They came in through the rear garden. Charlyyk was soon there, she knew James would rough her up. But she liked it from him. His large hands, hard and rough, but yet, can be so gentle.

'Well, how are we going to proceed with this?' Bryn asked.

James slapped Bryn on the back 'It's OK. We will be gentle with you. We have been discussing how...we have even brought the props.'

James walked out into the garden; Bryn followed. On the back of the trailer, logs and a large axe. James turned to Bryn, 'Have you got something to wear that would look rugged?'

Bryn went to his bedroom and pulled out a case from behind the wardrobe. The torn T-shirt, and cargo trousers were within, wrapped in plastic bags... just as he had stored them, still stained with his own blood. He donned the cargo trousers, but not the T-shirt. Instead taking another old T-shirt from bureau drawer. As he passed his study, retrieved the hacking blade he had brought back from that hellhole of a planet. Carrying the torn T-shirt, he returns to the garden.

Janet with help from Charlyyk had set up the lights, and reflector screens. Janet wanted to bring in one of the trees as a backdrop, using James as a model, to set up the cameras. When Charlyyk saw the trousers, she stood still, rooted to the spot, her ears and eyes, twitching with each other. She was not comfortable. James saw it, went to scooped her up. Helen was soon there. It was not Charlyyk's eyes that were troubling her, it was the smell from the trousers. When Bryn had slain the Feeng, its blood, had splashed on them and she could still smell it...faint, but it was there. Charlyyk's built-in fears were playing games in her head, warning her of danger. As James tried to take her away, she would not go. Struggling with him wriggled free from his hold. 'I must face it, I must conquer my fears, the Feeng is dead, it should not upset me, I am here, it is not.' Charlyyk anguish showing, she did need to control her fears. She then went to Bryn and wrapped her arms around him. even with smell of the Feeng, she knew she must be in control.

Helen made tea, to help settle Charlyyk. Then sat with Charlyyk while they drank, talking through her anxiety. Helen could tell she needed this, to give her confidence in herself. Once again this was for Charlyyk, nobody else but her. Charlyyk conveyed how those beasts haunted her dreams. To end her nightmares, she must find a way to banish her fear.

Meanwhile Bryn tried many poses, as he wielded the axe, cutting many logs for the right effects. James suggested that Bryn takes the T-shirt off. Steam rising from him.

James, dove into Janet shoulder bag, found a bottle of baby oil. James handed it to Helen. 'I would think you doing the honours, Bryn would enjoy it more?' Helen applied the oil to Bryn's body. The glistening sheen, gave him that hot and sweaty look. Although Bryn had thickened around the waist, did not have a great six pack, though the oil showed his physic was still good for his age.

Rachel watching with her mother at the door to the cottage, could see another angle to capture the right feel for the picture. 'Thomas! Those pyjamas I love to wear, that you don't like. Could you fetch them please?' He came back with them, Rachel took Charlyyk's top clothes off, the simple shift type garment of a pale lime green colour blended in with Charlyyk's complexion. 'Right, Dad put the axe down and wear the torn T-shirt.' Bryn did what was asked, put the t-shirt on. 'Now stand with your feet apart.' Rachel, guides

Charlyyk towards Bryn. 'Pass that weapon to me, James.' Putting it in Bryn's hands, 'Charlyyk kneels down between Bryn's legs... yes bend your right leg, in front of dad's left leg, put your hand around, above the knee, your left leg bent so your body is resting on it, now peer around dad, now look at me, Dad... place the weapon between your legs... that's it' Turning towards Janet. 'How about that Janet?'

Janet reeled off many bursts, Janet could see what Rachel was trying to do, started to see other ways for the shoot. 'Charlyyk grip your dad's ankle with your left hand your right hand above the knee.' The camera whirred as she burst off many more shots. Then asked her to look around as if looking for a beast. Margret was impressed with what they could do with the bare essential props, that they had come up with.

Janet downloaded the photos on to her computer, they gathered around to see the results. Each shot examined, four photos were selected and printed. Then the images re-examined. Janet sent digital versions of them to the Editor from her computer, then they waited. The reply came back. *'Great shots, thanks, that's a wrap.'* The relief on Janet's face showed this meant more to her than just another magazine. Maxim is the most prominent selling Magazine for men and is sold all around the world. Publishing something with them was another big scoop for Janet.

Bryn and Charlyyk had changed back into their normal clothes, as they returned. Margret was setting dates with Janet, for an interview. Janet had already made inroads to various magazines. The biggest one. '*The Art of Watercolour*' based in NAINTRE-FRANCE, will run the spread. Which I suggest we concentrate on as the main article. Then I will use some different articles to send to the other magazines. *The Art of Watercolour*, also wants some in-depth interviews with some of the Artist, would like one of their own writers to interview some of them. They will be in touch with us this week.' Janet thanked them. James had already cleared everything away, with hugs and kisses, they were gone.

Carpenters Cottage was a hive of activity. Rachel and her mother, had folders in front of them, discussing the upcoming schedules. Michel with Charlyyk on his lap, chewing the cud with Harold and Bryn. Gwen, Helen and Thomas, we're talking about the Mary Rose.

Over dinner, the photo shoot was widely debated. Gwen giving Charlyyk, a comforting hug. 'You poor thing, it must have been terrifying for you?'

Charlyyk conveying her need to conquer her fears. 'Auntie Gwen they don't live on this planet, so I must dispel that inner fear I have of them, then

I might not have the bad dreams about them. Waking up in a state of worry, that they are chasing me.'

Gwen understood her anxiety, as she had spent many early mornings cuddling her trying hard to settle her down, feeling the tremors in her body, having to unwrap the sheets that had tangled around her legs, as her claws on her toes dug in. When she was dreaming of running away from the beast.

Margret kept looking at the far wall. 'Gwen, that painting, the one where the little girl is holding the rabbit...'

Gwen made a hand gesture towards Thomas. 'Thomas gave that one to me, it's from an earlier sketch he had done of Catherine, which I liked, and as you can tell I still love it.'

Charlyyk left the table and took a closer look. 'That's from the sketchbook we found in the back of the wardrobe dad.'

Bryn agreed with her, as he was present that day Thomas gave it to his aunt, 'You are right Charlyyk, and your auntie Gwen will no doubt show you the painting, she has hanging in her bedroom, one day?'

Gwen turned towards Helen slightly awkwardly. 'The original includes Bryn and Kitty in an intimate position. Every time Bryn saw it, he needed time to get over the pain, it gave him. So, I have hung it where it was out of Bryn gaze. I think he will be all right with it now though.'

Helen reached over, and taking her hand, 'I want Bryn, to still be in love with Kitty. She was the love of his life. He should not just turn his back on such a wonderful woman.' Helen's look was sincere. Gwen knew she was not trying to push her out of their lives. 'Remember, she is the mother of his children, and what a fantastic job she did bringing them up, when you see how they present themselves...Gwen, I am prepared to share Bryn with you all. The memories of Kitty for you all is something you should all cherish.'

Margret was concerned that asking about the picture could cause a problem. Thomas needed to explain about the painting, 'It's a painting I did, from a photo, Uncle Harold took.'

Harold nodded, 'When Bryn came home on leave one summer, we all went to Dippers Meadow on a picnic. I had been taking photos of the children when I took a picture of Bryn and Kit. It was only when we had the photos developed did, we realise the tender moment they were sharing.'

Thomas turned to face Margret. 'My art teacher was showing us how to paint a picture from a photo. How you can leave certain irrelevant bit out to improve the composition. I took no notice of what mum and dad were up to, just improving the whole concept of the picture. It was later when my hormones started to be active, did I notice what I had overlooked...a rather sensuous, emotional photo.'

Rachel winking at Gwen, 'So that's why it hangs in the bedroom, a Gwen?'

Gwen's face flushed, 'Go on, make it sound worse than it is.' But the words had joviality in them, not malice. Margret listening to this family sensed the honesty they had with one another, never no hard feelings, no ill thought, they were a pull your sleeve's up, and get on with its family. At first, she was not sure how Michel fitted in, now she can see he is now a member of the family, not just a friend. He also pulls up his sleeves and gets stuck in with what is needed to be done.

Then looking at herself, her thoughts realising the position she was in. *'I'm going to be here for a year, I can feel that Bryn is tolerating me for Thomas's sake, but why? am I that bad?'*

Chapter 31

Home Truths

On Monday morning, Charlyyk checked that she had everything ready for school, before sitting down for breakfast. Helen busy cooking and packing her lunch at the same time, when Rachel came into the kitchen and saw Helen rushing about, stepped in to help.

The school bus was spot on time, they waved Charlyyk goodbye. Margret had been very quiet. Nobody had said anything about how quiet she was, but talked about how quickly the holiday had gone.

Then out of the blue, Margret asked, 'What is it that people have about me, I don't think I am a bad person? Or am I?'

Rachel changed seats, sat next to her. 'No mum, but you must loosen up a bit. Dad was a bastard to you, the way he cheated on you. But not everyone is like dad. You must try and climb down off that high horse that you sit on and meet the ones you like halfway.'

Margret face dropped, 'You are my daughter, I'm not like that to you, am I?'

Rachel placed her arm around her mother's shoulders. 'Yes, you are. And if you are like that to me, how about Thomas? If he was not like his mum and dad, he would or should have, run away screaming by now. I warn you now, if ever that happens, I will be with him mark my words.'

Margret looked distraught, 'I don't mean to be like that.'

Thomas came and sat the other side of Margret. 'You are Rachel's mother I must respect that. But my real duty is to Rachel, even more now she is carrying our first child, your grandchild. I have told Rachel if your manner does not change, after the birth. We would move away from you because our child is not going to live a life of worrying what it says to you. I have family here, who would love to have us here permanently.'

Margret, with her now ashen face, looked at Rachel. 'Yes mum, I will follow Thomas to the other end of the world, and leave you behind, if you put me in that position, that I would have to choose between you.'

Margret stood up and left the room tears streaming down her face. Rachel made an attempt to follow, but Thomas stopped her. 'Give her time to think it through. She has to understand, that we mean what we have said. Give in to her now, and you will always have to give in.'

Rachel did not have tears in her eyes, which told Helen they meant what they had said.

Bryn looked at Helen, who nodded back to him, then rose and left the table.

Helen tapped Margret door and walked in. Margret laid sobbing on the bed. Sitting beside her, Helen preceded to stroke her back. 'Come. Life is not easy, but to ease the pain, let's talk about it. Maybe we can come to an understanding that will allow you to find a way to keep your family together. We could start, by thinking about your new grandchild. My parent never thought that they would have any, now the fact that they have Charlyyk, that has given them a whole new purpose in life.'

Margret stopped crying, turning over to face Helen. A wisp of a smile appeared on her face. 'Yes.' She raised herself and sat by the side of Helen. 'Thank you.'

'Sort yourself out, and I'll go and make a pot of tea.'

Ten minutes later, Helen returned carrying a tray, 'I've brought some of Charlyyk's favourite KitKats.'

Margret had done some thinking, while Helen had made the tea. 'Was I that bad?'

Helen looked at her sympathetically. 'No, not that bad. It is a constant nag, nag like a dripping tap, that becomes a nightmare in the end.'

Margret winced at that thought, 'It doesn't sound good, does it?'

Helen took a bite of her KitKat. 'You could look at it, differently, think of all the pain and grieve that Bryn has suffered, does he take it out on everyone around him?' Helen smiled a gentle smile, 'You are still going to need some help, to get you through this, I think if you ask Rachel and Thomas to help, they would.'

Margret found herself, scoffing the KitKat. Helen offered her another, a sheepish smile spread across her face, as she accepted it. 'How do you think they could help me?' Margret enquired

'How about asking them?'

'What should I ask them?'

Helen waited for a moment, 'Ask them to tell you when you act act inappropriately. If it is only by a hand signal.'

Thomas and Rachel were in the lounge. Bryn had spoken to them when they were in the kitchen, 'You have to hit hard, some time to get the message through. Your mother can be nice, and for all your sake, I hope a solution can be found... I would love to be there with Amy all the time. But it would mean a strain on Cat and Brent's relationship. I must respect that you have chosen to make a life for yourself. Just like I did with your mother. Now with plane travel, we're never too far away, for us all to come and visit.' Bryn then went to his study.

Helen entered the lounge with Margret. 'Where's Bryn?' Thomas replied he had gone to the study. Helen left them and went in search of Bryn.

Margret sat down with Thomas and Rachel, 'Helen has been very kind to me. We have looked at the way, you might be able to help, when I forget myself. You have not too grin and bear it, but to let me know. Helen put my silly ways, down to, as like a dripping tap...nag, nag. So... I'm reaching out to you both, to give this silly old woman a second chance to redeem herself.'

Rachel kissed her mother, 'Mum I love you, and so does Thomas, but you must want to do this, if you don't get on a plane and go home now. Take into account you don't just lose me, but also a grandchild. This is not Thomas talking. This is me.'

Margret saw her daughter was serious and meant every word she was saying. 'Yes, darling I do want to change, I want what they have here...a happy family. I want to be a loving grandmother.'

Rachel taking her hand. 'Then let's give it a go Mum...Look when we told Thomas's dad, we were coming to stay for a year. His first words were. 'How about your mum, she would want to be with you, at the birth'. His first thoughts were for you. That how Thomas thinks, more about others than himself. That's why I love him, he doesn't look over his shoulder to see what I'm doing. He looks to see if I'm alright.'

Bryn was sorting out the paperwork, for his accounts. Helen brought up her bank details and checked them with the statements. A letter from the accounts office to notified her of the way her pension would be paid. A cheque would be in the post as a one-off payment in recognition of her service. She passed the letter to Bryn, 'My dowry kind sir, I do not come empty-handed.'

At lunchtime, Helen asked Margret, if she would like to go shopping with her. Margret jumped at the idea, and could not wait to go. Rachel helped Helen to finish the cores. So, her mother could go.

Thomas went through his art equipment. It had arrived in a large container; easels, brushes, and most of all, paper, handmade in different grades.

At the bottom, right-hand corner of the garden and very overgrown, was Thomas's old studio a large summer house, with lots of windows, for natural light, it was situated against the far end of the garden wall. Since he had moved to America, the trees and shrubs had overgrown and covered it.

Bryn had collected the hedge trimmer from the garage, and like a man on a jungle mission, attacked the overgrown bushes. Thomas pulled the debris away, as Bryn chopped. Once cleared Thomas took his key fob from his pocket, found the key and opened the door. Releasing the bolts that held the shutters, Bryn opened the shutters up.

Thomas looked around the inside of the studio. Rachel joined him there, old works scattered about the walls, and standing together, were two old chairs. Catherine had been an avid model, from all ages, even Kit had taken her turn, allowing him to mature as an artist. Many objects for props for still life works scattered about, Thomas with his arm wrapped around Rachel. 'We've a lot of work to do here, it so dusty.'

Bryn in the meantime had found the fuse in the consumer unit and switched it on, checking the RCD unit worked. When he returned to the studio, Rachel had started cleaning. Thomas removing many items to allow clear access.

Helen and Margret returned laughing, the kettle was soon on. Bryn told them that Thomas had opened the studio, Helen looked surprised. 'What studio?' Bryn walked to the window. 'That one.' The two women looked out of the window. Margret watching Rachel and Thomas working together could see they were a team, the interaction between the two of them, bouncing off each other, was heart-warming to watch. Margret went and poured two teas and took them out to them.

Now it was Helen watching them, a satisfactory smile on her face. Bryn put his arm around her waist, 'Did it work?'

Helen nodded, 'Oh yes, I got her to talk. Then she could not stop. It all came out, she was so demanding, he could not live up to the constant nagging. As an artist, unless you were famous, you struggled. And with Margret as a wife, you struggled, even more. He had already left her, before he knew she was pregnant.'

Bryn with a stern look on his face, 'So she knew what she was doing and still could do nothing about it?'

Helen walking away from the window. 'Knowing and doing is two different things.'

Charlyyk breezed in, aiming for the fridge. Bryn's voice was stern. 'Touch that fridge door young lady.'

Charlyyk reached the top of the refrigerator to a laminated A4 sheet with her diet on it. 'I can have a drink of milk, when I come home from school, look it's here.' Tapping her long finger on the sheet.

Helen watching from the door. 'We have it all under control, we've had a serious talk and Charlyyk agrees that it for her long-term health.'

When Charlyyk had changed, she soon had the scent of Rachel and headed for her.

She stood at the door to the garden, standing there wondering how the large studio had materialised at the far end of the garden, Charlyyk was soon there. Rachel showing her the inside of the studio. 'Thomas wanted to get this sorted because he promised to give you some lessons.'

***

The next day. Thomas spent most of the morning sorting out the studio, he had told Charlyyk, she could do some painting when she came home.

When she did come home, she ran to her room. She changed into some old clothes and was soon in the studio.

Thomas had to settle her down, 'Painting is about control Charlyyk.'

When he felt, she was ready, he wet some paper, and stretched it, laying it flat on the workbench. He sponged some more water on to the paper, showing her the technique, of wet on wet, to show what happens when you soak the paper. He had given her strong, vibrant colours: Prussian Blue; Venetian Red; Cadmium Yellow; primary colours. Putting a little of each into separate mixing bowls. Then adding a little water, he gave her a mop. 'Dunk it in the bowl then drop some from 30cm high above the paper.'

The paint hit the wet paper and explodes out, she yelped with glee, at the results. Dropping different colours with a massive explosion of colour splashes. He made her stand back and view what she had achieved, using just the three primary colours. Then before the paper dried, dabbed a tissue in the centre of each colour burst, then allowed Charlyyk to drop more different colour on to the paper for more affect.

While she had been doing her painting, Thomas had stretched another piece of paper. 'Right Charlyyk, we will let that dry, here is what art is all about.' Using just those three primary colours, he created a rainbow. First, a yellow strip straight across the paper with a broad brush, for the centre then while still wet, the blue to form the bottom. She could see how when the blue touched the yellow the green appeared, it explained the bottom part of the rainbow. 'Water is like a mirror it reflects, so if the sky is blue, the sea is blue, using nature's own colour system.'

Then Thomas applied the red to the top part of the rainbow, when the red touched the yellow, the orange emerged creating the complete image of the rainbow, the knowing nod. Charlyyk soft smile, and gentle nodding. She could now see how when the sun hit drops of rain, they reflected the natural colours to create the rainbow.

Rachel came in, to let them know dinner would soon be ready. 'That's pretty Charlyyk.' Giving her some encouragement, Charlyyk did not need to say anything, but the wide eyes and smirk of a smile did, she kept touching a corner to see if it was dry.

At dinner, Charlyyk could not stop asking a question about how Thomas started in art and what he found difficult to grasp. Thomas and Margret had different answers. But this did not confuse Charlyyk, she had noticed this was the same with the posse, each one finding a different difficulty to grasp than others.

***

Wednesday, Thomas and Rachel spent the day in the studio, with Helen, keeping them supplied with beverages and snacks. Helen was enjoying sneaking quick looks, watching Thomas at work, with three pieces on the go at the same time. He was using previous drawings and photos, as a reference, the theme 'Autumn in New England' but one was Dippers Meadow, this was for Charlyyk's bedroom.

Margret had spent the morning in Bryn study, going over the details for the layout of the first exhibits. She was delighted, the gallery had offered her some of their best Watercolour paintings to include in the exhibition, she was keeping her fingers crossed for the Brighton and Hove City Council to allow the painting of *The Chain Pier, Brighton*. painted by Turner to be shown.

Janet's request for an interview with Bryn had stirred more interest from the military chiefs about Bryn's exploits, the phone call he received from Major Carter, came as no surprise to Bryn.

'Hello Major, what can I help you with?'

The Major quite apologetic. 'Sorry Captain but the big chiefs, want to talk with you and Charlyyk.'

Bryn did not answer straight away, but gave himself time to think it over, 'When?'

Major Carter was quick to respond. 'I told them you would not like Charlyyk to lose more schooling, and it would have to fit in with her.'

'Where?'

The Major's reply was chirpy. 'I suggested the Chelsea Pensioner's home. The Royal Hospital Chelsea.'

This tickled Bryn, 'Why are the big chief's that old?'

The Major chuckled. 'This Saturday at ten, will Helen join you?'

Bryn beckoned Helen to join him and explained to her Major Carter's request. Helen took the phone from Bryn, 'Alan will this be a full weekend?'

The Major hearing Helen's voice, 'It could be Helen, would this create a problem?'

Helen spoke to Bryn, 'No later than Sunday midday, Charlyyk will need some rest.'

Helen gave the phone back to Bryn. 'Did you hear that Major, no later than noon Sunday.'

'I will convey your decision to them, thank you, Captain.'

Charlyyk burst into the cottage, grabbed a glass of milk, and headed straight out to the studio. Helen did not have a chance to say Hi but followed her.

Well, what you think?' Thomas was asking on the painting of Dippers Meadow. He pulled up a chair for her. 'I've about four hours more work to complete it.' Charlyyk just stared at it.

Helen stood behind her. 'Isn't it lovely?'

'No bulrushes, there in that area where the tree hangs down.' She knew every bit, every blade of grass, Dippers Meadow was her domain. This is where she drifts to, in her mind when she needs to shut the rest of the world away. Those first early days with Bryn her new dad, allowing the worry what awaited her in this new world, to be a distant memory, was here in Dippers Meadow. Laying down in the grass listening to the strange, beautiful sounds of birds and insects, bees busying themselves in their short lifespan of three months, collecting the pollen for the next generation. Her planet so quiet compared to the vibrant noises of this world.

At dinner, Bryn informs them that they would be in London, at The Royal Hospital Chelsea. Helen telling Charlyyk about the Chelsea Pensioners, and the charitable work they did. They must have served twenty-two years in the services to the rank of warrant officer, to be eligible to be a Chelsea Pensioner. Charlyyk knowing about Bryn's army career, 'So, dad you could qualify to be one.'

Margret confirmed she would be away for four Days as the shipment of paintings arrive tomorrow. She has booked herself into a hotel close by to the gallery. Thomas and Rachel with a satisfactory smile showing their approval.

***

Thursday, winter was here, it was freezing. Under Charlyyk's tracksuit was another layer of clothes. Jane Parsons had knitted Charlyyk some gloves, and a pompom hat, in pink wool for Christmas. And this was the day to wear them with pride, she was keen to show James, she had them on, as she waved to him, passing by the cow sheds.

At breakfast, with Helen guidance, Charlyyk checked her homework. That Mrs Butler had set her, she could not thank Helen enough for the help she had given her. More, what she had put in her lunch box. Rachel could only smile on the interaction the two had with each other, joined them to wave goodbye to Charlyyk as she left on the school bus.

Rachel walking back in doors, 'Helen, I just love the way you and Charlyyk have with each other, if that is motherhood, I can't wait to have it.'

Thomas and Rachel went to the studio. Bryn and Helen to the study to catch up on the evidence they may need at the weekend.

At the Academy, Mr Pearson pointing at the Smartboard, 'We have many indications on how Britain has changed, anyone would like to add to them?' Charlyyk was the only one to respond, 'It appears that progress in Electronics, has led the way: Fridges, Freezers, Television, Computers. It was fridges that allowed people to make food last longer. Washing machines and vacuum cleaners made household chores easier, that gave women more free time. Some women started to go out to work to supplement the family budget, this allowed ordinary families to be able to afford to buy cars and go abroad on holiday. With joint incomes, buying a house became possible.' Charlyyk had spent many hours on the Internet cross-referencing the Post war years from 1945/85 looking at all the changes that could have been the reason for such a dramatic change to the British way of Life.

This pleased Mr Pearson, this what he really wanted to hear. 'Anyone else?' Mike raised his hand. 'My nan said that the first luxury item they got, was wall-to-wall fitted carpets, they were made with a synthetic material and not wool.'

Mr Pearson entered on the Smartboard what Charlyyk had said, 'Yes it not always politics that changes people's lives, but mainly new inventions, and industry, that can have the biggest impact.' He made a few notes. 'Well done, Charlyyk.'

At the Cottage over some lunch. Thomas showed, his father and Helen the finished paintings. 'It was Rachel's idea to paint Dippers Meadow. It will give Charlyyk a settling effect when she remembers her own planet. She sometimes feels guilty that she is safe, and the group were not.'

Margret was admiring the two other paintings, 'I remember when we went there and saw you sketching those scenes. Thomas, they are lovely, I understand what you mean about Charlyyk how it will help to calm her, I'm getting the same effect from these paintings.'

Thomas and Rachel had already been to Town and purchased a picture frame for the painting of Dippers Meadow. They hung the completed picture, in her bedroom. When she arrived home from school, it was Rachel who was just as excited as Charlyyk just to see her expression on her face as Charlyyk admired the painting. And she was not disappointed. Charlyyk almost flipped as she did at Disney World meeting Olaf, then she just sat on her bed gazing at it. Her hands clasped together between her knees, her body forward, the longing look on her face, she was there in the painting, laying in the grass, listening to birds and the insects.

Friday, Margret said her goodbyes, Thomas and Rachel were driving her to the hotel, situated close to the gallery. She will oversee the opening of the container, that the artwork had been transported in, and check that they were in good health.

Thomas and Rachel then we're heading for Liverpool to set up the next exhibition.

Chapter 32

Chelsea Pensioners

Saturday, the drive to The Royal Hospital Chelsea did not take long. For Charlyyk it was another new adventure for her. It was just as exciting for the pensioners, that now stood to attention and saluted, when the Colliers entered the building from the Chelsea Gate Entrance. Commissioned by King Charles 2. Designed and built by Sir Christophe Wren, three hundred years before.

Major Carter welcomed them in and showed them to the room, where the interview on what Charlyyk had seen when she met Bryn on that planet, would take place. Many officers, were already known to Bryn and Helen. Many warm handshakes were in order, it was going to be an informal interview, because of the way the seating had been arranged in a circle.

Helen had influence with her military rank, and Bryn did not want no reminding of it.

Major Alan Carter opened the procedure by requesting they all dropped rank. 'Bryn would like for the sake of Charlyyk, for it to be informal. As this is our first meeting between us, about the abduction Bryn, we would like emphasize, that we and Britains Intelligence Services have had many meeting prior than today. Bryn's detailed report show us that you have not lost your understanding how important this could be. The Meeting in Interlaken was only about you. Today we would like to hear from you both.'

Bryn did not hesitate to tell his side of the story. Showing the evidence he had brought with him.

A rather young Brigadier Alex Hutton spoke to Charlyyk. 'The battleground, can be frightening even to harden soldiers, let alone a young girl like yourself, how did you see it, my dear?'

Charlyyk had thought these questions would be asked and had put much thought behind them. 'The time my group were trapped, we were gathering the fruit from the *Cruul tree*. Maarlyyk was keeping watch, while Taarlyyk and I were collecting the fruit. We had little time, as the beast would know that the fruit was our favourite food. Maarlyyk gave out the warning that she could smell the Feeng approaching. We made our move towards our home burrows. When suddenly a net fell on us, we were scooped up by many bear-like beasts. As the net tightened around us, we could not move, With the little restriction of movement we had, all that I could see, was we were carried for some way. Then we found ourselves on board the craft that transported us to the place, where I met Dad.'

Charlyyk took a moment to compose herself as the memories flooded back to her. 'Finding ourselves frightened...were unable to move in the holding pen. Then as one by one we were pulled out to be eaten, by those beasts, I had given up thinking about survival. I just wondered when death was going to happen?

One of the beasts, it plucked myself up as though I was an apple. But another beast, wanted myself too, so the one that had taken myself, took me away from the pen. I was stressed out, with the expectation of being ripped apart, remembering the screams the others made, I knew the outlook was not good for myself.'

Charlyyk's body was trembling. Bryn squeezed her hand.

'It started to pull at my arm. Then all at once, a body flew over us, grabbed at the head of the beast, I heard a crack from the neck of the beast. The beast had not stood a chance. As it let go of myself, and I dropped to the floor. I saw the reason for it letting myself go, the stranger that had saved myself was struggling to get to its feet. I just lay there, daring not to move waiting to see what was this strange being was going to do. It took no interest in myself, only looked closely at the weapon the beast had. I looked around to see if I could flee from there, but I was not able to do so, not on my own. It was the best place where we were, away from centre of the cavern where it was dark and could not be seen.

I saw the stranger was hurt. So, made my mind up, If I could help to protect it, it could help to protect myself.'

Helen poured her a glass of water, Charlyyk sipped from it.

'I could tell the stranger was struggling. It was common sense to give the stranger assistance, for the stranger was brave and together we could escape, Charlyyk took another sip of water and carried on telling her side of the story, how she struggled, to sew Bryn up. 'When I had done, the best I could, this Stranger fell asleep. It was so cold, so I took the covering from the dead beast that it was wearing, and covered us with it, then cuddled this stranger that had saved myself, that act was to keep us both as warm as possible. When later I heard the other beast, had started to crowd around, looking at their dead comrade. I woke this stranger up, to warn it of the danger we were in.'

Alex was more interested in what was seen in the arena. 'When you were in the arena, watching your dad fighting for your survival, did you see anything different?' Charlyyk thought for a moment and looking at Bryn. 'Dad had lost a lot of blood, and was struggling to maintain his strength, I kept an eye on what was near and the present dangers that were mounting. The beam of light kept dropping more and more severe problems at him. The furry alligators did not come from the beam of light, there was no flash of light, I would have sensed it. How he found the strength, to hurl a furry alligator at it, I do not know how he could do that.' Charlyyk looked at her dad with a lot of pride, she knew what he had done for her. 'It was the Feeng that caught him with a terrible hit to his chest, I was already clinging to his legs when the beam of light engulfed us, and then we were somewhere else.'

Alex looked at a sheet of paper, 'About the holding pen, can you tell us what you can recall of what went on there.

Charlyyk paused for thought, she remembered what Bryn had said how important it was for them to remember as much as they could about what had happened. 'When we were herded off the craft that took us there, we were pushed into a large crate, it smelt of other creatures.' She stopped and closed her eyes. Bryn knew the trembling in her body was her reacting the nightmare, then Charlyyk's hand reached out for his, her grasp was tight. 'We had been lowered down when the crate was opened, then we were there in that hellhole of a place.'

She was not happy with what she was recalling, when she looked at Bryn, 'I could smell something, that I had smelt before, I could not see it, but the scent was in my nose.'

Alex went to say something, but Major Carter stopped him. 'Be patient, Charlyyk is delving into her memory banks. Give her time.'

Helen could tell by how her ears and eyes were twitching, that she was at a different place... then her eyes opened. 'It was at the place where the group lived, it was there.'

She looked terrified. Helen took her hand then looking into her eyes Helen could see the eyes had changed to a mauve colour, this worried her, made Bryn's aware of what was happening to her. He too became concerned, seeing the different colour in her eyes, but he did not want to disrupt her thinking.

Charlyyk had found the piece of memory she needed. 'We found strange footprints, around the opening to our living burrow.'

Alex could tell by the way Charlyyk was behaving, that these footprints, were different than what they had ever seen before. 'How strange were they?'

Charlyyk held her hands up. 'All beings, on our planet, have four digits, these footprints had only two, wider than a cow's.' She took a deep breath. 'Knowing how Fuung and Feeng smell, I knew it could not be either of them.'

Alex could not understand why she was so frightened. 'What is it that troubles you?'

She looked at him, 'It had killed a Fuung and dragged it off.'

Bryn's head shot around to look at her. 'No wonder you were frightened.'

Alex still could not grasp what the meaning of what they were talking about, Helen showed him a drawing of a Fuung and of a Feeng, and the difference in their size, so that they could be related to. Then he realised why Charlyyk was concerned.

Bryn thinking about what Charlyyk had told them. He had that flash of memory of when he first found himself in that arena, it was not a flash of light he had seen, out of the corner of his eye, but a large dark form, moving away. But as hard as he could try, he could not tell what it was. The worry of what was happening at that same time with the Feeng concerned him more.

Major Carter had given the military chiefs a breakdown of what they had disclosed already, and the pictures of the aliens. The story that Charlyyk had told was new. Her statement brought in the likelihood of another alien. But with no description, it did not really give them anything. But if the new alien had only two digits, how could it kill? And drag a Fuung away. It did not make sense unless it was a vehicle for something else? 'Charlyyk, did you smell anything else, that time when the Fuung was killed?

'Charlyyk's eyes closed. Her ears were twitching. Her eyes moving under her closed eyelids. For a time, she was holding on to Bryn's hands, he could feel the tension coming from her, when she opened her eyes, she turned and looked at him. 'The Alien on the craft, not the pilot, but the second one, that was also there.'

Lieu-Col Jim Murthy was an old friend of Bryn's, 'What are you thinking Alan?

The Major, nodding his head with that knowing look. 'Like we would use a horse.' Then turning to face Charlyyk, 'How big were those footprints?'

She thought for a moment, then looking around saw a newspaper, on a nearby table. Taking a sheet of newspaper, she folded it to the size she could remember. Alan taking a good look at it. 'That's a lot bigger than a carthorse's hoof.' It was not much to go on without some description of the new alien beast, but with each little nudge, it had brought something new to the table.

The military officer was now in debate, with Charlyyk's new evidence.

Time had passed, a Chelsea Pensioner approached and announced that dinner was ready and escorted them to the dining hall.

Charlyyk sat among the pensioners, enjoying the old stories from these veteran soldiers. When Bryn was asked to retell a story, he had told leading his squad into their first mission, in the Kuwait, Gulf War. He started to explained how nervous they were, Sgt Brodie had asked him to give them words of encouragement.

Bryn obliged with a story. 'We were on the beach. The wind swept in from the sea, blowing the sand into our faces. A lone piper could be heard in the distance, with shots going off all around us. Bannerman pointed to the top, of a large sand dune. The time ten-past-eleven. 'We must be there by twelve.' he demanded. The sand was soft and made the going very hard. We formed a caterpillar, and pushed ourselves up the sand dune. Shots could still be heard all around us, men falling, were left where they fell. We achieved our objective and reached the top, by twelve. Just in time to see Nick Faldo and Seve Ballesteros tee off, on the ninth, at the Old Royal Troon Open.'

Major Carter could not stop laughing. He had heard it before, but he knew the calming effect it had on those young soldiers, going into battle for the first time. It settled their nerves, so when they hit the front line, they worked as a unit. Many Army training instructors, used Captain Collier's training techniques, because of the success they had with them.

Brigadier Alex Hutton, had heard of the deeds of Captain Collier. His men would never question him because they knew he always had their welfare at heart. He would never ask them to do something he would not do himself.

Charlyyk and Helen were separated by a robust pensioner, with a large white moustache, and wire-framed glasses, he spoke to Charlyyk.

'What do you think about your new dad, Charlyyk?'

She turned towards him, and with a soft smile, 'My Auntie Gwen, has a lot of faith in her god. I have the same faith in my dad.'

During the meal, some of the pensioners were asking questions from Charlyyk. She would leave the table, walk to those that asked the questions, and give her answers directly. Helen admired the time and patience she gave them all. Charlyyk had realised that some of the pensioners were hard of hearing, and Charlyyk did not like shouting. But it gave the other pensioners a chance to see her close up, and they appreciated her efforts.

When dinner was finished, they carried on talking. The Brigadier asked Charlyyk about her own planet. She was quick to point out that she did not travel far from the place where she lived, due to the danger of being eaten; Lieu-Col Jim Murthy, then asked, 'You have lived amongst us for two years, do you question yourself on how you can adapt to our ways?'

She looked slightly annoyed at this question, 'I have to adapt. I have no choice but to adapt. If you mean, did I find it hard. No, the guidance I have received from the family, have helped to make it as easy as possible.'

Jim Murthy then went on to ask, 'What sort of question do you ask yourself?'

She looked down into her lap, her hands clasped on her knee's. 'Why were there no older ones, in the group, and no babies. Why, were there only females, all of the same age group. Living amongst you, I see family units, we did not have that, but I must have come from someone, you don't just appear like magic, do you?'

Bryn and Helen just looked at each, they had not heard this before, and they wondered how they had missed not asking about her family.

Alex Hutton wrote down what had been said, 'What made you think along those line Charlyyk?'

She shifted in her chair making her tail feel more comfortable, 'Going to school and seeing the same age groups, but with mixed sexes. In our group, on my home planet, there were only Lyyk's. At that time, we were trying to survive, so we had no reason to give it any thought. Now it does not make sense, and no matter how I try, I cannot resolve it.'

Major Carter sat down next to Bryn, 'The more we uncover, just adds to the confusion, with more question unanswered.'

Helen looked around at them, the questions had dried up. 'I think we should call time on this, we are not going anywhere, and we need to give ourselves time to reflect on what has been said?'

Alex Hutton spoke with Jim Murthy, then said, 'Yes we agree, if we need to talk again, I suggest that we meet you at your house Helen, and thank you for assistance.' Alex also wanted to dissect the information that had been given before asking any more questions. He felt they needed a clear objective as to where the next questioning should be directed. 'We can tell by what has been said by both Bryn and Charlyyk, that the circumstances of them meeting was a hit and miss. To make anything from what we have heard, it will need careful consideration.'

***

On Sunday morning, a cold biting wind blew. It made the three of them push harder. The wind was holding back the chance of rain. Charlyyk had covered her head with the hood to protect her ears just in case it rained. The trumpet shape of her ears, could fill with water when it rained and made it uncomfortable for her. Gwen had made her some plastic covers for her ears so she could shower. But she did not like wearing them out in public. She felt a little self-conscience about them.

The shower, when she could feel the water flowing over her without worrying about her ears, was a sheer delight. Shampooing her hair was something else she delighted in. Michel had mentioned how her body had changed due to this world's bathroom pampering, her skin was leathery when she first arrived now was soft, her hair was straw-like now it glowed, smooth and silky.

Standing in front of the mirror, she loved feeling herself. Could not help herself from running her hands over her own body exploring the changes. She dressed in her new silk lingerie, and the dress she had bought at Christmas. She felt she had won the lottery.

Helen had wonder where she was and came to see if she was alright. 'Hi, there you Ok... I was getting worried?'

Charlyyk was sitting at her dressing table, admiring herself. She knew the changes she was going through, and she liked them. Helen stood behind her, took the hairbrush and gently brushed her hair. 'Thanks, mum.'

Helen smiled at her, bent down, and kissed the top of her head. 'Pleasure darling'.

At Carpenters Cottage, Bryn explained what had incurred at the meeting the day before. Harold and Gwen listened intensely. Harold mauled over the information carefully. 'So, at no time, did you not see any older persons in your group?'

Charlyyk pondered the question. 'No many times, I have asked myself that same question?' Then she paused for a second. 'Another thought keeps entering my head the thing that killed the Fuung was it protecting us?'

Helen listened to what Charlyyk was saying. 'That could mean all this could have been orchestrated by them?'

Bryn's face showed that the possibilities were there. 'It is feasible. It was set up very nicely, that anyone could have been chosen at random, was this not random?'

Helen could see Charlyyk was getting concerned. She placed her arm around Charlyyk, 'I'm so glad it was you, sweetheart.'

Looking up at Helen, the look in Charlyyk's face, 'I was worried you might have got angry?' Then a little gulp from her. 'Thinking you were set up.'

Harold made a motion with his hand. 'What could they be doing this for, there must be a reason?'

Gwen stepped into the conversation. 'Let's think about it, we have to be logical with the information we have to go on. To make a snap decision, could lead us astray.' Gwen, was watching Charlyyk, her expression looked as if she was thinking hard. Gwen who had spent most of her time getting to understand Charlyyk, and her special ways. She had seen this change in Charlyyk demeanour before, and it had led to problems. Helen and Gwen took Charlyyk into the lounge to settle her down.

Bryn and Harold filled their glasses and quietly went over much of what had been talked about. Harold collected some paper and strategically, started to put things in order of events...sequences that Bryn had described. It did not change anything. The matter still did not make any sense at all. He screwed up the paper and tossed it into the waste bin.

***

The morning run, during breakfast and then on the school bus, Charlyyk was quiet. The thoughts of the week-end at the meeting, running through her head would not go away. Mace tried hard to talk to her, but Charlyyk could not engage with anyone. At school, the posse allowed her a little space. After the first lesson with Mrs Butler, Mike spoke with Charlyyk, at first, she did not want to talk, he would not let her carry on taking her problems on her own. It was in Mr Waverly lesson that Mike made a plea to Charlyyk to speak to the class. She had helped so many of them when they needed help, he argued, it was her duty to allow them to help her. Mr Waverly was keen to help him to persuade Charlyyk to talk,

There were tears in Charlyyk's eyes. Mike took her hand and supported her, 'A trouble shared is a trouble halved.' He said to her.

Julia was the next one to give her encouragement. She took hold of her other hand, not saying anything, just giving her a squeeze.

As Charlyyk began to see the concern on all their faces, she took a deep breath, then told them, about what had happened at the weekend, and revelations that had been discussed.

Mr Waverly pulled a chair up and sat down in front of her. 'Charlyyk, you have done nothing wrong just a pawn in some other people game.'

Mace and Sandra, could not stand back and allow their friend to take the guilt solely on her own shoulders, approached her in a caring manner

But it was Mike who spoke, 'Charlyyk we all love you... You have given us great pleasure with your friendship. And in your own way, you have helped us all to look at ourselves more closely. Never expecting anything in return, this is our turn to support you. But if you are as you are with us now, what are you like to your new family? Talk with them, you will realise that they won't blame you, but love you, just like us.'

At lunchtime, the posse was in full support mode, giving Charlyyk enough space, but tried hard to keep off the subject of the morning.

Mr Waverly informed, Mrs Landon of what had happened, and she was soon on the phone to the Colliers. Helen answered the phone and assured Mrs Landon the headmistress that they had allowed Charlyyk a little time to be able to think through what she thought had taken place on that faraway planet. Her unique way of looking at problems usually resulted in a solution to them. Helen thanked Louise and confirmed her intention to discuss the matter with Charlyyk's father.

The school bus trundled down the lane and stopped at the cottage. Charlyyk stepped down from the bus, to see Bryn and Helen standing together, with warm smiles on their faces. As she walked towards them, they raised their hands to greet her. She rushed into their arms and buried herself in them. They could feel her body trembling with total emotion.

Bryn knelt down in front of her, 'Sweetheart we both love you very much, and that will never change. We are a family, and whatever happens, we will stick together.'

Inside the cottage, Charlyyk relayed what her classmates had said to her.

Helen picked up on her admiration of Mike, he had been instrumental in rallying the class around her to give her support. After dinner Bryn made an effort to sit with Charlyyk, giving her plenty of cuddles.

Later when Charlyyk was in her bedroom, she texted Janet explaining to her what had happened, Janet did not text back, phoned her instead on the landline, the conversation lasted for an hour. Charlyyk conveyed her fear that she had been used to in some way. She could not work out logically why the Aliens had done what they had done. Janet promised, she will return on Wednesday.

***

At breakfast, Helen spoke with Charlyyk. Bryn watched on, pleased with how Helen was handling the situation. As Helen walked with Charlyyk to meet the school bus. Charlyyk put her arms around Helen and gave her a big loving hug. As the bus door opened, Mace and Sarah were soon surrounding her. She turned and faced Helen, the warm smile she gave her from the bus, gave Bryn satisfaction that his two girls were now as one again.

At school the posse was soon in attendance, checking to see if Charlyyk was OK. She thanked them all for helping her. Then to Mike's surprise, Charlyyk gave him an extra big hug, and a long lingering kiss on his cheek.

'Mike, you persisted in helping me, and I am so grateful. I was so down in myself I could not see the truth...that when you have friends who care, you should listen to them.'

As the school bell rang, they preceded to attend their lessons. Mrs Landon asked Charlyyk to see her in her office. 'Charlyyk, Mr Waverly and Mrs Butler informed me how upset you were yesterday, and how it affected the whole class, so how are you?'

Charlyyk tried to smile but struggled, 'I've spoken with my parents, and I now see I should have been more open with them, and not bottled up my emotions. I thought I had let them down, that I would have been to blame if my dad had died on that planet. But my mum said how could I blame myself, if I did not know why it was happening.'

Charlyyk went on to explain the story in full to Mrs Landon, and how Mike had persisted in her talking to the whole class: Mrs Landon stood up and took Charlyyk hand. 'Come, let's take a walk.'

Leaving the office, they walked around the school. Louise Landon showing Charlyyk the importance of school life. Looking in on classes and the involvement of the teacher and students, and the interconnection between them.

'When you go, and see your aunt and uncle, and look at the photos on the walls, it tells you how we as teachers, get involved trying hard to get the best from you. So, you get the best possible chance in life. Any problem that you may have, can upset school life. We need the students to confide in us so we can help. You are fortunate to have such good friends, its good friends that bring out the best in each other, like yesterday, you brought out the best in Mike. Mr Waverly remarked on how he handled the situation. Mr Waverly said he was the most unlikely person to have done what he did yesterday. Such friendship you could not buy for all the money in the world, so value it with pride.'

At lunch the posse asked Charlyyk about the morning. They had observed her walking with the headmistress, and were inquisitive. Jan especially pushed for details, but Charlyyk only gave them a brief summary of what was said.

Back home at Oakleaves. Charlyyk was more forthcoming about what had occurred that morning. Helen did not tell her, about the phone call she had made to Louise Landon, informing her of the weekend revelations. Getting Charlyyk to talk about it settle her.

During dinner, Charlyyk remembered Janet was returning on Wednesday and informed her parents, Bryn agreed with Helen, it would be good for Charlyyk.

When they returned to Oakleaves after the morning run, the laughing, and the playful mood carried on through breakfast. Charlyyk was back to her usual self.

She ran to the bus, so eager to be with her friends. She hugged Sarah and Mace; Bryn and Helen with their arms wrapped around each other, with smiley faces waved her off. Life at the cottage was back to normal. The playful way Bryn grabbed Helen's hand left no doubts in Helen mind the good life had returned to Oakleaves.

Tim Pearson's class were studying the smart board. 'These are the points you have made in The Changing Face of Britain. I want you to write a speech about it. You should write only four paragraphs to explain your point of view. May I suggest, before you start to write, allow time to read your work and check your use of language before you finish. Plan your format. How will you open your speech? First paragraph: a direct statement of how you feel and why. Second paragraph: seeing other points of view. Third paragraph: the evidence for your point of view. Fourth paragraph: the effect of what you propose. And how will you close your speech?'

At lunchtime, the posse were gathered together, discussing the homework Mr Pearson had given them. Sandra and Peter now an item sat with Julia, next to Charlyyk. Mike was now a major player, since his big part, he played in helping Charlyyk. The rest of the posse in close order, the debate was orderly, each making notes on what was discussed. Keeping a close eye on them was Mrs Butler, she looked pleased with what she could see. Her report to Mrs Landon that all was well.

Janet was at Oakleaves when Charlyyk arrived home from school and was standing in the driveway waiting for her as the bus arrived, Charlyyk had so missed her, the embrace they gave each other, showed Janet had missed Charlyyk too.

Later after dinner, when Charlyyk had explained to Janet, the confusion she had got herself into. 'I felt that it was me that was at fault. I needed to put it right, but could not see how. The more I thought about it, the worst it became.'

Janet gave her a cuddle. 'Now you see what real friends are about. We are here to help when time get hard. Those that stay and help, are your true friends.'

Chapter 33

Analysing Charlyyk

Bryn trailed the girls on the morning run. The three were talking girl talk, and it was probably not for Bryn's ears. He did not mind. Seeing them all happy gave him an inner satisfaction. As it was becoming a nice family unit.

Helen was at ease when Janet was there. She found herself confiding in Janet, with the things she found hard too with Gwen. Although Gwen was no problem to talk to, she was still Bryn sister, which Helen had felt twinges towards awkwardness.

After Charlyyk had gone to school, the adults went to Carpenters Cottage. Over coffee, they discussed the situation that the weekend before had thrown up.

Harold seemed surprised how Charlyyk had reacted, but Gwen did not. 'No, I disagree, because of her love for Bryn. Any thought, that could have jeopardised him would have concerned her. Because she could not see the truth of it, it compounded itself. The more she thought how to solve the problem, the bigger the problem became. We have a lot to thank young Mike, for grasping the situation. Before Charlyyk had a total meltdown.'

Harold needed to understand, Gwen theory. 'But Charlyyk's logic has always served her well, she usually finds what she is looking for.' Harold was still in his own mind, still looking for clues to how Charlyyk would react to these situations. 'And if she can't find the solution she keeps trying. The tension she builds starts to increase till it creates a ticking time-bomb. If allowed to go on it would have led to a meltdown.' Gwen glanced at Harold with raised eyebrows, agreed with him.

Janet was with Gwen, on her theory, 'I totally agree with you Gwen. It's the way she handles most thing, with logical solutions. The problem was that she could not come to that way of thinking, with what evidence she had, for it was all conjecture with no facts.'

Helen asked Janet, was she going to use this knowledge in one of her articles. 'Definitely not.' Janet replied. 'I am now Charlyyk's friend, that brings responsibilities, to act as a friend. I told you all from the beginning I was not here to dig the dirt. She has vulnerabilities which I will not discuss. Charlyyk really isn't any different than us. She has a brain; she just uses it differently.'

Helen reached over and touched her hand, 'You are right. She really isn't any different, she just a young girl growing up on a different planet.'

Bryn had been quiet up till then. 'We are not condemning her. We just need to understand her. We know from past experiences she can be a little sensitive. As most people can be. She has feelings, just the same as us.'

Janet selected a biscuit from the plate in front of her. 'When James talks about Charlyyk, he has so much respect for her. He acts like a big brother towards her, and it beginning to rubbed off on me. When I think about her? I'm her sister, and want the best for her.'

Gwen just nodded her head, she wholly understood what Janet was saying, 'I feel like a mother duck towards her, always trying to shelter her under my wing.'

Helen gave a big sigh. 'Charlyyk calling me mum, just makes me go weak at the knees. And when she cuddles up to me, I could just melt. I never in my wildest dreams, thought this could happen to me. So when she was so troubled on Monday, I felt it too, and it really hurt... but like what Bryn has said, we do need to understand her, so that we can help her.'

***

Bryn and Helen waited for the school bus the next day. Sheltering under a large golfing umbrella, from the deluge of rain, stepped toward the bus as it stopped, giving Charlyyk cover, the laughing face of Charlyyk bringing out a laugh in Helen, 'What's the laugh for sweetheart?'

Charlyyk keeping as close to Helen as possible, because of the rain, 'Fred the bus driver, said you looked like a mushroom standing there.'

As they entered the cottage, to Charlyyk's surprise James appeared, 'Hi twinkle.' She rushed into his arms and kissed him, with as many kisses that she could. Janet poked her with her finger, 'Get off he's mine.' Then Janet tickled her.

Helen took Charlyyk's coat. Charlyyk sat with James and Janet, while Bryn and Helen started preparing the evening meal.

When James returned home, Janet and Helen sat with Charlyyk, discussing her homework for Mr Pearson. Bryn watched the interaction between them. It confirmed his theory of a good family unit.

The men's magazine for which Bryn posed in the Photo shoot, had sent him to peruse before General release. It was spread out in front of him. He was not sure he liked it. The article that was printed before the one of his, it featured a scantily clad girl. That looked younger than Charlyyk. But Janet had confirmed she was of legal age.

The editor had not made changes to the basic story, it was as Janet had written.

Another article on men's health had caught Bryn's attention, that he read with interest on prostate problems in middle-aged men. Although he was not struggling with it himself, but thought it would be good to keep an eye on it, just in case.

***

On Friday, the weather was damp. The trek up the Lane, leading up to the farm was very slippery. James had kept an eye out for them and came over to the gate to collect kisses from Janet and Charlyyk. Bryn could not help laughing at the little heel click James gave as he turned away, then as he landed slipped and found himself flat on the ground, with the two girls rushing back to check he was all right.

Janet collected enough material to write about the visit to The Royal Chelsea Hospital. She was finishing an article for a teen magazine, had based it on the fashion side of Charlyyk. She was expecting some more fashion shots of her at the weekend.

Mike had asked Charlyyk, to help him with his homework. He had completely messed up. Charlyyk went through it with the support of Julia. Afterwards, Julia said to Charlyyk. 'It wasn't that bad.' She had noticed Mike was more assertive, then he used to be, 'What do you reckon...do you think Mike is changing?'

Charlyyk thought for a moment, 'I believe we are all changing. We have all started, to look at life differently. Take Peter and Sandra for example. They are not stupid with their relationship, it is, so nice to see how they respect each other. Charlyyk sensed the vibes Julia was giving out about Mike had become stronger than before.

Sarah overhearing what they were saying, 'Do you sense something Charlyyk?'

'Well, my nose is picking up something.' Sarah and Julia leaned closer in, so Charlyyk could whisper, 'Jan is giving out vibes.'

Their eyes widen, and they closed tighter, 'Who with?'

Charlyyk lowered her voice, 'None of our age group, it happens every time Mace's brother is around.'

Sarah asked breathlessly, 'Is he responding back?'

Charlyyk smiled, 'Oh yes, it still early days, but there is a reaction from him.'

There was glee in their eyes, knowing something no one else knew. Charlyyk was quick to remind them, 'Now don't say anything. Otherwise, you could spoil it.' She looked at them both, very sternly, 'Now promise me, you will not say anything to anyone if you do, I will never confide in you again.'

They both gave their promises to her, that the matter would stay between them.

Charlyyk did not want Julia to know how, she was responding to Mike. Well, not yet.

Thomas, Rachel and Margret arrived at Oakleaves at three. There was a jovial atmosphere to them as they entered the Cottage. Bryn greeted them back, Helen was already making tea, and as usual, they congregated in the kitchen.

Margret was most pleased with what Janet had written for them. When Janet entered the kitchen. Margret spread her arms out to greet her, 'Thank you, Janet! Thank you so very much, the articles are fantastic.'

Bryn, still could not believe the changes that have happened in his life since his return to earth with Charlyyk. He had gone from obscure lonelyness to living in a beehive. Helen touched his hand, 'Come on sweetheart, the bus will be here soon.' He looked into her eyes, slipped his arm around her waist, pulled her towards him and kissed her. Helen sighed, then leaning back, 'I will give you, twenty-four hours, to stop doing that, kind sir.' Then kissed him back. 'The bus?'

With that they went to meet Charlyyk. Cuddling together under the golfing brolly. Charlyyk stepping off the bus with an enormous smile spread across her face, ran to them, given them one great big hug. She had already spotted the Picasso parked in front of the garage. Her jaunty walk towards the cottage, left Bryn and Helen in no doubt that they had their daughter back.

Inside the cottage, they were all waiting for her, with lots of hugs and kisses, but to all their surprises Margret produced a large carrier bag. 'Charlyyk, I saw this, and I thought of you. So, with all my love this is yours.' Charlyyk peered into the bag and gently took out an emerald green dress made in a fine wool knit. It was V-necked, with three-quarter-length sleeve, with a half collar that rose up at the back.

Janet looked at how Charlyyk received this gift, taking in mental notes. Trying to understand the emotions she was experiencing. 'Come, let's try it on.'

They both collected up the bits and went to the bedroom. Charlyyk was a little taken back, by this surprise from Margret, it still showed on her face.

Janet helped her to put it on, then opening the wardrobe doors, to allow her to see how it looked on her, Charlyyk admitted to Janet, that it looked better on than it did off. 'It looked a bit old fashioned when I took it out of the bag, but now, Wow, it looks great, it reminds me of Audrey Hepburn, in *Breakfast at Tiffany's.'*

She turned this way and that. She thrust her hands in the side pockets pulling the skirt out to the side, then letting it go. She looked at herself from the back and seeing how her tail behaved in the dress, 'Come let's show Margret what a great dress she has brought me.'

The family looked amazed how the dress had transformed her, it had put a few years on her, she did not look at all, as a little girl. Margret asked her to turn around. Then gave Charlyyk a hug. 'This is just as I saw it in the shop, with you in it. I am so pleased I bought it. You look fantastic.'

Charlyyk hugged Margret. 'Thank you so very much. It's such a lovely gesture, and I really do appreciate it.'

Janet was already taking in the photo shoot options for Charlyyk. 'Black shoes, a little heel, patent.' 'Yes, tomorrow morning, we are going to a little shoe shop I know.' Janet was pressing buttons on her phone. 'Tina, Janet Stokes, now listen... narrow fitting, size six, black patent, little heel, anything?' Janet waited for the reply, 'Good girl! See you early tomorrow.'

Rachel sidled up to Janet. 'Can I come?' Janet took her arm in hers, 'Of course, you can love to have you on board.' Then turning to Bryn and Helen with a guilty look on her face. 'Sorry, I hope you don't mind?'

Bryn looked at Helen they both nodded. 'Of course not, it is what Charlyyk needs to be able to do.'

The rest of the day, the cottage was a hive of activity. Margret going over the details of the exhibition. Thomas and Rachel explaining how the trip to Liverpool went. Janet, taking Bryn and Helen through the details of what she wanted to achieve.

Charlyyk in her bedroom on the computer with Julia on the other end, telling her of the emails she was getting from Mike? 'So, he needs to react to someone, so I told him to speak with Mace. Did I do right Charlyyk?'

Charlyyk agreed with her and signed off. Mike needed the help of someone and Mace fitted the bill perfectly. Charlyyk had watched the change Mike had been making, she also knew it was not intentional. They were just happening. Mace's quiet manner was what Mike needed.

***

Janet at the wheel of her red Mini, with One Direction beating out of her car stereo system. The girls sand along...well, the two women sang and Charlyyk howled. Making good headway towards Bourne End and the little shoe shop.

At the Cottage, Bryn was in conversation with Major Carter. Bryn had told him of the theory, that he had needed, to go over the details with him. The Major listened 'It definitely makes sense Bryn, but it throws open a lot of other question the top brass has been looking at.' They sat and discussed a few angles. Helen had made a detail report for him to give to the various Arm Forces. In the report, Helen mentioned what Charlyyk remarked on. The point that they were all females of a certain age, within the group that she lived with. Major Carter sighed. 'It's been a constant drip, drip, of information Bryn.'

Bryn looked at Alan, 'Yes but, it is usually what happens in these circumstances. You cannot remember anything then some little nudge, then you do remember, or see it in a clearer light.' Bryn suddenly stopped, looked towards the floor, closing his eyes, then looking at Alan, 'I saw a large shape, move in the corner of my eye, when I was trying to survive, but can I see it now? No, but one day, something will trigger that image, then it's back to the drawing board.'

Janet parked the car in the pub's car park just down the little side street fifty yards from Tina's shoe shop. Tina, the shop owner, was finding Charlyyk's feet a little troublesome, 'My, they are narrow.' Janet knew she would not give up on Charlyyk.

It was no surprise when Tina's assistant came back with four boxes. In the second shoe box, a lovely pair of black, kitten heel, multi-strap, court shoes. Then the Cinderella moment when the foot fitted the shoe arrived. As Charlyyk walked up and down, stopping and turning, she looked on happy bunny.

Also in the box was a little clutch bag, made of the same bookbinder leather, to match the shoes. Rachel and Janet just loved them together. Tina could not find a price for the shoes as they had been in the shop for many years. But Janet worked out an offer that Tina could not refuse. Neither Janet nor Rachel could resist picking up a couple of pairs themselves. The drive back was much the same with the full throttle sing-along with One Direction.

Major Carter completed his talk with Bryn and warned him that more meeting would be required as he was leaving.

Margret was with Thomas in the study finalising the set up for the exhibition. As they all enjoyed a cup of coffee. The trio arrived back, still in fine voice. Helen took an interest in Charlyyk's new shoes, but it was the little clutch bag that stole the limelight, as Helen remarked. 'It's the feel of the leather, it so soft.'

After the coffee's, Janet with the help of everyone, set up the photo shoot; the lighting, the white linen drapes, a few props dropped here and there. Charlyyk came in wearing the usual casual clothes she normally wore...tight jeans, casual tops, with her favourite white tennis shoes. She posed like the models in the fashion magazines. The white drapes, by altering the colour filters, created a different ambience.

Then Charlyyk changed into the Laura Ashley dress, with the Moreno cherry red tights. then the Burberry camel coat. Rachel and Helen doing the makeup, and her hair in between the shots, the dress she bought at Christmas and the dress Margret had brought her was also worn, with the black shoes and clutch bag. Charlyyk surprised them by posing in her silk underwear, and nightwear. Helen keeping a close eye on those proceedings. Especially when Bryn had quired the scantly dress girl in the Maxim magazine.

Time had flown by. They were all a little tired and hungry. Everyone was pleased to hear that Bryn had ordered a table at an Italian Restaurant.

Clearing up did not take long. They were all keen to go to the restaurant for dinner, the conversation was mainly about, how the day had gone. Harold and Gwen were already at 'The Restaurant Milan' an authentic Italian eating place, with long tables to accommodate families. This was a favourite of Harold and Gwen's, the head waiter Gino was already buzzing around making them feel at home, Gino's younger brother Alberto, was soon taking their coats, and helping to seat them.

Helen was liking her new life. She recalled lonely nights, eating on her own. What a change had occurred. She loved this family way of life. Yes, sometimes it was hard work, but God, it was worth it. Looking around at the family, with the cheery banter that they were all having, confirmed her reasons for marrying Bryn. Watching Charlyyk so involved with everyone, her laughter was infectious, for this was a party girl having fun. The smile broke out over Helen's face. She was so gratified finding herself in this inestimable position at this time of her life.

***

On Sunday morning. Rachel laying in a nice warm bed, felt contented as she pulled the covers up and settled herself.

Ten minutes later the door opened. Her Mother entered with a tray, bearing two large mugs of tea, 'Move over sweetheart and let your mother in.'

Rachel could not refuse. It had been a long time this had happened. It had been the morning of her wedding, and it felt special then. 'I have never stopped loving you mum, nor shall I ever stop loving you. But I love Thomas more, and now I'm with child, you stand a close third. But you are not out of my daily thoughts. It's not for me to give you a chance, but for you to earn it.'

Margret realised what Rachel was telling her, it would depend on what she does, not what they do. The onus was on her.

Rachel placing her empty mug onto the bedside cabinet. 'When you see Thomas, his dad, Harold and Michel. You see in them, what most girl's mothers, would love their daughter's husbands, to be like. But it does not mean that's what they will end up with. I am blest with Thomas, and I intend to keep him, whatever it takes. When Thomas's mum, came to our wedding. I saw how she handled Bryn. I vowed to carry on using her methods with Thomas. Yes, mum, it suits me fine, Thomas gets what he wants and I get what I want. I'm as proud as punch, doing just that.'

Margret saw herself in Rachel. The same determination, though Rachel endgame was so different to her own.

Rachel cuddled her mother, 'Come join us in our adventure. Don't walk away to be on your own.'

The door opened, and Thomas walked in. Seeing the two of them in bed together, made him smile, 'Hi this looks cosy, can I refill your mugs?'

The two girls pass their mugs to him, and with cheeky grins, 'Yes please.'

When Thomas had left. Rachel looked at her mother. 'See mum, I've caught the biggest fish in the sea, and he is in my keep net, where I mean to keep him.'

Margret reached toward Rachel's tummy and stroked it. 'That's one special keep net, darling.'

Rachel's wry smile and little snigger implied; she knew mothers meaning.

Breakfast was loud and buoyant, with much flippancy to it, the banter was how Charlyyk had performed the day before. They were comparing the different top fashion models, who did they think she had tried to impersonate. Thomas remarked, 'It definitely isn't Elle Macpherson. The Body.' Everyone named a different model, each one was subject to scrutiny, then Thomas brought the loudest laugh when with a haughty flick of the wrist, 'Of course it could only have been, Julian Clary.'

The phone ringing, took Bryn to his study, Thomas, Janet and Charlyyk went to the lounge to go over the photo pictures of Charlyyk. Margret, Rachel and Helen cleared the breakfast table.

Bryn picking up the phone was surprised to hear Brigadier Su Shi talking.

'Bryn, I can call you Bryn, not Brian?'

'Yes, Su Shi, Bryn will be okay.'

'Bryn, I have a report in front of me, from Major Carter, explaining, your theories, they leave us with many questions still to be answered?'

Bryn reached over to a folder, he had predicted, the calls would come, as soon as Alan Carter released the information in the report, that Helen had written.

'I have the report in front of me now Su Shi, is there any points, I can help you with?'

'Yes, how was it, we did not pick this up earlier, it puts an entirely new meaning, even a different route to go down.'

'We were casually talking, when Charlyyk was asked did she have any worries on her planet. Charlyyk started to speak about the group she was living with. She could not understand why they were all of a set age group, no old elderly, or very young. Like when she is at school, the students were off the same age group. This started a discussion between, my brother-in-law and myself.'

'Yes Bryn, I see we were only looking one way at this. Bryn, I will speak with Yuri, and Chad, probably I'll get back to you on this, Bye.'

When Bryn entered the kitchen, he let Helen know what was said, Helen asked did he sound annoyed at what was in the report. Bryn replied, 'No, he was his usual self, inquisitive to get the exact meaning of what was said.'

Janet seeing Rachel's baby bump growing was making her broody, her desire for James was becoming stronger. It was creating a need to hurry back to Parson's farm. Janet had phoned James to brace himself for her return; he was quick to instruct her to meet in the barn. This excited her even more. The roar of her poor Mini, as her pedal hit the metal, the back end of the car skidding as it left the drive.

Rachel nudged Thomas. They had seen how impatient Janet was getting, as she hurried to finish what she had started that morning. Then hearing the roar of her Mini, just brought up an urge in them, to rub baby oil on her bump. Their rush to the bedroom brought smiles to everyone else's faces.

Margret looking at Helen, 'And it's not even spring,'

Later at Carpenters Cottage. With the men in the kitchen, the girls in the lounge, each talking on their own favourite subjects. Bryn relaying the conversation he had with Su Shi.

Michel stroking his chin had the look of someone that had been asking himself the same question over in his mind a few time before. But now he was sure. 'Bryn would you bring Charlyyk to my surgery one evening.'

Bryn and Harold had the same expression written on their faces. 'Why?'

'Let look at it this way…if there was an alternative reason for Charlyyk to be here, could those aliens, have planted something in her to monitor her?'

Bryn and Harold's heads stared straight at Michel, not in shook but more with realisation.

Harold said slowly. 'It could be a possibility, Bryn?'

Michel still stroking his chin, 'The test I have carried out on Charlyyk, indicate that X-ray would not have any detrimental effect on her, so let's give it a go.'

Thomas asked, 'Are you sure it won't harm her, or set off a chain reaction in her?' Michel nodded his head, 'Better we do it, then the Government. At least we would know when to stop, but would they?'

Harold nodded. 'I'm with you Bryn, better us then them.'

Bryn nodded, 'When Michel?'

Michel sounded more eager, 'Tomorrow night, I will set up the surgery, so Charlyyk won't worry about it. I will tell her, it is essential we carry out these tests, tomorrow night.'

Over dinner, Michel slipped the matter of the Xray into the conversation, as though it was a matter-of-fact thing.' Charlyyk had complete faith in Michel, did not query his request. Gwen and Helen were the ones that their manner at looking first at Michel, then toward Bryn and Harold. Their concern faded as the men looked satisfied with Michel suggestion.

***

On Monday, the school bus dropped the students at the school gates. The mingling of friends talking about their weekend activities. Charlyyk, Sarah and Mace, strolling towards the area where the posse always congregated, exchanging hugs, high fives, and kisses as they met.

Charlyyk impressing them with photos of the fashion shoot when the school bell sounded. There was a surge to get into the warmth of the school. Mr Waverly for science, then Mrs Butler for maths. At lunch, Charlyyk enjoyed what Helen had filled her lunch box. Helen always made sure each days lunch had something different.

Bryn and Helen for their part was having lunch with Margret. Thomas had taken Rachel shopping, and they would not be home until late. The phone rang, Helen answered, but soon gave it to Bryn.

'Hi, Bryn… Chad… spoken with Su Shi on the report your Helen has given us. I agree with him…this opens a new can of worms. I do believe, another chat could be in order. I am in touch with your Home Secretary and Defence Department to come to you this time, if you don't mind?'

'No, we don't mind. We welcome it. Charlyyk has had enough up evils so far, and we have just settled her over this, so please come to us.'

Chad paused, 'Bryn, the computer guy from the Johnson Space Centre wants to come and discuss some of his findings with Charlyyk. Is there somewhere we could put him up?'

'Chad, bring him. I remember him well, and Charlyyk would love to see him again. We will sort him out.'

Helen listening in on the conversation. 'Harold liked him, let's ask him?'

In Miss Vasey class, they were watching Charlyyk apply wet on wet, just as Thomas had shown her. She switched brushes, adding strokes of paint, turning the splotches into flowers. There were no drips of paint. She looked so relaxed as she worked. She was enjoying the experience no end. Learning technique that had given new meaning to art. Alice Vasey showing her how to use sea salt and cotton buds to soak up some of the wet paint, and how to use the blunt end of the brush, making white strikes, to give a different aspect to the painting. Charlyyk now could see what Margret and Thomas were remarking to about learning different technics to gain different results.

That evening, on the drive to Michel's surgery, Bryn allowed Charlyyk to sit in the front so she could choose the music she liked. He did this to make sure Charlyyk was settled. He even tried to show an interest in what she wanted to play, again trying to relax her.

Michel welcomed them to the surgery. He had a Labrador dog, ready on the table, 'Come in, let me show you how it works.' Clare, Michel's prodigy, took the X-ray of the Labrador. Then a little wait for the results. They put the X-ray picture up on the screen. 'As you can see Charlyyk, he has swallowed his owner's car keys. Look where they are.' Pointing to the tell- tell sign of them on the X-ray picture. So, she could see the bone structure of Bruno. 'Now too many X-rays can be harmful to us. So, we must put in place, a few safeguards. Clare will guide you through the procedure.'

Charlyyk removed all her clothes and jewellery, she put on a gown then got on the table. Clare showed her what position she wanted her in, then she set the procedure in motion. Clare then moved her to achieve a different view and finished the X-ray session. Then they waited while Charlyyk dressed. The X-ray results were just as Michel had thought. The plate that was visible, the size of an old fashion razor blade. The two X-ray plates allowed them to see how they, the aliens had attached it to the base of the skull by to pins.

Charlyyk was not upset, though took a keen interest in it. 'Can you remove it, Michel?' She asked.

'No Charlyyk, as you can see, the pins that fix it to your skull could do you damage if we remove them, I would rather we get a specialist team to attempt that, we love you too much, to jump in like amateurs, and do you harm.' Helen put her arm around her, 'We will find the best people, to do the right thing for you sweetheart, and that's a promise.'

Clare touch Charlyyk's arm, 'I will enlarge these X-ray plates, so we can get a clearer idea what is involved. It will give us some indication why it was planted there in the first place.'

Charlyyk thoughts that were going through her head, were like anybody else who would be thinking. 'Why?'

In the car, Charlyyk sat in the back with Helen cuddling her. Helen could feel Charlyyk's insecurity, and vulnerabilities, a small child's weakness, holding on to its mother for safety. Bending and kissing the top of her head, hearing herself saying, 'Now, now little one, mummies here.' The tears welling in her eyes. Helen pulled her closer to her, both arms holding her, remembering what Gwen had said, how she felt like a mother duck, wrapping her wings around her young, to protect them. Yes, Helen felt just like that.

***

Tuesday, Charlyyk woke, finding Helen in bed with her, still wrapped in her arms. Charlyyk laid there not moving, recalling how she had asked her to stay with her. Knowing when Helen made a promise, she saw it through. It settled herself knowing she was loved. When Bryn later peered into the bedroom. Seeing Charlyyk laying there in Helen's arms, with the most contented smile on her face, looking back at him. She winked and blew him a kiss. He shaped his hands into the letter T, she nodded. Bryn headed for the kitchen. When he returned, Helen was awake sitting up on the bed with Charlyyk. Placing the tray on the bedside cabinet. So, he could give them both a kiss, then handed them their teas.

'How are you, sweetheart?'

Charlyyk looked at them both, and then she gave them each a long lingering kiss. 'I could not feel better than right now... you make me very humble to have you two as my parents, and I promise you both I will make you proud of me, as I am proud of you.' Charlyyk had thought on all the possibilities, she had come to a conclusion during the night. She had lived without any side effects. No headaches, she was fine. She even reflected on everything, she could remember, even to those terrible days trying to survive living with the group. It raised other issues, why did her memory only begin from that period she had no recollection of her earlier childhood, that Sarah, Sandra and Julia could recall.

There was no run that morning. It had been time to reflect on being a family unit, relating to each other what it meant to be as one. They talked for some time, reflecting on what had happened since they all had met, and how they now found themselves enjoying each other. Time had flown by quickly, and it was a rush to meet the bus.

Harold and Gwen had already spoken with Michel when Bryn and Helen arrived and immediately inquired about how Charlyyk was taking it. Bryn strolled off with Harold telling him of the evening events, Helen sat with Gwen doing the same thing. The conversation had not changed, as they sat around the dining table over coffees. Bryn informed them that Chad and Su Shi had spoken with him and planned to visit them here. Helen then told them of the computer expert, that had requested to come, Harold agreed that they would put him up at Carpenters Cottage.

Charlyyk did not indulge any information to the posse about her visit to Michel's surgery, but Mike asked her, 'You look particularly happy with yourself Charlyyk, is there any reason for this?'

Charlyyk gave him a kiss on the cheek, 'Yes Mike, and its thanks to you that I am.'

Mike looked really pleased with himself, 'Because of me?'

She placed her hand on the side of his face, and giving him a big smile, 'You made me realise the value of friendship, and I cannot thank you enough.'

Julia witnessed, what was said. Put her arm in Charlyyk arm, and watching Mike turn and walk away, 'I don't know, which one of you benefited most out of that situation' As they watched Mike, they both agreed, yes, he as certainly changed for the better, since he stood up and encouraged Charlyyk to except their help.

Later at dinner. Charlyyk was talking to Helen about Mike, and the effect of the past week has had on him. 'He has become cleaner, no stains of previous dinners on him, his hair is washed, and he smells nice, I'm hoping he and Julia get it together.' Rachel picks up on how she hesitated when she was saying smell, 'Do you get vibes from him Charlyyk?' With concern showing on her face, 'No he must not, I could hurt him, he will be better off with Julia.' With that Charlyyk leaves the table and hurries to her bedroom.

After helping Helen to clean up after dinner. Rachel knocks on Charlyyk's door, and enters, 'Sorry Charlyyk, I should not have said anything.' Sitting beside her on the bed, 'If you feel it's wrong, then make sure you don't encourage him, yet still keep his friendship.'

Charlyyk, holding Rachel's hand, and looking in her face. She could feel the same loving warmth, as she felt with Catherine.

Rachel went on to tell her about the boys, she had friendships at school and then at college. 'At first, they seemed to be the only one in my life I would want to live with. Then a new boy would come along, and so on, and so on.' Then looking at Charlyyk. 'If you get the drift?' Rachel laughed. 'But it is all a learning curve to understand what kind of feller we will one day, we would want to marry.'

Charlyyk had understood Rachel. 'But that is not going to happen with me Rachel, would it not upset the people. I need people to like me, not see me as threat.'

Rachel stood up and started to walk to the door. 'I was not thinking Charlyyk, seeing you the way I do, you are one of us. A girl like every other girl.' With those thoughts, Rachel walked towards the door. 'Night-night Charlyyk, sleep well.'

***

Wednesday, the girls striding up out front, Charlyyk telling Helen what Rachel told her, as they reached the cowsheds, James called out to Charlyyk, his hand signal of thumb and little finger, to her ear and mouth. And shouting Janet meant only one thing, she called back. 'Yes, I will.' And carried on running,

At breakfast, Charlyyk phoned Janet, 'Hi kid. You...OK?'

Janet's croaky voice told her she was not well, as she spoke, the croaky cough could be heard, 'Went down with flu on Monday... seen Doctor... working in bed the best as I can?' Charlyyk wished her well and promised to phone again.

Harold and Gwen arrived mid-day, for lunch and remarked on the anxiety Charlyyk had endured these last few weeks, Helen was quick to ask them, was this normal for a teenage girl, 'Is this what you were telling us some time ago Gwen, when this first started.'

Gwen nodded, 'Yes you are right we did.'

'We know Charlyyk can be sensitive.' Bryn remarked. 'Her feelings, are based on her fears, on what she could lose.'

Margret could not resist the temptation of voicing her opinion. 'She is so young, yet so old, her unique way of looking at problems can be her strength or her downfall. Much like your Margret Thatcher, this woman is not for turning, so she could not amend her mistake.'

Harold thinking through what Margret had said. 'So, what you are implying is that her thinking is so set in stone, that generally she can work out and find the right answer in a logical format. But when she can't find the answer, she can't stop thinking about it, and then it can only end in a meltdown.'

Margret nodded her agreement.

Helen listening to this line of thinking, 'So, how we use grey matter, to solve or ease a problem she does not. Helping with her homework she has it all mapped out in her brain, like it is indented with bullets and numbers.'

'When are you going to London, Margret?' Bryn wanting to change the subject.

'Friday, for four weeks, with Rachel and Thomas, I was hoping that Charlyyk could be there, for the opening on Sunday.' Helen raised her eyes. 'You had better ask her tonight.'

Gwen with a pleading smile, 'Can we come, Margret?' Thomas walked over to his aunt. 'We have already printed, your VIP tags.' And gave his aunt a big hug.

Dinner was busy. Charlyyk was in full voice. An intense debate had been going on in school, and she was given her accounts of it. 'Mr Pearson had to step in. Mike called Jan a social snob, and Mace called Peter a red in the bed. And I thought Peter had cut himself while he was in bed. Julia started laughing, Jan thought she was laughing at her. Peter stood up to Mace, it was utter chaos, but fun to watch.'

After a while, when everything seemed settled. Thomas asked Charlyyk if she would come to the opening of the Exhibition on Sunday, 'Many famous people will be there, and rumour has it a famous boy band member, who is a keen artist will also be there.'

Charlyyk had already made her mind up when Rachel had whispered a couple of days earlier. 'I don't know if I can go, Thomas. I have other engagements to attend to.' Looking at Margret's and Thomas's faces she could not keep up with the pretence, and burst out laughing, 'Course I'm coming.' And gave Rachel a high five, well in Charlyyk's world, a high four.

***

Thursday morning, Helen nudged Charlyyk, as they ran down Bishops

Lane, heading left pass, Dippers Meadow on the return run. 'I have lost ten pounds since I been jogging and doing the Pilates. That equals three inches off my waist.'

Charlyyk laughed, the impish smile she gave Helen 'So it's your bum, that you need to work on next then, is it?'

Charlyyk was getting used to the noises coming from her mum and dad's bedroom. The books that Catherine had shown her on childbirth, she now knew what they were doing, was perfectly reasonable for them. Although some nights she would wonder, what would be expected of her if she had not been on this planet, but on her own world. All she had seen were Lyyk's, she had never seen, or smelt a Haagh, the male of her species. This thought sometimes troubled her, how did she know their language, who had taught her, what is the purpose of the metal plate? That and many more things she could not explain.

Looking into her lunch box. Helen had kept to her diet, that Michel had set up for her. The array of fruit and nuts, and veggie wedges, with a hummus dip, was the strict routine diet, but not the KitKat chocolate wafer bar, neatly concealed under the vegetable wedges, 'Thank you, mum.'

Charlyyk sat there watching the posse. Mike was talking to Jan. Peter was talking to Mace, so no problems there. When she felt Julia slide in beside her. Julia looking into Charlyyk's lunch box, 'Swop you, my quarter of egg sandwich, for a celery stick, and a dunk in your hummus.' The swop was made, and two happy souls enjoyed lunchtime.

Charlyyk liked Julia a lot, the large red birthmark that covered one side of Julia's face, had made Julia insecure. Being with the posse they did not take any notice of the birthmark, she could be herself, like when she was at home, but away from them, and on her own, the insecurities flooded back big time. Now being around Charlyyk and seeing how she handled the constant attention, made her problem seem so small. Gradually finding it easier not to worry about her birthmark. Sandra's relationship with Peter had altered their friendship a little, though that is what Julia had expected it to do, had managed to find adjustments, in how they carried on being friends. Being friends with Charlyyk, she could feel the changes it was making. Her confidence was much stronger, pushing herself forward in school more, being more assertive. Her parents were much happier the effect of this was having on her, was rubbing off at home. Julia's smiles were bigger and warmer their little rosebud now was blooming into a flower.

In the Teachers Study, Mrs Butler commented on her assessment of the improvements Charlyyk's class has made since she had arrived. 'It's above normal, their grades have gone up.'

Louise Landon looked at Tim Pearson. 'Definitely, I agree with Wendy, the results are a grade higher, even the improvement in their homework, I'm receiving from them, has so improved'

Richard Waverly shrugged his shoulders. 'What can I say, she has had an effect on the whole class just being there, they have matured so much, Mike who I thought was a hopeless case, his head in the clouds, no concentration at all, has so changed. I'm at a loss for words for it. Am I happy? Oh, yes indeed I am, bring it on.'

Louise Landon cast her attention to Alice Vasey, who was reading a letter. 'Alice, are you with us?' Alice's head shot up, a broad grin smothered her face. 'Yes, I have been listening, it's not what Charlyyk does. But it's the role the rest of the class have taken on, it's like they have become her guardians, and that has made them mature, in the they have.'

Alice looked down at the letter. Charlyyk had given her that morning. 'This letter has invited me, to go with Charlyyk on Sunday, to the Watercolour Exhibition in London, as a VIP guest. I've never been given anything like this before.' She just sat there, reading the letter over again, as though she could not believe what was written.

Louise Landon showed interest, could this be a good thing for the school? The board of Governors meetings always produce something good for the school, if the school get a good mention in the local media.

At the Cottage. Margret, Thomas and Rachel were hard at it, getting all the confirmations established, then ticking off each one as done when confirmed. Bryn and Helen making teas and coffees, to keep the troops happy.

When Charlyyk arrived home, all was calm as though nothing had happened, Charlyyk went straight to the fridge and poured a glass of milk, under the stern eye of Bryn. Charlyyk knew he was watching her, raised the glass so he could see it, Helen who was hovering close to her, asked her about her day at school, 'It was good, mum.' Then reached up to kiss her on her cheek, then whispered in her ear. 'Thanks for the KitKat.'

Helen returning the kiss, 'My pleasure' Charlyyk then went to her room to change and to talk with Janet, to see how she was coping with her flu symptoms.

Friday, Alice Vasey had found Charlyyk at lunchtime sitting with Julia, swopping their lunch together. 'Charlyyk, thank you for thinking of me, I will be there. I'm so excited to be able to meet so many prominent artists. I'm tingling all over with excitement, so I will definitely see you on Sunday.'

Julia looked at Alice, as she walked away, it was more like skipped away. 'Well done, Charlyyk, you have made the most liked teacher in the school, very, very happy, well done you.'

Charlyyk felt so humble. She had thought about Miss Vasey when Janet who was on the VIP list became ill. When Margret asked her which one of her friends would she take her place. Charlyyk did not want to favour one, over another, but liking Miss Vasey's Art class thought of her instead. Now it looks like she was smart, but she was not thinking like that when she had made her decision.

Margret, Thomas and Rachel had already left for London when Charlyyk had come home from school. Harold and Gwen were there to greet her after Charlyyk had changed and spoken with Janet, she was happy to share herself, with the family. Gwen had mentioned that it was going to be a cold, wet weekend. 'What will you be wearing Charlyyk? These places can be draughty?' Charlyyk thought through her wardrobe, the dress she had bought at Christmas although had long sleeves, was too young for this occasion, the green dress that Margret had brought her the sleeve's too short and would make her look too mature. Her Laura Ashley Dress would not be warm enough.

Helen opened her laptop, and looked online, they scrolled down the pages, discussing all the possibilities, a tailored jacket and skirt were Charlyyk's choice, but in what colour. The outlet was a tailoring firm in Basingstoke. Helen phoned them and agreed to meet them tomorrow morning.

Chapter 34

The Scent of an Alien

On Saturday morning, the shop front sign said, *'Little and Large Tailoring.'* The traditional ringing of the bell when they entered amused Charlyyk, wanted to hear it ring again, Gwen stopped her. The middle-aged lady that greeted them was charming 'Hello, I spoke to you yesterday.' Helen said as she held her hand out.

'Oh yes, the tailored suit.' The lady said looking straight at Charlyyk, 'Yes we can help. We cater for large companies normally...airlines and others, who need to dress their staff in good quality uniforms of all shapes and sizes.'

This was not like any shop they had been into before. They stood in a reception room. Fashion posters on the walls. The middle-aged lady opened a door, and asked for assistance, a young girl took her place, and she invited them to follow her.

They entered a large warehouse filled with rack upon racks of clothes. At a table with various tailoring bits and pieces scattered about, the lady measures Charlyyk, then showed her the suits: Blacks, Whites, Blues, Greens, and more. Charlyyk took a fancy to a light maroon suit, the lady checked the size and selected one. 'Slip this on.'

Charlyyk slipped on the jacket and looked in the long mirror, the colour was right, but the Jacket was a bit baggy, she looked disappointed, the lady asked how she felt, 'It's too big.'

The lady did not seem concerned, 'Is the colour right...the material to your satisfaction?' Gwen stepped forward and felt the material, nodded, 'Right next stage.' She took the jacket of Charlyyk then the lady selected another one, slipping it on Charlyyk. Charlyyk noticed the jacket was not finished, the seams were open, and she started to worry.

The lady took out some pins and started to fit the jacket to her. When she had finished pining the garment together, Charlyyk could see how it looked. Charlyyk's smile telling everyone that she liked the look of the finished article. The lady then called out, and an elderly gentleman came and took it away. 'Now the skirt, any particular style, and showed them a style book, the women agreed to a two-pleated skirt. the lady collected a garment for her to try on, the skirt fitted her hips but the waist was not finished and the skirt too long.

Out came the pins, that was soon adjusted. Charlyyk, again liked what she saw, once again, the skirt was taken away. After a lengthy wait, the suit was ready. Charlyyk tried it on, could see what Gwen was trying to portray. Not quite a school uniform, still keeping the girl image.

On the way home, they stopped at Liza Martins, and asked her advice on makeup for her, she was going to be in the spotlight, and they were making sure she would stand out from the crowd, yet not making her look too old. Gwen had told Helen that Margret would milk Charlyyk's presence. The press coverage would be much higher than normal, since the press was usually restricted from access to Charlyyk.

***

Sunday Morning, Alice Vasey was like a cat on a hot tin roof. This was the third outfit she had put on and was still not sure if it was right, her flat was in disarray, and time was running out. 'This will have to do.' She headed for the door to meet the Colliers at Oakleaves.

It was going to be a tight fit to get everyone in the car, so the choice of car was the Discovery. Charlyyk sat in the fold-down seat, at the rear of the Discovery. When they arrived, Rachel was so pleased to see them. A steward parked the car. Thomas had soon whisked Charlyyk and Alice of for a quick tour, and to meet some of the artists.

Margret took the rest of the family, on a more selective tour. This was to get the best impact from the media when Charlyyk was introduce.

Alice who was in awe of Thomas, kept close. This was to learn as much as she could with so many great artists on hand, with Charlyyk in close attendance. Alice was making the most of the opportunities that was afforded to her.

Now and again, there was a camera pointed towards them. Alice notice how Charlyyk did not let the press attention get to her, giving them ample chances to take pictures. 'Don't you mind all this intrusion Charlyyk?'

'No Miss, Janet has agreed with what was to happen. I will have to do a press interview later, that too has been given a time limit, one question from each journalist, so it does not get into a media scrum.'

As the guest and VIPs started to arrive. Charlyyk was kept away to get the best effect they could when they introduced her. Charlyyk, was not nervous. Her nods, and hand waves, where all given with gentle smiles. Gwen had written an opening speech with help from Janet. The press coverage, was intense, but Charlyyk knew if she tried to hide, the press would give her a hard time.

The first reporter asked his question. 'Charlyyk, you seem to like art. What is the type of painting that you prefer?

'With so many styles it would be a few years before I would be able to answer that question. It takes so much dedication, and time to be able to attain such a high standard. Only then will I be able to truly understand how they could make watercolours, look like photographs.'

'Miss Vasey, you teach art to Charlyyk. What can you tell us about Charlyyk's artistic side?'

But before Alice Vasey could reply, Charlyyk waved her hand as if she had a paintbrush in it and was attacking an easel like a sword fencer.

Alice with a laugh. 'Yes, just like that. We are lucky we can wash the paint sploshes of quite quickly.'

This brought a few chuckles from the press.

The inner smile Charlyyk was having, knowing she had got the right response...laughter. She had watched a film on the Television of a robot that understood a joke, which made him seem Human. Could that be the way to get people on her side. By the reaction she had from the press, it looked good.

When they returned to the cottage. Helen invited Alice to stay awhile, which she accepted without hesitation. Charlyyk showed Alice, Thomas's studio, and some of his earlier works. She stayed late into the evening.

Gwen could see why the student liked her. She had a natural way about her. She listened intently to what was being said, and did not try to put anyone down.

Alice had remarked, that she reckoned that each student had a talent, that was trying to break out. 'Art is a good tool to judge the social problems in students. The subject they paint, too how they apply the brush strokes. We can detect all manner of mental attitudes, that could trouble them. I use all my knowledge to get the best from each student. Mrs Landon knows this can help her discover which students might be in need of specialist help. Please don't misinterpret that I'm a spy of some sort... as I only inform her when it is necessary.'

***

On Monday, in the teachers meeting room. Alice Vasey was in full flow. Louise Landon could not be prouder. Her school had been mentioned on the news, that a teacher from her school had been shown, as a VIP, at an important exhibition in London. This will sit well at the next governor's meeting.

'What do you think we could get out of this Louise?' Asked Wendy Butler.

Louise's brain was in overtime, 'I have a week before the meeting, to sort something out Wendy.' She had learned, you must not get too ambitious, least she ends up with is nothing. Louise knew that running a school needs teaching and management. Too many heads were teachers and not managers, many schools failed because of it.

Charlyyk was telling the posse about the weekend and showing them pictures that the family had managed to take. Sarah was keen to find out how the makeup went. 'Send me that one Charlyyk... mum would love to see that one.'

Then Julia spotted Miss Vasey in the photo, 'Well she looks so different.' The posse gathered around all giving their opinion on her.

Bryn was cleaning the car when Helen called him in. 'Phone sweetheart. Chad.'

Bryn entered the cottage and picked the receiver up. 'Hi, Chad, what's up.'

Chad did not stand on ceremony. 'First of February. Yuri, Su Shi, Arn and of course myself. Bruce Foster still intends to come. We will keep it simple; you know we must talk.'

Bryn was not surprised. 'That's fine Chad, we will see you then.' Helen heard everything, 'Saturday then.' Bryn returned to finish cleaning the car.

Later in the evening, BBC Channel 4 had an hour-long program on the Art Exhibition, and footage of Charlyyk was shown in full. Charlyyk took mental notes on what she did, and the visual look she portrayed. Helen watched her going through hand gestures, and facial expressions. When the program finished, Helen asked her how she felt she came over.

'My hands need improving, they sometimes look a bit...un-gamely. My walk has improved, the makeup gave me better complexion. I will inform Sarah tomorrow. Julia and Sandra are going to tell me what they think. But overall, much improvement on last time. I'm pleased.'

Helen liked what she had said. Bryn could only smile, he knew Charlyyk rehearsed her moves with Julia and Sandra, her personal coaches.

Tuesday, Sandra walked up and down in the school locker area. 'See what I mean, not too much on swinging the hips; you are not a fashion model. What if Kate Middleton did that the press would have made her life a living hell. Keep the walk natural.'

Julia spoke about her hands, 'I picked up on your hands, you are right. What if you have your sleeves longer, would they make your hands look shorter.'

Charlyyk thought for a moment. 'In the warmer weather, I don't think it would work.'

The other members of the posse were listening in on what was being said. Sarah looked at her own hands, as she opened and closed them. 'What if you half closed your hands in this manner.'

Mike stepped up. 'Like holding an imaginary tennis ball.'

Charlyyk opened and closed her hands. Peter took a recording on his phone, then showed it to Charlyyk, 'Yes that could work Peter. I will practise it in the mirror.'

Helen and Bryn started the task of getting ready for the weekend. It was in the afternoon, just before Charlyyk was due to be home when the phone rang. Helen saw the surprised look on Bryn's face. He had not expected this call. She moved towards him. He turned the sound up. 'Bryn, can I stay at your house, my wife would like to come with me. We will be there Friday if it is OK.' Helen nodded. 'Yes, Su Shi, we will be ready for you.'

Helen placed her arm around his waist, and nestled her head against him, 'Thomas's room?' Bryn gave her an unmistakable look. Helen's arm tightens around him, and with a playful punch with her free hand. 'Oh, come on... for Su Shi and his wife to stay... Bryn?' He tickled her till she wrapped her arms around his neck and kissed him hard.

***

Wednesday, the frost was hard, due to the high weather system. The sky was clear of clouds, in the east, the sun was beginning to rise, and a tint of red could be seen. The family group of three, were in close formation, discussing Janet's, extended recuperation from the flu, and the advent of Friday, when Su Shi and his wife were coming.

As they turned left at the bottom of Bishops Lane. Charlyyk, suddenly stopped. Her nose twitched. Her head moved side to side. She gently moved forward. Her nose taking in as much as it could.

Bryn and Helen likewise stopped. Bryn held Helen back, the commander giving his scout a chance to evaluate the danger signs. Then Charlyyk stopped sniffing. Whatever it was it had gone.

'What do you think it was Charlyyk?' Bryn's military training had kicked in, he knew by experience that Charlyyk had smelt danger. The threat of it written all over Charlyyk's face.

'I've smelt that scent before, on that planet we were on, Dad.' Charlyyk was looking at the ground. 'It was not here yesterday morning. Whatever it was, it was here last night, before the frost settled. There are no signs of prints on the ground.' Then she was up and running, with Bryn and Helen in hot pursuit.

Breakfast was quiet. Charlyyk was scanning her memory cells, did not want to talk. She moved from the table, with her dirty dishes, to place them in the dishwasher, then paused. She then put her plates in the dishwasher, closed the door. Charlyyk reached the kitchen door, paused again but longer, then she was gone.

Helen had been holding Bryn's hand and watching his face for any acknowledgement. Bryn's eyes had been on Charlyyk all the time. Now that Charlyyk had gone to her room he turned and spoke to Helen. 'The aliens had been there.'

Chapter 35

They leave their calling card

Helen's, startled worried expression showed, that she wanted to know more. 'How do you know that.'

'If it had been a beast, there would have been a footprint of some sort. But There was nothing, so if she has smelt it before, but can't recognise it, it has to be an alien.'

Bryn now was thinking, he got up and made himself a coffee, Helen knew he was thinking. Otherwise, he would have made her one as well. As she started to clear up Charlyyk came back in, dressed for school. Bryn and Charlyyk looked at each other, and at the same time. 'It was an alien.' With that Charlyyk kissed them both and went to meet the school bus. Helen now was the one thinking.

Bryn took her hand, 'What is it?'

The puzzled look on Helen's face was still there. 'When I first came here, this would have frightened Charlyyk to death. Now she has just dismissed it as though this type of thing happens every day.' Then looking directly into Bryn's eyes. 'This is scaring the shit out of me, and I'm not afraid to say it.'

Helen picked up the phone, punched in some numbers. 'Wendy...Helen, early last night before the frost, and at the bottom of Bishops Lane, was there any activity?'

Helen waited for the reply while Sgt Wendy Bailey read through the reports.

'Helen... yes. At five past seven. It showed a blip on the monitor for ten minutes, a car was dispatched, but nothing was there, they covered the area but nothing.'

Helen had the speaker sound up too full, so Bryn could hear. 'Thanks Wendy, it was something that Charlyyk smelt. We were not sure but you have confirmed it. She had picked a scent of something could be an animal, she has not come across before.' Placing the phone down. 'I trust Charlyyk's nose,' Helen said to Bryn, concern still in her voice. 'And once again it shows how good her sense of smell is.' Then looking at the garden door. 'Now no arguments, new bolts for the doors... Today, Bryn!'

Lunchtime at the Academy, Julia on the scrounge for goodies. Charlyyk was in a pensive mood. 'What's up, kid.' Julia asked. 'You're never this quiet, unless something is worrying you. So, cough up. What is it?'

Looking around to see if anyone, was within earshot. She whispered. 'Do not look alarmed, or say a word.' She paused to await Julia's nod. 'Last night, an alien was at the bottom of Bishops Lane. It was not there for long, but it had been there. I smelt it.'

Julia's head spun around to look directly at Charlyyk. 'You're not kidding, are you?'

Looking into her lunch box, Charlyyk selected a stick of carrot, then dunking it in the hummus. 'No'

Julia sat looking at her lunch box, but it was not for a tasty morsel.

After dinner, the three of them, sat down to discuss the weekend. Helen wanted to lay some ground rules down. But Bryn said. 'No, just be yourselves, then it should cause no problems' Bryn was more concerned, about what Charlyyk might have said at school.

'Julia won't say anything. She has been trustworthy, since I met her, and she won't change. We have made a pact to be honest with each other. I've told her things before about other students, and she has always kept her side of the bargain.'

***

Thursday morning, the three runners arrived at the bottom of Bishops Lane. Bryn and Helen stayed back. Charlyyk checked with her nose; the sent was old, with a shake of her head, she relaxed then carried on running.

Gwen and Harold arrived later and were soon helping to make ready for Friday. At three Michel turned up. He was here to sort out Charlyyk's diet, and to collect a blood sample. Talking to Bryn in Kit's clinic, he showed Bryn a scanner. 'We use this to check the chips we put in animals. Some give out more data than others. This might pick up something that the plate in Charlyyk's head is sending out?'

When Charlyyk returned home, she was pleased to see Michel, 'OK, which goodies am I allowed to sniff, and the ones I am allowed to eat?' She showed a lot of interest when Michel showed her the scanner. 'Let's do it' Though it resulted in nothing, not a blip.

Sitting around the kitchen table, drinking teas. 'It's possible that it's a different type of science, or maybe it just controls Charlyyk?' Michel was not sure what it could be. He used electrical gadgets to assist him, that's how far it went. Chemicals he knew about, pressing buttons he was alright with, but that was that.

Helen looking at Charlyyk could see she was deep in thought. 'It does not matter sweetheart, we will be stronger together, facing it, head on.' Charlyyk was not worried about that. Her mind was who's scent she had picked up. The traces in her memory bank were muddled in with other scents.

***

Friday morning, the garden door burst open. Charlyyk had tried not to be so boisterous, she had started to realise her strength was increasing. 'Sorry dad, I must do better.' Then rushed to her room.

The school bus, you could set your time by it, right on cue it arrived. Charlyyk got a hug and a kiss from them. Then they watched as the bus disappeared from view. Helen had settled into this idyllic lifestyle. She would kill to keep it.

Time drifted by. Tidying up, with a little dusting she was ready. Looking around the cottage, she gazed at the picture of Kitty on the wall, 'Thank you, it was your love that made this family, let me do you justice, and keep this house as happy as you intended it.' At two thirty, a large limousine pulled into the drive. The doorbell rang, Helen checked how she looked, Bryn nodded his approval, and they opened the door. Su Shi and his wife were standing there, wrapped up against the English weather.

Bryn welcomed them in. 'Lovely to see you again' Inside the lounge. Bryn took their coats. They were dressed in western clothes. She was slim, five feet six inches tall.

'Su Shi this is my wife to be, Helen.'

Su Shi bowed and shook her hand, then with great charm. 'My darling wife, Liu.'

Bryn shook her hand, Helen stepped forward, and by instinct, they kissed each other cheeks; 'Can I get you something to drink?'

Liu took Helen's arm, 'Come lets us talk, while the boys talk.'

Liu's English was excellent, and soon they were talking freely. 'I met Su Shi in Oxford. My parents owned a restaurant in London, I was studying economics. On hearing of the love, I had for Su Shi. My parents were not happy, they refused me permission to marry. When Su Shi went home. I felt terrible, so I bought an air ticket and never returned to England, until yesterday. My mother just stood at the door of their house and just stared at me. I turned and walked away. Twenty-three years have passed, and she still felt the same.'

Taking the tea tray into the lounge, the women continued the conversation with the men. 'I was taking a big gamble marrying Liu.' Su Shi observed. 'If she would disobey her parents, she was bound to disobey me.'

Liu was charming. 'Our two sons, are at Oxford. We will go to them after we leave here.'

Helen checked the time, the smile on her face had just got bigger,

Su Shi was quick to his feet, and was soon helping his wife to her feet. 'Where have we to go?'

Bryn took his arm. 'Just to the front door' As the door opened, the bus was stopping at the drive.

The bus door opened, and as Charlyyk stepped down. She saw them, and rushed to greet them. Su Shi greeted her like a much-loved uncle.

Inside the cottage, Charlyyk was introduced to Liu. When Charlyyk mention, she needed a drink, all the Women headed for the kitchen. Liu was making herself at home, and Helen was getting to like Liu more and more. 'Helen, I also cook western food at home, so don't be nervous. Su Shi has not stopped talking about Charlyyk, since he met her in Houston. He has been on tender feet, thinking of coming here. But don't think I've been dragged here. I really wanted to come. Su Shi's description of Charlyyk fascinated me too. I threatened him with divorce if he did not bring me, so no pressure.'

Charlyyk drinking her milk. 'But I'm not that special... I'm no different than any other of the girls at school.'

Liu looked at her. 'That's right, you are no different, but you are also only one of a kind, and that's what makes you so important.' Liu touched the side of Charlyyk's face. 'When our friends heard that Su Shi had met you, we were inundated with questions, from everyone. The picture he took of you and him, is his card to anywhere in China. My God doesn't he use it. He is treated like Britain's Great Queen.' Liu's all-knowing look told Charlyyk, she enjoyed the benefits as well.

'So, I guess you want your own photo of me?' Liu's open eyes look of 'please'.

'OK, when I change out of my school clothes' Charlyyk went to leave, then looked at Liu. 'Do you want to come?' Liu did not need a second invite. Helen watched as they left the kitchen together.

Gwen and Harold arrived, ten minutes later. Harold joined Bryn and Su Shi. Gwen went to the kitchen with Helen.

Liu sat on the bed, talking to Charlyyk. She asked about the life Charlyyk now lived. Charlyyk found Liu easy to talk to, just as Su Shi was. The ringtone, on Liu phone, starts to play. Her son was calling her. Charlyyk now dressed, sat by the side of her. Liu showed her son, the image of her and Charlyyk side by side. Liu Son was impressed with his mother's newfound stardom. 'Mum... you now as big as dad.'

Charlyyk listened to Liu's carefully worded questions about how she had adapted to life on Earth. 'Liu, I wanted to adapt...I needed to adapt. Bryn gave me a chance to survive, and I took it... Did I know what was going to happen? No... I did not know, but what has happened, and how it has happened. I cannot have any regrets. Hearing all the different ways my school friend's lives are played out. I now know how privileged my life has turned out to be, yet now and again it feels I have taken it for granted.' Charlyyk paused for a moment contemplating her thoughts. 'It is so easy to let yourself get too accustomed to a way of living, that it is how you believe everyone behaves. Then you hear the problems of others, then you have to re-access you own advantages on what I now take as my normal family life. Living here with Bryn, which you can see is rather nice. Yes, you can say I've been spoilt, and you will be right to say so. Michel tells me to not concern myself, but to join in with the family and help to make their lives as easy as possible so we can be a family. At first, I could not understand his meaning, but now I'm beginning to.'

Dinner time was busy with conversation. Liu proved she was no shrinking violet and held her own. Helen observed her, she had her unique personal style that worked for her. Her hand movements when explaining detail had an elegant flourish to them. Watching Su Shi, he gave her the room to talk, never once interrupting her at any time, nor her with him, a good paring. His views, on life, was a mixture of Eastern and Western cultures. Liu gave Helen, the view she had been a hands-on mum, no nannies for her. The little things that they did for one another, she could see were done out of love.

Helen started to reflect on herself. Before she had met Bryn, would only look for faults in people, now she finds, she is looking at the real people. Knowing she had changed; she liked the new person she has become.

Gwen and Harold had much to say, as most of the question associated with the very early days of Charlyyk being here, and the problems they had faced, trying to keep her concealed, yet still trying to educate her.

After dinner, Liu was persistent that she helped Helen, and the friendship had started to take shape. It was Charlyyk taking notice of them, her ears were moving in many directions. Su Shi had noticed how Charlyyk could keep one eye and ear, in focus to whom she was talking with, but the other ear and eye were on walkabouts.

Bryn as usual said nothing unless someone spoke to him. Gwen had brought her photo album, the nice happy one, and when Liu sat down, it came out. To Gwen surprise, Liu had brought hers. Her iPad was full of beautiful pictures, depicting where they had lived, and mostly of the children growing up.

Harold and Gwen left, when Charlyyk went to bed, leaving the four of them, carrying on with the conversation. Bryn had brought out a bottle of Balvenie Caribbean, this was his favourite single malt. Wally Blyth had introduced him to it. This brought out a smile from Su Shi, as Bryn poured out a shot of whisky for him, Liu had pushed her glass forward. 'I hope it is not just for the boys?'

Su Shi was quick to explain. 'Liu's flatmate at University came from Glasgow, and the three years together, something had to rub off.'

Liu gave a little chuckle. 'The secret of whisky drinking is how much water? You take a drop of whisky on the tongue, and count in seconds the tingling sensations your tongue feels, how many second, how many eye drops of water.'

Bryn smiling at her. 'What is your favourite?'

But it was Su Shi who answered. 'Any full bottle.'

Liu's chuckle was getting more like a laugh. 'Su Shi, looks at cars, to how many miles to the gallon, and me, how many bottles to the year?' The impish smile she gave, 'At four bottles a year, I am still cheaper than his cars.'

Saturday, Helen was surprised to see them fully kitted out in tracksuits as they entered the garden. After the stretching, they were off at a settled pace. The light was starting to show, and as usual, the girls were in front. Passing the cowsheds and arriving at the top of the hill, Liu could see the sheer splendour of the sun, hitting the tops of trees, the many colours laid out around them. 'I have missed England, so many times, it has a beauty all of its own'

Liu pacing on the spot, then looking down into the valley 'Dipper's meadow'. 'I can see why you love it here Helen, it's not Spring, yet it looks so lovely'

The bottom of Bishops Lane, Charlyyk pushed forward, sniffing the air. Helen's tension was noticed by Liu. Charlyyk shook her head and carried on running.

***

The first to arrive for the meeting was Brigadier Alex Hutton and Major Carter. Then Yuri with Arn. Later Chad. Alan Carter had requested lounge suits. It would not be imposing on Charlyyk. It would help her to relax and talk freely.

When all the introductions had been done. Helen took Liu to Gwen's. Charlyyk played mother, and soon had drinks, for them all. Helen had placed water bottles at appropriate places before leaving.

Alex made the first move. 'Charlyyk something was said at our meeting, to trigger this theory of yours, could you explain please?'

Charlyyk took a sip from her cup. 'Going to school meeting people of my own age group, listening to the stories of their families. I did not have that where I had come from. Then the question was asked, it triggers those nagging thoughts that lingered in my head, why were we sent here, back to dad's house?' Charlyyk could see that they all had recorders working but were still making notes. Alan Carter was making a video recording when they were ready, she proceeded. 'That night, other things started to niggle at me. On Sunday, the next day, we went to Gwen and Harold's for dinner, we got talking about, what had come up at the meeting. I mentioned about the Fuung that had been killed and had been dragged away from where my group lived, could the thing that had killed the Fuung, been protecting us. If, so WHY?' Again, Charlyyk waited, while they gathered the information, and chatted a bit. Charlyyk then collected the X-ray pictures. Sitting back down again, and checking if they were ready. She placed the X-ray images on the table.

Charlyyk waited till they had settled. 'The conversation on Sunday had led us to believe, that this whole thing was orchestrated. Michel, the vet that look after me, suggested that I might have been monitoring some message to whoever. So, he has taken these X-rays of me to see if they had.' They started examining the X-rays. The look of realisation on their face as to what Charlyyk was relating to bore truth. Bryn then went on to explain the pins that secured the plate to her skull, we have used a scanner on the plate, but it sends out no signals.

Chad punches some numbers into his phone, 'Bruce, when can you get here?' Bruce Jenner was dropping his bag at Gwen's when the phone rang. Chad asked how long to get to the cottage. The taxi Bruce had arrived in, had already left. Helen offered him a lift, and told Chad ten minutes. Listening to Chad he opened his case and removed a small tool case from it.

At Oakleaves, Bryn showed the military chiefs the enlarge X-ray of the plate the strange formation of fibres that seem to be flowing out of the ends of the pins attaching themselves to Charlyyk's brain.

When Bruce arrived, Charlyyk was the first to greet him. Chad asked Bruce to look at the X-rays, and while he looked at them. Chad went over the details of their theories; 'Bruce is that plate sending out any messages, what we want is a direct answer?'

Bruce opened his tool case and select a meter. Placed some probes into it, then asked Charlyyk to turn around. Taking bearings from the X-ray, the fine needle ends of the probe, sunk into the back of her head. She did not flinch, he turned the meter on, and the dial flickered. Chad eager to find something, looked pleased. Bruce then changed the setting on the meter nothing, three more setting changes later. Bruce confirms what readings he had taken, would not send a signal.

Su Shi sighed. Alex looked at him, he could see that Su Shi was happy.

'This means Charlyyk is no threat to us, and I am relieved.' Alex again shot a look at him. Su Shi stern look. 'Why I am pleased, if you thought she was a threat you would send her to be terminated, and that's the last thing I would want to happen to her. She has shown us only that she too would like answers, and she has put herself out to cooperate with us in every way possible. The x-ray plates Charlyyk laid down in front of us, so we could see what they had done to her. Is this not proof of her innocence in all of this.'

Su Shi meant every word he had said. 'Bruce that meter, what do you use it for?' Bruce instantly replied, 'Microelectronics. The sort we use in spy bugs.' He then showed him how it worked and the range it covered, 'No minute amount of electricity, could escape its sensitivity.' He then took the probes from Charlyyk's neck, then without hesitation stuck them into his hand, then showed the meter reading, 'We all have electricity running through us.' And as you can see Charlyyk's reading is so much lower than mine. The first reading was to calculate, her electrical impulse so I could tell whether she could have enough electricity to be sending out a message. There was not enough to be sending anything at all.'

The Military Chiefs sat around and debated, what had been discussed. While the Chiefs talked, Charlyyk took Bruce to the kitchen and gave him refreshments, and chatted, with him. 'Charlyyk, the Kepla Telescope, has discovered many more planets, and in the corner of one of the pictures I discovered this.' And from a side pocket, he took out a photo, of a formation of planets, nestled in amongst them a planet that Charlyyk thought she recognised. 'It was nowhere near the other planets, but feeding the right information into the computer, it fitted to a T what you told me.'

Charlyyk studied the picture. 'So where is this one situated on the solar map.'

Bruce took out of his pocket a solar map, unfolding it, he laid out the map on the worktop. Pointing to where it was situated. 'Charlyyk, it placed the planet millions of miles away from where we first had thought.

'What had you told them, Bruce?'

He looked at her. 'I haven't disclosed too much information just in case it was wrong. I will have to spend much more time on it to be sure. Talking to you personally was the best option open to me. Helen said you go to your aunt and uncles, for dinner tomorrow, let's meet there I have some better footage on my computer to show you.'

Bryn entered the kitchen. 'They are leaving Charlyyk.'

Charlyyk left Bruce in the kitchen, then said goodbye to those that were going. She walked back to the lounge. Su Shi was wanting to ask a question of Bruce. Bryn listening in with the conversation was taking mental notes as to what Bruce had replied. 'No Su Shi, all electricity is the same. These meters were designed for this special type of micro readings. Any real strong current could burn this type of meter out as it is so delicate. The plate looks like a circuit board for what purpose I do not know.'

Su Shi, needed to know, as each country's military attaché, would relay the Xray evidence back to their scientist to valuate. 'Bruce, we must protect Charlyyk, from anyone in wanting to harm her.'

Charlyyk putting on her coat. 'Dad I need some fresh air; would you like to walk to the village with me and Bruce?' Charlyyk was keen to find out what Bruce needed to know to find the right answers to his questions.

The walk to the village gave Bruce freedom to speak to Charlyyk. 'Every planet has a different colour it is one of those unique fingerprints we have to identify them. The minerals on these planets reflect light differently, even gases can reflect light in different ways. So, we use those as identity tags. These fit in with what you spoke to me about, the last time we met, relating to the information you gave me the colour fits the minerals, and the smells fit the gases, if you get my drift.'

Leaving Bruce with Gwen and Harold. The women returned to the cottage. Liu had persuaded Helen that she and Su Shi would order a Chinese dinner for tonight, and when they were in the cottage she was soon ordering, but not from a menu. The person she had phoned was a cousin, and he was coming to them himself. 'This is the traditional way we dine, Helen, the chef, cooks a large bowl of rice, and we sit around the table and each course he cooks, we eat them there and then. It is a great way of eating.'

When the doorbell rang, there were three of them; Chi, Liu's cousin; and his twin daughters, Pia and Liu. Who was so excited to meet Charlyyk?

Chi's wife was looking after the restaurant. Chi had not seen Liu since she had left England to marry Su Shi. He wanted to know as much of her life as he could. And what a lot of talking they did.

Harold, Gwen and Bruce arrived later. Harold bringing the wine, Bryn only had reds, which could be, much too heavy for some Chinese food. Charlyyk soon explained what she could eat and what she could not, to Chi. The whole boned chicken stuffed with all types of delicate thing had Charlyyk, drawling at the mouth. Traditional Chinese meal like this one, are long affairs, but most enjoyable.

***

On Sunday morning, Charlyyk needed this run, but at a slow pace. She had woken early to put down in writing what she had remembered in her sleep. Which everway this pans out she wants to know the truth.

The evening meal will have to be worked off, it had been delicious, she found herself stuffing the last morsels down her throat with her fingers. Her mouth watered even thinking about it. As the run reached the top of Bishops Lane, she was feeling better for it. She stopped, for in amongst the smell of the farm, there was that scent mingled with it. Helen and Bryn picked up on it, again it was eleven hours old, but it had been there. Charlyyk started to look around using her sense of smell had a trail to follow, and there just a couple of feet away from the highest point was what she had been looking for.

She removed a shoe and placed her foot by the side of it. Bryn came and knelt down by the side of her. The print was four inches longer. 'It's big,' said Bryn.

Helen peering over his shoulder. 'It's definitely the same shape as your foot Charlyyk.'

Su Shi was now looking at it, a footprint just like Charlyyk's but larger. Liu asked what it meant. Su Shi and Bryn, were getting and idea of the reasoning behind it. 'What time was it here Charlyyk?'

Charlyyk made a quick calculation, the little intake of breath she did as she spoke. 'About seven, last night.' Helen sensed how Charlyyk was feeling, and placed her arm around her.

Bryn weighed up the two times. 'So, about the same time, each night.' Helen had taken photos of the print, and they resumed the run.

At breakfast, Su Shi spoke freely, as he felt that this was just the start of the aliens making contact. 'If they were going to invade. I would have thought they would have done that already.'

Bryn agreeing. 'I believe it could be Wednesday night at seven.'

Everyone went quiet.

Charlyyk concerned. 'Dad, what should we do.'

Bryn could not ease her fears. 'Nothing sweetheart, we will just have to wait to find out.'

Liu spoke with Su Shi in Chinese. 'My wife said I should be here.'

Bryn could not agree. 'The fewer people, the better, we must set up some recording device; so, you know how it went, good or bad.'

When Bryn looked at Helen, her intelligence training had kicked in. She was already on her phone. Nodded at Bryn. 'Sorted they will be here tomorrow.'

Bryn returned his thanks, for what she was doing. 'Right, now we must wait.'

Liu was not happy. 'You are taking, so much on your own...Can we not help.'

Bryn gave Charlyyk's hand a squeeze. 'It was Charlyyk and I who were thrown into this unwillingly. The aliens must have their reasons, to have done what they have done. I feel the aliens need to explain what it is they are trying to achieve.'

Charlyyk's was now putting Bryn's thoughts together. 'I understand what my father is saying, they need me to be the intermediary in this, to play a part as a translator, sending me here to learn the language and your ways, to grow up amongst you, and to be trusted.'

Su Shi stroked his chin. 'A clever scheme, so the plan is not to invade, but what?'

Helen sitting next to Liu. 'The plate in Charlyyk's head, could that have something to do with it, will the aliens connect to it in some way?'

Liu's face showed signs, of confusion. 'How have you all, come to this conclusion?'

Bryn closed his eyes tightly then opened them. 'They must be observing us somehow to know our movements. The precise time, and the places they have left their scent...knowing full well Charlyyk would pick it up. The footprint, that is their calling card. The days between. That's letting us know when.'

The knowing looks on Su Shi's face showed he was up with Bryn's thinking. 'Whatever you need Bryn, I will back you, wholeheartedly. Please let us be comrades in body and soul. I am becoming to believe, we could be as friends, like family. You will have my complete trust.' Su Shi offered Bryn his hand. Then wrapping their arms around each other, embracing in a manly hug.

Later at Carpenters Cottage, they all began to go over Bryn's theory. Gwen started to worry. Harold put his arm around her. 'This has to be played out darling. If Bryn is right. This could be a blessing for us all and could well be our chance to get on with our lives. Being able to plan for the future.'

Gwen was not taken with what he had said, 'Harold, I cannot see it that way at all, I sense it far different than you do. It really concerns me. We have no idea what these aliens are capable of doing.'

Michel had listened to what had been discussed. 'Bryn...you could be right in your theory. The plate was to program Charlyyk to allow her to play the part they had orchestrated for her. Blanking out the bits Charlyyk should not know, to allow her to adapt here.'

Bruce had been quiet. Had felt as if he was an interloper, 'Can I help in any way, with my computer skills.'

Su Shi looked at Bruce, then at Bryn. 'Could you set up a computer link between the two Cottages?'

Bruce smiled. 'Like riding a bike' Then Bruce produced one of Apple's new wrist phones. I could connect this so we could have complete communications with Bryn, we will be able to tell where he is at all times. Then he opened his laptop, waited for it to warm up. He was soon punching data into it. Then the map of where they were appeared. 'Ok, Charlyyk put Apple watch on, go anywhere, just keep talking.' Charlyyk left the cottage, then walked to Sarah House. When inside with the Martins, she spoke with them, thanking Liza for the makeup she had given her to wear at the Art Exhibition last Sunday.

Bruce showing them what was happening on the screen and they could hear everything that was being said.

When Charlyyk entered the cottage. Bryn nodded at her. 'It worked a treat, we could hear everything being said, and knew where you were.' Bruce then opened another program. 'This is that group of planets, and as you can see, nowhere near, that other grouping of planets. I believe you were transported from, was from some distance. Charlyyk these aliens are quite advanced.'

Su Shi looking over Bruce Jenner's shoulders. 'Who else knows of this?'

Bruce took a deep breath. 'No one wants to listen, they want to take what was said before as fact, and not confuse it, with what I could tell them.'

Su Shi thought for a moment. 'We'll let them.' Helen looked surprised, so Su Shi continued to explain. 'We are at a very delicate stage with this, it could keep them quiet for the moment. I believe that Bryn is correct in his analysis of what is going to happen, that this is not an invasion. The aliens could need our assistance in some kind of way. At this moment, the least people know the better, so we give them a chance to make contact. The idea that we need electronic surveillance is sound, so if anyway...that it should go wrong...we all have evidence of what had happened, for it to have gone wrong.

Helen accepted what Su Shi had said. 'I must find an explanation for the need for the surveillance equipment that is coming tomorrow.'

Su Shi looked at Liu. 'We will extend our holiday, to see how this unfolds.'

Liu did not look upset. 'I should say so, we are not leaving here, until we know they are OK.'

Charlyyk went to Liu. 'That is such a nice gesture Liu, thank you.'

***

On Monday, the large black van pulled into the drive. Helen went to meet them, three men were soon, opening doors, and removing equipment. Helen explaining what was required of the leader a large, Afro- Brit man. His family originally from Ghana from his large round facial appearance. He quickly grasped what Helen's instructions were for. Helen left them to do what was required.

Su Shi spoke with his sons, to tell them that they were having such a good time. That he and their mother would stay to the end of the week. Liu promised to phone them with an update.

At four the van left. Bruce arrived and checked the equipment. 'That good.' He attached some hardware of his own, little toggles here and there. Then set his computer up, then he could see all the rooms, covering all different angles.

Su Shi was happy. 'Will we be able to see all this, at the cottage Bruce?'

'Yes, tonight I will check it through with Harold and Gwen. I will record what we see. and tomorrow playback to make sure it works.' The camera set up on Thomas's studio in the garden will tell them of the alien's arrival. Bruce checked that it played on Charlyyk's iPad, all was set, with some time for adjustment if required.

Charlyyk looked apprehensive. 'What's the problem Charlyyk?' Helen enquired

'What if, it wants to take me back?'

Bryn took her in his arms. 'That would be up to you. You are growing up, and have started to make your own decisions. It will be your choice.' Charlyyk looked so worried. Bryn seeing the anxiety with Charlyyk. With soft reassuring words. 'But I would not let them drag you away.'

Her face brightened, Charlyyk hugged Bryn. 'I love my life here dad, I won't give it up.'

Later at Carpenters Cottage, Bruce had set up his computer. Harold and Gwen watching intently what he was doing. As he scribbled notes on a notepad and adjusted a few settings. Bruce, wearing a satisfactory smile. 'All looking good and working well.'

***

Tuesday morning, the run was as usual. Bryn trying to keep the appearance of normality. If they the aliens were watching, he wanted to make them cognisant, that all is well. He needed to get this right, at all cost.

At school Charlyyk too kept up the appearance of normality. Joined in with everything that was going on, as if nothing was happening. When she arrived home, the pressure of it definitely showed her body movement was stiff with tension. Helen took her in her arms. 'Come, sweetheart, let's go and relax in a nice bath.' Charlyyk liked the idea of that, and they both went towards the bathroom talking about how the day went. Laying in the warm bath, she began to relax and started to drift into a dream, thinking of all the lovely thing that has happened to her.

She woke in a panic, having dreamed she was being chased by a Feeng. She looked around the bathroom trying to see where it had gone. Then the realisation it had been a dream, brought her sweet relief. In her bedroom getting dressed, she returned to her musings about the plate attached to her head. If it had programmed her to remember only certain things in her life. Could the Alien change it back? If so would then the new memories be more painful. She shuddered at that thought. 'I cannot go back. I have a Mum and Dad here.'

Charlyyk was in a state of confusion. She did not know what was going to be asked of her. There was not enough evidence attached to it allowing to base any theory on, or to ease her concerns.

She sat on the bed trembling, as Helen came in, Charlyyk rushed to her gripping on to Helen in desperation. 'Hey, what's the matter?'

Charlyyk's hold just got tighter. 'Don't let them take me away, I love you too much, I can't go back, I love it here with you.' The tears in her eyes wetting Helen's blouse.

Helen cuddling her, with both arms, with a little rocking movement. 'There, there, little one.' Helen's maternal instincts setting in, she kissed Charlyyk on the top of her head. 'There, there little one mummy loves you.' Again, the realisation of what she had said, brought tears to her eyes, she really did feel a mother's love, for her daughter.

In the lounge, the plans were being drawn up. Su Shi, Liu and Helen would go to Carpenters Cottage at five. Leaving Bryn and Charlyyk alone in the Cottage. Bryn will leave the garden door open...that leads into the kitchen. He will need to block the entrance to the drive, by closing and securing the gates, so no unexpected visitor could disrupt them. To be able to achieve this, he will need to check if the gates will move, since it's been a few years since they were last touched.

Liu was enjoying this sense of drama. This was entirely new experience from her ordinary world. But to be involved with her husband was so, exciting her. She watched Helen reactions, she was so calm underneath all this pressure, she began to admire her. Remembering what her husband's summary of her, there's more to her, than what is on the records they had on her.

Chapter 36

A Change of Mind

On Wednesday, the nervous tension could be felt, like an electrical storm brewing, all morning Charlyyk did not want to go to school but knew she must. She clung on to Helen that little bit longer, her kiss was with so much feeling. Bryn watched them both, the love they had for one another, the bond between them was deeper and firmer. The cuddle he gave Helen as the school bus disappeared from view was showing how he appreciated her. Helen did not want to look Bryn in the eyes. Helen's tears trickled down, though she tried to appear strong, it was all too much for her. She turned and buried her head into his chest. Su Shi and Liu were at the entrance door. Liu could feel for her, being a mother, she knew the pain mothers shared with their children. When Helen and Bryn reached them. Liu put her arms around Helen and shepherd her indoors.

Su Shi had already put the kettle on. 'Tea has a calming effect at these moments.' He said, and it had just that effect on Helen.

Bryn went and cleared around the gates, and with some WD40 he eased the rusty hinges. Soon had the gates lockable. He then went to his study and retrieved the weapon that was in the case.

Helen looked at it, 'What do you expect Bryn?'

Bryn placed it on the table. 'This is for show. I will place it in the centre of the table. If I am right. The alien will ignore it. Then we can take matters slowly. I believe it will show the alien that I mean business if it tried to act with any form of aggression towards us.'

Liu had not seen the weapon she only knew what Su Shi had told her about it. Now here it was in front of her. It was just how Su Shi had told her. She felt the edge. 'It's not very sharp Bryn.'

'No, I don't think it was a true weapon.'

Su Shi looked at Bryn. 'What makes you say that?'

'The hands of the beast that carried it were too large for the hilt. The weapon would not have sat well in its hands. I sometimes wake up at night, and these little things nag at me, this was one of them. Real soldiers carry weapons that sit comfortably with them. They check the balance. The feel is the most important thing on any weapon. This was a prop.

At the Academy, Charlyyk kept up the pretence that all was well, but inside she felt the nerves getting to her. So, she tried to laugh them off, but that almost backed fired on her because her humour made no sense to the posse. Mace sat and talked with her, he sensed that there was something amiss. 'What is troubling you?'

Charlyyk knew she could not lie to Mace, so she skirted around the issue with half-truths. 'I've been worried that the Aliens would come back and take me away from you all. This has been a cause of concern to me. As I would not be unable to stop them.'

Mace put his arm around her shoulders, pulling Charlyyk towards him. 'That would worry us Charlyyk, for you have been the making of us...we have grown stronger as a team, including you. We would hate for that to happen, so let's pray it does not.'

Charlyyk touched Mace's hand, the look she gave him with the baying nod telling him she appreciated his kind words

When Charlyyk returned home. Helen fussed around her. She had made dinner for them early and tidied up. At five-thirty, after an affectionate goodbye to Charlyyk. Helen left with Su Shi and Liu, for Carpenters Cottage.

Bryn closed the gates and locked them. Charlyyk showered and changed into the Laura Ashley Dress. When she came down, she looked really nice. Bryn cuddle her. Charlyyk had thought that if she dressed in something really nice, the aliens would leave without her. This was her biggest fear, for she knew she would be unable to stop them. They had the means to just beam her back to where she had been taken from. These thoughts spun around inside her mind. She would clutch at any item of flotsam for survival.

Bryn set the scene. He was a warrior, and he wanted to portray that image. With his tight T-shirt; and army combat trousers, this was Bryn ready for action, at five to seven Charlyyk's iPad showed the blurred image appearing in the garden. The door was open ready to receive it.

The golden main, of its hair, was the first they saw of it, then the rest followed behind it, standing up it rose to seven feet tall. It had the same features has Charlyyk. Its long hands again, the same as Charlyyk's. Its flowing robes, a creamy white that draped to the floor.

The nods the tall alien conveyed to Charlyyk, she returned...knowing what they meant. Bryn keeping a close watchful eye on what was being played out between them.

The Alien looked at Charlyyk and spoke in Charlyyk's native tongue, she spoke back and bowed. The Alien looked at the weapon on the table bent down, picked it up by the centre of the blade, then placed it in front of Bryn. Bryn nodded, allowed it to talk with Charlyyk.

Charlyyk turned to Bryn. 'Dad this is Drenghaagh. He is the leader of his group. He wants to put a headpiece on me. Is that OK.'

Bryn nodded. 'Yes.' He knew that this was an act that had to be played out. They had to find a level where they could discuss the meaning of this whole saga.

Drenghaagh, took two metal headpieces from his robes. He put one on his own head. Then gently put one on Charlyyk head. With a slight awkwardness sat in the chair opposite Charlyyk. He nodded to her, then he spoke. This time he spoke in English that Bryn could understand.

'My name is Drenghaagh. I have much to tell you. I knew eventually we would find the right paring, but it came at a terrible cost, that we had to afford. On our home planet our genetic genes have eroded us. Our civilisation has been around a million years longer than your civilisation. We have evolved so much it is causing our own downfall. We have tried to keep everyone alive through good living and medical care, but the faulty genes in us have started to erode us. Yet no one wanted to do anything about it. Now we must begin again. We have found a suitable replacement planet. We need to set the right system, so we do not make the same mistakes again. We see the same problem's, exist on this planet, and you too will self-destruct in time.'

Bryn was troubled by what he heard. 'So why have you let Charlyyk live amongst us?'

'The new planet we have chosen has the same bacteria present, that exist on your planet. We have lost four colonies due to them Charlyyk is an orphan of those past mistakes. We have placed a plate in Charlyyk, it has a few functions. First, it stopped Charlyyk's memory in the first stage of her life. Second to give her some immunity to your bacteria. As your planet has had two orbits of your sun, and Charlyyk has survived. It has increased, our belief's we could have solved one of the problems of colonisation of our new home planet.'

Drenghaagh reached across the table and gently stroked Charlyyk's face. 'You have changed so much Charlyyk.' He nodded to her. She nodded back. Drenghaagh turned towards Bryn. 'The plate also allows us to communicate through these headpieces.'

'We thought at first that is how you monitored her.'

'No, we have a place on your moon. We use your satellites, that you are crowding your space with. To see how your knowledge is advancing'

Bryn noticed how similar Drenghaagh and Charlyyk were. There was no mocking, just a matter-of-fact straight-to-the-point in their manner.

Drenghaagh looked carefully at her. 'You have settled here. Your new family treat you well?'

'Yes, I love my life here' Again the nodding between them.

Charlyyk rose from her chair and put the kettle on. Drenghaagh watched her carefully. She made a mint tea and coffee. Gave him the tea, Bryn the coffee. Charlyyk explains to Drenghaagh. 'The heating of the water kills the bacteria.' And then she makes herself a mint tea.

Bryn observing every movement. He was not worried he knew it was not here to do harm, it was a graceful creature. Charlyyk's brain was picking up the wavelengths it was sending out, and naturally responding to them.

Drenghaagh turned to Bryn. 'Have you any questions?'

Bryn answered. 'Yes many, but where do I start?'

It was Charlyyk that asked. 'The planet I was placed on, was it my home planet?'

'No, the planet was too arid. It was only a short-term solution the planet you found yourself on when you met your guardian, another one too arid to sustain long time life.'

'And those beasts that killed my group?'

'Placed there to serve the purpose of paring together. Either one of your groups, with the chosen male specimen, who now is your Guardian.'

Charlyyk placed her hands together on the table and stared at them, the memories of her group, flooding back, the screams of them that haunt her constantly, were there again. Bryn reached out, and she went to him sitting on his knee sinking into him for protection. It was Drenghaagh turn to observe, he saw the way the two of them connected, his eyes turned a different colour. His body moved, and he was standing up. 'I must leave.' He said, and was gone.

Bryn comforting Charlyyk, who's sobs had started to subdue as they could hear voices. Helen was the first one in. Soon was cuddling Charlyyk. Su Shi checking on Bryn.

Liu went to Helen to also check on Charlyyk. The iPad was given out noises. Bryn could see Harold's face appearing on it, asking if everything was OK. Bryn's mind went through what had occurred. He had not been in control of the situation, so why did Dreenghaagh leave? it was bugging him. Bryn racked his brain trying to fathom it out. Su Shi was talking to him, but Bryn was not listening. When he finally looked at Su Shi.

'Why did it leave in that manner Bryn?'

Su Shi carried on speaking to Bryn. 'We saw, Charlyyk go to you. We waited...then it rose from the chair. It was gone.'

Helen had Charlyyk settled, then sat down by the side of Bryn. 'There was a sudden change. Then its head twitched, and the eyes went a different colour--just before it left.'

Harold, Gwen and Bruce, entered the kitchen. Bruce carrying his computer.

Harold walking towards Bryn. 'Why did it, just get up and go?' He asked.

Bryn could not answer him. He did not know the answer for himself. Bruce had set up his computer, in front of Bryn, He watched it from start to finish. 'Bruce, can you get a closer look at those eyes.' Bruce zoomed in on them, but nothing.

Bryn shook his head. 'Don't know, it shows nothing,' Charlyyk asked Bruce to show her the recording and sat there watching it.

Helen, Gwen and Liu made coffees, all of them talking trying to find answers. They sat around the Kitchen table, looking for any conceivable conclusion, but could not find the right answers, and at the end, decided to sleep on it.

***

Thursday morning, as Bryn and Helen, sneaked a look into Charlyyk's room the bed was empty. A feeling of misgiving crept through Helen. She had feared the worst. Bryn's reaction was different. He just walked to the kitchen, there was Charlyyk drinking water. Seeing them a smile spread across her face. 'Needed to clear my head from last night.' Charlyyk was already dressed for her early morning run.

Liu was next to arrive, ready for the run and greeted Helen with a kiss. Then went to Charlyyk, a hug for her, 'How did you sleep?'

Charlyyk still in the warmth of Liu's hug. 'Not a lot Liu, need the run to put me in the right frame of mind for school.'

When Su Shi arrived, they were soon limbering up and set off at a steady pace across the field towards the road from the village up to the farm. The chill air, catching the back of their throat's; As they reach the top of Bishops Lane. The sun was peeping through on the horizon. Heading down the lane, Su Shi was now ready to talk with Bryn. 'Had you thought more about last night, Bryn?'

Bryn was still quiet for a moment. 'I could not sleep, so laid there with my eyes shut, something did not frighten it, the colour change in the eyes.

I've seen it on Charlyyk once before, and I am racking my brain trying to remember when and why it occurred.'

Liu running with Charlyyk. 'What was it that frightened you last night Charlyyk?'

Charlyyk thought for a moment. 'I was not frightened, the memories of my friends dying in the terrible way they did. And it was they the alien's...and let us not forget...who are my people. They did this on purpose. That's why, I was so upset. I have an inbuilt detest of violence that is similar to Gwen's. I sensed the same from Drenghaagh. So how could they have done, what they did to my group?'

During breakfast, they allowed Charlyyk to talk. Then Su Shi slipped in the question to Charlyyk, 'Why did the eye's change like that?'

Charlyyk picking up her dirty things just said, 'A sudden change of thinking.' Then placing the things in her hands, into the dishwasher then closing the door to it. 'Must rush, school!' then kissing them all, she grabbed her bag, and with Helen in hot pursuit she was heading to meet the bus, leaving the two men just looking at each other.

Liu was quick to pick up on it. 'A change of mind, so it was not scared?'

Bryn smiled. 'That's it, a dramatic change of thinking, that's what it was, with Charlyyk, when it happened to her.'

Su Shi now had a smile. 'It's not over, this is just the beginning.'

Helen returning seeing the smiles on their faces. 'What, have I missed?'

Liu reached up and took her hand. 'It was not scared...it just had a change of mind.'

Helen did not hesitate and was on the phone with Harold. 'Has Bruce gone?'

Harold was quick to reply. 'No, why?'

Helen in a calm voice. 'Don't let him, we need to talk.'

This made Harold curious. 'What has happened?' Helen was soon telling him of what had transpired that morning.

Later, Harold, Gwen and Bruce arrived and over coffees. Su Shi spoke to Chad on the phone, with Bruce confirming the action from the night before, sending him the download from his computer. Su Shi said he would drop into him, on his return home to China. Then he phoned his sons to say he would see them tomorrow and to book a table with their cousin Chi for a family meal.

Bruce set up Helen's laptop, so she could use the surveillance equipment that was installed, and a guide how to use it. 'I have to return tomorrow, to report on this, it gives me time to say goodbye to Charlyyk. She has given me enough information to resume my search, off her own planet. Now that we know it was not the one, she had initially thought it was.

Julia was keen to find out more, on what had happened last night. And at lunch, they found a secluded place away from the rest so they could talk... without being heard. Charlyyk explaining, giving Julia a described vision of Drenghaagh. Julia's mouth dropped at what Charlyyk had told her. 'Wow... were you frightened?'

Charlyyk did not lie. She told of her fear of being taken away. Julia saw tears well up in her eyes. She cuddled Charlyyk when she heard about Charlyyk's feelings regarding what the alien leader said they had done to Charlyyk's group.

Julie's calm approach communicated to Charlyyk that what was done was done and could not be reversed, helped Charlyyk to settle, before going to their next lesson.

After school and back home at the cottage. Charlyyk was pleased to see Bruce, had not gone. She was quickly in conversation with him. They were all sitting in the lounge, the question was asked. What does '*Dreng*' mean?

'Leader, Lord, Chief. *Haagh* meaning Male.' She replied. 'It is deemed an honour if called Haarhhaagh, a man of men. It is like, a soldier being awarded a Victoria Cross.

Then Charlyyk stopped, and Bryn saw her thinking, put his hand up to tell them all to wait. A moment later Charlyyk said. 'The headpiece...it has given me more information than I knew before.' Bryn still asking them to wait before asking questions. 'Some memories are returning, that had only been a mist at the back of my mind. I must not push too hard but give my brain time to adjust.'

***

Friday morning, Su Shi and Liu were packed and ready to leave. Their farewell to Charlyyk was warm and moving. Charlyyk had come to like them very much and was genuinely sorry to see them go. She was pleased to see them wave goodbye to her, as the bus drove off.

Liu was happy with the many pictures on her phone to show her friends, she had more bragging rights, to be able to move in all the right places.

At ten, mid-morning they said their goodbye's, to the rest of the family. The chauffeured car taking them to Oxford, to the student house they had rented for their son's university stay.

Harold, sitting with Bryn in his study, relating to what had taken place. 'Do you think the alien will return?'

Bryn was confident it had only just begun. 'If it has only a change of mind, yes, but how and when that is a different story, we have just to wait to find out how it will unravel?'

At the Academy, the posse had gathered together for lunch; the main topic was Charlyyk's new diet. The salad looked nice, the avocado dip Charlyyk thought needed improvement. Michel did not want her eating salt, and she missed it, but under the rye crisps, the tell, tell signs of a KitKat, brought a little comfort to her. Julia managed to find a friendly soul who had some salad cream, in a little sachet, and lunchtime took on another meaning for Charlyyk.

This normality was helping Charlyyk to keep a stable hold on how her brain was reacting to all that had happened. The new memories she was now having were confusing to her...like a dream a mixed bag of jumbled nonsense.

Chapter 37

The Light Consumed Them

On Saturday morning, the three runners passed the cowsheds, James, his customary blown kiss to Charlyyk, received and returned. They carried on, till they reached the top of Bishops Lane, to begin for the return home. The light consumed them...in a flash they were gone as if nothing had been there.

In a safe position, set just of the dark side of the moon a Space Craft sat concealed. Charlyyk saw Drenghaagh's hand, reaching down in a friendly nature. She reached up, and he helped her to her feet. He noticed her worried face. His eyes showed her that she was not alone. 'I have not brought you here, to take you away Charlyyk, so don't be alarmed.'

Two more aliens were helping Bryn and Helen, to their feet. 'Welcome, please make yourselves comfortable. You are our guest.' Drenghaagh said. He pointed to some seats. 'Let me explain myself.' Bryn could see that all the aliens were wearing headpieces on their heads. 'When I was with you, I could see the bond that you share with one another. The thoughts I was receiving showed that Charlyyk had made many friends, it would be wrong of us, to think of taking her away from you.'

Helen face changed the anxiety on her face had gone.

Drenghaagh with a reassuring look. 'But it has its problems, as you can tell Charlyyk is growing. She has a healthy appetite, if we allow her to grow, she will tower over every human, and would indeed pose a threat to them. To help Charlyyk, we need to adjust the plate in her head, to stop this from happening.'

Bryn saw more aliens, assembling. 'Come Charlyyk, let us proceed.' Drenghaagh showed her to a table. A female aliens *a Lyyk* with a light blue tint to her skin, helped her onto the table with Charlyyk lying face down. The Lyyk gently lifted Charlyyk's hair back, a large overhanging machine was lowered down and was gently positioned.

Helen gripped Bryn's hand, and hung on to his arm. She felt helpless, there were more of the aliens than her and Bryn.

Drenghaagh stood beside her and placed his hand on her back. 'She will feel no pain. A tingling sensation will travel through her body. The operation will do her no harm, we are going to alter the genes that we have gained knowledge of. This will restrict Charlyyk's height and allow her to grow fingernails and not claws. Some of us will also benefit from this.'

A Lyyk came to them. 'It is nearly completed.' We will have to give her chance to gather herself.' Then went back to the table.

Charlyyk was now sitting up. Looking at them, she gave a big sigh...then smiled. Two of the Lyyk's helped her to a seat, as her legs were a little wobbly, from the procedure. Then a Haagh brought her something to drink and offered Bryn and Helen some refreshments.

Helen was a bit hesitant to accept the offer at first. Bryn agreed and took a sip, to show Helen it was fine.

Drenghaagh started to speak again. 'This will allow her to live normally with you. We have an arm band to place on the top of her arm. This has away, of giving you an idea of how she is health wise. The person that looks after her will need this.' He gave Bryn a square object with rounded corners, the size of a cigarette packet. A Lyyk's stepped forward and lifted her garment, to reveal a band on her arm. Then Drenghaagh showed Bryn how it worked, placing the gadget to the band. It flickered blue and green lights, then it stopped flickering. 'That is all there has to be done, the body's own immunities will do the rest' The Lyyk then fitted the band to Charlyyk's arm, then using the gadget, watching it flicker, then it stopped, she gave back the device and left.

Drenghaagh explained the necessity of the two years, to make contact. 'We could not make contact earlier as we did not know if the immunity, we had placed in Charlyyk worked. Two full solar cycles would determine if it had.' Then with pause. 'I too would not know how safe it would be, even for myself.'

Bryn was most impressed with the way they had treated them, then he felt he had to say something about the way the Military was looking at the threat of an alien invasion. Drenghaagh summoned his aides, and for a moment they talked amongst themselves.

Bryn, notice it was not a heated discussion, one of the aides left, and when he returned, he gave Bryn a small metal disc. 'Place that on your communicator, that will allow us to be seen and to be able to talk with them. Charlyyk will be able to activate it. When required.'

Helen now felt relaxed and went to see how Charlyyk was. The other aliens watching the interaction, between them, the looks they were giving, satisfied Bryn.

One of the aliens came and sat with Drenghaagh. 'I'm Strenghaagh, my role, is as an analyst. We have studied your people and find they are unstable, excitable, and to act on impulse. So, could be highly likely to react at the slightest provocation. We would like very much to dispel their concerns and to remove any threat of them to feel they would need to retaliate with force.

Bryn picked on the nods they gave to each other. Drenghaagh smiled at Bryn observations, but before he could answer.

Charlyyk answered for him. 'It is a sign of friendship, like when you shake hands.' Drenghaagh, looking at Charlyyk spoke in her native tongue, asking her if she felt good about herself. She assured him she was fine. Then spoke to Bryn and Helen. 'Mum, Dad I am good.'

One of the Lyyk's came in and gave them a ring each, this will help you with your return to your planet, a little reaction from Charlyyk to the Lyyk. Helen remembered Charlyyk responding to Sandra the same way at Christmas, like a thank you gesture.

Drenghaagh showed them to the area where they had landed on the craft, as they positioned themselves. He nodded to them. 'We will meet again.' A flash, they found themselves back in their garden, this time they experienced no problems as they materialised.

There were two anxious people, inside the cottage. 'Do you know what time it is?' asked Gwen, wringing her hands together pacing the floor, 'I've been worried sick, wondering what had happened to you all.'

Helen looking at her watch, two-twenty. 'Wow, it did not seem that length of time.'

They sat down, around the kitchen table, explained in full detail what had happened aboard the spacecraft. Charlyyk showing the band on her arm, and Bryn the disc and the gadget that went with the armband as with the rings on their fingers. Harold wanted to see how the disc worked. But Charlyyk said. 'No, too early,'

Bryn called, Su Shi. He needed to explained that they had a meeting with the Laight's. Su Shi said they would return to the cottage on Monday. Su Shi mentioned he would drop in and see Chad on his way back China, so could explain to the American's precisely what had taken place. Bryn's Military experience knowing it is better to report than to keep quiet.

***

The Sunday morning run, had a different feel to it, Helen had checked her weight, and was pleased. Another three pounds lost, looking in the mirror she liked what she saw, and so did Bryn, 'A wedding dress would look nice draped, over those breasts.' Bryn remarked. She reached over and kissed him.

Life was feeling good for Helen and it felt right. This was not for Bryn this was for her and her own self-esteem. She felt like a butterfly, not a moth. She was now matching strides with Charlyyk and Bryn. This was definitely the girl in her, not the old lady.

Breakfast was taken casually, at a slow pace. Charlyyk showed no effects from Saturday and was in good spirits. *'Monday morning with Julia was going to be awesome'* she had thought to herself.

Bryn carried on as if life was just normal. Completely not fazed by the latest developments.

Later at Carpenters Cottage. As they all talked with Michel, at what had happened on board the Laight's spacecraft, he was very interested in what the Laight's said about the fingernails, and when Bryn showed him the gadget for the armband, and what it achieved, he remarked. 'Now that what we all want, something to kick starts our immunities into action.' When Helen told him what the plate in Charlyyk's head could do, he sighed a big sigh, 'Lucky we did not try to remove it.' Was his reply.

Bryn's update to Catherine and Thomas on the Skype connection, had mixed reactions from them. Both concerned that if it had gone wrong, what then.

Charlyyk was quick to reply. 'My people are a passive society they will not upset the balance of life by doing harm.' Though Charlyyk was still not happy what had happened to her friend, was looking not to allow the situation to escalate out of control; knowing Catherine line of work in the media spotlight.

***

Monday, the rush to the bus. Charlyyk could not wait to tell Julia, all what had taken place, and what changes that the Laight's had planned for her to exist on Earth.

Su Shi and Liu arrived at Ten. The conversation on all the latest developments, lasted to Twelve, the phone call to Chad, was next, a Skype connection was set up. Bruce could be seen with Mrs Lomax, studying his video recording of the first meeting of the aliens. Chad felt a bit miffed he had not been there. 'We must meet up again, and soon.'

Lunchtime, found Julia and Charlyyk huddled together. Julia's mouth gaping open, hearing what had happened to Charlyyk. The armband and ring on her finger sealed the whole story for Julia. 'How tall was he?'

When Charlyyk, told her 'See the door over there, well six inches taller, almost up to the clock.' Charlyyk pointing to the clock that was fixed to the wall above the doorway.

Julia's wide-eyed look towards the clock then back at Charlyyk, 'Too, that height! and they promised you they could keep your height at a more normal height to suit us. Wow, that clever.' Julia looked as if she had been smacked in the face, then Julia face lightened up. 'And you will get fingernail like ours, Wow.' To Julia, the fingernails sounded more important.

Yuri welcomed Bryn's, phone call. He kept Bryn on the line for some time, asking many questions. 'I will speak with Chad...Bryn, I will expect, that we will all catch up, on these new developments...So look forward to seeing you then.' Bryn, putting the phone down, the soft smile on his face. He liked this larger-than-life Russian who took life at a moderate pace. He was much like himself in many ways, said nothing, until he had thought things through, weighing everything up judging their actual value. It could also be said he was making sure his English he was speaking was correct. But Bryn was sure Yuri indeed was a good man. He did not complicate issues, he usually made sound comments.

Bryn had left Helen to speak to Major Alan Carter, who needed the same updates. And the detailed reports that Helen gave the Major. He did not need to question.

The arrival of Charlyyk at Oakleaves brought them all together, sitting with drinks in hands, started to look how their lives should start from now. Charlyyk made the first suggestion. 'My diet, this one suck!' Bryn and Helen just burst out into laughter. Charlyyk had brought the unexpected events back to normality.

After dinner, Charlyyk helped Helen, to tidy up, then went to her room, she needed, to talk with Janet. 'Hi, kid, how you feel?'

'Much better, thanks Charlyyk.' Janet, sounded better than the last time they had spoken. 'Mum and dad are here... Edward and Jane invited them to stay for the week. Dr Patel has said when people have a full-blown virus, it can really bring them down, and weaken their immunities... Edward has brought a couple of crates of Guinness, and I am getting used to them, find that I look forward to when Edward has poured another one for me.' Janet gave Charlyyk, a little chuckle. It was not what she would have thought she would like to drink, so looking forward to having another one was way out of her usual self.

'Janet much has happened, and we need to talk about it, will it be Ok, if we come to you?'

There was a pause, then James answered. 'What's up Charlyyk?'

Charlyyk took a deep breath, 'James, we have had developments here, and I do believe, we should tell you all about them, as you are like family to us.'

James felt concerned. 'Whatever could it be Charlyyk?'

Charlyyk felt a little awkward. 'Promise you will not tell anyone James!'

He was getting confused. 'Why what's up?'

Charlyyk voice became firmer. 'Promise me?'

James gave in 'Ok, I promise, now what is it?'

Charlyyk took it slowly. 'We have had a visit from my people.'

James did not answer straight away...but when he did it was slow and precise 'From your people?'

'Yes, from my people.'

James took a large intake of breath. 'Bloody Hell.'

Charlyyk heard mumblings between him and Janet. Janet's voice upped a pitch. 'Is that true Charlyyk?'

'Yes, Janet, with video proof.'

Janet sounded a bit gurgled over the phone, then the line went dead.

As Charlyyk tried to redial, the mainline phone rang. Helen answered Jane who was on the other end, as Charlyyk entered the lounge. 'Yes Jane, what a great idea.' Helen seeing Charlyyk beckoned her, to come to her. 'Yes Jane, she is by my side now.' And passed the phone to Charlyyk.

'Sorry for the confusion Charlyyk. But Janet dropped the phone, and they both bumped their heads trying to retrieve it, we will see you tomorrow.'

As Charlyyk replaced the phone, Helen put her arm around her. 'We are going there for dinner tomorrow.'

***

Tuesday evening, the drive up to Parsons Farm did not take long, and James was at the front door waiting. Charlyyk was first out of the car, and into his arms. 'Hi, twinkle.' The manly way he greeted her, brought out a couple of squeals from Charlyyk. Bryn and Helen followed.

Charlyyk went through to the kitchen to greet Jane, then went through the house to the back, where Janet was sitting with her parents and Edward, in the large conservatory.

Janet was very pale the flu virus had really taken its toll on her. Janet looked concerned for Charlyyk welfare. 'Don't come to close Charlyyk, I don't want to pass this to you.' Charlyyk just smiled, and pulled her sleeve up, showing the armband, a thin strip of metal in a zig-zag pattern shaped that allowed it to be expanded with the movement of the arm biceps. 'They gave me this to protect me.' Then bent down and kissed her.

Janet reached up and touch it. 'How does it do that?'

Charlyyk was keen to explain. 'It gives my immunities a kick start.'

James was standing right behind her. 'Can I see?' He touched it. 'Wow, it actually came from out of space?'

Charlyyk with a wry smile. 'Yes, James just like myself.'

Janet then introduced Charlyyk, to her parents. They both were hesitant at first. Charlyyk pushed herself forward, not allowing them any choice but to shake her outstretched hand.

Helen came in and showed them the recording of the first encounter. Bryn was soon filling in with the story. When they heard, that this had happened at the top of Bishops Lane where they were taken from on Saturday morning, they were gobsmacked. So near to the farm, yet they had not seen nothing. The rest of the details Helen gave them. Poor Janet was trying to get enthusiastic but found it hard to.

Charlyyk was more concerned about Janet, then telling her what had happened to herself. Then Charlyyk changed, her expression was deep and meaningful. 'All of you are like family to us, we must keep this in the family until it is allowed to be broadcast to the world. This will no doubt be looked at by all the different Nations Governing bodies before it is released. So please...just us.'

Edward remarked about the plate in Charlyyk head. 'And that really can alter the way Charlyyk grows? bloody marvellous.'

After dinner, sitting and talking, Jane asked Bryn about Thomas, 'When will they be back?' Bryn looked at Helen.

Helen answered. 'They will return in two weeks, stay for two weeks, then Liverpool for six weeks...We have a lot of material for Janet. When Charlyyk opened the Exhibition, we have held onto it until Janet is feeling better.'

Edward laughed with Bryn about the editorial in the Man Magazine they had published about him. 'I was taken back, with the girl posing in the earlier chapter. She looked younger than Charlyyk.'

Jane quipped, 'You sure, you were looking at her age Bryn.'

Charlyyk chirped. 'Helen would have blacked his eyes if it were anything different.'

Charlyyk sensed that Janet's parents were apprehensive of her, they had been so quiet, all evening. She managed to get James on his own. 'So, when are you going to ask them? although you are both old enough, to not have to ask.'

James looked at her with a forlorn look. 'I keep plucking up the courage, then it goes. The cat catches my tongue.'

When they were both back with the others in the conservatory. Bryn asked James how life was treating him. When Charlyyk, gatecrashes. 'Edward, when are you going to shoot the farm cat?'

Edward looked at her, he knew Charlyyk would not mention anything unless there were something behind it. 'Why have I to shoot the farm cat Charlyyk?'

She turned to James. 'James is trying to pluck up the courage, to pop the question, but that bloody farm cat, keeps catching his tongue. All the time, it is here, he will never ask.'

Jane took hold of Helen's hand. Both had closed their eyes. Bryn shot a look at Charlyyk. Edward looked at James. Janet took hold of her mother's hand. Her father placed his hands on his own knees. But nobody said anything. Then Charlyyk still looking at James. 'Well, that good. No one's objected. so, it's a yes then.' Turned and walked to the kitchen and poured a glass of water. Charlyyk knew what she had done, but wondered to herself would it have the right results. She would have handled this type of matter in a much more sensitive way. Yes, it was what she wanted, but she could have been more delicate how she had handled it. A smile broke out on her face remembering how James's face distorted hearing what she had said. She collected herself together, so she could go back to the conservatory.

On her return, they were all congratulating themselves. Janet seeing Charlyyk struggled over to her and hugged her. 'Thanks, sweetheart, you are a treasure.' Jane and also Mary Stokes, Janet's mother. The smile on their face said, they wanted this to happen.

Charlyyk looked up, saw the big smiling face of Helen. Giving her a wink of the eye.

The drive home was lively. Bryn was making faces at Charlyyk, in the rear-view mirror. Helen reminding him to keep his eyes on the road. Then looking at Charlyyk. 'What made you say that Charlyyk?'

'It was dads' fault. He asked James what was happening and the answer was nothing. James needed a kick.'

***

Wednesday, when Charlyyk came home from school, she spoke to Helen about what the girls were talking about at school. 'Valentine Cards, mum?'

Helen looked at Charlyyk with that, *do we need to go down this path* look on her face. 'When a girl or boy, fancies someone. They can send a valentine card anonymously, giving them clues to who sent it and hoping the other person respond likewise. Usually to get the romance started but many, just want boys and girls to send a card to brag how many cards they had received... it what known as bragging rights.'

Charlyyk thought it through, 'So I could send, someone a card, without saying it was me.' Then she stopped. 'That won't work, will it, as soon as I write something, they would know it was me.' She went quiet for a moment. 'Then that would cause more problems, I think it would be wiser, not to send any cards.'

Helen looked down her nose at her, 'Have you someone in mind.'

Charlyyk's face did not change in any way. 'No... No one.' Charlyyk started peeling the potatoes, her thoughts still on what they had been discussing. 'So, what would one write on a card?'

Helen putting chicken pieces, in a roasting tin, and adding a little stock to keep them moist. 'Most people write poems, or some type of verse, like an ode which I believe is normally meant to be sung.'

Charlyyk laughed. 'Well, that will be no good for me, with the voice I've got.'

Helen sensed that she had an issue with something. 'What's bugging you Charlyyk?' As she covered the chicken with foil and placed them in the oven.

Charlyyk putting the potatoes on to parboil. 'I feel the meaning of love... the love for all the people that have given me a chance to live here, the way I feel towards those that are closest to me... Well, that love gives me that warm inner glow that Gwen says, her God gives her. But when I see you and dad enjoy each other. Janet and James rampant love for each other, I wonder, will I miss that type of love? I don't know, or never will know, yes, I'm different, still I don't know what would be expected from me if I returned to my own kind... I just don't know what would be expected from me. Full stop'

Helen for a moment said nothing, she had noticed that Charlyyk eyes had stayed the same colour pattern so it was just casual talk. 'Charlyyk, I was brought up by nannies, it left me cold in my feelings, never looked at the other sex for pleasure, only if they were efficient to do a job. But your dad, well the more I saw him, the more I wanted him... could not stop thinking of him, I would do anything for him. If I never had met your dad, well I would have carried on being a nun.'

369

Charlyyk strained the potatoes and twirling them in the colander, emptied them into the roasting tin, and replacing them in the oven. Then placing the dirty dishes in the sink. 'What are nuns?'

'Well, they are women that give their lives to God. They give up material things, when they go through a ceremony of marrying God, accepting his ring.'

Charlyyk's face did not show any change, but said. 'Are there many of them?'

'Yes, thousands of them.'

Charlyyk checking the potatoes. 'With that many wives, it should keep him busy, no wonder he doesn't turn up to church on Sunday's'

Helen took a grip on the table, trying hard to stifle her laughter.

***

Thursday lunchtime at the Academy. Charlyyk with Julia had started to form a pattern. They had positioned themselves so that they could see all the posse. They could talk without being overheard; the sharing of their lunchboxes is what the posse thought is what they were doing. But that was not the reason, what their primary interest was, the interaction between them all. Who was getting on, with who?

Peter and Sandra were getting more and more closer, Though Sandra had the control. George was getting closer to Jan. Mace and Sarah the brother-sister relationship had not changed. Charlyyk could sense Mike's vibes for Julia were still showing, but very faint. Julia's vibes were the same, but Julia spending more time with Charlyyk. Had kept Mike at bay, for the moment. Spotty Paul who was self-conscious sat on the periphery of the team, prepared to be used by them. Stella who lived close to Jan was like Paul. Was also being dragged along, glad to be a part of the group, was treated the same as Paul. Charlyyk felt sorry for them and was looking to see where she could alter their prospects, to bring them forward into the group.

***

Friday, they had returned from the run, enjoying a glass of water in the kitchen. Charlyyk was giving her idea for the weekend. 'Let's take it easy. After what happened last weekend. We could do lazy, easily by just chilling out.'

Helen liked that idea. 'How about a movie, there must be something we could see?'

Bryn nodded his approval. 'Catch a bite to eat, then cinema sounds good.'

The doorbell rang, and Bryn made his way to find out the reason why.

Margret, the post lady, was standing there. 'Hi Bryn, this bag of mail is all for you, happy reading.' He thanked her, and returned to the kitchen, and emptied the bags content over the kitchen table. Bryn picking up a handful of letters looked at them and past them straight to Charlyyk. Helen doing the same.

'Well, you will see what I meant about, who sent them?'

Charlyyk opened a couple, laughed at their content. Then she went to get ready for school.

At breakfast, the piles of opened and unopened letters and cards, were placed in order. The good, the bad, as with the downright unreadable. Charlyyk took a hand full to show the posse; at lunchtime, while all the girls were reading the cards. One of Charlyyk's eyes were watching Stella, she looked so forlorn, it concerned her.

Getting up and sitting with her. 'Aye, you don't look happy.'

Stella tried to smile. 'I'm okay Charlyyk'

But Charlyyk sensed that, lump in the throat, in Stella's voice. 'Come on. You are one of a posse, so, if there is a problem, it's my problem too. Talk to me.'

Sandra who was nearest to them, sat on the other side of Stella. 'What Charlyyk has just said, goes for all us, so if you have a problem, talk to us all.' Stella looking down into her hands. 'I feel that nobody likes me, I feel different from all of you.' Sandra placing her arm into Stella arm, giving it a gentle tug. Charlyyk is different than all of us, yet she talks to us. To make friends Stella, you must meet people, take that big step forward and say, Hi. You will hear them say, Hi, back to you. It's as easy as that, just as we are doing now.'

Charlyyk took her hand in hers. 'Happy Valentine's Day Stella.'

The rest of the posse was soon there. They were checking what was going on, joined in with conversation. This was giving Stella, moral support. Her smile, showed just that.

As the bell sounded for lessons, and they started to move to their next lesson. Charlyyk spoke to Paul. 'That goes for you too Paul, don't stay on the sidelines, come into the middle, or you will fall out of the group.'

Paul's, pale, pasty face, smiled at her. 'Thanks, Charlyyk'

Sarah gave Charlyyk a hug, 'Good on yer kid, well done you'.

Charlyyk started to think what she had said, was due her to changing. *'Careful, don't look to mature, remember to act your age'.*

Chapter 38

The silent visitor

Friday evening Michel Henderson the Vet and Clare were writing their reports, at their separate desks, and discussing the schedules, for the next day. Clare had been with Michel, since leaving University, she loved Michel's natural, relaxed manner. He never panics. When she suggested some changes to the clinic, he would just smile, 'So when are you going to implement these changes then Clare?' He gave her the freedom, to express herself. She had told her parent, Michel gave her, that feeling, it was her clinic, she was working in, not his, Michel's openness with her when Charlyyk first arrived. Letting her know, what was happening, and why it must be kept secret at all times, meant he had her trust.

The presence of someone was in the room with them, made them look up, the very distinguished tall figure of the Lyyk, that had put the armband on Charlyyk. Was standing there, she was wearing similar clothes that Drenghaagh had dressed in, that had a soft hint of blue. The friendship nod of her head, then sitting in the chair opposite Michel.

'Please do not be afraid, I have come to explain the procedure of the armband, we have placed on Charlyyk's arm.'

Clare did not look concerned with this tall elegant Alien, just pulled her chair closer to Michel, and then clearing the screen on the computer, she was ready to dictate, what was going to be told them.

The Alien Lyyk's passive nature was why Clare had not panicked it was so relaxed that Clare just went with flow of the moment. 'My name is Klyklyyk. The armband we have placed on Charlyyk, will respond to the electronic signal from Charlyyk's brain, or from any sign given by the nervous system in Charlyyk's body. The meter that goes with the armband has two functions, the first is to tell you that the band is working properly, blue to green. Straight green, it is fighting a virus at that moment. A yellow light, this will tell you that the band has a conflict with the plate in her head. Take the ring on her finger, and place it on the next finger, then check the band, for a straight green. If still yellow keep moving the ring to another finger till the meter reads green.' Klyklyyk, looked at Clare to see if she had taken notes of all what she had told them. 'The changes that Charlyyk will experience happening to her. A slight tingling will be felt, then her claws will drop off. Her fingernails will have already started to come through this will take a few light moments to complete the procedure. The slowing down of her growth, at first there should be no problems, but in two solar cycles, she will feel some side effect. We will be on hand when that happens.' Klyklyyk rose from the chair. 'Thank you, for looking after Charlyyk.' She turned then she was gone.

Clare printed off two copies. 'I will laminate these, we will need, to place one in Kitty's clinic.' Michel took notice on the laid backed way that Clare had behaved, to seeing this tall stranger, for he did not feel so calm at first, but it was how Clare had reacted to the situation that settled himself.

***

Saturday, at the breakfast table the Collier family, were still reading the mail. Some of the letters were from teenagers, struggling to find their identity. Some asking, how she coped adjusting to life here in their world. Helen trying to explain the strained relationship, some families, find themselves in. 'It's not always the teenagers that are at fault. Some parents, are lazy parents, not expecting to contribute to bringing up their children. All ways blaming the government for their own failings.'

Charlyyk was keen to find out more. 'When looking at some of the student attitudes, when at school, that bordered on surly, aggressive, obstructive. I wondered how they could behave in that manner?'

Bryn listening to her. 'We call that having a chip on their shoulder. Sometimes it a way of trying to influence others to give into their way of thinking, or their want's. Weak parents are to blame, not being able to say no to them, at an early age. Some parents are like that themselves; it brushes off onto their children.'

Charlyyk listened carefully to what Bryn was saying, 'It sounds that all the parents are at fault one way or another.'

Helen, putting down a letter she was reading. 'No that's not quite true, the nanny state has some part to play in it. Education was about teaching children the basics of life, allowing the natural aptitudes to come forward. Those that were good at set subjects went on to study them at the university. Now the governments want to put all children into the same box, those natural abilities are being lost.'

She did not finish what she wanted to say, a knock on the door and Michel distinctive voice. 'Anyone at home?' Walked in, Clare was close behind him. 'Had a visitor last night. Klyklyyk?'

Charlyyk's smiled, 'She is nice.'

Clare asked, what her name meant?

'Silent girl, or quiet girl. It a name given to someone that tends to listen not to speak.'

Michel's turn to smile, 'Well she spoke to us. She explained the workings of the armband, with the explanation of the meter. Clare made a copy, and we need to leave it in Kit's Clinic.'

He passed it to Bryn, after reading it, with Helen over his shoulder, reading at the same time. 'That's detailed?'

Clare stepped forward. 'Can we test it?'

Helen was soon heading to the clinic. 'Come, Clare, let's go and get it.

On their return with the gadget in their hands, Charlyyk had soon rolled her sleeve up. Clare placed it on the band, it flashed blue to green. Then she took Charlyyk's hand, with the ring on its finger, and placed the meter on the ring; again, blue to green, then she noticed that Helen and Bryn were wearing similar rings. 'Can I?' She beckoned.

Helen lifted her hand, and the gadget flashed, blue to green. Bryn was intrigued, and offered his hand, Blue to Green, 'Interesting.' he said, 'I wonder what they do?'

Charlyyk offered them refreshment.

'Coffee, would be lovely Charlyyk.' Michel, placing his hand on Charlyyk back as they all headed for the kitchen.

Clare was pleased that Michel had insisted she came. She had never seen the cottage. Though how Michel had described it, she felt, she knew all about it. Michel then explained why he had brought Clare. 'I'm not getting any younger, Clare has been like a daughter to me. If anything, unduly happens, I want to know that Charlyyk will be taken care of.'

Clare turned, looked at Michel when he had said that, leaning over and kissing him on the cheek. 'More like you treating me like a daughter.'

Later that day the Colliers met Harold and Gwen at the Fish Restaurant. Charlyyk liked it here, the relaxed manner of the staff, then with the freshness of the food. It was situated on the outskirts of the town, so easy parking. Its basic furniture, comfortable. It was the relaxed style she liked best. Harold reckoned it was the chips. The conversation featured the visit of Michel and Clare in the morning, and their visit, of Klyklyyk on Friday night.

At the cinema, Charlyyk wanted to see 'Guardians of the Galaxy' With popcorn, and orange juice, she was ready. After the show, they all had enjoyed the film, and all had a favourite part they liked. Gwen had not liked the choice of the film at first, admitted she loved it, at the end. But Groot was hard to get her head around. A living tree took some believing, then so did Rocket the racoon. So, when Charlyyk mentioned she too was different. Gwen just nodded with closed eyes.

***

Monday morning Charlyyk sat down to breakfast. A pile of the sealed letter's, in front of her. Helen looked at the distance some were travelling. 'They are going to cost a bit to send?'

Charlyyk counted twenty letters, but half were going overseas. 'Those are the ones that had no e-mail addresses on them.' She felt that she should justify why she was sending them.

Helen said she will post them for her. 'How many did you answer to sweetheart?' Charlyyk checked her diary, 'One hundred and fifteen. Some had no reply addresses, so I could not reply to them.' Charlyyk then left for school.

Mid-morning Helen though now retired from her role in intelligence, had not stopped acting on behalf of Toby Scalon her successor. She had sent in her reports. It was after lunch when the first replies from the military came in. All saying the same, that they will convey the report to their superiors, would be in touch. They too relied on Bryn and Helen first-hand knowledge, as to what was happening.

Helen's phone call to Rebecca, Sandra's mother. Checking on Len's condition, gave Rebecca a good feeling, it was a distraction from what else was happening. Len had put on weight, and his strength was returning. They agreed to meet again next Wednesday.

***

Tuesday, the crisp chill air, showing the vapour from their mouths, as they hit the top of the hill. Charlyyk stopped, but running on the spot, looked around, she marvelled at the way the sun caught the top of the trees, the mist hung in their branches, she glanced towards, Helen and Bryn the smiles on their faces, this was a family, enjoying life.

Julia Peters, being woken by her dad. was someone else, who's life felt good. She reached for her father's hand, who taking hold, turned and sat on the edge of the bed. He was a teddy bear of a father...big and cuddly, always had a warm, loving smile for his daughter. He helped her onto his lap. His big arms wrapped around her. 'I've to go to work sweetheart, see you tonight. Have a lovely day at school.'

She stepped off his lap and kissed him goodbye. He may not be the most intelligent dad in the world, but to Julia, he was the most loving dad in the world. She stood with her mum at the door and waved him off.

Iris Peters, Julia's mother was as thin as her husband was big. The pain they both felt when they saw the large birthmark down the right side of their newborn daughter's face, only made them love her more, and being more protective of her. Like Charlyyk's first years on earth being hidden, so was Julia's. She met Sandra at Primary school, who did not worry about the birthmark, soon were friends in the first week of school. Now with Charlyyk as a friend, life was good. Over breakfast, her thoughts drifted back to when she first went to the Academy. Sarah, Mace and Peter soon became friends with them, but when Jan who was Sarah's friend, joined them she started to make fun of Julia. Sandra turned on Jan, so much that Sarah made Jan apologise, to Julia. Now they were all friends, and it felt good.

Julia had noticed that Sarah and Mace were at school. 'Where's Charlyyk Mace?'

Mace looked around. 'I don't know Julia she was with us when we left the bus.'

Charlyyk met them at the lockers. 'At lunchtime, we have a meeting with the Teachers.' They all looked quizzical at her. 'Don't look so worried! I have something to tell you all, I think you should all know.'

At lunchtime Charlyyk led the posse to the Teacher's meeting room, Mrs Landon welcomed them in and beckoned Charlyyk to speak. 'In these last few days, much has happened.' Charlyyk went on to tell them about the visits she has had, and what had occurred, the showing of the band, but stressed the importance of secrecy until it had been disclosed formally. 'I appreciate the way you have all protected me, since my arrival. I know when this is told to the world you would look at me and say why did you not trust us. So, this is me, putting my trust in you. So, it is for you to show me, that my trust in you is vindicated.'

Julia felt at ease, keeping the secret from the rest of the posse had been hard. Now they all knew the truth; she now could relax. But she still knew that the secret must still be kept at school. Charlyyk was displaying her respect for them and was making them aware the trust she had in them.

The nodding and reaching out of hands to her, with the kisses she received meant so much to Charlyyk.

***

Wednesday, Bryn went with Helen to see Rebecca and Len. Bryn soon set up a conversation with Len, while Helen gave Rebecca her full attention. The pastries they had brought went well with the coffees. Helen and Bryn left at one.

Rebecca cuddling up to Len, found them both in bed by two, Rebecca making all the play as Len was still not up to full strength. When Sandra, returned from school, her mother was still on a high, and her dad looked like the cat, that had licked the cream. The silly smirk on his face, that he could not help passing winks at Rebecca. After dinner, Sandra managed to gain some sense from her mother, soon had text Charlyyk, thanking her for what her parents had achieved.

Charlyyk showing Helen, the text, Helen could not help but show Charlyyk the reply that Rebecca had sent her. *'Helen, we are husband and wife again, thank you X.'* Charlyyk knew what the text meant, and the cuddle she gave Helen, left no doubt, that she knew what it meant. Helen was showing Charlyyk her trust in her.

Bryn received notice from No 10, to join them, to the United Nation's Meeting in New York. A car will pick them up at eight on Friday evening, Bryn relayed the news to Helen and Charlyyk.

Charlyyk immediately set up her computer. Bryn gave her the disc. Charlyyk placed it on the laptop, then turning the disc, till it changed to a blue colour, then put the ring that was on her finger, onto the disc. The image of Drenghaagh emerged. Charlyyk spoke in her native tongue with him. A nod, then he was gone. 'All set up and ready to go. dad.' Charlyyk gave back the disc to Bryn for safe keeping.

***

On Thursday, the posse crowded together, listening to Charlyyk explaining the latest developments, Mrs Landon and Mrs Butler, joining in on the latest news. 'Will you do the school proud and wear your school uniform Charlyyk?' Mrs Landon probed.

Charlyyk stopped and gave the request some thought. 'Yes, I think, it would be good to wear my uniform.'

Louise Landon was in seventh heaven, remarking on her thoughts. *'Wendy this will go all around the world, on many news channels, the next governors meeting will be a doddle.'* The two women walking away, looked as though they had won the lottery.

When Charlyyk arrived home, she spoke with Helen, on what she had agreed with Mrs Landon. Helen's thoughts *'it was a good idea,'* 'It would give the people around the world, that you are just a teenage girl.'

Bryn listening in on the conversation agreed too.

Helen's look of realisation started to turn to panic.

Charlyyk looking at her. 'What's wrong?'

Helen, throwing her hands down to her sides. 'Look at me, I've lost so much weight, I've nothing to wear!'

Bryn laughed. 'Then tomorrow morning a visit to Little and Large, is where we must go.' Bryn had been impressed with how they had supplied Charlyyk with her suit at such short notice. And the way they had accomplished with such high-quality tailoring, at the drop of a hat.

***

The plane waiting for them was one of the new aircraft with sleeping capacity. The Prime Minister was pleased to see Helen, and welcomed her with a kiss on the cheek. Bryn's introduction to the PM was warm. The PM asked him to sit with him during the flight as he had so many questions to ask of Bryn.

Then it was Charlyyk's turn, this was different the PM knew, so much about her, was soon laughing and joking with her. By ten Helen and Charlyyk had settled down to sleep. Bryn answered many questions from the PM, and my twelve, they too had settled down to sleep.

***

Saturday, the Colliers had been booked into a hotel ten minutes away from the UN buildings. There was an icy chill blowing down from the north. Charlyyk preferred to stay in the Hotel until called for. Major Carter was at hand, with four security personnel.

Charlyyk liked the Limo drive to the meeting. They were ushered into the building; where more security covered every entrance. Lieu-Col Chad Smitt had done his homework, gave Capt. Hanne the role of honour to look after the Colliers. When the time came to enter the general meeting chamber. Charlyyk strode in, flanked by Helen and Bryn. Helen in her black two-piece suit stood up to address the contingent of the leading heads of states.

When the mumblings subsided, Helen spoke. 'I hope you have all read the dossier that we have circulated, giving you the details of what has occurred so far. What you are about to see, is the first meeting of the Leader of the Laight's, Drenghaagh.' Bryn pressed the key to start the video clip, and the image appeared on the giant screen, the meeting hall was hushed. Helen waited for the video clip to finish of that Wednesday evening, then paused for a few moments for the interpreters to finish.

The hum in the Assembly Hall started to subside. Helen then carried on. 'Since that meeting, a few days later, we were taken on board their spacecraft, for further instruction, they wanted to make it clear that they were there to help Charlyyk. So, she will be able to live amongst us.' Helen gave precise details how this was to be achieved in a slow...regulated speech, so everyone could keep up with her. Then playing a video clip showing the armband, the X-ray pictures of the plate in Charlyyk's head. Once again Helen gave the interpreters time to finish. 'During our meeting aboard their Spacecraft. Brian Collier mentioned the threat they imposed to our World.' Once again pausing to allow the delegates to keep up with what she was relaying to them.

Helen sensing calm carried on. 'The Laight's leader Drenghaagh took Brian Collier's comments with concern and wanted to give you all assurances that their presence here is for peaceful reasons only.' Looking around the hall making sure she had their full attention. 'Drenghaagh wishes to speak to you directly.' Then a nod to Bryn to say she had finished.

Bryn placed the disc onto the computer, with the Wi-Fi connected soon portrayed the image on the large screens. Charlyyk was ready to set the wheels in motion. With a nod, Helen carried on, 'Ladies and Gentlemen. Drenghaagh.' Charlyyk touched the disc with her ring, then Drenghaagh appeared. Looking majestic in his flowing robes, and his golden locks. 'Please don't be afraid, we are at peace with you. We have been monitoring your planet for many solar cycles. We wish you no harm, as you have given us so much valuable insight for us to be able to colonise our new home planet which has many features as you have here on your own planet. We have placed a monitor station on your Moon this will have a minimum of our people to observe that Charlyyk is well...we would like when Charlyyk has grown to be as an ambassador, showing our good intentions towards you.'

Drenghaagh knew that he had to protect Charlyyk. 'Charlyyk has been innocent to what we placed upon her. Our intention of returning her back to her own people. Had to be reconsidered, as Charlyyk has a strong love for those she has lived with and wants to remain here with them. We understand the bond that ties her to them and respect her wishes. We hope you too respect her choice to stay with you, on your planet. Thank you for listening.'

The nod he gave, was to Charlyyk. Helen also noted a particular change of eye colour and ear twitching between them. Then another nod then the transmission was terminated.

The Collier family waited for any comments the activity around the meeting hall, was not of uproar, more like the sound of bees in a beehive.

France was first to ask a question. 'How long have they been monitoring us?' Charlyyk stood. 'Give and take a decade or two, about two hundred years.'

The mumbling became a little louder. Canada was next to speak. 'That fits in with the sightings recorded in our records, the first recordings were of a story from an Indian Tribe depicted on a dear skin dating back to 1840.'

Much discussions were being made all around the hall, though no more questions were asked of the Collier Family.

After many minutes, had passed, a UN aide asked if they would like to leave. 'This could go on for some time.' The Collier's, quietly got up and left.

Drinks were arranged for them. Helen asked Charlyyk about the eye contact, she made with Drenghaagh, 'We are expected to make contact with him when things are quiet.'

Bryn looked at her, 'You saw that in his eyes Charlyyk?'

'In a lot of countries hand gestures go with the language, it is the same with us. Eye and ear signals can mean so much more than words...like actors in a play, facial expressions can say so much more.'

As they waited, an elderly lady approached them. 'I'm an aide to the Secretary-General.' Looking at Charlyyk. 'Will the aliens be making contact with you again?'

Charlyyk did not flinch. 'Yes, of course.'

The lady turned and re-entered the Hall.

Waiting time always seems longer than it really is. Bryn hated this part...the hanging about...waiting for something to happen. Charlyyk reached over and took his hand. He smiled at her, but she could feel the twitching in his hands.

The lady re-immerged and headed towards them. 'Could you come this way?' Instead of going to the main hall she headed towards some other doors and along a corridor to an elevator. Three floors up, then showed them to an office. 'Please make yourselves comfortable.'

The Secretary-General came in after ten minutes and soon introduced himself, 'I am pleased how this has turned out. At first, I was most concerned that an alien invasion was about to happen, now I have never known a more peaceful conclusion to a United Nations assembly like this one.' He made himself comfortable in his chair. 'I, like so many of us, have followed your story with great interest. But it did have a very serious side to it. Major Arn Sigurdsson has assured me, that I should keep faith in you for the way you have conducted yourselves, in making sure you have told us everything you can tell us about what has happened.'

He smiled at Charlyyk, 'Looking at you today, in your school uniform. Makes us realise that you are a young girl, definitely not a threat. Who's ever suggested that idea I must thank, for it was the best way to stabilise calm amongst the delegation here today.' He then gave Bryn a sheet of paper, 'These are my personal telephone numbers, that you can reach me on, at any time, if you think necessary to do so.' The meeting then went on to more a personal note, asking Charlyyk on her views of living on this planet. The Sectary General slipping into a more direct question now and again just to make sure he knew all there was to know.

Later at the Hotel, the family were getting ready to have dinner with the UK delegation. Helen dressed in a black dress. Charlyyk in the green dress that Margret brought her, Bryn in a light blue serge suit. The large round dining table was set out majestically. Charlyyk stood by the side, just staring at it. The centre decoration of flowers, that looked good enough to eat, never mind their decorative effect. A waiter seated them at the table. If the PM was twelve o/clock, Helen was Three, Charlyyk was Six, Bryn was Nine. The delegation was interspersed between. No politics were discussed, but many more personal questions for the family to answer.

***

Sunday, the drive back to the cottage, Helen found herself cuddling a very tired Charlyyk. The whole weekend had really caught up with her, Helen was more concerned about school the next day. Bryn having to carry her into the cottage, then straight up to bed.

Earlier Charlyyk had mentioned about the funny sensation her fingers and toes were feeling. Helen undressing her, checked her toes the redness around the claws were signs of the changes That Drenghaagh had promised.

***

Monday morning, Charlyyk awoke to feel the strange effect, of losing her claws. The tingling in her fingertips, and the first signs of fingernails, she headed for Bryn's bedroom. At first, she had to hold onto the furniture for balance, to reach her bedroom door, gradually she managed to adjust.

Helen seeing her was quickly out of bed, to assisted her. Charlyyk sat on the bed, showing Helen what was happening to her. 'Does it hurt?' Helen could see the tips of fingernail just appearing.

Charlyyk smiled, 'No it just feels strange.'

Bryn lent over to look, 'They look tender, sweetheart?' Bryn gave her a gentle cuddle, 'Come, let's get into bed, and have a late morning.'

Charlyyk loved this side, of human life. Before she met Bryn, she cuddled for warmth, and protection, but this was different. The more Charlyyk did it, the more she liked it. As she watched Helen smooth her hands over Bryn. Charlyyk could see how he enjoyed it, then when he applied the same to her, how Helen enjoyed it. She understood the meaning of, endearment, love, and affection. That was what humanity was all about...the desire for the love of one and another.

Breakfast, found them laughing, as Charlyyk tried to hold a spoon. Helen phoned Michel, but he was out. Clare said she would come instead. Twenty minutes later Clare was holding Charlyyk's hand checking her fingertips, 'And they are not painful?'

Charlyyk showing the interest in how Clare was treating her. 'No, not at all.'

Clare then looked at her toes, 'Same again no pain?'

Charlyyk shook her head, 'No.'

Clare reached into her bag, a tube of antiseptic cream was the answer, 'This will just soothe the area.' Then she asked Helen if she had some cotton pop socks for her. Helen fetched them. 'The toes need more protection as they would be inside her shoes, the pop sock will help.'

As Clare tidied up, Charlyyk walked up and down, 'Yes, that feels better already, thank you, Clare.'

Clare asked Helen for the gadget, and when Helen fetched it and gave it to her. Clare rolled up Charlyyk's sleeve and checked, blue to green, 'Great that shows it's all working well.'

Helen gave Charlyyk a pencil, with a piece of paper, 'Write your name sweetheart.' Charlyyk found it, tricky at first, but soon had adapt to the changes.

Bryn came in, 'I've informed the bus driver we would take her to school later.'

Clare finished her cup of tea, 'I'm going that way, can I drop her off?' The drive to school. Clare talked about many things, mainly of herself. Charlyyk found this a nice change. From people always asking her questions.

Lunchtime the posse and Mrs Butler, found Charlyyk's weekend adventure fascinating but losing her claws, that was different, as there were lots of OH's and AH's. from them all.

Mrs Butler was quick to inform Mrs Landon, the success of the school uniform. The photo in the New York newspaper that Charlyyk had brought back, even mentioned the school. Twitter also covered the story. Mrs Landon smiled as she read the paper over and over again. 'Now let's see what the governors say to this.'

Harold and Gwen had been waiting for the school bus to arrive, 'Hello darling,'

Charlyyk accepting Gwen kiss. 'Auntie Gwen, look my claws have gone.' Showing her fingers.

Harold, giving her a squeeze. 'How are your toes?'

She gave them a turn, on the balls of her feet. 'Perfect...it's so much nicer already.'

Janet and James arrived after dinner. Janet looking more herself, grabbing Charlyyk in a bear hug, and smothering her with kisses, then showing her the ring that James had given her. 'Charlyyk, I love you.' she could not hide her feelings she was ecstatic with joy. 'I cannot begin to tell you what this means to me, and it's all down to you.'

James stood close by. With the look of a big loving brother gathered her up in his arms, giving her a long brotherly kiss. 'Twinkle, we both, love you and just wait till my Mum gets hold of you. Make sure you take a deep breath. You sure will need to, with the kiss she is going to give you.' The big cuddle all three gave together left Charlyyk speechless but proud.

Helen gave Janet the report she had written about the weekend, with photos, plus a video clip. Janet checked it through with Gwen, 'I can get much from this Helen, the photos and video clip tells me everything I need to know. I've checked the tweets on twitter. Some of the delegates have put their views online. There is, so much I can cross reference.'

The biggest reports were those that remarked on the close relationship the biggest power were applying to this UN meeting.

Bryn and Harold watching on. 'Remembering when Janet first arrived, now look at her she's family.' Harold looked up at the picture on the wall of Kitty. 'Do you know Bryn if that picture could talk it would say Kit would approve of what is happening here.' The two men looked at each other, Harold gave Bryn a hug, 'Don't wait too long. Marry Helen the sooner, the better.'

Later in Charlyyk's bedroom. Helen kneeling down in front of Charlyyk applying cream to her toes. Bryn sitting beside her could see how much in a day the toenails had grown. 'This morning, we could just see them, now they have grown, an eighth of an inch!'

Helen could see the holes, where the claws, had dropped out, were closing and the toenails were gradually covering. The pulpous ends of her fingers where claws had been, were also changing shape. Helen looking up at her, from the kneeling position that she was in. 'We should soon be able to apply nail furnish to them.'

The smile on Charlyyk face, was the girly feeling she was now experiencing.

Chapter 39

Setting the Date

Tuesday morning. Charlyyk was ready for her morning run. The three runners were in a line, the talk was about how the changes that could give Charlyyk a much better way of life. Not that she ever complained. Overnight the nails had grown another eighth of an inch. Charlyyk feeling with the excitement of being able to do her nails like all the other girls. She had always listened to Gwen, Catherine, Rachel and Helen discussing their nails. Their shape, how long they should be, what colour? Now she can join in with them. This was becoming the big thing in her life, and didn't it make her feel like a lady.

Lunchtime at the Academy the posse gathered around Charlyyk admiring the changes. The girls, also inspecting their own nails and making comparisons of each other's fingernails. As they started to attend their next lesson, Julia slipped her arm into Charlyyk's. 'How do you feel?'

Charlyyk tossed her head back, and with a satisfactory chuckle. 'Human.'

At Parsons Farm, Bryn and Helen, were sitting in the large conservatory with the Parsons and Janet, 'Have you set a date, Janet?' Bryn was showing genuine concern and was keen to know.

Jane reached across and placed her hand on his knee. 'Interested in a double wedding, Bryn?'

Helen took a sharp look at him. Her expression read. 'Well, are you?'

Bryn smiling back at her, 'We have yet to set a date?' with Jane and Helen sitting side by side both looking at him for some clarity from him.

'I would rather have it sooner than later?' Bryn said it with a determined look on his face.

The two women, looked at each other. 'So, do we'

Janet, looking at James for confirmation. 'We want to wait for a year, so we can plan our future together properly.'

Edward held Jane's hand. 'We agree with them. Planning a future, you need a little time to get it right.' Then with a stern look at Bryn. 'But you two, come on. Get your arses in gear and make it happen.'

Helen gave Bryn a hug. With a girlish smile, 'I'm ready when you are.'

Bryn and Helen arrived back in time for the school bus to arrive at the cottage. They were waiting for her as she stepped down from the bus. She started to walk towards them. Charlyyk could tell that there was a new air about them. Her nose was picking up different types of vibes, but they were good vibes. With a smirk of smiles on their faces. Helen's buoyant swing of her body. The sweat-with-sweat smell was not fresh, so it was not that. She looked into their faces, a searching look. 'You've made your minds up, you have a date?'

Bryn stared at her. 'How can you tell that... not your nose again?'

Charlyyk high fives Helen. Then holding hands. They did a ring a ring of roses. Bryn could not be happier. He had spoken with Catherine earlier. She had blown lots and lots of kisses at him from the Skype connection.

Preparing the dinner, Helen tells Charlyyk what they must do to be able to marry, 'We must get a Licence, call the banns, send out the invites, a wedding dress, flowers.' Helen spun around and around she was in heaven. Charlyyk watched on with a big silly grin on her face. Helen stopped turning, then taking Charlyyk in her arms and lovingly looking into her eyes.

Charlyyk, softly said, 'My mum.'

Helen with tears of joy, 'My daughter.'

Bryn watched this affectionate bonding these two girls were building with each other. Aware he had started the ball rolling. It is now entirely out of his control. The wedding witches will gather in their covens hatching their spells...plotting their magic, to make it an extraordinary day. He will be placed in a trance to agree to everything, they boil up in their cauldron. Yes, he has witnessed this. His own wedding to Kitty, then Catherine's and Rachel's. Though the women call themselves fairy godmothers, the result still remains the same.

***

On Wednesday. The fingernails were halfway out. Charlyyk kept looking at them, 'They won't grow any faster sweetheart' Bryn placing his arm around her shoulders.

'I know dad, but don't they look good, and to think, they will be fully grown in time for the wedding.'

Helen moving closer to her, 'The timing is perfect sweetheart.' Helen putting her hand around behind Charlyyk's head and gently pulling her face towards her and kissing her on the cheek. 'We will have time to shape them and make them ladylike.' Then rubbing of noses together. Two girls, with the same mission in mind.

The posse had already brought in samples of colours. This was to check if they could find the right colour match for her. Sarah had each finger a different tone, to show Charlyyk how it works. Liza her mother had done them especially for her the night before. But when Charlyyk let it slip that they would be fully grown for the wedding. It all took off: Bridesmaids dress, how to do her hair, who's going, Charlyyk threw her hands in the air, and screamed, 'YES, BRING IT ON!'

Helen, Gwen and Charlyyk, were talking with Catherine. Bryn and Harold just looked on, 'Now the plotting begins,' Bryn remarked with a heavy sigh.

Harold pulls out his wallet and takes out a ten-pound note. 'A pound, for every major change from now to the wedding.'

Bryn laughed, 'You don't think that will cover it, do you?'

***

Early Thursday morning, the first thing that Charlyyk did when she opened her eyes were to look at her fingernails. They were three quarters the way up. She lay back in bed waving her hands in front of her. The claws were history. Her hands still long, but that did not matter, not at this moment in time. Hearing Bryn moving about, she made a move to get up. She felt like dancing and skipped across the bedroom.

With her tracksuit on. She tied the laces on her tennis shoes, then met them in the garden. Did she notice the cold? Not at all. She was off? With Helen and Bryn in her wake. The skip in her stride showing this was one happy girl. Her little tail wagging. Helen and Bryn could only but smile, at how her tracky bottoms were behaving.

At breakfast the jungle drums were beating in the form of the telephone ringing. Helen's ecstatic talking made Charlyyk and Bryn head for cover. When the school bus arrived, Charlyyk had kissed Helen goodbye. Helen had not even noticed her. So much was going on inside her head.

Bryn kept in his study out of the way. The wedding witches were cackling their spells, and he did not want to be caught up in them. It soon became apparent that he had to play his part, when his mobile pinged, with a text message. *'Wedding car? Bill Symonds?'*

Bryn text back, *'When'.*

The reply was instant, *'Now, I'm outside.'*

Bryn settled next to Harold in the passenger seat. Harold took off, 'Just had to get away Bryn...Gwen has every issue of Vogue, with anything about brides, and weddings. Jane, Janet even Elizabeth, Helen's mother, the phone has not stopped... Gwen has even pulled poor Liza Martin into it.' Harold looked stressed, 'We went to bed, with the magazine, and woke, with magazines.'

Bryn nodded, 'You pushed me, to name a date, you must have realised what was going to happen?'

Harold's distressed look was in recognition of what he had started, but there was no way of ending it. They were going to have to see it out to the very end.

Bill Symonds seeing them drive in; stood there with his hands-on-hips, smiling as they walked up to him, 'What have you done Bryn?' Bryn just looked at him, 'Tina has not stopped talking about the new outfit she will need, hairdo, the works.' Bill turned, started to walk to his office, 'Come, we will need a stiff drink' then all three of them walked towards the office. Bill called out 'Ted you had better come too.'

Louise Landon and Alice Vasey headed towards the posse, 'Hello girls, can we sit with you?'

Louise sat next to Charlyyk, 'We know how excited you must be Charlyyk. Your auntie Gwen has informed me of the upcoming wedding.'

Alice looked as excited as Charlyyk, 'How do you feel, your first time being a bridesmaid?'

Charlyyk stopped and thought for a moment. 'When I was asked that same question, I was in Houston... I could not understand the meaning of it...It sounded illogical...all that fuss. Just to wear a dress. I was just glad to be getting a mum. But now, the whole buzz of it makes it magical. You know that Walt Disney type of magic, that tingle inside it gives you.' She closed her eyes, her facial expression, as if she was in a dream, her shoulders scrunched up, as she gave out a sigh.

Alice looking at Charlyyk could only sigh with her. Alice like the posse knew how Charlyyk was changing, they might be small changes, but becoming a significant change. The smiles that they all had on their faces as they all watched Charlyyk going through her febrile imaginative excitement.

Stella had noticed how Charlyyk's ears pointed forward when she was happy. And that was what they were doing now. She was waiting to see which way they would return, in their upright position, or straight backwards. Stella was beginning to understand how Charlyyk's eyes and ears, changed with her moods. The talk that Charlyyk gave her made her realise that she would have to start talking to the other members of the group. But what could she say to them? So she made her mind up to study them. She must talk about the things that they are concerned with, just not anything that would bore them.

Bill Symonds, listened to Harold's idea of a wedding car, looking at Ted, 'Alan Lyndd... he has the best selection of vintage cars, Roller's, Bentley's, Lagonda's, not forgetting the Mercedes Nazis Staff car. Leave it to me... I will talk with him.'

Charlyyk went straight to her bedroom after dinner, just to get some peace from the constant phone calls. A half-hour later, Bryn had joined her. He too needed to get away from the constant wedding banter. Charlyyk smiled at him, holding her hand out to him to welcome him to her little sanctuary. The smile on Charlyyk's face, that of an innocent child. He snuggled up to her.

**

The morning run was no different, 'Come on, it not that bad' Helen was trying hard to justify herself, 'They need to know the details about the wedding. Getting the right dress, matching hats...this is so important, and must not be taken lightly. The timing is so crucial!'

Bryn looked at Charlyyk, who was sniggering, 'So what's so funny?'

Charlyyk gave a light-hearted laugh. 'It's the same at school. The girls, even some of the teachers, they all want to talk about it.' Charlyyk had to take evasive action, to avoid a puddle, then got back in line, 'The girls are bringing in magazines to show me all of the latest fashions. It great, I love it.'

Bryn gave her a nudge, 'Turncoat, traitor.'

Helen pushed Bryn. 'Leave her alone, bully.'

At breakfast, the first phone call was not for Helen; Bill Symonds for Bryn. 'Alan Lyndd, said yes, if all of you would see him Sunday afternoon. Fret House' Bill gave Bryn the full details, with the phone number, to make contact.

Bryn wrote it down. 'Thanks, Bill I will make contact with him.'

Helen smiled at him, 'Wedding business?' Bryn explained about the wedding car. Helen perked up on hearing it could be a vintage model. The image of herself sitting on the backseat was pleasing. 'That sounds good. I would like that.

At the Academy, the posse gathered around Charlyyk, with more wedding items, to browse through. Julia showed her a copy of her mum's wedding list; something borrowed, something blue, something lucky, something new.

Charlyyk's quizzical look at the list, Julia explained what it meant. 'My mum's wedding dress was her sisters...something borrowed. The garter she wore was blue. She carried a horseshoe for good luck in her bouquet, her shoes were new. She matched all the criteria on the list.'

Sandra was quick to point out to her, 'It is supposed to be unlucky if you don't meet the right criteria?'

Mike chuckled, 'That's probably why my mum and dad keep arguing. They got married in a registry office, on the spur of the moment.' He moved his chair to make himself more comfortable, 'Mum put on a shift dress, put some flowers in her hair, carried the book of her favourite poems, and said I will. That was that.' Julia gave him a cuddle. Sarah took a sharp look at Charlyyk and winked.

The phone call to Alan Lyndd, that Bryn made that afternoon gave Bryn the understanding that Alan Lyndd was keen to meet the family. 'Come for dinner, then I can show my collection of motors, take a spin in some of them?'

Bryn agreed and set a time. 'See you and your wife at twelve, Sunday.' Then quickly phoned Harold, to inform him of the plans he had made.

After dinner, as they settled in the lounge, the doorbell rang. They were not expecting whoever this was. It was Father Stevens that was standing there. 'Ah, Mr Collier, with all the talk in the village, I have taken this opportunity to offer my services to you and your future wife to be.'

Bryn opened the door to allow him access. 'Please enter Father.'

Helen stood up when he entered. Charlyyk also stood up but position herself behind Helen. She still was not sure about him, so when they sat, she made sure it was the furthest she could be from him.

Father Stevens, was first to speak, 'Your sister Gwen, mentioned that you were thinking of getting married Bryn. I wondered what your plans were. I would love to offer you both, my service at our little church.' He then sat back on the sofa, looking towards Charlyyk. 'But with all the media attention that has been given to you all, the Dean has asked, would you like to be married in a bigger Church, with myself conducting the service?'

Helen smiled as she spoke. 'Thank you, father. We are still trying to work out the invitation list, to see what will be required...Our family and friends are quite extensive. You are right to point out the media attention. Everyone will be stretching their necks to see what Charlyyk will wear on the day... The village Church would be overwhelmed...Had the Dean any suggestion?'

Father Stevens, raised his hands as if to welcome them too him. 'There are four possibilities, but I would count them out, too far away, except for one. The Dean admired the way Charlyyk handled herself at midnight mass and thought that would be more suitable, for your big day. He would assist in the ceremony.'

Bryn gulped. 'I'm honoured at the suggestion, but it is a bit OTT... don't you think?'

Father Stevens smiled. 'The Dean believes that when it starts to take on momentum, it will probably be just right for the occasion...Trust him, he has a lot of experience in these matters.'

Helen's wide eyes and enormous smile, could not hide her feelings. She liked the idea a lot. Father Stevens, could see the pleasure it gave her, Charlyyk kept very quiet. 'Don't worry Charlyyk, you will not be gobbled up by our God. He is spiritual, not physical. He will give comfort in the mind. He won't give you a kick from behind. Then I will be there to protect you...that's a promise.'

Charlyyk saw the meaning in how he had said those words. She smiled back at him. He was not bad after all.

Father Stevens started to leave. 'Charlyyk come and see me, with your aunty Gwen one Saturday morning...I will explain our thinking about religion... but I promise not to attempt to convert you, only to explain, how it works...I saw how frightened you were, that first time you came to our church. That not how we would want you to see it. So, come, and I will explain it to you.'

***

On Saturday, the fresh buzz that had settled amongst them, Helen had this warmth inside of her, the thought of being married in a Cathedral, gave her that warm glow, it radiated from her.

Charlyyk felt more confident at being a bridesmaid now that Father Stevens had assured her their god would not come down on her.

Bryn was not comfortable. The wedding was getting too big; it was getting out a hand. But there was no going back, so he must face it head on. First, he must talk with Catherine, for she was the conscience, that sat on his shoulder, He would hear her say, 'Hu, Hu, listen to me Dad' That's what you must do.

When Harold and Gwen arrived, Charlyyk quickly spoke with Gwen telling her of Father Stevens and his request. Gwen agreed, she would go with her, promised that it was only to explain the workings of her God. That would be that.

Helen's excited news of them getting married in the Cathedral set Gwen of in raptures. The jungle drums were soon being beaten. Harold could only put his arm around his Brother-in-Law shoulders and remove him from the disaster zone.

A dark cloud had descended over Bryn. He looked a forlorn man. He hated to be the centre of attraction, He remembered Kitty how she paraded him around as if saying, 'Look he is mine'.

The sound of Margret's voice, soon had the girls rushing to convey the news to the new arrivals. Rachel soon had Charlyyk attention. Charlyyk's fingernails, were now longer, and Rachel was keen to get some shape to them. 'WOW! Look at them! Come let's see what we can do with them'

All the women were sorting through their handbags, for their makeup bags. Rachel did no shaping, just applying polish for a bit of colour.

Thomas only needed to look at the state his dad to realise he was suffering big time. 'Dad, let's go to the study.' Sitting in the study. Thomas consoled with his father, 'You must have known what you were starting, and that Auntie Gwen, Jane and Tina Symonds would encourage Helen, let alone Rachel and Catherine, so you had better let them have their day. Thomas wrapped his arm around his dad's shoulders, 'So what are you, going to wear dad? Your Dress Uniform, now that would look good.'

They carried on discussing what had been going on while they had been away. 'That's incredible Dad.' Bryn played the video recording, Thomas stopped it and replayed where Drenghaagh sat in the kitchen, 'You can see where Charlyyk gets her looks from.' Thomas using his artistic skills to see, the sheer magnificence of the alien...how graceful he was in his full height and the way he moved. His golden hair flowing with the movement of his head. The silken cloths swirled around him. 'But it was the colours in his eyes, and the way his ears moved. That made the biggest impression. Thomas remembered something Rachel had said about Charlyyk. 'There is so much to her, you don't see in us humans. Her eyes talk to you. Her hands move like a conductor's baton, orchestrating a musical concerto.' *Those were the early years, when everyone gave her so much attention, not knowing what to expect from her, and each movement she made, they analysed her minutely. That was when Gwen was so suspicious of Charlyyk in those early years, if it was not for Harold, Charlyyk's life would have been a lot harder.'* Thomas was taking his father's mind of the wedding and make him think of Charlyyk's early years.

Thomas was studying the video again, 'Do they all look the same dad?'

Bryn thought for the moment. 'No, there were many differences in how they looked. Drenghaagh who you can see in the video, had that look of a leader. Strenghaagh had a more passive look to him. His hair was lighter, and he was thinner in the face. There were two others *haaghs*, one looked older than the others, then there was the *Lyyk's*. There was one there, that was at least three inches taller, then all the others. Then there was Klyklyyk...she was the one that visited Michel and Clare. Her skin colour was greener than the pink of Charlyyk's.'

Charlyyk entered, carrying two mugs of coffee. She looked at the video recording playing Drenghaagh visit. 'He is like our dad Thomas...he was concerned that I was OK.'

Thomas moved his chair around and allowed Charlyyk to sit on his knee. 'What was your concerns, when you found yourself on the spacecraft?'

Her eyes changed colour, and her ears twitched. 'I was so frightened that they had changed their minds, and we're going to take me away. But when Drenghaagh showed me that Mum and Dad were with me I settled down. My fears evaporated. 'She cuddled Thomas, 'I love my life here, with you all. You are my family... my love... my life. They sensed it and are helping me to keep my dream alive. I now know, what I have endured was for a reason. I am not happy with the loss of those I had lived with before I met Dad. But I'm in a happier place then I was before.'

Thomas could not help but cuddle her, 'We would have been devastated if we lost you Charlyyk. You have made us a much better and closer family. We had been drifting apart since my mother passed away, and dad was stagnating. Now look at him, we could not be happier. Helen is the icing on top of the cake, now Catherine and I can build our dreams knowing you and Helen will keep dad happy.'

Bryn looked at his family. He felt so proud, seeing the love they were both sharing. The wedding seemed so right. He was telling himself to allow what must be, to be.

Charlyyk showed Thomas her new fingernails. 'Look Thomas, they are going to make my hands look so elegant.'

Thomas kissed her on the cheek, 'You are going to be the prettiest bridesmaid ever.'

Gwen had come into the study and positioned herself behind her brother. With her arms wrapped around him, she listened to Thomas praise Charlyyk. The contented look on Charlyyk's face gave Gwen much satisfaction. She kissed her brother's cheek. 'Margret has booked a table, at the 'Restaurant Milan' for later, would you all like a sandwich for now?' They all agreed. Then Charlyyk slipped of Thomas's lap and followed Gwen, to help with the lunch.

'Dad, so what was the meaning of your abduction?' Thomas queried.

Bryn paused for a moment before answering, 'Drenghaagh said that they needed to test, the genetic changes that they require to live on the new planet they had chosen. They needed to send someone to live here for a period, to test the changes they had made. They needed to find a way to have somebody to look after her. So, this very elaborate charade was thought up. Their new planet is like our Earth, with the same bacteria, that is where their problems were, so the plate in Charlyyk's head, were installed to allow the experimental genetic changes. Drenghaagh came to take Charlyyk back home, but when he saw the reaction of Charlyyk to myself, he had a change of mind, realised that taking her away, would cause her grief, he just got up and left.'

Thomas was taking great interest in what his father was telling him, 'So the second meeting, was to adapt Charlyyk to suit us?'

Bryn nodded, then showing Thomas the ring on his finger, 'These rings are to give us better stability when we are taken by the light source and returned, but what else we don't know? Charlyyk's ring has many functions. We do not know if ours have the same ability has hers, but the gadget that they gave us to check Charlyyk's health, works on these as well?'

Rachel came in to tell them that lunch was being served in the kitchen, Thomas taking her hand followed her, with Bryn close behind.

Around the table the discussion carried on, Thomas had got bitten by the story, and it had left its mark on him, He started to relate the story to Rachel and Margret. Rachel's eyes were wide with the explanations began to ask her own questions. 'Charlyyk was you not afraid of what they were going to do to you.'

'No Drenghaagh had explained that it would only cause a little discomfort, mainly a tingling sensation...Klyklyyk said I would be a little disorientated, would be there to help me afterwards to find my feet... which at first I could not feel, but when they put the armband on my arm... I was fine.'

Harold then asked, was it the same Craft, the one that you were taken, to the planet you met Bryn on?'

Charlyyk was quick to respond, 'Oh no, that was a completely different craft altogether. That belonged to the other aliens the Gaintt's. The flap to their nostrils was to protect them from the fine dust that exists on the Gaintt's planet, they are the same as us in every other form, except the facial changes, again to protect it from its environment.'

Helen, realising this was not known before, 'How did you know that sweetheart?'

Charlyyk's calm way of answering Helen. 'Oh, the headpiece, it had opened up memory cells in my head, and have started to recall some of my time before they placed me on that planet. But only little bits, it needs something to nudge it, and it starts to fit the pieces together. Like the other craft was of the Gaintt's.'

Bryn had been quiet; he was starting to get nagging thoughts in his head. 'How could I breathe the air on that planet?'

Charlyyk looked at her dad. Closing her eyes, her ears started to twitch. Standing up, then headed for the Clinic. She returned with the gadget. Went to Bryn and held the device between his eyes. The device blinked blue to green. She said nothing then went to her room and returned with the headpiece. Placing it on his head, she then spoke to him in her native tongue, he replied back to her, in her own language. 'I think a visit to Michel's Surgery could be in order?'

Helen looked at Bryn, her eyes wide, not quite taken the full meaning of what Charlyyk had said. 'You implying that your dad could be fitted with a plate as well?'

Charlyyk took a sip of water. 'Well, that could explain how he survived that ordeal.' Helen became concerned. 'How about me?'

Charlyyk removed the headpiece from Bryn and placed it on Helen. Then spoke in her native tongue, but nothing happened. Charlyyk removed the headpiece. 'The jigsaw pieces are gradually falling into place, each little nudge then another piece joins the puzzle giving a clearer view of the overall picture.'

Bryn had carried on being quiet, the headpiece had shown him the shadow that he thought he had seen, now there it was in his mind. Major Alan Carter was right. The Gaintt was riding a large beast, similar in shape to a T-Rex, but hooved feet. Its tail shorter but thicker, to balance it up, the neck thick, the head pulpous, its arms long with claw talons to them that could inflict severe damage to any animal. But how did it get there? Of course, the beam of light, but why? It did not make sense to him, so he said nothing.

The Restaurant Milan was so busy, the noise in the Restaurant made everyone shout. Each one trying hard to be heard, but this was the beauty of Italian food, also Italian's. Charlyyk just soaked it up loving the vibrant atmosphere and the food.

Sitting between Helen and Rachel, with Gwen opposite her next to Margret, it was girl talk all night, and she loved it. Rachel noticed how Charlyyk waved her hands about as if to say, just look at how beautiful they are. Charlyyk was becoming the woman, not a girl.

***

Very early Sunday, Charlyyk had tossed and turned all night the nag in her head was the welfare of her dad. What had they done to him? At four-thirty she got up and took her computer to the clinic, the disc was there. Setting it up she placed the disc on the computer. Then put her ring on the disc, it was not Drenghaagh but Klyklyyk that was there. They talked for some time. It was when Bryn sat down with her, did she realise how long it had been. He placed his hand on her shoulder, but said nothing, what surprised him he could understand everything that they were speaking to each other.

Klyklyyk soon dispelled Charlyyk's concerns. 'We needed to place the plate in his head to make sure he survived. We had made so many mistakes before, so this was the best way forward. No harm will come to him; in some way, will be good for you both, the gene changes were just so he could breathe and survive the time span. We had given him nutrients to sustain him for how long it was going to last for.' Klyklyyk's nod was to inform Charlyyk of a change of conversation. 'Helen's ring will only allow her the stability if we need to bring her on board with the light beam.'

Klyklyyk looked to her left, and an elderly Haagh sat down beside her. 'Charlyyk, I am Helmhaagh, it is nice to be able to talk to you and your new father. Please if you need to talk, contact us at any time, we will be here for you. We are on the base station on the Earths planet's satellite, the one they call the moon so don't be afraid, we have set up here, so we will be at your service at any time. We sense that there is something big that is coming up in your lives, we are very interested in what it could be?'

Charlyyk explained the importance of the occasion, how it will secure her wellbeing. Helmhaagh listened intently to what she had to say. 'It is quite similar to our joining together, although we have not a religion, a ceremony is taken place, with the custom of given each other a symbol of intent.'

Helen was now awake and concerned when she could not find them. She knew that they had not gone on a run, because their running kit was still there. A big sigh of relief when she did eventually find them.

Bryn explained how he had found Charlyyk, and the concerns she had about their wellbeing, and that being the reason Charlyyk wanted to know more about the plate they had placed in his head.

'So, are you okay with that Bryn.'

'Yes, it explains how I manage to survive for that length of time without food and water.'

After breakfast, Bryn put the address in the Satnav, and they were ready to go to Fret House. The drive through country lanes impressed Charlyyk. The beauty of the English countryside was in its full glory; small fields, with hedgerows of hawthorn and hazel. Charlyyk's head was moving around, taking everything in. They passed a stud farm, with Arabian horses that wandered about grazing in the fields. Large old oak trees, sprinkled about with a hint of buds just starting to appear on their branches. The large Georgian House could be seen ahead of them with its long drive, a metal fence with copper beech tree's bordering the driveway.

The drive up to the entrance had that stately house feel to it. A young girl stood by the large entrance doors, with the ornamental fanlight above them. The canopy protruded out three metres, with two tapered porch columns holding it up.

As Charlyyk stepped down from the car, the young girl came forward. 'Hi, I'm Annabelle, Mummy and Daddy said, come straight in.'

The 10-year-old daughter of the Lyndd's was very slim, with straight mousey-coloured hair. The braces on her teeth gave too an awkward smile. Charlyyk had warmed to her immediately as Annabelle did not concern herself about her awkwardness, and was not shy. She had composure; she walked with an air of self-assurance. Charlyyk quickly stepped up towards her and was soon talking with her. 'What a lovely house, Annabelle, the view of the countryside is fantastic.'

'Yes, it has been in our family since the Battle of Trafalgar.'

Helen and Bryn, admired the way Charlyyk had attached herself to Annabelle, as they walked behind them, and as usual in these occasions, were led straight to the kitchen.

Joyce and Alan Lyndd were busy preparing the dinner. Joyce had a full hourglass figure. She stood five feet eight inches tall, honey blonde, straight out of a bottle. It was tied back loosely, just how Catherine wore her hair. She, wore dark blue jeans, with a light blue long-sleeved shirt blouse, a black-and-white chef's apron, to protect her while cooking. Alan robust, with a rugby player's barrel-chested build. He was five-ten, fine sandy coloured hair, thin on top, his round face was warm, with intelligent eyes, his white chino trousers and light blue twill shirt. Here was a couple who did not stand on ceremony.

Alan met them with a firm handshake. 'Welcome to Fret house, my wife Joyce and I have looked forward to this meeting, since Bill Symonds contacted us.'

Joyce came forward, Bryn introduced Helen. The two women were soon in deep conversation and had turned to what was cooking. Alan collected a bottle of wine and was escorting Bryn to the lounge.

The two girls had already left for Annabelle's bedroom.

Bryn was already relaxed, he liked this type of man, he always felt comfortable with them. Alan Lyndd guiding Bryn towards the lounge and comfortable chairs. 'Bryn, I married into this; Joyce's family have owned this pad since the battle of Trafalgar. Her ancestor Philip Philpot, was an ordinary sailor, on one of the ships in Nelson fleet. The prize money they had received after the battle which was unusual, as the storm at that time many of the ships that were taken as bounty did not survive, with many of the crews not receiving any prize money. But Philips bounty was paid, it was burning a hole in his pocket. Then by chance, he found himself at a gaming table. The stakes were high. The contest was between him and a landed gentleman. On the table were this house and the gentleman's wife. The gentleman lost, Philip Philpot now had a large pot of money, this house, and a mistress to go with it.'

Alan pointed to a large painting hanging over the fireplace. 'And there they are. They produced four children and lived a long happy life together. The lady had accepted that she stayed with Philip Philpot or get thrown out. As women, did not have much to say in those days, she had been given no real choice but take the best option offered.'

Bryn studying the painting could see the Lady had given the circumstances her best effort for the way she was looking at Philip and held on to his arm she was enjoying the decision she had taken. Alan watching Bryn, sensed what he had been thinking. 'Yes, she made the best of her predicament, the story that the family told was that she turned Philip in to a gentleman. He turned the farms around and made them profitable. The win, win situation they both found themselves in was off the need to survive and to embrace whatever they could achieve from it.'

Bryn was thinking about his own situation, was it not the same in a funny sort of way. Each helping the other to survive.

Dinner was roast leg of lamb with rosemary and garlic, the girls had rainbow trout. Joyce told the story how she and Alan met. 'Four of the girls and I from Roedean College went grape picking in France, we were there to learn about wine...I met Alan who was there for the same reasons. We had a healthy romantic holiday, picking by day, singing around campfires at night, and love making when we could. Afterwards, we did not see each other for two years, then by chance, we met in Monaco, at a Formula One Grand Prix meeting. We married six months later... We started our own PR company, now life could not be better.'

Bryn told their story.

After dinner, the Lyndd's gave them a guided tour, ending at the garages. Which were initially the stables to the house. The cars were beautifully maintained, the gleam of the bodywork sparkled. Charlyyk loved the smell of them. An old Bugatti, open top in light blue stood there. Alan started it up, the noise was loud, but it was the sound of it, that old fruity roar it gave out, nostalgia written all over it. Joyce got behind the wheel and beckoned Charlyyk to join her.

Alan started up an old 1920 Bentley, open top, in dark green and black running boards, with large wire spoked wheels. Soon with Bryn, Helen and Annabelle sitting in the Bentley, the two cars were heading down the lane.

The afternoon was all about the cars. The 1920 Rolls Royce Phantom II. Black with Red side panels, with black leather, fold down roof like the coach-built prams of yesteryear. The gleam from it was majestic. Helen stood there drooling over it, it was magnificent.

Joyce put her arm in Helen's, 'So that's the one then?'

Helen nodded, 'Can we?'

Joyce smiled the biggest smile. 'Yes, you can.'

Bryn shook Alan's hand. 'Can we settle the cost?'

Alan looked at Bryn. 'This is payback time Bryn. Joyce had three bad miscarriages and Kitty your late wife helped Joyce through them all. We are allowing you the use of this car, to you and Helen as our thanks, and as our wedding gift.'

Joyce told Helen the full story, 'I could not have boys, we just kept trying, and now we have Annabelle, well worth all the pain.' The cuddle she gave her daughter, showed the love she had for her. 'Helen, we have been told by Bill and Tina, how you met Bryn, and how Charlyyk has come to love you. Although it was Kitty that helped me, we feel that she would approve to what was happening to Bryn.'

The drive back to Oakleaves, Helen seemed quiet. Charlyyk had noticed and asked why.

'The more people I meet, the more I find out how Kitty influenced so many families in this area, it really shows us what a wonderful woman she was.' Helen paused for a moment. 'These are mighty big shoes I am stepping into. I just hope I can do them justice?'

Bryn listened intently to what Helen had said. 'When you meet some people, they seem to be so eager to impress, try so hard to give an impression, that they are really better than they look or really are. But it is when you meet those that say this is me, take me or leave me, that how I took the Lyndd's. They did not try to impress, for we are what we are type of people. That's how I saw you, sweetheart. I felt something when I shook hands with you that first time at Gilmore's. Then later, I saw you change, it was not just me, but you realised that there was a new world you had not encountered before. It turned your head, and for a brief moment you went with it, then your old self-took over, and you ran away frightened, that you would make mistakes. But it niggled at you, and then bit by bit your defences crumbled, and the new you started to appear. You were always there. It just needed the realisation that there was a different you... and my was that not the truth.'

Helen stared straight through the windscreen, the truth of it. Bryn was right, she needed something to shake her out of her old self.

The voice of Charlyyk brought her out of her glazed trance she was in.

'No one is perfect, we see things that are set before us, it is normal to go on what you see, as being real. It is when you discover that you have misinterpreted it, is when you have to readjust... it is never easy. How we had been led astray on that planet, now as the truth emerges, we are making adjustments too.'

It was not an outburst, Charlyyk did not do outburst, she always spoke as she saw things.

Bryn nodded to what Charlyyk had said. 'Yes, but we should try and fit in the shoes we are wearing, and not try and wear other people's shoes. I married Kitty and loved every minute I was with her. But I also love every minute I am with you, Helen... Kitty was Kitty... but you are someone else, you might show the same qualities but so different from each other in many other ways.' As they drove into the drive. Bryn brought the car to a standstill.

Charlyyk reached across and touches them on their shoulders. 'Love comes differently to everyone, it depends on how you want to share it, how I see you two... you share it well.'

Helen reached up and covered her hand with hers. 'Thank you, sweetheart, that was nicely said.'

***

It was Monday, the morning light had started to appear through the window when Charlyyk opened her eyes. Her dream had been of nice things, and she felt good about herself. A slight tingling sensation she was feeling in her hands and feet, made her examine them, she could not see anything unbecoming, and dismissed it as a part of the changes she was going to experience.

During the run, she mentioned, it to them of what she was feeling, Bryn listened, but Helen, suggested that informing Michel, would be the better option.

Lunchtime at school saw Charlyyk and the posse, talking about the meeting with the Lyndd's. The drive in the Bugatti was the highlight, not only for Charlyyk but most of the posse. Top Gear, was what most of their parents watched, looking at new cars and how they performed.

Bryn's study had paper all over the work service. Helen and Bryn were trying to get a wedding list of guests sorted, and it just grew and grew. The arrival of Janet and Jane, was a relief to Bryn. He got up to make the tea.

Jane's level-headed attitude was what was needed, and cut the list by 30 per cent. The girls joined Bryn in the kitchen with the list, he nodded his approval. Now, where was the reception to be held, that was the next problem?

Janet laughed. 'The barn! there is parking, it could hold two hundred, no worry about noise, ideal.'

Helen looked at Jane, wrong time of the year with the lambing season, written across Jane's face. 'Gilmores.'

Bryn nodded. 'Yes, that sounds good, I like that. The date?'

Helen went through her diary. '5th April, onwards.' Jane looked at her. 'That's Easter weekend, would it not be better, the 12th April?'

Helen phoned Father Stevens. He said he would phone back with the Deans answer.

As they sat talking, and drinking tea. Janet was catching up on Charlyyk. She had given Bryn a couple of articles she had written, then she gave Bryn, the BBC's request for an in-depth interview. If they agreed the interviewer would be Fiona Bruce, for her easy-going unobtrusive style would suit this assignment.

The phone call was from the Dean himself, confirming the date, for the wedding, and the rehearsals? They could be done in the village church, to save travelling. Helen was in full control, and the phone call to Gilmores was next. Her to-do list was getting shorter, 'Invitations next' looking at Bryn. Helen's worried look had started to evaporate; she could see the finishing line, and she was feeling good. Jane sitting beside her made a list of what was next in preference of order.

Janet watching could see what was going to happen when it was her time to marry James. She made mental notes preparing herself for what was inevitable, when her time comes.

Michel and Clare arrived ten minutes after Charlyyk had come home from school. Charlyyk looked pleased to see them. In the Clinic, Clare took Blood samples from Charlyyk, and a new diet sheet was produced. Then Clare took the gadget and checked her armband, the familiar blue, green light appeared.

'Nothing to worry about Charlyyk.' But Clare still gave her an examination. Michel watched with a satisfactory smile, his protégé was doing good.

Michel explained the diet sheet with Charlyyk, explaining to her the reasoning behind it. 'We have had some concerning results, from the previous test, so this diet I must ask you to adhere to it. No KitKat's the sugar and chocolate contents are a definite no. no.'

Charlyyk's eyes changed colour, and her ears, moved backwards, she was in her sad mood. The nod of understanding, she gave Michel. He looked down his nose at her. 'It is for the best, until we can rule out the long-term dangers, it could do to you.'

Clare looked at Charlyyk, she stood there nodding. 'Michel is right, some people can eat anything and not have any problems. Other could eat a nut, and die. We just don't know enough to say, eat what you want to. So, these tests are important, for your long-term well-being, so bear with us so we can do the best for you.'

Bryn brought Michel up to date by explaining about the plate in his head that the alien had placed there, and the reasons why they had done it to him. Clare listening to him went and collected the gadget meter. She put it on the ring Bryn was wearing, the blue, green light appeared then she took the ring from his finger and placed it on the next digit. She held the gadget meter to the ring. A green, and yellow light appeared. Each finger had a different colour. She returned the ring to the first finger, the blue, green light showed. 'So, it is doing something, but what?'

Helen had come in on what they were trying to do and offered her hand. Clare, copied the same procedure, as she tried on Bryn. This time, each finger resulted in a blue, green light. 'So, as they said, just to give me stability.'

Chapter 40

Which Dress

Helen liked the lighter mornings. The fields looked fresh; the grass looked greener. The buds on the branches had that hint of green to them. The runs were having the right effect on her. Janet and Jane had shown her a picture of a wedding dress, the mental image of it draped over her pleased her. Running with Charlyyk, she described the dress to her. 'It was a combination of silk and lacework, ankle length, with three quarter length sleeves. Lacework covered over the breast, so a hint of skin showed through. The veil, in the same lace.'

Charlyyk looked excited about it. 'So, what will I wear?'

Helen smiled, 'We have yet to decide on that, but you will have your say, the final word is yours.'

Bryn was running with Thomas. 'We should make it back in time for the wedding' Thomas remarked. 'I have spoken with Brent and his mother who will be coming with them. Amy is looking forward to being a bridesmaid. Catherine has been tied up with the TV coverage of the Cricket, but she is up to date, with everything. Jo has kept her well documented, with the data Helen and Rachel keeps sending her. Even Margret has donated some time to her over the wedding details. Dad this is becoming quite an international thing. Australian TV companies have picked up on it, Brent said that he has had a request from the New Zealand broadcast stations to do interviews about the wedding.'

As they arrived at the turn, at the bottom of Bishops Lane, the girls waited for the men to catch up. Charlyyk remarked on the pace the men were taking. 'Come on you two, you are letting the side down here.'

Thomas caught up with them and gave Charlyyk a gentle tap on her bum. 'We were talking, about the wedding.'

Helen looked at Bryn. 'Were you, now?'

Bryn lifted his hand up and placed it on Helen's back. 'You look surprised?'

Helen laughed. 'Now what gives you that impression?'

Thomas broke in, 'I was telling dad, about Catherine coming to the wedding.'

Helen reached over and took Bryn's hand, 'I was just teasing' They carried on running hand in hand. Thomas reached over and took hold of Charlyyk's hand. 'Come on sis, let's do the last stretch together.'

Gwen and Harold arrived at ten, sitting around the kitchen table, some with coffee, others with tea and biscuits, the to-do list, and which order to be accomplished it in, was the main topic. Gwen was adamant that the wedding invitations were a priority. We must send them out as quickly as possible.

Bryn, Harold and Thomas, sneaked away leaving them to it. Bryn showing the boys the pictures he took on Sunday at Fret House. The 1920 Rolls Royce Phantom II, looked good in the photo, but Bryn was keen to point out, it seemed ten times better in the garage.

Margret was concerned what Charlyyk was going to wear. Rachel had picked up many Wedding and Brides Magazines she could lay her hands on. Gwen had an old issue of *Vogue*. A Vivien Westwood outfit was circled. It was in multi-coloured red material, looking though it had been made with offcuts, but still very stylish. Gwen laughed. 'Charlyyk had picked this out, when Bryn first proposed to Helen, saying she would wear this to their wedding.'

Rachel loved it. 'Yeah, I could see her wearing that, her rose gold hair would really bring those colours out.' Margret pulled the magazine toward herself. 'Actually Rachel, I agree with you, those colours, and the style of dress would really suit her. The model wearing it has that skeleton frame like Charlyyk has.' Helen took a closer look. 'Yes, it would suit her to wear in the evening, any other suggestions?' The magazines were fingered through relentlessly.

Thomas asked Bryn. 'Why Fret House. It a strange name?'

Bryn told them what Annabelle had told Charlyyk. 'The first owner was a local farmer. Tobias Fret, the family name had been altered by the Parrish Priest who had misspelt the name, at his christening, the original name being Prett. By law, it had to stay as Fret. It was very common in those days.'

The men wandered back to the kitchen and met up with the women.

Gwen and Harold then said goodbye. They were going to find some examples of invitations at the Stationers in town.

Helen had the to-do list in front of her. She looked more settled. Margret and Rachel were going through the Yellow Pages, for a florist. Gwen's favourite florist had retired, but she advised Gwen, that the best flowers were those in season...they give the best effect on the big day.

Later Gwen called Helen to say that the invitation cards have been organised. And that the stationers had a printer to do their special cards for them.

On Wednesday, the posse's main topic conversation was the upcoming wedding. What was Charlyyk going to wear? Sandra and Julia had put together colour combinations, to match Charlyyk's complexion and hair colour.

Stella sat listening with them. Julia explained, that the wrong colour could ruin the wedding picture. 'One must not upstage the bride, as it is her day, not yours.'

'Oh, I see.' Stella was getting to understand the thinking behind their advice to Charlyyk.

Sandra heard doubt in Stella's tone. she did not want her to misunderstand what they were trying to do for Charlyyk. If Stella was going to be a part of the posse. Sandra wanted to make sure she was not left in a state of confusion. 'Not the photos with everyone in, but the main ones. 'Bride and Groom photo's' but after at the reception she could change into what she likes, but it best to keep to the main rule, is you must not upstage the bride.'

Stella started to see why so much effort was being shown on what colour Charlyyk should wear.

Charlyyk showed them the Vivien Westwood Dress she liked. *Vogue* had four pictures showing different angles.

Jan quipped. 'Now you are just showing off. Do you know, how much it will cost? You could be looking in the hundreds.'

Peter looking over Sandra's shoulders. 'What! it looks like it's made out of bits and pieces. My mum could do you something like that, out of her scrap bag.'

'Peter, you have not a clue.' Sarah pronounced. 'This is art, look how it has been intricately put together. I love it Charlyyk, I agree with Sandra it would be fabulous at the reception, in the evening.'

Mike moved his position and stood behind Julia. 'I like the pattern and the colour. You would look nice in that Julia, it would bring the soft tone of your face out, and make your smile, even lovelier.'

Julia placed her hand on his hand...gently stroked it. Her smile was mellow. She liked his praise, but she still felt sensitive about her birthmark.

Sarah kept an eye on how Julia reacted to Mike. For Julia had not removed her hand. There was another stroke, then a squeeze. Sarah shot a look at Charlyyk, who saw that knowing expression... for Charlyyk had seen it too. Sarah could only marvel, at how Charlyyk could tell by her nose, how people felt about one another.

Sarah looked at Mace. She pondered why there was no chemistry between them. They had grown up and done so many things together. She knows he loves her...yet nothing. Then she searched deep into her own feelings. '*I know I love him.*' Then looking at Peter and Sandra. '*But not like that.*' Charlyyk was right, Brother and Sister love, still love, but not the love Sarah had in mind.

That evening at Oakleaves. Charlyyk brought up the question of the bridesmaid's dress, 'Will I have a say in it? Or have I to wear what you chose for me? It was not said in an indecorous way, more of 'just wanting to know' kind of way.

Helen knew Charlyyk's ways. She did not do nasty; it was just not her: 'I thought we could go to London...you know, a girl's thing. We could do the bridal stores, have dinner somewhere nice, and talk over dinner. In the afternoon... do more stores. What do you reckon?'

Charlyyk's grin nearly split her face in half. She was beginning to like London a lot, and this felt grand. 'Can we go by train again, Mum?'

Helen liked this mum thing, and with a big cuddle.

'Of course, we can.'

***

On Thursday, Bryn and Helen arrived at Carpenters Cottage, at one o'clock. Helen spoke with Gwen about the proposed trip to London. Gwen had already put some thought into the various stores, and where they were situated. Gwen stressed that they should concentrate on two main stores, one in the morning, and the other in the afternoon. 'Give yourself time to try on a few dresses in each store, if it means we must go back another weekend, it would be worth the effort in the end.'

The dress Helen had initially liked would be at the second store and not the first. 'We will do it that way, so you don't make rash decisions, we will have a little time to be sure we get it right,' Helen explained. She told Gwen what Charlyyk had asked her on Wednesday evening, about if she would have a choice.

Gwen phoned the stores and confirmed an appointment for Saturday. Helen booked a table at the restaurant. Everything was gradually falling into place

On Friday at school, Stella sat with Charlyyk at lunchtime. She was starting to talk with the posse, and she found they responded freely. 'Thank you Charlyyk I had always felt so insecure around other people, not knowing what to say to them. That talk, you gave me. At first, I was still at a loss to what to talk about, and still did not say a lot, so what I did. I watched everyone and tried to see what they were interested in, then I realised that you don't look at talking about set things, but what comes up at that time.'

Charlyyk chooses a morsel from her lunch box. 'That what happens. Life throws up different things every day. Sometimes there is nothing to talk about of any significant, so you can just relax. If someone says something, and if you feel you can contribute, then say something. If you want to be liked, people have to know about you. How are they going to be able to do that if you don't let them know who you are?'

Jan added. 'None of us are the same. That is a good thing, not a bad thing. We may have alternative views, by discussing together our ideas, it can open our eyes to the truth. When we debate different subjects in our lessons, we develop a clearer view of what we are trying to learn. That also comes from talking to each other.'

Spotty face Paul spoke. 'That's ok with you, but when Stella and myself, try to say anything we tend to be ignored as though we were not here.'

Sandra chirped up. 'Is that because you were not sure, in what to say, so you did not stand up for yourselves? When you feel strong enough and voice your opinion, like now! You are heard.'

Paul looked at Stella, the look she gave him made him realise it was true... they did not push themselves strongly enough.

Sandra listening to Paul, had a good idea to how he was thinking. 'You don't have to say anything Paul, unless you have something to say. When listening to what being discussed, to how you believe it was meant to represent. Then if you need to reply, give you reply with some commitment, you will find that you will be listened too, and more likely treated with respect because you have made a contribution to the debate. Mace has a quiet personality you don't often hear him say much, but when he does, we listen to him because he contributes to what we are talking about at that time. We know Mace would have thought through what he wanted to say, after he had listened to what he has heard.'

Paul nodded; he could see the truth in Sandra's words. He remembered Mr Pearson remarking during a lesson when Peter tried saying something funny in class. 'If you have no good words about someone Paul, then it is best not to say anything at all, for it is better to look a fool, then to open your mouth and be proved a fool.' Paul had taken that, in his belief, if he said anything. It would be him that would look the fool.

***

Saturday, Charlyyk could not get back sooner from the run, crashing through the rear garden door, rushing to get a hot shower. She was sitting at her dressing table trying to dry her hair, when Rachel came in, 'Come on, let me help.' Rachel soon was brushing through her golden strands glistening with the morning light.

The over-enthusiastic Charlyyk could not keep still, the trip to London was apparently on her mind. Her clothes already set out spread across her bed.

Rachel loved brushing Charlyyk's hair, seeing how it sparkled when the brushing brought out the natural oils in her hair. Rachel understood Charlyyk's eagerness to travel to London, this newly found freedom she was experiencing just made her want more...anyplace, anywhere, anytime. 'Bring it on' was how Charlyyk looked at it.

As soon as Rachel was finished. Charlyyk got dressed, her little tail flicking with erratic swishes. Charlyyk chooses the emerald green dress; that Margret had brought her. It would be easier to remove when trying other dresses on. She added the white ankle socks, and black patent court shoes, Rachel could see how much Charlyyk had started to get her dress sense right, wearing clothes to suit the occasion.

Breakfast was simple and quickly finished. Charlyyk was a girl in a hurry. Slipping her Burberry camel coat on, and with the little clutch bag, she was ready. The voice of Gwen, coming through the front door, and Charlyyk was off like a scalded cat. Sitting waiting for them all, in the Discovery. Rachel came to her. 'I think you might need this' and gave her, the purse she had left behind on her bedroom dressing table.

Charlyyk's smile broke out. 'Silly me.'

Rachel reached in and gave her a hug. 'Have a successful day sweetheart, see you when you get back.'

Helen and Gwen got into the car. Bryn was driving them to the Station. Then he and Harold went to collect his dress uniform. Bryn had left it in storage, at his Regimental Barracks at Grantham.

Charlyyk sat by the window on the train. She loved watching the countryside, as it passed by. Her fellow passengers took great interest in her but did not bother her. But the sound of I-Phones flicking as they took pictures of her, but none were in her face. *Julia and Sandra had remarked to Charlyyk, when they realised the media attention, Charlyyk was receiving 'You are in the News, that makes you a celeb. Everyone now will want a bit of you.'*

As she walked out of the station, people stopped and stared but did not mob her. She was feeling more comfortable going out and about. The taxi ride to Helen's mothers took fifteen minutes. Elisabeth Bennett was waiting by her front door with Anna. Elisabeth slipped in beside Charlyyk looking just as excited as Charlyyk was.

The first store was ready for them, the elegant middle-aged lady called Joan had soon measured Helen now was given Helen ideas on what type of dress she had in mind. The first three dresses after much discussion, did not suit Helen. Joan, the shop assistant showed Helen two more dress, but Charlyyk did not like them. 'Too young, mum!' Gwen and Elizabeth agreed with her, after four more dresses. Gwen decided to note what they liked, then they left the Store.

The restaurant was situated in a quite secluded back street, a young couple had started the business five years before. They specialised in fish. Helen had eaten there before, had liked it seclusion. The building had two floors, and the top floor looked out across a quaint Tudor building, that was otherwise hidden from view due to its location. They could discuss the dresses with no one bothering them. Charlyyk enjoying the company of Elizabeth, catching up on events.

When they were ready, the next store beckoned. This was the store that carried the dress Helen had set her heart on.

The twenty-something young lady with a French accent was soon in attendance. She pulled out eight dresses that fitted the description that Helen had conveyed to her. The dress that she had preferred Gwen put it to one side. After many dresses, Helen put on the dress she had come for, then walked up and down Helen looked breath-taking, the dress material dropped just right, it gave the right type of movement as it flowed when she walked. Elizabeth was so proud, at last, a mother's dream was coming true. Her watery glazed eyes were genuine. Was because of realisation of what was happening, was actually happening,

Elizabeth, had longed resigned herself that this was never going to happen for her. Her career had over taken her life, to that point that she thought time had robbed her of this ambition. Elizabeth knew that it was through Charlyyk's emergence that she had gained this joy, and she was going to cling to it.

She recalled how Edward had said, when he read the text message that Helen had sent him from Interlaken. 'Careful we must not push it, let us hope the relationship grows stronger'.

Gwen cuddled Charlyyk. 'Well, what do you think of your mum now?' Charlyyk looking much the same as Elizabeth.

'Fantastic, the dress makes mum look really beautiful.'

The sales assistant made Charlyyk hold her arms up and ran the tape measure over her. With a nod of her head, she left them when she returned, she placed four dresses on the rail. One after the other Charlyyk tried them on. Gwen was the more assertive dismissing each one. 'No, not right.' Charlyyk agreed with Gwen she did not feel right in them, not at all, another dress was brought in. A Jane Austin style dress, something out of *Pride and Prejudice*. Charlyyk walked up and down she sort of liked it but was not sure. Looking in the long mirror did not help either her hair did not go with the dress. It was not happening for her. She sat on a chair looking despondent.

Elizabeth sat beside her. 'There are other stores we can try Charlyyk, we have only tried two of them?' Helen had finished having the dress she liked checked for alterations, with close attention, given by Gwen. Helen settled up with the shop assistant, soon as Charlyyk was ready, they left. Helen hailed a cab. and gave an address.

The Taxi pulled up outside a small boutique. Elizabeth ushered Charlyyk inside, Gwen showed the shop assistant a copy of the Vivien Westwood dress. The assistant eyed Charlyyk up and down and was off. Soon she was back, a dress that Charlyyk recognised draped over her arm, her face beamed. And before anyone could stop her. Charlyyk disrobed. She stood there in just her silk undies dying for the dress to be put on. It did not take long, Charlyyk was prancing up and down twirling about. She loved it, and so did everyone else.

Helen took a video of the whole procedure. Sarah had been right; Charlyyk's hair colour brought out the colours, of the dress. It was if this dress was designed especially for Charlyyk.

Another assistant had brought a pair of gold ankle laced up sandals, with a little flat heel. They looked like something from classical Greek art. When Charlyyk put them on, they perfectly complimented the dress.

Elizabeth soon had settled the bill, without anyone else noticing. As they were too engrossed in Charlyyk.

Back at the Bennett residence, Anna was admiring the dress that Charlyyk was guarding with her life. Holding it up in front of herself, Charlyyk twirled around.

Edward looked on; with pride he had never seen his wife so happy. When she took hold of Edwards' arm, he could feel the pent-up excitement trembling through her whole body.

On the train, Charlyyk's grip on the bag had not let up. The one thought going through her head was showing it to her dad. She was in Neverland. Everything was spinning around; she was giddy with pleasure. There was no thought about a bridesmaid's dress, that was out of the window with the fairies. Today for her was what was in that bag.

Bryn stood in front of the long mirror in his bedroom. The dress sword was the last piece he put on. His Royal Gloucester dress uniform, fitted him to a T.

Harold moved around him. 'Bloody hell Bryn, how do you do it? It looks no different to when you last wore it, collecting your gallantry awards. You were forty then!'

His medals were impressive. Two of them had gold bars and oak leaves. The gold bars, he had already been awarded the same medal before. The oak leaves he had been mentioned in dispatches. Standing to attention he was the picture of manhood. From the crisp black trousers to the flat hat with a peak, He looked magnificent.

When Bryn and Harold collected the travellers at the station, Bryn had changed clothes. It was a good thing. The sight of Charlyyk rushing at him, the bag still held in a very tight grip, caused him to brace himself for the impact that was bound to happen. Harold took evasive action and kept three paces back. He knew how Bryn would have to swing her around when she jumped at him, just to dampen the impact of an over exuberant Charlyyk.

The conversation in the car was all about the shopping and Charlyyk's new dress. She spoke like a very young excited child, almost blabbering. They could only laugh at her incoherent enthusiasm.

Later in bed, Helen explained to Bryn the problems of getting a bridesmaid's dress for Charlyyk. 'They made her look like an Alice in Wonderland or a sugar plum fairy or an orphan from a Dickens book. The dresses just were not her. I could feel Gwen starting to explode with frustration.'

Bryn looked concerned. 'So where do we go from here?'

Helen sighed a long sigh. 'I really don't know Bryn.' Another sigh, 'I really don't know.'

***

Sunday, Mid-morning Janet and James arrived at Oakleaves. Charlyyk could not wait to show them her new dress. She was taking her clothes off before she reached her bedroom. James had seen this behaviour many times before and merely smiled.

Dressed in her new outfit, she paraded before them. Janet taking as many shots of her as possible. She loved the whole experience. Watching her friend experience such an ecstatic feeling brought out the emotions in herself.

Helen once again explained the problem choosing a bridesmaid dress. Rachel and Janet, sitting together started to discussed the matter. Then Janet text Sam, explaining the issue of the dress, the reply was simple. '*I'm staying with Chance.*' Janet showed Rachel and Charlyyk the Text, the look of realisation of the two being together. Rachel just had to show Thomas the text. 'Good for her.'

In Charlyyk's bedroom, the women were trying hard to find a style to suit Charlyyk. Janet had set up Charlyyk's computer and was bringing up various Fashion Houses, and their outlets. It was Charlyyk's thin frame, her hair and complexion that caused the problems. Helen wedding dress was brought into the girls thinking, but no definite style was found to suit Charlyyk.

Janet and James left at five. Rachel had enjoyed their company, and carried on the conversation she had with them with Charlyyk and Helen, at Carpenters Cottage.

Later, Thomas and Charlyyk launched a conversation with Michel. The diet test had proved that some of the foods that Charlyyk liked, were not good for her. Chocolate was one of them, saccharine had its problems too, but sugar she burnt off; it was a source of energy for her. But Michel was keen to stress, she was to be careful with how much sugar, it could still be a problem for her later. Salt was one of the things she should have, but moderately. He was worried about dairy products, as he could see that would not be in her regular life diet, on her home Planet. No issues showed up on her tests, but still felt hesitant. 'Keep your intake moderate for now.'

***

At the Academy on Monday morning, the pictures on Charlyyk's I-phone garnered much attention. Rachel had made an effort to include the shoes in the picture. Julia, Sarah and Sandra, were interested in the overall look of dress and shoes.

Jan sitting with Stella showed her how the dress gave Charlyyk's slim figure, shape and proportion. Julia pointed out. Now if Charlyyk had some backcombing on the top, it would lift her hair, and give it some body. Stella started to see how even simple things can make a big difference.

Julia pulled her hair back to show Stella the large birthmark that covered one side of her face. 'When I allowed my hair to grow long, then with some careful brushing to turn the ends, so that they turn under my chin, so it does not show so much, yes I feel uncomfortable for it to be seen. I cannot lose it so I have to make the best of it, as I can. Where Charlyyk does not worry, she just gets on with it. Her hair is her, that's how she accepts it. Just like her hands, they are there, we have to accept them as Charlyyk's, as there is nothing more she can do, than the improvements of the fingernails have done already.'

Charlyyk sat listening, she liked the attention they were all showing her, but one ear was pointing to the conversation, Mike was having with Paul. Mike had looked in Paul's lunch box. 'What food don't you like Paul?'

'Why do you ask?'

Mike pointed to his lunch box. 'There's nothing in there that's healthy, and you are what you eat.'

Paul's face had that look of doubt. 'My mum always said that what you like, does you good.'

Peter remarked. 'Don't you ever look in the mirror.'

'Of course, I do.'

Mike replied sternly. 'Don't you ask yourself, why do I look like I do?'

Paul was not happy with what was being said. 'But I enjoy what I eat.'

'But you kept telling us you don't like people laughing at you because of your appearance.' Peter pointed out to him. 'Yet you attend the same lessons with Mr Waverly as we do. He's always on about what types of food we should eat to keep us healthy. Are you asleep in those lessons?'

Paul pursed his lips angrily, he felt very awkward, looking into his lunch box he had suddenly lost his appetite.

Sandra who was sitting close to Peter gave a sideway nod to Charlyyk, who passed her lunch box towards her. Sandra then showed it to Paul, the pieces of vegetables, and lettuce leaves, rye bread, nuts, and dips. Julia passes her lunch box and the sandwiches with salad fillings. Paul started to get the message.

Janet arrived at the cottage at lunchtime, showing the article she had been working on, Margret liked the column she had placed in the *New York Times Magazine* on the Watercolour Art Exhibition in London.

But what Janet was most eager to get going were the interviews for the BBC. 'Bryn, next weekend, the production manager for Fiona Bruce, said she would like to come Friday night and spend some time with you all.'

Margret looked a little disappointed that once again, they would be away when something was happening. 'As we leave then something happens!'

Helen was looking in her diary. 'Sometimes it feels as though we are on a carousel. As someone step on, someone steps off. Though it seems that it is all quite necessary, when it is all happening.'

Bryn looked at Janet's articles and the photos that went with them. 'You can see the changes clearly. Look how the eyes, are taking shape, and the face has become a little longer.'

Margret looked carefully at the photos, 'You must make a drawing of her Thomas, a true artist sees the real person, and their pictures of them translate that. I remembered that first drawing you did of Charlyyk. We could compare them together that will show the real changes in her.'

Rachel touched her husband's hand. 'What a great idea, I would love to see that.'

Margret turned her attention to Janet, 'We leave Thursday morning Janet, for Liverpool. We will be back for the wedding. Is there anything we should discuss before then?'

Janet looked at her schedules. 'I have made all the necessary changes to the programmes you asked for. The printers have assured me that all the printing has been done and waiting for you. I hope the exhibition is a roaring success.'

After dinner, Thomas asked Charlyyk to pose. 'Just relax, this is going to be a ten-minute pencil drawing, very sketchy, then I will complete later with pen and ink.'

The rest of them carried on, as nothing was happening, Helen made coffee, and took it to the lounge. By the time she had seated herself. Thomas had finished his rough sketch of Charlyyk.

Charlyyk got up looked at what he had achieved. 'I like that, Thomas. You are so clever. You have not worried to get it right first time. But from all those pencil lines, I appear to be coming through the mist.' She placed her arms around his neck and kissed his cheek.

Thomas was finishing the drawing in sepia coloured ink on handmade paper. When he was done, Rachel produced the first drawing he made of Charlyyk, and placed them together. Even Charlyyk herself, could see the changes.

***

The next day, Charlyyk was allowed to take the drawing to school to show the posse. Alice Vasey could not help but join them for lunch. The fine pencil lines still showing in the drawing, giving it character. This she points out to the posse. 'We can see how Thomas has laid out his guide lines so to get Charlyyk's features in their true proportion's,'

Alice asked Charlyyk if she could show Thomas's drawing in her afternoon lessons, Alice had two of her most talented students in mind, that were in their last year at the Academy.

Peter examined Paul's lunch box. 'Now that's better Paul.'

Mike took a picture of Paul. 'In a month from now we will take another picture, and we will compare them to see what change there are. In the meantime, we will check what you are eating.'

Stella spoke up, 'What about when he is at home?'

'We need a programme of foods he should be eating at home.' suggested Jan.

Julia who did not live far from Paul. 'I will go and see his parents, and have a word with them, so we get it right.'

Miss Vasey listening in on the conversation. 'What's happening, why is Julia going to see Pauls parents?'

Sandra explained. 'Paul needs help, and we have made our minds up to see he get that help, whether he likes it or not. We are tired of his bleating of nobody likes him because of the spotty way he looks. Now he will have no excuses.'

In the Teachers meeting room after the lessons were over, Alice was talking about the posse's concerns about Paul, and what they had in mind for him. Tim and Wendy showed interested. Wendy, reflected on the changes in Stella during this last month. 'I wish some of the other groups of students took the same interest in their friends as the posse does. It would make our life so much easier.'

Louise Landon said. 'I agree with you Wendy, too many of them, just want to ridicule others, and not help. They seem to think life is just for laughs.'

***

Thursday, Margret, Thomas and Rachel said their goodbyes to Charlyyk, they were making an early start for their trip to Liverpool. The pen and ink drawing were going with them. Margret thought it would be good to put it on show alongside the first drawing that Thomas had done of Charlyyk. Some of Janet's Photos was also to go in a separate exhibit from the watercolour paintings.

Bryn and Helen had much to get ready for the weekend. With many adults in the cottage, it was a lot to keep up with the housework. Helen's life had changed, but she had met the challenges. With Bryn's help, it did not seem that bad.

Charlyyk put effort into the general chores. Helen always like what she had to say as they worked. Yes, there were days, but overall life was good for Helen. She kept Catherine informed through weekly talks. The wedding plans, meant that there was always something to do.

The thing that was most on her mind was the bridesmaid's dress. The weekend will be tied up, with the BBC interview, so time was becoming important. Taking a break with Bryn over a cup of tea. 'I don't know who else could help?'

Helen reiterated. 'Janet and Sam tried to work out something, but as yet nothing.' A worried frown appeared on her face, and her shoulders sank down.

Bryn gave a sigh. 'Yes, I notice the way you have been searching the internet, and talking with Gwen, that time is running out?' Bryn took her hand. 'Let's get this weekend over, then we will put all our efforts together to get this settled, no matter what the cost.'

***

During the Friday morning run, had the three of them in conversation about the interview with Fiona Bruce. Charlyyk was not worried at all, she will be her usual self and take it as it comes. Bryn also was not concerned, he knew Charlyyk better than anyone, how she would respond and the straightforward answers she would give to each question asked.

Helen started to relax, she had been getting tensed about the whole wedding affair and listening to them she realised, she must go with the flow or break under the pressure.

The posse also knew how Charlyyk would respond to the interview. They were more concerned about what she was going to wear. Julia was more into about how she would place her hands and practised with her to get the right pose.

Sandra watching for any other mistakes she could make. Like the angle of the body while sitting. 'Charlyyk, many of the female celebs, during interviews. Sit at an angle with the legs in a < shape, on a chair or sofa, its so the camera does not upskirt them and capture a delicate shot of you.'

Peter asked the question as if he was Fiona Bruce, Mike and Mace trying to think up questions for him to ask. Jan and Stella, looked on the procedure with some bemusement.

Charlyyk kept smiling she knew they had her best interest at heart, but when the time comes, she will act as it pans out.

At a few minutes to five, the doorbell rang. Bryn opened the door, and a tall, elegant figure, with a signature smile. was standing there. 'Fiona Bruce.'

Bryn shook her hand and introduce himself. 'Please come in.' He took her bags, and showed her through to the lounge. Helen was the most nervous, but Fiona had her soon at ease, with her natural, relaxed manner.

Then Charlyyk stepped forward. Fiona's smile increased. When Fiona invited her to sit with her, Charlyyk responded. Helen fetched some refreshments, and for an hour they soon got to know each other.

Charlyyk taking Fiona on a guided tour of the cottage, and showed her the guest room then Thomas's room. 'Please any one of these rooms that you may like?'

Fiona liked Thomas's Room. 'This will do me just fine.'

Over dinner, Fiona made many notes, 'I've read much of what Janet Stokes has written about you all. I am so pleased that the company gave me this chance to put my take on you.'

After dinner, Janet and James arrived, there was much to talk about. Fiona found it useful to get as much information she could so to ask Charlyyk the question she believed to be what her viewers would wish to ask, themselves.

***

Saturday morning, when Charlyyk returned from her run, she found Fiona already up and working on the sort of question she was going to ask. Over breakfast, Fiona had thought of some more question, and as the weather looked good, she wanted to see some of the places that Charlyyk liked.

A stroll around the area would be a good thing to do. As they walked through the village, Sarah and Mace met up with them. All four walked up the Lane to Parsons Farm to the top of Bishops Lane. Charlyyk showing them the copse of trees on the hill, where Bryn and Charlyyk had been delivered on her first days on earth. Then where they had seen the footprint, down to the bottom of the lane to Dippers Meadow. All the time Fiona asking questions, arriving back at the cottage. Sarah and Mace giving their view about their time at school. With all the laughing that was going on, everyone was enjoying the experience immensely. Sarah and Mace left at five.

The camera crew were arriving on Sunday to do the filming. In the meantime, Fiona was making the most of her time with Charlyyk. Her producer came at six and Fiona filled her in on what she had thought could be the best angles. During dinner, more talk about the life they have found themselves in and the challenges it had brought them.

Gwen and Harold arrived later; the rest of the evening Fiona questioned them on how events had affected them.

***

Sunday, Helen woke to find a card sitting on her bedside cabinet. It was addressed to her, with it was a box of Belgium Chocolates, the neat handwriting took her by surprise, for it was not Bryn's handwriting; opening the envelope, to find a Mother's Day card inside, from Charlyyk. '*Sweetest Mum, I hope every day you share with me, will feel like Mother's Day, every day. My love always, Charlyyk X.*'

Bryn now awake and sitting up in bed, put his arm around her. Helen soon cuddled into him. 'So, this is motherhood...Oh, how I love it.'

The morning run was just Bryn and Charlyyk, Helen did not like to leave their guest alone. The camera crew arrived at eight and were soon set up. The weather had held up with fluffy white clouds, it gave a good backdrop for some outside views. A walk down to the village was planned, Fiona casually dressed as like Charlyyk.

During the stroll, Charlyyk's answers to Fiona's questions were given in Charlyyk's usual direct way. She would pause think and answer, they would laugh and make fun, at some of the issues. Then returning back to the cottage the producer going over what had been filmed, with many discussions how they thought the next session should be taken. It was Fiona that wanted a shot of Dippers Meadow, and the crew were soon there.

A scene was set up by the stream Charlyyk and Fiona sitting under the willow trees, with the bulrushes as a backdrop. Some of the question being repeated. Then they set up the next interview indoors. Very relaxed, the whole subject was on Charlyyk's time at school, and how she found living amongst us humans. As Janet, had written so much about her, there was no new material. The novelty was hearing it said in Charlyyk's own unique way. The programme was scheduled to be shown over the Easter weekend before the wedding.

Gwen and Harold helped Helen with the evening meal, and much was discussed on how it all went. After dinner Helen managed to get Charlyyk on her own. Wrapping her arms around her. 'Darling that was the sweetest thing, you did this morning, and yes every day with you is a real pleasure.'

Charlyyk gave Helen a hug of joy and buried her head into Helen's breast to listen to her heart beat. There was no need for words. Helen felt the love Charlyyk had for her.

***

On Monday, the posse was anxious about how it all went. Sarah and Mace giving their account of what they witnessed. At lunchtime, the conversation was much the same.

Sandra inquired 'Any news about the bridesmaid's dress Charlyyk?'

'No, it still not been resolved.'

Stella nonchalantly. just said. 'What would you have worn if you were on your own Planet, Charlyyk?'

Charlyyk's eyes turned a different colour, and her ears twitched to a forward position. The posse watched carefully to how she was behaving knowing full well she was putting that thought into action. The little baying nod meant she had thought it through. Charlyyk looked around her and at their pensive expressions, the smile she gave eased their concerns, she had come up with the answer.

'Thank you, Stella. That was just what I had not thought about, I had been so adamant that Earth was my planet, it had marred my thinking.'

Arriving home to the cottage after school, Charlyyk spoke with Helen. 'Stella asked what I would have I worn if I were on my own planet. I was about to say, that I'm on my own planet when I realised it could be the answer to our problem.'

With that Charlyyk fetched her computer, and set it up. With the disc placed on it, she activated it with her ring.

Helen called for Bryn, and as they gathered around the computer, the elegant features of Klyklyyk appeared. Charlyyk's nods and eye contact that was taking place, she then explained the difficulties they were experiencing. Klyklyyk nodded with Charlyyk, and the connection was gone.

Helen waited to hear what had been agreed. Charlyyk just smiled, 'it will be sorted no more to worry about.'

Later that evening a text message from Catherine to meet them at the Southampton Docks on Friday, she will give them full details as to what time it will be on Thursday evening.

Chapter 41

The Intent

The days went quickly. On Thursday night they had received Catherine's text, the ship that the Leany's were on would be docking at eight in the morning. The Leany's had travelled by sea to give Catherine a little comfort and piece off mind. Jo Leany had expressed, because Cat was eight-months pregnant, a flight was not considered suitable. On the ship there would be a doctor on hand at all times.

Bryn arrived at Southampton docks at Ten. He could see activity but no passengers as yet disembarking. He parked the car, then made enquiries of the port officer. The officer said that the ship had just moored. He made some phone calls and then stated that he could go aboard to help them in thirty minutes, after immigration and customs formalities had been completed.

When Bryn finally boarded, he could see the size of Catherine, and her smile was as big as her bump. Amy was three now and was running around, giving Brent and his mother some headaches. Amy, seeing her granddad made a beeline straight for him. Bryn was one happy fellow.

The drive to the cottage took an hour. Helen was waiting at the door, introductions over, soon coffee in the lounge was the order of the day and gave Helen a chance to talk about herself. Amy was up and about dragging her granddad about as if he was a ragdoll.

Jo Leany was quick to ask for the local Doctor to be contacted. 'Catherine needs to be checked over, it has been a long trip, and these are delicate times.' Jo had an uneasy sense of maternal worry at this stage of the pregnancy. Her feelings for Catherine were as a mother towards her. She had come to respect Catherine for many things, her determination for Brent to be his own man was top of the list this had made Brent stronger. For Brent, had originally taken after his father, who had a soft attitude towards life. This had worried Jo. Now Brent was more the man he should be in her eyes...a true colonial man rugged, that could stand upright when facing the world.

Helen had already been told my Margret that a doctor should be notified of Catherine predicament. And Helen had already taken care of it.

Jo had previously been to the Cottage, and knew all about the clinic.

It was not long before she had checked to see if it had been kept up to the standard, that she expected to find it, as it should be.

Brent was aware of his mother's steely determination, when she felt it required it. When she was sure, all is fine, she changes to a soft loving mum. You just have to give her time to adjust.

The school bus arrived. Like a whirlpool Charlyyk burst in, entirely unashamedly loud. Brent managed to stand in front of Catherine to save her from being knocked flying, as Charlyyk was so excited, she did not know who to hug first. Amy was the prime target, Jo and Brent were amazed how Charlyyk had grown, the skype views did not do her justice.

Amy now had control of Charlyyk and was soon off on a new adventure. Charlyyk played with Amy until she tired falling asleep in her grandmother's arms. Now Charlyyk could be herself and be able to talk with the Leany's. Catherine's bump was the main topic, and Charlyyk's hand smoothed over it in a very gentle manner. The kicks she felt brought out giggles and looks of wonderment.

It was what Charlyyk could hear going on inside Catherine's tummy that had her attention most. The heart of the child beat at a regular pattern. Taking in the scent that the baby gave out was another wonder to Charlyyk.

Saturday morning, Charlyyk sat with Catherine and set the computer up. With the disc in place, she touched her ring to it. Brent stood behind Catherine looking at the screen. The elegant figure of Klyklyyk appeared, and Charlyyk introduced Cat and Brent to her. The usual nods and eye contact, then she was gone.

'Stay where you are,' Charlyyk told them, then opened the door to the garden. In ten minutes the tall, lean stately figure of Klyklyyk stood there. She entered the cottage. Amy did not flinch but went to her. She held out her hand in a gesture of friendship. Klyklyyk responded, as her very long hand reached down gently allowed Amy to take hold, one of her long fingers. Jo was mesmerised by her height.

To make them feel less intimidated by her height. Klyklyyk looked for a chair to sit down. Amy by her side. Another instrument was taken from Klyklyyk's flowing gown, then Klyklyyk pointed the device at Amy. After a nod to Charlyyk, she pointed it at her. 'This will give us the size to make the gowns.'

Bryn and Helen joined them. Charlyyk made refreshments, and for a while, they all talked general chit chat. One of Klyklyyk's eyes was on Catherine's bump all the time they were talking. Then rising Klyklyyk nodded and left.

Jo looked at Charlyyk. 'You would have grown to that height if they had not placed, that plate in your head?'

Charlyyk nodded. 'Michel said, that the amount I was eating I could have grown even taller.'

Jo touched her hair. 'When I first saw you, your hair... it was like straw. Now it so soft. Your skin was dry and leathery. Now that's also soft and smooth. I love your fingernails.'

Charlyyk took a lot of pride in what Brent's mother was saying. 'I spent luxurious hours in the bath with a lot of bath oils. I blame Catherine and Rachel for that. Her face took on a dream look and she sighed. She knew she had been spoilt. The face of Klyklyyk showed none of the same pamperings, the way Drenghaagh had reached forward and touched Charlyyk on their first meeting showed he had noticed how different Charlyyk was.

Catherine laughed. 'Are you purring Charlyyk?'

Charlyyk cocked her head to one side. 'You bet.'

The week had gone by quickly. Catherine and Amy could not have been happier. Bryn was a punch bag to Amy, as she could not stop jumping all over her Granddad. With the wedding witches popping in to make sure everything was running to schedule. The wedding dress arrived and checked to make sure it fitted. The florist confirmed that everything was ready, and the delivery was at hand.

Only Catherine was concerned as she could tell the bump was more prominent. Jo fuzzed, making sure she was comfortable.

Easter was loaming. The wedding would be the next weekend. Father Steven had arranged the wedding rehearsals, and Gwen had everything under control.

***

At the little parish Church, Father Steven, smiled at Charlyyk. 'So, you see Charlyyk, it is spiritual, not physical. It's more in the mind. We use his teachings to guide our lives, to be better people. We look on at our fellow man, as an equal, no matter what religion, our fellow man follows. If man only did was what right for himself, anarchy would inevitably follow. Laws are there to give people an even chance to live a good life. As you know some people don't believe in God, but it doesn't mean they are bad people. Some are more Christian minded, then some of those that attend Church. So that why we the humble parish priest, try to help those that walk an unsteady path, to give them guidance.'

Gwen was pleased to see Charlyyk listening so intently, to what Father Steven said. 'What do you think? do you see what we see in our Lord, Charlyyk?'

Charlyyk's pause, and the expression on her face. Gwen knew she had not been convinced. 'I can see the reason for laws. We have them at school, it controls those that only want to mess about, and disturb lessons. The Church made laws to hold its parishioners to their will, and to look after their needs. It's the praying bit I have the trouble with. If I cook a bad meal, praying won't turn it into a good meal, it will still taste like crap.'

Father Steven spoke. 'That's correct Charlyyk, you are so right. It would be silly of anyone to expect it would. When you saw your dad, defending himself against that beast, what came into your mind?'

Charlyyk did not need time to think, 'Where was I going to run to.'

'And If that situation came up again tomorrow?'

Again, no hesitation, 'I would attack the beast as well, for it would be better to die together, then one of us left alive, wishing the other was still here.'

Father Steven looked at her. He had thought he would have won her around, but now it was making him feel that it was not to be. 'How did you come to that conclusion?'

The thought, that I had put my dad's life at risk because he had been taken to that planet on the chance, he would rescue one of us...not specifically me, any one of the *Lyyk's* that were sent there to die. If my dad had died, I to would also have died. I would have perished, just because I did not know. So, at that crucial moment in time, it would have been about survival.'

Charlyyk had not changed her ideas, she still saw things, Black and White. Gwen could see that there was no way that they could modify the way she thinks.

'Come Charlyyk, we have stepped over the boundary, of what we originally came here to discuss,' Gwen remarked as she got up. Gwen offered her hand, but Charlyyk did not accept it. Charlyyk was not angry. It was those memories still flashing through her mind, and the recollection of those horrible moments and the painful cries that still haunted her. She had tried to bury them in the back of mind, but as before a little nudge, there they are again, as large as life.

When Gwen and Charlyyk arrived back at Carpenters Cottage. Harold was the one that always put things into perspective. This time was no different. A chocolate biscuit and a mint tea did the trick, and a cuddle settled the deal.

Charlyyk nestled up to him. 'Don't tell Michel.'

'If I would?'

Gwen was feeling guilty she had tried to convert Charlyyk, to her own way of thinking, and it had backfired. She should have let her be, for Charlyyk it must have logic to tackle any problem, so had to fit her criteria of facts before feelings. It is her natural way, the way her logic sets out the path before her. 'I'm sorry Charlyyk, it was wrong of me to have put you through that.'

Charlyyk took a sip of the mint tea, then turned and looked at Gwen. 'How can I be, something I'm not? Auntie Gwen. I see life so different to you at times, but no it does not make me angry. I love you for all you have done for me. You could strike me in anger, I will still love you. My people do not do anger but try to understand why, so that they can resolve any issue, with some dignity, not conflict. That is why they are no threat to this planet.'

Charlyyk placed her arms around Gwen and cuddled her. She gave her a tender kiss. 'I love you so much Auntie Gwen. I would lay my life down for you.'

Harold gave them both a cuddle, in a great big bear hug. 'Come, Charlyyk let's take you home.'

***

Sunday morning. Amy found Charlyyk drying her hair after her shower, and wanted to help. Yelps emerged from Charlyyk, as the brush in Amy's hands were handled like a tennis racket. Amy's forehand smashes smacked Charlyyk's head, but Charlyyk still allowed her to carry on. The fun they were having could be heard all around the cottage. Jo came to Charlyyk's assistance.

'Granny look, I'm helping Charlyyk.'

Jo could only smile. She liked the way that Amy and Charlyyk were enjoying each other's company.

Later Charlyyk took Amy for a walk to the village and ended playing ball on the village green with Mace, George and Sarah. Brian and Sgt Wendy Bailey joining in on the fun. While Harold and Gwen watched from the Cottage. Liza Martin waved to them from her front door. She had not seen this amount of fun on the village green for some time. Liza quickly took a video from her iPhone to show Jim later.

The Discovery pulled up outside of Carpenters Cottage. Bryn and Brent could not help joining in with the fun. Catherine sat in the car with the door open. Soon the noise, had many of the residents, coming out to see what was happening on the green.

Helen sat in the front of the car. She looked at Catherine sitting next to Jo Leany, she could see the pride in her eyes of her little family sharing each other. Then Cat reached between the car seats and took Helen's hand, and placed it on her bump. Helen felt the movement, and that particular feeling that she was now an integral part of this unique family. Could Charlyyk survived if it was a different type of family. Watching Brent tickling Charlyyk and Amy, then the two girls joining forces to tickle Brent. This was family life, and boy, how she loved it.

Father Stevens came out of the Church to investigate what was happening. He walked down the path and leaned against the tiled porch. He too was smiling at the raucous laughter that was being generated.

***

The Easter Holiday was here. The posse had made plans to meet up, have a day in town, and go to Charlyyk's for a BBQ. Helen had promised Rebecca, that they would have a day together shopping, the girls would stay and look after Len.

Thomas and his charges had returned from Liverpool, in time for Easter Sunday. That morning, Charlyyk, Catherine and Rachel, were staying at the Cottage, the rest were heading for Winchester Cathedral the banns were being read out.

Thomas sitting next to his father, 'The last nail in the coffin, Dad.'

Bryn knocked Thomas's knee with his knee, remembering that was the words he had said to Thomas when he was about to marry Rachel.

At the cottage, the two pregnant girls had found a nice comfortable swing seat in the garden. The sun felt hot and was getting uncomfortable for them. Charlyyk ran about looking after them, supplying their needs. Digging in the back of the garage. Charlyyk found an electric fan and had soon set it up to cool them. Charlyyk loved being able to help them, remembering what they had previously done for her. Accepting she was different yet, treating her with love and kindness. As the fan twirled from side to side, blowing a fresh breeze at them, the gap between them big enough for Charlyyk to sit. She was soon sitting there, a huge satisfactory smile spread right across her face.

Catherine looked different. It was not just the bump. Charlyyk closed her eyes, and let her mind drift. In her mental vision, as Catherine appeared younger. Catherine's cheery smile had put Charlyyk at ease. Charlyyk did not understand what was being said, but that did not matter. It was the manner it was spoken, with soft assuring tones.

Cat placed her arms around her and gave her a cuddle. It was nice... warm... securely warm. That had never changed. Cat had been her first mum in a way, someone to cuddle too when you feel threatened.

A gentle squeeze of Cat's hand brought Charlyyk from her thoughts. She turned to look at Cat. Who taking her hand, had placed it on the bump, the movement felt so lovely, now it was Rachel that picked up Charlyyk's other hand and places it on her bump, the moving sensation she was enjoying kept looking at them in turn? This brought her so much pleasure, feeling the two unborn babies moving about in contentment in their mother's tummies. Tucked between them she almost felt the same as those two little lives.

***

The morning of Easter Monday the sky was clear and looked as another hot day was in store for them. The runners made the best of the conditions underfoot. The new spring grass was breaking ground, and the showing of cowslip and primroses were looking magnificent in the early morning sun. Hazel catkins hung down from their branches, nodding springs arrival. Lambs skipped about in the nursery fields half way down Bishops Lane.

Charlyyk could see Janet working hard with James, keeping an eye on those bundles of fun. Janet looking more and more a farmer's wife. As Janet stood up, the sun caught the top of her head, and the orange glow that radiated from it was like a burning beacon. Charlyyk's over exaggerated wave towards them was returned likewise from them both.

The rest of the run, Charlyyk bounced about like those spring lambs. With the sun on her, her nose scented the delicious smell of spring, and her ears were filled with the buzz of insects, and the chirps of birds. Life was so good. She threw up her arms, and jumped high in the air, and gave out a loud 'Wheeee.'

Thomas caught up with her. Charlyyk jumped into his arms, and wrapped her arms around his neck and kissed his cheek. 'What have I done to deserve that?'

Charlyyk leaned back. 'Just being Thomas,'

Thomas pushed his nose up to her nose then wriggled it. She was happy.

***

On Tuesday, Helen was all fingers and thumbs. Excitement was building inside of her, and she kept making silly mistakes. Charlyyk would nudge her, still help to cover for her. Helen could not be more thankful.

Charlyyk knew that this was not Helen's usual behaviour. Charlyyk phoned Sandra and asked If she could bring Helen over to see them. 'It could settle her down and take her mind off the wedding.'

Sandra thought it was a grand idea. 'Just come, we are going nowhere. We will enjoy your company.'

Charlyyk pushed Helen to the car. 'Come on. It will do you good to talk with someone else, for a change.'

Rebecca and Len were so pleased to see her, and soon Helen was her old self again. Charlyyk sat with Sandra and Peter. Peter was spending a lot of time at Sandra's house, since they had become an item. Julia had started to see more of Mike, now did not feel, cut off from her best friend.

Charlyyk began to understand the changes that growing up brought about. She listened intently not what they said, but more to how they said it, which told a much different story.

Stella's name was mentioned, which to Charlyyk's ears was good news as her name was never mentioned before.

Peter started to talk on his Mobile. 'The posse is meeting in town tomorrow.'

Then Charlyyk's phone vibrated, Sarah and Mace texted. *'Meet at the Village Bus stop 8.am, we are all meeting in town tomorrow Luv u x'* She showed the text to Sandra and Peter then nodded. But the two of them knew what her nod meant. Even in the short time they had known her, each nod said something different, this was her approval nod.

By the time they returned to Oakleaves, Helen was back to her usual self. The sleeping arrangement had Catherine and Brent in the Guest room. Thomas and Rachel in Thomas old bedroom. Amy was with Charlyyk and loving it. Margret and Jo were sleeping at Carpenters Cottage. Cat and Rachel had so much to talk about, Brent reckoned it was almost impossible to separate them to get them to bed, and threatened Cat he would move in with Thomas.

After dinner Helen and Charlyyk cleared away the dirty things, discussing between them, of what was still required to do for the wedding. Suddenly Charlyyk just turned and opened the door to the garden. The tall figure of Klyklyyk entered. Helen approached her, and without thinking nodded. Klyklyyk smile broadened. 'Helen, you are almost one of us.'

'Thank you Klyklyyk.'

As they entered another *Lyyk* came in behind Klyklyyk, carrying the Bridesmaids dresses. 'Let me introduce Saarlyyk' remarked Klyklyyk. They gave their nods all round. Saarlyyk was a young *Lyyk* about seven years older than Charlyyk.

The two younger Lyyk's met amid a series of ear movement, eye colour changing, and many nods. Charlyyk called for Amy, and the three of them left for Charlyyk's bedroom.

Klyklyyk sat down with the rest of the family. Brent and Thomas were in awe of her. Cat and Rachel were more matter of fact and asked many questions. Klyklyyk was fascinated by the two girls pregnancy.

When the Bridesmaids entered, the family sat amazed. The silk-like material had no seams. The dresses draped over their small frames had style. The trail of material that flowed behind gave the impression that there were no restrictions and allowed freedom of movement when they walked. The bodice of the dresses, had that art nouveau look of intricate designs and flowing curves. The neckline was loose, not tight, again for comfort.

Saarlyyk explained. 'The material is spun from the seed husk of a plant. The condition it grows in, is so unstable this fibre helps to keep the seed at a constant temperature, so it will keep the girls warm when cold, and cool when hot. The headdress is a unique metal that comes from a planet so far away, it took sixty of your planet's circles of your sun just to get there. As you will see on the day, will make the whole dress radiate. I will wear something very similar when I give my intent to my *Haagh*.' The way her ears moved and her eyes changed colour showed how excited she was at the prospect of it.

Klyklyyk then spoke. 'Saarlyyk is my daughter, her father is Drenghaagh.' She gave a little nod to Charlyyk. 'Charlyyk and all the other *Lyyk's* were alone in their lives. You would call them orphans? We feel that Charlyyk deserves something she can hold on to, and we see that she has it here. We owe her our gratitude, for what she has achieved for us. This dress will be like her intent to you... as you say, our love to you. You are a part of our family, and if you need us, we will be here for you.' With that, the two *Lyyk's* nodded and left.

Cat felt the material it was so soft, Amy cuddled up to her mum, 'Can I wear it to bed?'

Cat looked into her eyes 'No darling, I don't think we should not until the wedding is over.' Brent was already on the phone with his mother, explaining what had happened.

***

Wednesday, the walk to the village gave Charlyyk time reflect on many things. Images flashed through her mind, at a hectic speed.

A police car approached her. Sgt Wendy Bailey in charge of it. 'Hi, Charlyyk, they are at the bus stop already.'

Charlyyk smiled at her. 'Hi Wendy, they must be keen.'

Wendy nodded, 'I see from the surveillance equipment you had another visitor last night.'

Charlyyk nodded, 'Yes Wendy, they brought the Bridesmaids dresses.'

They bade their farewells and head off in their separate ways.

The emergence of Charlyyk, soon had them waving as she crossed the green towards them, they met with hugs.

Mace was the first to speak 'You must have seen Mum she was heading for Oakleaves?'

Charlyyk acknowledges him 'Yes she stopped and talked.'

Sarah was quick to ask 'She said you had another visitor?'

Charlyyk's nod agreed with her but did not answer. George had stepped in between them and kissed Charlyyk on the cheek. The bus had arrived, they brought their ticket from the driver and sat at the rear of the bus. There were a few nods, and hellos directed to Charlyyk, but not the frenzy she had started to get used to. It was as Michel said to her this time last year. 'Once people get to know you and you don't pose a threat, they will accept you. You can be yourself; you just have to be patient.'

She felt the strong arm of Mace cover her shoulders. 'You okay Charlyyk?'

She smiled at him. 'Yes, I'm fine. It's so nice to be able to walk about with some freedom. So often I had to move quickly, so not to create a crowd. Now I find myself strolling at a more comfortable pace.'

Sarah moved to allow more space for them and the four of them settled down. 'You were going to tell us about the visitor.'

Charlyyk told them all about last night. As the bus pulled into the bus station, they could see the rest of the posse waiting. With so much to talk about, they strolled into town, laughing and fooling about. The group fell into pairs. Jan and George trailing at the rear. Mace was with Paul. Where Sarah was talking with Stella. There was a satisfactory smile on Charlyyk's face, when looking at the clothes in a favourite fashion shop.

Gwen felt the dresses. 'How did they make them? It looks as if they were spun by a spider. There are no seams.'

Amy did not mind getting dressed up again, it made her feel like a Princess. As she glided about, Jo looked on with pride.

Margret sighed a big sigh, 'How much would they cost if you had to make them?'

Cat was hanging on to Brent's arm. 'All night in my dreams, I saw Amy walking down the aisle with Charlyyk. The dream just kept going around and around like a carousel at a fun fair, and I did not want it to stop.'

Brent bent over and kissed Cat on the forehead. 'You have taken me on an adventure, which I don't want to stop, Darling.'

Cat looked at him. 'That was your fault, you should not have looked so bloody handsome.'

Thomas laughed. 'I thought it was the fault of you being in Hobbit Land.'

***

Thursday, the weather had changed a low front had pushed the high front away, but the weather forecast for Saturday was fair.

Liza Martin was expected. She was bringing a friend. He was a top hair stylist in the movie world. Though she had left the industry, they had remained good friends.

When they arrived, Helen was so surprised. He was a massive man with enormous hands, but his gentle voice when he spoke, was a complete contrast to how he looked. Liza introduced him as Stefan Lennard. He soon had Helen sitting. As he fingered through her hair. 'Yes, we can do plenty with this. Now I must see you in your dress.'

When Helen returned in her dress, he stood back, then circled her. 'Yes, we could do many styles, as you have left your hair to grow. Do you have a preference or do you need guidance?' He went to his bag and took a sketch pad out, the delft strokes of his pencil soon gained Helen's undivided attention… page after page, front and back elevations.

Cat and Rachel stood close, marvelling at how those great hams of hands could draw so gently with so much detail. The girls looked and discuss each style very carefully. 'Yes, this one, it looks lovely, and the veil will sit nicely' Helen could see herself in how Stefan had drawn her.

Stefan picked up his bag, and took out a bib. He covered her. Using a light spray of water, hairdryer and brush, he soon had styled her hair. 'There, something in that style.' He took the bib off, showing herself in the mirror. The others nodded their heads in approval.

Stefan had fun with Amy, but nothing too elaborate. 'She is only three.' He observed.

Then he looked at Charlyyk's hair, and with an excited voice 'Now this is something else!' The colour, the feel was so different. As it gave the top of her head more volume, and at the rear dropped corkscrews twirls. She felt very girly. Her little purple tongue poked out between her lips and moisten them. Looking in the mirror, tossed her head side to side seeing the curls bounce. the smile, it made all the difference.

Sitting around the kitchen table drinking coffee. Stefan talked about himself. 'I'm Canadian. I have four sisters. Some winters you spend a lot of time indoors. I found myself talking more about my sister's hair and the ways they could have it. And that is how I got into styling. Found my way into television, then films. That's where Liza and I met. We worked together on many productions. As if...like magic. You created other people's fantasies. With films...you unleash your imagination.'

Liza Martin confirmed his stories, 'I had just got out of college and found myself on my first production set. Stefan saw I was vulnerable and soon was protecting me...he became a father figure towards me.'

Stefan promised he would be there on the morning of wedding, with his team. He had created a new fan base. The girls loved his soft manner.

Bryn made his way to Carpenters Cottage, as all grooms, should not see their intended bride in her dress the day before the wedding. He had been into battle so many times before, but he had never been this nervous.

Gwen loved her brother, and to have him there was like living a dream. Soon they were going over old times. Harold broke open a new bottle of Balvenie whisky. He knew too well that it will make him feel at home...but there was no need, this had always been Bryn's second home.

***

Friday morning, Charlyyk, Thomas and Brent had a good run. The drizzly rain did not deter them, they had stopped to talk to James to confirm the stag do and were soon heading back.

Breakfast was noisy, due to the nervous tension that was building up. As they waited for the wedding gremlins to strike. Charlyyk had arranged to take Amy, and spend the day with Sarah, Mace, George and Jan.

Brent and Thomas were heading for Carpenters Cottage. The women will remain at Oakleaves.

***

Saturday was the day of the Wedding.

The morning sky was clear, and the warmth of the sun could be felt. The lone runner pushed hard, the lure to enter Dippers Meadow was too much for her. Looking around brought back those lovely idyllic times, for this was where her freedom began when the family were protecting her, from the outside world, she learnt so much here.

Charlyyk let her mind drift. New memories were starting to manifest themselves. many due to her being around her own people. The changes to her external body did not concern her, but she was excited how her brain was developing inside her. She knew she had two brains; otherwise, her ears and eyes would not have been able to have functioned separately the way they did. Now she could feel the differences with how she could manipulate them like she could not do before.

The smile she gave herself was not because she felt superior, was more how she could use it to keep her secure, staying here with those she has become to trust. This is the basis of the love she had grown accustom to, having the respect off her new family, for they respected her as much as she respected them. Reflecting on these last month's how Helen had concerns for her feelings, this was the reason that had made her own feelings resolute to stay here on this planet, then to return to her home planet. Those blurred memories of where she once lived were not that clear, but she knew those images will eventually come clearer to her in the passage of time. But for now, it was what was happening here.

Charlyyk's contemplation of the things around her brought a smile. She was a big part of this family, and they had shown her that they valued her. Being wanted and trusted was the key, that unlocked her heart to them all. The posse was also a big piece of this jigsaw. The puzzle that fitted neatly into place, making one large fantastic picture, just as Dipper Meadow had done when it weaved its spell on her the first moment, she saw it.

When back at Oakleaves. Everyone was up, breakfast was laid out. It felt strange to Charlyyk that no men were there.

Helen was pushing for everyone to finish breakfast. 'Stefan will be here soon.' No sooner she had said it, the doorbell rang. Stefan with two girls in their late-twenties stood waiting to enter.

'Morning everyone, I hope that Coffee is fresh?' He waltzed in and introduced the girls, 'This is Jackie and Toni...my girls' They found places to sit and were soon tucking into breakfast.

Breakfast finished Stefan set up his salon in the kitchen. Charlyyk watched, her mouth ajar, trying to take it all in.

Liza Martin arrived and was greeted by Jackie and Toni as if they were sisters. Liza set herself up, at the other end of the table. Stefan had made a list of the order of hairs, and as one hair was completed, Liza did the makeup.

Charlyyk found herself answering the door and bringing in the flowers and the Bouquet. Then it was her turn at the table, as Stefan's hands smoothed over her. Charlyyk watching in the mirror how each movement created a different effect on her hair. She saw the joy in her own face as Stefan showed her how the corkscrew curls bounced up and down. Then when Stefan placed the headpiece on top how it all radiated and sparkled.

Out of all this chaos, came calm. Alan Lyndd arrived with the 1920 Roll Royce Phantom II. With the white ribbons attached with enormous bows, it looked spectacular.

Harold arrived and picked up Cat and Jo. Brent was already in the car. Thomas took Rachel and Margret in the Discovery and then to collected his father from Carpenters Cottage.

Charlyyk waived them off. The tension in the air was growing and nobody could sense that feeling more than Charlyyk.

A taxi arrived with Helen's Father, it pulled into the drive. Helen greeted her father Edward with the loving look towards him, that Daughters have on their wedding day.

Edward had to wipe his eyes, knowing that his daughter had already grown into a woman and was not a young girl. He still could not believe this day had finally come. The smile he gave Charlyyk seeing her standing beside Helen. He kissed her cheek, then squeezed her hand, knowing this was her doing. He was so thankful to her.

During the drive to Winchester, Amy keeping Helen amused with the small talk of a very young person. As they arrived at the Cathedral, Helen was taken back by the crowd that was waiting to see her arrive. Press and TV media cameras in attendance.

Alan brought the car to a standstill, checked that everything was in order, then opened the door.

Charlyyk was first out of the car, she helped Amy then Helen's Father Edward, Helen being the last one out of the car, Charlyyk checking to see that Helens dress was in order, before she organised Amy so that Helen could take the arm of her father.

The camera flashes, and the OH's and AH's sounding all around.

Janet had made sure she had a free day, had acquired a good friend to take the wedding photos. The few moments taken to get the right positioning for those essential photos. The photographer just kept clicking away knowing Janet would not expect nothing less.

Charlyyk and Amy walked behind Helen and Edward. The metal headdresses that Charlyyk and Amy wore sparkled in the sunlight and made the dresses sparkle as well. The crowd gasped at the effect created.

As they walked towards the large entrance to the Cathedral, there were more gasp from the waiting spectators. Charlyyk's senses made her turn around. To her pleasure Drenghaagh, Klyklyyk and Saarlyyk strolled behind looking magnificent in their silken robes. The nods they gave her was showing their approval of how she looked. The crowd outside was now mumbling as they could see the true height of the Laight's, and how majestic they looked.

They entered the Cathedral to the sound of the Organ, playing Felix Mendelssohn's 'Wedding March.' The rumbling sounds of the assembled as they saw the wedding group appear, and realisation of the Laight's that were walking behind.

Gwen and Jane Parsons quickly helped the Laight's to find seats next to Su Shi, Liu and Major Carter.

As Helen stood next to Bryn the smile on her face radiated a warm glow, her eyes glanced at Charlyyk with that look of 'Hey what do you think of your dad'

Charlyyk approving nod saying, 'Looking good'.

Everything was going to plan. The rehearsals were working, Harold as best man stood beside Bryn.

Charlyyk looked around the Martins, the Baileys, the posse, Wendy Butler, Alice, Mrs Landon, then to the other side, the Parsons, the Stokes, Symonds, Michel, Clare. Su Shi and Liu, Major Carter, Chance, Sam and her brother Philip, and so many more. The smile just radiated from her face as she nodded to them.

Helen passed Charlyyk her Bouquet. The ceremony had started.

Charlyyk helped Amy to get through the long service.

When the ceremony had finished. Charlyyk nodded to Drenghaagh. The Laight's rose from their seats and made their way towards Charlyyk the Bride and Groom. Standing in front of the three of them, Drenghaagh held his left-hand palm-up to receive their hands. Taking the fingers on each of their hands that wore the rings and placing all the rings together, then set the ring on his finger, with their rings. Klyklyyk stepped forward, then she wound a silk band around them.

Drenghaagh looked them in the eyes and with a gentle nod. 'You each have given your intent, now you three are one, may your life together, be in harmony.'

He nodded again, and Klyklyyk removed the band.

'You are now and always, our family.'

Helen had started to understand the meanings of the nods. Looking at Charlyyk the sense of being as one, had sunk in. She could see the Laight's were as happy as everyone around them.

The signing of the registrar took place, then to peel of the Cathedral bells, the newly-weds made their way out. Charlyyk walked behind them the smile she wore telling everyone how proud she was. Amy looking around making sure her mother was nearby. Cat nodding to her daughter to keep up with Charlyyk. The wedding congregation started to leave their seats, and follow the happy couple. The wedding photos were going to be very special, as the three Laight's stood out from the rest of the congregation.

When the photo shoot had finished, the elegant Fiona Bruce stepped forward and spoke with Charlyyk. Charlyyk beckoned Klyklyyk to her. Klyklyyk explained to Fiona the reasoning for what took place. Then the three Laight's stepped into an open space and in a flash of light were gone.

Fiona Bruce facial expression as they evaporated showed the wonderment of how instant it was, turned towards Charlyyk and carried on with the interview with her years of experience in TV presenting. 'Charlyyk, did you know that your people were going to attend today?'

'No, but I am pleased they acknowledge us as a family.'

The vague images she had earlier at Dipper Meadows were now opening up and becoming even more clearer. Her brain was expanding, the restriction she had previously experienced were lifting and she knew much more than she had first thought she knew. What had held her memories at bay were now crumbling inside and the control of them she was now taking charge.

Charlyyk stood there, she took a deep breath, ignoring all the flashes. She now felt so contented, she has her whole family around her. A real mum and dad, brother and sister. Feeling the touch of Amy's hand, she bent down and cuddled her. Looking up and around, seeing everyone there she loved.

Was she happy?

You bet.